Praise for *The Whiskey Rebels*

"Compulsively readable . . . Edgar-winning Liss . . . channels early American history in a thickly plotted tale of conflicts between revolutionary idealism and fiscal skullduggery." —*Kirkus Reviews*

"Marvelous . . . educational, entertaining, and thoughtful . . . a fabulous new work of historical fiction . . . What distinguished Liss's first three novels in the suspense genre was the literary quality of his stories and prose. This quality is even more evident in [this book]. . . . Liss possesses talent that cannot be denied." —*San Antonio Express-News*

"*The Whiskey Rebels* is that increasingly rare find—a book that's a truly satisfying read. . . . [Liss is] a skilled storyteller, creating compelling characters and an absorbing narrative. . . . Saunders is a likeable hero, with enough flaws to make him truly appealing." —Fredericksburg *Free Lance-Star*

"Liss delivers a portrait of post-colonial Philadelphia and New York, as well as the western frontier, that is convincing and acutely detailed." —*Houston Chronicle*

"[*The Whiskey Rebels*] will give you an entertaining, detailed historical perspective on greed, financial mismanagement and political bungling." —*Contra Costa Times*

"A raucous mix of historical fiction and action-adventure thriller . . . Like all of Liss's novels, this one has a remarkably complex plot . . . rich in fascinating detail." —*Booklist*

"A thoroughly enjoyable novel . . . Fans of [Liss's] earlier books won't be disappointed." —*Library Journal*

"Liss deftly ties together two elaborate plots, displaying his familiarity with eighteenth-century financial history, and offers a fascinating look at the factions vying for power in the early years of this country's existence." —*Book Page*

Also by David Liss

The Devil's Company
A Spectacle of Corruption
The Coffee Trader
A Conspiracy of Paper
The Ethical Assassin

THE WHISKEY REBELS

The Whiskey Rebels

A Novel

DAVID LISS

BALLANTINE BOOKS

NEW YORK

2009 Ballantine Books Trade Paperback Edition

Copyright © 2008 by David Liss
Excerpt from *The Devil's Company* © 2009 by David Liss
Reading group guide copyright © 2009 by Random House, Inc.

Published in the United States by Ballantine Books,
an imprint of The Random House Publishing Group,
a division of Random House, Inc., New York.

BALLANTINE and colophon are registered trademarks of Random House, Inc.
RANDOM HOUSE READER'S CIRCLE & Design is a registered trademark of
Random House, Inc.

Originally published in hardcover in the United States by Random House, an imprint of
The Random House Publishing Group, a division of Random House, Inc., in 2008.

LIBRARY OF CONGRESS CATALOGING-IN-PUBLICATION DATA
Liss, David
The whiskey rebels: a novel / David Liss
p. cm.
ISBN 978-0-8129-7453-9
1. Veterans—Fiction.   2. Married people—Fiction.
3. Whiskey Rebellion, Pa., 1794—Fiction.   4. Pennsylvania—Fiction.   I. Title.
PS3562.I7814W48 2008   813'.54—dc22   2008000075

This book contains an excerpt from the forthcoming hardcover edition of
The Devil's Company by David Liss. This excerpt has been set for this edition
only and may not reflect the final content of the forthcoming edition.

Printed in the United States of America

www.randomhousereaderscircle.com

4 6 8 9 7 5

Book design by Dana Leigh Blanchette

For Eleanor and Simon

THE WHISKEY REBELS

Ethan Saunders

It was rainy and cold outside, miserable weather, and though I had not left my boardinghouse determined to die, things were now different. After consuming far more than my share of that frontier delicacy Monongahela rye, a calm resolution had come over me. A very angry man named Nathan Dorland was looking for me, asking for me at every inn, chophouse, and tavern in the city and making no secret of his intention to murder me. Perhaps he would find me tonight and, if not, tomorrow or the next day. Not any later than that. It was inevitable only because I was determined not to fight against the tide of popular opinion—which is to say, that I ought to be killed. It was my decision to submit, and I have long believed in keeping true to a plan once it has been cast in earnest.

It is a principle I cultivated during the war—indeed, one I learned from observing General Washington himself. This was in the early days of the Revolution, when His Excellency still believed he might defeat the British in pitched battle, Continental style, with our ill-disciplined and badly equipped militias set against the might of British regulars. It was the decisive military victory he wanted; indeed, in those early days it was the only sort he believed worth having. He would invite the officers to dine with him, and we would drink claret and eat roast chicken and sip our turtle soup and he would tell us how we were going to drive the Redcoats back at Brooklyn, and the unfortunate affair would be over before winter.

That was during the war. Now it was early in 1792, and I sat at the bar of the Lion and Bell in that part of Philadelphia euphemistically called Helltown. In that unsavory scene, I drank my whiskey with hot water while I waited for death to find me. I kept my back to the door, having no wish to see my enemy coming and because the Lion and Bell was as unlovely a place as Helltown offered—and those were mighty unlovely. The air was thick with smoke from pipes plugged full of cheap tobacco, and the floor, naught but dirt, had turned to mud with the icy rain outside and the spills and spitting and tobacco juice. The benches lay lopsided in the newly made hummocks and ruts of the ground, and the drunken patrons would, from time to time, topple over and tumble like felled timber into the muck. Perhaps a drinker might take the trouble to roll a friend over to keep him from drowning, though there could be no certainty. Helltown friends were none the best.

It was a curious mix there: the poor, the whores, the desperate, the servants run off for the night or the month or forever. And alongside them, throwing dice upon uneven surfaces or hunched over a hand of cards spread across ripped velvet, were the gentlemen in their fine woolen suits and white stockings and shimmering silver buckles. They'd come to gawk and to rub elbows with the colorful filth, and most of all they'd come to game. It was the spirit of the city, now that Alexander Hamilton, that astonishing buffoon, had launched his great project, the Bank of the United States. As Secretary of the Treasury, he had single-handedly transformed the country from a republican beacon for mankind into a paradise for speculators. Ten years earlier, with a single stroke, he had transformed me from patriot to outcast.

I removed from my pocket a watch, currently my only possession of value if one did not account my slave, Leonidas. I had, despite the decisions that had prevailed among the wise drafters of our Constitution, never quite learned to think of Leonidas as property. He was a man, and as good a man as any I'd known. It sat ill with me to keep a slave, particularly in a city like Philadelphia, whose small population of owned blacks numbered in the dozens, and one could find fifty free blacks for each bondsman. I could never sell Leonidas, no matter how dire my need, because I did not think it right to buy and sell men. On the other hand, though it was no fault of his, Leonidas would fetch at auction as much as fifty or sixty pounds' worth of dollars, and it had always seemed to me madness to emancipate such a sum.

So the timepiece, in practical terms, was currently my only thing of worth—a sad fact, given that I had removed it from its rightful owner only a few hours earlier. Its glittering face told me it was now half past eight. Dorland would have eaten his fashionably late dinner well over two hours ago, giving him ample time to collect his friends and come in search of me. It could be any minute now.

I slid back into my pocket the timepiece I'd taken on Chestnut Street. The owner had been a fat jackanapes, a self-important merchant. He'd been talking to another fat jackanapes and had paid no mind while I brushed past him. I'd not planned to take the watch, nor did I make a habit of such things as common theft, but it had been so tempting, and there seemed to be no reason not to claim it and then disappear in that crowded street, clacking with the walking sticks of bankers and brokers and merchants. I saw the watch, saw it might be taken, and saw how I might take it.

Even then, if that had been all, I would have let it go, but then I heard the man speak. It was his words, not my need, that drove me to take what was not mine. This man, this lump of a man, who resembled a great and corpulent bottom-heavy bear, forced into a crushed-velvet blue suit, had been invited to a gathering the next week at the house of Mr. William Bingham. That was all I knew of him, that he, a mere maker of money, nothing more than a glorified storekeeper, had been invited to partake of the finest society in Philadelphia—indeed, in the nation. I, who had sacrificed all for the Revolution, a man who had risked life in return for less than nothing, was little more than a beggar. So I took his watch, and I defy anyone to blame me.

Now that it was mine, I examined the painting in the inside cover, a young lady of not twenty, plump of face, like the watch's owner, with a bundle of yellow hair and eyes far apart and open wide, as though she'd been in perpetual astonishment while she sat for the portrait. A daughter? A wife? It hardly mattered. I had taken from a stranger a thing he loved, and now Nathan Dorland was coming to avenge such wrongs, too innumerable to catalogue.

"Handsome timepiece," said Owen, standing behind the bar. He was a tall man with a head long and narrow, shaped like one of the pewter mugs into which he poured his ales, with wheat-colored hair that curled up like foam. "Timepiece like that might go a way toward paying a debt." He held out one of his meaty hands, covered with oil and filth and blood from a fresh cut on his palm to which he paid no mind.

I shrugged. "With all my heart, but you must know the watch is newly thieved."

He withdrew the hand and wiped it on his filthy apron. "Don't need the trouble, but I ought to send you to fence it now, before you lose it at game."

"Should I turn the watch to ready, I would not use it for something so ephemeral as a tavern debt." I pushed my empty mug toward him. "Another, if you please, my good man."

Owen stared for a moment, his tankard of a face collapsed in purse-lipped indecision. He was a young man, not two-and-twenty, and he had a profound, nearly religious reverence for those who had fought in the war. Living, as he did, in such a place as Helltown, and moving through indifferent social circles, he had never heard how my military career had met its conclusion, and I saw no advantage in sharing information that would lead to his disillusionment.

Instead, I favored other details. Owen's father died in the fighting at Brooklyn Heights, and more than once had I treated Owen to the tale of how I had met his father that bloody day, when I was captain of a New York regiment, before my true skills were discovered and I was no longer to be found upon the battlefield. That day I led men, and when I told Owen the tale, my voice grew thick with cannon fire and death screams and the wet crunch of British bayonet against patriot flesh. I would recount how I had given Owen's honored father powder during the chaos of the ignominious retreat. With blood and limbs and musket balls flying about us, the air acrid with smoke, the British slaughtering us with imperial fury, I had taken the time to aid a militia volunteer, for we had shared a moment of revolutionary comradeship that defied our differences in rank and station. The tale kept the drinks flowing.

Owen took my mug, poured in some whiskey from an unstoppered bottle and hot water from a pitcher near the stove. He set it down before me with a considerable thud.

"Some would say you've had your fill," he told me.

"Some would," I agreed.

"Some would say you're abusing my generosity."

"Impertinent bastards."

Owen turned away and I opened the watch once more, setting it upon the counter, where I might stare at the tick of its hands and the girl who had meant so much to the merchant. To my right sat an animated skeleton of a man in a ragged coat that covered remarkably unclean linen. His face was unshaved, and his nasty eyes, lodged between the thinning brown hair of his crown and the thickening brown hair of his cheeks, stole glances at my prize. I'd seen him come in an hour earlier and slide a few coins across the bar to Owen, who had, in exchange, handed a small parchment sack to the ragged man. Owen did a brisk trade in that greenish powder called Spanish fly, though this man, his magic dust in hand, seemed content to sit at the bar and cast glances at me and my timepiece.

"I say, fellow, you are looking upon my watch."

He shook his head. "Wasn't."

"Why, I saw it, fellow. I saw you setting larcenous eyes upon my watch. This very one."

"Ain't," he said, looking closely at his drink.

"Don't you speechify at me, fellow. You were coveting my timepiece."

I held it up by the chain. "Take it if you have the courage. Take it from my hands while I observe you rather than skulking in the dark like a sneak thief."

He continued to gaze inside his pewter mug as though it were a seeing crystal and he a wizard. Owen whispered a word or two to him, and the skinny gawker moved farther down the bar, leaving me alone. It was what I liked best.

The hands of the watch moved. It was strange how a man could find himself in so morose a state. Only a few days before I had considered Dorland's pursuit of revenge as a vague amusement. Now I was content to let him kill me. What had changed? I could point to so many things, so many disappointments and failures and struggles, but I knew better. It was that morning, coming from my rooms and seeing the back of a woman half a block ahead of me, walking quickly away. From a great distance, through the tangle of pedestrians, I had seen a honey-brown coat and, above it, a mass of golden-blond hair upon which sat a prim if impractical wide-brimmed hat. For a moment, from nothing more than the color of her hair, from the way her coat hung upon her frame, from the way her feet struck the stones, I had convinced myself that it was Cynthia. I believed, if only for an instant, that after so many years and married though she was to a man of great consequence, Cynthia Pearson knew I now lived in Philadelphia, knew *where* I lived, and had come to see me. Perhaps, at the last moment, recognizing the impropriety, she lost her courage and scurried away, but she had wanted to see me. She still longed for me the way I longed for her.

It lasted but an instant, this utter, unassailable conviction that it was Cynthia, and then disappointment and humiliation struck me just as hard and just as quickly. Of course it had not been she. Of course Cynthia Pearson had not come to knock upon my door. The idea was absurd, and that I should, after ten years, be so quick to believe otherwise testified to how empty was my sad existence.

When Owen returned, I closed the watch and put it away, and then I drained my drink. "Be so good as to pour another."

Owen hovered before me, shaking his head, his mug handle of a nose blurring in the light of the oil lamps. "You can hardly keep yourself sitting. Go home, Captain Saunders."

"Another. I am to die tonight, and I wish to do it good and drunk."

"I daresay he is already quite drunk," said a voice from behind me, "but give him another if he likes."

It was Nathan Dorland. I needn't look, for I knew the voice.

Owen's eyes narrowed with contempt, for Dorland was not an imposing figure. Not tall, not broad, not confident or commanding "Unless you're a friend of Captain Saunders, and from the look of you, I'm guessing you ain't, I'd say this is none of your concern."

"It's my concern, because when this wretch is done with his drink, I mean to take him outside and introduce him to a concept called *justice*, with which he has been all too unfamiliar."

"And yet," I said, "I am familiar with *injustice*. Such irony."

"I don't know your complaint," said Owen, "and I know the captain well enough to trust you've got your cause. Even so, you'll not harm him. Not here. If you've a grievance with him, you must challenge him to a duel, like a gentleman."

"I have done so, and he has refused my challenge," Dorland said, sounding very much like a whining child.

"Duels are fought so early in the morning," I said to Owen. "It's barbarous."

Owen looked over at Dorland. "You've heard it. He has no interest in fighting you, and you must respect that. This man is a hero of the Revolution, and I owe him a debt for my father's sake. I'll defend his right to fight or not fight whom he wishes."

"Hero indeed!" Dorland barked. "I suppose when he is spinning tales of his time with Washington, he may have neglected to tell you the one in which he is cast out of the army for treason. Haven't heard that one? Ask him if you doubt it. Captain Saunders's career ended in disgrace, and as to the matter of your father, be assured he tells every tavern keeper in Philadelphia that he fought with his father or brother or uncle or son. Our friend here has given so many doomed men powder, he is like the angel of death."

Owen's eyes glistened in the light of the fireplace, and I shrugged, for I had been caught. I would not shy away from an untruth, but it seemed a contemptible thing to lie about a lie.

"I *was* at Brooklyn Heights," I said. "I might have seen your father.

And no matter what you may hear said of me, I can promise you I was never a traitor. Never."

My words only served to make Owen more teary. He looked over at Dorland. "Leave now. I don't want trouble, and nor do you."

"What does he owe?" I heard the ease of wealth in Dorland's voice. "I'll pay his debt."

Owen said nothing, so I spoke. "'Tis near eleven dollars." It wasn't true. I owed less than six, but if Dorland was going to pay for my death, at least Owen should profit from it.

I heard behind me the music of metal on metal, and then a purse landed hard upon the bar. "There's three pounds of British in it," said Dorland. "Near fifteen dollars. Now Saunders comes with me."

I nodded at Owen. "'Tis my time. Thanks for the drinks, lad."

I pushed myself off the rough wooden stool, and the room turned to a wild and topsy-turvy thing, with the floor leaping up toward me and bar stools taking flight like startled birds. I reflected on the danger of drinking so long without rising—that it is often hard to say precisely how drunken one has become if there is no new movement against which to test oneself. And then I believe I lost consciousness.

The rain fell hard and cold, rousing me lest I sleep through my own murder. My head ached along the temple from far too much whiskey and from what I judged to be a rather cruel kick delivered to an already fallen man. Very uncivil. Sharp pain jabbed into my ribs—from, I surmised, the ongoing kicks to my side, but in these I found less fault. What is there to do with a fallen enemy but kick him in the ribs? The head, however—that is bad sport.

I gagged on the metallic taste of my own blood and the soot of filthy snow, which was piled high against my face. The blood, I presumed, was mine, as I had no memories of biting anyone. I pushed my face, numb from the cold, away from the snow and saw the alley was wet with rain and mud and horseshit. My pants were wet too, and I could not be absolutely certain, but I had likely pissed myself.

Had this event transpired, it cannot be reckoned the result of fear. I believe this point worth making. I had decided that death was an agreeable outcome and was not only determined to be philosophical, I *was* philosophical. Life, death: I had no strong predisposition for one or the other. No, if I had pissed myself it was because one of those kicking feet had made contact with my abdomen and pressed into my full bladder. Nothing but anatomy, natural philosophy, human mechanics. There are diagrams in books to explain.

"Get up. You are a disgrace." The feet stopped kicking. In the heavy rain, Nathan Dorland's face shone spectrally in the sliver of moonlight that peeked through the cover of charcoal clouds. Dorland's features twisted into a snarling rage, simultaneously wolfish and petulant, sharp despite his plump, jowly looks. His nose was too long and carrotish, his chin too weak, his teeth unhealthy, and his eyes baggy. Nature had been unkind to him, and so had I. There was no victory in taking liberties with the beautiful wife of an ugly man, and had I known him before I met the lady, I would have restrained myself, for I am not unfeeling.

I managed to gain my feet in slow and awkward motions, my hand sliding in a pile of shit as I tried to gain leverage. A loose nail—rusty, by the uneven feel of it—cut into my palm. Once standing, I remained doubled over, unable to straighten. My hat had fallen off somewhere between the tavern and the alley, and now the cold rain ran down my face, washing the blood from my sundered lip.

There were four of them: Dorland and three friends, all of about his age—perhaps ten years older than I was—and all as plump, as uncomfortable in their bodies, as unlearned in the school of war. These were not men to fear, but I was drunk, they had the numbers, and, most significantly, I had no fight left in me.

Dorland held out his hand, and one of his companions placed within it a military bayonet. "In past days, men carried swords upon their person, but our times have decayed." He altered his grip upon the blade, weighing it in his hand. He drew close, as did his friends, two of them as near as he, though one hung back. "Have you anything to say before I end your life?"

I cleared my throat. "Dorland, I am sadly disappointed with the man I have become. I am drunk not only at this moment but perpetually. I have had no steady source of income in half a decade, and I am incorrigibly addicted to gaming, so that the money I steal or borrow or, on those rare occasions, earn, is gone as soon as it is in my hands. My clothes are old and tattered and frequently pungent to the nose, and above all of that I believe that during your attack I lost control of my bladder and pissed upon my own person."

"You think this should make me spare you?" Dorland asked. "Do you think your pathetic condition will stay my hand?"

"No, I only wished to make note of the sort of man your wife admitted to her bed."

For a moment, despite the dark, Dorland's face glowed white, a second moon, and then disappeared back into the blackness. I had seen faces contorted with rage before. I had killed men with such looks upon them, but that was war and this was murder, a crime even I considered too base for contemplation.

I'd wanted to anger him, of course. I'd wanted to seal my fate, but even then, having scorned his pride, having insulted him before his friends, I knew I could have altered events. It was but the work of a few words, well-chosen comments to appeal to their mercy, to make them feel grand and gracious. I'd saved myself from worse, for it was my particular talent. It was why Fleet, my mentor during the war, had chosen me to work with him, and it was what he had taught me to refine.

The blade rose high, and I fought hard to keep my eyes open. Better this had come at the hands of the British ten or twelve years ago, when I might have died a hero. Now I was much decayed, but that was the world, after all—a series of things that were not so good as we would wish. I awaited the blow, ready and determined if fearful of the pain. No blow came. Instead I heard a voice call out, "Stay your hand! You'll not want to commit murder before a witness."

There, not fifteen feet from our little confrontation, obscured by sheets of rain, stood the massive shape of a man, all silhouette in the downpour and darkness. He stood upon the prop of a broken keg, his greatcoat fluttering in the cold wind, and under the coat his arms were raised as to protect two pistols from the wet.

I knew the voice, but Dorland would not, just as I alone knew there could be no real pistols secreted away.

"This is a matter of honor and not your concern," Dorland called out.

"If it were a matter of honor, you would be meeting beside the Schuylkill at dawn," my defender said. "Here are four men setting out to kill a fifth, and I see no honor in it."

Dorland snorted and wiped rain from his eyes. "What will it cost to be rid of you?"

Poor Dorland, believing his money should answer all, knew nothing of how to regard an enemy, to measure his worth and his means. No, Dorland was a product of Hamilton's new America, standing in the shadow of the Bank of the United States, and Dorland's defiance came from wealth, from his utter assurance that it made him superior to any ball of lead, to any martial prowess. This man with his arms outstretched in the thunderous rain was but one more thing to be bought and sold. Like Dorland's wife—what was her name? Sally or Susan or something of that sort. Lovely woman. Very red lips.

All at once, the clouds shifted; the rain lessened and a full moon shone above, casting light upon all, including my rescuer, who towered above us, wild and demonic.

"'Tis but a nigger," said one of Dorland's friends.

"Hear me," said Leonidas, for it was indeed my man. "I am a slave, and you threaten the life of my master. I've a rare opportunity to kill white men and be excused for doing so."

I would not have chosen to save myself, but Leonidas was involved, and now I had a duty to him. He would not rest until I was safe, and I would not risk his life.

"'Tis but one man," said his friend again, "and only a nigger."

"Begging your pardon," I interrupted, "but there are, in fact, two men." This point might have given my enemies greater pause had I not punctuated it by vomiting on my shoes.

"Reckon how you like, then," Dorland said. "You are yet outnumbered. We are four to your two."

"Are you certain?" asked Leonidas, his voice quite arch.

"What the devil do you mean?"

"I mean look at me when I speak. Yes, over here; that's right. What, a

Negro is not worth your attention? I mean you miscount." I could not see his face, but I knew his tone. He spoke slowly, and he drew Dorland's attention for a purpose. Something had turned. "We are three to your one."

It had not been so, and yet now, impossibly, it was. I had not seen the third man arrive, nor note what he did—granted, the rain beat loudly, and I was distracted by pain and the rush of blood in my head and a bit of vomiting—and had I not later come to know him, to see what he could accomplish, if I had only known him from this one act, I would have believed him a ghost, some phantom from Hell untethered by earthly laws. He was not there, and then he stood by my side, but it was more than that. Dorland's three companions were now in the mud.

One lay on the ground clutching his middle. Another pressed a hand to his throat. A third lay flat on his back, his eyes wide, the stranger's boot on his chest. He held a thin knife, not particularly long, yet I did not doubt its deadliness in his hands.

I stared at this man who stood still with his shoulders wide in a stance of readiness, a bound coil ready to spring. He was slight of build, evenly proportioned, but a little inclined to be short, and, even stranger, he was bearded. I could not be certain in the poor light, but I thought he might be dark of skin, a lascar-looking fellow.

Dorland shook his head at the scene before him, having no greater understanding than I. He set down his bayonet and backed away, his hands out to make clear he would offer no more tricks. "Let him go," he said, looking at his friend writhing under the stranger's boot.

Dorland, however, was now no longer in a position to negotiate. Without taking his foot off the chest of the fallen man, the stranger had lashed out and pulled Dorland to him, the way a frog pulls in an insect with its tongue. He pressed Dorland's back tight to his chest with his left elbow, left hand gripping Dorland's right hand. The stranger's own right hand now held his knife to Dorland's thumb.

"You're going to feel a hot sting," he said, "and then excruciating pain."

He had done so much and so quickly, and I did not know him. I could only presume he truly meant to cut off Dorland's thumb, and I could not allow it. Yes, Dorland was a fool, and yes, he had thought it a fitting thing to kill me, but he was hardly the first to think that. And I *had* done him harm. I'd injured him and then refused to meet him on the field of honor. Having his thumb cut off in a Helltown alley struck me as a bit more than he deserved, or, if not, then at least more than I wanted upon my conscience.

"Better to let him go," I said to the bearded man.

"I think not," the stranger said. "He'll likely return to make another attempt."

"I must insist you let him go," I said, this time more strongly. "It's my rescue. I'd like to think I have some say in it."

The bearded man pushed Dorland away. He stumbled but did not fall.

Perhaps it was the darkness, but the stranger's expression seemed to me coldly, even frighteningly, blank. He had not been out for blood before, and he was not disappointed now. He had judged mutilating Dorland the best course, and he would have pursued it had I not insisted otherwise. Now, with Dorland away, he released his foot from the friend's chest and took several steps back from his victims, who were apparently not so badly hurt that they could not struggle to their feet. These were dandified gentlemen with no stomach for street brawling in the mud and rain. A little taste of violence and pain proved sufficient.

"There you have it," I said. "You may flee."

Dorland gazed upon me. "Saunders, don't think our business concluded," he said, apparently eager to prove the stranger's point.

"You did not find this encounter decisive?" I asked, then vomited once more.

"You are repulsive."

I wiped my mouth with the back of my hand. "Ladies are known to find me charming."

He took a step forward but one of his friends, the one who had been struck in the throat, held him back. Dorland grabbed his fallen weapon, and he and his friends hurried off.

Leonidas hopped down from his broken pedestal, sending out a splatter of cold mud, and placed an arm around me, for he sensed it was only with great difficulty that I remained on my feet. "Let's get you dry and warm," he said. "Then I'll present this gentleman, and we shall all have a talk."

I found the stranger's coldness unnerving, but I knew a worthy fighter when I saw one, and I owed him my politeness. "I am in your debt," I said to him.

The man grinned—the first sign I'd seen that he possessed anything like human feeling—and it was a wide, open, likable sort of grin, but also strangely false. It was not precisely insincere but rather had the air of being an afterthought, something he had to remember to do when interacting with human beings in such a way that involved no violence.

"Entirely my pleasure," he said, and I did not doubt him.

With the stranger lagging behind, perhaps making certain our enemies attempted no late ambush, Leonidas led me limping back into the Lion and Bell. We took a table near the fire, attracting no little attention as we did so. My man shrugged off his greatcoat, hanging it to dry, and then his hat, revealing a round head of closely cut hair. Next he took his pistols and checked the powder. The sight of this big Negro examining firearms caused a few men to gaze upon us with apprehension. Philadelphia white men are more at ease around Negroes than those in southern climes, but the sight of a muscular and broad-backed African checking his pistols is never a comforting sight. No one dared say a word, though—in part because it is unwise to be rude to a large man with firearms, but also because there was something in Leonidas's countenance that allayed suspicion. He was black as midnight but handsome as Oroonoko, possessed of a natural dignity, and if there was but one Negro in the country you wished to see with primed pistols, surely this was he.

"You did have weapons," I said. "I thought you were posturing."

His mouth twitched in the merest hint of a smile. "I should have hated to shoot a hole through my coat. 'Tis a fine bit of tailoring."

"Why do you have pistols?" I demanded.

"I have to do something with my money, as I am not permitted to purchase my freedom."

I often had no need of his services, and I let Leonidas hire himself out as a laborer down by the docks. He had saved enough to purchase his freedom at a fair price should I wish to permit it. It seemed to me an unnatural cruelty to ask a man, made a slave through no fault of his own, to have to pay for his freedom.

While I dried myself and let the pain wash over me and crystallize, Leonidas fetched for me more whiskey, for the events of the evening had created a void within me that wanted filling, and soon. He handed me a mug and sat down next to me.

All this time, the stranger stood by in a pantomime of anonymity. He shook off his coat by the fire. He patted his hat against his forearm. He rubbed his hands together.

"Again I thank you," I said to him. "I never asked for it, but still— very kind."

He nodded, and I had the distinct impression he grew weary of gratitude.

"You're fortunate we arrived when we did," Leonidas said. "You looked quite defeated."

I met his eye. This notion that you cannot look into a man's eye while dissimulating is, of course, an utter falseness. I could stare into the eyes of Jesus and tell him I was John the Baptist, and should the chance ever arrive to do so unlikely a thing, I meant to try it, just to see how it would go. "A few more minutes would have set things right. Still, I am always grateful for timely assistance."

Leonidas turned to the stranger. "May I present to you Mr. Kyler Lavien."

"Lavien," I said. "What sort of name is that? Are you a Frenchman?"

The stranger met my gaze with something hard and unflinching. "I am a Jew."

I suppose he might have been prepared for some unkind words, but he would not get them from me. I have nothing against Jews. I have nothing for them, of course, but nothing against them, nothing against anyone—not Papists, Presbyterians, Lutherans, Methodists, Menno-nites, Moravians, Millenarians, or Mohammedans. I have nothing against members of any religion—except Quakers, whom I despise, with all their sanctimonious peace-mongering and property-owning and *thee*s and *thou*s.

"And what is your business with me?" I asked him.

"That is rather the question, isn't it?" said Leonidas. He looked pointedly at Lavien when he spoke, and I felt very much a stranger to events in which I ought to have been central.

Lavien cleared his throat. "I was outside your boardinghouse when this good fellow left in search of you, because in the capacity of my work I followed someone to your rooms."

"Whom did you follow, and what is your work?" I said. "My head is too hurt for circuitous answers. Say what you mean, sir."

"I am employed in the service of your old acquaintance, Colonel Alexander Hamilton. I serve him now in his capacity as Secretary of the Department of the Treasury."

Despite my pain and drunkenness and general confusion, I felt my senses sharpening. I had suffered a decade of ignominy because of Hamilton, and now here was his man to save me from a vengeful husband. It made no sense.

"What does Hamilton want with me?" I asked.

"That is the wrong question," said Leonidas. "Ask him whom he followed to your house."

"Enough of this nonsense," I said. "Tell me what you do not say."

"In the capacity of serving the Treasury Department," said Lavien, "I followed to your home a lady who wished to deliver you a message."

"What of it? Ladies like to send me messages. I am a good correspondent."

"This lady," said Lavien, "I believe is known to you, though you have not spoken with her in many years. Her name is Mrs. Cynthia Pearson."

All pain, all confusion and disorder, were gone, and I saw the world before me in sharp detail—fine angles and defined colors. Cynthia Pearson, whom I had once intended to marry, the daughter of Fleet—my dead and much-abused friend—betrayed, as I had been, by Hamilton himself. I had not spoken to her in ten years. I had seen her, yes, glimpses upon the street, but never spoke. She had married another man, married for wealth, I believed, and our paths were forever diverged. Or so I thought, for Leonidas and this stranger now told me that this very evening she had come to my house.

"Why?" I spoke to Leonidas, forming my words slowly and methodically, as though being careful with my question might help him produce a more lucid response. "For what reason did she come to see me?"

Leonidas met my gaze and matched my tone. He had been with me almost as long as I had been apart from Cynthia, and he understood the importance of this question. He understood what this must mean to me. "It has something to do with her husband."

I shook my head. Never had I believed that Cynthia Pearson even knew I lived in Philadelphia, and now she had come to my home, at night, to speak to me of her husband.

Seeing the confusion upon my face, Leonidas took a deep breath. "She believes her husband, possibly herself and her children, to be in some danger. She came to see you tonight, Ethan, to beg for your help."

Joan Maycott

Summer 1781

I wanted to produce one sort of story, and I found myself producing one entirely different. Much of what transpired was born directly from my own decisions, my own actions. If I had not been what is called willful in women (it is called energetic or ambitious in men), my life might have unfolded quite differently. When we make decisions that lead us down a difficult path, it is easy to imagine the untaken course as peaceful and perfect, but those neglected choices may have been as bad or worse. I must feel regret, yes, but it does not follow that I must feel remorse.

I shall therefore tell my story and explain how I came to be an enemy to this country and the men who rule her. I do so with the full expectation that even if these words are read, they will find few sympathizers. I will be called a base and treacherous woman, diabolical in my unnatural resistance to the paternity of nation. Even so, there will always be those who have lived through what I have, similar or worse—for I know there is worse—and they will understand. It is small compensation, but there is no other for me.

I was born under the name of Joan Claybrook, and I lived on lands near the town of Albany in New York. My mother was one of six children from a poor family, and my father had come to this country from Scotland an indentured servant, so they set out upon the adventure of life with few advantages. But they struggled, and land was cheap, and by the time of my birth they were possessed of a moiety of property upon which they farmed wheat and barley and raised some cattle, occasionally pigs, and always a prodigious number of fowl. We would never have, and never aspired to, true wealth, but my family had reached a state in which we had no fear of starvation, and, at least before the war, we managed to save more each year than we spent.

I had one older brother and two younger, and, the family being well situated—quite overstocked, really—with heirs and farm hands, my parents, and my brothers too, were most indulgent of my whims. I was disinclined to farmwork and, as the only girl child, found my family tolerant—unwisely tolerant, some would say—of my wishes. It was not that I did not have responsibilities. By my estimate, I had far too many, but they only asked of me what they could not do without. I tended the chickens and collected their eggs. I kept them fed and cleaned their coop. I did a bit of spinning and sewing. Beyond that, I read.

It is to be expected, I suppose, that simple folk such as my parents, who grew up with little more than their letters, who had neither time nor money for reading, would have discouraged these pursuits. Perhaps they ought to have, but they were kind people and they found my love of books and reading charming—perhaps as Dr. Johnson found charming the dog that walked upon its hindquarters. They bought for me what they could and cultivated friendships with people of means in Albany, people who would be willing to lend me books of history and natural philosophy and political economy. I hardly cared what it was, so long as it imparted knowledge. I would sit outside on fair days, by the fire in foul, and I would forget there was a far smaller world around me.

By the time I was twelve I had read Hobbes and Locke and Hume. I knew Adam Smith's *Theory of Moral Sentiments* enough to quote chapter and verse, and his *Wealth of Nations* nearly so well. I had read Macaulay's history, and Bolingbroke's essays, all of *The Spectator*. I had read—in translation, of course—Herodotus and Thucydides and Homer and Virgil.

My father quizzed me, though he was little read himself. Over meals I would tell him of the follies of Xerxes or of how Zeus suffered when made to stand by, powerless to stop the death of his son Sarpedon. He found these tales—those from classics and histories—far more interesting than the thoughts of Hume or Berkeley, and this desire of his that I tell him stories might have colored his choice of books for me. So it seemed when I was sixteen, and he brought home a book that changed everything. Of course, I knew all about fanciful tales; I had read the epic poems of antiquity, and I had read Milton and Dryden, the plays of Shakespeare and Marlowe and Jonson. But this—this was something else entirely.

Even today, though I've read it more times than I can count, I sigh a bit to name it. It was called *Amelia,* and it was a novel. Inevitably, I had come across references to novels in my reading—in magazines and occasionally in pamphlets and works of philosophical discourse—but they were always dismissed as frivolous things for silly women, composed by silly women or disreputable men. So conditioned was I to regard novels as trivial nonsense that when my father put Fielding's three volumes in my hand, borrowed from a merchant he knew in town, it took considerable will to smile and act, in some small way, appreciative. My efforts proved insufficient, however, for my father's countenance fell.

"Don't ye like it?" His eyes went wide and slightly moist. He was a proud man, broad-shouldered, with strong though strangely flat hands and more than his share of physical courage, but he found my reading mysterious and vaguely frightening. I could see he thought he had made a foolish error, embarrassed himself before his clever daughter, perhaps even offended her, or even—for who knew how these matters of books worked?—done her harm.

"I—I don't know, not having read it," I said. Then I smiled at him, smiled as he deserved. "I shall let you know anon."

Had he not looked so sad, I should almost certainly have set it aside as something unworthy of my notice and returned it unread after a few days. Now, however, I felt obligated to give Fielding my attention. So it was I began to read. Perhaps it was my good fortune that the first novel I read should be so unusual of its kind. Novels so often concerned women looking for husbands, but in this book, the principal couple was already married. The hero, William Boothe, endures debt, imprisonment, the temptation of lust, and the guilt of adultery, while Amelia, his loving wife, struggles to preserve her family in the face of ruin and reprobation. I wept for its pathos, and I wept upon its conclusion, not only for the depth of the emotion it produced in me but because it was over.

By the time I finished reading, my father knew he had brought me something I loved. I recall that I sat in the field behind the house, the sun warm though not hot on my face, the completed final volume on my stomach. I stared at the misty blue of the sky, and I had the strangest thought of my life. Never before, as I read books produced by the ancients, books of philosophy or history, essays written by men of this very century, had the notion of writing myself ever possessed me. What could I write about when I knew nothing but what I read? Now everything was different. Why could I not write a novel? I could not hope to produce anything of *Amelia*'s majesty, but I could surely produce *something*.

I set my too-willing and indulgent father upon his task. He was to borrow every novel he could find. I read them all: Fielding's other, lesser works, *Joseph Andrew* and *Tom Jones*; Richardson's *Pamela* and *Clarissa* and *Sir Charles Grandison*. I read the bawdy humor of Smollett, the social explorations of Burney and Heywood and Lennox, the sentimental nonsense of Henry Brooke and Henry Mackenzie. I made copious notes on each, quantifying what I loved and what I hated. When my empathy for a character led me to weep or laugh or fear for her safety, I spent hours determining by what means the novelist had effected this magic. When I cared nothing for suffering and loss, I dissected the want of craft that engendered such apathy.

By the time I was seventeen, I believed myself ready to write a novel of my own. The only obstacle was that I had not, myself, experienced enough of the world to describe life with the novelist's verisimilitude. I had read, but I had not lived. I was determined that I should do so, not only for the sake of my craft but because I was now old enough to understand that books might not, by themselves, be enough for me forever.

One afternoon, near the end of the war, before the peace was made official but subsequent to the surrender of Cornwallis, I was in town with my father and Theodore, my elder brother, when I happened to see a pair of gentlemen emerging from a tailor's shop. One was older, clearly the father of the younger, for they shared the same long face, patrician nose, and penetrating eyes—though I could not see their color from the distance, I marked their glowing intensity. The younger man moved stiffly and with the aid of a cane. He seemed to wince with each step. Despite these grimaces, however, I knew he was the most beautiful man I had ever seen, with his fair hair and kind face, angelic in its proportions, both revealing and reflecting the world around it like a cold, still lake. Granted, when I say his beauty exceeded all others, I own my life had been sheltered, having come of age during a war in which many young men had been off fighting, or hiding that they might not be made to fight, or imprisoned upon suspicion of fighting for the wrong side. I had not seen many young men, and fewer still in other than a state of desperation, but this one was indeed beautiful, and had I gazed upon a hundred thousand of the finest specimens of the sex, I do not know I should have seen one I liked better.

I asked who he was.

"That," my brother said, "is Andrew Maycott."

I remembered him, for their farm was not far from ours. He had been four years younger last I saw him, hardly seventeen, and I had been thirteen, no more interested in men than I was in military tactics. He had matured in those years, and I even more so. Perhaps he felt a stranger's eyes upon him, for he turned to look at me across the street, and our eyes met. He leaned upon his cane and tipped his hat to me—to us—and I felt—well, I hardly knew what. I became light-headed and weak and terrified, and yet I was determined to know him better.

I thought to speak of it to my father. He was indulgent and should no doubt have done all in his power to arrange a meeting of the Maycotts and our family, but I had no wish for that sort of introduction. I had no mind to make small talk with his farming parents. More to the point, such a conjoining of two farming families did not seem to me sufficiently *novel*-like, at least not in the best sense. I did not want my story to begin with a quotidian gathering of Squires B, and Western. Far better I should do something of note, something replete with adventure and strong feeling and new sentiment.

To that end I took Atossa, a spotted mare who was my favorite, and rode the five miles to the Maycott farm. Perhaps I ought to have been apprehensive, for I knew what I planned was quite scandalous and would anger my parents. I was calm, however, for even at its worst my parents' anger was mild, and I spent my time imagining how, when I returned home, I would makes notes that would later provide detail for my novel.

I arrived at the farm and approached the house. The Maycotts had more land and wealth than we did, and if it was not a great deal more, it was enough for them to hold themselves above us and for us to consider ourselves humbled in their presence. The house itself was a large and handsome thing of two stories, all recently whitewashed, neatly tucked in a sheath of sheltering maples. None of us had fared well during the war, for it was hard to profit when there was so little money in circulation, and it was a sorry thing to grow crops when they might be appropriated by the enemy to feed its army or appropriated by our own troops and paid for with worthless promises. Nevertheless, the Maycotts had kept up appearances, and as I approached the house I felt like a frumpy rustic approaching the lord's manor. My dress, a homespun nut-colored thing, was clean enough, and my plain bonnet was neat and not overly discolored, but indifferent for all that. I had longed for a new ribbon to wear on such an auspicious occasion, but there were no new ribbons to be bought—and if there had been, we would not have had the money. Under my bonnet, such as it was, my mass of unruly brown hair was pinned as neatly as nature and impatience would allow. I had been careful to wash my hands before leaving, and my fingernails were free of dirt.

I had planned a speech to give to the servant who answered the door, but I was never afforded the opportunity. I had not yet knocked when I heard footsteps behind me, and I turned to see Andrew Maycott himself, hand upon his cane, coming with some difficulty up the path.

Leaning upon the cane, he bowed slightly. "Good afternoon, miss." His smile was correct and polite, and there was nothing ungentlemanly in his words or his manner, and yet I felt his eyes linger upon me. I enjoyed the feeling.

I straightened my posture. "You are Andrew Maycott, the very man I've come to see."

"Why, I believe it's Joan Claybrook," he said, shifting his head this way and that, like some collector of curios who has come upon a new and exciting specimen. "I remember you when you were a little girl."

"Which I am no longer," I said, hoping to sound more confident than I felt.

He made no effort to hide his amusement. "I don't think there is any room for discussion on that score." There was nothing lecherous in his tone, but he flirted, I could have no doubt of it. His attentions distracted me, and I did not wish to be distracted. I wished to be the one who distracted, who made the rules, but now, so close to him, I found it hard to keep my thoughts clear.

"Does it hurt—your wound?" I kept my voice calm and even, no easy thing when my pulse pounded in my ears.

"It is painful sometimes," he said, "but I will not let that keep me from doing what I like, and I am told it shall abate by-and-by."

I smiled to best disguise my anxiety, and then, taking what I hoped was a surreptitious deep breath, I said, as airily as I could, "I shall not wait for by-and-by. Let us take a walk."

I astonished him, I could see as much. He shifted a bit, and did a charming stammering thing, and then swallowed hard. "Miss Claybrook, I do not think it would be proper for me to take a private walk with a young lady."

Perhaps I might have been stung by this rebuke. I might have attempted to retrench, to recast what I had said, but I felt no shame or remorse, and the absence of regret gave me courage. "Oh, rabbit proper. You'll walk with me, won't you?"

"I do not think your father will thank me for it," he said. "Why do you not come in for some maple wine with my sister?"

I did not like this suggestion, and my tone revealed my irritation. "I haven't come for your sister. I came for you."

"Then you shall prosper," he said, "in having the both of us."

All at once, I found I was no longer performing. I did not act bold, I *was* bold, and I liked it. I put my hands on my hips. "Mr. Maycott, I have no interest in stilted conversation with your sister. I wish to talk to you, and I am sorry to see you are afraid to walk with a young lady."

"I merely consider your interests," he said, both surprised and amused, "even if you do not. Perhaps the impropriety of what you propose has not occurred to you."

"I believe, sir, in making my own propriety. If you do not come with me, I shall tell the world you did, so there is nothing to be gained by demurring."

He laughed, and his blue eyes mirrored the sky. "I see you have quite defeated me. Let us take a short walk along the road, then."

"I should prefer privacy. The woods."

"And I," he said, holding up his cane, "prefer to depend upon well-packed earth."

I could not argue with this requirement so I compromised, happy, so very happy, that I would now be walking with this beautiful man who had been, I must think, charmed and not appalled by my speech. We took a few steps, and Mr. Maycott began to comment on the fineness of the weather, on how even now he could not quite believe he was safe from the terror and tedium of war. Then, perhaps feeling awkward at his own seriousness, he changed to more agreeable topics. He spoke of how good it was to be home, of the simple pleasures of living upon his family's land—and, he said, of resuming old acquaintance.

Of course I found all of this interesting, and I loved to hear him speak, and in particular I loved to hear him speak of his feelings. He was more open and direct about such things than any other man I'd known. And yet, I was impatient. I wanted to speak of the two of us, of this moment, of what I had done to make it possible. At last I said, "You do not seem shocked by my addressing you as I've done."

"Would you rather I were shocked?" he asked.

"No, of course not. I am only surprised. Pleased, of course, but surprised."

"There has been a Revolution," said Andrew. "A king has been replaced by the people. It can hardly be surprising if other changes follow."

He looked at me, calm and easy, and yet his eyes were distant, as he considered the implications of his own words. Later, I would come to see this as the moment I fell in love with him. He was so glorious to look at, so strong and well formed and elegant, and yet contemplative. He took me seriously, regarded my words as thoughtfully as I could want. I felt no one had ever before truly listened to me.

I searched for the right words. "Sir, I am in need of a sentimental encounter. I saw you in town, and I thought I should like it if you were to begin courting me."

He had seemed beyond shocking, yet this shocked him. "Miss Claybrook—"

"Given our new familiarity, it would be better to call me Joan."

"Miss Claybrook," he repeated, "if I did not know better, I should think you had just arrived here from some distant island, or newly freed from captivity with the Indians. If I were not a man of honor, you would be placing yourself in grave danger."

"Then I depend upon your being a man of honor. I do not suggest anything untoward, Andrew. Men court women with a great deal of regularity, and it is perfectly acceptable. It is possible that, once we spend some time together, we may discover that we do not like each other well enough, so that will be the end of it. I only propose we find out."

"But this is not the way it is done. You are obviously a clever girl and know that."

"What happened to the Revolution?" I asked.

He laughed. "Perhaps you have outsmarted me."

"Oh, there is no *perhaps* about it, but I have no doubt you will have your revenge."

He bowed. "You are too kind."

"I am just kind enough." I was thoroughly myself now. He and I were comfortable, and his beauty ceased to frighten me. It charmed me and thrilled me, but I began to feel at home in its presence. "The truth is, Andrew, that I hope someday to write a novel, and I thought it might provide for an interesting experience if I were to make bold with you."

He blinked at me, like a sleepy cat. "You speak to me this way so you can turn our conversation into a novel? You do not really wish me to court you?"

"Oh, of course I do," I said. "But my being so direct was, I admit, a sort of experimentation, for I require some experiences. I have had too few. Come, pray don't be cross. I should not have spoken to you thus if I did not like you."

"But what sort of novel?" It was not a question I had anticipated, and it delighted me.

"The one I like best is Mr. Fielding's *Amelia.*"

"That's a good one," he said.

"You see? Already we are compatible. Not only do you read novels, which I'm told most men do not, or at least do not admit to, but your taste in novels is sound. Do you not think that courting me would be a good idea?"

"Miss Claybrook, I do not believe there is anything anyone could say that could possibly dissuade me from courting you." With this he began to walk again upon the road, bringing his walking stick down more jauntily than before.

We spent some moments in comfortable silence. Then he said, "Would you be so good as to tell me about your novel?"

How like him, I thought—though I hardly knew him and had no business deciding what he was like or unlike—to get so quickly to the heart of it. "That's precisely the difficulty. I haven't a notion of what to write about."

Andrew laughed.

Perhaps it was childish, but I felt wounded. "You think my difficulties amusing?"

"Not at all," he said. "I only like the thoughtful way your brow wrinkles when you wrestle with them. But, pray, tell me why you have such trouble telling your story."

Even as I had been studying his face, glorying in his handsomeness, it had not occurred to me that he would regard me the same way, and I felt myself blush. "If I am to write a novel, I wish for it to be an *American* novel, not a mere imitation of what is done in England. I don't want to move Tom Jones or Clarissa Harlowe to New York and set them to running about with Indians or fur trappers. The book must be American in its essence, don't you think?"

Again he stopped and stared at me. "You are a clever woman and, if I may say so, a true revolutionary. I believe the war would have been over three years ago had you sat in the Continental Congress."

"You tease me," I said.

He looked me in the eye so I could see his earnestness. "I do no such thing, I promise you. You, on your farm, in isolation, have understood more about the Revolution and the new country than half our politicians and generals. We cannot do things the old way but must make our own new way. Though, to be honest, I am not entirely certain what an American novel would look like."

"English novels are almost always about property," I said. "Estates miraculously inherited or diabolically stolen. There are marriages, of course, but these marriages, regardless of protestations of affection, are ever about land and estates, holdings and rents, not about love, not really. I don't want to write a novel about property. Here, in America, property is abundant so it is held cheap. It is not what it is in England: precious and scarce and hard to retain."

Andrew stroked his chin and then nodded, as though listening to a voice only he could hear. "The American novel, if it is to be honest, must be about money, not property. Money alone—base, unremarkable, corrupting money."

The moment he spoke, I knew he was quite right. I would write a novel about money. The notion contained such power over me that it was as though we were already married, and I took his arm and pulled him toward me. His brilliant suggestion, I knew, would be important, but I could not yet know that it would change everything.

Ethan Saunders

Cynthia Pearson had come to my home to ask for help. So many questions, so much confusion, and yet this fact stood out. This fact and one other—that it *had* been Cynthia I'd seen hurrying away from my house that morning. I was not a deluded fool dwelling pathetically on his past. The past, it seemed, was coming back for me.

I drained my whiskey and turned to Lavien. "Why were you following her?" I did not like the thought of someone so ready to slice off a man's thumb slinking around in the dark after Cynthia Pearson.

His expression was calm and easy. "I have been looking for her husband, Jacob Pearson, but with no success."

I remembered Jacob Pearson well. During the British occupation, I'd been in Philadelphia for nearly three months, attempting to infiltrate an enemy spy ring. Richard Fleet—my friend, my teacher, my fellow spy, the man who had recruited me into the business—had asked me to look after his daughter, then living in the city. He had not asked me to fall in love with her, granted, but these things often come unexpected.

During those months I'd met her future husband, Jacob Pearson, a successful dealer in properties, who managed to remain in the city, avoid the taint of royalism, and grow even more wealthy after the end of the war by snatching up properties from British sympathizers who were forced to flee. Pearson was perhaps five years older than I, not unattractive in person, and while he and I had never been friends, I had never had any reason to dislike the man. Not until circumstances forced me to flee Philadelphia, to leave Cynthia for her own happiness, and Pearson so successfully took my place.

"Why are you looking for him?" I asked Lavien.

"So I might speak to him," he answered, holding my gaze a moment longer than he needed to, as if daring me to treat his answer as anything other than illuminating.

"Speak to him about what, Mr. Lavien?"

"Speak to him about things that do not concern you, Captain Saunders."

"Once you start slinking about in the shadows, following people who come to visit me, it becomes my business, does it not?"

"No."

I cleared my throat. "Well, you've quite thoroughly demonstrated your inscrutability, and now I know that if there is to be give-and-take between us, you wish to maintain always the upper hand, but you *are* going to tell me more of what you know, so let us not pretend otherwise. You came to find me, sir, and if you came to find me, it is because you want something from me, and since you shall not get it without telling me more, we might as well move forward to that part of the conversation."

A faint smile crossed his lips. "For a beaten drunkard, you know your craft."

I liked him for saying so. "Now, you work for Hamilton, and you want Pearson, and Cynthia Pearson herself is looking for me. Tell me what I need to know."

"I can't and won't tell you why I want him. I have taken an oath of silence to reveal what I learn to none but Secretary Hamilton or the President, and I'll not break that oath. I can tell you that the man is missing, and has been for several days. I believe that is why his wife wishes to speak with you. She knew you from the war, I believe."

"Her father and I worked together. He was my friend."

"I see," he said, evidently seeing a great deal. He was no fool, this Lavien.

"You've already spoken to Mrs. Pearson, I imagine."

"Of course," Lavien answered. "She was kind enough to grant me an interview, but she claimed total ignorance of her husband's whereabouts."

"Did you believe her?" asked Leonidas. He and I had been together a long time. He knew what to ask.

Lavien nodded. "I did. Mrs. Pearson did not at all strike me as a woman dissembling, only as a woman uneasy. A woman whose husband is missing may very well display concern, but she struck me as agitated. I believe there were things upon her mind she did not speak of, but I doubt if she lied about knowing where to find Mr. Pearson."

"So you followed her to my home tonight. Then what happened?"

"After she was admitted, she emerged a few minutes later in the company of Leonidas. She proceeded to return to her carriage, so I inquired of Leonidas the nature of her business."

"And you told him?" I asked Leonidas.

"He serves the government," he answered. "I saw no reason to withhold what was said, especially since he already knew many of the particulars. Mr. Lavien asked if he might accompany me to find you."

"It was my hope," said Lavien, "that, in your company, Mrs. Pearson might be more forthcoming and say things she had withheld from me."

I took a moment to consider everything he said and to make myself comfortable with these surprises. Then I asked an obvious question. "Why does Cynthia believe herself and her children in danger?"

"That I cannot say," Leonidas answered.

I pushed myself to my feet. Pain exploded within my head, and I had to grasp the side of the table to keep from falling over, but I steadied myself, and the worst of it soon passed. "Time to find out," I said to Leonidas.

"May I join you?" asked Lavien.

"And what if I should say no?"

Lavien's mouth twitched. "Better not to explore that possibility."

I looked at him, prepared to let him know that his company was provisional, and if I did not like what he did or said, I should banish him at once. I said nothing, however, because I'd witnessed him in a flash of lightning, in the blink of an eye, overcome and disable three men. If he wished to join me against my will, I had no notion of how I might stop him.

By the time we left, the rain had mostly abated and we walked through the muddy ruins of Helltown. The walk did me good, set my blood to flowing, worked the pain out of my system. I've never been particularly good at fighting, it being a rough sort of work best left to rough men, and I'd learned long ago how to handle a beating with equanimity. Also, I had more important things to consider. Cynthia was in some sort of trouble, and she came to me. I'd only been in Philadelphia for four months, following my flight from Baltimore and a misunderstanding involving a cousin or niece or some such. Cynthia somehow knew I now lived here, and in her time of trouble she'd turned to me. No pain could compete with my curiosity, my buoyant and irrational enthusiasm at the thought of having, once more, some contact with her. I was not so ready to disregard reason as to believe that somehow, against hope and propriety, we might be together. I only wanted to see her, to hear her, to have her near.

As we moved, silent and huddled in the cold, toward the center of the city, the landscape metamorphosed from an outlying camp of poverty and debauchery to the height of American propriety. The streets, as if changed by magic, were all at once bricked, with lamps lit on walkways and watch houses occupied. The homes were no longer makeshift affairs, serviceable and expedient huts of castaway wood and thatch, but Philadelphia redbrick, stately and handsome, with stone fences that hid clever little gardens.

Jacob Pearson's house, at the corner of Third and Shippen, was one of these. It was no great monument to American wealth like the Bingham house, or like the Morris mansion where the President resided, but it was a large and stately home of three stories, surrounded by denuded apple and—appropriately—pear trees, shrubs, bushes, and plots set aside for flower gardens when the weather turned warm. Pearson's home was made of the same redbrick as the house where I rented, yet here was wealth on an order I could never hope to attain. Looking upon this fine building, could I wonder why Cynthia had married him?

During our walk, I'd heard the church bells strike ten, but Pearson's home was bright with lit candles, and from the outside it looked a hub of activity. The rain, light though it had become, undid my time before the fire, and we were quite wet by the time the three of us approached. I stood upon the porch and contemplated the knocker. There was, I understood, no way to prepare myself for what must happen next, no way to make myself ready. There was nothing to it but to move forward. I wished I could face Cynthia in a clean suit, unbloodied and neatly ordered, but it was not to be. She thought herself in danger, and I would not ask her to wait while I made myself fit for presentation.

"Do you require that I knock for you?" asked Leonidas, having apparently noticed the gravity with which I regarded this moment.

"No, I believe I can manage."

"I am quite willing to bear the burden," he said, "and, with the rain beginning to fall harder, I am even eager to undertake the physical labor required to bring a servant to the door."

"He's very cheeky," I said to Lavien, and then knocked myself. I was, after all, capable enough, requiring only a little browbeating from my Negro to make it happen.

A footman soon opened the door. His livery was rumpled, as though a dirty set of clothes had been thrown on hastily, and he had dark circles under his eyes. I'd seen the look before, and I had no doubt this was a household in distress.

"Captain Ethan Saunders to see Mrs. Pearson," I intoned with an importance my hatless wet head belied—or at least contradicted.

The footman, tall and rugged in build as was common for his species of servant, looked to me like a stage actor who had only been waiting for another player to speak a line that he might speak his own. Practically biting off my words, he said, "I'm afraid Mrs. Pearson is not accepting visitors at this hour."

"Of course she is," I assured him, "as she went to the trouble to summon me, and I have gone to the trouble of answering. You need do no more than go to the trouble of inviting us in and presenting us."

He looked me over, perhaps for the first time taking in my deplorable condition. "That shan't happen, sir. Good night."

The fellow was actually going to close the door in my face. Once a door is closed, it is not an easy thing to get it open again, so I stepped forward, pressed one hand upon the door, and strode directly toward the footman. The primary responsibility of such a servant is to see to the safety of his employers, so he ought to be possessed of a great deal of courage. Nevertheless, surprised, and faced with my alarming appearance, he took a fatal step back. This proved enough for my pair of worthies to move past him. It was an effective ploy, but I had no doubt that, had it not worked, Lavien would have dispatched him with little trouble. I was glad to avoid that outcome, however, as I did not wish to begin my reunion with Mrs. Pearson with the hobbling of her footman.

Regaining his confusion, the serving man stammered a moment and then managed to utter a coherent sentence. "I must ask you to leave. At once."

"My God, man, have you never had a wet drunk, a Negro, and a Jew call upon Mrs. Pearson before?" I said. "Don't just stand there. Tell her we're here."

"Get out or there will be trouble you shan't like, violent trouble, sir."

If this fellow thought he and a handful of kitchen boys were a match for Leonidas and Lavien, he was sadly mistaken. Nevertheless, it all proved unnecessary, for at the end of the front hall a figure emerged, silhouetted by the light of the sconces behind her. I could only see a shadowy form, but I knew her at once.

"It's all right, Nate, I shall tend to this."

The vibrating in my chest reverberated through my body. I could feel my pulse in my fingertips. My breath came in short bursts. After ten years, I stood in the same room with the woman I had once loved, once believed myself destined to marry. I wished to rush to her, and I wished to flee. Instead, I held my ground and attempted to conduct myself with the greatest possible dignity for a man so befouled and ill used as I was.

I attempted an awkward little bow, though my middle sections pained me considerably. "Mrs. Pearson, you have summoned me, and here I am."

She advanced a step and at once became visible. She wore a gown of pale green, perfectly chosen to match the shade of her eyes. Her hair was piled into a bun, from which a few delicate golden-straw wisps escaped, and she wore a prim little bonnet that did no more than suggest the possibility of a head covering.

Once, a month or more ago, near the covered market, I chanced to observe Mrs. Pearson upon the streets as she went shopping with her maid, her two children—a boy and a girl—in obedient tow. It had been fleeting, for I dared not let her see me. In ten years I'd not had the chance to gaze upon her face. When I'd known her, she had been a mere girl of nineteen, but now she was a woman, and the soft features that had made her so pretty had sharpened into beauty: her eyes, wide and liquid; her lips, full and red; her nose, sharp and distinguished. If her loveliness were not enough to move me, I should have been undone by the sadness overlaid upon it, for it was apparent that Mrs. Pearson was a melancholy woman and, indeed, a fearful one. I had not been a student of human nature for so long—it was what distinguished my service during the war—without being able to see such things.

"Captain Saunders, I am sorry to have troubled you, but it would appear I have made a—oh, dear God, what has happened to you?" She stepped into the far superior light of the foyer, and I was pleased to observe that her beauty was unharmed by greater illumination. "You are hurt, sir. Is this because—what I mean to say, are these injuries the result of my having—"

She did not know how to finish, and were she anyone else, I would have let her dangle upon her own words, to reveal what she feared, and I would have as much information as I could. But this was Cynthia Pearson, once Cynthia Fleet, and I would not be the cause of her suffering. "I have had an unfortunate encounter with some rough men," I told her, "but you may be assured that it has nothing to do with your circumstances. Indeed, I may owe you my life, for had you not sent my man to fetch me, I cannot say how things might have concluded. But that is not important. You must tell me why you summoned me."

She shook her pretty head. "It is nothing," she said, and attempted a weak little smile. "My husband has gone away on business and neglected to inform me of where he visits and when he returns. I grew worried and called upon you, as the only person I have ever known who might be able to find him. But now I see that I am foolish. I have no reason to fear for him, and certainly no reason to trouble you."

"You have assured me several times that your husband's disappearance does not trouble you," said Mr. Lavien, "and yet you sent for Captain Saunders, a man with whom you've had no contact for more than ten years?"

Mrs. Pearson spun and gave Lavien a most terrible look. I believe she had not seen the little man, for he stood near the door and had—no doubt intentionally—obscured himself behind Leonidas.

"Mr. Lavien, I've indicated our conversations were finished." She turned to me. "I would never have called upon you if I had known you were an associate of this gentleman."

"We never met before tonight," I assured her, "and though I owe him a debt, if he is odious to you, I shall remove him at once." I did not know how I would do such a thing, but I hoped he would not take too much offense at my offering to do so.

She forced a smile. "He is not odious, merely persistent, which can be rather tiresome."

Lavien bowed. "I do not mean to be so, but I serve a demanding master."

"Hamilton is your burden to bear, not mine," said Mrs. Pearson. "And Captain Saunders, you have obviously had a difficult night and would be much better served by going home and resting. I am a silly woman to have begun this business, and I hope you will forgive me."

"I will forgive you," I said, "as long as you are being perfectly direct."

She looked away. "Of course I am."

"Then why," asked Mr. Lavien, "did you wonder if Captain Saunders's injuries were the result of your attempt to enlist his help?"

"I said no such thing," she said to him.

It was true that she had not, but she had certainly implied it. It was clear, however, that she did not wish us to stay and that no amount of badgering was going to alter her opinion on the matter. There would be time for further contact.

As though seeing my thoughts, Mrs. Pearson retreated a few steps. "I must ask you to leave, Captain Saunders, and not return."

"Very well." I thought it wisest to agree as quickly as possible before promises were extracted. The more said, the less able I would be later to pretend to have misunderstood. "Come, Mr. Lavien. We need not belabor the point."

I held the door open for Lavien and Leonidas and turned back for one last look. "Good night, Mrs. Pearson."

"Good night," she said. She caught her breath, as if to say something more, but stopped herself. She blinked once and looked at me very directly. "And, Captain Saunders, it is good, very good, to see you again."

Was it my imagination, or was there something pleading in her tone, in her looks? I did not think she longed for me or my company but for something else, to communicate something of import. I had loved her father as though he were my own, and he and I had been brought low together because of Alexander Hamilton. I had loved her, and perhaps still did, and now she was married to another man. Those children in the house, sleeping their quiet childish dreams, were meant to be my children. I could not have her or this life, but if she were in danger I meant to resolve it, and I pitied anyone who would stand in my way. I was not like Mr. Lavien, capable of miraculous feats of martial prowess, but I had my own methods, my own tricks, and I was eager to use them.

Joan Maycott

Autumn 1788

Andrew and I married. Not immediately, of course, for there was all that courting to tend to, which was interesting and emotionally reward- ing enough that I did not wish to rush it, particularly not when it pro- duced such excellent notes in my journal. All those sweet and awkward moments wanted describing: the long talks; the vibrancy of stolen mo- ments in barns, and kitchens, and under a vast summer sky. I enjoyed one marvelous first after another. Less enjoyable, but perhaps equally novelistic, was the tedious gatherings of our families, full of forced con- versation and compliments on cheeses and pastries, the excellence of eggs or the sweetness of apples. My mother, delighted at the prospect that I should marry into such a family, with so handsome a man, snapped at me constantly to remove my nose from my books and cease my endless writing in my journal. Andrew, however, loved me for these things. He admired my learning and my ambition. My mother said I was being foolish, for Americans—and particularly American girls—do not write novels. Why, Andrew asked her, should his Joan not be the first? This was a new beginning for a new country, and there was no reason I could not be the foremost woman of letters in the new republic.

At first I worried that I had somehow tricked Andrew into offering to marry me, that I had been too forward with him, that I had confused his emotions. Time, however, soothed these fears. He would greet me always with a decorative carving or a piece of jewelry he had made for me, a bouquet of flowers or even, on occasion, a new ribbon with which to trim a hat. At family gatherings he would contrive some means to secrete me alone, if only for a minute, to steal a kiss, full of passion and desire and a yearning to have me to himself, to take from me all I would yield. When we parted, I saw the yearning in his eyes, and I felt it too. I had begun my dealings with Andrew as a kind of girlish experiment, but it had changed, truly changed, into womanly love.

We spent two years in courtship, attending family gatherings, dinners, and dances in town, once he was able to make do without the cane, though he continued to limp in damp weather or when much put upon. Concerns of money wanted sorting, but his parents did not insist upon a dowry that my family could not afford, for they saw his affection for me and were content that their boy, who had seen so much horror in the war, should enjoy a portion of happiness.

Andrew was the third of three sons and so was not to inherit his family's farm. This fact caused him some sadness, for he loved to work the land. He had spent little time in cities, but what he knew of them he did not like. Yet I, for my part, had always longed for city life, though I knew it only from novels, and it was my firm opinion that we should move to New York. Prejudices from the war, when New York was the British capital, colored Andrew's opinion, and he at first resisted, but he had never been an unreasonable man. We were only six weeks married when we arrived in New York City, where Andrew hoped to set himself up as a carpenter—a trade he knew well from the farm and which he had honed during the war, building bunkers and fortifications and redoubts, and then, once he had studied under more capable men, furnishings for officers' tents.

Our plans met with trouble almost from the first. We had less money than would have been ideal for such a venture, and we could not afford to live in any of the charming old Dutch homes off the Broad Way. Instead, we rented a house between the Collect Pond and Peck's Slip. This was low-lying land, inhabited by immigrants and the desperate. The streets were muddy, often choked with dead dogs and cats. The horses did not last long before they were stripped of their hide and flesh and hooves. Sometimes, when it was dry, piles of bones could be found stacked alongside the decaying wooden houses. When it was wet, the streets were thick rivers of slow-moving mud that flooded our house. It was a poor place for a carpentry shop, but we could pay for no better. We had, however, our own house and our privacy, and though we could afford only the scrawniest of chickens and the thinnest of cheeses, we made do, happy to be alone and together.

New York had suffered under the occupation, and remaining everywhere were signs of careless treatment of a place that was never to the British more than a campground and a plaything. Much of the city had been burned, and even now some buildings were but charred beams; others had been left in terrible conditions of decay, and the people—so many of whom had sided with the British—were now reduced to penury. Those royalists who had not fled wandered the city as though dazed, unable to believe they had bet upon the wrong horse and lost everything.

Yet, for all that, New York was a city on the rise. Though the dominant argument in the air was whether or not the new Constitution would receive ratification by the states, many New Yorkers were so convinced that they were to be the center of a new imperial experiment that they had already come to think of their city as the "empire city," their state as the "empire state." Everywhere, decayed streets metamorphosed into rows of charming brick houses with tiled roofs. Great boulevards of shopping—Wall Street, the Broad Way, and Greenwich Street—became almost daily more refined. In the distance to the north were quaint villages and farmland and, beyond that, sublime outcroppings of mountain and forest. We walked the cobbled streets of the new imperial capital, the rivers filled with forests of merchant-ship masts, yet we were surrounded by the untouched sublimity of nature. There could be nothing more American.

Though I lived in this city of commerce, I continued to have trouble writing my novel, principally because I still did not know what I wished to say. I sat, when I could find the time, with my books on finance: Postlethwayt's *Universal Dictionary of Trade and Commerce,* Thomas Mortimer's *Every Man His Own Broker,* Smith's *Wealth of Nations,* and a thousand bone-dry pamphlets arguing on all matters from free trade to taxes to tariffs to pricing. Somewhere in all that reading, I was certain, was a novel.

Though women were not welcome, on a few occasions I made my way to the Merchant's Coffeehouse on Wall Street, where commodities, bank issues, and government loans were traded in a kind of organized frenzy. Men shouted out prices, while others attempted to buy to advantage or sell before the price further declined. Here I thought was something else uniquely American. In England, jobbers traded their issues in London; in France, they traded in Paris; but in America, we traded in Boston, New York, Philadelphia, Baltimore, and Charleston. What effect did a decentralized market have upon prices and upon a trader's ability to profit? It seemed to me, even then, that an unscrupulous jobber with a few fast riders in his employ could exploit the system and profit handsomely. This too seemed to me fundamentally American, for we were a land where cleverness and ingenuity bled quickly into chicanery and fraud. How easily, I thought, in an untamed land did the steady energy of ambition become the twitchy mania of greed.

That we had no child also lay heavily upon me. I became pregnant three times in the five years we lived in New York, but always I miscarried before the fourth month. The surgeons and midwives gave me all manner of medicines, but none served. As the years passed, I began to grow despondent. For no want of effort, I could produce neither book nor child.

I wish to make it clear that Andrew was perfectly capable as a carpenter and equally so as a man of business. He was thrifty and hard-working, skillful and exacting, and could we have afforded to establish ourselves upon a better street, I have no doubt he would have risen to prominence, but we were trapped in the horrible cycle of poverty made inevitable by our neighborhood. Andrew offered his services cheap, and we had business enough, but once we were done paying our rents and our bills, there was little left. Some months we earned less than we spent, and after years of trying to make the carpentry business pay, Andrew began to wonder if it would not be better if we gave it up and attempted something new, though what this would be, neither of us could yet say.

Like many soldiers, Andrew found that after his service the Continental government had no funds with which to pay him, but he had long held on to his promissory notes rather than, as had many others, sell them to speculators at a fraction of their face value. Then late in 1788, Andrew came home one evening in a thoughtful mood. After a spare meal, he told me he had something of great importance to discuss. He had met a man named William Duer, an influential merchant in the city and an associate of Alexander Hamilton, who was rumored to be the new Treasury Secretary when General Washington took office as the first president in April.

No one knew what future, if any, there might be for war debt held by the various states. Some said the federal government planned to assume these obligations and pay all promissory notes. Other said it would declare the debt void with magisterial apologies, and soldiers like my husband would be forced to accept that they would never receive their due. There was no way to tell, this Duer had said, but there were men who were willing to hazard the risk. They had acquired land inexpensively in western Pennsylvania, near the forks of the Ohio, and they were willing to trade this acreage for war debt, assuming the risk of its future payment.

I knew nothing promising or inviting of western Pennsylvania, but Andrew had always regretted leaving farming behind, so was this not our opportunity? The western land, Duer claimed, was wondrous fertile. Once we had been willing to put farming behind us, but after years of struggling in the city, perhaps what we required was something familiar.

I always believed Andrew to be more innocent than I and said I wished to meet with this Mr. Duer myself, so the next day we had him in the sitting room, such as it was, on the second floor of our little house. It rained outside, and all the while I was in a fret that the first floor would flood while there was company there to witness it.

Duer was a small man in build and stature, in his forties, well groomed, with delicate features that made him look vaguely girlish but not effeminate. He was too fussy for that, like a squirrel worrying a nut. His pale brown eyes darted rapidly but lingered on nothing for long. Andrew and I sat on a cushioned bench, while Mr. Duer sat in a finely crafted chair—Andrew had made it himself—across from us, sipping tea and smiling with a small mouth full of very small teeth. With the cup in his hand, he rocked slightly with what I supposed was enthusiasm or an excess of energy. "It is a considerable undertaking," he said. His voice was slightly high-pitched, slightly whiny. It cracked upon long vowel sounds. "You must decide if you will move to western Pennsylvania, a land you have never visited, and start anew. The journey west is long, and it is far from everything you know. However, it is also a marvelous opportunity for many people, people who were never paid by the country they served, to exchange their intangible notes for land of real value."

"If the land has value and the notes do not, why do you propose such a trade?" I asked.

He raised his teacup to Andrew in salute. I noticed the cuffs of his sleeves were unnaturally white. "This is a clever woman you have here, clever and observant. There are some small-minded men who regard a clever woman as a curse, but I am not one of them. I admire a clever woman prodigiously, and I congratulate you upon her."

"And yet you have not answered her question," said Andrew.

"My own wife, Lady Kitty, is also such a woman, and cousins, you know, with the wife of Colonel Hamilton."

"You clearly have an excellent domestic arrangement," I offered.

"Yes, thank you. Most excellent. Now, you see, Mr. Maycott, western land is fertile, but cheap because it is so plentiful; there is far more land than there are people to settle upon it. The land is cheap for me to buy, but for those who wish to live, to farm, to have a life of plenty away from the city, it is of real value, for the land will grow nearly anything and livestock will thrive. Winters there are mild; summers are long and pleasant, without being oppressive and unwholesome as they can be here."

He handed Andrew a pamphlet entitled "An Account of the Lands of Western Pennsylvania," which, we discovered when we later read it, described an agrarian paradise. Rows of corn and vegetables that grew almost without husbandry. Because the land was so easily worked, families there had more free time than they did upon other farmlands, and balls, with fanciful homemade gowns and suits, had become something of a passion. It was a place of rural refinement, unlike any other in the world, for only in this new country, where good land remained unclaimed, could there be such independence and success. The dream of the American republic might have been born in the East, but it was reaching full flower in the West.

"I shoulder the risk in this investment," Duer said. "Should the new government decide to assume the war debt, then I will profit. If it chooses not to—well, the land was got cheaply, and the loss will not do me great harm. In any exchange of this sort, each side makes a wager that he will be better off than he was before, but a speculator must also look at the consequences of losing. In my case, I will be poorer for the loss, but I must lose sometimes, and I do not chance what I cannot bear to part with. In your case, if you hazard and lose—which is to say, you do not like your new circumstances—you have parted with paper notes, perhaps worth some cash someday, perhaps not. On the other hand, you will still have your lands, your wealth in food and crops, and your independence."

Andrew wore a serious expression, but I knew it belied his enthusiasm. He would be imagining the farms of our youth, a table on which a suckling pig steamed, surrounded by bowls of cabbage and carrots and potatoes and warm bread, all arising from the work of his own hands. Maybe the land would not be worth much to sell, but that was now. What of our children? Andrew believed the city air unhealthy. We would have children in the country, and they would inherit the land, which, as the nation moved west, would increase in value.

I was not, however, so eager. "I am concerned about Indians," I said. "I have read more than one account of Westerners set upon by them. Men killed, children killed or abducted, women forced to become Indian brides."

"It is a clever woman," Duer said to Andrew, "who thinks of such things. And she is well informed, I see. I congratulate you, sir, upon her excellence."

"Perhaps you should congratulate the lady directly," Andrew suggested.

Duer smiled very politely—at Andrew. "Yes, the savages were a menace during the war, but that was owing to the influence of the British. Now the Indians have been run off—all but those who've embraced our savior. Just as their pagan brethren can be savage beyond imagination, the ones who accept religion become like saints. They live upon the most Christian principles, never raising their hands in violence. All say they make better neighbors than the white men. Not that white men have excessive faults, but the novelty of Christianity inspires the Indians to take its teaching to heart and to keep its doctrines foremost in their minds."

"Perhaps we could go look at the lands," I said. "Then we will let you know."

"Your excellent wife proposes an excellent idea," Duer said. "Many prefer to do so. I know of a group traveling out that way in two weeks. It should take them no more than a month and a half to make the journey, though it may take you some time more to return, for you will need an eastward-heading party. In the lands we speak of, the Indians have been quite quelled, but in the wilderness between it is still safe only to travel in large groups."

Andrew shook his head. "I cannot afford to keep my house and yet not work my shop. I do not see how we can travel out there to inspect our property."

"If we cannot see the land, we cannot buy it," I said. "I am sure you understand that."

"Absolutely. If you cannot see the land, then of course you cannot buy it." Mr. Duer began to collect his things and spout pleasantries about how if we needed anything of him, we should not hesitate to call. Then he stopped himself in mid-sentence. "A thought occurs to me. It is the very germ of an idea. Hold." He held out one hand in a gesture directing us to halt while he collected this notion from the ether. "Would it have some effect if you could speak to someone who has seen the lands—who has lived upon them?"

"I cannot say for certain," Andrew said. "It should very much depend upon the person."

"It *should* depend upon the person, I agree. And it *would* help to speak to such a man. As it happens, I know of a landowner who is in town this very week," he said. "Perhaps I could persuade him to take a few moments to answer your questions."

We agreed it would be a worthwhile conversation to have, and two days later he was back in our parlor, this time accompanied by a rough-looking fellow called James Reynolds. He was perhaps no older than my Andrew, but his face was cracked and wind-beaten and sun-blasted. Across his right eye a scar stretched from his forehead down almost to his mouth, half an inch wide, a deep gulf of violence that had mysteriously left his twitching eye intact. He wore homespun clothes of a rugged material, but they were nicely tailored and by no means out of fashion. Indeed, he carried himself with the rigid posture of a proud gentleman planter, though his manner was a bit more coarse. His teeth were sepia from a tobacco habit, and he was inclined to wiping his nose with the back of his hand.

He sipped at his tea, holding the whole cup with a strange caution, as though he might forget himself and crush it like an empty eggshell "So, Mr. Duer here wants me to tell you about Libertytown." His voice was thick, as if his throat were coated in gravel.

"Libertytown," Andrew repeated.

Reynolds smiled. "Most of us served in some way or another, during the war."

"Are you satisfied with your life there?" Andrew asked.

"You have to understand, I wasn't born to money. My mother was a seamstress, and my father died young. In Libertytown, I work my own land, and I take orders from no one. I grow more than I need, trade some of the surplus to the other farmers, and the rest we cart back east. I've got a little bit put away now. I didn't have that much debt to exchange, not so much as you, so I'll never be rich off my land. But I'll tell you this: I won't never be poor neither."

"In your opinion it is every bit the paradise that Mr. Duer describes?"

He ran a hand through his hair, which fell freely to his shoulders, was unevenly cut, and was very black but flecked with gray, or perhaps ash. "I wonder," he said to Mr. Duer, "if you could give us a few scant minutes alone."

"Come, sir," Duer protested. "There is nothing you can say that I may not hear, surely. We are all friends to be honest with one another."

"Only a moment, if you please."

"Only a moment, then." Duer stood, offered us a bow, and left the room. In but a moment, I could observe him out the window, pacing upon the street. He did not seem to me particularly uneasy, but more like a man who had other things to do with his time and did not care for matters to run longer than he had expected.

With Duer gone, Mr. Reynolds let out a sigh of relief, like a man who has overdone himself at feasting and now unbuttons his trousers. He set down his teacup and leaned forward slightly in his seat. "Here's the truth of it. Duer there, he's as straight as they come. Even so, you have to understand, he wants to exchange land for war debt. That's his business, and so he puts things in a particular color."

"It is not paradise," Andrew said.

"Ain't no paradise on this earth, Mr. Maycott. Nothing even close, so don't believe those stories. The winters ain't as mild as he might suggest; we get big snows just like everyone else. Summers can be hot and muggy and full of flying things that you sometimes think will drive you mad. We've had problems with bears from time to time. Couple years back, a friend of mine was mauled to death when his rifle misfired, hitting the thing in the leg instead of the head."

"Do you regret exchanging your debt for the land?" I asked.

"Not for a moment," he said. "It ain't perfect, but I ain't never had a chance at anything better. The land is wondrous fertile, and the crops nearly grow themselves. The society—well, you couldn't ask for better folk. He told you about the dancing, I reckon. He loves to talk about the balls. There's all sorts of societies and clubs. We get newspapers and pamphlets and books—we get them late, but we get them."

"And the Indians?" Andrew asked.

He appeared amused at our silly question. "The bad ones been run off, the good ones are like children to look at them. They don't do nothing but work and pray. You ask them to trade you one of your ears of corn for their six, they'll take the trade and thank you for it. To some folks the redskins are a bit unsettling, but they don't never do harm."

"Do you feel that most people out there share your sentiments?" Andrew asked.

"There's always some that don't take to it. There's some that never worked land before, even easy land, and they find they don't care for the labor. Or they come from Philadelphia or Boston or New York and find they don't like our simple houses and simple clothes. There ain't nothing in this world that's good for all folk, and that's the truth, but when someone wants to leave, there's always been a neighbor who's done well and is willing to buy him out."

"I thank you for your candor," Andrew said.

Reynolds shook his head. "No more than I ought to do. We ain't that big a settlement, Mr. Maycott, and we don't want people who don't want to be there. But a patriot like you, I can promise that you'd find yourself most welcome. And I'll tell you another thing," he said, looking about our parlor, his eyes falling to the shelves of books we could ill afford. "I see you got books, so be sure to bring them. You'll get a better price in the West, if you're looking to sell, and if you're willing to lend, you won't find no better way to make friends."

Mr. Reynolds left, Mr. Duer returned, and we talked more. When we were alone, we said nothing of it, merely going back to our respective duties, but the next morning I woke up with Andrew holding my hand and studying my face in that way he did when his love felt fresh and new. I understood then that all was decided. Andrew, after struggling to keep his shop profitable, could return to the independence of working the land. I, for my part, had become convinced that this was the opportunity for which I had been waiting. If I wished to write an American novel, what better opportunity could I have than to experience a uniquely American way of life? I would go the frontier, live among settlers, write of their ways, of land-clearing and farming, of Indians and traders and trappers, of western folk who lived by their strength and wits and force of will. I would write the novel that would define, for years to come, the very nature of its American form. My enthusiasm grew so great that I could not have imagined the land would fall short of our expectations in any way, yet I would soon enough learn we had been tricked into trading the hope of our future for nothing but ashes and sorrow.

Ethan Saunders

The rain had mercifully abated, and so the three of us strolled away from the Pearson house with at least some comfort. I did not know what to make of this strange experience. How had Mrs. Pearson learned I was in Philadelphia? Why had she chosen to contact me and then sent me away once more? Did she truly think that, upon seeing my injuries, they were somehow linked to her husband's disappearance?

Yes, all these questions raced through my mind. Old habits, the ones Fleet had taught me, die hard. Silently I made lists and checked fact against fact, weighed theory against knowledge, proposed notions and dismissed them almost as quickly. Yet while I did this, one thought dominated: *Cynthia Pearson called for me.* She was in trouble, and I was the one to whom she turned. This filled me with hope and joy, yet at the same time I found myself wracked with bouts of unspeakable melancholy.

I would have to wait until I was secure in my own rooms, bottle of whiskey in hand, before indulging my sadness. While the stranger walked with me, there was work to be done.

"How long has Mr. Pearson been missing?" I asked Lavien.

"Perhaps a week," he said, his voice neutral, even distant. It was the voice of a man who wished to reveal nothing except, perhaps, his wish to reveal nothing.

"Why would she change her mind about wanting help?" Leonidas wondered.

"I don't know," said Lavien, "but I cannot believe her when she says she has dismissed her concerns as silly. Perhaps, Captain Saunders, I can call upon you tomorrow and you can tell me more of your impressions. Knowing Mrs. Pearson far better than I, you may have some useful insights, but I believe we are all too tired to be very productive tonight."

"Of course," I said, not at all certain I would share anything with him. I believed I liked him, but I did not precisely trust him. He knew, or suspected, far more than he was willing to share with me, and I found it irksome that he expected my notions to be given gratis while his were tucked safely away.

"I shall make my own way home," he said. "It is but a short walk to Third and Cherry."

I thanked him again for the service he had rendered me earlier, and so saying we parted ways. Leonidas and I, meanwhile, turned toward the river and my own lodgings at Spruce and Second. "What is your impression of him?" I asked Leonidas.

His face assumed a series of lines—eyes squinted, lips pressed—as it did when he grew thoughtful. "I don't know. He is certainly competent. When we came upon your trouble in the alley, he immediately—or I should say instantly—began to set forth a strategy, telling me what I must do and how I must do it. And I had no difficulty doing precisely what he said, such was the confidence and authority in his voice. But that matter with Dorland's thumb. He is cold in a way that is almost unnatural."

"A kind of stoic efficiency," I said. "Like a surgeon."

"Exactly," Leonidas said. "He knows his business, I've no doubt, but I don't think he is telling us everything. It's strange. I would think he'd want your assistance in finding Mr. Pearson."

"Why should I wish him found?" I asked. "I'd rather he went to the devil."

"It would be very pleasant if Mrs. Pearson were to become a wealthy widow in search of an old love, but I would not depend upon it."

"You are ever a delight," I said to Leonidas. We now found ourselves outside my boardinghouse, so it was time for my man to take his leave. My rooms were cramped, and Leonidas did not choose to lodge with me. Had I larger and more spacious rooms, he still would not have chosen to lodge with me. Like many Philadelphia slaves, he had his own home, which he rented with his own money. I had in the past, for reasons not entirely clear to me, arrived at his door late at night, knocking loudly, calling out, once crying like a child. Leonidas had responded quite soundly by changing his address and neglecting to inform me of where he now resided. Indeed, all local taverners, merchants, peddlers, and landlords knew not to inform me should I come asking.

This sense of independence was my own doing. I won Leonidas in a long and vicious card game not five or six months after my ignominious departure from the army. I was living in Boston at the time, and his owner was as compassionate and caring as a slave owner might be. Prior to his purchase, and therefore through no fault of his owner's, Leonidas had been separated from his parents when he was little more than an infant and had no recollection of them. His Boston owner had seen to his education, and when he came into my hands he was eleven, clever and already large for his age.

I thought it best to continue his education, and, until he concluded his studies at sixteen, I always found the means to pay for his tuition at a Negro school, even if I could pay for little else. The young Leonidas had been inclined to dark moods, and I could not blame him. Even then he expressed with hot eloquence his hatred of slavery, so I agreed to free him in ten years' time, when he turned twenty-one. That milestone had come and gone the previous summer, and though Leonidas had been so good as to remind me of my promise, I was reluctant to let him go. I had been prepared to do so when events conspired against me and I had to make a hasty retreat from Baltimore. Then I had to establish myself in a new city, and I hated the idea that I must be made to do it alone.

Once we reached my boardinghouse, I sent Leonidas home and

knocked upon the door. My landlady had never seen fit to trust me with the key, yet she was always majestically resentful when I awoke her upon returning. There is no reconciling with some people, and I was, admittedly, disinclined to reconcile myself to this one. She did not care for me much, though I did not know if it was because of my general habits, or because I did not pay rent, or that during my late-night returns to her house I would sometimes behave unquietly. Once, while too full of drink, I had reached out and pinched her nipple.

It was now nearly midnight, so I was surprised that my knock was answered so rapidly. My landlady, Mrs. Deisher—a stout German thing—was in the habit of answering my late knocks with a taciturn scowl, clad only in her dressing gown. Tonight she was fully dressed, and though she opened the door she did not stand aside to let me in. Indeed, she blocked me, holding a candle, her hand trembling slightly.

"We must speak, Mr. Saunders," she said, in her heavy accent.

"*Captain* Saunders," I told her. "Must I always remind you? Do you not value patriotic service, or do you perhaps mourn for some Hessian officer?"

"I am sorry to say to you this, but here there is a difficulty with your rent."

My rent. There was always a difficulty with my rent, perhaps because I was so very undisciplined about paying it. "Then we shall discuss it in the morning, but I must now sleep."

She grunted. She winced. She shook her head. "You owe me for three months, and I must have payment."

What nonsense over a mere ten dollars. I have ever been good with words, good with the gentle art of persuasion, but I rarely could summon the will to speak to this creature with a smooth tongue. Instead, I took a step forward and gave her my most charming smile. "Mrs. Deisher, we have ever been friends, have we not?" Never wait for an answer to such a question. "We have ever been on excellent terms. I have always been your admirer. You know that, do you not, Mrs. Deisher?"

"Have you the money?" she asked.

"A mere ten dollars? Of course I have the money. I shall have it for you tomorrow. Next week at the latest."

"But not only for this month, sir. You owe for the past months. You must pay thirty dollars to clear the account."

My mind had only been half engaged in this conversation, for it was a dance we had danced before, and we knew each other's moves as well as old lovers. Instead, I had been turning over thoughts of Mrs. Pearson and, to a lesser extent, Lavien, while I absently charmed my way into my unpaid rooms. The demand for thirty dollars arrested my attention, however.

"Thirty dollars!" I said. "Mrs. Deisher, is this the time to speak of such things, in the cold darkness when, as you can see from my face, I have suffered great injury tonight?"

She shifted her squat weight and squared her squat shoulders. "I must have money now. There is a young man with wife, a baby, who can take your room in the morning. You will pay me, or you will go. If you don't do either, I will summon the watch."

"Are you trying to ruin me?" I demanded. My irritation caused me to forget, if only for a moment, the value of good manners. "Can this not wait until morning? Can you not look at me and see I have had the very devil of a damnable night?"

Her face settled into hard woflishness. "Do not use such language. I don't love it. Tell me only, have you money now?" She asked the question through trembling lips.

"It is clear that there is more to this than meets the eye. What is this about? Has someone paid you to cast me out? It was Dorland, wasn't it?"

"Have you the money now?" she repeated, but with less self-righteousness.

I had hit upon something and thought to test my theory, so I said, "Yes, I do. I shall pay you, and then I shall go to sleep."

"Too late!" she shrieked. "It is too late! You have used me ill, and I do not want you no more. You must pay me and go."

This was Dorland; it had to be. And yet I did not quite believe it. It was not that he was above such mean tricks, just that I did not think he had the wit to conceive of them. "If you are going to cast me out, you can hardly expect me to pay you," I observed. "You'll not get a penny."

"Then you get out. You do it or I'll call the watch."

By itself, the watch was nothing to me, but I feared public knowledge of my eviction. Should word spread that I had lost my rooms, my creditors would descend upon me like starved lions on a wounded lamb. I could not disappear into the airless bog of debtor's prison just when Cynthia Pearson had reappeared in my life.

It was not the first time I'd been cast out of a lodging, nor the first in the middle of the night. I had done what I could and would not humiliate myself by prolonging the argument. "Very well. I shall collect some things, and I shall quit your miserable house. Be so kind as to pack what I do not take now, and keep your fingers off what does not belong to you."

"I keep your things as surety, and if you try to get them I'll call the watch. The watch." She'd seen it in my eyes, sensed my fear with her low animal cunning, and now she held forth the word like a talisman. "I call the watch and they take you away. Forever!"

Forever seemed a bit extreme, even for a flight of fancy, but I did not dash her dreams. I was too angry, and she must have seen that too in my eyes, for she took a frightened step backward. In response, I offered her a very stiff bow and set out once more into the rain.

It is a sad thing for a man to realize that once he has lost his home, he has nowhere to go. My life in Philadelphia, brief of tenure, was such that I knew many men, but had no friends I dared approach this late at night to request shelter. I could not go to any of the ladies who were generally kind to me, even the unmarried ones, for if I were to appear in my current sodden, beaten, and hatless state, I believe the spell I had once cast might dissipate. As for Leonidas, I would, this one time, violate his desire for privacy and throw myself on his mercy, if only I knew where he lived.

As if in accompaniment to my bad humor, the rain had begun once more. With the cold numbing my fingers, my boots nearly soaked though with melted snow and mud, I trudged back to Helltown and the Lion and Bell. I asked Owen to let me have a room and to put it upon my account, which was now, ironically, in excellent order. If not precisely warm, Owen was at least agreeable, recognizing that, in what I had believed to be my dying moments, I had deceived my way into doing him a good turn. Surely this act of kindness undid my early misrepresentations.

He would not allow me a private room but sent me to a mattress of sack and straw on a floor in a room full of drunk, farting, belching men who smelled as though they had never seen the inside of a washtub. I was one of these creatures, and I fell asleep regretting that Dorland had not killed me after all.

Morning came, as it insists upon doing, and my head ached from drink and violence. My ribs were purple and inflamed. My ankle was swollen as well. I hadn't noticed it the night before, but I must have given it at least a minor twist during my adventures with Dorland.

I had no time to nurse my wounds, however, for I had money to earn. And how does a man such as myself fill his purse in a pinch? Unfortunately, the secret involves a clean and handsome appearance. Even were my face not in its current contused state, I would still need to bathe and gain access to better clothes, now held hostage by my ogre of a landlady. Were I in possession, however, I should proceed with the confidence of one pleasing to the female eye. I am told it is so. I am tall and manly in stature, and I know how to direct a tailor to shape clothes to advantage. My hair remains thick and dark brown in color, and I continue to wear it in the rugged queue style of the Revolution.

Once I am properly appointed, it is off to a public place, perhaps a park or a walk or skating pond, where I find a group of promising women, preferably a gathering in which all or most wear wedding bands. It is far easier, and less vexing to my sense of propriety, to convince a married woman to compromise morals in which she no longer believes than an unmarried woman to abandon a purity to which she yet aspires. So I fall in with a set of ladies, conducting myself as though I already know them, so that each will presume that she has met me and ought to recollect me or—far worse—that she alone has been omitted from the frolics where the others first had the pleasure of my company.

Once at ease with these ladies—perhaps walking arm in arm with two of them for a time to introduce them to comforts of physical proximity—talking with them, flattering them, bringing them to unseemly convulsions of laughter, I begin to drop hints of my past. I make allusions to my time as a spy (though I never use the word, because of its ungentle-manly connotations), serving General Washington, risking life and free-dom behind enemy lines. There is always at least one lady who expresses a wish to hear more. And though I plead reluctance to dwell on those dark days, I can, in the end, be convinced to speak—but, pray, not in public. No, it is a hard thing to talk of here, in the daylight, in so beau-tiful a place. Perhaps a quiet chocolate house, just the two of us? No? Your home? Yes, that is much better; we may speak there without a spec-tacle being made of my pain.

From here it is a simple thing. A story or two of danger, of friends lost, of torment in enemy camps. A bit of a choke in my voice. A sympa-thetic caress of the hand.

That is what I would do were all means open to me. The thirty dol-lars I needed to retrieve my goods were nothing and would be mine by the end of the afternoon, should I put my mind to it. Without my good clothes, and with a bruised face, and smelling like a dead dog in an out-house, I had no such options.

I sat in Owen's tavern, enjoying a breakfast of stale bread dipped in whiskey, followed by a refreshing draught from the mug. I could not mistake Owen's gaze, nor the distance granted to me by the other morn-ing patrons. In a state of agitation, I took a piece of thick twine I'd dis-covered in my pocket and rolled it over my bunched fingers, unrolled it, and proceeded again while Owen stared at me.

"What is it?" I demanded. "Is it my twine? Do not think to take from me my twine."

"I don't want your twine."

"A man ought not to be without his twine," I told him.

"Forget the twine. You look like bloody death," he said to me.

"I but need to clean up a bit. And to do that, I will need—oh, what is it? Ah, yes, a bit of cash. What say you, Owen, to lending me thirty dollars?"

"Get out," he said.

I decided it was time to move on. I took leave of the good barkeep, re-trieving from the insensible head of one of his inebriated customers a hat of indifferent quality. Even after a quick reshaping and delousing it sat poorly upon me, yet a man cannot endure to be hatless.

Dorland would be out with his business. This being Tuesday, his wife would be hosting her weekly luncheon, a salon with ladies of her acquaintance. I had never observed the ritual myself, but she had spoken of it while we lay together, and I would pretend to find it interesting.

On the way, I grew thirsty from the day's cold, and I wished to make certain my credit had not been harmed by rumors of eviction, so I stopped to quench my thirst and test my luck. Three whiskeys, a mug of ale, and a less than fortuitous game of dice (my wager on credit) later, I concluded that my reputation was in good health and so resumed my mission.

At Dorland's house, I pulled the bell, and the servant who answered regarded me with considerable disdain. Now, I am not an unreasonable man. I knew I appeared poorly, but I firmly believe that servants ought to regard every gentleman as though he were perfectly appointed. I suppose I could be a vagabond, but I could also be a wealthy gentleman just come from a carriage mishap. It was not for him to judge.

"I should like very much to see Mrs. Dorland," I said. "I am Captain Ethan Saunders, though I do not have a card upon me. No matter, the lady knows me."

The fellow, quite old, with a face cracked like dried tar, stared at me. "Sir?"

"What do you mean, *sir*? What have I said that requires clarification? There is no call for *sir*. Have you no manners, no respect?"

"Sir? I am sorry, sir, but I'm afraid I cannot understand you, sir. Your words are running together somewhat." He licked his lips thoughtfully, as though working hard to determine how best to render his thoughts into speech. "From drink, perhaps?"

I had no time to bother with servants who cannot comprehend spoken English, so I pushed my way past him. He was old and frail, and it required no great effort, though I could not have guessed how easily he would be knocked to the floor. Many times before I had been in the house, so I made my way to the sitting room, where I believed I should find the lady. And there she was. She and seven or eight friends sat about in handsome little chairs displaying themselves to one another, dressed in a stunning array of blues and yellows and pinks, looking like a sampling of exotic birds, like French royalty. They sipped coffee, nibbled upon dainties, and discussed I know not what. I know not because they ceased discussing when I made my entrance, a bit too abruptly, I admit. I lost my footing as I pushed open the door, tripping upon the rug, stumbling forward, catching myself on the sideboard, and, finally, bouncing a bit, righting myself only by grabbing hold of a portrait upon the wall. This came off, having been hung improperly. It fell to the floor, where I believe the frame may have cracked. I, however, remained aright.

The ladies stared at me, their coffee cups suspended in an eerie tableau of fashionable life. Finally, Mrs. Dorland spoke. "Captain Saunders! Lord, why are you here?"

Note she did not ask what had happened. Here I was, looking as though I'd clawed my way out of my own grave, and yet she did not come running, hug me, caress my injuries, ask me how she might be of service. Could she get me anything? Could she put me to bed? Could she call a surgeon? No. She wanted to know why I would interrupt her gathering.

"Susan, my dear, I have been laid low by unfortunate circumstances." I gesticulated like a stage performer and knocked over a vase, though I have excellent reflexes, and so caught it and returned it to its place. "I am afraid, Susan, I am in a bit of a difficult situation. I should be most grateful, Susan, if you might offer me some assistance."

She gazed upon me with disgust. I wish it were not so, but there is no other word.

"Why do you look at me so, Susan? Have we not been friends? Has not our friendship brought me this state? Will you not help me for what has been between us?"

Then she spoke four of the most withering words I have ever heard. "My name is Sarah."

I clapped a hand to my forehead. "Of course. Sarah. It is what I meant. Sarah, things have grown a bit difficult for me. A few dollars would help me smooth over my troubles. You have always been a generous woman. I have need of your generosity now."

I looked at her, my eyes wide and moist, masculine but also childlike in their raw, naked need, but it was all for naught. She only turned away in horror. It began to occur to me that visiting the lady while she had guests was not a sound idea. It may, in fact, have been a poor one. I had hoped to charm her and her friends. I had hoped to have many women offering up coin and sympathy, but I now saw that I had only embarrassed Mrs. Dorland, and she wanted nothing more than that I should leave her be. And not only that lady. The others looked away as well. One held her head down with her hand raised, so that I could see nothing of her face, only her mass of copper-colored hair.

It was a distinctive color, and I began to think at once that I knew it. I took a step closer and stooped a bit to get a look upon the shaded face. "Why, it's Louisa Chase!" I cried. "Lovely Mrs. Chase. I know I can rely upon you for a few dollars. It shall not be missed by so magnanimous a creature as yourself."

Louisa Chase did not raise her eyes. She and I had enjoyed some lovely afternoons together some months before. I had no notion that she and Mrs. Dorland were friends. I had the notion now, and I saw that things had turned out very, very badly.

"I beg you, leave," said Mrs. Dorland.

"I want only fifty dollars," I said. "That is all. A mere fifty. It shall not be lost to you. Come, good woman, a pittance for a patriot, a soldier of the Revolution, a man upon whose back the republic was built."

Her eyes had reddened considerably as I spoke, and now tears were flowing freely down her cheeks. "Get out," she said, "I hate you!"

Knowing when I am unwelcome, I took my exit no better than when I had arrived but surely no worse, and I chose to count that a kind of triumph.

Since the previous night I'd given a great deal of thought to what had happened with Mrs. Pearson. She had summoned me, taking the trouble to travel to my rooms—which meant she must have made an effort to discover where I lived. I had been in Philadelphia only a few months and had never been upon the social scene. I did not believe we had acquaintance in common, unless some ladies I had known were friends of hers. Even so, I never took such companions to my own rooms.

Nevertheless, she had found me, and when I obeyed the summons, she sent me away. She had lied, and done so quite badly. She had wanted me to come, but, once there, she had an even more pressing reason for sending me away.

Now, as I walked along Spruce Street, I contemplated the possible reasons for her behavior. The first was that circumstances had changed. Either she had obtained intelligence of her husband or had reason to believe he and her family were safe. The second was that her disposition had changed. She had either concluded or been convinced that, whatever her concerns, they did not justify renewing an association with a man she once intended to marry but whose companionship was not now appropriate. The third, and the one that had me moving in the direction of her home, was that she had been forced somehow, against her will, to tell me that she wished me to leave: a threat against her husband, herself, or perhaps even her children.

It was that possibility, that and my desire to look upon her face in daylight, and perhaps even a desperate knowledge that I had nowhere else to go and nothing else to do, which brought me once more to the Pearson house. In the light of day it seemed even more luxurious and stately, though the leafless branches and empty gardens gave it a forlorn appearance, dignified but terribly lonely.

I knocked upon the door and was addressed almost at once by the same footman with whom I had dealt the previous night. He appeared neater and better rested, but I supposed I did not look better for the time that had passed. My injuries developed into bruises, and while I might be certain that the light of day would only elevate Mrs. Pearson's loveliness, I knew it served to make my own appearance even more dreadful—beaten, rumpled, and tattered. Given that my clothes bore the odors of my recent adventures, I must have seemed no better than a vagabond, a pitiful unfortunate, and though this footman and I had locked horns not a day earlier, he at first had no notion of who I was.

"Beggars are dealt with at the servants' entrance," he intoned.

"And I'm sure they are grateful," I answered. "I, however, am Captain Ethan Saunders and would like to speak with Mrs. Pearson."

He studied me again, attempting to contain the disgust so visible upon his face. Yet the typical sneering so common among footmen when confronted with those beneath their masters' station was not evident. Indeed, he took a step forward and spoke in a low if sympathetic voice. "Sir, I believe the lady herself asked you to go and not return."

"She did, but I doubt she meant it. Please tell her I am here."

"She will not see you."

"But you'll tell her?"

He nodded but did not invite me in. Instead he closed the door, and I remained upon the front porch, cold in my insufficient coat. Light snow fell upon me, and I watched as gentlemen and ladies traveled along Spruce, glancing up at my vigil with dismay.

In a moment, the man returned, his expression neutral. "Mrs. Pearson will not see you."

I could not argue this point with him. If I was refused, nothing I could say would alter his mind, and unless I was prepared to force my way inside, which I was not, that would be the end of it. "You seem like an honest man," I said. "Is there something you would tell me?"

He opened his mouth as if to speak but then shook his head. "No. You must go."

"Very well, but if you—"

This little speech was interrupted, for he reached out and pushed against my coat. "I said go!" he cried, rather more loudly than necessary. "Leave, and return no more!"

I turned away, slouching in a performance of shame, feeling the stares of passersby upon me. On the surface, I should have been dispirited by these events, which might now appear as one more disappointment and humiliation in a string of such since the previous night. That was on the surface. Look beneath and you may find several things that surprise you, such as a footman with more cleverness and dexterity than that for which perhaps you gave him credit. You may also find a piece of paper, cleverly secreted inside the coat of Captain Ethan Saunders, a piece of paper from the lovely and once-beloved Cynthia Pearson.

Though I may have been eager to tear open this piece of paper, I knew better than to do so. If the footman had taken the trouble to disguise the delivery of the note, it suggested he believed the house was under scrutiny. The streets were populous enough that there might have been someone following me at that very moment. I knew I had to read the note at once, but I had to find a way to do so without betraying its existence.

I crossed the street and turned to look at the house. On the second floor, a curtain was parted, and there stood the lovely Mrs. Pearson, her children by her side, looking out at me. Our eyes met, and she did not look away. We looked upon one another for half a minute, perhaps longer, and in that time I saw her as the woman I had loved, fully and entirely, and I saw in her too her father's face, proud and wise. Then the curtain closed, eclipsing an expression unspeakably sad.

She had her father's bearing and dignity and earnestness, and it was for his sake as well as hers that I would do what I must. He had been the most resourceful and clever man I'd ever known; I cannot say what would have become of me if it hadn't been for Fleet. For good or ill, he'd made me what I was. I'd grown up in Westchester, New York, the son of a successful tavern keeper who died five years before the Declaration. My mother's second husband was of a staunchly Royalist bent, and politics proved a useful means of separating me forever from my inheritance. I had graduated from the College of New Jersey at Princeton, and once the war began, my education was sufficient reason to grant me the rank of lieutenant when I enlisted in the cause. Yale and Harvard men generally became captains.

I made a poor officer, however, and often incurred the anger of my superiors for disorderly behavior—and once for slipping behind the lines to occupied New York to learn if a favorite whore had survived the famous fire that nearly destroyed the city. It was suggested to me by the captain of my regiment that it might be in everyone's best interest if I simply ran away from the service, but I had enlisted, and no amount of regimental displeasure would make me break my word.

Then, one afternoon when we were encamped on Harlem Heights, Captain Richard Fleet came to see me. Tall and slender, white-haired, serious, yet with an unmistakable look of mischief in his eyes, he was unlike anyone I had ever known. He was one of those men whom others instantly like, and as determined as I was not to fall under his spell, it took no more than a quarter of an hour before I thought of him as a trusted friend. We sat in a tent while he poured us wine and said he had heard I found some difficulty in settling into the life of a soldier, but General Washington needed men with skills such as I possessed.

What skills were they? I wished to know. Why, I was told, my ability to lie and smoke out a liar. My ability to slip across enemy lines and then back across our own, all without detection. My ability to ingratiate myself with women, with strangers, with men who thought, only a moment before, they found me most detestable. In short, I was a man like Fleet himself, and General Washington wanted me. He wished to make me, the son of a Westchester landowner, into a *spy*.

I was young and brash and proud of my honor and was not eager to adopt a way of life scorned by gentlemen as disreputable, but Fleet was persuasive. He convinced me that I could not be but who I was, so I might as well be that in the service of my country. Yes, he said, spies have long been despised by gentlemen, but was this war not proof that the world was changing, and who could not say that in its aftermath spies would not be embraced as heroes? The first step, he said, was for us to see ourselves as such.

It was all as he had said. We became heroes, up until the time we were disgraced, up until the time Hamilton had broadcast that disgrace. That man had ruined my life and essentially killed Fleet. And now here was Fleet's daughter, afraid and desperate. I felt the note that had been slipped to me and swore an oath to myself too primal, too raw, to find form in words.

I walked north to Walnut Street and turned west, moving through increasingly thick crowds of people: men of business, men of trade, women about their household duties and less savory business as well. Carts moved this way and that, hardly knowing how to get past one another and the pedestrians and the animals that crowded the street. In such chaos, I might perhaps have risked taking out my letter and reading it, but I did not do so. I dared not look back to demonstrate that I searched for someone upon my trail, but I felt him there.

Once I reached Fifth Street, I turned north and walked quickly up the stairs and through the front door of the Library Company building, directly across from the Statehouse. It was a new building, envisioned by an amateur architect who had won a design contest, and it was a glorious thing to behold. The massive redbrick structure boasted two stories, columns, and, above the front door, a statue of the late Benjamin Franklin, the library's founder, in classical garb.

Inside, all was marble and winding staircase and books. Books upon books upon books lined the walls, for the Library Company, though a private organization, had become the official library of the Congress and so considered it its business to acquire virtually everything. Once through the doors I was struck by its stately appearance. In the lobby a half dozen or so men, all of whom were finely dressed, turned to look at my unpleasant intrusion upon their cerebral seclusion.

I had not long, and I hoped it was not a lengthy message or I should run out of time. I turned to the gentlemen staring and said, "Yes, I know I am too unseemly to be here. I do not wish to stay. Give me but one minute."

So saying, I took from my pocket the note and broke the still-soft wax seal. Inside, in a hasty hand, I found the following:

Captain Saunders,
I am sorry to have sent you away last night, but I had no choice. My house and my person are watched, which is why I could not see you. It has not long been so, and I can only wish you had responded to one of my earlier notes, but there is no helping that now. The die is cast. You must not come again or attempt to contact me. I do not know who they are or what they are or what they want, but they are very dangerous. My husband is missing and I believe in danger, and that danger may extend to me and my children. I wish I could tell you more, but I know nothing other than that it has something to do with Hamilton and his bank. I beg of you to help me. Find my husband and discover the danger to which he has exposed himself and his family.

I have no right to ask this of you, but I know of no one else, and if I did, I would still want you, for I know of no one better. For the sake of the memory of my father, please help me.

Yours &c,
Cynthia Pearson

Nothing could have been more shocking. Jacob Pearson missing, and Mrs. Pearson herself in danger, her house watched? A connection to Hamilton and the Bank of the United States. Most troubling of all, however, was the fact that she had sent me notes previously. I had not received any, which meant someone had intercepted them. I could not contact her again, that much was clear, for I would not expose her to more danger, not for the world, and yet I must help her. I knew not how to do it, but I must.

I crossed Fifth until I reached the grounds behind the Pennsylvania Statehouse, across Walnut Street from the jail and, perhaps more ominous for me, the debtor's prison. The Statehouse offered handsome gardens, full of trees, even if they were devoid of life in the heart of winter. With no better thing to do, I brushed snow off one of the benches and sat alone in the growing gloom, the cold jabbing its sharp needles into the armor of my tattered clothes and the dimming warmth of drink. The park was near empty, but not entirely. Here there was a small group of boys playing with a lopsided leather ball that made an unappealing wet noise whenever it struck the ground. There an old man watched his trio of dogs folic. Closer to the Statehouse, only yards away from the courtyard where this nation declared its liberty, a young man attempted to obtain the liberty of a young lady's petticoats. Behind me, on Walnut Street, a steady stream of pedestrians and carriages passed. I was tired, and despite the cold, I thought I might fall asleep.

"Captain Saunders. A moment, if you please, sir."

I opened my eyes and saw before me a tall man with long reddish mustaches and a wide-brimmed hat that sat high enough upon his crown to reveal his apparent baldness. He spoke with the thick brogue of an Irishman, and was—I guessed from the lines upon his face—perhaps fifty years of age, but a rugged fifty. He had the look of a man used to hard labor, physically imposing but not menacing.

"Do I know you?" I asked.

"We have not yet met," answered the Irishman. "But I've a feeling we're to become excellent friends. May I sit?" He gestured toward the bench.

I nodded and moved to give him more room, but I was on my guard and already thinking through my options.

He removed the rest of the snow, sat next to me, and reached into his beaver coat. "I am told that you are a man who enjoys whiskey." From the coat came a corked bottle, which he handed to me. "It is the best produced upon the Monongahela."

I pulled out the cork and sampled the contents. It was, indeed, quite good. It had a depth of flavors I had not known before in the drink, a kind of sweetness I found surprising and pleasing. It hit my empty gut hard, though, and a warm feeling built there to near hotness. I bent over hard, holding out the bottle so as not to spill it.

"Too strong for you, lad?" the Irishman asked.

I shook my head, once I'd sat upright again. "'Tis a mite powerful, but that's not it. The stomach is a bit queer these days."

"Powerful or no, I can see by your face that you enjoy it."

"It's good stuff, quite unlike any I've had before." I took another drink, bending over only slightly this time. "Now, tell me who you are and what you know of me."

"I am an admirer," he said. "I have heard of your acts during the war."

My guard was up. "Those who have heard of me are generally not admirers."

"I, for one, do not believe the charges leveled against you. I know the taint of falseness when I hear it, and I know a patriot when I see one. You see, I fought in the war myself, sir, serving under Colonel Daniel Morgan."

I was now interested. "You were at Saratoga?"

He grinned. "I was, lad. In the thick of it, with Morgan's riflemen. Have no doubt of it."

"I congratulate you, then. And I think, as one soldier to another, you perhaps can tell me what you wish of me."

"I know you have come upon hard times. I believe I can help you."

"And how can you do that?"

"You require money."

I looked at the Irishman. He had a ready grin and the sort of face that most men would find easy to trust, but I was on my guard. "You want to give me money? For what?"

"You are concerned about Mr. Pearson, though I know he is no friend of yours. Mrs. Pearson may be another matter, and perhaps for her sake you would search for her husband. I want you to understand that he is in no danger. None of them are. We only wish for you to no longer trouble yourself with Mr. Pearson's whereabouts. If you do that, you shall find many of your own difficulties will be gone. They will vanish like smoke. Mr. Pearson is in no danger, but it is vital that you not pursue him."

"You convinced Mrs. Pearson that I ought not to pursue him," I said.

"She understands what is at stake."

"And what is at stake?"

"The future of republican virtue," he said. "Nothing less, sir, nothing less. Do you want to stand with the virtues of the Revolution, or do you submit to Hamiltonian greed?"

"I am no Hamiltonian," I said, not failing to note the significance of his name appearing in this conversation.

"I thought as much," he answered. "I can tell you little, but there will have to be trust between us, as we are both brothers of the Revolution and patriots."

"Mrs. Pearson is concerned for her husband, and perhaps even for her own safety. You would need to convince me that her family is in no danger."

"I promise you, he is unharmed. They are in no danger from us."

"And yet you watch her, threaten her."

"Never," he said. "We would do no such thing."

"And you have seen fit to have me cast from my own home."

He shook his head. "I have heard of that but, again, it is not our doing. You have enemies unconnected to us, Captain Saunders; you would be better served cultivating friends. Think on it. Why should we harm Mr. Pearson? We do not seek to harm you, only to aid you in your current embarrassment. Were we villains, were we interested in doing violence to those who oppose us, we could simply kill you."

"I'm hard to kill," I said.

He laughed. "No one is any harder to kill than anyone else, and that's the truth."

I knew otherwise but saw no point in saying so, not when I might offer a demonstration. I took a deep drink of the whiskey and then doubled over once more, coughing and gagging. From the corner of my eye,

I could see the Irishman looking away politely, pretending to watch a pair of antic squirrels rather than listening to the prolonged sounds of my retching.

At last I sat up and wiped my mouth with the back of my hand and took another drink of whiskey. This time, I remained upright.

"You see?" I said to him. "Hard to kill."

He took from his pockets a piece of paper sealed with wax. "You need only trouble yourself with these matters no longer. Fifty dollars in notes to do nothing. A good bargain."

I held out my hand, and he gave me the paper, which felt warm in my ungloved hand. "Suppose I take the notes and continue to look for Pearson?"

"You do not want to do that, Captain."

"Oh?"

"We are not people to cross."

I put the notes into my coat pocket. Why should I not? I was not a person to cross either.

"I do not fear you, Irishman, and I believe you have erred significantly. The lady is frightened, for her husband and for her children, and I believe she is frightened of you. I shall find out who you are and what you've done with Pearson, and put an end to whatever you plan."

The Irishman folded his hands together, and a ghost of a smirk appeared under his orange whiskers. He was very confident, that one. "You'll do all that, will you? Have another drink, lad. Vomit once more upon the ground. That's what you're good for now, and not much else. You won't help your lady friend by pretending to be what you were before you became a ruin of a man. Now, if you've no mind to behave sensibly, agree to my terms or return to me my notes."

"And what shall happen if I don't choose to?"

He grinned again, showing me a mouth full of even brown teeth. "Look across the street, upon the roof of the prison, near the cupola. There is a sharpshooter, another of Daniel Morgan's men, so you know what that means. You're in his sights, and if I give the signal, or if he thinks me in trouble, you'll be heading home tonight without your head. If you had a home to go to, I should say."

I looked over my shoulder and saw, upon the prison roof, the unmistakable flash of sunlight against metal. I estimated the distance at near 150 yards. If the rifleman was good enough to have served with Daniel Morgan, I doubted not he could make the shot.

Only the day before, I had surrendered; I had regarded death as a thing of no consequence. Now I wished to live, and I was fully alive. These men, whoever they were, with their schemes and bribes and intrigues and efforts to buy my loyalty—and, most insidiously, their willingness to underestimate me—had awakened a slumbering dragon, who would now unfurl to show his might.

I turned away from the prison building. "You think me an idiot, Irishman. Whoever you are, whatever you do, you crave secrecy. That is why you do not wish me to seek out Pearson. Go ahead. Signal your man that he must kill me over fifty dollars. You see I do not move."

His face darkened. "You've made a mistake. There are more of us than you suspect, and we are in places you would not credit. We are determined, and we cannot be defeated."

"Then you will have to know triumph with fifty fewer dollars." I rose from the bench and strode away. Alas, for form's sake I could not watch what happened next, though I heard it clear enough. The Irishman pushed to his feet and attempted to pursue me, but he took only half a step before something suddenly jarred him, shortened his step. A moment of disorientation, in which he could not account for all that happened, and then his falling upon his face. I heard the satisfying thump of aging Irishman upon snowy earth.

It had been but a little thing to pretend to vomit while encircling my piece of twine around his ankles. It would not keep him entangled for long, but it would be enough.

I now looked back to see him force himself up and back to the bench that he might examine my little trick. His hat had fallen off, and I saw he was indeed hairless, his skull like a tanned and leathery egg. He dusted the snow off said hat and replaced it. It did not afford him the dignity he had hoped.

"I believe you're the one who has made the mistake, Irishman," I said. "I fear neither pain nor death. The only thing in the world I feared this morning was that I should not be able to find thirty dollars anywhere in this world." I took out from my coat the gathering of notes and held it up. I waved it at him. I mocked him with it. "Now I have twenty dollars to spare. So get gone under cover of your sharpshooter, I care not. I'll find Pearson and then I'll find you."

I actually did not get to the end of that sentence, for at some point around *I'll find Pearson* a third party crashed into my back, knocking me to the ground so that I struck my head. Once I was down, the Irishman cut himself free while his friend pulled the banknotes from my hand, and the two men ran off, leaving me down in the snow, cold and despondent, happy only that he had left me his very good bottle of whiskey.

Joan Maycott

Spring 1789

We were told that we must limit our belongings to necessities. The roads, they said, were not serviceable for wagons or carts, and all we needed would be provided for us once we arrived at Libertytown. We sold nearly everything, taking a few clothes, Andrew's tools, and some favored items, including some books—though not so many as I would have liked.

We convened in Philadelphia, where we were to be guided by Mr. Reynolds and two others, who sat astride old horses, tattered and slow, with rheumy eyes and puffy red sores that jutted out through their hair like rocks at low tide. There were mules to bear our packs, and we traveled at their sluggish pace on dirt paths sometimes wide and clear, sometimes little more than a hint of an opening in the forest, sometimes so soft and marshy the animals had to be aided to keep from stumbling. In the worst places, logs had been set down to make the road passable. On the steep paths through the Alleghenies, the beasts were often in danger of falling over entirely.

There were twenty of us, excluding our guides. Reynolds wore somewhat rougher clothes than those in which we had first seen him. These were undyed homespun, and a wide-brimmed straw hat that he kept pulled down low. In our parlor, Reynolds had seemed a kind of rusticated country gentleman, the sort of rude clay that the American experiment had molded into republican respectability. Now he was revealed as something far less amiable. He showed no friendly familiarity toward us and acted as though he did not recall our previous meeting. Andrew's efforts to converse with him were met with rude barks, and at times I found him staring at me with cold predatory intensity. The scar across his eye, which I had taken as proof of his revolutionary duty, now appeared to me more the mark of Cain.

Of the other two, Hendry was of some forty years, slender of form, high-pitched of voice, with a long nose, narrow eyes, thin lips, and a face that appeared designed for spectacles, though he did not wear them. In attire, Reynolds cut the form of a hardened country farmer, but Hendry seemed a parody of a stage-play country rustic. Yet I was to learn that this was the true garb of the border man: a raccoon hat and buckskin leggings and an upper garment called a hunting shirt, a fringed tunic made of doeskin that came down to his thighs. On some men, these clothes would look manly, even heroic. On Hendry, with his foxlike face, they looked absurd.

In New York or Philadelphia, he might have, with different clothes, passed for a poor scholar. In the wilderness, he looked to me nothing but a cunning low creature, cruel and heartless, and more foul-smelling than any other species of man. Like the majority of the tribe of the West, he either did not approve, or had not yet been made aware, of the functions of the razor, but his miserly face yielded only a scraggly outcropping of pale whiskers here and there. Clearly visible under this sparse growth was a most lamentable skin condition, cursing him with a reddened and scabby appearance. It must have caused him considerable discomfort, for he scratched at himself almost incessantly, sometimes with absent interest, other times with the repetitive fury of a cat with an itchy ear.

The third of their number, Phineas, was but a boy, or what should have been called a boy in more civilized climes—fifteen or sixteen, by my reckoning, with fair hair and sunburned skin and a narrow blade-shaped face. He dressed in frontier clothes, but his gaunt frame left him aswim in his hunting shirt, which came down so low on him as to be almost a gown.

Phineas took to me at once. Perhaps he saw me as a kind of mother, or perhaps he merely noted that I looked at him with compassion. He would often ride alongside me a portion of each day, and if he did not speak, he took some pleasure in the companionable silence. At meal-times he made certain that I enjoyed a superior portion, and he often reserved the softest and most secure spot for me. He looked at Andrew with indifference but not hostility. For Phineas, it was as though Andrew did not exist.

Of the settlers, eleven were Americans, the rest were French. Andrew had learned serviceable French during the war and so was able to discover that these people had sailed all the way from Paris, lured by agents of William Duer into settling the lands of western Pennsylvania. These French pilgrims gave us our first true cause to wonder about Mr. Reynolds's veracity. He had told us that all the inhabitants of Liberty-town were veterans. Who then were these Frenchmen? He had told us that crops they grew on their fertile lands had made them comfortable, but whence came the money? If there were no roads that could support cart or wagon, how were the crops brought to market? They could not be sent east without spoiling; they could not be sent west, for the Spanish did not permit American traffic upon the Mississippi.

For the first few days of our journey, Reynolds listened to our questions, though he would not answer but only grunt or shrug or shake his head. When we were a week or more out, he began to exhibit signs that this reticence was, for him, the height of patience and manners. When I asked him about the means of transporting goods, he looked at Andrew and spat. "Does that bitch ever shut up?"

Andrew, who had been walking alongside me, only a few feet from Reynolds's horse, rose to his full height. "Sir, step down and say that to my face."

The boy, Phineas, turned away, but Hendry let out a shrill laugh, shockingly like a tiny dog's bark.

"You ain't challenging me, Maycott," Reynolds said. "You live and die as I please, so keep your mouth shut, and that goes twice for that woman of yours. She's pretty enough, but, by God, does she ever stop talking?"

"Sir!" called out my husband in his most commanding voice. I had no doubt that, during the war, such a tone would have made even the highest-ranked officer stop in his tracks, but here it meant nothing. As he called out, Hendry rode astride and kicked Andrew hard in the back, just below his neck. He lurched forward and fell into the dirt.

Hendry let out another burst of shrill laughter, and a horse whinnied, and then all fell silent. The horses had stopped, the mules held still, the settlers milled in place. I knelt by Andrew, making certain he was unharmed, and heard nothing about me but the endless singing of birds. Once I had found it melodic, but suddenly it became cacophonous, the unnerving music of chaos, the orchestra of Hell. Andrew looked up at me. His cheek bled from a cut of some three inches below his left eye, but it was not deep and would heal well enough. The wound to his pride was another thing. I met his gaze and shook my head. Honor demanded that he not let this pass, but I demanded he did. He could not hope to defeat these men, and even if he did, then what? We were at their mercy for another month or more of hard travel. The luxuries of pride and reputation were no longer for us.

"Listen to me," cried Reynolds. He held up his rifle by the barrel, pointed to the sky, like a brutal general rallying his barbarian troops. In his rage, the scar across his eye had turned as pink as the inside flesh of a strawberry. "This ain't the East. You've left the lands of manners and justice. There ain't no law here but force, and while you're in this traveling party, that law is mine. If I choose to call your woman a whore, then a whore she is until I say otherwise."

He unlocked the catch upon his rifle's flintlock and pointed it at Andrew. Then he swiveled around and pointed it at one of the French settlers. "I don't care who among you lives or dies," he said. "It ain't my trouble to care. I'll kill one of these Frenchers to make my point unless you"—here he glanced at Andrew—"get on your feet and start walking and keep from looking at me for the next few days. Maybe until we get to Pittsburgh. So up with ye and keep your tongue still."

How can a man be made to endure such a humiliation? I did not think Andrew could have been made to bury his pride and his rage to save himself, but he did it to save the stranger. He pushed himself to his feet, and, keeping his eyes straight ahead, he began to walk. In so doing, the entire procession began to move. I put my arm about Andrew, but he did not respond. I do not know that he could have made himself speak.

Reynolds returned the catch on his rifle and lowered it. Hendry rode alongside us and laughed softly, as though he recalled a joke from a long time past. Then he scratched at the rash under his beard. "Next time you forget yourself, Maycott, you'll be sorry for it. Reynolds might like to kill Frenchers, but I think I'll fuck your wife instead."

He did not wait for an answer but rode ahead, leaving us to our silence and to watch Phineas glower at Hendry for the rest of the day.

The weather, at least, was fair. We made our trek in the first full bloom of spring, and the sun, wreathed with unthreatening wisps of cottony clouds, was warm but not hot. At night, the cool was refreshing rather than uncomfortable, and mosquitoes were not out in full abundance. At times it rained, but a little wetness did us no harm, and it did not persist long enough to make the roads, such as they were, unbearably muddy.

Far more distressing was the tense disposition of our guides, who clutched their rifles perpetually, keeping them taut and ready like the muscles of a crouching beast. Ceaselessly they scanned the tree line for signs of danger, though they never spoke of what form it might take—bears, panthers, Indians? One of the Frenchmen attempted to inquire of Hendry, but he only told him to shut his Frencher mouth.

One day followed another with blunting drudgery, and though the memory of Andrew's conflict with the guides lingered, the wound grew less hot. Reynolds or Hendry would, from time to time, make some trivial comment to Andrew, perhaps to make him feel that all had been forgotten.

Three weeks in, we had begun to make camp for the night in a grassy clearing. We sat huddled by a small fire that danced in a strong breeze and ate what the guides had hunted during the day—a medley of rabbit, squirrel, and pigeon—and a porridge made of cornmeal. We rarely spoke to the other settlers, and Andrew and I, who had so often passed count-less days and night in easy conversation, now spoke to each other with increasing infrequency.

While we ate I looked up and observed emerging from the trees an Indian woman and a little girl. The guides raised their weapons, and I believe Hendry would have shot them as they approached, but Reynolds stayed his hand. He bared his teeth like an animal. "Don't be an idiot," he said, and Hendry lowered his weapon, grinned a largely toothless grin, and spat tobacco onto the dirt, near a Frenchman, his wife, and their little boy.

The Indians approached tentatively. The woman walked with a limp. She wore a ruined dress of animal skins, perhaps once quite pretty but now soiled and torn and, as we found when she approached, rank to the nose. The girl, not above ten or eleven, wore a cotton shift, formerly white, now the color of all things unclean. She had been the victim of a burn; her face was scorched, and she was missing her entire right eye-brow, there being only a horrific red welt.

The woman might once have been a regal squaw, but circumstances had brought her low. Her face was filthy, smeared with mud and hard-ened, I had no doubt, by much violence, for her lower lip was split, as if by a fist. It took little imagination to see that these poor wanderers had walked through chaos and might yet trail it behind them. Andrew must have felt it too, because he took my hand and held it in a firm grip.

Once the Indians were no more than ten feet from our little camp, the woman moved her hand to her mouth, making signs of eating. She had, I observed, lost several fingernails, and a fresh cut on her thumb bled freely.

Though we could have spared enough for a meal, charity would no more occur to Reynolds than would sprouting wings and taking to flight. He waved his weapon at the poor creatures. "Git on," he said.

"We cannot let them run off those unfortunates," Andrew said.

I felt my stomach lurch. Andrew was anxious to restore his honor, if only in his own eyes, and I knew he could not remain still while these refugees were sent away. Yet I knew full well that he could not challenge our guides on this matter. There was nothing he might say to persuade them, and he would only make them more determined to be cruel.

"They know their business," I said, hoping for the best. "We know nothing of Indians."

He would not be moved. "We know of human beings, and these are in want."

He began to rise, but before he could do so, I pushed hard upon his shoulder, forcing him down and rising myself. Andrew had no time to object before I was several paces away and had begun talking to Reynolds. "Perhaps we can be charitable and spare some food."

Hendry laughed his unpleasant laugh. The veins in his neck began to bulge.

I did not let my attention waver from Reynolds. "It is the Christian thing."

"They ain't Christians," said Reynolds. "They'll repay your kindness with blood."

The boy Phineas nodded his young head, showed his teeth, and made a trigger-pulling gesture with his finger. His stringy hair fell into his eyes, and he did nothing to brush it aside.

"Even that burnt girl'll kill us if she gets a chance," Reynolds said, "'Tis what they do."

"How can you be certain they are not Christianized?" I said.

Both men laughed the way adults laugh at the whimsical wonderings of children. Phineas looked down, as though the notion somehow embarrassed him.

The woman pointed at her neck, and then made the eating gesture once more. I saw now that she wore a necklace, an elaborate and filigreed carving of bones in the shape of a beautiful starburst. She said something, which sounded not to me like the language of savages. I realized only once Andrew had cocked his head that she was speaking in a kind of broken French, yet I required no translation to understand.

"She will trade her jewelry for food," I said. "I doubt she has anything else of value."

"I think she's got sommit else," Hendry said. "Sommit I'd trade for."

"Shut up," said Phineas, surprising everyone.

"What, you don't want that nice jewelry?" he said to the boy.

"Shut up," said Phineas. "Just shoot 'em. That's all."

"I'd rather wait till they do something I don't care for and then shoot 'em," said Hendry. "But I might take that pretty thing she's got round her neck."

"Surely," I said, "you are not so base as to let her give up the only thing she has in the world for a few morsels—not when we can spare the food."

"Maycott!" Reynolds shouted. "Sit your woman down. She's come off her leash again."

I would not give Andrew a chance to respond, for any response would almost certainly be incendiary. "They may be savages but we are Christians. We shall feed them, and if you don't like it, you may certainly shoot us."

Andrew blanched, and I knew what he feared: that he would be humiliated once more and then be given no recourse to preserve his honor. Yet Reynolds seemed untroubled by my speech. He picked up a rabbit bone and stripped it of its boiled meat. Then, after due consideration, this Solon of the West nodded his head, his ruminations complete. "Green idiots," he pronounced. "Let 'em stay, then, but 'tis on yer head."

I gestured for the two to sit. We understood they were not to be given their own food and that Andrew and I would have to give of our own portions. Some of the others did as well, but many of the settlers steered clear, not wanting to stand with us against Reynolds. The Indians sat by our fire, hunched over the food we'd given them, eyes darting about like wary animals. They ate with their hands, smearing dirt and blood on their food. The woman was missing two fingers on her left hand, and the wound looked recent and raw.

I had thought Phineas a sensitive boy, but he watched the two Indians from the outskirts of camp, hands on his gun, never taking his eyes off them, waiting for some menace that never manifested itself.

Andrew tried to make conversation with them, but the woman said nothing more and the child, if she could speak—our language or her own—never showed a sign of it. They ate their pigeon—it was what he liked best, so of course it was what Andrew had volunteered to first give—and corn pudding, and when they were done they moved some fifty feet from the rest of us, curled up upon the ground, and went to sleep without delay. Andrew said nothing to me of what I had done for the Indians—and for him—but when we went to sleep he wrapped his arms about me, I about him, and we slept together as lovers in a way we had not since leaving for the West.

I awoke in the night to the sound of two gun reports in rapid succession. It was distant, but I knew the sound. I sat and looked about me. The fire burned and no one was disturbed. I convinced myself that I had dreamed it, but in the morning I knew better. The Indian woman and child were gone when I opened my eyes. Reynolds and Hendry acted as though nothing had happened and offered no comment, but Hendry, I saw, wore the elaborate bone ornament around his own neck.

He leered at me, evil delight in his narrow eyes. "The boy done it. Woke 'em up, dragged 'em off, and done it. Like Reynolds told yer, 'tis on yer head." He walked away, laughing as though it were the greatest joke in the world.

Andrew and I chose not to speak of the incident. Instead, I rode by Phineas. The suggestion that he might have shot those Indians in cold blood terrified me, but it fascinated me too. What, I wondered, would drive a boy to so unspeakable a crime?

"They say you hurt the visitors," I said, after a period of quiet. I had already observed that, in the West, conversations often began with a respectful period of silence.

"I ain't going to speak of it."

"You may speak of it to me," I said, hoping my face showed warmth I did not feel.

Phineas said nothing for some time, and I thought better than to repeat my inquiries. Yet he surprised me by finally breaking his silence, perhaps an hour after I had first raised the subject. In a flat and lifeless tone, like an oracle whose mouth is but the instrument of a remote spirit, he told me he had lived, since the age of seven or eight, in a settlement some twenty miles from Pittsburgh, the great metropolis of western Pennsylvania as Mr. Duer described it. "Hain't no Philadelphia," Phineas told me, "but 'tis big. Biggest place I ever saw afore I come east. Maybe a full thousand people there." He and his father traveled to Pittsburgh five or six times a year, and Phineas had grown up knowing how to read the ground, the leaves, the sky. He was a tracker, as I saw every day we were on the road with him. He tasted the earth and sniffed the air, as much beast as human being, as much Indian as white man.

One day he traveled the road not only with his father but with his mother, little brother, and older sister as well. Both his mother and little brother were ill—feverish and vomiting—and were in need of a physician. The only one in hundreds of miles was to be found in Pittsburgh, or so they thought, but when they came to town, they discovered that he had been killed three weeks earlier in an argument over the best way to dress a roast duck.

They had no money to remain in town, not even for a single night, and so with an ailing woman and child, they returned to the woods to make their way back to their cabin. They were not a mile and a half outside of Pittsburgh, however, when they were set upon by a trio of Indian braves. It was late autumn, but it had grown warm in what is called Indian summer, for it is the season when Indians go on the warpath one last time before spring. Accordingly, these men were near naked, their heads shorn and shaved into savage designs, their faces and bodies covered with demonic symbols that made them seem creatures of Hell. Indeed they must have been, for they paused hardly a moment before one slit Phineas's father's throat. That atrocity was hardly complete before a brave held Phineas's mother so she would be made to watch, then another picked up her younger son by his foot, twirled the toddler about over his head, and dashed his skull into a tree. Only then did they do her the mercy of slitting her throat.

One brave grabbed Phineas, the other took hold of his sister, each man clamping a hand over the mouth of his prisoner. At this time Phineas was but nine years of age, his sister eleven. They had witnessed the death of their parents and of their sibling, and they were not permitted to cry out in grief and terror. While one of the Indians held his sister, the other began to cut off her clothes with a fierce knife, long and twisting and gleaming in the flicker of sunlight. The one that held Phineas, entranced by this orgy of violence, let slacken his grip upon his prey, and Phineas managed to stomp hard upon the brave's moccasined foot. It was too futile a blow to do serious damage to so strong a creature, but it was sufficient to loosen his grip. Phineas was free, and he fled into the woods, leaving behind the bodies of his parents and his brother, and consigning his sister into the hands of monsters, where she most likely remains today, presuming she was not burned alive, as is sometimes the custom.

He made his way back to Pittsburgh, where he told his story, and men ran out into the forest armed with guns and hatred of the Indians. The idea that Indians might be human beings with souls, capable of good as well as evil, is disregarded as romantical rubbish. Every evil the white men have done the Indians is forgotten, but every crime against the white men by Indians is branded into their souls. These men hate Indians with a passion hardly to be understood if not felt, and no opportunity for taking an Indian's life must be neglected. Phineas's story was the sort of thing that unleashed their most feral passions. They muttered curses, blaming not only the savages but also the men back east who would spare no money for the protection of the West. They had no choice, they said, but to take matters into their own hands.

In the woods, they found nothing, not even the bodies, but their blood was up, and they could not let the incident pass. Instead of killing the fiends who had committed these crimes, they marched back toward town with Phineas in tow, to a small cabin just outside the city full of Christianized Indians—seven in all, including two small children of their own. The Indians did not resist. They had no weapons to fight with, but the men barricaded them inside their home and set it afire. As the flames rose, Phineas could hear their voices rising in song, calling upon the Lord to carry them home.

Phineas told me this story without inflection or emotion. It was as empty and hollow as an old legend, one from a stranger's childhood, without connection to his own experiences. When he finished, he turned away from me. At first I thought it was shame, but I soon decided it was something far more visceral. The story had been like phlegm that lodges in the lungs. It must be expectorated and, once gone, is thought of no more.

After a long silence I said, "Did you kill those Indians last night?"

He did not look at me. "I ain't never going to let an Indian live if it's in my powers to kill it. I aim to be a great Indian killer, like Lou Wetzel. You ever hear of him? He's killed more Indians than any man in the West."

"Is that truly what you wish?" I asked, not knowing what else to say.

"Wishing don't signify. 'Tis what I am. Now you know what I done you won't be my friend no more, but there's no helping it. Not now. You'll see, though. The West changes you. It don't let you be a Christian. I'm what the West made me, and you'll be what it makes you."

It was now near the end of the day's travel, and soon he was occupied in the business of making camp. I left the poor boy and made my way back to Andrew, who asked nothing of what Phineas had told me, and I told him nothing. I told him nothing because I sat there lamenting the horror that was now our lives. We had traded what little we had in exchange for a passage to Hell, and I could not end the question that repeated itself in my own mind: *What have I done?* I would not have Andrew asking the question of himself.

As for Phineas, he was never again kind to me. In truth, he grew hostile, even predatory. He had regarded me before as a mother; now he joined with the other men in gazing at my body with hungry interest. He glared at me if I walked too slowly. If I stumbled, he pointed and laughed. I grew fearful of him and kept my distance. The men were fiends and I could hate them, but his youth made Phineas's hardness far more frightening.

Ten days later, days filled with tension and fear but no further incidents, we arrived in Pittsburgh, though only with the greatest of difficulty. We could not simply stroll into town, the way being made near impassable by great mountains of coal. Instead, for the last few miles, we were piled, beasts and all, upon a great flatboat that made its way down the Monongahela, propelled by burly men, muscled and bearded, mostly shirtless, who thrust great poles into the riverbed to force the lumbering conveyance forward.

The landscape was both rugged and beautiful, certainly sublime in its untamed majesty of undulating hills and thick forest. The city itself was another matter. Even before our flatboat docked, I could see that to call Pittsburgh a town would be like giving the name of feast to a moldy crust and a sliver of hard cheese rind. It was but a muddy clearing with the most uneven and haphazard log cabins, all stained with coal dust. There were no roads to speak of, but mud passageways that were, to the credit of the city founders, arranged with a Quaker regularity. The people looked more savage than civilized. The better sort wore rough homespun in cuts that were a mockery of fashions some five years past, though I looked with relief upon even the most outdated satin petticoat or laced waistcoat. Otherwise it was naught but buckskins and hunting shirts for the men, rough burlap gowns for the women. The men were all bearded and rugged, and a disproportionate number were missing an eye. The women, for their part, were often misshapen and hunched, with faces ravaged by weather, hands clenched and arthritic like demonic claws. It was the rare citizen who possessed even half his teeth, and all the people, like the buildings, were black with coal dust.

We trudged through the muddy streets of Pittsburgh, looking at the ramshackle houses in stunned silence, growing more filthy with each step. This, we knew, was going to be our dream from now on. This dirty, muddy grid of rude shacks would come to seem to us, as weeks turned into months and months to years, as a glorious metropolis. How long until this decrepitude came to seem like the glories of New York? How long until we lulled ourselves to sleep with the fanciful notion of what we would do once we arrived in this city of delights?

Duer had arranged for us to lodge separately with different residents of the city for the night. In the morning we were to be led to our plots of land. Andrew and I were given a space on the floor—naught but dirt packed hard and smooth—of a miserable cabin, somewhat larger than most others but cramped and cold and smelling like a tannery. This room, which seemed to me little better than a ranger's tent, was shared by a couple with three children, and, indeed, a pair of pigs, which wandered in and out of the house at their leisure. It had a single room, though there was a separate bed for adults and offspring. They had rough furniture, made from barrels and shipping crates and hewn logs, and the meal that night was a stew of Indian corn and potatoes, cooked with a sour meat from their freshly slaughtered old milk cow. Only later did I learn that our hosts were one of the most prominent families in town.

The meal was served not with water or wine or tea but with liquor, a kind of western rum, of which I had never yet heard. The husband, the wife—even the children—drank it as though it were sweet nectar, but I could hardly manage a swallow. It tasted to me like poison set afire, but

Andrew, perhaps savoring the distraction of something novel and un-threatening, sipped as though it were a prized claret. "How is it made?" he asked. "With what varieties? How is it aged?"

"Aged?" our host had asked.

"Yes," said Andrew, who had some limited experience making wine in his youth. "Like wine, it is aged, is it not?"

Our host laughed. "'Tis aged from the time we put it into the jug to when we drink it. Don't last that long. Around here, you see, there ain't no money. Where would money come from? Ain't no roads back east, and the damn Spanish won't let us use the river. You want to buy some-thing, you buy it with whiskey. You want to sell something, you get whiskey for it. This here is our money, friend, and ain't no one can be bothered to turn money into prettier money. There's nothing to be gained by doing so."

But there *was* something to be gained. Andrew saw it—not yet clearly, but I believe an idea was already forming in his mind. He now knew how the locals did their business, and he already sensed there was opportunity for a man willing to do it a little differently. He had never in his life made his own whiskey, never even considered doing so. He was, nevertheless, already mulling over in his mind the things he would do that would, in the vicinity of the four counties, elevate his name from obscurity.

Ethan Saunders

Evening descended, and Cherry Street was full of middling people in their middling clothes going about their middling business, exchanging with each other their very, very middling sentiments. They stepped with manic precision, avoiding mud and filth and mounds of snow, piles of manure, clusters of animals—chickens, cows, goats, pigs—being driven here and there by angry-looking minders waving their sticks. They ignored the looming blackness of chimneys spewing soot. They bustled and bumbled and bumped about, returning home, attending to their evening meals, engaged in conversations so quotidian I could scarcely comprehend. When shall I mend this pillow? What thought you of that piece of ham? No, the other piece. Have you had a moment to speak to Harry about the crate of salt cod?

I do not condemn these creatures for living their own little lives and discussing the things in them, but the smallness of it pained me. Yes, I was brought low, but what of it? Had I not lived fully? Such a full life does not allow for the petty and trivial concerns of domesticity. That was the palliative I applied when I thought of how fate had robbed me of Cynthia all those years ago. Even then I understood that I would never have conversations with her about salt cod and pillows. Men who had lived as I had, with dirt and blood and death, were not made for the comforts of domestic quiet.

Mixed in with the sooty air lingered the scent of hearth fires and stews and soups and roasting meats, and I recalled that I had eaten nothing since breakfast. Here, where Cherry intersected with Third Street, near the Hebrew house of worship, was where Lavien had told me he made his home, so it was here I looked for him. I saw a pretty young Jewess and thought that if I were in better form I should surely present my question to her, but now—tattered and filthy and bruised, wearing a poor and stolen hat—I feared I would frighten her. Instead I found an Israelite peddler, pushing his cart of rolls, and asked him if he knew a man named Lavien. He directed me to a house in an alley, half a block away, with a bright red door and said, in heavily accented English, that I might find him within.

I knocked at this narrow two-story house, and a servant at once appeared. She was aged and unappealing, with that distinctive and unpleasant old-person smell, and yet she sat in judgment of me.

"Go on," she said, with a wave of the hand. "We have nothing for you."

"How can you know what you have for me when you know not who I am?" I asked.

"Get gone, you with your fancy talk. We have given to beggars enough today."

All at once a woman appeared behind her, and she was like the sun rising against the black sky. This was a very pretty Hebrew, with a wide round face, large black eyes, and arched eyebrows.

"I beg your pardon, madam," I said, directing myself to this new and infinitely more pleasurable creature, "but I am an associate of Mr. Lavien, and I must speak with him."

"He's a beggar, missus," the servant said, "and drunk, by his smell." Here was a woman whom clearly no one had ever married, and I could not blame mankind for not asking for her withered and mean-spirited hand. For shame, old prune, to speak to me so.

The wife, however, demonstrated her superior perception. "He's no beggar but something else." Then, to me: "You know my husband?"

"I do, madam, and I apologize for my appearance, but things have gone hard for me this last day, a story with which your husband is familiar in part."

"Show him in," she said to the servant. "I'll fetch Mr. Lavien."

The house was narrow—as was common, for in Philadelphia, houses are taxed according to their breadth—but it was also quite deep. The crone led me through a well-appointed hallway, with a handsome rug and several fine portraits, and into a sitting room that was very full of books for so modest a home. I sat in a slightly low-backed but well-cushioned chair, and there the woman left me without offering refreshment, which I thought rather uncivil.

Lavien was apparently at hand and had no interest in impressing me by making me wait. I had hardly had time to study the pale green wallpaper, flecked with bits of pink, before the Hebrew attended me and was good enough to present me with a glass of Madeira. I drank deeply from it—very good stuff—and we settled down together.

"You are bleeding from your head," he told me.

"Prodigiously?"

"No, only a little."

I shrugged. "Then it is no matter. I shall come to the point, sir. I need you to give me thirty dollars. Perhaps another twenty for comfort. I need you to give me fifty dollars."

He made little effort to mask his amusement. "I have no such sum to spare. My position pays well enough, but I am hardly a rich man."

"I thought all you Treasury men were wealthy," I said.

He snorted. "You have been listening to the lies disseminated by that rascal Jefferson."

"You are not one of those men so blinded by Hamilton that you are set against Jefferson?" I asked.

Lavien clucked like an old woman. "Jefferson is a liar and scoundrel and, in my opinion, an enemy of the state."

"I think he is, in fact, *Secretary* of State," I suggested. "Common mistake, though."

His eyes narrowed, and his expression darkened ever so slightly. I suspected he was attempting to measure my sincerity, my level of enthusiasm for Jefferson and his republican followers. Lavien struck me as the sort of man who always measured a man's opinions, who felt for strengths and weaknesses. He was the sort who could not step into a room without noting the location of every door, which windows he might jump through in a pinch, which tables might be toppled for a shelter from bullets. I knew the sort. I had spent the war as just such a man.

"Hamilton has had cause to lament that Washington puts his faith in that man," he said. "Soon enough, Washington will regret it. Jefferson has opposed us at every turn. And he will stop at nothing."

"Perhaps Hamilton wants opposing," I said.

"You cannot defend Jefferson. In his wretched newspaper he even insults Washington, calling him old and feeble of mind."

I knew it, and I hated that Jefferson did not have the sense to leave Washington's reputation alone. "That ought not to be," I admitted.

"But despite all that, you are against Hamilton's great achievements, Captain Saunders? You were against the Assumption Bill? You, an old soldier, opposed paying out the debts the states incurred during the war? And the Bank Bill? You think it a mistake for a nation to have a bank upon which to draw funds in times of crisis?"

The Bank Bill. The act of Congress that had established Hamilton's pet project, the Bank of the United States. Cynthia's note said that her husband's disappearance, the danger to herself and her children, had something to do with the new bank. Best to take this slowly, I thought. I would not show too much interest. I would listen.

He spoke very calmly, but each syllable landed like a hammer blow. The entire world knew that Jefferson hated Hamilton and his Federalist policies, but Hamilton and his supporters were generally much quieter. I suppose they had the advantage of success, since Washington so often sided with Hamilton, and the Congress, though it grumbled, had voted his policies into law. Hamilton and his followers did not need to spit venom in the press the way the Jeffersonians did, for they were instead making laws and shaping policy. But if Lavien was any measure, it seemed the Hamiltonians were filled with just as much resentment as the Jeffersonians.

"I opposed the Bank Bill in my own way," I said. Indeed, I distinctly remember sitting in a tavern and cursing it very colorfully.

Lavien shook his head. "I am sorry to hear that, but it hardly seems the time to discuss policy. What has happened to you, Captain Saunders?"

"My landlady has very suddenly cast me out," I told him, providing a description of events from the previous night, and hinting that perhaps my expulsion was linked to his inquiry.

He pointed to my head. "That new injury of yours. Is that related?"

"Very likely," I answered, not quite ready to tell him about the Irishman. When he shared what he knew, I would consider dispensing my little store of knowledge.

"It is as I told you last night," he said, perhaps noting my skepticism. "Pearson has been missing a few days, perhaps a week. I would like to find him. And, lest you ask, I cannot tell you why. I am not to share information regarding my inquiry with anyone uninvolved. You would need to speak to Colonel Hamilton."

"Do you hold everything you do in such secrecy, or just this?"

"I can't tell you that either," he said, without irony.

"You must know I don't want state secrets. My questions are about Pearson. If you won't tell me why you seek him, tell me at least if you believe his family to be in danger."

"In danger?" he repeated. "No, I don't think so."

"But you cannot say for certain?"

He shook his head. "There is so little of which one can be certain."

I made an effort to hide my frustration by refilling my glass. Though he was a small, swarthy, bearded man, I liked Lavien, and while he certainly was possessed of some rather significant abilities, he did not strike me as a gifted spy. He was alert, and no doubt was possessed of a kind of cunning, but did he have the sort of expansive intelligence, the curiosity and openness, that is required of the best of those in the trade? I doubted it.

"I wonder if there are things of which you might be more certain," I said, "if you went about your affairs in a different way or had the benefit of more experience."

At once it all became clear to me, like a vision: Lavien and I working side by side, his curious physical prowess and my abilities as a spy. I'd had too much to drink, I suppose, and had been confronted by the past too unexpectedly. I had not thought of being in service for some time now—years, perhaps—but suddenly it seemed close enough to touch. Were I to find myself a coequal with Lavien, would that not erase the tarnish that had been placed upon my name all those years ago? Could I not appear in better circles without the whispering and pointing and awkward conversation? The encounter with this remarkable man, in service to Hamilton, and my contact with Cynthia Pearson, who made all things seem bright and wonderful, left me with the unexpected notion that I could rejoin the brotherhood of respectable men, that I could be useful once more. The thought of it was every bit as intoxicating as the wine.

"You misunderstand me," he said, "I have been sworn to secrecy on this matter, and on all matters relating to my work for the Treasury Department. I am sorry, Captain Saunders. I understand that you have a personal interest in this, but I cannot tell you much, not without the express permission of Colonel Hamilton."

"But he shall never give me permission. Hamilton despises me."

Lavien looked distraught, like a child told there were to be no sweets. "I am certain you are mistaken. I have heard him speak of you, and he has had only flattering things to say. He tells me you were an exceptional spy."

"What else has he told you?" I could not help but suspect that Lavien was lying to flatter me or for some other deceptive end.

He smiled. "He said you were remarkably clever in your dealings with people—that if you wished you could talk the devil himself into selling you his soul."

These words surprised me. Perhaps Hamilton had spoken of me after all, and in these flattering terms. Still, it did not change things. "Nevertheless, he dislikes me."

"I suggest you visit him, put your case to him yourself. In the meantime, Captain, if you know of anything that can help me find Pearson or aid his family, I hope you will tell me."

I thought about the note in my pocket, the one from Cynthia. I thought about my encounter with the Irishman. Surely he would like to know these things. If he were unwilling to aid me, however, I would not share with him. Indeed, it seemed increasingly necessary that I conduct my own inquiry. I would find the wretched Pearson, and I would protect Cynthia from whatever dangers lurked around her.

"Where did you learn to do such things?" I asked. "To move so quickly and silently?"

His eyes moved this way and that, a sure sign that he considered a fabrication, but in the end his words sounded like truth. "I was in Surinam, sir. The Maroon uprisings."

I am not a man easily impressed, but here was something. The Maroons—with their mixture of African and Indian blood—were said to be among the most vicious fighters in the world, ruthless in their quest for land and liberty. They lived by a rigorous code of honor, but any man they called enemy would die and die hard.

"Good Lord," I said softly. "You fought the Maroons? You must have seen Hell itself at the hands of those godless savages."

"You misunderstand me," he said. "I fought *with* the Maroons, for their freedom. It was they who taught me to do what I do."

Had he told me he fought on behalf of the moon in its war against the sun, I could not have been more surprised. I had never before heard of a white man siding with the Maroons. I had never even heard of a white man being allowed to live by the Maroons. "You fought alongside those dusky savages?" I managed.

"Neither their complexion nor their degree of civilization interested me," he said, his voice rather flat. "Only that they were wronged."

There was nothing to say, not to a man who would help a pack of cannibals slit the throats of white men. Yet I do hate a silence, so I rose and refilled my glass from the decanter. I drained it and filled it again before returning to my seat.

"As for my difficulties," I said.

Lavien, perhaps eager to change the subject himself, waved me off. He told me he had no sums of money to give away, but he would be honored to have me as a guest for his evening meal and to spend the night. He would have his woman make up the garret for me. If I wished to refresh myself with a washbasin, that too could be arranged. He managed to make the suggestion sound generous and not an unkind comment upon my state.

I took him up on his offer and cleaned myself as best I could.

In the meantime, his sitting room had been turned to a dining room, with the table assembled from its various pieces. The old crone laid it out quite elegantly, with fine silver and handsome drinking glasses. The room was well lit, and the food was plentiful. Yet, for such refinement, Lavien conducted himself like a peasant by bringing his children to the table. We sat with a pretty girl with fair hair whom I guessed to be seven years of age, and her younger brother, no more than two. The food was of the Hebrew variety, filled with strange spices and flavors but by no means unpalatable to a man open to alien sensations. The wine was superb, for Jews ever have connections for good wine. The conversation was quite lively, for the little girl, called Antonia, was a champion conversationalist and bade me speak at length about my wartime adventures, interjecting quite often with her own opinions upon all matters political.

It astonished me that Lavien, whom I had judged to be so hardened and cruel, cut off from human society by his past and by his skills, was a different creature altogether with his wife and children. He was open and easy, obviously delighting in their company. Once, when his daughter made an unusually mature and earnest observation, he and his wife burst into peals of rich laughter. Lavien had seen and drawn blood, hunted white men for Maroons, eaten human flesh for all I knew, and yet found comfort in domestic quiet. The envy I felt for him made my heart ache.

After dinner, once the women and children departed, Lavien poured more wine, and I inquired as to how he came to stand with the Maroons, and what he did with them, but he demurred, saying that he would tell me some other time; he did not like to speak of it, particularly not in his own home. Yet he did provide me with the most skeletal of explanations.

"I did things which I am now ashamed to own," he said, "though I am not ashamed of the cause. I believe that all men, African, Indian, and European alike, are equal in the eyes of God and of nature. It is only in the eyes of one another that inequity lies. I grew up in the West Indies, upon the island of Nevis, and, pressed into the family business, I visited Surinam. There I was abducted by the Maroons, who thought to use me as a hostage, or perhaps they would have killed me out of vengeance. I convinced them, however, that I was of a different tribe, one as despised by their oppressors as their own, and through a series of circumstances I shall not now relate, I remained with them for two years, embracing their cause, though at the same time attempting to temper it."

"It must have been trying to live among them," I said.

"At times it was, but I did not live wholly among them. I would travel to white settlements, where my connection to the Maroons was unknown, and I would learn of the outside world. I became enchanted with what I read of your new country. After so long in the jungle, I knew I must live in a land founded upon the principle that all men are created equal. So I came to Philadelphia, for it has a large population of Jews, and here I met my wife."

"How is it that you came to work for Hamilton?"

"Having done what I did with the Maroons, I did not wish to return to a life of trade, though that is how I first supported myself. Once the government moved to Philadelphia, upon a whim I presented myself to Hamilton. He has since found work for me serving the country, though this is the first time I have served him directly."

"Why Hamilton?" I asked. "Why did you seek him out of all men? Is it the West Indian connection?" Everyone knew that Hamilton had been born a bastard on the island of Nevis. His mother had been a French strumpet, his father a penniless younger son of a Scots family of more puffed-up pretension than means.

"It was more than our geographical connection. Hamilton's mother's first husband," Lavien said, "was my uncle, Johan Lavien."

This was a greater surprise than his past connection with the Maroons. "What? Hamilton has Jew kinsmen?"

Lavien shook his head. "They had no children. My uncle was a monster, and the lady was right to run from him. Hamilton has every reason to dislike me for my name—and my face, I suppose; I'm told I look a bit like my uncle. Yet Hamilton has been nothing but kind."

I found this hard to believe but did not say so. "As Hamilton admires you so much," I suggested, "perhaps you might come with me when I speak to him. You might try to persuade him to let me in on your secrets."

He shook his head. "I do not like to visit Hamilton at Treasury. I prefer other venues."

I smiled. "Of course. Hamilton was always uneasy about his lowly origins. It would not do to so remind the world, let alone to parade his Hebrew near-kinsman before subordinates."

"He does not like to be reminded of his origins, it is true, but there are more complicated matters at work here."

I sipped my wine. What could these more complicated matters be? My thoughts were clouded by drink, but even so I found the truth in the thicket of obscurity. "Jefferson doesn't know about you, does he? You do not visit Hamilton at Treasury because you do not want it known that you work for Hamilton or what sort of work you do. If the Jeffersonians were to put it about that the Jewish nephew of Hamilton's mother's first husband was slinking about the city looking into the business of wealthy families, they would piss their pants with glee."

"You see right to the heart of things," he said. "It is no inconsiderable skill."

"One you could use," I said.

"If that is Colonel Hamilton's will, then I think so."

"You understand that Hamilton hates me, don't you? It was he who exposed my supposed treachery to the world. He promised he would hold the accusations against me secret, but he could not spread the word fast enough."

"Why do you say so? Have you evidence to prove it?"

"It is what I heard, and I believe it."

"Did Colonel Hamilton tell you that he would protect your reputation?" Lavien asked me.

"Yes, and he lied."

"If he said he would protect your reputation, then he did. Colonel Hamilton was not the one who maligned you, sir, and unless you have proof otherwise, I will not believe it. It is not something he would do."

"I knew Jefferson had his worshipers, but I did not know Hamilton was also blessed."

"I am not a worshiper, but I know the man, and I have too much respect for the truth to believe an obvious falsehood when I see one. If you like, I could use the resources my position offers to launch a full inquiry into what happened those years ago."

Something uncomfortable twisted inside me. "I should very much prefer to keep the past where it belongs," I said. "What is done cannot be undone."

He nodded. "Then let us turn to the present. I wonder if I ought to send someone to look for Leonidas? You may fear to seek him out, but I see no reason why I may not do so."

I sat up straight in my chair. "Why, I would be most grateful. Very decent of you."

Lavien excused himself, and when he returned perhaps half an hour later, he said that he had sent a boy from a nearby coffeehouse with instructions to ask about Southwark for a man of Leonidas's description, and that, should he be found, he would meet me the next morning at a nearby tavern.

After I'd had my fill of wine, I told him I wished to retire, and Lavien bade me good night, saying he had work yet to do that evening. I assured him I could find my own way to my room, and so, taking a candle, I ascended the stairs, steep and narrow as in a Dutchman's house. When I reached the second-floor landing, Mrs. Lavien emerged from her children's room.

"I heard Jonathan fussing," she told me, as though some explanation were necessary. "I hope you find your room comfortable."

"Oh, very," I told her. "I never mind a garret, and it is made up quite elegantly for a room of that species. Yet, Mrs. Lavien, there is something of solitude I do not like, and I cannot but think how much brighter the room would be with your company."

She glanced back and forth and then, to my delight, ascended the stairs to my room. I followed her, my single candle providing scant illumination, but enough to watch the delicious movement of her form under her pretty yellow gown. She had a commanding presence, a recklessness that reminded me of Cynthia Pearson as she had been all those years ago, when she was Cynthia Fleet.

Here, too, was a woman who craved excitement, who delighted in the pleasures of the illicit. Why should I not accommodate her? Yes, her husband had done me a kindness, but had she not done me a kindness too, and would it not be mean of me to demur from returning the favor? She had acted the proper wife all evening, devoted to children and husband, managing her home both with earnestness and good cheer, but what Lavien did not understand—it was quite apparent now—was that she was also a woman with complex desires.

We reached the top of the stairs, and though my sensations were fuzzy from all I had drunk that night, still I felt the excitement rising inside me. My heart pounded and my pulse beat in my neck. I closed the door behind me and set the light upon a small writing desk in the corner.

"Indeed, I was right," I said, "for in being here, you do make the room so much more—"

"How very broken you are," she said. Her voice was soft, confused, and even a little sad.

"I beg your pardon?" I felt the prickling of something ill—not danger but yet unpleasant.

"You heard me, Mr. Saunders." Her voice had an icy edge I did not like at all. "You must be broken in your soul. My husband and I invite you to our home, taking you in when you are in need of shelter, and in response to this kindness you choose to offer me insult. I wish to know what portion of your heart, of your soul, is so damaged that you would do such a thing."

"I must point out that it is *Captain* Saunders."

"The time when I might be impressed by your rank has passed us," she said, "and I do not reject it for any accusation of treason. I reject it for how you act here, tonight. You think your honor, your chance to be an honorable man, is in the past, and so you befoul the present."

"And the future!" I added brightly.

"I understand that your wit keeps you sane, sir, but you must set it aside now and again, or you shall ever remain a wretch."

I suddenly felt very sober. And ambushed, I might add. It was cruel to lead me into a position of vulnerability, only to take advantage of my open nature. That was what I told myself. "If there has been some misunderstanding between us—" I began.

"There is no misunderstanding. Do not try to pretend that either of us can believe it. Have you no decency?"

I was prepared to answer sharply, but I suddenly saw things with a starkness I would have preferred to avoid. "No," I told her. "At times, I haven't."

She must have heard something in my voice, for even in the frail wash of candlelight I saw the pity in her eyes, and pity was a thing I could not endure. "You are a very sad man, are you not, Captain Saunders?"

"Do not speak to me so. If you like, you may cast me out, but do not speak to me so."

"I shan't cast you out," she said. "It is what you wish, I believe. You wish it far more than you wish me to yield to you. Who was she, Captain Saunders, that so hurt you? Was it long ago or recent? Long ago, I think."

"Don't act as though you know my heart."

"How could I not, when you wear it on your sleeve?"

"I am sorry to have offended you," I said. I looked about the room to collect my things, though I had no things to collect. "I shall go."

"You will stay the night, and in the morning you will go see Hamilton."

"Your husband speaks to you of his business?"

She laughed. "Should he not? You who love women so well do not think to speak to them of your work?"

I stared at this woman. Lavien, with his beard and slender shoulders and unimpressive stature, had wed a mighty creature.

"I would be grateful," I said, "if you would not mention this incident to your husband."

"It was he who advised me on how best to conduct myself when you approached me." In the dim light her gaze was dark and magnetic. "You have fallen very low, have you not? Perhaps there is nothing to do but rise. Tomorrow is something entirely new, entirely unwritten, and full of possibility. Won't you use it?"

She turned away, and the power of her gaze snapped, like the thinnest of glass rods. She opened the door and descended the stairs. I closed the door and sat upon my bed, my head in my hands. Who were these people? What manner of being were these Laviens, and with what had I become involved?

Joan Maycott

Spring 1789

In the morning, our hosts gave us a breakfast of whiskey and corn cakes served on mismatched pewter plates, a luxury we would not fully appreciate until we were, as we would be soon, without any plates at all. While we ate our meager portions, Reynolds arrived to inform us that prior to visiting our land we were to speak with Duer's local agent, Colonel Holt Tindall. Though much abused by Duer and his people, we thought it best to present ourselves to advantage, so Andrew wore clothes he had not touched for the journey, looking dignified in plain artisan's breeches, a white shirt, and a handsome woolen coat. I wore a simple dress, far more wrinkled than I would have liked, but it was clean at least.

Though he had eyed me with open lasciviousness through our journey, when I was dirty and tired and blunted by exhaustion, Reynolds hardly looked at me now. There was something quite different in the odious man's manner. Even as he spoke of this Colonel Tindall, something like respect, or perhaps wariness, spread over his features.

Duer's man in Pittsburgh or no, I expected another makeshift shack, but Holt Tindall was of an entirely different order of being. Reynolds pointed out to us Tindall's handsome two-story structure on Water Street, recently whitewashed and looking within this primitive city much like a diamond in a barrel of coal. This, however, was not where we were to meet him. Instead, Reynolds led us once more across the river and some miles out of town to Colonel Tindall's country estate, a vast southern-style plantation called Empire Hall. Here was a large wood-frame house, very like the one in town only larger and more stately for being surrounded not by shacks and mud but by fields of crops and barns of livestock, all of which were tended to by a dozen or more Negro slaves.

Indeed, I saw no one but Negroes. Reynolds seemed to read my thoughts, for he said, "He ain't got a wife; he lives only with the niggers. But he takes to company."

If the outer countenance of the mansion was surprising, the interior made us gasp. I don't know when it happened, when we decided that we had passed from one world to another, but I now recognized that I expected never to see again such signs of civilization. From the inside of the house, one would hardly know that this was not some elegant New York mansion. The walls were lined with fine paintings and tapestries, the floors with excellent coverings that produced the most faithful imitation of tile. While Pittsburgh smelled like a necessary pot, this home gave off the fragrance of baking bread and cut flowers.

A pretty young Negro girl, light in color, met us at the door. She would not look directly at us, and so I did not notice at once the severe bruise upon her eye. Perhaps she wished to hide this from us, or perhaps she feared Reynolds, who studied her with naked desire while fingering his scar. With a torpid gait, as though unwilling herself to approach, the girl took us to a massive sitting room. This chamber boasted not only a fine rug—for here only guests without mud on their feet would be admitted—but, beyond all the handsome chairs and two sofas, a large pianoforte was propped against the far wall, where it was bathed in the light of the morning sun. It was now nine, for the tall case clock rang cheerily, echoed by chimes throughout the house and the church bell from the distant town.

At the far end of the room, before the fireplace, sitting upon an isolated high-backed armchair—looking much from its form and placement like a throne—was a stout and rugged man in his sixties. His white hair was long and tangled in the back, though he balded considerably, and he had wild gray eyes and a rough stubble upon his cheek—features that clashed with his tailored breeches, ruffled shirt, and embroidered waistcoat. All of these things contributed to give him the look of a deranged surveyor who has spent too much time alone in the wilderness. If his countenance had not given that impression, I suspect it would have been provided by the fowling piece he clutched in one hand, its butt resting against the floor, like a brutal frontier scepter. Above him hung a string of hairy things attached to bits of leather. It took me a moment to recognize them as Indian scalps.

The servant had not admitted Reynolds with us, and we were alone with this old man, who bore himself with the silent dignity of a savage chief. He opened his mouth to show us two rows of dark teeth, which he clamped together in something like a grin.

"I am Colonel Holt Tindall of Empire Hall, and I am Duer's partner on this side of the Alleghenies." As he spoke, I felt the heat of his gaze as it settled upon my body. He looked at me as no man should look at a woman not his wife. "Reynolds said I'd want to meet you, and he knows my business, I'll say as much as that." He spoke with the heavy accent of a Virginian, but it had an additional drawl, a kind of laziness I had already begun to associate with Westerners.

"Care to sit?" he asked.

"Thank you," said Andrew.

Tindall banged the butt of his fowling piece upon the wooden floor. "Not you. A man stands in the presence of his betters. I address the lady."

I could not endure that Andrew should be again debased for the sake of something so trivial as my appearance. I gazed upon this Colonel Tindall with hatred and contempt, lest he think I mistook his rudeness for authority, and remained standing.

"You must suit yourself," he said, in response to my silence. "Stand, sit, don't matter."

He might have been a Virginian once, but evidently he had forgotten the culture of extreme politeness cultivated in those climes. All at once I knew precisely what he was—a hybrid creature composed of a Southerner's sense of privilege and a Westerner's brutality. There is a name for a creature that is part one thing and part another: monster.

My pulse quickened and my breathing deepened. I was afraid. I had been living for weeks in perpetual fear—fear for what would become of us, fear for our safety—but this was something much more urgent, something sharper. I looked at Andrew, and his lips curled in a reassuring smile. If he too was afraid, he would not show it.

Andrew stepped forward, inclining just enough toward a bow to be polite without actually offering obeisance. "I am Andrew Maycott, and this is my wife, Joan. We are anxious to see our land, so please state your business."

The colonel's old face darkened at Andrew's words. He sneered, again revealing his tobacco-stained teeth. As if to demonstrate the origins of this discoloration, he pulled from inside his coat a twist of tobacco and bit off a considerable piece.

Just then the doors to the chamber opened and a Negro woman of great girth and indeterminate age—but surely neither young nor very old—entered the chamber. "I see you got company, Colonel. You want tea, or maybe that cake I done baked this morning?"

The colonel banged his fowling piece upon the floor. "Did I call for you?" he demanded. "Do not come unless I call. Now get you gone, Lactilla."

I was later to learn, as a point of gossip, that this Negress had been the colonel's property for near twenty years. When first making her way into Tindall's household, her breasts had been large with milk, for she had been separated from a child not yet two years old, owing to the death of her previous owner. The colonel found this condition amusing and had taken to calling her Lactilla.

Now the woman stared brazenly at this beast of a man. "Don't you use that tone with me when I ain't done nothing wrong but only my duty, which is to serve tea and cake."

Tindall raised his fowling piece. "You'll go back to your damned kitchen, nigger. The only question is if you do it whole or filled with shot."

She waved a hand and let out a guffaw. "Look at him. Old man with a gun." She turned to me. "You come by the kitchen when you done, honey. I give you some cake, you and that handsome husband of yours." She shrugged her massive shoulders and heaved herself from the room.

Tindall set the gun back down with a thud, but he kept his hand upon it still. "Damn that old bitch." He looked at Andrew. "As for you, don't hope I've forgotten your impertinence. You don't much care to mind your place, but you'll come to understand your error. You ask around, Maycott, and you'll hear the same thing from everyone. I am generous to the town and its poor. I am free with my money, and I believe those with means ought to help those who have none. I do not, however, suffer insolence gladly."

"And how is it not insolence on your part when you ask us to stand while you remain seated?" Andrew asked.

"Because this is my house and my town, and the land you are to settle upon is my own."

"I believe," said Andrew, "it is mine. I bought it."

"There'll be time for you to examine that belief. For now, it would be well for you to listen to what I say and to think no more of the sort of leveling foolishness that comes from misunderstanding the late war. I am familiar with the principles of the Revolution, for I fought in it."

"As did I," said Andrew.

"What of it? One cannot empty a workhouse, a jail, or a brothel without uncovering a passel of veterans. You would do better to attend to more immediate concerns. Such as your land, for example." He held up two scrolls of foolscap, both clutched in his left hand, clearly unwilling to let go of the fowling piece. "One of these is the deed to your land, the contract that you signed, cleverly written by our friend Duer, who is quite adept at these things. It is, I am afraid, not a favorable piece of property."

I took a step forward. "Mr. Duer assured us that it was very fertile."

"Duer lied, pretty thing. The land might be fertile to corn for all I know, but you will have to clear it of trees and rocks and then see what it yields. If you had a team of mules and a pack of niggers, you might do it in as little as two years."

"You wait a moment," Andrew said.

Tindall showed us his teeth again. "I ain't got to wait. Duer deceived you. You know that by now. He spoke to you of the glories of Liberty-town, but you've seen Pittsburgh, and you wonder how the settlement can be a paradise if Pittsburgh is so wretched. Your allotment is not farm-land but wild forest, and taming it will likely be your death."

Neither of us spoke because, terrible though these revelations might be, they were not shocking. As Tindall had suggested, we had long since understood Duer's deception, though we were not yet aware of its extent. We did not speak because of our of pure, sharp, numbing surprise. It was one thing to trick a person but quite another to glory in being a cheat.

"Now," he continued, "the other deed I hold in my hand is more like the sort of thing Duer suggested. Not quite, you understand. It won't be what you were told, but this one is very much nearer. 'Tis cleared land, already a cabin on it, such as it is, and the land's been farmed somewhat in the haphazard ways of western rabble. It is a better piece of land—much more workable. Perhaps you would like to consider trading what you have now for something more agreeable. 'Tis equal acreage, so you need not concern yourself on that score."

Andrew said nothing. What was there to say? We were hundreds of miles from our home, abused and deceived, in the hands now of a de-ranged border despot whose greatest pleasure seemed to be abusing those in his power. Tindall had every advantage over us, and the only power we had came from withholding our acknowledgment of that power.

"I have come to these terms with other settlers, who have always found them advantageous," Tindall said. "Would you care to come to terms with me, Mr. Maycott?"

"That would depend upon the terms, would it not?" His voice re-mained steady. I knew he was frightened, for me and for our future, but he would not show it.

"It is not what I asked you." Tindall's voice shifted from syrupy to hard. "I did not ask about the terms, I only asked if you would like ad-vantageous terms. Answer me yes or no."

"I shall listen to your offer," Andrew said, "and if I think it sound I shall consider it. I am not going to agree to any theoretical proposal. To do so would be foolish."

Tindall pounded the butt of his fowling piece against the floor several times, like a judge banging his gavel. "Enough of your insolence. I ain't got the time for it. Here is what I offer you, though you're fortunate I still give you the chance to take it. I wish that Mrs. Maycott may attend me here once a week, and maybe stay the night. 'Tis no great thing; it's an insubstantial thing, if you know that word. In exchange, a substantial thing may be yours."

Andrew remained silent a moment longer. I could not imagine that anyone faced with this blunt and diabolical demand would surrender to it, that there were men and women so low in the world, and in their sense of their own worth, that they would agree to these terms as though they had agreed to the price of a pound of flour. Images of the blunted and weathered inhabitants of Pittsburgh came to my mind, and I wondered if these people were capable of agreeing to anything at all. It seemed to me that, once so defeated by life, they would do nothing more than submit the way a lamb submits to be shorn.

Andrew stepped toward the colonel, and so bold was his determination that the old man set down both deeds and tightened his grip upon his fowling piece. "The proposal you make concerns my wife. Why, then, do you present it to me?"

Tindall at first did not stir and then he cleared his throat. With his free hand, the one not clutching the gun, he stroked the stubble on his chin.

He let out a little bark of air, something like a laugh, I suppose, in the same way that a drab brown moth is something like a resplendent butterfly. "How modern of your husband. What say you, Mrs. Maycott?"

Andrew looked at me, but I did not meet his gaze. Instead, I smiled at Tindall as though he were a peddler who had not yet shown us his best wares. "I am sure the plot of land for which we have contracted will prove sufficient."

"You and Duer may have cheated us," Andrew said, "and you may relish that fact, but that does not make us your slaves nor you our master. We shall turn dross into gold and never depend upon the favors of men like you."

Andrew walked back to me, took my arm, and led me toward the door.

"You may not later change your mind," Tindall said. "I won't have my tenants switching their plots. It would cause"—he waved his hand about in the air—"discontent."

"I am not your tenant," Andrew said, turning to him. "I have purchased this land, inferior though it may be, outright. You and I are both landholders and so equals."

"And perhaps we would be *if* you owned the land. I do find it sad, so very sad, when low people who know not their way around a contract sign one without first inquiring of a lawyer. You are, I am told, a carpenter by trade, yes? You would despise someone, I think, who attempted to construct an armoire out of his own imaginings of how it must be made without seeking experienced advice. You have *not* purchased the land. You have purchased the right to occupy the land and pay me ground rent."

I looked at Andrew. Could it be true? Ground rents were generally inexpensive, and held for very long periods of time. Ours, I would later discover, as was typical of the sort, was for ninety-nine years. Each quarter for that period we were to pay our landlord ten dollars, rather expensive for a ground lease, let alone one in so remote a location. So long as we paid, we retained possession and could sublease or even sell the right to occupy, though at the end of the ninety-nine years, ownership would revert to the landlord.

I now saw the extent to which we had been deceived. We had given up all we had, not to own land but to occupy and pay rent upon a worthless plot of forest. To make it yield value, and so be able to raise the money needed to pay our rent and not lose our property, we would have to clear the land and increase its worth. Tindall and Duer had discovered a way to profit while turning worthless holdings into a valuable estate. And surely we were not the first. Others had been cheated thus, for there was a whole community of victims under Tindall's command. None who had been cheated had found redress, for Tindall and Duer continued their scheme, and that could only mean one thing: that the law, the principles of the republic for which Andrew had fought, had already been abandoned. The men back east could not or would not protect us.

"You'll be taken to your plot," Tindall said. "You may have occasion to wish you had accepted my offer. As I said, it will not come again.

There is, however, the matter of quarterly rent, and if you find that you cannot pay, and you risk losing your land, we may then talk again."

It was as though he were a candle that had been blown out. He remained in his chair, his weapon in his hand, but his eyes went cold and empty, and I had the strange feeling that Andrew and I were now alone. We opened the door and departed without escort.

Ethan Saunders

Wearing tolerably clean clothes, washed in my basin and then dried by the fire, I slipped quietly down the stairs early the next morning. The sun had just come up, and if I could avoid the serving woman, I had no doubt I could escape the house without enduring awkward conversation with its inmates. The memory of my encounter with Mrs. Lavien still felt as raw and vulnerable as a new wound. It was not simply the shame of having been exposed, of having treated so shabbily my hosts' kindness, it was the notion that these antics were somehow alien to me now. Something had changed. My new proximity to Cynthia Pearson's life made my behavior unseemly even to myself, and Mrs. Lavien's cruel words still rang in my ears.

My plan was a simple one: I would obtain a few coins from a careless gentleman on the street, take my breakfast in a tavern, and meet Leonidas as planned. When at drink, I can be clumsy, but that morning I moved as quietly as a cat on the hunt. No floorboards creaked under my weight, no stairs groaned at my descent. Even so, when I reached the ground floor, Mr. Lavien leaned forward in his chair in the sitting room. He saw my position—hands out for better balance, feet at sharp angles to test the stairs for weaknesses that would betray me—and met it with one of his thin, vaguely predatory smiles. I had accepted his hospitality, allowed him to feed me, serve me drink, introduce me to his family. I sent him out into the cold night to hunt down my slave. In return I had attempted to seduce his wife, and now he sat grinning at me, looking like a serpent before it lashes out at a cornered and frozen mouse.

"Shall we go take some breakfast?" he asked.

In a nearby tavern, crowded with laboring men in early morning silence, I sat next to Lavien at a poor table—too close to the door, too far from the fire. He ate buttered bread and pickled eggs. I made an attempt at some bread as well, but concentrated more upon the beer.

I took a deep drink. "I suppose you want to speak about the incident last night."

"What, the one with my wife? What have you to say?"

I let out a sigh. "Look, I apologize for attempting to take liberties."

He shrugged. "It is no more than I expected. Your reputation in such matters precedes you, and there was never any danger of your doing anything but becoming embarrassed, which I see has occurred."

"You don't care that I might have seduced your wife?"

"Oh, I would have cared about that. It is not what happened. You thought you might seduce my wife, and that is another matter, for in reality you could have achieved nothing."

"You know that, do you?"

"I know my wife," he said. "And I think I begin to know you well enough too. The sting of your disgrace years ago still hangs over you, so you look for new disgraces. But we can put a stop to that. When I prove to the world that your reputation was so unjustly injured, you will have a chance to begin your life anew."

"I told you I do not want you looking into my past."

"You did not say not to, only that you prefer the past to be left alone."

"Then now I shall tell you not to."

He studied me. Then at last he spoke. "Ah, I see."

What could he see? What could he know? Perhaps he had heard fragments of the story, or perhaps Hamilton had told him all he knew, though Hamilton's version of events would be slanted and ill-informed. The short of it was that, in the weeks before Yorktown, Fleet and I had been stationed with Hamilton's company and had just returned from making a series of runs between the main army and Philadelphia, visiting our Royalist contacts along the way. We had been sitting outside our tents, playing at cards, when an officer I had never before met, a major from Philadelphia, rode into our camp and demanded from Hamilton permission to search our tents. I had been outraged upon general principle, but Fleet had outright refused.

Fleet was a tall man, slender, more serious in bearing than he was in character, with a full head of cottony white hair. He was a man born to be a spy. One moment he could be either serious, or a doting father to his Cynthia, or as good a drinking companion as any man might wish. He could also be studious and sober and precise.

That afternoon, as we stood outside our tents, the air still and lifeless, I would have expected Fleet to tell me to endure the outrage with good cheer; that there was little that could be done, so it must be suffered without resentment. But not that day. He swore that this man, this Major Brookings, would lose his hand before he would touch any item in Fleet's tent. At last, Colonel Hamilton was called upon and, in his stiff, magisterial manner, ruled that as Major Brookings acted upon good intelligence, he must be allowed to search, but that he, Hamilton, would oversee the matter to make certain all was done properly. Indeed, he even demanded that we be allowed to remain present, though he asked us not to speak.

Fleet's tent was searched first, and when suspicious documents were discovered tucked into the lining of his travel pack, I could hardly believe what I saw. It had to be planted falsely, I thought, for, beyond any unthinkable doubts about his loyalty, Fleet would have known far better than to hide something in so obvious a place. Yet the look in his eye, that of distant terror, left me unable to speak.

The knife was to twist once more, however, for, when my own pack was searched, documents of a similar nature were found in a similar position. Appearances may have been sufficiently against Fleet to make me doubt him, my best friend, and yet now they were also against me, and I had no doubt of my own innocence. It was hard to focus my rage on this Major Brookings, for he hardly looked pleased at his discovery. Indeed, his face was cast in an expression of distant sadness. Neither Fleet nor I knew him, and that made it unlikely he came upon some errand of personal vengeance.

Fleet and I were placed under guard while Hamilton reviewed the materials, and in a few hours' time he came to see us. The documents, he said, letters between an unnamed American and a British agent, suggested we had been selling low-level, inconsequential secrets. To an outsider it would appear that we had been in the business of making money while not precisely compromising the American positions, though certainly coming close to doing so.

Given, he said, that the army was in motion, it could ill afford the distraction of the discovery of treason among two well-placed officers. It was his decision, therefore, that we resign. We both resisted vehemently, but in the end it became clear that we had no better option, and we surrendered to our fate.

Hamilton would not permit me to examine the documents myself, so I could not see the hand in which they were written. It hardly mattered. Fleet and I both knew how to disguise our penmanship. I could not imagine that Fleet would do something so base as to sell the British secrets, even useless ones. He hardly needed the money, and even if he had done such a thing, why would he have hidden some letters among *my* things? And yet, how else could they have gotten there? Was it possible that the letters were from an earlier time in the war? Perhaps they were from months or even years before. I did not place items in the lining of my travel bag, but neither did I make a habit of checking to see if anyone else had inserted something.

I was troubled because Fleet hardly spoke to me on the subject. I proposed all the most obvious questions. I asked how he thought the letters came into our possession, if we were being made to look like traitors by some other person. He would not answer. He never struck me as guilty, only as too thoughtful to speak. He would fall into such moods at times—as he pieced together a puzzle or connected disparate facts or decoded a message—when he would allow no conversation, sometimes for days at a time. He needed time to think.

Then he left camp without speaking to me. While I awaited his return, Hamilton came to see me and put a hand on my shoulder. "There's something I think you should know," he said. "The war has been hard for Fleet, hard on his finances. I believe he is quite ruined."

I removed his hand from me. "What of it? We've all suffered."

He shook his head. "You and I came into this fight with little of real value, but Fleet was a rich man in Philadelphia. Now he is near penniless."

"He would not allow his daughter to slip into penury," I said.

"Before the war he settled separate property on her, in anticipation on this. But his business is gone. I am only saying that he might have thought it not wholly wrong to make some money selling worthless secrets to the British. He might have thought it his due."

I came close to striking him. Nothing could have convinced me of such a thing, and I turned away without another word. I suspected Fleet had gone to Philadelphia to be with his daughter, and I rode out the next morning intending to follow him. Instead, I decided that it would be best to have some time away from him first, so I went to visit my sister in Connecticut for two weeks.

When at last I arrived in Philadelphia, I received the shocking news that Fleet was dead. Cynthia was in mourning, the house shut against almost all visitors. Her father, she told me, had returned from the war a different, nearly unrecognizable man. He had spoken to her infrequently, and then only a word or two at a time. He had turned aggressively, uncharacteristically, to drink, and had become very belligerent when drunk, only slightly less so when sober. After a week of such behavior, he was killed in a barroom brawl by an assailant never found. And there was more, she said. People whispered. They said he had been cast out of the army in disgrace.

I told her all I knew, disguising as best I could the degree to which appearances implicated her father—implicated both of us, really. I vowed I would find for her the man who had killed her father, but it proved impossible. I could go nowhere without fingers pointed at me in suspicion and hatred. No one would speak to me or answer my questions. Not only was it said that Fleet and I were traitors but that the accusation came from an unimpeachable source, Hamilton himself.

It was for that reason I left Cynthia behind. I could not ask her to be with someone labeled so blackly as I was. Fleet was dead, and people soon forgot that he had ever been involved in the scandal. I could go nowhere, however, without the rumors following me. These accusations had killed Fleet, and they destroyed my life. They were never forgotten, but time, at least, had softened the bitterness felt toward me. And now Lavien wished to unearth it all.

I kept my gaze hard and cold. "You cannot know what it is like to be labeled a traitor, and so you cannot understand why I want it left alone."

"I think I understand," said Lavien. "You have proclaimed your innocence, and I believe you. That means there can be only one reason you do not wish the past unearthed."

"And why is that?" I asked, though I wished I hadn't.

"Because you believe your friend, Captain Fleet, was indeed a traitor. He, your best friend, father of the lady who is now Cynthia Pearson, whom you intended to marry—it was he who sold secrets to the British. That is what you know—or what you believe. It is a great and noble secret that allows you to revel in your own suffering, for each time someone marks you as a traitor, you know that you bear this burden for love—not once but twice."

It is not an easy thing to be laid bare in this way by a man who is little better than a stranger, a stranger to whom you are indebted and whom you have wronged. He had seen things as they really were, and had done it at once.

"You must let it alone," I told him. "When Fleet died, the world chose to forget his part in these crimes. His name was allowed to be spoken without taint."

"You allow your name to remained blackened for her sake?" he asked.

I nodded. "For her, and for Fleet. I do not say he was guilty, but if he was, it was trivial. Empty secrets were sold—lies and worthless information only. Whatever the truth, Fleet was a good man, a hero who did a thousand courageous things for his country. I'll not have it said about him now that he was a traitor."

"It is said about you."

"I am here to defend myself. He is not." I stood up. "I have asked you to leave this alone. I will say no more of it."

"Sit down, Captain. I am sorry if you feel imposed upon, and I shall heed your words."

I sat. I wanted to press him into more vigorously worded promises but at this point I observed Leonidas enter the tavern. I waved him over, and he called for bread, butter, and small beer. I finished my ale and called for another.

After a moment, Lavien excused himself, saying he had things to do, and wished me good luck with Hamilton. He and Leonidas shook hands, and I watched the little man leave. Once he was gone, I informed Leonidas of all that had happened since I last saw him—being cast out by Mrs. Deisher, the note from Cynthia, and the encounter with the Irishman.

Leonidas listened, nodded, but said little. Finally, he commented upon the most practical of matters. "What shall you do about lodgings?"

"I have not yet made a determination on that."

"Do not think you will come live with me. I'll not have it."

"It would only be for a few days."

"No."

"It is really unkind," I said. "I would not have thought you so unkind."

"I must have a place that is mine."

"And I must have a place," I said.

"That is your business and none of mine. However, if you would be so good as to free me from bondage, as you promised to do, I would happily lend you the money to get your things out of surety and to rent a new set of rooms."

"Why, that is the most villainous blackmail I have ever heard," said I.

"Ethan, do you mean to hold me forever? You are not a man to keep a slave, and I am not a man to be one. I know not what you mean by it. You agreed to free me when I turned twenty-one, which was six months ago."

"I agreed to free you when you *were* twenty-one. I didn't mention anything about the specific moment of that year. I wish you would attempt to be a little patient, Leonidas. All this casting about for favors does not become you."

I could not free him. That was what he did not know and could not understand, though the reason would have surprised him. I could not free him because he was already a free man. I'd simply neglected to inform him.

It was really no more than a curious series of events. Once Dorland began stalking me, I grew concerned for Leonidas's future. I owed him his freedom and thought it best to secure it at once. Accordingly, I'd gone to a lawyer and paid ten dollars to have the appropriate papers drawn up, freeing him not simply upon my death but immediately and irrevocably. As I sat across from him, Leonidas had been a free man for nearly a week.

If Dorland had killed me, he would have found out then. He was to be freed in my will, but I arranged with the lawyer to contact Leonidas and make sure he knew I had freed him before I died. I did not die, and I surely would have mentioned all of this to him, but then I'd heard from Cynthia, and suddenly there were more complicated issues requiring my attention.

Were I to tell Leonidas that he was free, he would likely continue to help me, but perhaps he would not. There was so much about his life I did not know. I should have liked to have taken the chance, and if it were merely my life, my happiness, in the balance, I would have done so. I would not take that chance when Cynthia Pearson told me she was in danger. Leonidas would have to believe himself a slave for a few more days—or weeks.

Do not think this decision was an easy one. I could imagine the joy of leaping up there in that tavern and informing him that I had already freed him and required no more of his pestering to do what was right. But as much as I yearned to be open with him on this matter, I dared not. I therefore sacrificed not only the immediate relation of the news of his liberty but my own chances for obtaining a place to live.

We walked to the offices of the Treasury upon Third Street at the corner of Walnut. Leonidas was clearly still harboring resentment over our conversation, but my thoughts were already elsewhere. All around us hurried clusters of men who appeared too big for their suits. Walnut Street was the center of finance in Philadelphia, and of late it had been a place where clever and ruthless men could easily fatten themselves a little further.

Hamilton had launched his bank the previous summer, using an ingenious system of scrip—certificates that stood not for bank shares but for the opportunity to purchase those shares. Scrip holders could later, on a series of four predetermined quarterly dates, buy actual bank shares, using cash for half the payments and already-circulating government issues for the other half. These issues—six percent government loans—had been performing poorly in the markets, attracting little interest, so Hamilton's method promoted trade in the six percents, since scrip holders needed to acquire them in order to exchange their scrip for full ownership of the bank shares. In addition to strengthening a market for already existing government issues, Hamilton's scheme created a frenzy for the new Bank of the United States shares; the act of delaying gratification fueled the mania, and in a matter of weeks speculators were earning two or three times on their investment. Then, just as manically as the price soared, it crashed to earth, producing a panic. Hamilton had saved his bank only by sending his agents to the major trading cities—New York, Boston, Baltimore, and Charleston, as well as here in Philadelphia—to buy up scrip and settle the market. Many unwary investors lost everything they had, but clever men made themselves richer.

No harm done, one might say, but there were those who thought otherwise. Thomas Jefferson, Secretary of State and Hamilton's great enemy, argued that this mania proved the bank was a destructive force. Jefferson and his republican followers believed that the true center of American power must be agriculture. A national bank would empower merchants and traders and turn the nation into a copy of Britain—that is, a sink of corruption. I'd been inclined to side with the Jeffersonians on this point, though in truth I'd not given things too much thought. I merely chose to be opposed to anything that Hamilton desired.

The center of this new American trickery and greed was the Treasury Department, now located in a complex of conjoined private homes, roughly converted for the purpose of housing the largest of the federal government's departments. We stepped through the front door and were

met not by an austere and magisterial lobby but by a frenzy of excitement, hardly less riotous than the jostling of traders outside. Men scrib-
bled away furiously at desks or rushed to bring one meaningless stack of
papers to a place where an equally meaningless stack would be taken instead. Everywhere were clerks, busily writing and tallying and, many believed, plotting the downfall of liberty. I gave a clerk near the door my
name. He looked at me most unkindly, but soon enough we were directed to Hamilton's office.

Not until that moment had I considered what was about to happen.
Hamilton had cast me out of the army and made free with my name, letting the world hear the lies that I was a traitor. His actions had led directly to the death of my great friend. Now, ten years later, I was about
to present myself to him, red-eyed and haggard, in a wrinkled and
stained suit, and beg that he make me privy to what he seemed to regard
as state secrets. I felt anger and humiliation, and I wished to run away,
but instead I marched forward, as a man marches forward to the noose
that is to hang him.

I took deep breaths and attempted to anticipate the scene that lay before me. Since returning to Philadelphia I'd seen Hamilton a few times
upon the street, but I had kept my distance, wanting no discourse with
him. I'd not had an opportunity to see him close since the end of the war,
and I was now pleased to observe that he was not looking his best. He
was a year or two older than I was but looked as though the span were
closer to ten years. He had grown plump in office, jowly in the face,
saggy under the eyes. His nose was as long as ever, but it seemed to be
growing, as the noses of old faces do, and he had begun to lose his hair,
which must have displeased his vain and libertine nature. Clearly the duties and difficulties of being one of the most hated men in the nation had
begun to affect him. They had affected his clothes too, for his suit looked
faded and shiny in spots. Perhaps the Treasury Secretary ought to present
himself to better advantage, but then even I knew the rumors of his enriching himself off government funds were false. The less popular truth
was that Hamilton had so dedicated his time to promoting his policies
that he had allowed his own finances to suffer.

If, however, he looked less than his best, he was certainly formal. He rose when we entered his spare-looking office—short upon decorative flourishes, but long upon filing cabinets, imposing-looking financial volumes, and writing desks filled with ledgers and charts. As for his own desk, it was as neat as though no one used it. Hamilton, I recalled, from his days as Washington's chief of staff, loathed a cluttered workplace.

Once upon his feet, and thus revealing his short stature, he approached us. He took my hand and shook it warmly, and such was my surprise that I could not but allow this to happen. "Captain Saunders, it has been many years." He appeared—and I found this shocking—pleased to see me. It is usual that a man hates no one so much as a person he has wronged. But here was Hamilton, smiling, his eyes crinkling with pleasure, his cheeks rosy. Perhaps my presence recalled to him fond memories of life as a young officer in a momentous war. Perhaps he merely rejoiced to see me looking so poorly.

I let go of his hand, for I did not love his touch. "It has, in fact, been many years."

"Many years," he repeated, not knowing what else to say. He looked at Leonidas and then brightened, no doubt with the hope of easing the tension. "Please introduce me to your colleague." He said it with no inflection, but I knew his motive was only mischief. He did not approve of the mistreatment of Negroes and opposed all slavery.

"This is my man, Leonidas."

Hamilton now shook his hand and applied his charm, justly legendary.

"I trust you will sit," he said, with a gesture to a cluster of chairs before his desk. "I am astonishingly busy. You cannot imagine the demands upon my time, but I can take a few minutes for an old comrade. I should like to say I hope you are well, but I presume, if you will excuse me for observing what is obvious, that you are in some distress. If you have come for assistance, we shall see how we can help you."

I credited his presumption, making polite observations on my appearance and suggesting that he was available to assist me. Did he forget that it was he who had ruined my life, expelled me from the army, and made certain the world heard the tales of my supposed treachery? Was it of so little import to him that it slipped his mind? Had he done harm to so many over the years that he no longer even recalled the particular instances of his perfidy? Or did he merely enjoy playing the munificent despot?

Leonidas and I sat in two chairs before his desk. Hamilton returned to his own seat. He took a detour to a sideboard and I thought he meant to offer us drink, but then he glanced at me and changed his mind. Instead, he sat and placed upon his face a look of important expectation.

I waited a moment, the better to make him slightly uncomfortable, to feel slightly less in control. "I have had a difficult few days," I said at last, "as my appearance will testify, and I believe it has some small relation to an inquiry you are running out of your department. You look into the affairs of Mr. Jacob Pearson?"

He hesitated a moment and then nodded. "It is not commonly known, nor would I have it so, but as you seem already familiar with some general facts, I will admit it but ask for your silence."

Ironic, I thought, coming from him. "You need not concern yourself with that. But, as it happens, my path has crossed with your kinsman Mr. Lavien."

"He is not my kinsman," said Hamilton, with some force. It was hard enough for him to have the world know he was born a West Indian bastard, but if the world were to think him a Jew he would die from shame. "He is, however, a remarkable man."

"I should like to assist him in his case. In short, I should like the government to employ me to use the skills I honed during the war to serve you in this and other matters."

Hamilton kept his face remarkably devoid of expression. "I see."

"Captain Saunders is already materially involved," said Leonidas. "He has suffered physical attack and the loss of his home. He is personally caught up in the matter, and he is also possessed of certain skills, relatively rare as I understand it."

"And you are certainly a strong advocate, Leonidas," said Hamilton, who apparently delighted in having someone to speak to who was not me. "But it cannot be."

"Why can it not be?" I asked.

"I am not ignorant of the past," said Hamilton. "You had a connection to Mrs. Pearson once, did you not?"

"She is Fleet's daughter," I said. *You recollect Fleet, whom you hounded to death.* I did not say it, though. I am not so foolish as that.

"I am well aware of that, which alone would make it a difficult matter. But it was commonly said that you and she were once engaged to marry."

"It was never so formal as that, though who can say how things might have gone had you not cashiered us out of the army and then ruined my reputation? Of course, had you not done so, Fleet might yet be alive."

"Captain," he said gently, "you do your case poor service with these accusations."

"Is there anything I could say that would do my case good service?"

"No, my mind is quite made up on this matter."

"Then I feel quite at my liberty to call you the rascal you are," I said.

Leonidas put a hand upon my arm. He turned to Hamilton. "Captain Saunders does not intend to be so harsh, but his need is great."

"Oh, I think he intends it. I have become a convenient object of hatred and blame for him over the years—don't think I haven't heard that you say so, doing no small injury to my own reputation, I might add—but I must clarify a point or two. You know well, Captain, that dismissing you from the army was the only way to save your life. You were under my command when the charges were leveled against you and Captain Fleet. Had I not agreed to a discharge, you would have been court-martialed and likely executed."

"I ought not to have let you talk me into destroying my own reputation."

"The evidence against you was strong," he said. "It might have been a British sham. They may have had enough of your tricks and decided to let us deal with you by allowing us to find false evidence. But remember the mood of the army in those days, the exhaustion and setbacks we'd suffered. Men were still raw from Arnold's betrayal, and at that crucial hour another pair of officers in league with the British would not have been treated well."

It was perhaps unfair to blame him for Fleet's death—by all accounts

Fleet had initiated a fight and come out the loser—but I blamed him anyhow. And, of course, there was more. "What of my reputation? You promised me then that no one would hear of it, yet by the time I returned to Philadelphia it was common knowledge."

"I know," said Hamilton softly, "but I was not the one who made it so. I swore to keep it a secret, but in an army nothing can be a secret for long. I spent the better part of a week trying to find out who had spoken out of turn—I need not tell you how serious a thing that is before a major battle—but I could learn nothing. If you like, Captain, I can parade before you a dozen officers who will recall, ten years later, the fear I put into them over this matter."

"Then you are not the one who ruined Captain Saunders's reputation?" Leonidas asked.

"Of course not," he said. "Why would I? You have wasted your time hating the wrong man. My God, Saunders, why did you not simply ask me? You were always a man who could sniff out a lie. You would have known if I had tried to deceive you."

I *could* sniff out a lie, he was right in that. It was why I sat in astonishment, for I believed him now. His voice was so free, so easy, so empty of guile, I could not help but believe him. For the past ten years I'd cursed the name of Hamilton, considered him a villain and an enemy, and now it seems he was not. I felt sick and foolish and drunk. And, much as I had the night before with Mrs. Lavien, I felt ashamed.

I remained silent, trying to think of everything and blot out all memory and to do both these things at once. While I considered this revelation, too astonished and angry to speak, Leonidas made polite conversation. I looked over at Hamilton, hardly knowing what to make of the long patrician face before me. For ten years I had hated this man as the author of my ruin, and when the country, at least the Jeffersonian part of it, began to hate him as well, to make him the central agent of corruption in our government, I could not help but feel that, at last, the universe had aligned itself with my perceptions of it. Now, it seemed, I hardly knew anything of the man.

When I turned my attention to his conversation with my slave, it seemed they were talking of my troubles with my landlady.

"And this happened the same night Mrs. Pearson contacted him?" Hamilton was saying. "That does sound suspicious. Captain, I cannot pay your way in the world, but I can send a representative to speak to your landlady and ask her, on behalf of the government, to give you three months to set your affairs in order. Will that be sufficient?"

"It is kind," I admitted grudgingly, though I attempted not to sound sullen. One never likes to see a man he is used to hating prove himself magnanimous. "I am grateful, but I must ask you again to put me to work, to make use of my skills."

"Your skills are formidable, and I could use a man like you," he said, "but I cannot have you inquiring into something involving these people to whom you are so nearly connected. Not only will I not engage your services, I must ask you to have nothing to do with the matter. Stay out of Lavien's way."

"You cannot expect me to ignore Mrs. Pearson's distress," I said.

"You will stay away from her," he answered, his voice becoming harsh.

"I understand there is a gathering in a few days at the Bingham house," I said airily. "I'm sure the lady will be in attendance, for she and Mrs. Bingham are good friends. Perhaps I shall tend to her there."

"Damn it, Saunders, you will stay away from Mrs. Pearson in this inquiry. This is not a game. There are spies everywhere, and there is more at risk here than you can imagine."

"Spies? What, the British? The Spanish? Who?"

He let out a long breath. "The Jeffersonians."

I barked out a laugh. "You are afraid of a member of your own administration?"

"Laugh if you like, but Jefferson's ambition knows no bounds, and he would do anything—destroy me, the American economy, even Washington's reputation—if it meant advancing his own ends. Have you never looked at his vile newspaper, the *National Gazette*, written by that scoundrel Philip Freneau? It is full of the most hateful lies. Have you so forgotten the past that you think no ill of maligning Washington?"

"Of course I have no patience for insults against Washington," I said. "I revere him as a patriot ought. But that is beside the point. As near as I can tell, you wish me not to help Fleet's daughter because you fear Jefferson. Perhaps I should speak with *him*."

"Stay away from him," said Hamilton. His voice was now nearly a hiss. "Stay away from Jefferson, from Mrs. Pearson, and from this inquiry. I will not allow your curiosity to risk everything I've attempted to accomplish."

Everything he had attempted to accomplish? There was clearly much more happening here than he would admit, and I knew I could not convince him to tell me. Instead, I tried to show myself reasonable. "Then put me to use on another matter," I said. If he did so, he would pay me, which would be of great benefit, and then I could inquire into whatever I liked.

He shook his head. My willingness to change the subject appeared to ease him considerably; the redness in his face lessened and his posture became less rigid. "Captain, I wish I could do so, but look at you. It is not ten in the morning, and you are already besotted with drink. You are terribly disordered. Give me a few hours to clear up the business with your landlady, and then go home, rest, and consider your future. In a few months, come see me. If you are in better order, we can talk about a position at that time."

"I am hardly the only man in Philadelphia to take a drink in the morning," I said.

He leaned forward. "I am not a fool, Captain. I know the difference between a drinker and a drunkard."

I thought to rise and announce my indignation, but I did not feel it. I could be besotted with drink and still best Lavien or anyone else he thought to employ over me. I had no doubt that events would soon prove it.

Joan Maycott

Spring 1789

Our meeting with Colonel Tindall left me feeling as though the earth itself had been taken apart and set back together, though not precisely the way it had been before. We came out of his house, stunned and stiff, as though from a funeral. The sky was shockingly blue, the way it so often seems in its brightness to stand in counterpoint to our own inner turmoil, but over Pittsburgh a cloud of smoke and coal fire hung like a vision of perdition. To add to this effect, we found Reynolds waiting by a pair of mules, which had our possessions already loaded. He looked us over, perhaps attempting to evaluate how we had chosen with Tindall. Then he laughed.

"Hendry and Phineas'll be here soon. They'll take you out to your plot. I can't go with you." He looked out to the expanse of wilderness. "I ain't made to feel welcome."

Andrew said nothing, allowing the silence to cast its own withering retort.

"I got to get back east to my wife," said Reynolds, as though we were all old friends. "She's pretty, like yours. It don't suit for a man to be too long away from his wife."

Andrew remained silent.

"Look here, Maycott. Let me give you some advice. I know we ain't got along on the way out here, but I had to keep order, and that's what I done. Don't mean I got anything against you. And the way things are with Tindall, don't think I don't know. I say, so what if he wants your wife? What does it signify? He's an old man, probably can't do much anyhow. Why not give him what he asks? You get something for it, and it don't really cost you anything."

"Would you prostitute *your* wife?" Andrew asked.

He shrugged. "Depends on what was in it for me. If I was in your shoes, it's what I'd do. I ain't been put up to this by Tindall. I'm just telling you what I think."

He put out his hand for shaking, and when Andrew did not take it he shrugged and walked across the grounds, disappearing into the stables.

We waited there an hour until Hendry and Phineas appeared on horseback. They provided ragged horses for us to ride, and soon we were upon a dirt track through the wilderness, well beaten and pocked with hoof marks and old manure.

We rode through barren landscape for more than half a day. The land was thick with oak and sugar maple and chestnut and birch trees, surrounded by brambles and boulders and rotten logs as large and ornate as monuments. Animals too; we saw deer scatter and bears off in the distance, and the occasional wolf loped along our path, mouth open in lazy defiance. There were other wild things too. Along the barely discernible path, from time to time, we passed clusters of cabins and dirty, ragged people who stopped their toil to watch us. One-eyed men looked up from their fieldwork or tree felling or tanning. The women stared like feral things, their faces sun-blasted and soulless, their bodies twisted and bent, far more terrible in appearance than the most wretched creature I'd seen in Pittsburgh. I understood without being told that, though life in the West might be hard for men, it was doubly so for women. Once the hunting and farming and clearing were done, a man might settle down with his whiskey and his twist of tobacco, but a woman would still be cooking and mending and spinning. I feared in my heart that I should become one of those broken, horrid things. I did not tremble to lose what men called beauty, but I feared the loss of my spirit and humor and love of living, the things I believed made my soul human and vibrant.

Finally, and seemingly without cause, Hendry called for us to stop. We were upon a spot of the forest no different, as far as I could tell, from any other. While he picked at a scab on his face, Hendry gazed about, taking stock of tree and rock and sky.

"Looky there," he said, pointing to a large boulder up ahead, maybe a quarter of a mile. "That's the north border of your land," he said. "Them thick trees we passed back there, the ones with white paint on 'em, that's the southern border. Lotta rattlesnakes near there, if you care to mind 'em. Don't matter to me. The rest of it runs from here to the creek on the east and west to the other creek. Unload the mules, and good luck to ye."

"What?" I cried out. I wanted to be as stoic, as sturdy, as Andrew, but I could not help it. "You're going to leave us in the wilderness with no roof over our heads?"

"Shelter ain't my worry," he said. "My worry is getting the animals back. This is your land, what you bargained for, so here it is. Do with it what you want. You don't like living on it, go find a room in town. It's nothing to do with me, though I'd advise you to be on your guard for painters. Too many of them about this spring."

"What is a painter?" asked Andrew.

Hendry looked at Phineas and they both laughed.

"They don't know about painters," Phineas said, with an unmistakable tone of cruelty. "Guess they'll find out."

Hendry's nose had begun to run as a consequence of his mirthful snorting. He wiped it with his forearm. "You talk smart, but you'll get a good schooling, won't you, maybe in its jaws? A painter is like a cat, if you know what one of them is, but about ten times bigger, and it likes to eat fresh and tender eastern folk."

I'd had quite enough of Mr. Hendry. "I believe you mean a *panther*. If you wish to mock people for their ignorance, you ought at least to say what you mean."

"Call the critter any name you like. It'll tear the bubbies right off you all the same."

"Enough. You are going, so get gone," Andrew said. He put a hand on my shoulder.

"That's a good thankee for one what's brung you home." Hendry snorted.

Phineas eyed me unkindly. "Don't signify. They'll be dead 'fore end of winter."

"You can't leave us here." How I hated the tears that welled up in my eyes, but I could endure it no longer. "Are we to sleep on the ground like animals?"

Andrew shook his head. "I know how to make a shelter and endure far worse than this. We'll make do, never you mind."

"I cain't say what you brung in your packs," Hendry said, "but from the looks of you I reckon you come with nothing and expect the spirits of the woods to raise you up a wigwam. Well, good luck, I say, for yer on yer own now."

"I don't doubt they'll do fine," said a voice from behind us, "but if you please, my good turd, they won't do it alone."

I turned and saw two dozen men and nearly that many women, some of whom had children clinging to their skirts or babes in their arms. There were beasts—a quartet of sturdy horses, a pair of mules, and half a dozen frolicking dogs. Nearly all the men wore western attire, and they carried guns and knives and had tomahawks looped to their belts. They looked like white savages, clad in beast skins and furs, and yet for all that a humanity shone through.

The one who'd spoken stepped forward. He was a tall man, almost a giant, I thought, and looking every bit the frontiersman in western garb and reddish whiskers, which were, if not long, then at least ornate. His mustaches, in particular, drooped down from his face with a curious flourish. This man removed his raccoon cap to bow, revealing an entirely bald head.

"Lorcan Dalton at your service," he said, his voice redolent with the tones of an Irishman. Returning the hat to his head, he said, "We'll get to more introductions soon enough, but first let's get these villains back to their master."

"Hain't no call for unkindness," said Phineas.

"You want kindness, you quit Tindall," Mr. Dalton said.

Hendry turned his horse to face Mr. Dalton. "You act like we ought to fear you, Irisher."

Mr. Dalton grinned, showing a mouth of regular brown teeth. "Reynolds used to bring out the new ones. He doesn't do it now, does he? Guess maybe that pretty wife back east don't like the scar."

Hendry said nothing. He and Phineas tied together the horses and mules and rode off without a backward glance.

"I never lament seeing the back of Hendry," said Mr. Dalton, "and I'd only relish the front if there were a bullet in it. He's worse than any two Indians and only makes amends for it with his lack of cunning. Now, then, let's let the women start making us some repast while we men get to working. Lot of folks come out here, Mr. Maycott, who never got their hands too dirty before, but you don't look like that sort. You look like you're equal to some hard work."

"I reckon I am," Andrew said. "But what work is that?"

"They bring you out here," Dalton said, "and they leave you here. And why not? Tindall and Duer—they don't care if we live and would rather we die, for they can then turn about and pass the land along to another victim. It's why they don't trouble themselves to do aught about the redskins. But we look after one another here. Many folks on the border have turned savage, hardly better than Indians, but we don't let that happen. New folks get the help they need, and all we ask in return is that you do your share when the next new man arrives."

"Of course," said Andrew. I saw he was moved by the kindness. Perhaps back home he would have made free with his emotions, but the western frontier was no place to be a man of feeling.

"Now, you'll need a place to sleep," Dalton said, "so we've come to build you a shelter. And we had better get to work if we're to make any progress before the sun goes down."

So it was that our first day upon our new land showed us both the lowest depths of human greed and evil and the great generosity of the human heart.

They were wondrous in their skills, felling trees, cutting them to size, and, with ropes slung across their shoulders and feet dug in like horses, dragging them to where they might be of use. My innocence, coupled with their single-minded labor, in which they were more like buzzing bees than men, led me to believe that they might build a cabin entire upon the spot, but such luxury was not to be ours. Their design was instead what is commonly called a half-faced camp—a shelter made of logs, composed of but three walls, with a fire built on the fourth side to keep the inhabitants warm and the beasts at a distance. The roof was made of a combination of crossbeams and thatching and would be of limited value in any great rain, but it was far superior to the wild nothingness to which I had believed we had been consigned.

Andrew had brought with him the tools of his trade, and the hardened frontiersmen were pleased and impressed by his carpentry. It seemed he possessed some special new way of bracing the logs together, and they were glad of his addition to the community, if that term could be used for such isolation.

While the men worked, the women provided me with instructions on how best to build a fire and fetch water and regaled me with more information than I could hope to absorb on the spinning of flax, the preparation of bear meat, the uses of bear fat, and a thousand other things I could not recall the next day.

Our rude shelter was completed shortly before dark, and I thought we should be left alone to our first night in the woods, but it seemed that the assistance they provided was, in part, an excuse to gather. The fire that burned outside our shelter was joined by a series of others, and soon the women were roasting meats, boiling porridge, and teaching me to make a kind of western bread called johnnycake, made of nothing but corn flour and water and grilled into flat pieces useful for taking in a travel bag.

These women were helpful but reserved—suspicious, I believed, of what they saw as eastern refinement: my education, my manner of speech, my obvious fear of the West and its environs. Yet they did their best with me and explained about the settlement, a rough and loose confederation of cabins, bound together by little more than vague proximity and a few points of social contact: the church, which lacked any sort of clergyman unless an itinerant wandered through; a rough imitation of a tavern called the Indian Path; a mill; and Mr. Dalton's house. He owned the whiskey still, which made him something of a grandee.

I struggled to feel at ease, but Andrew seemed to have no difficulties. These Westerners valued competence above nearly all else, and he impressed our neighbors with his skills that day. Of these men, two in particular interested me. One was a man my own age, not yet thirty by my estimate, one of the few to keep his face free of whiskers, though it was possible that he could not grow them. He was handsome in a rugged sort of way, with wide eyes that seemed forever lost in thought. He had assisted in the hard labor of building the half-faced camp, and in so doing he had exhibited extraordinary strength. More than once he had been called over by some great bull of a man who wanted this smaller man's assistance in rolling a log or pulling an unmovable lever. Yet, though he exhibited in a thousand ways signs of great strength and no aversion to using it, his interactions lacked the open ease that most men exhibit with one another. At times he and Mr. Dalton exchanged a quiet word, but mostly he kept to himself. Now that the time of merriment had come, he neither ate nor drank as much as the other men but only sat by Mr. Dalton's side, sipping his whiskey while others gulped, smiling politely at jokes while others guffawed and brayed laughter.

The second man piqued my interest also because he was so different. He was no older than Mr. Dalton, but while the great Irishman's power rendered him ageless, this man had something of a scholarly look about him and seemed to me almost old. He wore not the rough clothes of a border man but the practical breeches and shirt and coat of a successful tradesman of the middle rank. He kept his gray hair long and his beard short, and perched upon his nose was a pair of little round spectacles.

He sat upon the ground with the other men, and he drank his whiskey with them, but I observed that on several occasions he turned to look at me. When our eyes met, he turned away and reddened slightly. I have been gazed upon by men before, sometimes in the predatory manner of a Colonel Tindall, but here was something else. I did not know what it was precisely, but it neither frightened nor offended me.

The other women noted his interest as well, and while they talked and gossiped, one creature, a rugged and meaty woman they called Rosalie, with hair somewhere between straw and white, let out a snort. She told me she was not yet forty. She had once been, perhaps, pretty, but now her face had been leathered by the elements, her hands calloused and sun-spotted. "That Scotsman should learn to keep his eyes to himself or I reckon your husband will relieve him of one of them."

"Who is he?" I asked.

"He was a schoolteacher," said another woman, older and thicker than the first and with but three or four teeth in her head. "In Connecticut, they say. But there was a scandal with a married woman. And now here he is, gawking at you like you ain't got a husband right before him."

"He don't belong here," said Rosalie, "and would never have no companionship neither if it weren't for Dalton. He and the Scot make their whiskey together and are friends, like. But then Dalton has his own way with friends."

All the women tittered at this, and I suppose if I had felt more at ease with their company I should have asked about this secret, but as they did not volunteer I did not inquire. I think they did not like my reserve, and one of these women whispered something in the ear of another, and she, in turn, looked at me with face frozen for a long moment before she burst out in laughter.

I loathed this feeling of being unwanted and longed to join the gathering of men. I would have even consented to drink their whiskey if necessary. As I lamented my state, the Scottish gentleman, whom they called Skye, rose from his seat and approached our fire. The women began a fresh round of whispering and laughter but fell into an awkward silence as the man came toward us and took a seat in the dirt next to me.

"I beg your pardon, Mrs. Maycott," he said, in a Scots brogue that reminded me of my father, "but we haven't met. I am John Skye."

"You've met her husband, I'll wager," said Rosalie, igniting a general laughter.

"Maybe she'll take it kindly if you give her your Shake Spear," said one of the others.

"Lord knows Annie Janson weren't impressed," cried a third, to much amusement.

"Might I have a private word with you?" he asked of me.

I looked at the faces about me and knew they disapproved, but I could not live my life for their favor. I pushed myself to my feet and he followed, and we walked away from the women's fire, listening to their cackles and their hooting. We did not step far, remaining close to the men's fire. Andrew looked at me and smiled and then returned to a conversation with Mr. Dalton. Never had there been any mistrust between us on this score, and certainly he could not have mistaken my interest in Mr. Skye and found it inappropriate. Andrew would have seen the thing for precisely what it was and found amusement in it; here, among the rough and unlettered folk of the West, I had found perhaps the only person of a literary turn.

"Your husband tells me you are a great reader of books, Mrs. Maycott," he said. "I wished to let you know that I am lucky enough to possess no small number of volumes, and I should be happy to lend you what you wish."

"You are kind," I said, "though I am not sure a roofed patch of forest floor is the best place to bring so precious a thing as a book."

"You'll have your own home soon enough. Your husband will fell some seventy or eighty good trees in his spare time, and when these are assembled we will have a cabin-raising party. If he is industrious about it, you should be inside doors within a month or two."

I laughed. "A month or two sounds to me like a long time to be outside-of-doors."

He coughed into his fist. "I am fortunate enough to be in possession of a large home, in which I live alone. I have two stories and several rooms. You may, if you wish, pass the time there. I have already made the offer to your husband. The two of you may stay with me."

I sensed that he wished to add that if I chose to stay while Andrew worked about the property, I should be most welcome, but he did not yield to the temptation. Instead, he offered me a crooked smile in which his teeth, very white for a man his age, glistened in the light of the fires.

"It is a funny thing, is it not, people such as ourselves cast adrift in a place such as this?"

"How can you be certain that you and I are people of the same sort?" I asked him, though not unkindly. He addressed me with an attention that was not entirely appropriate, but the great difference in our ages, and the proximity of my husband not many feet away, made me feel there could be no danger in it.

I looked over at the beardless young man, who continued to sit with the others and yet somehow hold himself aloof. "Pray, who is that gentleman?" I asked Mr. Skye.

He let out a guffaw. "Mrs. Maycott, there are no gentlemen in the West. That man, however, is Jericho Richmond. He is Mr. Dalton's friend."

"Does he have but one? I thought I had observed that you are Mr. Dalton's friend."

"Indeed I am. My life should be far more difficult without his friendship. Jericho, however, is Dalton's very *good* friend. They live in the same home."

"He is a handsome man. Does he not have a wife? I was led to believe that people married quite young in the West."

Mr. Skye cleared his throat. "He and Dalton are *very* good friends."

I then understood the nature of the connection, and that it was to be spoken of only obliquely. In some strange way, these ruffians of the West were more tolerant, out of necessity, than men of the East. Jericho Richmond, from what I had observed, worked with every bit the vigor as any other man, and that was, no doubt, all that was required of him. It was Hell we had come to, there could be no doubt of it, but it was turning out to be a curiously complex sort of Hell.

The scene was almost merry. One fellow named Isaac, who worked for Dalton—he called his men whiskey boys, and they ran his spirits throughout the four counties—played a tolerable fiddle. Another whiskey boy, a one-eyed fellow, entertained the children with the story of how he had, fifteen years earlier, been transported to America for the crime of catching a two-pound trout in a squire's pond. Andrew stood with his arm around my shoulder, staring at our little hut, made by his labor and the community's, and I knew he was in some small measure happy or, at the very least, satisfied.

The frolic, as such parties were termed, had been under way many hours, and the men had swallowed a river of whiskey, before trouble showed itself. One of the men who had done much of the work had struck me as the most unsavory of this western lot. He was, like Andrew, a carpenter. As with many western men, it was hard to guess his age, concealed as his face was beneath hair and grime, but I imagined him to be near forty and hardened by his years in the wilderness. He wore an old hunting shirt, much in need of mending, and had a wild prophet's beard near as black as midnight, soiled with food and wood shavings and, I suspected, his own vomit. The other men made no secret of their dislike for him, but they tolerated him for his expertise. Indeed, I suspected that one reason Andrew had been so instantly embraced was because his carpentry skills meant the settlement would be less dependent upon this vile man.

Andrew had taken his measure early on. There had been a dark anger in his eyes when Andrew had mentioned his trade. The bearded man, Mueller, by name, had spat and shaken his head. "Lot of eastern men call themselves what they like. Out here they ain't nothing; no one calls himself carpenter till I give leave." Rather than take offense or give challenge to this bumptious boasting, Andrew had instead given the man the respect he craved. If Mueller was nearby whenever Andrew performed some operation, he would ask the ruffian his opinion. He watched Mueller work and asked questions or made observations upon his skill— which, he informed me, was really quite impressive. "I hate it when men are full of bluster but without merit," he said, "but I hate it more when they actually know of what they speak."

This show of respect did its business, and soon enough Mueller was putting his arm about Andrew, drunkenly shouting that this city dweller would be a man yet. Dalton had informed us that Mueller lived some distance away and had little to do with their community except at those events where his skills could not be done without. Andrew understood that the best course was to pretend friendship and then send him on his way.

At the frolic, however, Mueller would not leave Andrew's side, and his company—along with his stench, his belligerence, and his propensity for physical contact—began to grow wearisome, even oppressive. Westerners drink whiskey as though it were beer, but even by those standards Mueller drank great quantities. When he'd had enough to kill two ordinary men, he began to stagger on his feet and speak so he could hardly be understood. His beard became a great greasy tangle of gristle and tobacco and once, though I did not know its origin, blood.

All night I'd feared he'd been racing toward confrontation, and at last I was proved right. He approached Andrew and gave him a shove in his chest. "You got a nice woman there, Maycott!" he shouted, though they stood but inches from one another.

Andrew offered a faint smile and then shrugged, gesturing toward the crowd of people who gathered around while the fiddle player scratched at his instrument. A dozen or more Westerners sang along to "Lily in the Garden," and Andrew wished to communicate that these conditions made conversation difficult.

"I wouldn'ta thought you could land such a pretty thing, to look at you," Mueller shouted. "Maybe she wants to sit on *my* lap. One carpenter's as good as another, eh?"

Andrew forced a weak smile. "I do love your good cheer, friend." He cast me a glance, which I understood to mean he wished me to disappear from the drunkard's sights.

I had been delivering a dish of roasted turkey to the gathering, so I set it down and turned to make my way back to the cooking fire. Mueller, however, reached out and grabbed my wrist.

"Sit on my lap, I said."

Andrew stepped between us. It was one thing to placate such men when they were merely boorish, but here was something else, and he would not let it pass unchallenged. "You grow too warm," he said, in a voice firm though not yet challenging.

Mueller let go of me and rose to his feet. "And you forget your place."

Andrew appeared to all the world placid, but I knew a fire raged inside him. "My place," he said, in the softest of tones, hardly audible over the music, "is looking to my wife's honor. You know that. If you must challenge me for doing my duty, I stand ready. It is no more than I did in the war."

Isaac still fiddled and the singers still sang, but this conflict had attracted no small attention. Mr. Skye, who from his expression indicated he had expected it all along, was standing now at my side. Mr. Dalton and Jericho Richmond were there too, and I saw from the former's face that he wished to save Andrew this fight. He opened his mouth, ready to speak, but Mr. Richmond whispered something in his ear, and so Mr. Dalton held his tongue.

Mueller gazed upon the onlookers and then at Andrew. There was a pause, and then Mueller lurched forward and wrapped his arms around Andrew—but not in attack. There was a gasp among the onlookers, and several took steps back. Mr. Dalton and I both stepped forward, but there was nothing to do. Mueller had embraced Andrew in a hug.

"You are in the right, friend Maycott. I beg your pardon." I thought at first he sobbed, but no. He let go at once and smiled through the foliage of his filthy beard, and he clapped a hand upon Andrew's shoulder. Once more he said, "Friend Maycott," as though they had been through many adventures together, and no more needed to be expressed.

I did not care for it, however. A man like Mueller might a quarter hour from now decide he had been humiliated and come upon Andrew without warning. I had not been dwelling on this thought for more than a moment before Mr. Dalton appeared at my side.

"You're not easy, are you, missus?" he said.

"No," I agreed. "That man is barbaric. I think he is hardly sane. He could be about murder before Andrew had a chance to defend himself. Can he not be cast out?"

Mr. Dalton shook his head. "That's not what you want, Mrs. Maycott. It's best he be got rid of, but you don't want him making you and yours the object of his anger."

"Then who?" I asked, though I believed I already knew the answer.

"I'll tend it. We've got a new carpenter now, and a better one. I'll ease your husband's way." He said nothing else for a moment, only shifted away from me and toward Mr. Richmond, with whom he began a private conversation, keeping one eye the entire time upon his target. After a moment, Mueller looked over and Dalton pointed to him and said something to Mr. Richmond, who responded with a hearty laugh.

That was the bait, and it was quickly taken. Mueller was at once upon his feet. He strode four or five steps over to the two men and kicked dirt upon the younger one. "You have something to say to me, Richmond?"

Both men met his gaze, but it was Dalton who spoke. "Sit back down, Mueller. Maybe this time you can leave the frolic without a fight."

"What if I don't? I ain't lost one yet."

"You haven't fought *me* yet, have you?" Dalton said, his Irish inflection exaggerated.

"Not yet, and maybe not tonight. 'Tis your good wife I heard laughing at me." He flicked his hand contemptuously at Mr. Richmond.

Dalton took a step forward. "What say you?"

Mueller laughed. He raised his mug to drink, but it missed his mouth entirely and sloshed down his thick neck, soaking his hunting shirt. "I guess Miss Richmond's afraid to fight. The Irisher, I don't doubt, is the man of the house. I reckon every morning—"

This was as far as the speech progressed, for Dalton, who'd had in his mouth a thick wad of tobacco, spat it into Mueller's face. Remarkably, he missed the beard near entire, and the shot landed true in the ruffian's eye.

I watched in stunned silence, clutching Andrew's hand. These men were about to engage in brutal, bloody, maybe deadly combat, but I could not regret it. Better Mueller should fight Mr. Dalton upon these terms than fight Andrew. Even so, I had the uncomfortable feeling I had done something if not precisely wrong then at least improper. Dalton made the choice to put himself at risk, but I could not shake the feeling that he did so for me, not for Andrew, and that I had somehow, without meaning to, convinced him to act.

Mueller stood still, his face red in the light of the fire, the wet of Dalton's tobacco shimmering on his forehead. The crowd stepped forward. One mass of hands pulled at Mueller, the other Mr. Dalton. In my innocence, I believed that the people wished to stay the hand of violence, but that was not the western way. It soon became clear that there were rules to be obeyed. In an instant, the fiddler was done playing, and the singing and dancing had come to an end. Here was the real entertainment of the evening.

Andrew was soon at my right side, Mr. Skye remaining at the other. One of Mr. Dalton's men, the unnaturally tall fellow, Isaac, stepped into the ring of onlookers, circling some fifteen feet across.

"What's it to be, boys?" he called.

Dalton did not hesitate. "Eyes."

Something dark, very much like fear, crossed Mueller's face, still slick from the tobacco. He might have resented the insult, but apparently did not mind the substance enough to wipe it away. Now he squinted narrowly and gritted his teeth. "Aye," he said. "Eyes."

This all sounded confusing to me, which Mr. Skye observed. "Surely you've wondered why so many men here are missing an eye," he said. "'Tis a common challenge. They fight until one man takes the other's."

"But that's monstrous!" I had been pleased that Dalton had been so willing to fight Mueller, but I had not wanted this. If Mr. Dalton were to lose an eye, I would be responsible.

"'Tis the West. But fear not. Dalton's never yet lost, as you can see from his face. And he's been yearning for an excuse to shut Mueller's mouth for two years now."

"It appears that Mr. Mueller has clearly never lost this challenge either," said Andrew.

"He don't often take it. He can't afford to lose an eye in his trade, which you'll no doubt understand. And, at the risk of revealing a partiality, he's never fought Dalton before, and Dalton, you might have observed, is angry. He don't take too kind to remarks about Richmond."

I looked over at Jericho Richmond, who stood on the sidelines, arms folded, watching without agitation. Indeed, there was a little smirk upon his lips, satisfied and a bit impatient, as though the outcome of the contest was already decided.

The two men were released. Dalton at once leaped into the air like a panther and landed hard upon Mueller. The two crashed upon the ground, and I heard something crack, though I could not say if it was twig or bone. The crowd of Westerners grunted their approval. A few men cheered, and one little boy laughed like a shrill madman, but none moved closer. The circle remained still and solid, as if this were some sacred place of Druid worship.

Dalton now lay upon Mueller, his knee pressed across the carpenter's chest, his thick left arm keeping Mueller's own arms pinned. It was a matter of balance, the result of the momentum of Dalton's leap, and it could not have been more than a second or two before Mueller forced Dalton off and changed the balance of momentum. The Irishman's face grimaced with determination and understanding. He bit his lip like a concentrating child as he examined the field of battle and quickly, in an instant too fleeting to be called thought, saw his opportunities and formulated his strategy.

He raised up his right hand, his thumb stuck out like a man beginning an ostentatious count. It hung still, no more than an instant, but I saw that hand like an icon, like a standard, glowing orange in the light of half a dozen fires, and then it plummeted downward, with the fury of a hawk seeking its prey. Mueller let out a piercing cry of surprise, which changed in an instant to a howl of pain. I felt myself tremble with fear and pity and disgust. Mr. Dalton then stood. His face and shirt were covered with blood, which also dripped copiously from his hand as though he had cut open his own flesh. Mueller lay upon the dirt, curled up so I could not see his face, but he emitted a horrible, chilling noise, a lamentation for his life as it had been, as dark blood pooled about his head.

Mr. Skye *tsk*ed like an irritated upper servant. "You can't call the man inefficient." He looked at Andrew. "Dalton's a good friend to have."

Andrew nodded, too numb from horror and surprise to say much. "It's well he seems to like me," he managed, though he spoke hardly louder than a whisper.

"He likes you both," said Mr. Skye, "and he don't take to strangers that often." He glanced back at Mueller's pathetic form. "I guess that's the lesson, though. You can't be friends with everyone, not out here. You make your friends, but you make your enemies as well."

Ethan Saunders

Having given Hamilton enough time to work whatever magic he intended to work, I returned to my rooms at Mrs. Deisher's house that afternoon, where I found that stout German lady ready and willing to receive me. Once her girl opened the door, the landlady herself forced her massive bosoms past the servant and thrust them toward me.

"Mr. Saunders," she said, "I your pardon beg. I mean to say *Captain* Saunders. I trouble myself for the misunderstanding, but the man from the government has everything made clear. Are you hungry? May I make for you something to eat?"

"Be easy on the matter of food," I said. "I am, however, much in need of a wash and a change of clothes, not having had access to fresh linens in well over a day."

She colored. "I must beg again your pardon, Captain. Now I shall send my Charlotte to bring for you the waters."

I smiled benevolently at her, for now we were good friends. All was easy between us, and we had nothing but love in our hearts. "Oh, and one more thing, Mrs. Deisher. Before I send you away, please be so good as to mention why, precisely, you chose that night to cast me out."

She cringed a bit at this. "It was just a notion, a terrible foolish notion. You must forgive."

I continued to smile, but my voice was icy. "I shall forgive you when you tell me the truth."

"Oh, I would never lie," she said, to her shoes.

"Madam, you have seen how friendly I am with the government. If you do not tell me what I ask, I shall have you arrested for a foreign spy—let's say French, since the notion of a German spy is absurd—and you will be cast out of the country forever. Perhaps, as reward, I shall be given your property for my own. Leonidas! Take a letter for me. *Dear Secretary Hamilton: It is with grave concern that I must report to you the presence—*"

"Enough!" she called. "I will tell you, only you must not say I did. He promised to hurt me if I did not remain quiet."

"I shall protect you with my life," I said, "if you but tell me."

"It was a very uncivilized-looking man," she said, "with a gray beard and long hair. He gave his name as Reynolds. He paid me twenty-five dollars and said he would burn down my house if I did not do as he says."

"Did he say who he was or why he wished me gone?"

She shook her head. "No, but I believed him. He seemed to me like the sort of man who might a house burn."

I nodded. "Be so kind as to give me the twenty-five dollars. I think I've earned it."

"I have already spent it," she said.

"Then give me a different twenty-five dollars."

"I have not got it."

"Perhaps she could apply it to what you owe," suggested Leonidas.

It was not as good as having twenty-five dollars in my pocket, but it would have to do. I turned to Mrs. Deisher. "I accept those terms. Now, let's not forget about my bath."

She stood and shook her head. "It don't make sense."

"What is that?"

"He say, this Reynolds, that he throw you out behalf of Secretary Hamilton, but he must lie, for it is Secretary Hamilton that make me take you in."

I felt something, like a dog catching a familiar scent in the air. Leonidas turned quickly, but I caught his eye and gave him a most subtle shake of the head. Long ago I learned that when someone inadvertently stumbles upon something important, you do not draw attention to it. "How interesting," I said, in order to say something. "Now to the bath." There could be no further progress without washing off the accumulated filth of my trials.

At last I was able to remove the grime and humiliation of the past two nights. The warm water was a balm, the clean clothes as good as a full night's sleep. Once I had cleaned myself and had Leonidas shave me, I felt free to examine my reflection in the mirror that hung over my fireplace. In truth, I was not entirely displeased. My face was a bit contused. There were bruises and a few wounds, which were healing far more slowly than they had in my youth, but in my newly scrubbed state, these now bespoke manly combat and not impoverished desperation.

Able to enjoy the calm of my room, I sat in a well-padded chair near the window in the fading afternoon light. Across from me, Leonidas put away the shaving things. Once finished, he took one of the chairs and gave me a meaningful look. "Perhaps," he said, "it is time to consider your next move. Do you truly wish to squander your time attempting to find Mr. Pearson?"

"Of course I intend to find him."

He leaned forward in his serious way. "Ethan, you should think about this. You have little money right now, and I understand that you care for Mrs. Pearson, but caring does not mean you must sacrifice yourself to her memory. If Mr. Lavien does not wish your help, perhaps the matter is in hand."

"To begin with, I would never turn my back on an old commitment."

"I am not convinced of that," he said, with much bitterness. "I've seen it happen."

I was not about to get dragged into another conversation about his emancipation. "On top of that, I have been personally injured. Men have sought to intimidate and harm me, to have me cast from my home. I cannot simply turn my back. And what is most amazing to me is Hamilton. All these years I believed it was he who chose to ruin my reputation by putting it about that I had committed treason, and I hated him for it. Now, it seems, I was mistaken. Hamilton turns out to be a fairly decent fellow, and he went so far as to say that he values my skills."

"What of it?"

"Don't you see? If I can find Pearson first, if I can beat Lavien at his own game, Hamilton will bring me back into government service. I will be of *use* again, Leonidas. I cannot let something like that slip between my fingers."

"How are you going to best a man like Mr. Lavien, who has his own impressive skills, is younger than you, and enjoys the protection and power of the government?"

"I believe we shall do so not by pursuing the obvious but by pursuing lines of inquiry that are ours exclusively. What do we know that Lavien does not?"

"We don't know what Lavien knows, since he won't share anything."

"But we can operate on certain assumptions. Let us assume, first of all, that Lavien and Hamilton don't know about the Irishman, they certainly don't know about the note from Mrs. Pearson, and it seems to me likely that they don't know about this Reynolds man pretending to be one of their own. Lavien has been looking for Pearson for nearly a week now, but he does not seem close to finding him; otherwise he would not have followed Mrs. Pearson to my rooms. I'm sure he is going about it the usual way—speaking to his family, his friends, his business associates—but this method has yielded him nothing. We shall try it my way, Leonidas, the old Fleet and Saunders method, and we shall see who finds the man first."

"And what does that mean?" he asked.

I took out my stolen timepiece and checked what o'clock it was. "Let's return to see Hamilton. I have an important question for him."

Leonidas shook his head. "He won't like it."

"I know," I said. "It's why we need to find a newspaper first. I will require something to persuade the secretary to be amiable."

"A newspaper," he repeated.

I was on my feet, reaching for my hat. "You were not so privileged as to be in my company when I served the nation during the war, Leonidas."

"No, but I have heard the stories," he said, his tone implying that they were somehow tedious. I must have misunderstood him.

"This is your lucky day, then. Now you will, at last, see how business is done."

It had surprised me how quickly Hamilton had seen me that morning. It did not surprise me that he made us wait well over an hour that afternoon. We sat in a vestibule outside the front office, which was, in turn, outside Hamilton's sanctum. Anxious-looking clerks hurried in and out, avoiding eye contact with us. It was daylight, albeit of a gray and cloudy sort, when we entered the treasury buildings, and darkness fell while we awaited Hamilton's pleasure. A pair of young Negroes came around lighting candles and lamps, and as they passed through our room they nodded at Leonidas, who nodded back. Did they know one another, or was this merely the recognition of race?

At last a clerk ushered us into the Treasury Secretary's office, which in the darkness had a far more dour and constricted feel. Hamilton sat at his desk and hovered over his oil-lit work like an angry bear in its cave. "I had not expected to see you so soon," he said.

"And you do not sound happy to do so. No matter, we won't waste your time. Just a quick question and we'll be on our way."

"I believe I was clear," he said. "I do not want you inquiring into Pearson's disappearance."

"And what makes you think I am doing that?"

"Look at you. You are like a dog on a hunt."

"Only one question," I said.

"No, Saunders, I'll not play games with you. You may wait there as long as you like, but I'll not start answering your questions." He turned to his paper and began writing.

"I anticipated this," I said. "Leonidas, please hand me that newspaper I asked you to bring along. I expected we would have to wait, and so I brought reading material. It is the *National Gazette,* which you mentioned to me earlier."

Hamilton looked up, clearly unhappy that I would read a paper whose single purpose was to attack him.

"I do love this paper," I said. "And its editor, Mr. Philip Freneau. Clever fellow. Now that I think on it, I have an excellent idea for an article. Take a letter, Leonidas: *Dear Mr. Freneau: You may not be aware of this stunning fact, but apparently Alexander Hamilton is currently employing his own Jewish half brother to inquire into the mysterious dealings of a noted Philadelphia gentleman.*" To Hamilton I said, "I know the half-brother business is false, but it will get his attention, and I'll let him sort the rest out himself. You know how scrupulous these journalistic fellows are about their facts."

"Enough!" Hamilton slammed his hand against the desk. "You would not dare."

"Just a simple question, Colonel. Much easier that way."

"Damn it, Saunders, what is this about?"

"It is about Fleet and about his daughter. I would think you, of all people, would understand. It was always said that you were a man for the ladies."

His eyes narrowed in anger. "If you think—" he began to bark.

"I don't mean you are a scoundrel, as your enemies like to cast about. I mean you understood the old ways, that a man must do what is right to protect a woman, a woman who, however incidentally, has crossed under his protection. So long as I think there is any chance of Cynthia Pearson being in danger, I will try to protect her. You may as well settle in for a long siege."

He shook his head sadly and slumped slightly in his chair. "Very well. If it will make you go away."

"See? Nothing simpler. My question is fairly simple. Does the name Reynolds mean anything to you?"

I had anticipated denial or obfuscation or genuine confusion. I did not anticipate what actually happened. Hamilton leaped to his feet. His heavy chair toppled behind him. Even in the poorly lit chamber I could see his face had turned red. "What do you mean by this?" he shouted. "Do you think to push my endurance to its limits?"

I exchanged a look with Leonidas, who was as confused as I. To

Hamilton I affected calm, always the best way with a man in a rage. "I mean nothing, Colonel. The man who paid my landlady to cast me out said his name was Reynolds. I merely wished to see if you knew him. Apparently you do."

Hamilton blinked at me several times and then at Leonidas. He turned around, righted his chair, and sat down again. He dusted off a spot on his desk. "I don't know the name. It means nothing to me."

"Just so," I said. "I thought as much, for your ignorance of the name effectively explains your outburst. Well, I'll just post a letter to Mr. Freneau. Perhaps he can do a bit of digging into the matter for me."

"Oh, sit down." Hamilton suddenly sounded tired. "I'll tell you, but you must promise not to pursue this. And I don't want you coming to my office and threatening me every time you have a question."

"Absolutely," I said, knowing full well I meant to take the information on any terms now and worry about the meaning of those terms later.

"Since you are such a close reader of Mr. Freneau's paper," Hamilton said, "you are undoubtedly familiar with the name William Duer."

"From the war as well. He supplied the army, didn't he?"

"That's right," said Hamilton. "He also served as my assistant for the first few months of my term at Treasury, but Duer, despite his patriotic impulses, was always looking for a better opportunity. He and I were once close friends, but things have been strained between us. I did not like the way in which he executed his duties while he served as my assistant, and he has also shown a coarse side at other times.

"As you know, the Bank of the United States launched last summer, and the price of shares soared astronomically. Duer invested heavily, but his investment became not only a sign but a symptom. He is so wealthy, he invests so much money, and his choices are of so much interest that Duer's actions not only reflect or even moderately affect the market, they directly shape it. When he buys, everyone buys. When he sells, everyone sells. Try to understand what I am telling you. Ours is a unique economy, unlike any in the history of the world, for two reasons. In most nations trading is centralized—in London, Paris, Amsterdam. In our country, a man is used to thinking of his state as an autonomous entity, and the first reason is that trading is decentralized—in New York, Philadelphia,

Boston, and so on. The other reason is that the nation is new and, in terms of the number of major participants, very small. One man, a single actor, can alter the shape of the market if he is careful."

"Or careless," observed Leonidas.

Hamilton nodded. "Precisely. Duer, I fear, may be both. He uses his undue influence—understand me that he has an influence unlike any other single man in any single market in the history of finance as we know it—he uses this power to manipulate prices to his advantage, sending up the price of shares. He planned to raise them to their limit and then sell at an enormous profit, crashing the value of bank shares as he did so. Before things could get so far out of hand, I let it be known that I thought the trading price of bank shares was inflated—and in doing so depressed the market, costing Duer a great deal of money. He was very angry with me."

"Go on," I said.

"This Reynolds works for Duer. I believe he may have been exacting some revenge on you in order to get to me."

"Colonel, you and I have not spoken in ten years. Why would he use me to harm you?"

"He may have made assumptions. He knows of you from the war. Perhaps he thought I would use you to conduct my inquiries, such as the one involving Mr. Pearson. He wished to thwart me for the sake of vengeance."

I took a moment to let the silence do some work. "So, Duer is angry with you over an incident last summer and chooses to inconvenience me now as a way of extracting revenge?"

"Revenge," said Hamilton, "or merely to push back at me and show me he still has power, yes. That is my theory, in any case. Now you need but let the matter alone, and I will see to it that you are not troubled any longer."

"Very kind, but you know, I think I'd like to speak to Duer myself. I presume I can find him with the other speculators at the City Tavern?"

Hamilton sighed. "Duer lives in New York. He comes here on business but has not been in town for some weeks. I believe he has some business in New York that absorbs his attention. You see, there is nothing for you to do, and this matter has nothing to do with Pearson. I am asking you to let it alone."

I stood up. "Of course. It is hardly worth a trip to New York over something like this, and I have other things to do besides hunting down Duer's man. I am sorry to have troubled you. Good night, Colonel."

We strolled out of the office and past the clerks stationed outside.

"Surely you did not believe any of that?" said Leonidas.

"Of course not," I said, "but it was hardly to our advantage to push him further. He did not want to tell us more, and he would not have done so. Pressing him would have only made him angry. For now we take what he has given us and see where it leads us."

Leonidas was about to speak when a thunderous roar erupted from inside Hamilton's office. "Damn it!" cried the Secretary of the Treasury. This cry was followed by the sound of glass breaking. Several of the clerks looked up from their work, hesitated nervously, and then returned to their business.

For our part, we hurried outside and toward our next destination.

The Crooked Knight was a decidedly Jeffersonian tavern on the cusp of the Northern Liberties, a wretched place on Coats Street near the Public Landing, frequented by workingmen full of private rage masquerading as political anger. These were the sorts who read Freneau's *National Gazette* aloud, jeered at each mention of Hamilton, and cheered at every reference to Jefferson. Indeed, off in one corner a spot had been roped off for a cockfight between one bird, stout and muscular and resplendent with shiny black feathers—this one called Jefferson—and another, scrawny and weak and pale—called Hamilton. Each time the larger bird attacked the lesser, the crowd cheered and cried out in praise of liberty and freedom.

This was, in other words, a tavern wholly dedicated to men of a democratic republican turn of mind. These men believed the American project to have been already tainted by venality and corruption. These were men who worshiped George Washington as a god but were willing to damn him to Hell for admitting Hamilton into his inner circle. These men had rioted against the ratification of the Constitution without having troubled themselves to read it—if they could read at all. They would only have known that some petty John Wilkes in their number had cried out that their liberties were in danger; if there was beer enough, they were always ready to answer the call.

It was not the sort of public house I frequented with any regularity. I prefer taverns where I may game or drink in quiet or talk in peace with those to whom I wish to speak, not cheer while a man I hardly know gives voice to a resentment I never knew I had.

The owner, however, was an old acquaintance, if not precisely a friend, and I had a reasonable expectation of obtaining some little help in that quarter. The Irishman outside the Statehouse had identified himself as a man of the Jeffersonian faction, and, if he drank in Philadelphia, it would likely be in the Crooked Knight or someplace like it. It was my hope that there I could find some means of learning his name or location.

It was far less wet and cold than recent nights and, as the tavern was the sort of place not likely to make a Negro feel at his ease, I asked Leonidas to wait outside. Pushing open the wooden door, I walked into a long low-ceilinged room filled with tobacco stench, wood smoke, and the scent of sausages roasting in fires. The men sat in small groups, huddled around low tables, their feet pressed into the dirt of the floor. Conversation, which had been boisterous but a moment before, at once tapered down as all inside stared at me. The Crooked Knight was the sort of place outsiders sought to avoid.

I went at once to the bar, where a man of exceptional shortness stood upon a box, polishing mugs. I knew him as Leonard Hilltop, a humorless sort with deeply lined skin that looked like carved stone and hollow eyes dark in color and bright with thick swaths of red, visible even in the poor light of that room. In his youth, he had been part of a network in occupied Philadelphia that had passed intelligence, often to me. It did not make us friends but it made us familiar, and there was undeniably trust and respect between us.

"Go back to your drink, you sods," called the little man. "He's all right, this one."

The men did as they were told, and at once the space was filled with the hum of conversation.

"Well, now," said Hilltop. "That was my first lie of the evening."

"Let us hope it is the last," I said.

He snorted. "What is this? You run too big a debt in every other tavern in town, and now you must drink here? A bit of a risk, isn't it? The men here might not know your face, but they know your name and what you're said to have done. If I were to tell them who you are, you'd be torn to bits like that there Federalist chicken." He waved a hand toward the cockfight.

"It's well I can trust you to keep quiet then," I said. "In any case, you know the truth. My reputation was fouled by Federalists. Indeed, you told me so yourself those many years ago. You said it was Hamilton that exposed me. How precisely did you hear that, Hilltop?"

"Christ, I can't recall," he said. "It was a long time ago. It was just what I heard. Everyone said so."

I was not hopeful he would remember, but it did no harm to ask. "In any case, I'm sure you can spare a drink for an ill-used patriot. Perhaps that most American of elixirs, which we call Monongahela rye, that drink of border men, hideously taxed by the nefarious Hamilton. Just a single glass of whiskey shall serve my purpose."

"As you put it so," said Hilltop with a grimace, like a man who had been outplayed at cards and now must accept defeat. He poured a hearty quantity into a mug and handed it to me undiluted. I tasted it and found it remarkably like that which the Irishman had given me.

I set the glass down. "It's good, this whiskey."

"Aye, the best there is."

"Where do you get it?"

He grinned. "I've my sources."

I took another sip. "Is your source a rugged Irishman with a hairless and leathery skull?"

Had I knocked Hilltop off his stool I could not have astonished him more, and that was certainly my goal. I might have worked the matter over slowly, like a tongue in search of the precise location of a vaguely aching tooth, but I saw no point in it. Hilltop was a suspicious sort, and a direct approach seemed best.

Hilltop had aided spies in the war, but he was not a spy himself and had no training other than to hope what he did went unnoticed, and this was often enough crudely practiced. I noticed his eyes shift to a table where a man sat alone. He was of about forty years, with dark receding hair and a flat, long-mouthed, froggish sort of face. He sat hunched over a piece of paper, quill in hand, and did not so much as look up. Hilltop next glanced near the fire where two men sat in close conversation, working hard to pretend they did not see me. I took in this scene without giving hint to the men or to Hilltop that I did so. Indeed, I was able, over the course of the next several minutes, to reposition myself so I could keep a perpetual eye on these men without letting them know I did so.

"What do you know of him?" Hilltop asked me.

"I know you know him," I said, "as you've not troubled to inquire of whom I speak. I'd like a word with him, and I should very much prefer if he did not know I was coming."

"What, do you work for Hamilton again?" Hilltop asked me. "After all he done to you?"

It was uncomfortably close to the truth, and I could not afford the luxury of believing I was the only clever man in this conversation. "I have my own business with him."

"I ain't seen that man in here in some time," Hilltop said. "Few months back, he sold me a dozen barrels of this whiskey, and I was happy to get my hands on it. He ain't been in since, though I did hear tell of him not two weeks ago."

Hilltop certainly had my attention, though it was not so full as he believed, but thinking me riveted by his intelligence he gave the slightest of nods to the two men by the fire. One of them, the taller and younger of the two, handed something to the shorter and older. Then the first of these men rose and left the tavern. I hated to let him go, but I could only attempt to apprehend one man, and I thought it might as well be the one who had whatever item had been passed off.

"Haven't seen him," Hilltop was saying, "not personally, but a week ago a patron of the Knight says he saw him coming out of a boarding-house on Evont Street, near the corner of Mary, down in Southwark. I don't know if the Irishman lived there or was visiting, but this man said it was him, all right. I hoped to find him myself on account of wanting to buy more of his whiskey."

"You know who he is?" I asked. "His name, his business?"

Hilltop shook his head. "Didn't say much, but he'd been hurt by Hamilton's whiskey tax, that much is certain."

The whiskey tax had been approved by Congress as a simple means of helping fund the Bank of the United States. What better way to raise revenues, it had been argued, than to tax a luxury, and a harmful one at that, that many enjoyed? Let the men who would waste their time with strong drink pay for the economic growth of the new nation. This had become a major cause of resentment among the democratic republican types who liked to pass their time, as fate would have it, by drinking whiskey.

The shorter and older man, the one who had been given something of import, now pushed himself away from his table and began to head for the door. Hilltop must have noticed my interest, because he said, "Let me pour you another one, Saunders. Even better than the first, I'll warrant."

It was tempting, but I thanked Hilltop, and told him I would be back to collect it soon enough. I moved to the door. The man had his eye upon me, and there could have been no way to move without attracting his notice. He opened the front door and broke into a run. I began to run as well. A large man immediately stepped forward into my path, but I dodged past him, more lucky than skillful, and was out of the tavern and into the cold.

Leonidas was already on alert, and I needed only to point to the running man to send him off in a mighty sprint. I checked behind us, and while the drinkers at the Crooked Knight had been willing to block my passage, they were not willing to venture out into the night in an adventure that did not concern them. Seeing that no one pursued us, I redoubled my efforts. I felt a stitch in my side, but I pushed onward, not because I thought I could overtake Leonidas, but I wished not to be too terribly far behind when the man was brought down.

They turned north on St. John toward Brown Street, where the man headed west. As he reached the corner of Charlotte, Leonidas gave a great leap and tackled the man. He landed flat, with his arms outstretched, and I arrived upon the scene just in time to observe the stranger attempt to slip something into his mouth. I could not see it well in the lamplight, but it was small and shiny. Leonidas did not notice, for he was too occupied in keeping the man down, so, though I was still twenty feet away, my side ached, and I feared I might vomit up the whiskey I'd been drinking, I found strength to dash forward and stomp my foot down upon the man's wrist.

It did the business, for his hand opened, and out rolled a silver ball, about the size of a large grape. I had not seen one since the war, but I knew what it was immediately, and I felt a chill of terror run through me. Whatever I was now involved in, whatever Cynthia Pearson had become trapped in, was far more dangerous than I had imagined.

I had only just secured the ball when things happened in an astonishing succession. Leonidas slumped forward, letting out a loud grunt. The man under him scrambled backward and ran off down Charlotte Street, and I was once more surrounded by Nathan Dorland and his several friends.

It was Dorland and the same three men who had assaulted me outside the tavern in Helltown. I could not imagine how they had found me, but they must have followed us to the Crooked Knight and then out again.

Without taking more than a cursory glance toward Dorland and his men, most of whom had pistols, I slipped the silver ball into my pocket and leaned down to see if Leonidas was hurt. He had been struck in the head with a pistol, and he bled, but not egregiously. He stirred now and rubbed the back of his head and then rose, slowly and deliberately, like a great monster rising from its lair.

"Who struck me?" His voice was calm but full of quiet, coiled menace.

"What, shall you return violence to a white man?" asked Dorland. "Consider yourself fortunate I did not shoot you on sight."

"Hold," I said.

"The time for holding is done," said Dorland. "You'll not have anyone to rescue you this time, Saunders. You are finished."

I did not want to be finished. I had Cynthia Pearson to protect, and I had, not quite at my fingertips, the prospect of redemption, of returning to the service of my country. I had the silver ball in my pocket, and I could not guess what mysteries it contained. I had important work before me, and I could no longer afford this game with Dorland. Once his rage and inept thirst for revenge had amused me, because I could pull upon his strings and he would dance. Now it stood in my way, cropping up when I would have quiet and calm. Leonidas had been hurt and might next time, were I to escape to find a next time, be killed. It was all this, and there was another thing. It was what Mrs. Lavien had said to me the night before, that I had become something shameful, but that each new day brought the promise of a new path. Her words reverberated now like a cold blade against my skin, making me awake, alert, terrified. It was for all these reasons, and perhaps others, that I turned to Dorland and said what I said.

"I have wronged you and then ridiculed you for that wrong. I apologize, though I know an apology will offer you little satisfaction. Instead, I offer you what you have long wished for. I shall meet you in accordance with the code duello at the time and place of your choosing. Dorland, I accept your challenge."

"Well, now," said one of his friends.

"I never would have thought it," said another, at almost the same time.

Dorland, however, held up his hand in silence. "Do you mock me?"

"Not anymore. I am done with that, and I won't place my friends in danger any longer."

He shook his head. "I don't believe you, Saunders, and if I did, it would still be too late. You had your chance for honor. Now it is time for an ignominious end."

"That is not your choice," said Leonidas. "You must honor the code."

"I'll not take lessons in honor from a nigger," said Dorland.

"Then take the lesson from me," said one of his friends. "He has accepted your challenge. You cannot refuse to meet him on the field of honor."

"He has no honor," said Dorland.

"That doesn't matter," said another of his friends. "He has accepted your challenge."

"You must do it," said the third.

"One moment," said Dorland. "You are supposed to be with me on this. Macalister, you swore you would aid me."

"Because he would not duel," said the first man who had spoken. I recalled him kicking my side in the Helltown alley. "You asked me to be your second, and I agreed. Now he says he will duel, and you must agree."

Dorland's plump face quivered. "But he is a veteran of the war. I would have no chance against him."

"You mean you will not duel?" asked Macalister.

"Let us deal with him here and now," said Dorland.

And then the most astonishing thing happened. The one called Macalister walked away, and the others followed. Dorland called after them, but they did not look back. There had been four of them, and suddenly it was a dark alley, and Dorland stood alone with me and Leonidas.

"Well," I said. "This is what I believe is called a reversal."

Leonidas took a step closer to him, and Dorland ran fast and hard. I cannot even begin to guess when he noticed that no one ran after him.

In the war, it often happened that messages of vital import would need to be carried through dangerous lines. Various methods could be employed to preserve the secrecy of the message. It could be written in code, it might be carried by an unassuming courier, it could be well hidden away. But what happens when the courier is captured, as must sometimes transpire? One method was to carry the message, written in a tiny hand upon a tiny piece of paper, housed within a little silver ball. If the courier was captured, he could swallow the ball and then, once free of the British (for he would have nothing else upon his person to incriminate him), could retrieve the ball at his own unpleasant leisure.

That the people involved in this scheme, whatever it might be, used such methods frightened me. Whom did they fear? What must they communicate that required such secrecy?

I dared not open the ball in public, but once Leonidas and I returned to my rooms I pried it open and looked at the tiny parchment inside. It read:

W qcas tfca R. ozz cb eqvsrizs vsfs. Ies qcbhoqhe hc qcbtwfa voa eiegsqhe bc-hvwbu. Kwhvcih vwe wbhsftsfsbqs, PIE kwzz tozz pm aofqv.

"It's nonsense," Leonidas said.

"It's a cipher," I told him, "and a fairly simple one. This is quite clearly what is called a Caesar code, so named because it was allegedly invented by Julius Caesar himself. Each letter stands in place of another. If you can break one letter, you can usually break them all."

"How can you do it?" he asked.

"It can always be done, merely by finding patterns common in writing," I said. "Given time, a simple Caesar code can always be broken, which makes them of limited value. This one can be broken more easily than most, however. The people writing this code are not nearly so clever as they wish to think themselves, and they made a number of mistakes. There are, for example, a limited number of words in our language that consist of two letters that can be reversed to make another word. I am guessing *on* and *no*. And look at this: a word of a single letter. It must be *A* or *I*. And all these words end with two identical letters. It is likely that *Z* is an *S* or an *L*. Bring me a pen and paper. There you go. Also, they are foolish enough to use *I* as a discrete word, which gives me everything I need to break the code."

With pen, ink, and paper at my disposal, I began to set up my key, matching the words I believed I could crack with those I could not, substituting letters as I went. It was tedious work, and the whiskey made my vision waver, but I drank it all the same. Soon the puzzle pieces fit together, and I looked at the message. I could scarce believe what I saw, yet there it was.

I come from D. All on schedule here. Use contacts to confirm Ham suspects no-thing. Without his interference, BUS will fall by March.

I stared at the note, hardly daring to comprehend it. Leonidas looked over my shoulder.

"What is BUS?" he asked. "Who is D?"

I had my suspicions about D—Duer?—though I was still too early in the game to say for certain. BUS, however, was another matter. It was the institution that was upon everyone's minds, upon everyone's lips. It was the thing that had elevated Hamilton to unimaginable power and made him, to some, an unspeakable demon. It was the thing that, it now seemed to me, for good or ill, defined our moment in time, much as the Revolution itself had defined the world half a generation ago: the Bank of the United States. What I held in my hands changed everything, for this was not a matter of a missing gentleman and a pushy Irishman. Cynthia was right. Whatever had happened to her husband had something to do with the bank, but it was a far more sinister something than I could have suspected. There was a plot at work, a genuine plot to destroy Hamilton's bank. It was a plot to alter, for good or ill, the future of the American government.

Joan Maycott

Summer and Autumn 1789

The half-face camp built that day proved but a poor shelter, yet shelter it was, and though we endured a few rain showers that rendered it near useless, it was, at most times, not so terrible. To be sure, our difficulties were eased by the help of our new neighbors. Mr. Dalton developed a particular attachment to my husband that first night, and he proved to be a good friend. We learned that his companion, Mr. Jericho Richmond, was generally praised as one of the great marksmen in the region, and in that period of adjustment we would have starved had it not been for their regular gifts of game. Two or three times a week, as sunset approached, we would see the two of them enter our clearing, some great beast stretched over Mr. Richmond's shoulders or, if too large, dragged in a cart. They brought us deer and bear and once a small panther, quite sleek in form and beautiful in its tan color.

"Can panther be eaten?" I inquired, skeptically eyeing the felled beast.

"Panther's good," answered Jericho Richmond, in his terse and soft-spoken manner.

"What does it taste like?" I asked.

Mr. Dalton considered this question. "Tastes a lot like rattlesnake."

I laughed aloud. "You cannot expect me to know what rattlesnake tastes like."

Dalton answered by strolling toward the thick growth of forest. Richmond stared at his back, and then, when Dalton was gone from view, Richmond stared at me. He seemed to have nothing to say, and yet his look held an accusation I did not understand. I attempted conversation—nothing of great complexity, for most of what I said involved speculation upon what Mr. Dalton might be doing—but Richmond would not speak to me. And so we stood there, Richmond as quiet and inscrutable as an Indian, I confused and not knowing how to excuse myself. So we remained until Dalton returned ten minutes later, the limp body of a rattlesnake dangling from one hand, its lifeless head peeking out from above his fist. He held it out to me.

"Roast it on the fire. Don't boil it. Boiling's too tough." He winked at me as I, with some effort, reached out and took the thing from him. Later, when I examined it, I found it had not a scratch upon it, and that, for all I could tell, Mr. Dalton had reached out, grabbed it by the neck, and strangled it. Not precisely Hercules in his crib, but near enough to astonish me.

Richmond said nothing during this exchange, but he shook his head once in a way that made me feel as though I had walked into a disagreement between the two of them.

Dalton was equally useful in selling us supplies that we required, including seed for our first crops and ropes for land clearing, giving us a pup to be raised as a hunting dog and, most useful, an old work horse whom he called Bemis. I later learned that the beast had been named after the skirmish at Bemis Heights, the pivotal encounter of the battle at Saratoga, in which both Mr. Dalton and Mr. Richmond had served under Colonel Daniel Morgan. Mr. Dalton told us that Mr. Richmond was the marksman who dispatched the British general Simon Fraser, a shot that changed the course of the battle and thus of the war itself, given the victory's influence on France's entry into the conflict. It was something I loved about my country. In a war with countless turning points, one never needed to look far to find the men who had worked the levers upon which all depended.

With the occasional assistance of our new friends, Andrew managed to fell eighty trees within three weeks, and so the call went out that there was to be a cabin raising. I had thought our camp building had been a significant gathering, but a cabin raising turned out to be an event of an entirely different order. Mr. Dalton had it put about that he wished everyone to help, and as a prominent distiller of whiskey for the region and an employer of more than ten men—his whiskey boys, who traded his wares—his wishes were always obeyed. From as far away as twenty-five miles, dozens of men arrived for what was to be a four-day frenzy of work and merriment. When it was completed, we had a home and we had friends. The house was rough, and so were the people, but life seemed much easier than it had at first.

Through Andrew's skill and industry, and with the aid of our new friends, we managed to improve upon our uncouth cabin week by week. Though there was much to do outside the house, Andrew found time to construct for us a bed, a dinner table with chairs, and a tolerably comfortable rocker, and to set to work on a wood floor, though this would be a long and ongoing project. He could make simple household furnishings quickly, so he was soon trading for other necessities: blankets, plates and cups, and even a tablecloth and some rough flaxen napkins. These were difficult times but sweet ones. Never had Andrew and I spent so much time together alone, without visitor or distraction, and we delighted in taking refuge in each other, a soft relief to our hard surroundings. The world was only unfamiliar challenge, but in our cabin we could find familiar delight.

Those early weeks now seem a blur to me as, with the warmth of spring turning to the heat of summer, we spent our days engaged in little more than the business of surviving—or, perhaps more accurately, attempting to understand how we were to survive. Andrew cleared land—backbreaking labor which I feared might be the death of him and his horse. Even with all his strength poured into the work, it yet confounded him, as he pulled saplings from the ground and chopped to the stump a near forest of oaks and birches and sycamores. They gave up their earth grudgingly, and Andrew would return from a day's work covered in dirt, his hands caked with blood. I would gaze out upon the land and be unable to see what his efforts had yielded.

Yield it did, though, and at last enough land was cleared for a small planting. I would spend my mornings tending to corn and vegetables in the hopes that enough would grow for us to have some food in the fall. Many in the West planted Indian style, sowing the seeds upon the earth in a formless scatter and hoping a sufficient number took, but Andrew and I were more methodical, tilling the earth, planting in rows, giving each stalk room to breathe and grow.

The purchase of an old spinning wheel—it required significant repair at Andrew's clever hands—allowed me to spin flax, and my needle was often busy in repairing our clothing and making new from the cured skins of Andrew's hunts. Only a few months in the West, and with his beard, hardened muscles, sun-reddened skin, and buckskin clothes, my husband had become a true border man. He would come home at night, exhausted and hungry but content to eat the meager repast I could provide—corn pone from our stock of meal and meat from what animals he had hunted, given what flavor we could by an always diminishing supply of precious salt. Venison was a rare treat, for he had little time to hunt deer, but almost without effort he might kill a turkey or bear or even a rattlesnake, which were ever lurking; no trip to our own gardens could be conducted without vigilance. In some strange compensation, the woods afforded a species of pigeon so insensible to danger that to kill it one need only walk up to one and hit it with a stick.

This was our life. After his dinner, Andrew lay down upon our rough bed while I lit candles (which I learned to make with my own hands from bear fat!). Perhaps I might spin awhile or, if I could steal an hour, pore over my copy of Postlethwayt's *Universal Dictionary of Trade and Commerce* or James Steuart's *Inquiry into the Principles of Political Economy.* Even in the wilderness, I still sought inspiration for my novel, now little more than scraps of dead characters walking though their fictional lives like ghosts—empty and evacuated, present but incorporeal. Despite my bone weariness, I knew that this book resided somewhere inside me, wanting only its time of quickening, awaiting the right alchemy of idea and story and setting. The West, or perhaps the scheme by which we had come west, held something for me, but I could not say precisely what. I could not name it, but it was there.

We were often enough called upon by what was there styled neighbors, though the nearest lived more than half a mile away; these visits were often a strange mixture of backwoods civility and the hostile curiosity with which outsiders are often regarded.

Mr. Dalton and Mr. Richmond sometimes ate the evening meal with us, and I sensed that they imposed upon us not only because they had taken to Andrew but also because our hospitality allowed us, in a small way, to compensate them for the pains they had taken on our behalf. Dalton and Andrew talked at great length about land clearance. Mr. Richmond said little, but he did not seem uneasy or resentful of Mr. Dalton's interest in us. I surmised that Mr. Richmond was simply a quiet man, who rarely found in the routine of ordinary life circumstances that required speech.

While Andrew and Mr. Dalton talked—of how we were neglected by the East, of how the government in New York (and then Philadelphia) would not send soldiers to fight the Indians, and of how Hamilton's schemes in the Treasury Department would destroy the poor man for the sake of the rich—Mr. Richmond would sometimes aid me in washing and replacing the dishes. He might sit with me while I spun or sewed, content to sip his whiskey and look as though he thought about significant things. Once, however, he turned to me and offered me a rare smile of crooked teeth. "Andrew is a great friend to him."

There was something more than his words to what he said, but I did not understand it. I only replied simply, "I am glad of it. You have both been good to us."

Richmond said nothing, and then, after a moment, "Dalton is a good friend to have, but not to take advantage of."

"I can assure you, Mr. Richmond, that Andrew would never—"

"I know Andrew would not," he said.

I could not have been more surprised had he struck me. Did he accuse me of in some way abusing Mr. Dalton's kindness? I turned to him, but he only shook his head, as if to say that the subject had been exhausted, and with that he left the room.

One night we sat with Mr. Richmond and Mr. Dalton, this time joined by Mr. Skye, the five of us enjoying some precious tea and sweet corn bread following a meal. Skye happened to glance over to a little round table next to our rocker upon which sat my copy of Postlethwayt. This interested him at once, and after rising to inspect its edition and condition, he inquired of Andrew what he did with such a book.

"'Tis not mine," he said. "In truth, it's too dull for me."

"You, madam?" asked Skye. "You have an interest in finance and economical matters?"

"I do," I said, feeling myself redden. I was not quite ready to reveal myself to be a budding authoress.

It was fortunate that he spared me a request for further explication. "Then perhaps you have some thoughts upon the latest news, just arrived in a mule train from the East this very day?" His gray eyebrows raised in amusement, or perhaps anticipation. "I spent the afternoon reading through the newspapers, and I cannot credit what I have discovered."

"Then tell us," said Andrew.

He smiled, clearly pleased to be the one to relate it, yet I could see it troubled him too. "The new treasury minister, Alexander Hamilton, has appointed an immediate assistant, the second most powerful man at the Treasury. With the influence that department is gaining over George Washington and the federal government as a whole, it makes him well near one of the most powerful men in the entire country. Can you guess of whom I speak, for he is known to us all?"

Dalton snorted. "We have no idea, so out with it, man."

Andrew smiled. "I have no idea, but look at Joan. I think she knows."

I had opened my mouth, but I had not yet spoken. It seemed to me impossible, but I could think of but one man who met the criteria Mr. Skye had outlined, and I could not, at first, bring myself to say his name out loud. "No," I managed at last. "Not William Duer?"

Skye nodded. "How ever did you guess it?"

"She didn't guess it," said Andrew. "She merely drew the only logical conclusion. I did not myself, but now I see how she did so. He is, after all, the only man known to us all, and he did speak of his close ties to Hamilton when we met him."

Dalton actually snarled in disgust. "It makes me ill to think that a man like Duer, who has made his living by cozening patriots, should be rewarded with such power and influence."

"He shall do well for himself," said Skye. "It seems that his good friend Hamilton has convinced Congress to pay in full the states' debts from the war. All our promissory notes that Duer got in exchange for land are now to be paid at full value."

"He knew!" I cried. "He and Hamilton must have plotted it out all along. They would trick patriots into surrendering their debt, and when they had enough they would get the American people, through their taxes, to pay off that debt, enriching themselves. It is the most monstrous abuse of power imaginable."

"That is how things are done in England," said Dalton, "but it is not how they are supposed to happen here."

"No, but it is the way of things," said Skye. "It hardly matters what principles are foremost in men's minds. Those men are still men, and they will either be too idealistic to maintain power or too corruptible not to seize it."

"You judge human nature too harshly," said Andrew. "For what did we fight if this country is doomed to be no better than the one from which we won our independence?"

Dalton regarded him with the greatest seriousness. It seemed his orange whiskers stiffened, like the ears of a cat going back. "You do not submit to a harsh master because the next master may, for all you know, be no better. You fight, and that is what we did. We fought for the chance, lad."

"And do we not fight now?" I asked, looking up from my needlework. "Is the fighting all done? We fight against England for oppressing us, but when we do it to ourselves, when our own government places men like Hamilton and Duer in a position to destroy the soul of the nation, do we take our ease and do nothing?"

"There's nothing to do," said Skye.

I was not so certain. I could not think what we might to do push back against the interests of greed and cruelty that had so clearly gained ground, but that did not mean I could do nothing. I thought of my book once more and considered that perhaps this novel, this first American novel—could I but write it—might be an instrument of change, or at least part of a movement for change, a movement of sincere citizens hoping to keep their government free of corruption. If this news about Duer so troubled me, it would trouble others. All over the country, honest men and women must be looking on with horror as corruption wound its way into the hearts of the political men in Philadelphia. Alexander Hamilton, once Washington's trusted aide, had turned the nation in the direction of British-style corruption. I knew I must find my voice, and soon.

These thoughts were upon my mind as I stepped outside to clean dishes in the stream. The men, or so I believed, were still within, drinking whiskey and speculating upon the evil plans laid back east. To my surprise, Mr. Skye stepped out with me. He appeared slightly, only slightly, uneasy, with his hands in his pockets, stepping with a gait too casual.

"I observed to your husband that it might be best to have an escort with you as you went about your chores," he said, with a slight simper. Were I unmarried, I might think from his tone that he wished to declare himself.

"I do it often enough," I said, but not unkindly. It was a cool evening for summer, and a light breeze made the air pleasant. The night sky was cloudless, and the thin crescent of a newly waxing moon underscored the brightness of the stars without overshadowing them. Together, Mr. Skye and I strode the short distance to the creek, where, setting down my sack of dirty dishes, I squatted by the cool water and plunged in the first vessel.

He took another dish. We worked in silence for some minutes until Mr. Skye said to me, "I did not mean to make you uncomfortable before. You blushed when I first spoke of your interest in economical books. I am sorry if I stepped upon something."

He was not sorry, he was curious. If he were sorry, he would not have pursued the subject, but I could not fault him for it. Even so, I hesitated for an instant, for I did not like to speak of my ambitions to just anyone, but I sensed in Mr. Skye a man who would embrace and not scorn my project. I took a deep breath. "I plan to write a novel. Perhaps the first American novel."

It was dark and I did not look upon his face, but even so I sensed a look of interest and respect. "The first, you say. I believe it may be too late for that. Our own Mr. Brackenridge in Pittsburgh has set his cap at the same thing."

I felt a twinge of disappointment, but it would not last. I had long been determined to write my book and had not done so. Surely someone with more resolve would succeed where I had only delayed. Instead of dwelling upon this point, I determined that I would have to meet this worthy. "Well, it is not vital to me that I be the first, but that it be particularly American. I know not what Mr. Brackenridge's novel might be, but I doubt we intend to write the same thing."

"I have seen part of it," said Skye. "It is a picaresque—a sort of American *Don Quixote,* or perhaps an American Smollett."

"Then we have very different projects," I said, and saw no reason to say more.

"Should you ever require a pair of eyes to look at it, I hope you will call upon me."

"You are very kind," I said, and turned to my dishes. A moment later, because I sensed my words had so pleased him, I repeated myself. "Very kind."

Andrew began to spend a great deal of time with these men. They helped him with the land clearing—at least Dalton and Jericho would, for John Skye avoided such work where he could, pleading age and back pain. Instead, he would aid me with the farming or join me in the cabin and ease my isolation while I prepared the evening meal. The five of us would eat together and then pass the evening with whiskey and conversation, or perhaps Andrew would join them, riding out to one of their cabins. Then, so slowly I did not notice, the land clearing diminished until it ceased entirely. Andrew would leave in the morning and come home in the evening. He would more often than not smell of whiskey, but he did not seem inebriated and I had no concern that he had found another woman. Even so, there was something furtive in his looks, as though he had been about something not entirely wrong, but certainly something he chose not to reveal. I did not love it, but I would not ask him to speak before he was ready.

Indeed, Andrew appeared happy, self-satisfied. Though he would approach the cabin with a secretive lightness in his step, I had not seen him appear to be so pleased with himself in a long while. I was lonely, yes, and missed the company of the men, Mr. Skye in particular, but I could not protest. I was a woman, and my presence was expendable so long as I did my duty. I would have to endure the solitude even while Andrew enjoyed company.

It was not only the company of Mr. Dalton and Mr. Skye that drew him in, however. He would sometimes spend his evenings at the Indian Path tavern, where women were not welcome. There the men would talk of the things that plagued Westerners—how the politicians of the East wanted us to tame the land but cared not to help us fight Indians. They spoke of the fear of foreign agents combing Pittsburgh—the British, the Spanish, the French—looking to stir up trouble. They talked of the new government back east, their hatred of Duer, and how all must be set squarely at Hamilton's doorstep.

So it was that, with Andrew gone so much from the cabin, my novel began to take shape in my mind—slowly at first, but the characters gathered around me, moths drawn to the flame of my mind. In the quiet, I spent the day making notes, examining the contours of my story, and, soon enough, beginning the writing process itself. I would write, I decided, a novel about our own experiences, about the evil men who defrauded patriots to line their pockets. I would write about the Duers and Hamiltons and Tindalls of the world, and about a group of Westerners who decide to exact their revenge upon them. Perhaps it was the thrill of confronting these men, if only on paper, but the words came to me as they had never done before.

This is how our time passed for two months, and then, as summer began to turn to autumn and a coolness settled over the land, Andrew spoke to me.

"Have you never wondered," he said, "where I go each day? Where I spend my time?"

"I have wondered," I said, "but I thought you would tell me when you were ready."

"It is not like you to restrain your curiosity."

"'Tis not like you," I countered, feeling somewhat chastised, "to be secretive."

"You have your novel," he said. "You do not have to tell me it goes well, for I can see it upon your face. Can you not see from my face that something goes well for me?"

I could not help but smile. "I have seen it."

"And shall I tell you what it is?"

"Do not tease me, Andrew. You know I wish it. Tell me if you are ready."

"It is better that I show you."

And so we set out across the rugged path to Dalton's large cabin, some two miles away. It was a pleasant afternoon, the air filled with the buzz of insects, and we strolled in easy silence, my hand upon his arm. Somehow we were happy. Somehow in the midst of our ruin we had each found something, some part of ourselves we had been missing, I in my writing and Andrew in his secret.

At Dalton's cabin, which I had never before visited, the large man greeted me, Mr. Skye beside him, at the door, and they both had the foolish look of boys who have done something both wicked and childishly charming. Behind the house, Jericho Richmond worked in the field. He raised his hand at us as we approached, but at once wiped his brow with his sleeve and returned to his work. Mr. Dalton invited me in, sat me near the fire, and set before me a small glass of whiskey, which I began to lift to my lips.

"You've come to enjoy your whiskey," Skye said, before I could drink.

"I don't think *enjoy* is the right word," I said. "But it is part of life here."

I took a sip of the drink, but I immediately took the cup away in astonishment. I'd had whiskey before, in quantities I would not have credited in my former life, but here was something entirely different. It was darker, I saw by the light of the fire, amber in color and more viscous. And its flavor—it was not merely the sickly sweet heat of whiskey, for there was a honey taste to it, perhaps vanilla and maple syrup and even, yes, the lingering tang of dates.

"What is this?" I asked.

"To answer that," said Skye, "to fully answer your question, we must first make sure you understand what whiskey is. Do you know why we make whiskey? Are we merely hard-drinking men, reprobates who cannot live without their strong drink?"

"Would you catechize me?" I asked.

He smiled. "Oh, yes. You see, I've been planning this conversation in my mind, and I mean that it should go as I wish. Now, tell me. Do you know why we make whiskey?"

"It is the only way to profit from your harvest."

"A woman who reads the *Universal Dictionary of Trade and Commerce* misses very little," my husband observed.

I took another sip, attempting to dissect its intricacies. "You grow your grain, but beyond what you need for your own use, there is nothing to be done with the surplus. There are no good roads, so the voyage east is too long and too difficult, and ultimately too expensive to transport large quantities of grain. You cannot use the Mississippi to travel west, since the Spanish will not permit it. So what is to be done? The most logical answer is to turn your surplus grain to whiskey."

"Quite right," said Skye.

"There is always a market for whiskey," I continued. "It becomes popular back east, and the army is increasingly replacing rum with whiskey, and though it is cumbersome to transport grain, it is far less to transport whiskey by the barrel. That is why whiskey stands as a substitute for money. At some point it may be exchanged for specie and thus is useful for barter."

"And that," said Mr. Skye, "is where your husband has become so useful." He pointed at Andrew. "He almost at once recognized that there was more flavor to be got into the drink. 'Tis a barter economy, but right now all whiskey is held equal. No one's drink is lauded above another's. But what if we could produce something that was better than what anyone else had?"

"Of course," I interrupted. "You introduce something more scarce; it generates more desire; you get more for your trade."

"Exactly so once again, lass," Skye said. "Now, Dalton and I have been in the whiskey trade for some time, and we thought that Andrew here, with his skill as a carpenter, could be of use to us. We've long known you get more flavor out of whiskey by storing it in barrels rather than jugs, but the difference is not significant. More flavor, but the flavor is not always good, and an abundance of bad flavor does not add much value. Beyond that, the barrels are harder to transport, and the wood absorbs some of the whiskey, leaving you with less product for the market."

"But sometimes barrel storage is desirable," said Dalton. "Jugs can be hard to come by in large quantity, and wood is plentiful. If you have enough surplus, it is better to lose some to barrel storage than have no place to store it at all. When we explained all this to your Andrew—well, he had other ideas than mere coopering."

I looked at him. "Is that right?"

He smiled, somewhat sheepish.

"Let's show her the still," Dalton said.

We exited the cabin and went to what Dalton called the outhouse, though it was a cabin twice in size to the one he lived in, a kind of rusticated warehouse or factory. In it was a profusion of pots, jars, and tubes that jutted out from one another and crisscrossed the room in a fowling-piece blast of confusion. Wooden barrels lined the walls, small fires burned in contained furnaces, steam boiled out of pots in tight little puffs. It smelled rich and rank in there, a kind of sweet and decaying smell, combined maybe with something less pleasant—like wet waste and fleshy decomposition. It was enticing and revolting.

"The principle is fairly simple," Dalton said. "You start with a kettle full of fermented corn, what we call the wash. Then we boil it there, over that fire. The lid goes on the kettle. You see that tube coming out of it? That catches what burns off, since 'tis the strong stuff that burns off first—the spirit, if you will, which is why we call strong drink spirits."

"So the drink that comes out of that tube is whiskey?" I asked.

"No," Skye said, "that's what we call low wine, which is run through the still once again. Now it comes out in different strengths. The first of it, the foreshot—well, that ain't for drinking, let's say that. 'Tis nasty and foul and strong. You can add a little bit of that to the final produce to give it some strength, but no more. After the foreshot comes the head, which you can drink, but it still ain't good. Then comes the clear run. It looks like this."

He handed us a glass bottle, and inside was a near-colorless liquid.

"That is more the whiskey I'm used to."

"Aye, it is," said Skye. "The flavor and color of ours come from the barrel. The longer it sits in the barrel, the more flavor and color it gets, but there was more to it than that."

"It seemed to me," said Andrew, "that more of the barrel's flavor could be brought out by charring its insides. And so it is. The whiskeys we've been experimenting with the past few months are more flavorful than any we'd ever tasted before."

"He's done more than that," said Mr. Dalton. "He's been meddling with the recipe too, adjusting the proportions of the grains, adding more rye than corn to the mash. We've made your husband a partner in our still, and unless I'm mistaken he's made the lot of us very rich."

Dalton took out a bottle of the new tawny whiskey and poured us all a glass, with which we toasted our future. We had come west as victims, but now, it seemed, we would be victors. It was what we believed at the time and what we ought to have believed, because this was the America we had fought for, where hard work and ingenuity must triumph. We did not know that at that moment, back east, Alexander Hamilton and his Treasury Department schemed to take it all away from us.

Ethan Saunders

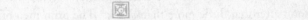

The previous night I had not been so abstemious with drink as might be desired of a man in pursuit of reform, but I nevertheless awoke early and with an eagerness I had not known in years. I had before me a remarkable day because I had things to do. I had not had things to do in years. I'd had things that needed doing, that ought to get done, that had better be taken care of, but they were usually of the *if not today then fairly soon* variety. I had safely hidden away the stolen message inside an orphaned second volume of *Tristram Shandy;* the silver ball itself sat upon my desk like a monument to all that had changed in my life. I was alive and vibrant and I had things to do, monumental things, and I intended to do them.

Of the greatest importance was a visit to the City Tavern to begin my quest for William Duer. It seemed to me he was at the heart of everything. It was his man, this mysterious Reynolds, who had arranged to expel me from my home. Hamilton had identified him as a mischief maker, and the note I had recovered the night before seemed to allude to him. Granted, the *D* might well have been another man, but I did not think so. Hamilton had assured me Duer was not to be found in town, but I was not confident Hamilton had been honest on that score, not when the mere mention of the name Reynolds sent him into spasms of rage.

Trading would not begin at the City Tavern for several hours yet, however, so before going there I thought it best to visit the address Hilltop had given me. Thus, at ten, Leonidas met me at my rooms, and together we made our way south to the boardinghouse on Evont Street. The voyage from the heart of Philadelphia to Southwark was like witnessing, all at once, a youthful face wither into age. The redbrick houses, first stately and well-maintained, were, a block later, turned ramshackle and ill-kept. A block or two after that they became wood frame, and, soon after that, little more than shacks. The prim men of business and frenetic speculators and wealthy Quakers gave way to the laboring poor, to Papists and Presbyterians, to curious foreigners from Poland or Russia or other alien lands, to free Negro cart men crying out oysters and pepper pot. Some of these were dressed in the same plain garb one might find on a white man, but some of the women wore brightly colored and curiously patterned scarves upon their heads, the vestigial remain of savage origins.

Leonidas kept his head straight ahead, but I had the distinct impression that he knew some of these people and the odd feeling he did not like being seen with me. Indeed, we were not three blocks from our destination when a Negro boy of fourteen or fifteen, wearing heavy green woolen breeches and a ragged outer coat, came running up to him. "Ho, there, Leon, this man that own you?" he asked, in a sort of singsong voice.

"Run along," Leonidas said, very quietly.

"Hey, white man, why you not let him go when you promised?" the boy asked me.

Leonidas made a shooing motion, and the child, mercifully, ran off.

Evont Street was wide and well traveled but unpaved, and thus full of filthy snow and mud and animal leavings. Pigs roamed freely and grunted their courage at passing carriages. The boardinghouse—poorly kept, with peeling paint and splintering wood—was on the corner, facing the far more quiet Mary Street, but that offered it no air of repose or peace. It was a wretched place for wretched people, with boarded windows and a visible hole in the roof.

The woman of the house answered our knock. Here was a haggard creature of some thirty years, quite old-looking, with gray hair and heavily bagged eyes that bespoke her bone-weariness. Her three small children stood behind their mother and gazed at us with the empty expression of cattle.

"We seek an Irishman who may live here," I said. "Tall, hairless, red-whiskered."

"Ain't no one like that lived here," she said.

"Then you've never seen him?" I asked.

She said nothing and had the distinct look of a woman attempting to make up her mind. Leonidas pushed ahead of me. "Have you seen him, Mrs. Birch?"

Her face did not exactly brighten, but it became a degree less sour. "Didn't see it was you back there, Leon. Is this him, then?" she asked, pointing at me.

"Yes, it's him."

She eyed me critically.

"Have you seen him?" Leonidas asked again. "It is important."

She nodded. "I seen him. He come by here looking for my landlord, but he ain't been by for a while, and so I told him."

"And who is your landlord?" I asked.

"Who *was* my landlord, more like: a wretch named Pearson. Almost cost me my livelihood too, with him losing the property, but the new fellow is letting me stay on at the same rent."

I nearly took a step back in surprise. "Let me clarify, if you please. Pearson owned the house but owns it no longer?"

"He sold it, and right quick too, like he was in some sort of hurry," she said.

"When did this happen?" Leonidas asked.

"Two weeks ago the new landlord arrives, telling me he now owns the house and that Pearson has been selling off his properties."

This was the sort of matter I could better investigate back in the heart of town, perhaps even at the City Tavern. I thought it unlikely that this woman would know the specifics of Pearson's finances, but it seemed to me interesting that he was selling off property. "What of the Irishman?" I asked.

"I don't know if I should tell you anything," she said. "Pearson ain't my landlord no more, but even so he's not a man to cross."

"A moment, if you please, Mrs. Birch," Leonidas said. He stepped forward into the house with her, and I heard them speak in hushed tones for a moment. Once I heard her say *missing!* in a loud and gleeful voice, but I could make no more of it.

When they emerged, Leonidas turned to me and announced in a businesslike manner that Mrs. Birch would be happy to tell all in exchange for one British shilling.

"I have no money, so you pay her, Leonidas. Be so good."

He reached into his coat, but the woman stopped him. "Is he going to pay you back?"

"Very likely not."

"Don't forget I've reformed," I said.

"Very likely not," Leonidas said again.

"Then don't pay me nothing," she said. "I don't want to take no money from you."

I looked at Leonidas. "Why are people so nice to you?"

"Because I am kind to them," he said.

"Fascinating," I muttered, and it was. To the woman I said, "Now that we've worked out these pesky money matters, can you tell me what I wish to know?"

She nodded. "Pearson would use one of the rooms in the house. He discounted my rent on account of me not being able to rent it out myself. He kept it for a delicate kind of business, and though I didn't much care for it happening under my own roof, I was in no position to object, if you take my meaning."

"He brought a woman here?" I asked. "He strayed from his marriage vows?"

She laughed. "He invented whole new ways to stray from his marriage vows. He only came here with one girl; Emily Fiddler's her name. I told the Irishman too, 'cause he come looking for Pearson. I tell him that

Pearson don't live here, don't even stay here, he just uses the room for his special girl."

"And what is so special about this Emily Fiddler?"

A distressed sort of grin crossed her face. "You'd have to meet her to understand."

She directed us to a house not far away on German Street. It was a better sort of place than that from which we'd come, in superior repair, not so reeking of desperation and decay. Seeing me look upon it, Leonidas said, "I suppose Pearson never owned this one."

We knocked upon the door, and the serving woman, upon hearing our request, sent me (without Leonidas, who was sent to the kitchen) to a sitting room, where I was met by a not unattractive woman in her early thirties. She had dark hair, large emerald eyes, and lips of unusual redness against pale skin. She was a bit plump perhaps, and her nose a bit too thin, but she must have been spectacular ten years earlier.

"I am looking for Miss Fiddler."

"I am she," the woman said, with the charming tone of a lady who knows her business. "Have you been referred to me?"

"As it happens, we have," I said.

"Then by all means let us talk business. Let me call for tea."

There was something in her tone, something jaded and eager, like the crier at a traveling show, that put me on my caution. The room, which had seemed perfectly charming to me, now took on a less agreeable cast. The furnishings, which were neat, were also quite old, and not in the best repair: chipped wood, tattered upholstery, fringed pillows. The windows were covered with gaudy red curtains, laced with gold chintz. I had the strangest feeling that we were children playing at being adults.

"Miss Fiddler," I began, "I have just come from a Mrs. Birch, who formerly rented her home from a Mr. Jacob Pearson. I am told you know him."

She smiled, quite lasciviously, I thought. "Of course. I know him well. He is always a good man with whom to do business."

"Is that so?" I asked.

"And would you care to do business as well?" she asked.

Were I less used to female charms, I would most certainly have blushed, so saucy was her tone. "I will certainly discuss business with you."

"I speak for her when it comes to matters of money, but in the end I cannot influence her when it comes to preference. You understand me. You are a handsome man, Mr. Saunders, but you are also bruised in your face, and that may frighten her. In the end, the arrangement must please her, or there can be no business at all. I must also tell you that in order to indemnify all parties, money may be exchanged in my house, but the business, shall we say, must be transacted elsewhere. You must have somewhere to take her."

A lesser man would have inquired what, precisely, the deuce she was talking about, but I had ever thought it best to let these things unfold upon their own terms. "May I meet her?"

"Of course."

She rang a bell.

I had already surmised that while this lady might have been *a* Miss Fiddler, she was not *the* Miss Fiddler with whom Pearson had a relationship. My guess was that this lady was a relative—an older sister or cousin or aunt—who functioned as the younger woman's bawd.

In a moment a pretty young girl entered the room, looking like a younger version of our hostess. The girl had the same dark hair, the same eyes the color of brilliant summer grass, the same red lips and snowy skin, the same too-narrow nose. She, like the older lady, was a bit inclined to plumpness, but she wore it well, for her weight was well located in precisely the places a man likes a woman to accumulate herself. She wore a simple white gown, low cut to expose her large breasts. She curtsied, saying nothing, gazing upon nothing with a kind of amusement, as though nothing were a perpetual show staged for her entertainment.

I rose and bowed. "You must be Emily. May I ask you some questions?"

She smiled but said nothing. There was nothing rude or defiant in her silence, rather a kind of uncomplicated absence. The serving girl now wheeled in the tea things, and the cart was rickety and squeaked and rattled, producing an atmosphere at once comic and ominous.

"May I ask you some questions about Mr. Jacob Pearson?" I asked the girl.

She curtsied again, but the older woman shifted in her seat as though she too was uncomfortable. She sent her serving girl away with a flick of her hand. To me she said, "Did Mr. Pearson tell you much about Emily?"

"He only spoke of her great beauty," I said quickly, "and he did not exaggerate."

"You are a man of taste, sir. You may direct your questions to me."

The girl now said something that sounded very much like *Peah-soh*. Her voice was deeper than I would have anticipated, and the sound was low and nasal, as sad and dull as a cow's mournful lowing.

I turned to her. "I beg your pardon."

Her face opened into a wide grin. "*Peah-soh,*" she keened.

All at once it was clear to me, and I cursed myself for a fool for not seeing it sooner. "My God. Is the girl a simpleton?"

Miss Fiddler did not respond to this vehemence. "I thought you knew. Yes, she was born that way, and when her parents died last year and left her in my care, I knew not what to do with her. But as you can see, she is very pretty, and she does not object to her duties." She leaned forward and said in a conspiratorial whisper, "She rather relishes it. You are not going to be one of those men to lecture me, are you?"

There was a depth of inhumanity here that even I found too diabolical to contemplate, but this was not the time for useless lectures. I was getting close to learning something, and along the way I was both elated and horrified to discover that Cynthia's husband was more of a beast than I could have imagined.

To the elder lady, I said, "I am not one to judge. One man's monstrosity is another man's diversion. For my part, Miss Fiddler, I would delight in bedding an idiot—vastly amusing and all that—but that is not why I've come. It is on government business, and I do hope that when I come to report my findings to the President and his advisors I have only information to tell him, not the nature of the people who could not help us. You understand me, I think."

She nodded, now of a more sober deportment. "I see all too clearly what you are after." She waved Emily out of the room. "Ask me your questions."

"Did a tall hairless Irishman come here looking for Pearson?"

"He came," she said, "but there was nothing to tell him. We never do business here, as I told you, so Pearson, other than our first meeting, was never a guest in my home. I explained that to the Irishman, and he left almost at once."

"Almost," I said.

"He asked if I would hold a letter for a friend," she said, "He gave me five dollars to take the note and said I would receive another five when its rightful owner came to collect it."

"I am the rightful owner," I said.

She laughed. "I doubt that, as you did not know of the letter before now."

"Miss Fiddler," I said, "I presume you will have no objection to giving that letter to representatives of the United States government."

"Of course I would not, were I still in possession of it," she said. "But I gave the letter away three days ago to the last gentleman who came in search of it."

"The last gentleman," I repeated.

"A slender young man with a beard who also claimed to work for the government. Lavien, I believe he called himself. Is he a colleague of yours?"

Joan Maycott

Winter and Spring 1791

They let the whiskey age in the barrels all winter and then much of the next spring. In summer, while Andrew tinkered with the stills, experimenting with new ways to bring yet more flavor to his drink, Mr. Dalton and Mr. Skye traveled the county, letting men sample their new whiskey. Mr. Dalton's whiskey boys went even farther to spread the news of this new distillation. They rode from settlement to church to trading post, uncorking their bottles for eager settlers to taste. When autumn came and the rye and corn were harvested, mules and horses laden with grain began to make their way to Mr. Dalton's operation.

Stills were expensive things. Most men could not afford one, not even a small one, and so the custom was for farmers to bring their grain to a third party who would distill it in exchange for a portion of the proceeds. Virtually everyone who tasted the new whiskey understood that they must have this drink and no other or their grain was wasted. It would trade for more or, for those who wished to make the venture east, sell for more. In turn, Dalton, Skye, and Andrew amassed increasing stores of grain to turn to whiskey, which they could sell or use for trade. Whiskey was the coin of the realm. Like a creature from a child's tale, they had learned to manufacture precious metals from baser materials.

Dalton and Skye soon found their stills used beyond capacity. More machines had to be purchased. Men said they would wait as long as it took, if only they could have their grain distilled to be so full of flavor. It was not only that the new whiskey was desirable but that the old was now depreciated. Why turn your straw into silver when you could turn it into gold?

For my part, I was busy too. Once I decided that I would place a fictional version of William Duer at the center of my novel, I filled up page after page. The story centered around the evil speculator William Maker and his scheme to defraud war veterans of their pay, and in it I mocked the greed of the wealthy, celebrated the ardor of the patriotic, and bemoaned the conditions of the frontier. Yet the frontier of my novel was peopled not only with ruffians and miscreants but noble souls, patriots swindled by a government tending only to the cares of the wealthy. These fictional men found a way to strike back and set the country to rights. I felt certain, utterly certain, I was doing what I had longed to do, inventing the American novel, writing a new kind of tale, whose concerns and ambitions mirrored the American landscape.

Autumn turned to winter, and we spent our second cold season in the West. It was hard, for our fireplace and stove could sometimes do little to stave off the brutal western chill, but it proved easier than our first winter, for now the whiskey bought us food and blankets enough to increase our ease. Sometimes Andrew would join Mr. Dalton and Mr. Richmond in a search for desperate winter deer or in a far more ambitious bear hunt. This was a dangerous business—waking a beast from its winter sleep—but at least it yielded us fresh meat. During these excursions, Mr. Skye would often invite me to pass the time at his own home.

Visiting Skye's house was always a delight, for he had the finest cabin in the settlement. It rose two stories, and having no one to spend upon but himself, he had troubled to furnish it, if not elegantly, then at least comfortably. Through a set of circumstances that were never entirely clear to me, he had purchased the lease for this land from a man who'd been desirous of leaving the area quickly, having incurred the anger of both Colonel Tindall and a band of Shawnee braves. Mr. Skye had come west with more ready cash in his pocket than most men, and he had been one of the few settlers in the region capable of buying the lease for any amount of real specie. Now, each season, he hired four or five workers—usually slaves lent out by their owners—to help him grow wheat and rye and Indian corn for whiskey and vegetables for his own use. He had, in addition, several cows and chickens and half a dozen pigs, and he worked hard each winter to keep them all alive.

While the others hunted—a sport for which Mr. Skye said he'd had no enthusiasm, even as a young man—I would sit with the white-haired gentleman, the only person with whom I could discuss my novel in any detail. I would not let him read any of it—not yet—but I would tell him of the story and its actors, and he would offer useful suggestions. He also presented me with roasted meats and fruit preserves and even eggs, all served with samplings from his precious store of wine. I will not pretend it was not good to taste such things again.

I am not foolish, and I also cannot pretend, particularly when we took wine, that I did not feel Mr. Skye's eyes upon me in a way not entirely appropriate. But I saw no harm in it. I knew to my soul he would never act upon whatever impulses he might feel, and I enjoyed his hospitality and his conversation. It would have been wrong to deny one another the pleasure of our meetings because he harbored feelings about which he would remain forever mute.

One afternoon, perhaps a bit too warm with his excellent wine, I turned to Mr. Skye, who sat next to me, explaining to me his understanding of the evils schemed by Hamilton and Duer back east. His argument was a convoluted business, not Skye at his best, and while I wished to comprehend his meaning, my thoughts were too jumbled, my disposition too relaxed, to take in his words. Instead, and rather rudely, I said, "Do I remind you of someone, Mr. Skye?"

I had my answer at once, for he turned red and looked away, rubbing his leathery hands at the fire until he could regain himself. "Why do you ask it?"

I had been too free. I drank deep of my goblet of wine, to hide my discomfort, and took some pleasure in the feeling of numbness that spread through me. I finished what I had, and Mr. Skye refilled, and I could not say I was sorry. "It is only that you look at me with a certain recognition. You have from our first meeting."

"Perhaps I recognize in you a kindred soul," he offered.

"I have no doubt you do, but I think I recall to you someone from your past."

"You are perceptive, which I'm sure you know." He smiled at me, a sad sort of smile, and though I had always seen him as an old man, in an instant I had a glimpse of him youthful and beardless, charming if not precisely handsome. "When I was a young man at St. Andrew's I had a connection to a young lady in Fife. Her father was a wealthy laird, extremely well placed in society, and my father—well, he was not. It was not a usual thing for someone in my family to attend university. I was very much in love, Mrs. Maycott, but the situation ended in scandal. There was a duel, you see, and the young lady's brother died. It was for that reason that I fled my native land and came to this country."

I blame the wine, for I said what anyone would think but few would speak. "They say it was scandal that sent you west once more to our settlement."

His face revealed nothing. "I am, perhaps, prone to scandal. It is a poor trait, I know."

"I rather think it depends on the scandal," I told him.

He blushed, which I own I found rather charming.

"You and I are friends," I said to him, "and so I hope I may ask you something, as a man. I fear I cannot ask my husband, for it might be too uncomfortable for him to be honest."

"Of course, Mrs. Maycott."

"It concerns the attraction men feel for women, something I must understand for my novel."

He took a sip of wine. "You have raised a subject about which I know a great deal."

"I know about courtship and love. I understand these things. Your feelings for your lady in Fife, for example. What I cannot comprehend is the attraction felt by men like Tindall or Hendry. They look at a woman with desire, yet they do not love her or like her or even regard her, as near as I can discern, as a person. If it is mere physical release they want, would not one woman do as well as another?"

He sipped more wine. "I wonder if perhaps this is a conversation best not had."

"We have come so far. We must finish. Do you not think so?" I do not know that I thought so. I knew the impropriety of the subject, but that was what I loved about it. Why should I not speak of what I like with a trusted friend? I knew I could depend upon his goodness, and I saw no reason why I should not take some small thrill in something as harmless as it was illicit. Even so, I knew there was a more selfish reason I pursued this subject. The people I wrote of in my novel held no propriety as sacred, and though their transgressions were far greater than anything I contemplated there in Mr. Skye's home, I believed I needed to know some small measure of it. I wanted to know the thrill of doing what the world must condemn.

Mr. Skye nodded at me, and I took that as agreement, so I pushed forward. "Do all men desire women they neither know nor like? I understand attraction, being drawn to a face or a shape, but for women, I believe we must always engage in fancy with such an attraction. If we see a man we like, we imagine that he must be good and kind and brave or whatever thing it is we most treasure in a man. It seems to me men like Tindall and Hendry don't trouble themselves with such fancies. They merely desire and wish to take. Are all men thus?"

Mr. Skye cleared his throat. "A man will always be drawn to a pretty woman, there can be no stopping that, but each man alone chooses how to shape that interest in accordance with his heart. If you will forgive a crude analogy, every hunter must have his dog, but when the dog is not hunting, some men will allow it to lie by the fire and feed it scraps from the table. Others will curse it and beat it if it so much as wanders where its master does not want it. Can you conclude from these two examples how men, taken as a whole, treat dogs? No, for though the desire to hunt with a dog may be near universal, the method of keeping the animal is different from one individual to another."

"Do you mean that some men long for affection whereas other men yearn for conquest, and these are unrelated desires?"

"I think all men desire conquest of some sort, but the ideal differs from man to man. One might wish his affection returned. He has thus *conquered* the indifference a woman might feel toward him. Another prefers conquest in its basest form. In this, I think, women are different, which is only right. Men will yearn for any willing heart, so women must be the gatekeepers of desire in order to prevent a general anarchy."

By now, I had pushed the subject as far as I dared, and as far as I wished to. I had made him uneasy, and I had made myself uneasy, but we had both persevered, and, if I was not mistaken, we had both enjoyed the challenge. And perhaps not coincidentally, he opened for me another bottle of wine and sent me home with half a dozen eggs.

Winter at last relented, and in the spring of 1791 it seemed that, despite the despair we had known only a year before, life was a delight. Our cabin had become a home, with wooden floors and warm carpets, the walls papered with birch bark, covered with prints Andrew had himself framed. We had such material things as any Westerner might desire, and if we wanted something—food, tools, linens—we need only trade whiskey to get it. We had gone from being outsiders to occupying a pivotal place in the community, and there was hardly a man west of the Ohio Forks who did not know Andrew's name. My pile of completed manuscript pages grew, and I believed that in a year's time I should have the book that had been my life's ambition.

Once the snows had melted and the paths were cleared, Andrew planned a trip to Pittsburgh. We had not been since the fall, but such visits were not particularly pleasant. The cooler weather offered a lessening in the scent of rot and decay, but the city grew even more filthy with soot and coal dust, and though we might ride into town well appointed, we should ride out looking like chimney sweeps. The city was populated by the worst of western rabble—rough trappers and traders, drunken Indians, lazy soldiers for whom a gun and a uniform gave them leave to confuse liberty and license. Even more, I loathed the wealthy of the town. They walked about in outdated eastern finery, pretending the streets were paved, the buildings made of stone, and that they were in Philadelphia, or even London, rather than the last outpost of civilization. All was dirt and muck and filth, coal dust that descended like black snow, rooting pigs, fluttering chickens, defecating cows. It seemed to me less an attempt at a city than a preview, for so many of its inhabitants, of Hell.

Andrew, nevertheless, needed supplies to experiment with new whiskey recipes, so I went with him. As we often had different tasks in town, we made a habit of tending to our separate business, and so we parted, planning to meet again outside a grocer's. Andrew went in search of what his whiskey trade demanded of him. I went in search of a lawyer.

The man I wanted was Hugh Henry Brackenridge, a prominent figure in town, famous or infamous, depending upon who described him and upon his most recent case. I was interested to meet him for a number of reasons, not the least of which was that Skye had told me that he wrote a novel of his own, but there was more to it. I was fascinated by what I'd heard of him—principally his willingness to accept the causes of the penniless, from murderous Indians to squatters upon Tindall's lands.

Brackenridge kept his office in a street not far from the crumbling remains of Fort Pitt. Outside his doorway, two shirtless men wrestled with a kind of drunken desperation that bordered on the amorous. They hardly noticed me as I slunk past to knock upon the lawyer's door.

I was shown immediately into his office, furnished in the rustic western style, and found him to be a strange-looking fellow in his forties, graying and pointy, in respectable if somewhat rumpled clothing. He was perhaps the most birdlike man I'd ever seen.

"Mrs. Maycott!" he cried, as though we had long known each other. "My dear, dear Mrs. Maycott, how is it I may serve you? Here, have some biscuits." He shoved a plate before me, then took one and popped it into his mouth. "You must tell me how I might be of use." The food was not entirely chewed when he spoke, and bits flew out, but it seemed to me more charming—in the way of an exotic animal—than boorish.

He was not only birdlike in his appearance but in his manner. He spoke in a high voice, and was in his manner as nervous and twitchy as the creatures he resembled, flitting from here to there, jumping up at a moment's notice, hardly able to speak of one topic before hopping to another.

"I am always eager to meet those who settle the lands hereabout. I don't often meet the wives, you know. The husbands? Oh, yes, often the husbands. But the wives? No, not so often."

For all his queerness, he did not make me uneasy. The world is full of unusual people, and though some may scorn them, I had ever believed that a bit of kindness would earn an enduring loyalty. "How is it you know me?" I asked.

"You gave your name when you called," he said. "And your husband is quite famous for his whiskey. I have sampled it, and it is indeed something special. But please, sit, sit, sit."

I did so and thanked him for the compliment he offered my husband. Then, wishing to move things forward, I explained to him my business, for true business I had—that of examining our lease, for I had concerns about our responsibilities and obligations. "There are not so many legal men in town," I said, "and it is well reported that you alone will stand against Tindall."

"He and I are not friends," he said, "but neither are we enemies. I take upon myself causes that have merit, that is all. And it need not be the merit of the particular person at the center of the case. That is what people do not understand. I've been much criticized for taking the part of that Delaware Indian Mamachtaga—got himself drunk and killed a white man and that was all there was to it. With every ounce of will, I defended him, though it earned me many enemies among those who could not understand why I would stand with a murderous Indian over a white man." He grinned at me and then, perhaps needing something in the way of punctuation, bit into another biscuit.

"But why did you defend him? Why anger your neighbors to defend a man you knew to be guilty of so terrible a crime?"

For an instant his features—the darting eyes, the flaring nostrils, the quavering lips—all settled. He was like a monument cast in stone as he met my gaze. "I did it because someone must, because even the guilty must be defended, or the system of law has no meaning. I did it, Mrs. Maycott, because I am a patriot, and if a man loves his country he must uphold the principles of that country even if doing so may make him uncomfortable in his own heart and odious to his neighbors. A patriot does not make the principles of his country conform to his own ideas."

"You are a clever man, Mr. Brackenridge."

"Too clever for my own good, if you must know the truth of it." Perhaps dismayed by his own gravity, he offered me a curious smile and then ran a hand through his hair. "Now, let us look at your contract with Colonel Tindall. And never fear, I shall not tell him you came to see me. He would not like it, though I presume you know that."

He took the document and sat at his desk, a glass of wine in one hand, his glasses slowly sliding down his nose like the slow melt of mountain snow in the encroaching spring. He traced each line with his finger and mumbled, like a clerk in a stage comedy, and I believe he did so consciously. Mr. Brackenridge was not only a quirky man, I decided, but a man who enjoyed his own quirkiness. He would nod, sip his wine, find his place, nod again, mumble, shake his head, point, wave his hand in a circle, and find his place again. In the end he looked up and discussed the parameters with me. It was much as I had expected, and the explanation was clear. When he was finished I felt my color reddening, and I turned away from him.

"There is another matter I would like to discuss," I told him. "I hope it is not too personal."

"Come, Mrs. Maycott, we are friends now, are we not? Not such great friends, I suppose. I would not, for example, lend you any great sum of money. Not that I expect you to ask. A small sum, perhaps. Yes, a small sum is not out of the question. A few dollars? Will that do?"

I laughed. "Sir, I have not asked you for money, and I do not intend to. You have done me a service, and it is I who owe you."

"Oh, yes, of course."

"It is something else. You see, I have heard that you are writing a novel."

His face brightened, like that of a child upon the mention of sweets. "Most people consider the endeavor very silly, but then, this is Pittsburgh and hardly a center of letters. Yet, I do write a novel. Are you a lover of novels, Mrs. Maycott?"

"I am." I looked away. "I am also, I hope, a writer of novels."

"Oh, my dear, how exciting," he said. He did not hesitate but took from his desk a large manuscript and began reading to me from his book, *Modern Chivalry*. It concerned the adventures of Farrago, a kind of American Don Quixote, with his faithful and hapless servant Teague. It was very, very funny, and I laughed several times, both at his quips and at his wonderful enlivened performance, for he spoke in the voices of his characters and even, as best he could with papers in his hand, acted out scenes as he read. It was also, I was relieved to see, nothing at all like what I was about. I wished to write something new. Mr. Brackenridge wished to write something old. My mind was put at ease.

"Perhaps you would care to share some of your book with me."

I would not have asked him to look at it, but he offered, and I had come prepared with a fair copy of the first few chapters, some sixty pages written in my best hand. This was no whim, for paper was expensive, and it cost me much to spare these pages, and yet I knew I must have someone's opinion, and someone who had no interest in pleasing me.

"I have not the time to wait while you read it, so I shall leave this with you, sir, trusting that you will show these pages to no one. But as you are a man of letters, I would value your impressions. Should I continue with my work or abandon it? I beg you will promise to tell me your true opinion and not stand upon politeness. When I come to town again in a month or two, I shall call upon you to hear your verdict, and you may return the pages."

He agreed to my terms, and so I left. It was out of my hands, and I should have thought about it no more, except the next day, back in my own cabin, I heard the sound of approaching hooves as I prepared the evening meal. I went outside to see who came, and there, riding toward me, was the owlish Mr. Brackenridge.

He came down from his horse, reached into a saddlebag, and returned to me my pages. "It could not wait a month or two," he said. "What you do is remarkable! New and important. I beg you to finish and finish quickly. The world needs novels such as this."

Perhaps a week after my meeting with Mr. Brackenridge, while I served an afternoon meal to Andrew, Mr. Dalton, and Mr. Skye, our dog began to bark wildly. This was followed by a violent knock at the door, and all three men took hold of their guns at once. It was the way men behaved in the West, though I thought it silly. A raiding party of savages would not knock before entering. Andrew nevertheless motioned me to the back of the cabin and stepped forward toward the door, which he opened slightly. Then he opened it the rest of the way.

Standing there, in the thin light of the late afternoon, the sun blindingly behind him, were Tindall's men, Hendry and Phineas. Hendry grinned at Andrew and scratched at his scabby face while he dug at the dirt with his boot. In that light, his face looked not red, but blazing scarlet. "You done good for yourself." He licked his lips as he studied the inside of the cabin.

"Good afternoon, Mr. Hendry, Phineas," said Andrew.

Hendry pushed his way inside, and Phineas followed close behind. I'd not seen him in more than a year, and he'd grown since then, broader about the chest and shoulders, more stubble upon his face. Phineas had made the transition from being a brutal boy to a brutal man.

Andrew stood aside, ever mindful of the push and pull of violence. Men such as Hendry were wont to set traps, daring others to step into them. Andrew would not be so prompted. I presumed I could count on the same restraint from Mr. Skye, but I did not know about Mr. Dalton. Both men eyed the intruders and clutched their muskets but did not raise them.

"No one's invited you in," Mr. Skye said. "Mind your manners here."

These were not men made to mind their manners, and they did not like that they should be asked to do so. Phineas spat on the floor, that his contempt might be better visible.

Hendry watched Skye's face darken, and he responded with a grin. "I guess we can't all be schoolteachers like you. We can't all know about our p's and q's, but then, some of us are still men and don't hide behind the skirts of an Irisher, so there it is. You have something to say to me, stand up, set down your piece, and say it like a man."

"One moment," I said. "This is my husband's house, not your camp. You, Mr. Hendry, must be the one to restrain yourself."

"Shut up!" It came from Phineas, and we all stared, even Hendry. He eyed me with such hatred, I feared he might leap upon me like a savage and slit my throat. More than that, I feared Andrew might confront him, and such a confrontation would lead to disaster. Perhaps not today, for these men were outnumbered and outgunned, but soon enough.

"Phineas, what have I done that you would speak to me so?" I spoke quickly, my words rushing together, but I needed to get them out before Andrew could speak. I would make this a woman chastising a boy so that it would not become a conflict between men.

"Muzzle your woman, Maycott," Hendry said. "She's brung you enough troubles already, hain't she? Talking to lawyers and such. That's right. You thought no one saw you going to speak to that troublemaker Brackenridge?"

I felt a jolt of fear run through me. Had I done this? Had I brought this trouble upon us?

"I only wished to discuss with him the writing of novels," I said, pleading my case to Dalton and Skye, not Hendry.

"You may speak with whom you like," said Andrew. "It is no concern of Tindall or his bootlicks. You've been tolerated long enough, and now you are warned. Leave my cabin."

"The colonel don't like to see a man so used by a woman," said Hendry, who would not do Andrew the honor of hearing his words. "I come from the colonel and I speak for the colonel and I hear for the colonel, and the colonel don't like to hear women speaking out of turn. Makes him angry, is what it does. I don't much care for it, neither. I beat my own wife, and I don't see no reason not to beat yours."

Dalton rose to his feet. "You must be mad to speak so. You'll not leave here with your tongue in your mouth."

"I'm from Colonel Tindall, and if I don't return, and return whole, the lot of you will be fitted for a noose."

"Yes, you come from Tindall," Andrew said. "We all understand you believe it protects you. You speak foully to my wife to show your power, and I do not kill you for your words to show you that they are meaningless. Now say your master's bidding and spare us more bluster."

Mr. Dalton scowled at what he perceived as conciliation on Andrew's part, but Mr. Skye smirked with approval. Andrew had granted Hendry permission to state his business but humiliated him at the same time. It was perhaps as good an arrangement as could be hoped for.

Phineas appeared lost in a different exchange, one that took place in an overlapping, ghostly realm. He spat on the floor again and looked up at me, his eyes dark and frightening.

Perhaps sensing things could yet go badly, Hendry sucked in a breath and pushed forward. "I'll say my bit then, as ye beg me." He stepped over to the table and examined the bottle and the mugs. He picked up one of the pewter vessels and sniffed at it. "Is this it, then?" he asked, looking directly at Andrew. "Is this the new whiskey that's got folks talking?"

"'Tis the whiskey we have been making," answered Andrew.

Hendry drank back the mug. He looked inside it. "Tastes like the same pig shit to me. Looks a little different, but it don't taste like nothing new. Maybe all you done was piss in some of the old sort. Is that it, Maycott? You been pissing in the whiskey? That's what it tastes like, piss drink. Pisskey maybe you'll call it. Be more honest that way."

Mr. Skye let out a guffaw. "Spoken like a man too familiar with drinking piss. Is it your own or Tindall's that you suck down so often?"

Something hot and dangerous began to form on Hendry's wreck of a face.

I think Andrew must have understood that we found ourselves in a powder keg, and he wished to douse all fires. "Thank you for your critique," he said. "I shall certainly keep it in mind as we make the next batch, which perhaps you will care to sample."

"I would," he said. "I would like to, thank you so very much, but I don't think I'll be able to on account that there ain't going to be a next batch."

"You're done with it," said Phineas.

"Think ye so?" Dalton took a step forward, and he was a fearsome sight as he did.

"It come from Colonel Tindall," said Hendry. He picked at a scab on his flaking chin. "He don't like it. He's heard that Maycott here ain't clearing the land none. It won't serve, so you," he said, jabbing a finger in Mr. Dalton's direction, "you'll make your pissy whiskey the way you used to. I don't want to see nothing like what you done with Maycott again. I want to hear people complaining they can't get it no more."

"We will do as we please," said Andrew. "You've had your say, and we've tolerated far more than we ought for the sake of keeping peace, but I won't keep it forever. Get gone. I'll hear no more of you."

"Well, that's where you're wrong. See, Colonel Tindall is your landlord, and he wants you clearing land. If you don't, there'll be trouble."

"Tindall's got his own distillery," said Mr. Skye. "and he doesn't much care for us eating into his business. That's all there is to it."

"You think so, is it?" Hendry asked, as though he knew something we did not.

"I shall tell you what I think," I said, stepping forward, "should you care to hear a woman's opinion. I did visit Mr. Brackenridge, as you say, for I wondered if a man who cheated once might not wish to try to cheat again. I wanted my contract examined very closely, to make certain we did nothing the law did not allow. There is nothing in it that grants Tindall the right to tell us what we must or must not do with our land or with our time."

"Shut your mouth!" Phineas barked at me.

Dalton lifted his weapon, though he did not yet aim it. "That boy's lost his mind, Hendry. Get him out of here before something untoward happens."

I put a hand to my mouth. I did not want bloodshed, and I certainly did not want it in my home. And yet, I did not fear. I believed Mr. Dalton had the control not to lose sight of himself.

Hendry did not flinch. He put a hand on Phineas's shoulder and spoke gently. "Let's keep our heads, boy."

He spoke as though everything were easy, and that made it possible for Phineas to believe it. It seemed that even vile Hendry had things to teach me.

He looked at Andrew and grinned. "You can see my point now, I think. All this business with women and lawyers, it won't come to any good. It ain't wise to go against the colonel."

"I think it's time for you to run." Mr. Dalton raised his gun.

Hendry shook his head, as though saddened by the depravity of those whom he tried to help. "I guess you're gonna make it hard 'pon yourselves, hain't you? I can't say I'm surprised. Told Colonel Tindall it would be that way. Harder on you for all that, but it was never going to be otherwise. Let's take our leave, Phineas."

The two left and closed the door behind them. The men began at once to speak to one another in excited tones, but I paid no attention. Of course I was interested, but I was distracted by the scene out the window. Directly before our cabin, Hendry was taking a leather strap to Phineas. He'd made the boy lift up his hunting shirt, and he whipped at the exposed buttocks. Phineas faced the window, but his eyes were tightly clenched. Then, at once, he opened them, and saw me watching. I ought to have turned away, but I did not. Phineas met my gaze, bold and un-flinching, and, despite Hendry's lashings, his manhood began to stiffen, and his eyes bored into me with pure malice. I should have looked away, spared him his humiliation and myself the raw nakedness of his fury, but I kept looking all the same. I found it terrifying and terrible, and yet it was the darkest, truest thing I had ever seen.

As we walked to City Tavern, I explained to Leonidas what had happened with Miss Fiddler—that Pearson kept a simpleton as a whore, that the Irishman had been searching for Pearson there and had left him a note, and that the note had been picked up by Lavien, who seemed not only to know what I knew but to be well ahead of me. I should not have been surprised, given that he had been looking into this matter for weeks, but I was nevertheless disheartened by losing what I had imagined to be an advantage. On the other hand, if Lavien knew all I knew, perhaps he knew of this alleged threat against the bank, which meant I would no longer be burdened with keeping the secret.

We walked the distance back to the heart of the city and to Walnut Street, where we stepped under the enormous awning of the three-story City Tavern, the principal location in the city for business. No city in the United States had a genuine stock exchange, and perhaps taking its cue from the British model—where there was, indeed, a proper stock exchange, but all real business was transacted in nearby taverns and inns—the trade in government issues, securities, and bank shares transpired in public houses.

The City Tavern was but the most principal of trading taverns, where the most powerful and reputable speculators plied their trade, but one building was not enough these days to house the mania that had infected the city of late. At virtually any tavern within two or three blocks of the Treasury buildings, men might be found buying and selling securities, stocks, loans, and bank issues. The success of Hamilton's bank had created a frenzy for bank stocks of all sorts, and the trade in Bank of New York and Bank of Pennsylvania issues was brisk. Much of this new business sprang from a general sense of possibility and euphoria, but much was merely because the Bank of the United States had millions of dollars to lend and did so at easy rates to help promote the economy. Hamilton believed in making credit widely available and making it cheap. The end result was trade, frenetic trade. Men bought and sold with wild enthusiasm but also created: new businesses, new ventures, and yes, new banks. These sprang up almost monthly, and though most were mere opportunistic adventures, occasions for selling worthless shares to men who hoped to sell again before the bubble burst, the trade appeared unaffected by the common knowledge of worthlessness. Hamilton had hoped to invigorate the economy with his bank and he had done so, but his enemies argued that he had not merely given the markets energy, he had rendered them mad.

I asked Leonidas to wait outside and stepped through the front door. In doing so, I thought I had stepped into the middle of a brawl, for in the front room some two dozen men were upon their feet, shouting most vociferously and waving papers at one another. Each man appeared to have with him a clerk, who sat by his side, frantically scribbling down the devil knew what upon pieces of parchment or in ledger books. Their pens moved with such rapidity that ink sprayed in the air like a black rain.

I stared at the chaos, hardly knowing how to respond. I must have remained there a few moments, transfixed by the lunacy around me. At last I heard a whisper in my ear. "Curious, is it not?"

It was Lavien, and he wore a look of extreme satisfaction. "I wondered how long it would take you to find your way here. Come sit for a moment."

He led me to a table and called for tea. I called for porter. Our drinks arrived with relative dispatch, and Lavien leaned back, to watch the confusion of the room around me in which men in fine suits acted as though they had been possessed by devils. I could make nothing of it, but my companion watched the proceedings as though it were a race conducted with horses whose skills and particulars he knew well.

"What brings you here?" he asked me.

"Once again, you hope to get information from me yet offer nothing in return," I answered. "But I will be more generous than you. I look for a William Duer. Do you know if he is in Philadelphia or has been recently?"

He pointed. "The one waving papers in both hands—that is Duer."

Hamilton, who evidently had not troubled to inform Lavien of his lies, was now exposed, and I looked over at the man the Secretary of the Treasury was so anxious I not meet. The madman in question was not very tall. He had narrow shoulders and delicate, nearly feminine features, though he had a high and balding forehead and hair cut short with a dandyish curl to it. He wore a crushed velvet suit, dark in its blueness, almost purple, and he would have appeared comical had he not conducted himself with the most astonishing seriousness. I found nothing compelling in him myself, but the men in the room appeared to attend to his every sound, his every gesture. A mere shift in the direction of his small eyes was enough to change the course of whatever lunacy took place before me.

"Why are you looking for Duer?" Lavien asked me. His expression betrayed nothing.

"Oh, this and that," I said. "Any thoughts on why Hamilton would tell me that Duer was not in Philadelphia and had not been for some time?"

Lavien paused, but only for a blink of an eye. "I doubt Hamilton remains informed of Duer's comings and goings. Tell me how the two of you happened to discuss him."

"How odd. I don't recollect. But what can you tell me about him?"

"He is the king of the speculators," Lavien said. "He is both daring and reckless, caring for nothing but his own profits. In my opinion, he is plotting something this very minute."

"What?"

"I don't know precisely, but I have seen him consistently shorting six percent government issues—that is, gambling that they will lose value. He is important enough that when he predicts stocks will decline, others presume the same and follow suit."

"Is that illegal?"

"No," said Lavien. "Merely interesting."

After another hour of commotion, the frenzy died down. Men settled at their tables. Clerks ceased their writing. Most of the speculators now turned to the business of drinking tea or left the tavern altogether. Duer sat at a table speaking with a pair of speculators Lavien did not know. All appeared easy and jovial.

"You very obviously want a word with him," Lavien said. "Let me introduce you."

"Why are you helping me? I thought you and Hamilton wanted me to keep my distance."

"Merely showing some respect for a brother of the trade," he answered, his face typically, troublingly, blank.

I did not believe. I think he knew Duer would prove uncooperative and I would learn there was nothing I could accomplish on my own and that attempting to meddle with a government inquiry would prove a waste of time. It is what I would do, were I in his place.

Duer was in the midst of some tale about how he had extricated himself from the decline of value that the Bank of the United States scrip had suffered the previous summer. According to the little I heard, the value reached a low point and would have caused financial disaster throughout the country had Duer not convinced Hamilton to take action. Once Hamilton did so, the value of scrip rebounded. It was, in other words, the precise opposite of the version Hamilton had told me: namely, that he, the Secretary of the Treasury, had refused to be swayed by friendship and had defied Duer for the benefit of the nation.

The story came to a rather abrupt end when Duer noticed us standing within earshot. He coughed rather ostentatiously into his fist and sipped at his coffee. "Mr. Levine is it? Have I not told you I have no more to say to you?"

"It is Lavien, sir, and I am not here to speak to you myself but to introduce this gentleman. Mr. William Duer, may I present Captain Ethan Saunders."

"Captain Saunders? Where have I heard that name? Nothing good, I think." He waved his hand, as though I were a fly to be shooed. "Wasn't there some business about betraying your country? I've no time for traitors."

"And yet here I am, making time for traders. Ironic, don't you think?"

He did not answer.

"And what of Jacob Pearson?" I asked. "Have you time for him?"

"Is he here? What of it? He has more to fear from his creditors than I have from him."

"His creditors?" I said.

Duer clucked like a schoolmaster reviewing some unsatisfactory work. "Have you not heard? Pearson is in dangerous straits. He's been selling off his properties all over the city, though it shan't be enough, I'll warrant. A reckless man, and reckless men always stumble."

"And what is your connection to him?" I asked.

"I know him from about town, of course. He has proposed business with me on more than one occasion, but I cannot work with one such as he, and his current crisis merely proves my earlier suppositions. Now, I've given you more time than you deserve. I must go."

"One moment, Mr. Duer. Are you familiar with a large Irishman?" I asked. "Bald-pated, red-mustached, muscular?"

"You must have mistaken me for a juggler," he said, "or perhaps a bearded circus performer. I know no one of that description. Good day."

He began to walk away from us, and I immediately pushed after him. "Hold," I called.

He quickened his pace. "Reynolds? Your assistance, if you please."

I started at the name, for it was that of the man who had paid my landlady to cast me out, and it was the name that had so upset Hamilton. From the corner of the tavern came a rugged fellow, rather tough-looking in his stature and homespun clothes, a large wide-brimmed hat draping over deep-set eyes. The hat shaded his face but did not entirely obscure a massive scar that reached from his forehead, over his eye, and descended to his chin—a wide pink swath of old injury.

He stepped between us and Duer and grinned in a most feral manner, showing us rather pointed teeth. Reynolds was large, in need of a shave, and possessed of an evil breath. "Mr. Duer requests the two of you would be so kind as to fuck off."

While we were so charmingly engaged, Duer and his friends hurried away, leaving us alone with his ruffian. I might have pushed the issue—with Lavien present, it would have been safe to do so—but there seemed to me no point. I wanted to speak to William Duer, one of the wealthiest men in the country. He could not simply disappear. If I did not get him today, I would soon enough. In any case, I had business enough here.

"Tell me, fellow," I said, "why would you have me cast from my home? It was the name of Reynolds that the villain gave when he paid my landlady to put me out."

"Fuck your landlady," Reynolds offered, by way of helpful explanation.

"While I appreciate your advice," I answered, "it does not answer my question."

"Then you must live with confusion," he said.

Sensing he meant to give me no more, and that he was the sort to delight in crude resistance, I turned my back on this Reynolds and retrieved my porter. I raised it in salute to the ruffian. Content that his master had made his escape, he glowered at us, meeting my gaze and then Lavien's, making certain to communicate his fierceness before stepping out the front door.

Certainly Reynolds was possessed of no uncommon name; there might be a dozen such or more in town. And yet I was not satisfied this was coincidence. The man who had run me from my rooms called himself Reynolds, but this man looked nothing like what my landlady had described. That man had worn spectacles and possessed gray hair and a gray beard. This man had brown hair, no beard, and no spectacles. Something curious had happened here, and given Hamilton's violent reaction when I mentioned the name to him, I thought it best to find out.

At once I set down my drink. "Hold here," I said to Lavien, and left the tavern. When I reached the street, I saw the back of Reynolds, who was already half a block distant. Leonidas sat on a bench out front. I tapped him on the shoulder.

"That man there, he's important. Follow him, find out where he lives, and anything else about him."

He nodded and hurried off. I turned to reenter the City Tavern. As I did so, I pushed past a man who appeared, in some distant recess of my mind, familiar. When I turned, I saw he was the frog-faced gentleman I'd observed the previous evening in the Crooked Knight. He had been sitting alone the night before, watching me with his froggish eyes. Now he looked at me, smiled in a knowing way I did not like, and touched the brim of his hat. I had not a moment to think of how to respond, and before I could stop or ask him who he was, he was gone. I had not the luxury of time to dwell upon this man, who might be of no importance at all, only a familiar face, so I headed inside the tavern.

Many of the financial men, having concluded the morning's trades, were gone or leaving, drifting off to their various homes and offices or retiring to different taverns to conduct more particular business. I rejoined Lavien, who sat sipping his tea, looking pleased with himself.

"Duer," he said, "does not like to make himself available to men who are not of immediate use to him."

"He is a speculator and Hamilton is Secretary of the Treasury. Good Lord, he even used to work at Treasury. Cannot he be made to cooperate?"

"With you?"

"Well, ideally, but at least with you. He seems to treat you rather contemptuously."

"Hamilton's powers here are limited," Lavien said. "If Duer does not wish to speak, Hamilton cannot compel him. Of course, Duer takes certain risks in rebuffing Hamilton, but Duer may believe himself too powerful to care."

"Then they are no longer friends?"

"Oh, I think they are friendly, and Duer will always seek favors and information from Hamilton, but there is a lack of trust. They are like old friends who find themselves on different sides, not precisely during war but certainly during a time of increasing hostility between two nations. Duer wants the United States to emulate Britain, where men of influence have always had their way before the public good."

"And what does Hamilton want the United States to be like?"

"He wants it to be like itself," Lavien said, "and that is an ever more challenging goal."

Lavien was being surprisingly forthcoming, and I could see no reason to withhold any longer the secret I had uncovered. "I suppose so, particularly in light of the threat to his bank."

He nodded his approval. "You learned of that quickly."

"How long have you known?"

"We've been aware that there may be a plot against the bank for a week now."

"What sort of plot?"

He shook his head. "We don't know. The bank itself is located in Carpenters' Hall, and it could be a threat against the physical space, though I find that unlikely. A move to take over the bank through acquisition of the shares, perhaps. A move to devalue the shares and cause a run. It could be anything."

"And Duer's involvement?"

He shrugged. "Likely none that he is aware of. Duer has borrowed a great deal of money from the bank, and he no doubt intends to return to that well again and again. He would not do anything to stop its flow."

"But you said he owes the bank a great deal of money. Might he not want to see it fail to avoid repayment?"

"That would be like a man setting himself on fire to avoid paying his surgeon's bill. If the bank were to face some major crisis, all financial instruments would suffer, and that would destroy the market and so destroy Duer. But the fact that he is not involved in a plot does not mean he does not know something. He may know more than he is aware."

"Again, I must point out that you are being remarkably cooperative."

"I hope for a trade," he said.

"Of what sort?"

"Well, I depend upon your honor, for I have already given you what I have to offer—information about Duer and the bank—and now I want something from you, though in giving it to me, you will also be helping yourself." He took from his pocket a piece of paper and showed it to me. It was written in code, one that looked, on first glance, identical to the simple one I'd cracked the night before.

Lavien whisked it away, before I could even begin to effect a decoding.

"Retrieved from the enterprising Miss Fiddler," I said.

He nodded. "I could take it to someone at Treasury, but the fewer people who know about it, the more comfortable I will be. It is probable that Jefferson has spies at Treasury. Duer may have men loyal to himself as well. I may not want you involved, but I *do* trust you."

I nodded, and he handed me the paper again. Without my asking, while I continued to look it over, he brought me a fresh piece of writing paper, a quill, and ink, but I did not need them. I had worked through the code just the night before, and it was fresh in my mind. It took me but a moment to read the following:

WD. JP suspects efforts with Million B. I took action as discussed. D.

Was WD William Duer? JP Jacob Pearson? Who then was D if not Duer, and, perhaps most important, since it appeared to be the heart of the message, what was Million B?

I posed that question to Lavien.

"The Million Bank," he said, looking thoughtful. "I have not paid it much mind, but it is an effort to capitalize on the current enthusiasm for banks. It will be launched in New York City within the next week or two, but it is regarded by almost everyone as a foolish venture. I cannot think that either Pearson or Duer would have anything to do with it."

"And yet, here is this note," I said.

"This note, written by we know not who and intended, if we are to be honest, for the same. It is easy to imagine it is for Duer, but we have no real evidence."

It was true enough. "Then Duer will have to answer my question," I said.

"He has made a point of avoiding me. You think he will be less elusive for you?"

"No," I said. "But I mean to catch him all the same."

Later that evening, I quenched my thirst at the Man Full of Trouble, ate a dinner of cold meats and potatoes, and most likely would have passed the night there had not the barman come to me with a piece of paper.

"Just delivered. It is a message for you."

I grabbed the paper from his hand. "Very kind," I murmured. I opened up the note and saw by the dim light of the tavern that it was from Leonidas. He wished to meet me at the corner of Lombard and Seventh. He said it was urgent. I finished my drink and set out.

Leonidas was leaning against redbrick, puffing upon a pipe, sending up thick clouds of smoke against the light of the streetlamp. "You took your time," he said.

"I was upon important business."

"So I smell."

"You can't expect a man to reform instantly. Now, what are you doing upon this corner?"

"Expanding the boundaries of our inquiry," he said. "Keep your eye upon that building." He pointed to a house three doors in from the corner, on the other side of the street.

"What shall I see?"

"Something interesting, I hope. I was afraid you might miss it, but this is the house belonging to the rough man, Reynolds. He lives there with a woman—his wife, according to the neighbors. I've not looked upon her, but everyone says the same thing—that she is the most extraordinarily beautiful woman they have ever seen."

"Do go on."

"I followed Reynolds here. He left after an hour, and I continued to follow him, but though he did not see me, he seemed to sense there was someone watching him, and I was forced to let him go. He returned later, and now he has another visitor, which is what I wanted you to see."

"Who is it?"

"There are some things," said Leonidas, "that a man must see for himself."

We waited in the darkness. I wished I had taken the time for another drink before leaving, for it would have been pleasing to pass the time in a kind of numbness, though I suppose I achieved something like that anyway, watching the orange glow of Leonidas's pipe flare and fade.

At last I saw silhouettes pass before the curtains of the front room. Then the door opened, and two men appeared against the dim interior light. Reynolds seemed to be almost a different person, for he bowed before the second man, whom he evidently considered his superior. I could not at first identify him, though he seemed familiar in his shape and stature.

The stranger came out of the house, walking with his shoulders stooped, his gait quick but not sprightly, like a man rushing to get indoors during a storm. He cast his gaze back and forth, as though wishing to make certain no one would see him, and then stepped out into the street. He kept his head down and walked with sharp lashing strides like the jerky thrusts of oars into water. Only briefly did he pass into a splash of lamplight, but in that instant I saw his face, hard and set in anger, or possibly despair. It was Hamilton.

I let out my breath in a long steady stream and waited for him to pass. Then I spoke in a whisper. "Hamilton tells me he is on the outs with Duer, so why would he personally visit the home of Duer's lackey?"

"It is about money," Leonidas said. "Hamilton handed Reynolds a heavy purse."

Hamilton giving this man money? I had no idea what it meant, but for the first time since I'd taken on the search for Pearson, I began to feel unequal to the task before me.

It is only natural to feel anxiety when circumstances are larger than a man's ability to manage them. I learned this during the war, just as I learned that the only cure for such feelings is action. A man might not always be able to do all he must, but he can do something. There was no action for me to take, not right now, but at least there was always movement, and so, dismissing Leonidas, I walked through the streets of Philadelphia, keeping to the better neighborhoods, avoiding the taverns where I knew I might find drink to help me forget. I did not want to forget, I wanted to understand.

I had stumbled onto a dangerous situation, one I had no business involving myself in except that it concerned Cynthia Pearson, and that meant I had no choice. So what was it that I knew? I knew that Hamilton feared a plot against his brainchild, the Bank of the United States, an institution designed to invigorate the American economy, and which had set off a frenzy of reckless trading. The man in charge of inquiring into that threat, Kyler Lavien, was the same man who inquired into the disappearance of Cynthia's husband. It would be foolish to imagine that these two things were unconnected. My inquiries into the matter had so far led me to an unknown Irishman and to William Duer, Hamilton's former assistant, and to Duer's own underling, Reynolds, who bore the name of the man who had urged my landlady to cast me out of my rooms. And now, it seems, Reynolds was involved in some kind of secretive dealings with Hamilton himself.

All these things were bound together, but that did not mean they originated from the same point. Another thing I had learned during the war was that unrelated threads become entangled because important men can be important in more than one sphere at a time. Hamilton's secretive dealings with Duer's man might have nothing to do with the threat against the bank or Cynthia's husband's disappearance. On the other hand, just because these things might begin as unrelated didn't mean they stayed that way, and it would be best to assume connections even when there could be no logical reason for them to exist. Mysterious actions and unknown plots are uncovered not by understanding motives but by understanding men.

So I told myself as I returned to my boardinghouse. I walked with my head down, murmuring to myself like a drunkard, though I was perfectly sober. I felt it useful to speak aloud everything that troubled me, to give each difficulty some dimension in speech that I might comprehend it better. I hardly looked where I walked, for all that interested me was inside my mind. I was on the stairs to Mrs. Deisher's house, lost in thought and strategies, when the fist struck me in the stomach.

My attacker must have been crouched, hiding in the shadows of the stoop, for I had already begun to climb to the door when I saw movement in the darkness, a shifting of dark clothes, a glimmer of reflected light upon a button, a pair of eyes, teeth behind lips pulled back in a grin or perhaps a grimace.

I had no time to react, only to see it coming, this human form uncoil, and when the blow struck, it struck hard. I felt my feet actually lift from the stairs and I fell backward, landing hard upon my arse. I fought not to fall over entirely, but the force of the blow drove my head down. My skull struck with a jarring force—an angry thud that sent pain halfway down my back—but I hit not brick but dirt, the little circle of earth surrounding a tree. The pain ran down in a spiked wave, followed by a sprinkling of silver lights, but I knew at once I had not taken a deadly blow. Even in that moment I felt a foolish relief that the damage was all to a place that would be invisible to others. It would not do to have further wounds upon my face.

Now all at once I saw what I should have seen before. The lamp outside Mrs. Deisher's house was out. The lamps by the neighbors' houses were out. Were I not so out of practice I would have sensed the ambush, but I could not undo what had been done. I could only move forward.

The dark figure—a big man, stocky, probably muscular, wearing a wide-brimmed hat; I could see no more—stood over me on the stairs, perhaps savoring his moment of advantage. He reached into his belt for something and held it up. In the dim light of cloud-covered moon and dim stars and distant lamplight I could see the faint twinkle of polished steel. It was a blade, and rather a long one. From where I lay, even with the wind blowing between us, I could smell him: the rank sourness of unwashed clothes, old sweat, and the peculiar acrid scent of wet, moldy tobacco.

I knew several things now. This man, whoever he was, had not come to kill me. Had his first blow to my stomach been made with that knife, I would now be dead or dying. The blade was to frighten me or to hurt me without killing me. Even so, I knew if I was not careful I might yet end up dead.

My head ached, and I felt a dull, painful heaviness in my gut, but I ignored it. The man loomed closer, only three or four steps away. I was on my back, propped up on my hands. He would think me helpless and at his mercy, but it wasn't quite so.

Any encounter such as this one is like a game of chess. He had his moves to make and I had mine. We could go only certain ways. Each move creates a new series of possible countermoves. Most important, perhaps, victory goes not to the player who is stronger or more ready to attack but to the player who can see and anticipate the farthest into the future, who can map out the multiplying strands of possibility. This is what I told myself.

He had made his first move, and now it was time for mine. Under the circumstances, I needed to buy time and distract him. Asking him who he was or what he wanted, begging for mercy, telling him I could pay him well to leave me be—none of these things would do. Not because they had no chance of working, but because they were all too predictable. I chose to speak nonsense, but nonsense that would make him stop to think.

"I began to think you would never make your attempt," I said.

In the dark, I saw the outline of his head shift in birdlike curiosity, as though he took a moment to consider. He took a step toward me, and I believe I as much as saw his mouth open, though I know not that he would have spoken.

He never had the chance because at that moment Mrs. Deisher slammed open her front door and stood there, a dark and billowing figure in her dressing gown, a candle burning behind her, holding something long with a comically flaring end. It took me a moment to identify it as an ancient blunderbuss.

The weapon must have been a hundred years old at least and, from the look of it, would best serve as nothing more than a decorative wall hanging for a hunting lodge, but the stout German lady wielded it like it was Excalibur. My assailant was prepared to take no chances, and he immediately leaped from the stoop and began to run down the street. To my surprise, Mrs. Deisher jumped after him. She launched herself into the air, and her gown ballooned out. Her feet spread wide, she landed upon the cobbled walkway with a crack as wooden shoes struck brick. Taking not even a moment to think of her own safety—or, I might add, to aim—she raised her antique weapon and fired. It exploded like a cannon and belched out a great foul cloud of black smoke. She had fired high, for I heard only the cracking of brittle winter tree branches, the echo of the report, and, finally, the distant slap of feet as my assailant vanished into the night.

Mrs. Deisher tossed her smoking weapon to the ground, put a hand on my forearm, and pulled me to my feet. "I wrong you once," she said to me, "but not twice. You friend of government, and so friend of me. I save you for America."

"And America thanks you," I said, pushing myself to my feet. I pressed a hand to the back of my head, and it came away dry, which was a rare bit of good news. I gave Mrs. Deisher a little pat upon her hand and then looked down the street at the empty darkness, expecting to see nothing and finding all my expectations, for once, fulfilled.

I could not criticize her for having saved me, though I thought that if the encounter had lasted even a few moments longer I might have learned something of my attacker. As things stood, I had not seen his face or heard his voice. And yet there was something familiar about the man. I had no idea who he was, but I believed this was not the first time I had been close to him.

Joan Maycott

Spring 1791

We had wanted to believe that Tindall had sent his men to our cabin as an empty threat, and at first it did appear that way. The fame of their whiskey, and Andrew's skill as a whiskey maker, continued to spread throughout the four counties, and, as our profits increased, we congratulated ourselves on our success. Andrew and his friends had bested Tindall, who, far from attempting to duplicate the new method of making whiskey, continued to produce cheap spirits from his stills. Perhaps he believed that quantity must win out over quality, but it showed no sign of doing so.

I continued to work on my novel, which I wrote and revised and perfected, as Andrew did with the whiskey, until it was closer to what I wished for. I was not done, not near done, but I began to sense that it might someday be finished—that completion was no longer an elusive goal but an inevitability.

With winter over, there was more cause for happiness. I was not yet ready to say anything to Andrew, but I had missed my monthly courses now two times, and though I felt on occasion sick, and the scent of foods I had once loved now sent me to retching, I knew this time would be different. We were healthy and strong and rugged, and this baby would live and thrive.

If our lives in the West were far happier than once we would have dared to hope, events back east turned ominous. With the melting of the snows we had received our first dispatch of news, and we learned that Hamilton and Duer had only increased their power. Having enriched themselves with the Assumption Bill—a slap in the face to every patriot who had traded his debt for western Pennsylvania land—the money men in the government had convinced the Congress to charter a national bank. This project, all in the West agreed, was but a scheme to tax the poor, so that monies could be provided for the rich. The bank was upon everyone's lips. It was the harbinger of doom, the sign that the American project had failed. In breaking away from England, we had become but an imitation, a model of its injustices. Hamilton, in our estimate, was the architect of American corruption, and Duer his principal agent. What had been done to us as individuals would be visited upon an entire nation. We of the West, it now seemed to me, who had long been America's unwanted stepchildren, might be forced at some future time to pick up arms against Philadelphia, much as we had done against England.

For now such a cataclysm seemed a distant prospect, perhaps a battle to be fought by our children or grandchildren, but tyranny crept upon us sooner than I could have imagined. Perhaps a week after learning of Hamilton and Duer's attempt to sow corruption, Andrew and I were interrupted in our cabin. It was after dark, and we had only just sat down for supper when the door to our cabin opened. My first thought was that it must be Mr. Dalton and Mr. Skye, though they were not in the habit of entering without knocking. It was neither of them.

Three Indian braves faced us with the blank and unreadable expression so typical of their race—faces hard and stony, as though they had never known emotion and, at the same time, as though that lack of feeling was the very apex of some human experience. In recent weeks the air had remained rather cold, so they wore deerskin breeches and jerkins.

Their hair was long and unrestrained, their faces unmarked by war paint, and they had the slovenly look of redskins too long living among white men, too accustomed to strong drink and unsavory habits. They set their guns by the side of the door and then sat down at the table without a word.

I had heard of such things happening before. The guns by the door were a sign that they meant no harm, but I remained uneasy. We dared not attempt to force them away or make them feel unwelcome, but I cannot fully describe the great fear I felt upon seeing them. It seemed to me the confined space of our cabin could not contain the mounting energy of their silent anger, violence, and, yes, carnal urges.

Andrew cleared his throat. "Well, friends, it seems you'll be joining us for our meal, then. I'm afraid the offerings are meager, as we did not know to expect company."

If they understood him, or had even heard him, they made no sign of it. They stared into nothingness and waited to be served, blank eyes straight ahead, soulless and soulful all at once, the centuries of hatred for our race written into their very skin. Serve them I did, giving each a plate of venison stew, a salad of field greens, and a piece of corn bread. Their eyes did not move as I set the food before them. It seemed I could have tossed stones on their plates, sending their food splattering, and they would not have responded.

I dipped my spoon in my stew, but only because I feared not doing so would upset the braves, make them believe that there was something untoward in the meal. My cooking since coming to the West was none the most sophisticated, but now it tasted like sand in my mouth, and it took every effort to swallow. I hoped the braves would be satisfied, however, eat their fill—and go. One dipped his fingers into the stew and put them in his mouth. He made a sour face, the first semblance of human expression I'd witnessed, and spat toward the fire. Another brave bit into the corn bread and let the food tumble from his mouth the way a baby does when first learning to eat. The third, unwilling even to sample what his friends found so distasteful, lifted his dish and allowed its contents to slide to the floor.

I expected Andrew to offer some kind of rebuke. In my mind I could see him gently scolding the braves, explaining that if they were to visit a white man's house they must behave in accordance with the white man's customs.

He merely sat with his hands in his lap. He blinked but otherwise remained motionless.

I stared at him. Andrew was no coward, but even so he was only one man, and here were three braves. What could he do? What could I expect him to do? I did not know, but oh, how I wanted him to do something!

The braves rose now, all three standing across the table from us. One took from his belt a knife. "We take your wife, we let you live," he said.

"You are not taking my wife anywhere." Andrew remained in his seat, looking like a clerk before a supplicant. He blinked again and again, as though trying to get something out of his eye, but he did not lift a hand to rub it.

"Not take *away*," the brave corrected. "*Take.* You watch, we take."

A second brave clarified his meaning, taking the index finger of his left hand and moving in and out of the circle of finger and thumb on his right. The gesture was so foolish, so much like that of a puerile apprentice, that I repressed the mad desire to laugh.

"We take your wife and you both live," said the brave with the knife. "You fight us, you both die. This the deal."

"I see," said my husband, still the calm of a man who considered whether or not to buy a mule. "It is a rather unusual deal, is it not?"

"It the deal," the Indian insisted.

"Does this deal come from Colonel Tindall?"

The braves exchanged looks, and then the one with the knife nodded. "From Tindall."

"Very well," said my husband.

There was then the loud report—louder for being so unexpected—of a pistol shot from nearby, followed almost immediately by a thud upon the table and then by another pistol shot. The air at once was singed with the bitter scent of powder, and our little cabin was full of stinging smoke. I looked around in terror, not knowing whence the shots had come, but the brave with the knife sank to his knees, his stomach darkening with blood. He clutched the knife so tightly, the skin of his hand turned white, but as he did so, he fell forward onto his face.

The second shot had struck another brave in the knee. He collapsed upon the floor and clutched his wound with his hand, but he made not a noise. The third brave bolted for the door—to get his gun, I presumed. Andrew let go of the pistols, and I now realized why he had been sitting with his hands under the table. I remembered Dalton's warning, and I could only think that Andrew had taken it to heart but had said nothing lest he upset me. He sprang to his feet, and I could see that his hands were stained with powder. His pants had been blackened by the shot, and it looked as though the fabric had caught fire and been put out. Andrew, however, remained utterly calm—focused and determined, but not hurried. Taking the hunting rifle mounted upon the wall above the fireplace, he turned, aimed, and fired.

Once more the scent of powder burst into the cabin, and smoke choked the air. Only after the ball struck the brave's back did we see that the man had not been running for his gun, he had been running for the door. He had been trying to escape. I looked at Andrew to see how this would affect him, the knowledge that he had shot an unarmed man in the back while he fled. I did not see the man I knew there. Musket in hand, eyes hard, he looked as remorseless as had the braves.

Andrew reloaded the gun, grinding down the ball with a kind of mad calmness, and then handed it to me. "Keep it trained on him. Shoot him if he makes any move toward you." He then fetched a piece of hemp rope and began to bind the brave's arms behind his back.

"What are we going to do with him?"

"Tie him up while we fetch help. We need to speak to Dalton and the others."

"You know they will kill him," I said. I was not protesting or suggesting a course of action. I merely made a statement of fact.

"Probably. And then we go deal with Tindall."

I should prefer to believe that it was the Indians who were the savages, while the white men bore the standard for civilization. It was not true. When we reached Dalton and told him our tale, he immediately sent word to others in the community. It was not long before a group of two score men, women, and children arrived at our cabin. They took possession of the brave. The bleeding had abated somewhat, but his leg remained atop a bloody patch of floor I would later have to cover with ashes and sawdust. I was, at least, spared witnessing what came next. The Indian was taken out to the woods to be beaten, tortured, and, in the end, scalped. His body was left to rot.

The Indians, however, were not the main source of consternation. Indians had ever been a problem, ever would be. Though I dreaded their violence, I felt sympathy for people who wanted only to protect their ancient rights and lands. These dead braves, however, had struck a bad bargain with a man who could not be their friend. They had agreed to do a terrible thing, for what I did not know. Maybe they thought it would gain them freedom or privacy or peace, but violence could never yield such things.

The next day the bulk of the community met in the large cabin that served as the church and sat upon rough-hewn log benches that wobbled upon an earth floor. There were sixty or more packed inside, men, women, and children, faces dark with filth and anger. The air smelled of bear-fat candle and smoke and spat tobacco juice, and the faces around us were hard and set and angry. In truth, I thought they would be angry with us, as though we had visited this upon ourselves and, in doing so, visited it upon them. It wasn't the case. We had not been living in the settlement two years, and yet these people took this assault upon us as an outrage. Some wanted to take up arms and attack Tindall's house at Empire Hill, to set the whole city on fire. Some wanted to send envoys to treat with him that we might find some sort of peace.

There had been much shouting, but it was Mr. Dalton who brought the meeting to order. He rose, and his mere presence, great and wide and bald-headed, quieted the agitated gathering.

"This attack upon the Maycotts is an attack on all of us, make no mistake," he said. "And 'tis a mighty low thing to get redskins to do what you won't do yourself."

The crowd, which hated Indians above almost every other thing, heartily agreed.

"But while we each have reason to take it to heart," said Dalton, "I have more than most, and so does Skye, here, for this is about our whiskey. You all know Tindall has his own stills, and he sees he stands to lose money if we keep on with what we're doing. For his loss is your profit. You have more to trade than anyone else in these parts. You all get richer. Tindall don't like that."

"That's right," shouted Mortimer Lyle, who worked a plot of land down by the creek. He was short but squat and muscular and was missing his left eye. "That's it, all right. And that's why we've got to go burn him out. Burn him out, is what I say."

This got a general cheer of approbation, and though Dalton tried to quiet the crowd, he could do no good. Then Andrew stood and waved the men down, and slowly they calmed. My gentle Andrew soothed this group of border rioters. It was something to behold. Of course, he was known by now as a reasonable man, generous with his carpentry tools and eager to lend a hand to aid a neighbor. That he was the creator of the best whiskey in the four counties only added to his reputation. Yet that was nothing compared to what had just happened. He was new, a soft man from the East, but he had dispatched three murderous braves on his own, and that meant the floor was his if he wished it.

"I have fought in one war," he said to the group, once it had been quieted, "and I have no wish to fight in another, even less so if it is unnecessary. Yes, we might kill Tindall and burn down his home, but what should that get us? The men back east won't send soldiers to fight the Indians that terrorize us, but I can promise you they will send soldiers to fight rebels who visit violence upon the wealthy. You men read the newspapers. They say Hamilton wants to consolidate the power of the Federalist government—not to mention his own power within that government—and an insurrection in the West would give him what he most wants: an excuse to exercise his power. We could never win. It would be a victory for our enemies if we even showed up to fight."

This produced a murmur of agreement.

"Then what do you suggest?" asked Walter Gall, the miller.

"I suggest," said Andrew, looking rakishly handsome as he grinned his devious grin, "I suggest that we go have a talk with him."

"A talk?" Gall answered with indignation. There was general uproar. Andrew, it seemed, was soft after all. He would respond to violence with palaver.

Yet he calmed them once more. I looked upon him with admiration, and I saw Mr. Dalton and Mr. Richmond did so also. They knew his worth, and it made me proud.

"He thinks to provoke us into a fight. It's what he's counting on. I think he needs to see that we are resolute. Steady and firm, but not quick to violence. He'll not back us into giving him what he wants."

It was a simple argument, but it was met with general approbation. They would talk to Tindall and they would let it be known they would not be so used. So it was they began to put together a delegation of men to go into town and confront the man who had yet again attempted to ruin all our lives.

Ethan Saunders

I could not long delay speaking with William Duer. I had already learned this would be no easy thing. He did not wish to speak to me, and he employed a vicious tough who could see that he did not have to do what he did not wish to do. My only option, then, was to get to Duer where he dared not refuse me and where he could not call upon Reynolds. As it happened, I believed I knew just the place.

All Philadelphia had been discussing the upcoming gathering at the Bingham house. William Bingham was one of the wealthiest and most influential men in the nation, friends with anyone of any significance. His wife, Anne, was considered to be one of the most charming and beautiful women in the world, and it was said that much sympathy in Europe for the American cause originated with that lady's tour of foreign courts. Needless to say, it was inconceivable that I would be welcome in, let alone invited to, their home. It was as well, then, that I did not limit myself only to those places where people might wish me to be.

———

It was impossible for me, as I passed the day, not to dwell upon the fantasy that Mrs. Pearson would attend the gathering that night. For many years she and Anne Bingham had been particular friends. Had Cynthia's husband not vanished, she would certainly be in attendance. Under the circumstances, it would be impossible, but even so, I imagined what it would be like to meet with her in such a setting, in polite company, where we could stand near each other, make polite conversation, and imagine that all was as it should be.

I had met the lady at such a gathering. When I had traveled to Philadelphia during the British occupation to infiltrate a British spy ring, Fleet had asked me to keep an eye upon his daughter and make certain she wanted for nothing. I never after discussed with him my attachment to her for fear he would think I had taken advantage of the girl, though she and I intended to reveal all to him after the conclusion of the war. Later, after Fleet's death, I could not help but wonder if I had been silly, if Fleet had thrown us together in the hopes that we would develop those feelings we found so irrepressible.

Young Cynthia Fleet was active in Philadelphia social circles, and it was at the home of Thomas Willing, Anne Bingham's father and now the president of the Bank of the United States, that I met both Cynthia and her future husband. The latter I found utterly unremarkable and could easily have never thought of him again, had fate not continually thrown him in my way. Of my friend's daughter, I could not cease to think. Cynthia was a fair-haired beauty with eyes of the palest, most transcendent blue. Her figure was arresting, her skin unblemished, her face a model of symmetrical loveliness. In her manner there was all that a man could find delightful and refined, and even before I heard her lively and clever conversation, I believe I was a little in love with her. Yes, it was something as shallow as beauty that made me love her, before I knew that our minds were perfectly formed for one another, before I even knew she was Fleet's daughter.

I allowed an acquaintance of mine, a man of decidedly British sympathies (for such were the sort of men with whom I was forced to traffic), to introduce us, and I detected nothing significant in her reaction when she heard my name. Obviously Cynthia did not know I worked with her father or that I was in the service of the patriot cause. Nevertheless, she took a particular interest in me, allowing me to continue to address her for some length of time. What I found was that this lady was not only beautiful but clever, accomplished, and exceptionally well informed in matters political. She did not hesitate to offer me opinions on the most important men of the day, what they had done and written, of battles won and lost, of strategies failed and successful. She spoke quietly, for my ears alone—and I could not regret that she did so, for it was an invitation to lean in closely—but I feared for her safety. In an occupied city, she ought not to have been so free as to praise Americans and condemn the British, not to a total stranger.

At last I put a hand upon her arm and leaned toward her close. "Miss Fleet," I said in a low voice, "do you think it wise, in such company, to speak so highly of the rebel cause? Do you not know you are surrounded by Royalists? Do you not know that the man who introduced us is a Royalist? You must assume me to be one as well."

"No, I mustn't," she said, with a mischievous smile. "Not when you are my father's associate."

I could not keep from barking out a laugh. "If you knew that, why did you not tell me?"

"I wished to know if you would tell me yourself," she said. "I suppose only an hour's conversation is not enough to know what you might say in future, but I believe it shows a certain amount of restraint on your part. It will have to do."

"Do for what?" I asked.

"For us to continue to be friends," she said.

Not a week later I met her at a ball hosted by a British colonel, and though she was promised to an unpleasant officer for the first two dances, she and I managed—much to this officer's displeasure—to find many opportunities to dance together and even more to speak. It was soon after the dance that I received an invitation to dine at the house of her late mother's sister and husband—people of Royalist sentiments with whom she lived—and I did not hesitate to use all my charms upon these people, that I might become a regular fixture within their circle. Cynthia and I soon found other occasions to be together. We strolled the streets, took tea, or visited the sights. She had an almost insatiable appetite for tales of my adventures, and though I often had to withhold particulars, I told her enough to thrill her.

I was no stranger to female companionship, yet I could not believe I had been so fortunate as to secure the interest and affection of Cynthia Fleet, a woman who seemed molded by nature for the sole purpose of being my companion. We lived in such happiness for two months, but then the man whom I followed left the city, and I was forced to do the same. Cynthia and I exchanged vows of love and determined to marry upon the war's conclusion. I could not say when I would return to Philadelphia, but we would write. Indeed, we did, and on many occasions, after the British gave up the city, I managed to find my way back to visit her. The last of these was but three months before Fleet and I were accused of treason. A decisive battle was coming, and as I kissed her goodbye I believed in my heart that the time would soon come when we could declare ourselves and commit to law what was already in our hearts. The next time I saw her, however, all had been altered. Her father was dead; a malicious fate had made it impossible we could ever be together. I would live with the false accusation of treason if I must, but I could not endure casting such a stigma upon her.

Two hours before the Bingham gathering was scheduled to begin, Leonidas informed me that Mr. Lavien was below and wished to see me. I was already dressed and had no objection to passing time in his company, particularly if he might impart to me some useful information.

He came into my rooms and shook my hand with his usual reserve. I offered him a drink, which he declined, and I was glad of it, for if he took one, I would have been forced to join him, and I wished to remain clear-headed as long as I might.

Once we were seated, Lavien said, "You are rather well dressed this evening."

"A man cannot dress poorly at all times," I answered.

He knew my evasion for what it was, but he did not pursue it. Instead, he leaned forward, and there was something rather lively in his eyes. I believe this was what passed for excitement in a man of such rigid control. "I have learned something interesting," he said, "and I wished to share it with you at once."

"About Duer?"

"No," he said. "About Fleet."

A chill came over me, as though I'd heard a whisper of a dead man's voice. I now wished heartily I had taken a drink, with or without him. "I told you to leave the matter be." My voice, not nearly so steady as I would have liked, betrayed my agitation when I wanted cold anger.

"I know you did, and I meant to do what you asked, but then one thing led to another and I ended up doing what I wished to do instead. I don't know how it could have happened. In any event, you will want to hear what I have to say."

"No, I won't." I rose to my feet.

My disposition had no effect upon him. He remained seated and still, as though we were still engaged in a friendly exchange. "Information once learned cannot be unlearned, and I believe you will not be easy until you hear what I now know."

I sat, for there was no denying what he said.

"I troubled myself to call upon General Knox, who I thought, as the Secretary of War, might be able to assist me. Indeed, he directed me to some archives that proved useful. You recall, I am sure, Major Brookings."

I nodded. Of course I remembered him. He was the man who had uncovered the damning evidence in the linings of our travel packs.

"It seems that even after the war's close, Major Brookings remained interested in your case. He became increasingly convinced that you and Fleet were done a terrible wrong. His notes show that he had found some evidence to at least suggest that the case against you had been fabricated by an enemy—likely British—who wished to see the most effective American spies removed from the field."

I swallowed hard and did my best to master myself before speaking. "If he thought so, why did he never tell anyone?"

"Based upon what his notes tell me, he wished to form a definitive conclusion and uncover the names of the perpetrators before announcing his suspicions, but he died before he could complete his task."

"Murdered?"

Lavien shook his head. "Nothing so mysterious. This was two years ago, and as you will recall, he was not young when you met him. His heart apparently failed him while he was riding with his children. There can be no thought of murder, only ill luck, for him and for you. It is not enough to clear your name absolutely, but it is enough for us to begin making further inquiries."

"I want you to let it be," I said. My voice was quiet, and at first I feared he had not heard me. I attempted to speak more forcefully. "You must not pursue this."

"Is it because you fear Fleet will not, in the end, be proved innocent," he asked, "or because you cannot endure the knowledge that you have suffered all these years for nothing?"

I did not answer him. I would not, and waited for him to excuse himself and leave me be.

Joan Maycott

Spring 1791

Three days after the meeting at the church, we set out on the ride to Colonel Tindall's home at Empire Hill. It took several hours by horse, so we left early in the morning, that we might be there well before midday. Mr. Dalton thought it dangerous to stay overnight in town; he wished to see Tindall, say what needed saying, and return to our homes before dark.

The journey was tense, and Dalton never once eased up his grip upon his pistol. For my part, I vowed I would not be entirely at their mercy. Since the encounter with the braves, I had made it a point to hide a primed pistol in my skirt or apron. I had learned from Andrew, and I would imitate him if called upon to do so.

We arrived at the estate in a timely fashion and were admitted to a sitting room on the first floor, much more primitive than the room to which we'd been invited on our previous visit. There the floor had been covered with a painted tarp to mimic black and white tiles, but this room

had much more rugged furnishings—all wooden—and I quickly surmised that Tindall used this space when dealing with men of the rougher
sort. Society friends were invited upstairs.

We took seats in the various chairs and awaited Tindall's arrival,
which happened soon enough. "Good morning, men, Mrs. Maycott,"
he said, as he came in the room. "Fair weather we are having, do you not
think so?"

"You may keep the pleasantries to yourself," said Mr. Skye. "That
don't interest us."

He smirked as though Skye's response was precisely what he had
hoped for, as though we were already falling into his trap. "Then what
does interest you?"

"You know why we're here," said Mr. Dalton. "Now let's have your
end of it."

Andrew, during all of this, remained quiet. It had been agreed that it
would be wisest to let the others do the talking, for once Andrew or I
spoke Tindall could easily accuse us of letting our emotions lead us to
rash conclusions.

"Listen to you, putting on airs," said Tindall. "You may strut around
all you like, but I can't say I have any inkling of what you want. I am a
busy man, but as you wish to speak with me, I've made myself available.
Now it seems you answer my kindness with insult."

"It is you who insult us," said Mr. Dalton. "We know perfectly well
that you sent those three braves. Had Maycott not shot them, I don't
know how far the incident would have progressed, and I do not care to
know."

"The killing of Indians is a serious business," said Tindall. "You don't
want to provoke the local savages to violence."

"I can't agree," answered Mr. Skye, "that refusing to be killed is a
provocation."

"The Indians may see it differently," said Tindall.

"You may end the nonsense," said Mr. Dalton. "You got no right to
tell us what we can and cannot do on that land, not so long as the rent is
paid. This kind of insult can't go unanswered."

Tindall slammed the butt of his gun upon the floor. "Then answer it!" he roared. His voice was sudden, loud, a challenge so blatant and naked it seemed to me obscene. In the face of it, the three men—Andrew, Dalton, Skye—stood silent and humbled. I saw quite clearly that with me in the room there would be no violence, and Tindall might continue to taunt us as much as he liked.

No one spoke. The silence was thick and full of menace, going on longer than I could have imagined. At last the stalemate was broken when the door opened and the plump Negress whom we'd encountered on our previous visit entered the room. "I see you got yourself some guests, Colonel," she said. "How come you don't ask old Lactilla for refreshment? I got biscuits, I got cake, I can make some tea right quick."

"Good God, gal," cried the colonel, "if I wish for refreshment, I'll call for it!"

"Well," said the woman, "you got that lady here again, and looks like you're being none too kind to her husband and their friends. Seems to me, if you're going to be unkind to folks, you might as well give them some tea to make it go down the smoother."

Tindall clutched his fowling piece. "If I wish for advice from a nigger, I will certainly call for it. Until then, I'd advise you to shut up and get gone."

She put her hands upon her massive hips. "Don't you talk to Lactilla that way."

"Gal," Tindall said, half rising from his seat, "get gone before you regret it."

"I ain't going to regret nothing but letting you talk that way. It ain't right."

My eyes were upon this woman, so I did not see what Tindall did next. From the corner of my eye, however, came the red flash of flame and the smoke and the crack of the discharged fowling piece. All at once, Lactilla's face was covered with blood. There were small holes in her plain white dress, across which erupted rosettes of blood like crimson fireworks against a night sky.

Tindall had fired the weapon from a distance of fifteen feet, and I presumed it contained birdshot. It was plain the poor woman would not die of her injuries, though she was lucky to have escaped blindness. I knew

Tindall had missed her eyes, because they were wide with surprise, her mouth open and slack. Then, understanding what had happened, she let out a shriek and ran from the room.

Tindall set down the smoking gun, returned to his seat, and smiled at us. "I beg your pardon for the interruption. You were saying?"

It was Mr. Skye who spoke first. "You're mad."

Tindall shrugged. "I will not be challenged in my own home. There is no serious harm done, but I believe that nigger should be well behaved for a little while at least. When she forgets herself, I shall know best how to remind her."

Andrew shook his head. "You have convinced us that you are a villain, but you have done nothing more than that. You may own our land, but you do not own us. We did not fight in the war to be slaves here at home."

"I am sick to my death of the war as an excuse for every beggar who wishes to prop himself up. You tell me that you did not fight to be a slave. Well, I fought that I might *keep* my slaves, so that puts us rather at odds, doesn't it?" He pointed at Andrew. "You allege I sent red men after you but now stand there silent. Did you fight in the war so you might enjoy the luxury of being a coward later?"

Andrew began to move forward, but I put a hand upon his arm.

Tindall grinned at me. "I see you are governed by your wife. I cannot blame a man for wishing to please so pretty a lady, but he must also know when to be his own master."

My heart quickened, and I feared that in the end he would goad Andrew into doing something foolish. "You may try to provoke us," I said, "but it is your deeds and not your words I hate."

"Don't be so eager to dismiss my words," he said. "I've not yet finished speaking."

There was something in the air, and we felt at once that Tindall had been playing games with us.

"You think that because I am against your brewing whiskey I am somehow threatening you? That I have no better things to do with my time than to toy with my poor insignificant tenants? You fools. I am only looking after your interests. You, in your little hovels away from the world, have no knowledge of what is happening back east. You don't know what the government says of you, or that indeed it says anything at all."

Mr. Skye took a step forward. "If you have something to say, then say it."

Tindall smirked. "I don't know if you are familiar with the plans being orchestrated by Alexander Hamilton, the Secretary of the Treasury. His most recent project is to establish a national bank, separate from the government but closely allied to it. The revenue for launching the bank will have to come from somewhere, so Hamilton has decided to place an excise tax upon unnecessary luxury items, those people desire but can do without. There is no better way to raise revenue, he has argued, than by putting an excise tax on something no one actually needs and only hurts the fabric of American life."

"And what is this luxury?" Mr. Dalton asked.

"Why," said Tindall with a grin, "'tis whiskey, boys. It has been planned for some time, but I have just received confirmation by fast rider that Hamilton has convinced Congress to pass the whiskey tax, and what you owe will be based not upon how much you sell or how much you earn but on how much you produce."

Mr. Dalton rose from his seat and took a step forward. "They cannot do it!" he cried. "We make no true money from whiskey but use it for trade. We have no money to give."

"You need not shout at me," said Tindall. "I did not devise the law. No one consulted me. It has been passed, and nothing can be done about it."

"And that is why you were so eager to see us?" asked Andrew. "So you might gloat over imparting the knowledge that the government has passed a tax designed to ruin us?"

"No," he answered. "Not at all. I wished to speak to you to inform you that my old associate General John Neville has been appointed local tax assessor, and he has secured my services to make certain the money owed the government is collected. In the weeks to come, I will determine how much each of you owes, and I mean to collect your debts. If you refuse to pay, I shall take what you owe in land or equipment. It is the law of the land, and I mean to enforce it. That will be all, gentlemen." He looked at me. "And lady, of course."

Ethan Saunders

All the world wished to be at the Bingham gathering, and I was not invited. This was of no moment, for I had no doubt getting in would be the easiest thing in the world. As I approached on Market Street I observed the lanterns lit all along Bingham's mansion. Here was one of the jewels of the city, a private residence of remarkable splendor and taste, hardly less massive and grand than the Library Company building. For those Europeans who believed America to be a country of fur-clad man-beasts, possessing nothing of arts or subtlety, I should defy them to see our finest architecture, of which this house was certainly an example—a monument to American sturdiness, modesty, and opulence.

A queue of coaches made its slow, important way through the circular path along the front of the house, but I would not join with them. Instead, Leonidas and I went around back to the servants' entrance. Much to our surprise, this was locked. I had anticipated a busy stream of servants moving in and out, among whom we could be lost, but apparently the Binghams had prepared long in advance.

Leonidas asked not my plans nor made snide remarks upon my lack of preparation. He knew me too well to think I would regard this locked door as any sort of impediment. I reached into my right boot, in which I kept a hidden pouch containing several useful lock picks. I found the one best suited for the device before me, and within a minute the lock sprang and I turned the knob. Replacing the picks in my boot, I pushed open the door. Here we found a dozen or more cooks, chefs, and servers hurrying about not in chaos, but with a kind of mechanized determination. Upon the stoves, steam billowed forth. From the ovens came fiery blasts of heat. One woman set pastries upon a white porcelain tray. Another used a massive pair of tongs to pull small fowl from a pot of boiling water. Into this fray we ventured, and I commenced a lecture to Leonidas on the proper placement of cheeses, a lecture that lasted the breadth of our stroll through the kitchen. If anyone considered it remarkable that a man should walk through this room lecturing a Negro on the art of serving food, no one mentioned it to me. Thus, emerging from the kitchen, we found ourselves in the massive house, where we had only to follow our ears and ascend a set of stairs to reach the main body of the festivities. Thus settled, I sent Leonidas to find where the other servants were gathered.

There were several dozen guests in attendance, and in addition to the room that had been cleared to create a space for the dancers, the revelers were spread throughout three large rooms that appeared to have been furnished with such gatherings as this in mind. Each room contained pockets of chairs and sofas, so guests might sit and converse, and every chandelier, sconce, and candleholder was stuffed with a fat taper, lighting the room so that it seemed almost daytime. In one room, several tables had been set out with cards for gaming. Wine and food was served freely, a trio of musicians played in one corner, and our beautiful hostess, the incomparable Mrs. Bingham, beautiful and elegant, enfolded in her massive nimbus of golden hair, flitted from guest to guest. In the ballroom, the great and important and pompous of the city, and so the nation, turned about with elegance or clumsiness.

I minded neither the candles nor the food nor the fiddlers nor even the dancing. I was less comfortable with the company, for here was nearly every man of substance in the city. There was Mr. Willing, president of Hamilton's bank. There the great windbag John Adams, the vice president, with his agreeable wife, Abigail, by his side. Missing, much to my simultaneous disappointment and relief, was the great man himself, Washington. It was said he avoided such gatherings, for he alone had to forge the public role of the President and knew not if it would be too frivolous for the leader of a republican nation to attend a gathering of this sort. It was for the best, I decided. In my fallen state, how could I face a man revered by all, and by me more than any other?

However, there was Hamilton, standing next to his wife, Eliza. I had flirted with her many years before, but if she recognized me, she made no sign of it. She was still vaguely pretty, but she'd grown a bit plump and dowdy, having given birth to so many children I believed even the parents had lost track. The two of them bred Federalists like rabbits. It was an easy enough thing to mock him, but when I observed the happiness with which she looked upon her husband and the comfort he took when he held her hand, I felt keenly why I was in that room. I was there for Cynthia and for all I had lost, all that had been denied me.

I took a goblet of wine from a passing servant and acted as though there were nowhere else in the universe I belonged so well. I wished above all things not to be noticed, for there were many men in that room whom I did not know well but who might yet recognize me, might yet recall my name, my face, and the crime of which I had been accused. I wanted to do what I must before being generally seen.

I was not to be so lucky, however. I had only begun to scan the room when I felt a hand on my shoulder and turned to face Colonel Hamilton himself, with Eliza still by his side. Diverting her gaze for a moment, she smiled at me. "Captain Saunders, it has been many years."

I bowed to her. "Far too many, and yet while I have aged, you look no different than when last I saw you. I trust you are well?"

So went our exchange of nothings. She, politely, made no mention of my having been disgraced since I last saw her. Very polite woman. After a moment of this, Hamilton excused himself from his wife and pulled me a few feet away. "What are you doing here?"

"I did not mention I was invited? It's strange. You know, sometimes I think we are not so close as we used to be."

"Saunders, I don't want you muddling things. You have no business here. I don't want you making enemies."

"What do you care if I make enemies or no?"

"I don't want you making enemies for me," he clarified.

"Oh," I said, noting that his eyes moved past me to nearly the other end of the room where stood a man of about the same stature of Hamilton. He had red hair and a handsome face that beamed with pleasure, in no small part, I thought, because he was surrounded by a small group of men who appeared to hover over his every word.

"Why, that's Mr. Jefferson," I said, more loudly than Hamilton would have wished for.

"Please leave," Hamilton said.

"You know," I said, "if you did not wish Jefferson and his minions to associate the two of us together, all you had to do was ignore me. Now here we are in close conversation. Looks quite bad for you."

"That is the least of my worries," he told me. "I want you to go."

Across the room, Jefferson appeared to note Hamilton's attention, and the Secretary of State offered the Secretary of the Treasury a stiff bow. As Hamilton returned it, the hatred between the two seemed to me an almost physical force, as solid as steel, as hot as the sun. If a man had stepped between their searing gazes, he would surely have been incinerated.

Jefferson looked away, and I turned to say something to Hamilton, but he too had walked away, having wasted, perhaps, enough energy on me already. I could not help but think there was something of a kindness in his words, as though he had asked me to leave for my own good rather than his own, and I wondered if I ought to take it to heart. I continued to wonder as I crossed the room, and I might have kept on wondering to the point of departure if I had not observed the man I had come to molest.

Huddled with a small group of men was Mr. Duer, and his rugged associate was nowhere to be seen. I took a glass of wine from a passing servant, finished it, found another, and began to approach the speculator.

I had not gone more than a step or two before I was joined by Mr.

Lavien, who moved along as though we had been by each other's side all night. "Shall we?" he asked.

"I did not think you were invited," I said.

"I know for certain you were not," he answered.

We strode toward Duer, who was engaged in conversation with a trio of men, two of whom were unfamiliar to me, though I recognized the third as Bob Morris, perhaps the wealthiest man in America, in whose Philadelphia mansion George Washington lived and worked. An unapologetic speculator, Morris had grown rich off the Revolution and even richer in its aftermath. Even this capacious cormorant hung upon Duer's every word.

Now that I had a chance to study him, Duer appeared even smaller and more fragile. He was as delicate as a statue made of glass, and his little body suggested smallness the way the night suggests darkness. I had the distinct impression of towering over him, though he was only slightly shorter than Lavien. Finely dressed in a trim suit of navy blue velvet with bright gold buttons, he was a dandyish-looking fellow, whose hair was cut into one of those unnatural short bobs then fashionable. It looked for all the world as though someone had dropped a pyramid of hair, from a great height, to land upon his head.

Upon seeing us, Duer turned to his companions. "Gentlemen, if you will excuse me. Even at such a pleasant gathering as this, there are unpleasant duties to which I must attend."

His courtiers disappeared, and we had the great speculator to ourselves. He prepared himself to say something dismissive, something intended to introduce and conclude our conversation in a single stroke. I understood the look of determination upon his face, and I jumped in just as the corners of his mouth twitched. I would not let him take a position from which he would find it hard to retrench.

"I am sorry," I said, before he could utter a sound, "if I approached you too abruptly the other day, sir. Allow me to say I have long admired you, if only from afar. I am also sorry if you have been troubled in the past by this fellow Lavien. He is troublesome, I daresay."

"In the capacity of serving his master, yes, even though his master is an old friend of mine. Even so—"

"Even so," I interrupted—always a risky move, but I aimed to show

Duer I was more his man than he was himself—"there is a time and a place for everything and this is not the time for pushy Hebrews to be troubling men at so glorious a gathering. Do you know, Mr. Duer, that he has not even an invitation to be here? I know, it is scandalous. Oh, don't look that way, Mr. Lavien, if we were to insert ourselves into a secret gathering of the high Pharisees, I am sure we would be made to feel as unwelcome as we must, alas, make you under these circumstances. So be so kind as run along, there's a good fellow. Find yourself some unleavened bread and perhaps something porkless to put upon it."

Lavien, who never betrayed a feeling without first calculating its efficacy, now wore upon his face a mask of anger and humiliation. We had discussed nothing in advance, but he allowed me to pursue my course without hesitation, and I could not help but think how well it would be if our partnership could be formalized. What great work we could do for our nation! I watched as he wandered off, demonstrating his fictional chagrin with countenance and body language. I, for my part, set aside my glass of wine.

"What is your connection to that man?" Duer asked me.

"Oh, it is a silly thing, really," I said. "I have, through a series of obligations with which I shan't trouble you, decided to look into the disappearance of Mr. Pearson—a favor for a friend of a friend of the gentleman—and that man Lavien has set himself as my rival. I believe he attempts to curry favor with Colonel Hamilton, and it is a most irritating thing to look upon. Now, I admire Hamilton as much as the next man, but he has been curious in his choice of whom to employ and, if I may be so bold, whom not to. Those first few months, when you were taking charge of things at Treasury, were the most productive, I think."

He bowed. "You are kind to say so."

I was quite astonished to discover how prone he was to flattery, but I knew it was a hand that must not be overplayed. "Not at all, not at all. Now, if you don't mind, a question or two. I promise to make it quite painless, and you may always decline to answer. An easy thing between gentlemen—Christian gentlemen, I should say." That we together could have the joy of drawing a circle on the ground in which Lavien could not step was enough to satisfy Duer.

"I shall do my best to help you," he said.

"So good of you, but no more than I expected. Now, to the matter of Pearson. Can you tell me more about your dealings with him?"

"Oh, it is no great secret," said Duer. "He and I did some little business together, and though Pearson was desirous of doing more, he was never to my taste. Our paths crossed most significantly over a matter of property. He had some investments in a project of mine to buy and sell and hold leases on the western border of this state."

"You two dealt with war debt, did you not?" I affected an easy attitude, concealing the disgust I felt for a man who would cheat veterans out of their promise of payment when they had held on to their promissory notes for a decade or more.

"Among other things," he said. "The profit in war debt has, of course, diminished since the Assumption Bill passed, but it was a way to make a little money a few years back. Now the money is to be had in government issues: bank scrip and other ventures."

"Like the Million Bank in New York," I proposed.

He studied me closely. "I have heard of that bank and I suppose it may be as good as any, but I have no specific knowledge of it. How came you to know of it?"

"A cousin in New York is an investor and urged me to invest there as well. He said it was a significant opportunity."

"Any bank, if it prospers, is a good investment, and now that Hamilton has launched the Bank of the United States and plans the opening of more branches, I presume we shall see many more such institutions in this country. But while they can be an excellent investment, they can also be quite treacherous, like anything else. Witness your friend Jack Pearson. Nothing can be sounder than government six percent issues, but he has ruined himself in them."

I thought about what that woman, Mrs. Birch, had said, that the house she rented from Pearson had been sold precipitously. I could not affect surprise, however, lest I alert him to my ignorance. Instead, I chose a kind of easy familiarity. "Is not *ruined* a bit strong? I understand there have been some reversals, but surely nothing so bad as ruin."

Duer smiled, showing his canine teeth like a victorious predator. "Oh, he's quite ruined. The world doesn't know it yet, and if you count yourself a friend you shall not put it about, but it is the truth of the matter."

What could it mean? What could it mean for his disappearance, for the efforts directed against me, for the unknown agenda; perhaps most important, what could it mean for Cynthia that her wretched husband, whose only worthwhile quality was his money, was ruined? To Duer I said, "Is that why he has vanished?"

Duer made a strange noise in the back of his throat. "It's not a good vanishing he's effected. Is that not Pearson over there, speaking to that very fat gentleman?" He turned slightly, and it seemed to me he did so in order to avoid being seen.

I glanced across the room to where Duer had been gazing and saw that it was indeed Jacob Pearson, drinking a glass of wine and nodding solemnly, but in no way gravely. He looked nothing at all like a man under a cloud of financial ruin. Standing only a little way removed, attached to the conversation but in no way a participant, was Cynthia.

I looked at Pearson, then Duer, then Pearson again. Duer must have sensed my dilemma, for he tittered almost girlishly. "You want Pearson, I know, but you are not done with me. I see I've misjudged you, Saunders, but this is not the place to discuss business. Come see me tomorrow at the City Tavern. You may, upon the conclusion of trading, ask me what you like." He bowed and withdrew.

I hardly heard what he said. There, before me, was Pearson. Cynthia had been threatened to protect whatever secrets he held. Hamilton had unleashed the monstrous power of his man Lavien to find him. Now, here he was, in the most elegant private home in the city, and I could not think what to do about it. Even so, I must do something.

I had not even found a way to take a step forward when Lavien appeared by my side. "I saw him first," he said, and began walking. I roused myself and began to walk as well, unable to catch up. It felt to me like a metaphor.

Joan Maycott

Spring 1791

The response to the whiskey tax was universal: We would not pay. The tax was foolish and ill-conceived, and sooner or later the politicians in Philadelphia must recognize that fact. When Tindall sent Hendry to our cabin to tell us that we owed a hundred and fifteen dollars, Andrew shook with rage, and Mr. Dalton, who owed an equal amount, was tempted to take his gun to Empire Hall that day, but Mr. Skye talked sense into both of them, or what we thought was sense at the time.

Another meeting was held at the church, and little was agreed upon but that this was more eastern indifference to the plight of men upon the border. They let Indians murder us and refused to send their soldiers, they allowed speculators to toy with our lives, and now we must pay them to do it. Anyone with a still—anyone who brought his grain to a still—would suffer from this tax. What was immediately clear was that the tax would drive smaller distillers out of business and the only bene-fits would go to wealthy men back east and large-scale distillers like Tindall, who had cash and could shoulder the tax. The excise had been promoted in Philadelphia as hurting none and benefiting all, but it benefited only the wealthy, and it did so upon the backs of the poor.

Amid all this, life went on. I continued to withhold from Andrew the news of my pregnancy, preferring to wait until my fourth month—a milestone I had never before reached. I worked on my book, kept the house, and prayed that the whiskey tax would somehow disappear. Two or three times I slipped onto Tindall property to help nurse Lactilla, who returned to health remarkably well. I felt not precisely guilt, but I believed that Tindall might not have been so quick to anger had I not been in the room. In a strange way, I believed he had shot her for my benefit. I said none of this to Lactilla. I brought her fresh cheeses and milk eggs, though she needed none, and cloth to change her bandages. She lay upon her bunk, her face a collection of red welts. She would smile at me and say, "Missus Maycott, you just nothing but goodness," but I knew it was not true. I was not goodness at all. I was something else. I tended to Lactilla not because I thought myself responsible, but because I could not endure the thought of a world in which this poor creature must undergo such suffering without a commensurate response in kindness. It wasn't goodness, it was a kind of rage, a burning need to do something before things slipped into a darkness from which none of us could ever emerge.

I was by myself, preparing a stew for our evening meal, when the dog began to bark excitedly. We kept it tied up near the entrance to the cabin, lest it run off, but the disadvantage to this system was that it could not prevent a stranger from entering. I heard the alarm, however, and prepared myself just as the door to the cabin swung hard inward, and there stood Tindall, flanked on either side by Hendry and Phineas.

Hendry observed my expression of surprise and disorder and laughed cruelly. "Looks like we caught her making us some dinner, don't it?"

Tindall came in after him, clutching his fowling piece and grinning as well, and never had the two of them looked so much alike. Phineas closed the door and sat in the rocker by the window, his rifle stretched across his lap. He had not met my eye since entering.

Tindall strolled about the cabin with an arrogance only to be found in a man taking what is not his. He looked into the pot, he looked at the pantry. He peered at our bed and smirked.

"Where is your husband, Joan? He ought not to leave you alone like this."

"It is Mrs. Maycott, and he is about the property. He will be home shortly. I shall inform him you called."

"If he is to be home shortly, my dear, I'll just make myself comfortable right here and wait awhile. You want to get comfortable, Hendry?"

"I believe I do. I take my comfort where I can get it."

Something was different now. They were not here to bluster or to frighten but for something else. I dared not to consider what.

"I must ask you to leave now," I managed.

"Well, that's a funny thing," Tindall said to me, lowering himself into a chair. "Your husband owes more than a hundred dollars, don't you know."

"Every man with a still in the four counties owes you now," I said. "I have not heard anything yet of you trying to collect."

"Your husband is a special case, making trouble with his new methods. Now, I've been so good as to apply some of his rent money to that debt, but then you know what happens? It means he hasn't paid his rent. And if a man hasn't paid his rent, then do you know what happens to the land he's renting?"

"Get out," I said again.

"No, that's not right, Joan. That's not it at all. The land goes back to the landlord, and that landlord has a right, some might even say a responsibility, to toss that man off his property so he might learn to be industrious. Do you know what happens to the land he's renting?"

"Get out," I said again.

Phineas continued to look out the window. "Bitch," he said, without turning his head.

"An industrious man might have been clearing this land, doing something useful with his time, rather than making whiskey, which can't make him money and can only bring him debt."

I took several steps closer to him. "You think your money and your toadeaters are going to keep you safe if you stir the ire of the settlers here?

These are rough men with nothing but their strength and pride and resentment, principally for you."

Phineas did not move, did not turn, though he continued to mutter. Hendry took several steps toward me. I do not know what I thought he was going to do, but he appeared to me a monstrous face, the red skin under his scraggly beard glowing in the light of our fire, his eyes moist with excitement.

"This's been coming," he said. I could not react quickly enough to prevent it. He balled his fist and struck me directly in my belly. The pain hit me like a wall of water from a broken dam—it was vast and overpowering, and for a time I was lost in it. I fell to my hands and knees, gagged, vomited upon the floor. My bonnet fell off and hair fell about my face.

"Careful," Tindall said. "We've spoken about your temper."

The smell of my own vomit overwhelmed me. I gagged again, but nothing came forth. I had been expecting something terrible, yes, but not brutal unadorned violence. If they would do this, they would stop at nothing. Ugly lights danced before my eyes. "Please," I gasped.

"What is it?" Tindall asked me. "You talk like a man, but you don't know what pain and fear are. I reckon you're finding out, though."

"Please," I said again. "I am with child." This, I thought, could not but excite their mercy, or at least their pity. Tindall was a monster, but he could not be such a monster as to assault a woman with child.

"Ain't that something?" Tindall asked. "Well, a woman with child won't want another blow to her belly, I suppose. That would be what I imagine. Do you imagine that, Hendry?"

"I don't know if I do," he said, his foxlike face seeming to grow sharper. "But maybe."

"Git her dress off," Phineas said. "Git it unbuttoned, like you said."

I pushed myself to my feet. I felt the heat of tears in my eyes, the sourness of my purging in my mouth. "What kind of devil are you?"

"I'm a devil from Virginia, my good lady, and I take what I want if I can. That is the true vision of America, the one I fought for. The principles of the Revolution have made me a king in Pittsburgh."

"You go too far," I said.

"I go where I like. Now, should I ask Hendry to strike you once more?

Maybe we can do something about that troubling thing that grows within you."

Involuntarily, I put my hands across my belly.

"Or," said Tindall, "we can make a different arrangement. I'll allow you and your husband to remain here, and I will make certain Hendry strikes you no more, but in return I must ask you show me some consideration. You know what I speak of, don't you, Joan? Let us go from here, the two of us. We shall leave your husband in peace, let him tinker with his whiskey. I shall overlook his rent in arrears. I shall even wink at his whiskey tax for him this year."

"Why?" I gasped, my voice low. I struggled to keep myself calm. "Why do you do this to me? Why me above others? I cannot believe that I alone have caught your eye. Why me and not another?"

"Because the others have already given me what I like," he said, his voice cold. "You defy me. Your husband defies me. Your friends defy me. I cannot have it, and I won't have it. All of you must taste what it means to defy me, and you shall be the first."

"I would rather die," I said, and I may have meant it.

"Oh, I don't think so. In a moment or two, you will be imploring me to have you on the terms I mentioned. But if you vex me, if you are impertinent, I may have to alter the terms."

I forced myself to stand erect, to thrust out my chin, to show him my pride and my anger. "Not on any terms."

"I do like how she thrusts out her bosoms at me, but it shall not be enough. Hendry, would you please show this woman that I am not a man to be taken lightly."

I put my hands inside my apron. "Please," I said.

"I'll have my turn too," Hendry said. "When the colonel's done, I'll have my turn. And Phineas. He's been waiting."

"I been waiting," he said, staring out the window.

Hendry had only taken three steps toward me when I pulled the trigger. I was not so foolish as to take out my gun. I was outnumbered and could not compete with their strength. Even with the firearm, my chances were not good. If I wished to live I needed to depend upon trickery. I fired through my apron, and the ball struck Hendry in his neck.

I could not imagine how Andrew had so calmly fired his pistol under the table at the braves. The weapon bucked wildly in my hand, jerking back and striking my hip almost hard enough that I feared I'd broken bone. Heat burst around my hand. My apron caught fire, but I patted it out quickly. I staggered two steps back and looked up and saw Hendry put his hand to his neck, slapping it as though a mosquito had landed upon him. Blood flowed heavily through his fingers, thick and almost black. "That ain't right," he said. Then he fell.

Tindall stared at me for a second. His expression was one of monstrous, impossible disbelief, as though the sun had sprouted legs and walked from the sky. His face went red, and he lifted his fowling piece, and I knew all too well he would not hesitate to use it.

I leaped into the air to take shelter behind our evening table. I hit the floor as the gun roared, and a rain of birdshot hit the wood, a sudden and nearly simultaneous series of wet, hard, smacking noises. Above me glass shattered, and whiskey trickled down. He had struck our only piece of porcelain, a flour jar, and the room was covered with shards and white powder. I was unharmed, but I knew I had not much time. We had both spent our weapons, and neither could take the time to reload. In a contest of strength, though he was an old man, Tindall would certainly best me.

Only then did I recall Phineas. More than half a minute had now passed since I'd struck Hendry. If Phineas were to fire upon me, surely he would have done so by now. I dared to peer out from behind my table, but I saw no one in the cabin but Tindall, and the door was open. Phineas had run off. It was hard to believe that a boy who would kill Indians in cold blood would flee from this, but perhaps the scene was too close to his own past. Perhaps, despite the hatred he felt toward me for knowing his heart, I still reminded him too much of the life he had lost, and he could neither go against Tindall nor strike out at me.

I could afford no time to sound the depths of the boy's soul, however. I had to get away from Tindall before he reloaded, or came after me with a knife, or simply used his strength of body to overtake me. I lay but a few feet from our fireplace, and, having no other recourse, I reached into the fire and pulled out a burning branch. It was hot, but I grabbed an end as yet untouched by the fire. Gripping it tight, I pushed myself to my feet, using my free hand for leverage, and charged at Tindall. I suppose I must have been an unnatural figure, disheveled, blackened with powder, whitened by flour, red with anger, eyes wide with determined rage.

He maneuvered around me and made his way to the hearth. With two or three quick kicks he dislodged the logs, which spilled out and tumbled near our dining table. The flame from the logs began to lick at it, and I would have to act quickly to prevent the spread of fire.

It was what Tindall depended upon, because he used my moment of confusion to rush out the door.

I should have let him go. The cabin needed tending to, but I did not think of it. I had no reason to charge after him, and yet I did. I was so full of hatred for what he had done, what he had threatened to do, what he had made me do. The part of myself I knew as me, where my soul resided, retreated and shriveled. All that was left was a white-hot demon who yearned to do some unnamed, unknown, violence. At that moment, the thought of life, the thought of continuing to breathe upon an earth where Tindall still lived, was unsupportable. He ran to his horse and I chased him hard and fast, waving my burning branch and screaming I can hardly say what.

Coming down the path now was Andrew with Dalton and Skye, approaching from the path on the other side of the tree where Tindall had tied his horse. I saw them, though I did not think about what I saw, or I would have left Tindall to them. Little can I suppose what they must have made of this scene, Tindall running frantically, me chasing him with a club of fire.

Andrew came running to me. He did not care about Tindall, and he would have known that if there was violence to be done, Mr. Dalton should have been happy to do it. He only wanted to come to me, and if I had only wanted him, to be safe and in his arms, then all would have been different. I should have turned and dropped my weapon and gone to Andrew. Instead, I ignored him and continued toward Tindall. I had killed one man, and I wanted nothing more than to kill another. Phineas had said that the West would change me, and now I knew it had. I was so changed I did not even know myself.

Tindall reached his horse but did not mount. He looked and saw me, then looked past me. I was a crazed woman with a stick, he an officer beside his mount. He saw Andrew running, and that was another matter. He did not know that Andrew would not harm him, that he only wanted me, to make certain I was unharmed. Tindall might simply ride away. Instead, he took a pistol from his saddlebag and turned to Andrew.

I saw it happening, and I opened my mouth to call out, but I could make no noise. My voice betrayed me, though I know not what I should have shouted to make a difference.

Tindall fired the pistol at Andrew, discharging it at a distance of no more than ten feet. Andrew was thrown back and fell at once to the ground, striking hard and flat and with sudden force. He landed not like a living man but a lifeless weight.

I found my voice and let out a scream as I dropped my torch and rushed to Andrew, ignoring now the murderous Tindall. That Andrew was struck need not mean his end. He was young and strong and resilient. It is what I told myself, but it was all deceit. Even from a distance I saw the ball had struck his heart, and I believe he was dead before he fell. He lay there, eyes wide and lifeless. I reached him and knelt. I cradled his head in my arms, I stroked his hair, I called out to heaven, though heaven would not answer. I felt a heat upon my skin, and though I did not look up, I knew it was the cabin, awash in flames I had not troubled myself to extinguish.

Tindall knew he was in danger now, and he acted quickly. He climbed onto his horse and rode off. Dalton fired his rifle after him, but he had no clear shot. I hardly heard the crack of the weapon, the cries of anguish around me.

What did I lose that day? It pains me now to speak of it, for I lost everything. I lost my darling Andrew, who wanted only that I should live the life of my innermost desires. I lost his child, which died inside me, though I know not if it was from Hendry's violence or from my shock at the events that unfolded. I lost my freedom, for Tindall put it about at once that I had murdered Hendry in cold blood and sought to murder the colonel too. And though it sounded trivial in my own ears, I lost my novel, taken by the flames that scorched my cabin. This too I lost—my innocence, for I had killed a man, and I could not regret doing so. Surely that made me into someone I was not before.

Everything I had desired and dreamed of and wanted in life was taken from me. Can it be wondered that I set myself against my enemies, and if my enemies were the first men in the nation itself, can I be blamed for seeking justice? The shape of that justice was not formed until later, and not formed alone, but even as I sat with my beloved husband's body in my arms, the ghost of it was there, haunting me from the spectral realm of notions not yet conceived.

Ethan Saunders

I had considered it a possibility that I might see her—not a realistic possibility, but within the realm of the conceivable. Yet, upon seeing her, I could not imagine a response other than to stand frozen, staring, then to look away, then to stare. Her gown, sky blue with swirling yellow designs, revealed her still-marvelous figure to advantage, having a low neckline and sleeves to just above her elbows, exposing her fine white skin. Her pale blond hair was piled high in the fashion, and atop it rested a prim little cap with yellow feathers stretching upward, a blue ribbon, which matched the gown itself, billowing down.

I had seen her in fine dresses before, of course, though when she had been younger they had been less stiff, less formal; they had been the simple if elegant dresses of a lovely girl, not complex fabric cages of European origin. Then she'd been a soft and charming young lady, a foot still planted in girlhood, but now she had turned into a woman, stony and commanding in her beauty.

Lavien walked toward them, came within ten feet, and then turned back to me. "I'll not speak to him here," he said.

"Why not?"

"It cannot be done here. For now, it is enough that he is returned. If he were in hiding, he would not have come to this house. Pearson is back, and that is all that matters. If you will excuse me." Lavien hurried off, careful, it seemed to me, to avoid being seen by the Pearsons. Across the room, he approached Hamilton and whispered in his ear.

This could not long hold my attention, not while Cynthia was in the room. She did not see me. Jacob Pearson, however, did. He looked up and met my gaze, and turned, most desirous of speaking to his wife. It had been many years since I'd seen him, but I had no difficulty in recognizing him. He was perhaps six or seven years older than myself, though the years had been more unkind to him than I flatter myself they had been to me. His hair had turned white, and lines had exploded around his eyes. Deep crevices had formed in his cheeks, and his teeth were yellow—those he still had. For all that, he retained some of the rugged handsomeness he had possessed a decade earlier, and though he was clearly Cynthia's senior, the two of them together did not have the comical aspect of some couples in which the husband is significantly older than the wife.

Pearson looked at me, and there was something cloudy in his brown eyes, bloodshot and tired-looking. I watched while he pretended not to have noticed me and reached out with his hand—thick with veins and unusually large—to grasp Cynthia's arm, digging into her flesh with his yellow fingernails. I saw her white flesh turn whiter and then red. She blanched, closed her eyes for a moment, and then nodded very briefly.

I was too far away to hear what he said, but I could see from the cruel shape of his lips that he said terrible things. I knew too that his soul was tainted with a blackness that frightened me. It is easy to look at the man who has married the woman you love and see only evil, but this was not simple prejudice. I knew what I looked at, and I hated it.

I was stepping up before I knew it, and I understood at once that had I not caught myself, had I not reestablished communication with my own mind, I would have strode forward and pushed him down. For an instant I imagined the room full of politicians and dignitaries would delight in seeing this man fall to humiliating injury, yet I realized at once that to find pleasure in this scene a man would have to know that Pearson was a fiend. To the uninformed, it might appear as though I simply delighted in knocking men over, and in such circumstances the world would no doubt turn against me.

Before either of them saw me approaching, I turned away. I grabbed a glass of wine from a passing servant and drank it down angrily. Then I went to do what I did best: I would set things in motion.

Think you it is easy to get a well-known and beautiful woman alone, away from her husband, at so public a gathering? Think you that, in the company of dozens of guests and nearly as many gossipy servants, a man can just pull such a woman aside into a private closet? It would not be easy for any ordinary man—at least I suspect it would not. I cannot say how ordinary men go about their business.

Here is how I went about mine: I had Leonidas request one of Mrs. Bingham's servants to inform Mrs. Pearson that the lady was needed most urgently in the library. It would work, I thought. All would be protected by a buffer of supposed Negro ignorance, each servant claiming to believe that he or she had only passed along what was believed to be true.

I sent the message and went to the library to await the arrival of the lady. I stood by the fire, leafing through a volume on the late war, until the doors opened and a troubled-looking Cynthia Pearson rushed inside.

Upon seeing me, she was struck still and silent. Then she opened her mouth and would no doubt have called out her surprise, but recalled the doors were open. Instead of saying something, she closed the doors. I believe it was good that she did so. It gave her time to think, or perhaps it gave her time to cease thinking and allow her heart, and the memory of past emotions, to, if not eclipse, then at least take the stage along with other more reptilian designs.

"My dear God," she said.

With the door closed, she took three or four purposeful steps toward me but stopped well short of the usual conversational distance. She folded her hands before me, as though she were about to sing an Italian aria. "I was told I was required for an urgent matter."

"You have been told the truth," I said.

Cynthia's blue eyes flashed something meaningful, though I knew not what, and she turned away from me. She strode purposefully toward the doors. Before pulling them open, she turned back to me. "I asked you not to contact me. I begged you not to. You cannot have been invited to this house. Anne would never have asked you without informing me. You must go."

"What does it matter? All centered upon your husband's unexplained absence, but he is absent no more."

"He returned last night and would say nothing of where he'd been— only that he had traveled on business. I tried to tell him that the government man, Lavien, was looking for him and that others had come, told me terrible things—"

"The men who warned you not to speak with me?"

She nodded. "I don't know what transpires with my husband. I don't know who it is that threatens me, but I know my duty, even when it is to those who do not deserve it. Why have you called me here like this, in so improper a manner? What is it you want of me?"

"Cynthia, you asked for my help. That you have been threatened into retracting your request does not relieve me of my duty."

"Have you been asked to speak to me in these familiar terms?"

"No," I admitted. "That was entirely my idea."

She shook her head. "What is it you hope to accomplish, Captain Saunders?"

What indeed? I hardly even knew. Did I want an apology or an explanation or a return to those days when I was young and had so much before me? I said, "I want to know why you married him."

She turned quite pink and her mouth formed a delicate O. I cannot say what she was expecting, but it had not been this. I watched as she took a deep breath to collect herself. She glanced about the library and her eyes fell upon a decanter of wine. She poured herself a glass and then, to my surprise, poured one for me. "It was more than ten years ago. You are not a child. Can you not put it behind you?"

"Is it the mark of maturity that one sets love aside?" I took the glass with much gratitude.

"Yes," she said. "It is."

She said it with such venom that I felt foolish and ashamed to have put her in so difficult a position, and I was prepared to tell her so. I knew not why I was there—in that house, in that city. I knew not why I had not been able to live my life since the close of the war, but I would not be so base as to drag this lady, this stranger, into my sadness.

When I looked at her, prepared to offer some tepid apology, I saw that something had changed with her—softened, perhaps broken. Her chin was lowered toward her chest, a hand raised to her face. She was crying. Tears ran down her face in slow, thick globes. She wiped at one eye with a delicate hand. "You were gone, Ethan. You left, and I knew why you left. You could not bear for your shame to taint me. I don't know if that was noble or selfish, or if those things can even be distinguished, but I was alone. You were gone and my father was dead. Jacob was kind to me, he wanted nothing from me, and he was—he was like a father to me. He was so much older that I did not even notice when his interest became something other than fatherly, and I was already so used to depending upon him that marriage, when he proposed it, seemed inevitable."

I ought not to have said it, but I was full of drink and had no will to control myself. "He does not seem to me paternal but cruel."

She turned away. "You embarrass me."

"I am sorry," I said.

"No, don't be sorry. You must never be sorry after what you've endured. My God, Ethan, what have you done to yourself? You did not have to let the blame attach itself to you."

"You know the reason. I could not bear the cost of extricating myself."

"I could have. You tell yourself it was the right thing, the glorious thing, to do, to sacrifice yourself for a great cause, but did you stop to think of those it would hurt? Did you think of what your nobility would cost *me*?"

I took a step closer to her. "You must leave him, Cynthia, before it is too late."

"Leave him? How am I to leave him? Am I to take my children and flee penniless into the street? And to what? Shall I come live with you, Ethan, in your boardinghouse, and be a fallen woman?"

"Cynthia," I said.

She stopped. "I am sorry. I have no business venting my rage on you, but I am trapped, and I rage like a trapped creature. I cannot go, so I must stay."

I had no heart to tell her that her husband, whose money alone now offered her solace, was likely ruined.

"You cannot think I am content to abandon you to that devil," I said at last.

"I have been with that devil since I was a girl. You are too late to rescue me. You are impulsive, but there is nothing for you to do."

"I am not prepared to leave you, Cynthia."

"You must leave. Only . . ." She looked away.

"Only what?"

"Only, you must see me again." She set down her empty glass and left the library.

Back at the gathering, I tried to make sense of our conversation. What did Cynthia want from me? Perhaps even she did not know. I hardly knew what I wanted from her. A dalliance? I could not ask her to compromise her position so. She was not some pretty housewife of an obscure gentleman farmer or merchant. She was a prominent lady, close friends with the most known and beloved woman in the city. Because of her friendship with Anne Bingham, if not on her own account, eyes were upon her, and the risk to her would be too great.

Not so far from where I stood, Cynthia's radiant face showed no sign that she had wept. Indeed, she now laughed most heartily in a small circle of people, including her brute of a husband. He hung upon Cynthia's arm—no signs of cruelty now—and smiled at this comment or that, occasionally dared a rasping laugh that sounded like dry leaves rubbing against one another.

I saw no sign of Lavien—or Hamilton, for that matter—which was just as well. I strode about the room, trying hard not to take another glass of wine. I think I would have surrendered to temptation, but I looked up and saw a familiar-looking man, plump and red-faced, and knew him at once, though I could not say how. I continued to study him, his little eyes and blunt nose—all so porcine—and perhaps would still not have known him if it had not been for the girl next to him. She was equally porcine, though younger and less plump, and with a mass of yellow hair. She was the girl in my stolen timepiece and he the owner.

I walked over to him, bowed, and held out the watch. "Sir," I said, "I believe I saw you drop this in the street several days ago. I attempted to run after you to return it, but my way was blocked. I have carried it upon my person ever since in the hope of finding its owner."

He took the watch from me, his fat fingers moving with surprising gentleness. "Why, I never thought to see it again. I must ask your name, sir, that I may know who to thank."

I bowed again. "Ethan Saunders, at your service."

"What? The traitor?" He must have regretted his words, for his red complexion now purpled.

I bowed again. "I am not he. That man and I merely share the same name."

He wished to make more conversation, but I demurred and excused myself to wander more. There, standing by himself, looking morosely at a portrait upon the wall, was Jacob Pearson. With little to lose, I approached him, probably with more boldness than clarity.

"Why, 'tis Jacob Pearson!" I cried. "Good heavens, man, it has been years."

He turned to me and smiled reflexively. In an instant his smile faded and then returned, this time quite false. "Sir, I am afraid you have me at a disadvantage. You look to me familiar, but I cannot place your name."

It was a well-executed lie, I will grant him that. "It is Ethan Saunders. We knew each other during the war."

Pearson glanced across the room until he found Cynthia, locked in conversation with her friend, Mrs. Bingham, and another woman, also quite striking, whom I did not know. They did a passable job, I thought, of pretending not to observe me and Pearson together.

"Yes, of course." He let go of my hand. "I heard you were dead. Or was it disgraced?"

"Disgraced," I said. "But enough of *my* ignominy. Tell me, Mr. Pearson, where have *you* been this last week?"

"Why does everyone wish to know? Not ten minutes ago Hamilton himself was troubling me with his questions. I see not why it is the world's concern. You do not like my saying so? It is rather bad for you, then, for it is my custom to speak as I like. For what does a man rise to consequence if he must guard his own tongue?"

"I can think of no reason."

"And why are you here at all? Can it be a man like you has been invited here? I must ask Mr. Bingham what he means."

I saw no need to answer this implied threat. If he wished to issue a challenge, I could certainly answer it. "There's been considerable speculation about your absence," I said. "Some have talked about your properties in Southwark, and others of your interest in the Million Bank. Surely you can shed some light upon the subject?"

"I suppose my wife has been talking. Let me tell you something." He put one of his enormous hands upon my shoulder. I did not like the feel of it. "There's more to wish for in a wife than beauty. That is my advice to you."

My stomach clenched at this mention of his wife. I could not let it go unanswered. "You have strangely large hands," I said. "It's as though they've been flattened by a great stone. You'll forgive me for talking freely, but I also like to say what I feel. What is the advantage of being disgraced if a man cannot speak his mind?"

He studied me, looking me up and down, his sharp nose bobbing like a blade. "I think this conversation has taxed me long enough. Now I must away to look for Mr. Duer."

Pearson wandered off, and it occurred to me that I had not seen Duer since our conversation. Could it be, I wondered, that he did not want to see Pearson? Duer appeared to have no interest in or respect for Pearson, yet Pearson spoke of seeking out the speculator the way one speaks of seeking out a friend. Those answers would have to wait, for here and now I could pass the time in gazing openly upon Cynthia.

I watched her now speaking with Mrs. Adams, the Vice President's wife. My brief conversation had only confirmed to me how hateful was Pearson and how unhappy Cynthia must be in her life with him. She was right, of course, that I could not simply take her away, but neither could I leave her. I would have to conceive of some alternative, and I would have to do so soon, because each day she spent with him would be a torment to me.

"You appear lost in thought, sir."

I looked up, and there was the woman I had seen with Cynthia and Anne Bingham. She wore a much simpler gown than did Cynthia, looser, longer arms, higher neck. The material was of a plain pale red, but it looked marvelous well upon her. She was a brown-haired beauty with large eyes, penetrating in their gray intensity, like clouds threatening snow.

She stood next to a man of my own age who, though not very tall or very distinguished, with his receding hair, yet held himself in an admirable manner. Here was a man the ladies enjoyed, and who enjoyed the ladies. He had something of a swagger I could not help but approve.

"Captain Ethan Saunders, at your service," I said to them both.

"A pleasure to meet you, Captain," said the man. "Colonel Aaron Burr, though now I suppose I am to be addressed as senator."

"Ah, yes," I said. "Senator Burr. I have read much of you in the papers. You have made quite an enemy of our Secretary Hamilton in New York."

He laughed. "Hamilton and I are friends from many years back, but he is every inch the Federalist, and New York is increasingly republican and anti-Federalist in its outlook. Nevertheless, I like to think that men might be opposed politically and friends socially."

"I do love an optimist," I said. "And is this lady Mrs. Burr?"

"Mrs. Burr is not here at present. I am afraid I only just met this delightful lady, yet I will take the liberty of introducing you to Mrs. Joan Maycott."

I bowed.

"Now that you are in good hands," the senator said to the lady, "I must beg your leave to speak to some of my brothers of the Senate. I hope I shall see you more, Mrs. Maycott."

He took his leave and left me with the woman, and I could not say I was displeased. She had that vivacious look that suggested she should be good company. There was more to her too. She had a command in her physical presence, a kind of authority that, in her own feminine way, reminded me of the most accomplished and successful of military men. Strange though it might be to say, I had never met anyone, man or woman, who so immediately put me in mind of Washington himself.

"You did look lost in thought, you know," she said to me.

"I am a thoughtful man," I said.

"Was it something to do with Mr. Pearson? You will forgive me for asking, but I saw you in conversation with him. Is he a particular friend of yours?"

"I know him from many years ago," I said. "Is he a friend of yours?"

"I am friends with his wife," she answered.

"Then you know he's been missing."

"Oh, he told me he was in New York," she said. "But perhaps I ought not to have said as much. I was under the impression he did not wish people to know it."

"Then he has been thwarted. How sad for him."

She laughed. "I enjoy my pettiness with a dose of wit. You do not like him?"

"I love wit and may endure pettiness, but he strikes me as cruel, which I cannot abide," I answered.

"I think perhaps you know his wife from many years ago too." From another person this might have seemed impertinent beyond endurance, but there was something so clever and endearing in how she spoke these words that it doused all impropriety.

"She and I are old friends." I turned to look at this beauty full on, and she met my gaze most boldly. Here, I thought, might be an agreeable consolation to my confusion with Cynthia. "Do you live in Philadelphia, Mrs. Maycott?"

"I live here, though I travel much."

"You enjoy travel—with Mr. Maycott, perhaps?"

She looked directly into my eyes once more, as though leveling an accusation. "Sir, Mr. Maycott is dead."

"I am sorry for that, madam."

"That is merely something one says."

"Mrs. Maycott," I said, to my strange interlocutor, "I cannot help but feel you believe we have met before, or that you expect me to have some knowledge of your circumstances."

"I don't believe you do, sir. Mr. Duer tells me, however, that you inquire into Jacob Pearson's business, and that you do it for Hamilton. Is that so?"

I did not pause. I did not wait so much as an instant, for I would not show surprise that she had previously spoken of me or knew anything of my business. I would act as though it were the most natural thing in the world. "You know Mr. Duer?"

"There are so many here," she answered. "One may meet everyone. But I must ask you, as there is much consternation about Hamilton's policies: Are you an enthusiast of his?"

"I do not work for or with Hamilton, though my interests may be intersecting with his."

"Tell me, Captain. Have you any thoughts on the whiskey excise?"

"I am no friend to excise taxes," I said, keeping all inflection from my voice. Nevertheless, I set down my glass on a nearby table and scanned the room for Lavien. Pearson's disappearance and the whiskey tax were bound together—there could be no doubt of it, not when my inquiry into the matter had faced opposition from the hairless western giant, the man with superior whiskey as his calling card. I did not know if therein lay the link to the threat against the bank, but I hardly cared about the threat against the bank. I only cared that this woman appeared to be telling me that she had some knowledge of Pearson's disappearance and thus a connection to Cynthia's safety.

"I believe we have much in common, sir," she said. "We are both caught up in events larger than ourselves, and we must make choices that we sometimes find unsavory if we are to do what is right."

I attempted a smile. "What events are you involved in, madam?"

She leaned closer. "I cannot speak of them now. Not here. It is too soon and too public." She gazed across the room and, indeed, William Duer was looking at us most pointedly. "Would you be willing to meet with me again, sir? Have I given you sufficient reason to do so?"

"A man need never look too hard to find a reason to meet with a pretty lady."

"I do not know that I am vulnerable to flattery," she said, not unkindly.

"Shall we make an effort to find out?" I asked.

"That sounds most delightful."

"When shall we talk again?"

"Have you an engagement for two nights hence?"

I bowed. "I am yours to command."

"I am so pleased." Coming toward us once more was Jacob Pearson, now alone, Cynthia being across the room speaking with the beautiful Mrs. Bingham. Mrs. Maycott reached out and grabbed Pearson's wrist. "Mr. Pearson, would it be an imposition if I bring a dear friend to dinner the night after next?"

He looked at me and was unable to contain his surprise, but then seemed to recollect himself, or perhaps Mrs. Maycott. "You may, of course, bring anyone you like. Unless it is this man here. I cannot like him."

"Such wit," she said. "Certainly it is Captain Saunders. We both look forward to the evening." Mrs. Maycott paused not a moment, but took my arm and led me away. "You see, nothing is more easily effected."

"I am not certain I will be made to feel welcome," I said.

"And I am not sure either of us cares. I, however, will have the pleasure of offering consternation to a man I do not like, and you will have the opportunity to pry further into his business. We shall both, in the end, be made happy."

Joan Maycott

Spring 1791

There were days lost. I do not apologize for that weakness, though when some remnant of clarity returned to me, when I escaped the deepest fog of grief, I vowed I would never again give in to such madness, not on any account. They were days when my enemies ate and slept and prospered and advanced their goals, while I did nothing, and in doing nothing I aided them, for that is how it is when faced with evil men. One must either resist or, in varying degrees, collaborate.

The day after he was murdered, we interred Andrew in the churchyard. Several men from the settlement unceremoniously hauled Hendry's body to town and dumped it in the mud of Pittsburgh, as it deserved. I took no pleasure in the contrast. After Andrew's funeral, my friends guided me to the isolated hunting cabin shared by the men of the settlement. They told me it was important not to remain in my own home, that it had been damaged, though not destroyed, in the fire. I was too lost in my own confusion to inquire of the details.

At first my grief was so great I was like a woman sleeping with her eyes open, seeing all about me, understanding none of it. Then at last, after some days, I began to emerge from this first numb stage of grief, though what came next was worse by far, for I understood the enormity of what had been wrenched from me. I had lost my Andrew, I had lost our child, I had lost my work, my home, my purpose. In this whole universe, nothing was left that meant anything to me. It was as though some great hand had come and wiped away all that had ever given me cause to take a breath.

I could do little more than weep and clutch my knees to my chest and lament. Mr. Dalton and Mr. Skye, for reasons I did not yet understand, spent long periods of time in the hunting cabin. When not out in search of game, the Irishman stomped about the cabin in a rage, swearing vengeance, clenching his fists, ripping off bites of his tobacco twist as though he could rip off Tindall's flesh by doing so. Mr. Skye, in his far more subdued manner, sat by my side. He made perpetual efforts to feed me venison broth and bits of buttered corn bread, and it was by his efforts that I did not starve.

When Mr. Skye grew too tired or restless to tend to me, Jericho Richmond sat in his place. I took comfort in his silent company, yet there was a darkness in his gaze too. His brooding wood-colored eyes hung on me—in pity, yes, but something else.

Once I turned to him and said, "I am dead now. I have lost everything."

"You are not dead," he said. "But you are different."

I looked away, for I did not wish to hear more.

"Be mindful of it," he said. "You have sway over these men."

I had no wish to be careful or thoughtful or anything else, and after he spoke these words I found I did not love Mr. Richmond's company. It was Mr. Skye who proved my most attendant nurse. I welcomed his presence but refused, at first, his ministrations. I would shake my head and push away his spoon when he tried to feed me. Oh, I was cruel to him. I called him names, a withered old man who knew nothing of what I had lost. Unlike him, I could not simply sail to distant shores when my life lay in ruins. I felt nothing but regret and self-hatred even as I spoke the words, yet I could not stop them, and so I only wept more. Mr. Skye, that good man, nodded in understanding and offered me another spoonful of soup. In the end, I ate.

On what I believe was the third or fourth day, I began to shake off the greatest torpidity of grief. That is not to say I no longer felt grief keenly or was no longer weighed down by it. On the contrary, I knew it would kill me, and I would welcome death, if I did not find some means of converting my sorrow to something of purpose. I sat up straight and looked at Mr. Skye, who had been sitting and gazing out the little cabin's window. "Something must be done about Tindall," I said.

"It is not for you to do," he answered.

"And why not? Did he not take everything from me? Am I to be content to lie quiet? I will travel to Pittsburgh and swear out an arrest on him."

Mr. Skye's lips were colorless, though he'd been biting them incessantly. "You cannot go to Pittsburgh. There is a warrant out for you for the murder of Hendry." He paused to take in a deep breath of air. "And Andrew."

I threw off the blanket that covered me and leaped to my feet. I had been abed for days, in the same dress I had worn to Andrew's funeral, and had I been driven by anything other than the most vivid of rages, I might have fallen over from dizziness. "Do not say it! He cannot dare to accuse me of his own crime, of killing my beloved Andrew!"

Misunderstanding my outrage for unendurable sadness, Mr. Skye moved to embrace me, but I pushed him away—more cruelly than I would have wished, but I suppose I already understood I might be as cruel to him as I liked without risk of his resentment.

"Don't try to comfort me. How can you sit here, feeding me soup, while the man who murdered my husband blames his crimes on me? What sort of man are you?"

He looked into my face full on, something he rarely did, and I saw precisely what sort of man he was. I saw it in his unwavering eyes of cold gray, how he showed neither surprise nor anger. I did not know what I would do with him, but I already knew I would do something.

"What kind of man am I? A wanted man. I am here because the warrant has been sworn for me as well. And for Dalton, aye. Tindall means to use his crimes to end our distilling, and that's the truth of it. Now, have you anything else you wish to say to me?"

I sat back down upon the rugged bed with its rough straw mattress and said nothing. I did not weep. My mood was too dark for that. Instead, I searched my mind for some answer, some response to this horror that would not end.

"How can he do it?" I asked finally.

"'Tis but greed, Joan," said Mr. Skye, in his quiet and gentle voice. "That's all. We fought the British so we would not be slaves to their greed, but we've greedy men enough of our own to take their place."

"Might I trouble you to fetch me a bucket of hot water?" I asked him. "And a cloth to wash myself and a bit of privacy?"

"Aye, Joan. With all my heart. I'm glad you're of a mind to see to yourself."

"I don't even know precisely where I am," I said to him. "Will I need a horse to get to Pittsburgh? Is there a horse if I need it?"

He narrowed his eyes as he studied me. "You haven't heard me. You can't go to Pittsburgh. They'll arrest you."

"I am certain they will try. The water, if you please, John."

He squared his shoulders, really quite broad for a scholar of his age, but then frontier living left no man scrawny. "I can't let you do that."

I somehow managed a smile. "You can't stop me. Your task is to help me. Now, go fetch Mr. Dalton. I will need both of your consents in writing for what I must do."

Already my plan had begun to take shape. It was bold and large and audacious, and to accomplish what I wished, I would need the loyalty of these men. To have that, I would need to show them I was not to be underestimated.

When Dalton returned, we sat at the cabin's rude table, sipping whiskey, while I told them the first part of my scheme. It would not do to tell them more. Skye was willing. Skye was always willing, but Dalton looked to his friend before making any decision.

Richmond shrugged. "Do it if ye want, but not without thinking. Don't do it because she says it's to be done. Be your own man."

"Don't make trouble," Dalton answered. "We've trouble enough."

Jericho shook his head but said no more. Really, I could not blame him. Though I asked them to trust me, to trust me beyond all reason and wisdom, they gave me what I asked for. It was but my first inkling of what was to come. I had always been bold and audacious with men, and I had, in the end, never been denied anything from a man well disposed toward me. Only now did I begin to understand how such a power might be used to save a nation worth saving or, perhaps, destroy one too corrupt to save.

It was a rough road, and though I left while it was still morning, I was not in Pittsburgh until well after noon. I had no notion that I was so well known, but once I stabled my horse and began to walk along Market Street, passersby stopped to stare at me. Men streamed out of Watson's Tavern as I passed. I was infamous. I was an outlaw. I suppose the notion would once have filled me with horror, but a strange sensation of mastery came over me now. I was the subject of scrutiny and, yes, fear. It was good, I thought. They *should* be afraid.

I knocked upon the door to Mr. Brackenridge's house and was greeted by a woman significantly younger than he, yet far too finely dressed, in a handsome gown of printed cotton, to be a servant. I could only presume this to be the lawyer's wife. She was pretty, with a mass of blond hair bundled under a saucily propped bonnet. The lady looked at me, smiled, and prepared to inquire of my business until she saw a group of two dozen or more onlookers creeping forward to watch the proceedings. She ushered me inside and closed the door. After pausing for a moment, she slid shut the bolt.

"Better to be safe, yes?" Her voice betrayed a slight German accent. "Now, you've business with my husband, I'll wager."

"Yes." Under the judgmental scrutiny I'd suffered on the street I'd felt a kind of jagged strength. Now, subjected to this stranger's kindness, I had to fight hard to swallow my tears. "My name is Joan Maycott."

The lady's eyes widened in surprise, and she moved to put a hand to her mouth but stopped herself. "I'll show you to the office, and then I'll fetch Hugh."

I followed her in silence. Mrs. Brackenridge had known my name at once, just as the people on the street had recognized me instantly. I could only imagine what lies Tindall had cast about to turn me into so well-known a personage.

At Mrs. Brackenridge's direction, I took a seat in her husband's disordered office and waited only a moment or two before the lawyer came flitting in, taking a step toward me, then one toward closing the door, then changing his mind and performing the whole dance once more. At last he settled upon closing the door and then taking my hand.

"Mrs. Maycott," he said, his voice solemn for one who was used to speaking in such high and sharp tones. He then bowed and let go my hand and moved toward his desk chair as though he would sit, but instead walked over to the window, parted the curtains, and examined the crowd of people gathering outside. "You seem to have gained a great deal of notoriety since last we met. Have you come to me for assistance in surrendering yourself?"

He asked the question with a great deal of uneasiness. Perhaps he thought I might kill him too. How absurd it was. Here I was, a woman brought as low as any in history, deprived of all. How could I be a greater victim? Yet, the world feared me.

"Mr. Brackenridge, I'd heard rumors that charges had been set against me, but until I came to town I could not believe they were anything more than stories. Do you mean to say that I am truly called to account for"—here I paused, for I did not believe I could speak Andrew's name and refrain from weeping—"for what has happened?"

Something in my tone must have soothed him. He removed himself from the window and took his seat. From under his writing desk, he brought forth an old wine bottle filled with whiskey and poured himself a drink into a pewter cup. Then he poured me one, as well, and slid it across the desk. "The sheriff has issued warrants for your arrest, along with Dalton and Skye." He looked at his shoes.

I drew in my breath. I must say what needed saying and do what needed doing. The weakness must end or there was no reason in living. "They dare to accuse us of Andrew's death." It was somehow easier to speak in the collective, but still I clutched my cup of whiskey and drank deep. I knew it from its darkness and rich flavor to be one of Andrew's batches, and its warmth gave me strength. Speaking without weeping gave me strength. Holding Brackenridge's gaze—yes, that too gave me strength. There was so much out there, all for me to take, if only I would grasp it. Weakness was easy and comforting, and action tore out my very heart, but I would do it. Why else live if not to do it?

Brackenridge studied me, as though he could see something changing inside. "Yes, they accuse you of that, and of killing Hendry. Colonel Tindall claims to have witnessed it himself."

"You must know I would never have harmed my husband, and neither would his friends."

"It has been cast about that there was an argument, fueled by whiskey. There was some talk—well, I am loath to say it, Mrs. Maycott, but as your lawyer I must. There was talk of a matter of impropriety between you and Mr. Dalton."

I believe I shocked Mr. Brackenridge by laughing. "That accusation could only be made by someone wholly unfamiliar with the man in question. Sir, I know we have not been long acquainted, but do you believe that I was a party to these things as Colonel Tindall has alleged?"

He dared to gaze at me. "No, I do not. I have seen many horrible things in the West, but I have never once seen any person, man or woman, so coldly dissimulate about murder. There is little wealth here, and most crimes are those of passion, and those passions are ever on display afterward. So I do not believe things transpired as we have been led to believe. I don't know how much time we have before the sheriff arrives, so I suggest you tell me what really happened as quickly as you can."

"And then I will need you to do something for me, sir. It will require me to place a great deal of trust in you, but you will see I have no choice."

We had more time than either of us imagined, the better part of an hour, before the knock came. The time proved sufficient for me to tell a much abbreviated version of what had happened at our cabin. I could not have told him a more detailed one, for to do so would be to reduce me to the weeping woman I'd been in the hunting cabin, and I would not permit that. Mr. Brackenridge suggested that the boy Phineas might yet be found to serve as witness. I did not think it likely. Even if he saw every-thing, I did not know I could depend on him to speak truthfully, so great was his irrational hatred of me.

We had no time for anything but my original plan. Thus, I told him as much as he needed to know and convinced him to transact my busi-ness. A hasty contract was drawn up and signed, with Mrs. Brackenridge and a literate serving girl as witnesses.

We were not done five minutes before they arrived. When Mr. Brack-enridge opened the door, the stout and hateful Colonel Tindall stood there, clutching his beloved fowling piece, the very one he had fired at me minutes before killing my husband. Next to him stood a man I had seen but never met, who I knew to be the sheriff. He was nearing sixty, I supposed, but looked as fit and rugged as any frontiersman. Tall of form, wide of shoulder, he wore a plain hunting shirt, from which rose a thick and corded neck. His face sported a short and reasonably well trimmed beard, its orderliness perhaps a nod to his office. His dark and hooded eyes rested on me from under a tattered beaver cap.

There were now a hundred or more townspeople crowding the street in an effort to witness the apprehension of the horrid criminal Maycott. They blocked the muddy roadway, pressing in close for a glimpse of the evil woman.

The sheriff stepped forward, though he did not cross the threshold. He looked past Mr. Brackenridge and addressed me directly. "'Tis Mrs. Maycott I presume I'm talking to."

"I am she." I met his gaze, but I would not look at Tindall. I did not trust myself to do so, for I feared I must spring upon him and prove my-self the creature they believed me to be.

"That's the shameless whore who killed my man!" Tindall cried.

A gasp arose from the crowd, and I first believed it was owing to the cruelty of his words, but I soon realized it was in response to the fierce-ness of my expression. Perhaps they believed I might strike again, and any of them could prove victim.

"I'm afraid you'll needs come with me, madam," said the sheriff, at-tempting a civil tone.

"I don't believe that either necessary or advisable," said Brackenridge.

He stepped forward, and now he was in his most lawyerly mode. He still appeared birdlike to me, and his eyes flitted here and there, but he had a kind of regal quality to him that I had not previously witnessed, and I imagined he must be a formidable presence in the courtroom.

"Advisable be damned!" Tindall shouted. "And you be damned too, Brackenridge! Are you so desperate for money that you will take to your bosom a woman who would slaughter her own husband? Murderous Indians are no longer enough for you?"

"It is not advisable," repeated Mr. Brackenridge in a stately tone, "and I say that for your sake. I can conduct our business in the full light of day, before all these witnesses, if that is what you wish, sir. I think if we do so, it will be much harder for you to choose a favorable outcome. Now, I beg you both come into my office, where all may be set out in private."

Tindall must have understood the note of triumph in Brackenridge's voice, for he assented. In a few minutes, the two of them sat in Mr. Brackenridge's office across from the desk. The lawyer sat facing them, and I stood behind him, too agitated to do otherwise.

"I don't much see the meaning of this," said the sheriff. His cap was off and resting in his lap. Mrs. Brackenridge had offered to take it, but he assured her it was too crawling with lice to be welcome upon her hat rack. "There's a warrant sworn, witnessed by the colonel himself."

"I have a great deal to say," answered Mr. Brackenridge. "To begin with, there are witnesses who will contradict the details that Colonel Tindall has provided."

"Witnesses," barked Tindall. "No doubt the woman's co-conspirators. No one will credit anything such men say."

Mr. Brackenridge smiled. "They are among the witnesses, but not the only ones. We spoke with a group of Indians who say that you hired them to harass this lady and her husband." Brackenridge, I must point out, did not lie, but repeated a lie I had told him.

Tindall snorted. "That's nonsense, sure enough. Those Indians are dead."

The sheriff now turned to observe Tindall. "I am sorry, Colonel, but precisely *which* Indians do you believe to be dead? You do not deny hiring the dead ones?"

Tindall now blanched and cast me a gaze of unrestrained hostility. Perhaps it was meant to frighten me, but with what could I be threatened?

"I know nothing about them. This woman's lies will come out in court. I shall see her and her fellows prosecuted, and when they are convicted I will confiscate their property."

"You may wish to take your chances in court," said Mr. Brackenridge. "It may strike you as a reasonable gamble, but there is no chance of confiscating anything. I have personally overseen the sale of these properties and the goods upon them."

"They cannot be sold," said Tindall. "They belong to me."

"As you well know, title to the ground rents can be sold and, given the improvements made to the land, can be sold at considerable profit. I'm afraid there is nothing left for you to confiscate. You will receive your rents from the purchaser, but the stills and equipment—and, indeed, the secret to making the new whiskey—belong to the new owner." He now turned to the sheriff. "If you must take the lady into custody, then do so. I insist upon a speedy trial, however, for I believe that information to be revealed will lead not only to my client's acquittal but to an arrest warrant sworn for Colonel Tindall."

The sheriff studied Tindall and then Mr. Brackenridge. My thought apparently hardly mattered in this exchange.

"Who holds the lease?" asked Tindall.

Mr. Brackenridge shook his head. "I do beg your pardon, but I cannot tell you that. It is confidential, as my client wishes."

Tindall pushed himself to his feet. "You dare cross me, Brackenridge. The day will come when you will wish you never had."

"But today having crossed you yields such a delightful feeling," he answered. "Rather warm inside, like a good glass of exceptional whiskey. I believe I shall savor it. Am I correct in assuming that you are withdrawing your complaint against Mrs. Maycott?"

"Damn you, yes!" he shouted. He abruptly stormed from the room and then from the house.

The sheriff sat in silence for a moment, occupied in no more complicated an operation than the removal of lice from his hat, which he nervously cracked between his teeth. Finally, he turned to me. "We still got two dead men, missus."

I swallowed hard. "Hendry shot Andrew. Before Andrew died, he shot Hendry."

"Mr. Brackenridge suggests Colonel Tindall might've had a hand in it."

"That is not what I saw," I answered. This wasn't the time to pursue Tindall. We could not prove his complicity in a court of law, for it would be our word against his—and his word had the power of wealth behind it. I would have to take him on in another way.

The sheriff nodded. He replaced his hat and nodded to us both. Then he went outside to disperse the crowd.

Ethan Saunders

The new day brought much to think about and reflect on, but the first order of business was to finish my conversation with Duer. He had promised to meet me at the City Tavern, so that was where I traveled in the morning. There I found the trading room in an uproar of chaos that made my previous visit seem a scene from Easter prayer. Men were on their feet shouting at one another, red in the face. Two rather bloated gentlemen stood close enough that, in the heat of their exchange, they made each other's faces slick with spittle. Clerks scrambled to keep track of trades, but the quick trades and angry progression made their task impossible, and most were filthy with hastily applied ink.

I watched, not knowing what to think, like a street gaper watching the aftermath of a terrible accident. I stood that way some minutes until I noticed someone now next to me, a bespectacled older fellow with gray hair and a gray beard.

He looked at me with some amusement. "Not certain what to make of it?" he asked, in accents that betrayed Scottish origins. "If this is your first time at trade, and it might be from the looks of you, you've chosen a bad day."

"Not my first time, and I'm not at trade. I'm merely curious. What has happened?"

The Scotsman gestured with the back of his hand toward the room in general and at nothing in particular. "Bank shares are down, for the first time in some months. They were trading at 110 just a few days ago, but today they've dropped. They were trading at under 100 for a while, but there are some bargain hunters that have raised the price to 102, last I saw."

"Are you a trader in bank issues?" I asked.

"No." He shook his head. "I am merely an observer, like you, lad."

I looked at the fellow again. There was something familiar about him I could not place, as if he was a man I'd never met but heard spoken of more than once. He, like Lavien, was bearded, and that was unusual enough, but otherwise he seemed unremarkable, a serious, scholarly-looking fellow in a gray suit—none the best, but not terribly bad.

"Do you know Duer?" I asked him.

"Oh, I know him."

"Where does he sit? I don't see him."

The man laughed. "He's not here. The rumor is he's gone back to New York on the early express coach. He has fled, as they say, the scene of his crimes."

I felt myself tense as disappointment and anger coursed through me. I ought to have made him speak to me last night when he'd been in my grasp. It seemed to me that Duer was a most effective liar. He had, after all, fooled *me*.

"He owes you, doesn't he?" the Scotsman said. "I can see the disappointment."

"Not money, only his time," I said, affecting calm. "You mentioned he fled his crimes. What crimes do you mean?"

He gestured at the room once more. "This chaos. Before leaving, he let it be known that there are some who have borrowed from the Bank of the United States who won't be able to pay what they owe. He cast a bomb of chaos and then fled the explosion."

"Why?"

The man shrugged. "Perhaps he is shorting bank stock. Perhaps he wishes to buy cheap. Perhaps he merely likes to keep the markets unpredictable, since a man of Duer's sort thrives upon chaotic markets."

"But he's not here."

"Some of these men act secretly as his agents. It is not necessarily a good thing to be, but when the most powerful trader on two exchanges asks a man to be his agent, he cannot say no. If he refuses, he turns his back upon opportunities. But to Duer, these men are no more than firewood—to be used, burned, and then swept away."

I looked around the room once more and saw no one I knew, no one who could help explain these matters more clearly. The man with the beard was now engaged in watching some trades, and I troubled him no more. Indeed, every man was now trading or watching with rapt attention as men sold their shares of bank issues or bought in the desperate hope that the price would recover. All were standing and talking and trading. All but one. It was the frog-faced man in his brown suit and sour countenance. He traded nothing but sat hunched over a small piece of paper, writing something—I could not see what—in a small hand, as pinched as his expression.

I did not like this fellow showing himself, again and again. And it was then that something occurred to me—why the gray-bearded man had seemed to me familiar. I stepped outside, where Leonidas sat with a group of other servants, and called him aside, telling him what I needed of him.

"She won't like it," he said.

"It is of no moment. Bring her."

He nodded and departed at once. I had no watch any longer, but it was yet early. Trading would continue for the next hour and a half, so I returned inside, all the while keeping my eyes upon the man with the gray beard and the man with the frog face—two figures who seemed to be of increasing importance in my life, though in both cases I could not say why.

Half an hour later, Leonidas returned, telling me he had brought whom I had asked. I went to the door, and my landlady, Mrs. Deisher, stepped inside the threshold, but no further. I did not want her to be seen, and I received a bit of good luck here, for the bearded man was absorbed in watching a trade.

"Sorry to trouble you, Mrs. Deisher, but this is important."

"I am ready to give help, but I never like to have your Negro, to have him drag me from my home, as though abducting me."

Leonidas shrugged. "Insisting is not abducting."

"Leonidas apologizes," I assured her. I gestured to the gray-bearded man. "Have you ever seen him before?"

She opened her mouth, raised her arm in a point, and was no doubt about to scream. In a single movement, I lowered her arm and clamped her mouth shut. "Let us be subtle, my good woman. Do you know him?"

"Yes," she said. "That is Mr. Reynolds, the one who came to my house and paid me to admit you no more."

I sent them both away and waited, drinking my porter, watching. The man with the frog face glanced over toward me now and again, but the bearded man did not. At noon, when the trading came to a conclusion, the bearded man took a fresh piece of paper from the leather envelope in which he stored his things and proceeded to write out a lengthy note. He then folded it into a small square and placed it inside something, though I could not see what. He rose and left the building.

In a moment I stood and left as well. Out upon the street, Leonidas remained where he had been before, sitting with the servants, but he pointed right, and so I proceeded to follow, just in time to see my quarry make another right upon Walnut Street. I remained distant, and the streets were sufficiently crowded and chaotic, with their usual press of people and beasts and wayward carriages, that to survive a man must look ahead of him and could not afford to look back. Thus I tracked him easily and observed again that he made another right upon Fifth.

This street was far less crowded than Walnut, and I hesitated as he approached the entrance to the Library Company building. I thought he might go inside—and, if so, I don't know what I might have done, for there could be no way to follow without revealing myself. But he passed the entrance and then stopped for a moment by a large tree on the far side of the library. He leaned against it for a minute and then hurried on. I knew enough of human nature and instantly ducked behind a watch house, for no sooner had he taken his first few steps than he turned around and looked behind him. He had, I knew, deposited something. He might have stifled the urge to look around while walking toward his goal, but, once having completed it, he could no longer resist the temptation. Fortunately, I had anticipated this move; I saw his body stiffen, I saw him begin to pivot, and so I hid myself effectively. I waited a moment as he went on, and then I did nothing more than take a seat upon a nearby wall.

I let a full half hour pass and then approached the tree I had observed the gray-bearded man molesting. It had a hole in it, and when I gently reached inside I found something that seemed to be the size and shape of a rock but was infinitely lighter. When I pulled it out, I saw it was a cunning container meant to look like a rock but made of painted wood, with a sliding device upon the bottom. When I opened it, I found a piece of paper, no doubt the one I had seen him write on before leaving. It was another message in the eminently breakable code but far longer than the others I'd seen, and I had no choice but to retire to the nearest tavern, where I called for pen, ink, and paper.

The code had changed, and I could not simply apply the letters I previously recollected, but it was still a Caesar cipher and quite breakable. In the end, it was well worth the effort. Much had been mysterious to me, but now vast amounts were laid open, and at last I had some inkling of what was transpiring. Almost certainly, I knew far more than Lavien.

I read and reread the message. Its contents meant I had to do something I would almost certainly have preferred to avoid, for now I would have to go see Hamilton once more. But before that I would have to deal with the note itself.

I met with Leonidas at the Man Full of Trouble and showed him the message, which I had transcribed for him.

Being unable to communicate with you directly is becoming increasingly difficult, as there is much to report. Fortunately, I am growing adept with the codes. As you must know by the time you read this, P has returned to Philadelphia; he pretends that nothing has transpired, but

Duer used him monstrous ill, and it cannot be undone. The BUS will feel it soon enough, and Hamilton has no notion of it. As for L, he is a dangerous physical presence, but he is not nearly as clever as he believes. He thinks the business is isolated, and he will not learn otherwise until too late. You were overly concerned about S, who is a blunderer and a drunkard. He knows nothing about P and shall learn nothing. As for Mrs. P, she knows nothing of the impending ruin, and, once faced with penury, I am certain you may have her to use as you like.

He stared at my transcript for a long time and then at me. "What does it all mean? There is some plot here, but I cannot even begin to fathom it."

"Neither can I," I said. "As near as I can tell, there is a scheme to hurt Pearson, and consequently the bank. Somehow Duer is involved, but it is hard for me to determine if he is a primary actor or some sort of unwilling victim."

"Yes, yes, yes. But that is nothing. The bank and Pearson and the rest be damned, Ethan. This is about you, somehow. Whoever these people are, they mock you, call you names, and plan to make Mrs. Pearson a whore."

"Are you saying you think I ought to go to Lavien with this?"

"By no means," said Leonidas. "This is yours, Ethan. This is your burden to bear, and you must see it through as you see fit. If there is a conflict between your needs and the Treasury's needs, you may be sure Lavien will not give a fig for yours—or about Mrs. Pearson's, for that matter. I say that with respect for him, for I do think him honorable, but his honor, his sense of duty, must put his service to Hamilton above service to you—or to Mrs. Pearson. You know it. Whatever is to be done, you must do it alone."

"Entirely alone?"

"It is not as though I have a choice, but you know you may depend upon me."

"And if you did have a choice?" I asked. "If I were to free you right now, would you continue to stand by me in this until the end?"

"You won't," he said.

"But if I did." I don't know why I chose to press the point at that moment, but his concern for me placed me upon the precipice of informing him that he was free already.

"I don't know," he answered earnestly. He met my eye and did not waver.

I appreciated his candor. How could I not? Yet he put me in a difficult position, for he was the only man I could trust entirely, and I could not do without him. So long as this crisis continued, I would have to keep the truth from him. He could not yet know he was a free man.

Leonidas sensed I was lost in thought and leaned forward to distract me. "What shall you do about the note? Do you plan to watch the tree?"

I shook my head. "It's not practical. Someone would have to watch it at all times, and there are only two of us."

"Then you'll put it back before they discover you've taken it?"

"No," I said. "I want them to know I've found it." I took a fresh piece of paper and wrote out a short note to replace the one I took. My note said only, *I am coming to find you.* "Let them ponder that," I said.

"What if they come to find you first?"

"Then they shall save me a great deal of trouble."

I did not know if Hamilton would see me again. Once was charity, twice a nuisance; a third time might prove an outrage. I had no illusions about my reception, but then he could have no illusions about me. If I wanted to see him, I would see him. Perhaps I would wait for him on the street or visit him in his home. He knew me. He knew if I wished to speak with him, I would make it happen. For that reason, he admitted me right away.

He sat at his desk, which was covered with four or five high piles of neatly stacked papers. He had a quill in one hand and a near-empty inkpot by his side.

"I am very busy, Captain Saunders," he said.

"So am I. It's terrible, isn't it?"

He set down the pen. "What can this be about? Mr. Pearson has returned, so I know you don't visit me upon that score."

"You know I do, and that Mr. Pearson's return is not an answer but another question."

"I seem to recall asking you not to involve yourself in this matter."

"I recall that too, but you and I both know you did not mean it. You would much rather I ran an inquiry parallel to that of Lavien. You will yield far better results if you have two men competing for the same ends. I will not say you engineered this competition, but you cannot regret it. Now let us end this dissimulation. You wish me to proceed, don't you?"

He looked at me directly. "No."

"Of course you do. There is too much in the balance. Perhaps it is time for you to tell me why you wished Lavien to find Pearson in the first place. Why is he of interest to you?"

"It is a private matter."

So he said, but I began to think it must be a public matter. There was no personal connection I could divine, so there was but one obvious reason Hamilton might take an interest in Pearson. Given what the bearded Scotsman had told me this morning about defaulted bank loans, I could but conclude one thing. "He has borrowed money from the bank, hasn't he?"

Hamilton blinked and looked away. "I suppose he may have."

"How much?"

"The bank was, in its conception, my idea, and I take an interest in its operation, but I do not run the bank, and I do not take an interest in its day-to-day operations. I doubt that even Mr. Willing, the bank president, could tell you about individual loans without resorting to files. You cannot expect that I, who am far more removed, can summon such information instantaneously on any possible borrower."

"No, I don't expect you to know any possible borrower. I do, however, expect you know about this one. How much?"

He sighed. "He has borrowed fifty thousand dollars."

"Good God, you give that much to a single individual?"

"It was for investment and development. You have seen how the city thrives under bank money. Pearson is a respected dealer in real estate, and he presented us with a specific plan for developing land to the west of the city."

"But he hasn't done it, has he? You received word that not only was Pearson not buying and developing land, he was losing the properties he already had. You don't keep an eye on the day-to-day minutiae of investment, nor does the bank president, I'll wager. No one was going out to Helltown to see if Pearson was developing it. He was a respected man of business, and it was safe to assume he was doing what he said. But then you receive word that his properties are being foreclosed, and you learn that no one knows where he is. Suddenly fifty thousand in bank funds may have vanished. Can the bank withstand such a loss?"

"Of course it can. It is a serious loss but there are systems built into the bank's charter to enable it to weather defaulted loans."

"Easily?"

"It is never easy."

"It is never easy," I said, "because what you fear most is Jefferson and his faction getting word of this. That is the issue, isn't it? Your bank has just launched and endured a rocky first half year with wildly fluctuating share prices. Now, it will be said, it is granting loans to the personal friends of the bank president, loans that will not—cannot—be repaid. You know what they will say: that the bank is an engine of the northern money men to feed their own greed."

Hamilton nodded. "That is, indeed, what they will say. That is part of it."

"There is more?"

"You will keep this quiet?"

"Of course."

"There is also the method of the bank's funding, the whiskey excise. Jefferson's faction will waste no time in saying that we tax the poor men of the frontier to pay for the irresponsible spending of the rich. That is what they will say."

"And the truth?"

"The truth is that the Bank of the United States is a large bank that makes large loans, so of course it is of direct benefit to the rich. There are smaller land banks that benefit small landholders, and that is what they should do, but projects that benefit the rich also benefit others. Had Pearson done with the money what he was supposed to do, he would have built properties, which would have employed men and caused goods to change hands. Those buildings would have provided housing, space for shops and services, for the growth of the economy. That bene-fits all, rich and poor."

"Clearly that is not what happened with Pearson. Now he has returned, what has Lavien learned about the fate of the money?"

"Very little. Pearson won't answer any questions."

"And, I suppose, you haven't given Lavien permission to break his elbows or cut off his feet. Not with someone so prominent."

"Pearson is clever," said Hamilton. "He has openly refused to appear at the bank to explain the status of his loan, and he knows we dare not press the matter, lest it become public knowledge that a loan of this magnitude is in danger. I'm sure Pearson knows that that scoundrel Philip Freneau, who writes Jefferson's newspaper, has been sniffing about, asking questions. If Freneau learns the truth, he will use it to ruin us all. Jefferson and his men would gladly sacrifice the national economy if only to prove I am wrong and they are right."

"Which is why the bank has not seized Pearson's assets. To keep this from becoming a scandal?"

"Yes. While there is the chance of a quiet repayment of all or even some of the loan, we prefer to avoid a public fiasco that will only feed Jefferson's public animosity toward the bank. Until we know more, we will have to find other means of discovering what Pearson is up to."

It seemed to me that, whether it was what he intended or not, I was those other means. There was no reason not to press it. "What of Duer?"

"What of him?"

"What is the link between Duer and Pearson?"

"None that I am aware of," he said.

I thought about the note I had found in the tree stump. *Duer has used him monstrous ill, and it cannot be undone.* That was, in itself, of no consequence. Let these men ruin one another to their heart's content; it was nothing to me. And yet there was obviously more to it. *The BUS will feel it soon enough, and Hamilton has no notion of it.* All this was a scheme to harm the bank. Pearson was but a tool, Cynthia but a casualty.

"Who would like to destroy the bank?" I asked.

Hamilton sighed. "Destroy it? Jefferson, I suppose."

"No, not malign it, or see it fail, or rejoice in its adequacies. Jefferson wishes to find political advantage. Who wishes to destroy it by his own hands?"

"No one," he said. "No one who could."

"And if anyone could, who would it be?"

"The rabble," he said. "The rabble prompted by Jefferson would see it destroyed. The western rustics, filled with democratical ideas by Jefferson, would rather go to war than hand over a penny in excise taxes. Things are not so complex as you imagine, and you cannot see that only because you have been out of the game too long."

It seemed to me they were far more complex than I could imagine. That was the difficulty.

If I was going to attempt to chip away at this complexity, the first thing I had to discover was the nature of the secret and financial relationship between Hamilton and Duer's man, Reynolds. I might well have told Hamilton more if I could have better trusted him, but so long as he was secreting purses of gold to men of this sort, I would have to hold fast to my secrets. More to the point, I needed to know why the men who acted against me, and acted against Cynthia, wished to point me toward this man. Reynolds worked for Duer—that much was certain—but it now seemed to me that the bearded Scotsman, who was so clearly involved with the threat against the bank—wanted to make certain I noticed Reynolds and perhaps was set against him.

It was time to approach directly. Thus, that night I walked to Reynolds's house and knocked on the door. It was later than good manners generally allow for a stranger to call, but this was an unsavory neighborhood, and lights were on. I would take my chances.

When no one answered, I knocked again, and then a third time. At last I heard footsteps upon stairs, and a woman's voice cried out from inside, asking who called.

"Captain Ethan Saunders, on behalf of the United States Department of the Treasury," I responded, with only slight exaggeration. This was no time to be shy. "I must gain entrance."

The door opened. Standing there, in a state of very appealing dishevel, was possibly the most beautiful woman I'd ever seen. Yes, I know this narrative is crowded with beautiful women—Mrs. Pearson, Mrs. Maycott, Mrs. Lavien, Mrs. Bingham. We might form a cricket team of beautiful women. I cannot help it if they are the ones who excite my notice and so trouble myself to describe. Yet how beautiful are they? Mrs.

Pearson is undeniably lovely, but it is my feeling for her that elevates her to so exalted a level. Mrs. Maycott is a bit weak in the chin, to tell the truth, but she is mysterious and poised. Mrs. Lavien has that Hebrew look about her which some may find unappealing.

This lady was beautiful, and not because her demeanor or exotic race or a longing heart provided an added advantage to elevate her. No, here was a creature of perfection, like Milton's Eve, the ideal of female loveliness. Her fair hair was wavy and in a state of wild disorder. Her eyes were large and so blue it was almost shocking. Her cheeks were red and round and molded to perfection. Her teeth as white as new snow, her lips the color of roses. Shall I go on? It is tedious, I know, but it is important that I make it clear that in part and in sum this was a woman, I believe, utterly without equal in the United States, possibly in the world. Those who would, in years to come, judge the frailty of a man enchanted with her, knew nothing of her astonishing charms. The man did not live who, given the opportunity to love her, would have turned aside.

"Madam, will you marry me?" I asked.

She laughed. She wore a loose gown, quite recently thrown on. It was rather generous in its presentation of décolletage, and her bosoms, large and full, moved very agreeably.

"I am afraid I am already married, sir."

"Then I shall take my own life," I said. "Before I do so, I would speak to a Mr. Reynolds. Does he live here?"

Her face darkened just a little. "That is the name of my husband, sir. He is not at home."

That slovenly brute with his scarred face and lupine demeanor was the husband of this creature? How did she endure it? How could the world endure it? Under normal circumstances, I would almost certainly have inserted myself in this lady's life to better her state, but I had other things that demanded my attention, foremost being Cynthia. I would focus on the beast and not the beauty. "I must find him."

"He is not in town at all," she said. "May I ask what this involves? Did you mention the Treasury Department, sir?"

"I work for Colonel Hamilton at Treasury." Reform does not extend to lies of this sort.

"And what will you with my husband?" There was now something rather unkind in her tone, and I did not like it. I wanted her to be charmed again.

"I merely wish to talk with him about Mr. Duer," I said, grinning amicably. "It is about that gentleman, and not your husband."

"I see."

"When will he return?"

"I cannot say."

"And where has he gone?"

"He doesn't tell me."

"Perhaps," I said, "you would care to invite me inside, and we can discuss this further."

"Another time," she said, as though she did not mean it, and closed the door.

Joan Maycott

Spring 1791

Mrs. Brackenridge insisted that I spend the night in her house, and in the morning I made my way back, not to the hunting cabin but to my own. I'd not told anyone of my plans to do this because I knew they would attempt to convince me of its imprudence. There was first the practical matter of my cabin's condition. Much of it had been destroyed in the fire; Skye had told me as much. I found the walls scorched, and such furnishings as had been saved were blackened. The curtains, table linens, our clothes and papers—including my novel, but Skye had prepared me for this too—were all gone. The place stank of fire and dampness, but it was where Andrew and I had lived, and I would not leave it until I must.

The other principal objection to my returning was that I no longer had any right to the cabin, though I did have permission from its owner, Mr. Brackenridge, to stay there as long as I liked. It would not be long.

I did not wish to remain, and doing so would be unwise. I understood, almost as soon as I'd understood anything, that Tindall had pursued us because he wished to deprive Andrew, Skye, and Dalton of the means of making whiskey. I also knew that there were more than a few wealthy farmers in the region who would be willing to buy our leases, with our equipment and instruction on the new method of distilling. For now, Hugh Henry Brackenridge held the ground rents to our lands. He assured me he would do his best to sell them to the highest bidder and to do so for no more than a 5-percent commission, though, if he wished to cheat us, we could do nothing to prevent it. It was a gamble, but I never doubted that he was worthy, and circumstances would prove me correct.

Thus it was that things settled into relative calm. Tindall, for the time being, would not risk harming us. His efforts to have me jailed, and his cowardly retreat, would make any attempt on the well-being of me or my friends far too suspicious. He might hope to evade the law, but he would not risk an all-out uprising from the populace. When Mr. Brackenridge sold our ground-rent lease and I received my share of the whiskey revenues, I might hope to return east, perhaps to my childhood home. It seemed a respectable way to engage my widowhood.

Yet I could not do those things. Jericho had said it changes you when you kill a man, and that was part of it. I had killed. I had faced Tindall both in physical combat and in a legal duel, and I had bested him both times. What else, then, could I do if I set myself to it? I was an unassuming woman and, men often said, a pretty one. My appearance led men, civilized men, to trust me, defer to me, and, often enough, overlook me. If I embraced these truths, if I used them, I could accomplish a great deal. What I wished to accomplish was revenge. Not pointless, hollow, bloody revenge, but revenge that would destroy those who had made a tragedy of my life and would, at the same time, redeem me and my friends.

The outlines of my plan were clear to me, but to proceed I would need the assistance of men like Skye and Dalton and at least some of Dalton's whiskey boys. If I were to have them, they must trust me, even be in awe of me, the way his soldiers and officers were in awe of General Washington. If I were to effect that, I would have to do something bold.

When she came into the dairy barn to milk the half-dozen cows, I was waiting for her. Dawn had only just struck bright and cloudless, filling the grounds with sweet possibility. I'd had to trek through the forest at night to meet her, but I'd carried my rifle and walked noiselessly in soft moccasins. My legs never tired, and though I made certain to watch every footfall, my mind wandered over what I would now do.

The door opened to the east, and when she came in she was nothing but a large silhouette, the skirts of her plain dress undulating in the breeze. But she did not see me, and so closed the door and reached for the milking stool. She'd healed well since I last saw her, but there were still red welts on her face and hardened scabs, and in some places the flesh had settled into a vaguely pale scarring.

She had just set down the stool and begun to talk to the first cow when she saw me. "Lord, Mrs. Maycott, what you doing in the dairy barn?" It all came out in a single breath.

I had not precisely been hiding, but standing in the shadows in the corner. I now walked forward, and it seemed to me that I was stepping through a door. I was about to become someone else. Here. Now. Under these circumstances. I must be a woman others follow. I must take command and make events unfold to my liking.

I looked at the woman. "What is your name?"

"Oh, Lord, grief done disordered your mind. You don't remember old Lactilla?"

"Of course I remember you." I took her hand. "I want to know your name."

It seemed to me that, all at once, this woman who had been rendered property, the plaything of a cruel master, understood everything. Not only what I was asking, but what I was doing and why. An understanding passed between us, two women shaped and blasted by a world who cared nothing for us but as playthings for its amusement. "I'm Ruth," she said, in a quiet voice.

"Do you know what I hate most about slavery, Ruth?" I asked.

"You gots to choose just one thing?"

"What I hate most is how we allow it to not signify. We tell ourselves we have produced this great experiment in republican government. We have launched a new era of human liberty, the culmination of two thousand years of the republican dream and centuries of philosophical ponderings. It has all led up to this glorious moment, this glorious nation, an exemplar of the greatest potential of the human soul. But never you mind about those Africans held in bondage. They don't signify. That is what I hate most."

"It's worth despising, but I'd place it something down on the list. For me, I'd rather reckon my baby which was took away. And with it I'd number getting shot in the face with fowling piece." She smiled, and I could see a scar where a piece of bird shot had grazed her lip.

"At some point," I said, "those things—the philosophical and practical—must come together."

She studied my face with a mixture of horror and understanding. "Is that point now?"

"Tonight it is," I told her.

She sighed and brushed off her skirts, as though my words rained down dust of disobedience and she wished not to be tainted. "What you mean to do?"

"I'm not certain, but I must do something, mustn't I? Everything begins with someone who either does something or does nothing, and I won't be the person who does nothing."

She shook her head. "You ain't gonna kill him, are you?"

The depth of her concern surprised me. "Would it trouble you?"

She rose to her feet and walked to the barn door. Then she walked back. "It simple for you. Tindall's a devil, that true. You want to kill him because he deserve to die. That true too. But you kill him, most likely the slaves get sold off."

I understood the fear of change, but here I thought it madness. "Ruth, are things so good here that you fear to find yourself elsewhere?"

"Things here are bad," she said, "but they always worse somewhere else."

I nodded. "I have no intention of committing murder." It was not entirely true. I could not say precisely what I intended to do to Tindall. Murder was certainly one possibility.

"All right. What you need?"

"I need everyone out of the house tonight. I want it free of servants and slaves."

"All right. I get that done for you."

I waited in the dairy barn the rest of the day. Ruth, who had been mocked with the name Lactilla for decades, brought me an afternoon dinner and an evening supper. Thereafter I fell asleep for some hours, but when I awoke it was the full of night, and there were no lights in the main house of Empire Hill.

I'd made arrangements with Ruth, and the front door was left unlocked. It was no great matter to make my way across the grounds, enter the house, and proceed to Tindall's bedroom, the location of which Ruth had also explained to me. I told her I only wished to frighten him and rob him, make him feel as helpless as I had been made to feel, but I had not told her the truth. I pitied her, for she feared being sold if Tindall died, but Tindall was not a young man, and he must die sometime.

It was not that I wished him dead so much as I wished to kill him. Or, more precisely, I wished to see that I could kill him. I had killed Hendry, but that had been in the heat of violence, and it had been the instantaneous decision of a moment. For what would happen in the months and years ahead, I wished to know that I could kill, and that if I were called upon to do so I would be ready. I hoped all could be effected without more bloodshed, but I knew that if I pursued my plan, the time might well come when I would have to make that decision, and I believed it would be easier if I had made it already. I could think of no better subject for the experiment than a man who deserved to die—and deserved death at my hand.

I climbed the stairs, delicately pressing my moccasins to the wood so it did not squeak. At the top of the stairs I turned right and went to the second door, as I'd been instructed. Inside it was light, but I heard no noise, not breathing or the turning of pages or rustling of sheets. I pushed open the door a little farther to gain a better view.

The room was roughly furnished, as though the delicacy of Tindall's receiving rooms was but posturing and here was the true man. A large oaken wardrobe, an inelegant side table, a plain bed, a bearskin rug upon the floor. Across the ceilings, rafters were exposed, built at an arc, almost as though we were in the hold of a ship. The walls were adorned with a few paintings of hunters upon landscapes. At the far wall, a dying fire burned in the fireplace.

From the rafters, near the center of the room, hung the body of Colonel Tindall, motionless, not even swinging, upon a monstrous thickness of rope. His dead face was near black, his tongue protruded, his eyes were strangely both bulging and closed tight. He was dead and had been dead for a few hours at least.

I stared, feeling astonishment, disappointment, and relief all at once. How had it happened that the very night I was to confront him, possibly kill him, he had taken his own life? I did not believe he was the sort of man to be so racked by conscience that he must choose oblivion over guilt. Yet here was the evidence before me.

I had been robbed of the chance to test my mettle, but I had nothing to gain by standing and staring, so I decided to search the house for anything of value I might take.

I took two steps into the room when I heard the boyish voice.

"I followed you." It was Phineas. He sat in a high-backed chair that faced the fire and so had been invisible to me at the door. Now he rose and turned to face me, rifle in his hand. He did not raise it, but it was only a matter of time until he did. I had a pair of primed pistols in the pockets of my skirts, but I thought it too soon to reach for them.

"Why?" I asked, not knowing what else to say.

"I seen you coming through the woods, and I knew you was coming here, and I guessed why. When I saw you hiding out with the niggers, I knowed it for sure. So I come here first and I hit Tindall in the head with the back of my gun, and then strung him up like the pig he is."

"Why?" I asked again.

"So you wouldn't," he said. "You come to kill him. I knowed it, and I didn't think you should." He laughed.

I had the strangest feeling of not being there, as though I watched these events unfolding from some distant place. Relief and disgust and terror swirled through me. "What is so funny?"

"I remember you when you first joined up with the party heading west. You was just a green gal from the East. Now look at you, killer of men, housebreaker, thief, who knows what else? I told you the truth, missus. The West changes you, I said, and by God it changed you good. But I ain't gonna let it change you that much."

He wasn't going to kill me. I began to feel it, and my muscles loosened. I took a deep breath. "What do you mean?"

"You killed Hendry 'cause you had no choice, so now you think you can kill when you choose. You think it's not so different. I did too, once. I'd killed some Indians when I was with a scouting party 'cause they ambushed us, and it felt good. I thought of my family when I fired my rifle right into those redskins' chests. I didn't mind at all. Then, a year later, I was coming through the woods at night and I come across a single Indian who'd made camp, asleep by his dying fire. I figure, I killed one Indian, why not another? I didn't know if there was more nearby, so I didn't use my gun. Instead I snuck up on him real quiet and tomahawked him right in the face. I done his mouth first, so he couldn't scream none, and then his whole face until he was dead, and then I took his scalp. I was covered with blood at the end, but that didn't matter. What mattered was that when I was done, I knew killing 'cause you could was a different thing from killing 'cause you was made to."

"You didn't like it," I said.

"Nah, I loved it. I love to kill Indians. Killing Tindall was pretty good too. But I don't love myself no more, missus. That's the thing."

"Why would you do this to save me? I thought you hated me."

"I hate me, missus, not you. I just get it confused sometimes."

I looked at Tindall, and I could now see the back of his head. The hair was matted with blood. "They'll figure out he didn't hang himself of his own choosing."

"Don't matter," he said. "I already wrote up a note, which I aim to bring to that lawyer, Brackenridge, in town. Then I'll go."

"But they'll hunt you."

"They'll hunt me, but they won't find me. I'll be an outlaw, which I reckon I'd like." He gestured with the rifle to the side table near the door. "There's some notes there, a pretty good amount. Three or four thousand dollars. I don't know what to do with paper, so you can have it. I'll take the coins, probably six or seven dollars' worth; they'll think I took it all. But you best get gone."

"Thank you, Phineas."

He shrugged. "I'm sorry I said those things to you, missus. I never had no choice in it. I had to say them, you understand, but I'm sorry all the same."

"I understand," I said, though I did not. Perhaps I did not want to.

"None of it meant nothing, and that's the truth. Now, you get gone. Then it'll be my turn. I need to get to Pittsburgh, deliver my message, and then get to killing Indians." He waved his gun at me. "You best go. I cain't always help what I do."

I gathered up the notes he'd assembled and hurried down the stairs, considering how best to frame these events to Dalton and Skye. I had not been quite the woman of action I'd wanted to be, but I did not see why they had to know that.

Ethan Saunders

The next morning I awoke to the emotional toll of knowing I must, that night, dine with the woman I had always loved and do so alongside her husband, a man whose improprieties had embroiled not only his own family but perhaps the nation itself.

By the time I awoke, a servant of the Pearson house had already delivered a note to the effect that I was expected at seven of the clock. I had come, in my mind, to see this evening as an opportunity to answer many outstanding questions, so there was little for me to do that afternoon. I may have fallen, therefore, into some old habits, and I spent much of the day in a few comfortable taverns, and yet I did not arrive to the Pearson house more than half an hour late. It had warmed a little and snow had begun to melt, so I should not be ashamed to own I slipped on my journey and was damp when I arrived, but as most of the damage was upon my greatcoat, I presumed my hosts would not know of it.

This house—or mansion, I might style it—was on Fourth Street, just north of Spruce on a fashionable block. The exterior was of typical Philadelphia redbrick, remarkable only for its well-appointed bushes, shrubs, and trees, the true beauty of the gardens not being visible in the winter or after dark. Inside, however, I was treated to the finest of floor coverings in imitation of exquisite white tile, a handsome silver-blue wallpaper—cunningly textured to evoke the impression of the water of a nearly still lake—and numerous portraits, many of the illustrious house of Pearson. A lower servant of some sort, a kitchen boy perhaps, offered to clean my shoes, for, unknown to me, I had traversed through horse leavings. After my grooming was so tended and I was dusted off like a freshly sculpted block of stone, I was at last permitted to ascend the stairs to the inner sanctum of excellent company.

I was shown into a large sitting room where Mr. and Mrs. Pearson sat next to one another on a settee. The gentleman of the house held himself stiffly and formally and waved his oversized hand about as he held forth on some matter of trade. His thinning white hair was wild and unkempt, and though his tone was voluble, his eyes appeared dim and hollow. Next to him, his wife wore a dress of sea green, with a flattering cut. She looked at me as I entered, turned away, then looked up once more and rose.

"Why do you rise?" asked her good husband. "I am speaking and you rise, as though no words come out of my mouth."

"Our guest has arrived," she answered, her voice flat.

"Our guest? Oh, Saunders. Hide the state secrets—ha-ha. He has kept us long enough, hasn't he?" Pearson at last rose to greet me and I shook one of his big hands. His grip was loose and absent, as though he could not remember why he took my hand or what he was meant to do with it.

Also rising was the widow Maycott, who had been sitting in a high-backed chair. She wore a much plainer dress than Mrs. Pearson, ivory in color, high-necked and remarkably charming. Upon another settee was a couple of some fifty years apiece, handsomely if uninterestingly appointed. The man was a bit on the short side, and plagued with that curious sort of fat which accumulates only in the belly, the rest of his body remaining gaunt, so that he appeared great with child. His gray-haired lady, attired in a modest black gown, had pleasing features and must have been acceptably comely some thirty years earlier; probably not so, ten years later.

"Captain Saunders, I am happy to see you once more," said Mrs. Pearson, her face the very mask of control. I suppose she had a great deal of practice.

"See him at last, you mean," said Pearson. "It is a dreadful thing to make a man wait for his own supper."

I bowed. "I do apologize, sir. I was detained upon government business." I told this lie not only to excuse myself but to excite a general curiosity.

"You must tell us of it," said Mrs. Maycott.

"What government business could you be about?" asked Pearson. "The kind with beer and rum by the smell of it. In any case, I would think the government is by now done with you."

Mrs. Pearson, blushing charmingly, made some sort of conversation-changing spouse-scolding noise in the back of her throat. "Mrs. Maycott tells me you already know each other and was the one who invited you here tonight, so I need not introduce you."

"I have indeed already had that pleasure," I said, bowing to the lady.

Did I detect a flash of jealousy upon Cynthia's pretty face? She turned to the older couple. "May I present Mr. Anders Vanderveer and Mrs. Vanderveer, Mr. Pearson's sister."

After making the necessary introductory remarks to the good man and wife, in whom I had no interest, I took a chair matching Mrs. Maycott's, separated from hers only by a small table of dark wood and oriental design. A servant arrived to present me with a glass of wine, and I accepted most gratefully. And there I sat, Mrs. Maycott smiling upon me, her red lips turned up with delightful impishness, and Mrs. Pearson, looking away.

"You work for our government, then?" asked Mr. Vanderveer, in a deep and booming voice. "Do you know the President?"

"I knew him during the war," I said. "Currently I am engaged in a project for Hamilton at Treasury, however, and have no contact with General Washington. I am led to believe, Mr. Pearson, that you have had some contact of late with Hamilton, or perhaps his men?"

"Not at all," he said. "Why should I?"

"I'm sure I cannot speculate. I hoped you would enlighten me."

Mrs. Vanderveer was still, in her mind, upon the topic of Washington, and had no interest in my sparring with her brother. "Do you not long to see him again?" she asked, her voice full of the worship only Washington could inspire among those who had never met him—and probably half who had.

I bowed from my seat. "Those of us who serve are not permitted to choose the terms upon which we serve."

"How they fuss," said Mr. Pearson. "I dine with Washington two times a month, and I may ask him to pass the salt as well as any man. He is like me, no better and, I pray, no worse."

"How is it that you are on such good terms with the President?" asked Mrs. Maycott. Her lips were upturned and her eyes sparkled.

"How should I not know the President?" Pearson returned.

"I do not know exactly how to respond," she said. "I only meant that, from my understanding, his inner circle is composed of government men, men he served with, and gentlemen from Virginia. It is my understanding you are none of those."

"I am from this city, madam," said Mr. Pearson in a loud voice. "A man need not be from Virginia to associate in the best company, and I might say that of Washington as well as he might say it of me. As for serving in the government, it is meaningless. Anyone may do so, as I am certain this fellow will inform you." He gestured toward me. "I dine with Washington because we are both men of consequence, so we must dine together or with inferiors."

Pearson spun his head so quickly I thought it might fly off entirely and pointed one of the stubby fingers on his oversized hand toward his brother-in-law, jabbing back and forth like the blade of an assassin. "What is it you say?"

"I said nothing, Jack," the gentleman answered, his voice a study of calm and reason.

"I heard you. You said *Bingham,* you rascal."

"I said no such thing," answered Vanderveer.

"May not a man say *Bingham* now and again?" I inquired.

Pearson was too far gone in some sort of fit to even hear me. "You suggest I dine with Washington because of my wife's friendship with Mrs. Bingham."

"Really, Jack," said the man's sister. "It hardly matters to us. We think it very grand that you know such people as the Binghams. We would never belittle such a connection."

Mr. Pearson now turned to Mrs. Maycott and attempted something like a smile. Perhaps at some earlier time in his life, before he allowed a pretty wife and fine house to convince him he was the emperor of the universe, he might have charmed a woman or two with that smile. If the day had been foggy or the candles dim, anything was possible. Now he appeared grotesque, a mask of human skin atop something diabolical and unsavory. Yet he clearly believed himself to be the embodiment of charm and sought to shore up his position by bringing to his side the only unattached woman in the room, always the jewel of greatest value in any gathering.

"Do you hear, Mrs. Maycott?" he said, his voice now a calm, unctuous vibrato. " 'Such people as the Binghams,' says my sister, as though she, the wife of a lawyer of but indifferent reputation, can sit in judgment of the first families of the nation."

"I think," answered the good lady, "that in this republic, there is no one family that may be elevated above another, as all are equal before the law."

From another, less charming, set of lips I supposed this comment might have launched an entirely new course of outraged oratory, but not so now. He merely smiled his death's-head smile. "A good joke, Mrs. Maycott. A very good joke."

"I should like to hear more of Captain Saunders's connection with Colonel Hamilton," said the widow, in a neutral tone.

"Oh, yes," said Mrs. Vanderveer, a drowning woman wrapping her arms about a piece of conversational flotsam. "Such exciting times there, I should think, with the bank and such."

Mr. Pearson would not be soothed. "Yes, yes, you must always flatter," he said to his sister. "You flatter me, you flatter my guests. What shall it get you?"

"I believe I was merely making an inquiry," said the lady.

"You've never *merely* done anything in your life, Flora, so let us not pretend otherwise." He turned to me. "Shall I tell you what it means to serve Hamilton at Treasury?"

"You may attempt to do so," I answered, "but as I'm the one who is so engaged, and as you are not, I cannot imagine you have much to say that will enlighten me."

Mrs. Pearson laughed and then covered her mouth. Her husband grimaced, as though this mirth had caused him physical pain. He then turned back to me. "Hamilton is a worm. Did you know that?"

"Once I cut him in twain," I said, and then leaned forward to whisper theatrically, "and now there are two of him."

"He is a worm, but he is a worm who does the businessmen's bidding. His bank is a ruse to trick the nation into funding a scheme to make Hamilton and his friends richer, but you may be sure I've taken advantage of it. Because of the bank, there is an excess of credit, and that means a man of significant commerce, such as myself, can find the money to invest in government issues when before it might have been difficult. I do not like Hamilton, but I will use him. What do you say to that?"

I sipped my wine. "It's all very interesting, but it does not precisely tell me what it means to serve Hamilton at Treasury."

"My partner in business once worked for Treasury, and he informed me in no uncertain terms that Hamilton is a prig with no imagination and no spirit."

I sat up straight. "Who is your partner?"

"William Duer. I thought all men knew that—or all men of substance, I suppose. Once you are drummed out of the army, you no longer hear the same things as the rest of us."

"Jack," said Cynthia.

"I say no more than the truth," Pearson said. "If he does not like the truth, let him stop up his ears. We have no shortage of candles. Where is the footman? Nate, bring us some soft wax for this gentleman's ears. He wants them stopped at once."

I closed my eyes and turned away, trying to shut out the noise, though I would not resort to candle wax to effect this aim. Pearson's words did not trouble me, not in the way he intended. If he wished to rub salt in the old wound, I could endure it. I turned not in pain but because I needed to think. He believed Duer was his partner, and yet the communication I had intercepted informed me, in no uncertain terms, that Duer was his enemy. And Duer had, most clearly, attempted to avoid being seen by Pearson at the Bingham house.

I understood then that there would be no answers to these questions without speaking to Duer, and Duer had returned to New York. I would have to follow him there. Cynthia was here, and Cynthia needed me, but I could no longer avoid the simple truth that I must go to New York to protect her.

I had turned away from Pearson and his harsh words, and then I had set my face in determination. It must have looked like pain, for I felt a hand upon mine, and when I looked up Mrs. Maycott was smiling at me with warm sympathy. Who was this good woman, I wondered, to feel so strongly for a stranger in what she thought was distress?

I cast her a glance and I smiled, hoping to show she had misunderstood my mood. Then I turned to Pearson. "What is the nature of your business with Duer?"

"What concern is that of yours?"

"I believe he is inquiring to be polite," Mr. Vanderveer said.

"I believe you are a fool," Pearson answered. "Well, Saunders, why do you wish to know? Did Hamilton send you to ask me? The Jew gets nothing, so he sends a drunken traitor, is that it?"

"I was invited here," I answered. "Hamilton did not send me, and this gentleman is correct. I merely make conversation."

"Make it about something else," Pearson said. "My business with Duer is private. We are engaged in a new venture, and we play it quietly. That is all you need to know."

It was not all I needed to know, but it was something. The entire world speculated on Pearson's declining capacity. What were the chances that William Duer would trust him with a secret venture?

Any further questions were forestalled by the arrival of a plump, buxom, and not unattractive serving girl. She informed us we might remove ourselves to the dining room. I was pleased to find myself next to Mrs. Maycott and not next to Mrs. Pearson, for I should have found that awkward. That lady did her best to avoid looking in my direction the entire evening, and though Mrs. Maycott made much polite conversation with me, we said nothing of further import—no matters of government or Washington or even accusations of malicious flattery. Mr. Pearson was the sole arbiter of conversational topics, and he chose to speak only of the excellence of his own food, the comfort of his dining chairs, and then, toward the end of the evening, the gripping narrative of his rise from son of the owner of an importation business to the exalted heights of being himself the owner of an importation business. Mrs. Maycott and Mrs. Vanderveer both gamely attempted to join the conversation, but Mr. Pearson would not have it. As for the lady of the house, she had, I could only presume, long ago abandoned all efforts at civil discourse.

I therefore endured pea soup, boiled potatoes with bacon, roasted pig, chicken in wine sauce, roasted apples in sugar, and a whipped syllabub—all of it without a single pleasant exchange. The wine, however, flowed. Mr. Pearson seemed unduly interested in his wife's consumption, commenting rather loudly when she finished her first glass and accepted a second, which went sadly unfinished. More than once, our eyes met over the embrace of this communion. She looked away. I did not. Mr. Pearson made the occasional unkind observation, but it altered neither conversation nor behavior. When Mrs. Pearson accepted a glass of port with her baked apples, her husband began such a paroxysm of tuts and clucks he sounded like a henhouse at feeding time.

"Have you not had enough to drink already?" he asked.

She now met her husband's eye, and her expression was dark and foreboding. Perhaps she had indeed had too much wine. "I believe I am the best judge."

"I think, of all possible judges, you may not be the best. The wife of one of the first men of the city ought to conduct herself with more sobriety. For all the world it appears as though you and that rascal are engaged in a tavern drinking contest." The reader may be surprised to learn that he gestured toward me when he spoke.

"Really, Jack," began Mr. Vanderveer.

"I'd advise you not to interfere," said Pearson. "It is a foolish thing for a man to wedge himself between another and his wife. In addition, that great belly of yours tells us you know nothing of when a person has had enough. Another baked apple, Anders?"

"There is no reason to be cruel," said Mrs. Vanderveer quietly.

"What is this? An entire sentence empty of flattery? All the toad-eating in the world shan't help you in the matter of my will, so be easy on it."

Mr. Vanderveer slapped the table. "I do object. That has never been our intention."

Pearson waved a hand in the air. "Yes, yes, don't be tedious." He pushed himself to his feet. "Well, it has been very good company. Now I am tired, and I must to bed. Good night to the lot of you." With that he left the room, leaving the rest of us in stunned silence and the unfortunate Mrs. Pearson with the responsibility of determining what must come next.

I, however, was not yet ready for the festivities to end, and I rose from my chair, excused myself to the company, and hurried after my host. He had stepped only a few paces out of the room and was on the landing at the stairwell, where only a single candle illuminated the gloom, when I caught him. He contemplated the darkness and had turned to call for a servant, when he saw me instead.

"What, Saunders? What is this?"

"I wanted to speak with you in private for a moment, if you will."

"I've nothing to say to you. I ought never to have had you in my home. I shall speak to Mrs. Maycott about what manner of person she claims as a friend."

I stared at him, his face—aging and on the very cusp of becoming elderly—in the dim light, the yellow flame reflecting off the yellow teeth. He was frightened to be alone with me.

All I'd had to drink rushed about in my head, and I forced myself to focus. "I want to know about you and Duer."

"I won't speak of it. I am to say nothing, and I shall say nothing."

"What of your properties in Southwark? You've lost them or sold them. And then there is the matter of your loan from the Bank of the United States. I understand your payments are past due, and you won't even appear when summoned. Are you unprepared to talk about that?"

Pearson's face twisted into a grotesquerie of hatred. All signs of the rugged man, the handsome man he had once been, were blasted away by an explosion of fury that altered, in a single flash, the landscape of his countenance.

"Do you mean to have your revenge, Saunders? All those years ago, you fled Philadelphia and I happened to marry the girl you once set your cap at. So now you must hound me?"

I could not show how bitter his words made me, and I would not dismiss my feelings for Cynthia—not for his satisfaction or my advantage. I said nothing.

Pearson seemed to grow calmer. He said, "Mrs. Maycott seems fond enough of you, and she's an excellent widow to catch. Put your mind to that, if you dare, and leave me and my family alone. You are not welcome inside this house again—or any longer, for that matter. I go to bed, but I shall tell my servants that if you are not gone in a quarter hour you are to be removed forcibly."

Pearson now turned from me and ascended the dark staircase. He did not pause to say good night, which was rude.

When I returned to the sitting room, Mr. and Mrs. Vanderveer were rising and thanking their hostess for an enjoyable evening. Perhaps it was a different, earlier evening they mentioned. They spoke as though the meal had come to a natural and pleasant conclusion. They spoke of the lateness of the hour, the goodness of the food. They thanked the hostess and departed.

Then it was Mrs. Maycott's turn. "You are a lovely hostess, Cynthia. Thank you so much for having me."

"Joan." She cast her eyes downward.

Mrs. Maycott raised a finger to her lips. "It need not be said. We are friends. I shall show myself out. I hope you have no objection if I first speak to your cook. That chicken was marvelous, and I would learn how she does it."

"Of course."

The two ladies embraced, and Mrs. Maycott allowed me to take her hand, which was very smooth for the time of year. Then she was gone, leaving me alone with Mrs. Pearson. We were both standing, looking to where Mrs. Maycott had gone, not quite sure what to say.

"She is charming," said Mrs. Pearson. "And they say her husband left her wealthy."

"It is good to know that husbands may be good for something," I said. "Such as leaving money to their wives."

I feared I may have exceeded my limits, but Mrs. Pearson burst out into a shrill, girlish laugh such as I never thought to hear again.

"Captain Ethan Saunders, let us take a drink in the library."

"Mrs. Cynthia Pearson, your husband has informed me that if I am not gone in a quarter hour, I shall be tossed out by the servants."

She smiled at me. "I've learned a thing or two after a decade of marriage. The servants are loyal to me. And the library is well removed far from Mr. Pearson's room. There is no better place to go in the house to avoid his notice."

"Then, Mrs. Pearson, let us go by all means. I do love a good library."

Her pretty plump girl led us to the library, where a fire already burned. The girl lit a number of candles and provided us with an excellent bottle of port. She was good enough to pour a glass for each of us, and equally good enough to disappear afterward.

Cynthia let out a sigh and sat in a high-backed chair across from me and, just like that, something changed. That one small gesture did it. It was as though a master carpenter presented two pieces of wood and they fit together with such preordained snugness that they clicked upon joining. So it was that Cynthia, in her good-natured and indulgent sigh, in her uncomplicated slide into a high-backed chair, put me at my ease. I was not an unwelcome intrusion from her past but something far more pleasing.

"It was wrong of Joan to invite you here tonight," Cynthia said, studying her port. "I think she is mischievous."

"Such old friends as we are might be in the same room without mischief."

"It was not what I meant. I wish you had not seen Mr. Pearson in one of his moods."

"I understand, and yet I have seen it. Mrs. Pearson, you asked for my help before. You asked me to find your husband because you believed yourself and your children in danger. I cannot believe you wished me to find him for his own sake."

"You mustn't say that," she said. "We cannot be together if you speak to me so."

"Then I won't speak to you so. It will be all business. I never mind a deception or two if it is to cover one's own tracks, but you must own up if discovered. Did you ask Mrs. Maycott to invite me here and to do it publicly at the party so all could see it was not of your doing?"

She blushed deeply. "How did you know?"

"Only a feeling. It was a clever maneuver."

"Thank you. I did learn a thing or two from you during the war. I always loved to hear of your tricks and schemes, and at last I had a chance to put into place a little scheme of my own."

"To what end?" I asked. "I would like to flatter myself that you wished no more than my company, but I cannot think it so. Can you not tell me more of what you know?"

"It began some six weeks ago," she said. "Mr. Pearson has never been the most even-tempered of men, but he grew much more irritable than usual. And he began to have around the house a very uncouth sort of man, very western-looking, with a scar upon his face."

"I know who he is. He works for William Duer. Have you met Duer?"

"Of course. Several times. Philadelphia society, you know. When he worked for Hamilton and lived in Philadelphia, our families came into contact often."

"When did your husband start doing business with Duer?"

She shook her head. "I don't know."

"And the reason you contacted me?"

"When Mr. Pearson disappeared last week, I hardly thought anything of it. That man Lavien came around, wishing to ask questions. He'd been around before, and Mr. Pearson had refused to speak to him. Now he wished to know where my husband was and what I knew of his business. It was uncomfortable, but nothing more. Then a man calling himself Reynolds—a tall bald man with an Irish accent—came to see me. He said I must tell Lavien nothing, and if I wished to preserve the safety of my husband, my children, and myself, I would not trouble myself with things that did not concern me."

The tall Irishman. Yet another man pretending to be Reynolds and making himself conspicuously my enemy. I had no notion of what it could mean, but it made me uneasy. "And that was when you sought me out?" I asked.

She nodded. "I would hardly have concerned myself about Mr. Pearson's absence. It was not his first, after all. But once the matter involved my children, I did not know what to do, and yours was the only name I could think of. I am sorry to have troubled you with all this."

"You must not say so. It is my duty to help you."

"And," she said, "it is good to see you after so many years."

It was at this point that the door opened and Mr. Pearson entered the room, red in the face, red in the eyes. His vest was unbuttoned and his shirt disheveled, and his mouth was twisted into a sneer. In one hand he held a silver-handled horsewhip. In the other, he dragged along a boy—perhaps eight or nine years of age—by the collar of a dull cotton sleeping gown. The boy's hair was mussed from sleep, but he was wide awake. And terrified.

The boy looked very much like Cynthia, with his fair hair and even features and a nose the image of hers. He looked like Pearson too, particularly in the eyes, though his were red with fear and confusion, not his father's diabolical mania.

Mrs. Pearson stood. "Jeremy," she said.

"Mama," he said, very softly, seeming both tired and terrified.

"I told you to leave," Pearson hissed at me.

I rose to my feet slowly, careful to observe everything with crisp clarity. I saw the whip in Pearson's hand, I saw the fear in the boy's eyes, I saw the faded burn mark on the boy's wrist, and the matching scar on his mother's. Someone was clearly fond of burning wrists.

"I shall leave the moment I know all is in order here."

"The ordering of my house is not your concern. My whore of a wife has bewitched the servants. They cannot confront you, for all are injured or frightened or unable to be found. I have therefore taken the trouble to awaken the boy. I shan't threaten to hurt you, Saunders, since I hear you are too pathetic to mind a sound beating, but the child is another matter. If you are not gone from this house in one minute, I shall whip the boy bloody."

"He is your son," I whispered.

"And so I may do as I like."

Cynthia was pale and trembling, and she held out her hands ever so slightly, from stiff vertical arms. Tears fell down her cheek. She bit her lip. I thought she must be a madwoman by now, gone into some lunatic maternal world of fear for her child, but she looked at me, and when she spoke, her voice was steady and strong and rational. "You must go." The last word came out smooth and easy, not a command, as in telling me I must leave at once, but as a qualifier. I must leave in this particular instance. The future was another matter.

"Well," I said to Pearson, "don't mutilate your heir on my account. I've things to do, you know, taverns to visit. The life of a drunkard traitor. Very busy."

"See that you do busy yourself with your wasted life," said Pearson. "You were far better off vomiting in alleys than troubling yourself in the affairs of gentlemen. You are too unrefined to travel in the circles you covet."

"It is interesting you should say that," I answered, "for when I spoke of that very topic to Miss Emily Fiddler—I mean the aunt, of course, not the niece, for there is no talking to that one, as I need not tell you. In any event, do you know what your good friend Miss Fiddler mentioned to me about the refined circles in which you yourself—"

I made it no further, for Pearson grabbed his son's tousled hair and yanked hard and mercilessly. The boy let out a horrible cry of pain, and silent tears, to match his mother's, poured down his face. His face then turned dark and angry, a juvenile reflection of his father's, but there was more there too. A silent resolve to endure his suffering in silence.

"You will leave my house!" Pearson did not cry or shout or bellow. He screamed. It was the voice of lunacy, of a man who has no sense of proportion or propriety, and it terrified me, for I had no alternative but to abandon these innocents to his insanity.

Then came another voice.

"I am so sorry. I did not mean to intrude."

We all stood, suspended in time for a moment, as though this mad tableau were something deeply private and personal that had been exposed. The voice had come from the doorway, but it was no servant's voice. I turned to look at the figure, pretty and perfectly composed, her red lips pursed in the most wicked of smiles, as though she knew exactly what she saw, exactly what she did. No argument, no violence, no reason could have diffused Pearson's rage. But shame was another matter. She understood the power of shame and wielded it like the whip in Pearson's hand. It was the widow Joan Maycott.

"I am so sorry to trouble you," said Mrs. Maycott, now acting as though she had ventured into nothing more troubling than a casual acting out of a scene from a Jacobean revenge play. "I spent rather more time with the cook than I had intended, and upon hearing voices I thought I would take my leave once more."

Pearson muttered something that might have been "Yes, yes, very good," or something to that effect. Then he let go of his son's hair.

"Well, then, I go. Captain Saunders, I have a coach outside, if you require transport. It is considerably colder than it was earlier."

I looked over at Cynthia, who offered me the slightest of nods. She knew her husband better than ever I could, and I would have to trust her as to whether my absence or presence would offer her greater security. For the moment, she seemed to believe herself best served by my departure.

I stepped forward, passed Pearson and his poor, terrified child, and stood by Mrs. Maycott. Then I turned around once more. "One of these uncooperative servants you mentioned will give me my coat and hat, I trust."

"At the door," Pearson hissed, a voice like air escaping a bladder.

I hardly cared about my coat and hat—but I had turned to take one last measure of Mrs. Pearson. Her husband was facing me and could not see her face, could not see her red lips as she silently mouthed her parting words: *Help me.*

Once outside, I saw that it had, indeed, grown brutally cold during my time in the Pearson house. I was used to the cold, and it was not such a long walk to my rooms, but I could hardly refuse the offer from Mrs. Maycott. I thanked her once more and helped her into the coach, and we began to ride through the empty night streets, populated only by the watch and drunks and whores and, mysteriously, a man driving a small group of goats, possibly not his own. I was not entirely certain what to say, but Mrs. Maycott saved me from awkwardness.

"I do not envy you," she said, "being caught in the storm of Mr. Pearson's fury. I have heard more than once from Mrs. Pearson of his temper, but I never before witnessed it."

"Nor I. I wish I never had, for I know not what I can do."

"I have no doubt you will do what you must."

"And what is that?"

"You cannot leave that lady and her children at the hands of that beast."

"There is nothing I can do for her. I can offer her no refuge, and she would not take it were I capable. Imagine the damage to her reputation. No one will care what Pearson has done, only that his wife has left him."

To this she said nothing, as though I were too foolish to engage seriously.

I thought it a good idea to raise another subject. "You mentioned the other night that you know Duer. Do you understand the nature of his business connections to Pearson?"

"No, but I do not know him well. It is, however, possible that it may have something to do with the Million Bank. That is one of Duer's new ventures, and it takes up much of his time at present."

"The Million Bank. Do you mean Pearson is going to invest in it?"

"Very likely," said Mrs. Maycott.

"So he will take the money he borrowed from the Bank of the United States to help launch a rival bank?"

"It is possible," she said. "Why do you care? You said before that you work for Hamilton, but I know that's not true. You were merely attempting to rouse Mr. Pearson. And yet I cannot help but wonder if you are a supporter of Hamilton and his bank."

"You sound so astonished. Would it trouble you if I were?"

"We live in astonishing times," she said, and her tone suggested she was not answering my question at all, but one she wished I had asked. "We have witnessed the most remarkable revolution the world has ever known, and the establishment of a republican government that has the chance to be the glory of mankind. How can I not be troubled by something that threatens to undermine our national good?"

"You will forgive me if I suspect your interest runs deeper than mere admiration for the cause of the nation."

"Then you are mistaken. I care about nothing so deeply as the nation. It is for that reason I am suspicious of Hamilton, who, I believe, does not love republican government. I believe he favors a British system, one of monarchy and corruption."

"I have heard such things before, and while I do not doubt that Hamilton is overly fond of the British system, I have seen no evidence that this fondness represents a threat to ours."

"This government was formed as a means of confederating the several states," she said, "but Hamilton uses his influence to strengthen the federal seat at every turn. States must now bow before their masters in Philadelphia."

Here was a much different conversation than that which I would have chosen. I could not yet guess what Mrs. Maycott was, nor how to measure her interest in these things. I believed she knew something, but I did not see the value of rehashing the debate from several years past on the validity of the new Constitution "Yes, this is the old anti-Federalist argument, and I know well its merits, but only time can tell which side is correct, and I am disinclined to rail against the federal government until it has tried the experiment. The anti-Federalists like to rage against the danger of centralized power, but I've seen no evidence of any harm coming from it."

"What say you then to Hamilton's whiskey excise, which has unduly oppressed poor farmers, forcing them into debt and ruin that he might fund his speculative projects?"

The whiskey excise again. "I wish you would speak plainly. What is this to you?"

"I am a patriot. That is all you need to know. I love my country, and I know you do. I do not think Hamilton does. I only ask that you be open to that possibility."

I though of Mr. Reynolds as she said this, and Hamilton's secretive dealings with him. Hamilton was not all he seemed, that much was certain, but I did not believe him to be the enemy of the nation that the Jeffersonians—and apparently Mrs. Maycott—painted him. "I am open to all possibilities," I said at last.

"That is why I trust you. Oh, here we are at your house."

How convenient—particularly as I had not told her where I lived.

I opened the door on my side of the coach. "I thank you for the ride, but I must say something. I can't guess the nature of your involvement in these matters, and I do not expect you to tell me. I can only say that if you know anything of import, I hope you will let me know."

She smiled at me, the glowing glory of her lips illuminated by the streetlight. "You must not suspect me of all people, Captain Saunders. I believe that as of this moment I am the best friend you have."

Joan Maycott

Spring 1791

The following afternoon, Mr. Dalton and Jericho Richmond gathered in the sitting room of Mr. Skye's house. Our host had prepared a meal of pigeon and dumplings, and though I ate but little I took more than my share of whiskey. Even so, I could not feel its effect. Only a few days before, I had been a grieving widow, a victim who had lost everything. I had, since then, done so much. Why could I not achieve things seemingly impossible? I had done so already.

I was tired, having had so little sleep, and my hand was cramped from writing past the dawn. After leaving the main house I'd gone to find Ruth, who would never again be called Lactilla. She, at my request, gathered together the other slaves. With quill and ink and Tindall's heavy paper, I'd written out individual false traveling papers, identifying them by names and description as free Negroes. To each I'd given fifty dollars. It was no small portion of the wealth I'd taken from Tindall, but I could hardly have sent them off into the world penniless. I'd taken away their

master and, unwilling to bear the burden of sending them off into a hor-
rifying unknown, I had instead taken on the burden of helping to make
for each a better life. At least a freer one.

Now, though I had not slept the previous night, I was fully awake
with the friends who had helped to shape my life here in the West. The
three men could talk about but one thing. Word had spread throughout
the settlement, probably throughout the four counties, that Colonel
Holt Tindall had hanged himself. No one had yet heard of Phineas's confession, and perhaps no one had troubled themselves to observe the blow
upon Tindall's skull. I believed there would be discoveries yet to come,
but not yet, and I hoped I might use them to advantage.

"It's hard to believe," Skye said, "that a man like that would suddenly
take upon himself a conscience." He was bent forward in his chair, holding his glass of whiskey between the palms of both hands, and he struck
me as a man hunkered down upon the fringes of a battlefield. Great and
cataclysmic things were coming, and some part of him knew it.

"I don't believe him a man apt to take his own life," Dalton said.
"There must have been something else—a painful illness, perhaps, that
would kill him in the end. This might've been his way of beating the
thing. It would be more like the old bastard."

"Something will come out," said Jericho. "You may depend upon it."
And now he looked at me, hard and cold. He knew something, or suspected it, which I did not like. I wished the information to be mine alone
to control.

It was time to speak. "Tindall did not hang himself," I said. "He was
executed for what he did to Andrew. I could not depend upon the law,
and so I depended upon myself."

All three men stared at me.

"Come now," said Dalton. "You don't expect me to believe a woman
was capable of forcing Tindall to put a noose around his neck, let alone
hoisting him up over the rafters? I'll wager you don't know how to tie a
noose."

I did not know how to tie a noose, but as for the other, I did not know
why it was so unthinkable. Phineas was not so much larger than I, and
he had done it all. If I were a man, the question would not have been
raised. Yet I saw no reason to pursue this now. There might be much to

be gained if I could make them see how others liked to aid me. "The boy, Phineas, helped me."

"Phineas?" Skye said. "I thought he hated you."

"Phineas is confused. Not yet a man, no longer a child, he's been through more than anyone should be asked to endure. But, in the end, he knew who his true enemy was."

"Why is that?" asked Jericho. "Because you told him? You said, *Let's kill Tindall,* and he did it? Or did you have to cast your witch's spell first?" Dalton began to say something to silence him, but Jericho held out a hand in defiance. "And now what? We wait for him to be caught, so he can link you to the murder, and then us?"

Perhaps I ought to have hated being so challenged, but I did not. I liked it. All three of them would have their doubts; better they should be voiced, and better if the questions were asked harshly by Jericho so the others would feel inclined to aid me. Perhaps neither would challenge him. Dalton might prefer to keep an open mind, and Skye might not wish to confront Jericho directly, but it was of no matter. They would counter his arguments in their own minds. They would silently resist him, resent his harshness to a grieving lady, and that, it seemed to me, would make them all the more agreeable.

"Phineas has gone off to the wilderness to kill Indians," I explained, "but first he left a letter with Mr. Brackenridge confessing to the crime and making himself the sole actor in it. He seems enamored of the idea of being an outlaw."

"This is fantastical," Jericho said. "I am sorry, Mrs. Maycott. I know you've suffered, but you've also sold my home out from under me, and I must speak the truth. How do we even know you were there?"

I set forth on the table what remained of the banknotes Phineas had given me.

Skye picked them up and looked through them. "It looks like she was there," he said.

"Colonel Tindall thought he was above the law," I said. "Now he is not."

"And what about you?" Jericho asked. "Are you above the law?"

"I am in the right, which is much the same thing. Mr. Richmond, you act as though I somehow put you in this situation. I am not the one who passed an excise law or enforced it here with blood and murder. I have been made a sacrifice to the greed of men back east—men like Alexander Hamilton and William Duer, who have turned their backs on the Revolution in order to fill their purses."

"Listen to you," he said. "You are putting yourself in the middle of affairs that are not your concern."

I slapped my hand hard against the table, rattling the dishes. "I believe, sir, I have been thrust into the middle of these affairs, and that makes them my concern. Did not William Duer himself lie to my husband to convince him to trade his war debt for land—land he knew to be useless and debt he knew to be valuable, and yet he told us just the opposite? Someone might object that we ought to have known better, that we should not have been so easily cozened, but he claimed proximity to Hamilton himself. He claimed to speak nearly on behalf of the government."

"No one doubts his villainy," Richmond said.

I would not let him continue. "We come here, to this wasteland, and find that Duer's man Tindall rules over us with a tyrannical fist. And then Hamilton's whiskey tax, enforced by Tindall, drives us all to ruin. It is a network of greed and evil and oppression—all we stood against in the war. All the evil we have suffered can be set before those three: Tindall, Duer, and Hamilton most of all. He is the master whom the others serve. It is he who would turn our republic into an oligarchy. Duer and Tindall are but the hands. Hamilton is the mind, and so I hate him above all others."

"It's a pretty speech," Skye said, "and what you say is nothing but truth, but I don't believe you say these things only for truth's sake. You obviously have something on your mind. Best you let us hear it now."

I steeled myself, for what I was about to propose was certainly madness, yet I believed it could be done. "Mr. Brackenridge believes he can make a sale within the next month. Perhaps even sooner. But thanks to Tindall's generosity, we need not wait before deciding what to do."

"We will find somewhere else to set up," said Mr. Dalton. "Buy a new still and begin production once more."

Mr. Skye spooned a portion of the stew into his mouth and then wiped his lips with a napkin. "I don't see how. No matter where we go, we will still face the excise. Even if we flee the four counties for Kentucky or Virginia, we will face the whiskey tax and there will be established distillers to resent our intrusion into their business."

"This money from Tindall is to be split among us. I cannot tell you what to do with your portion," I said. "I can only tell you that for my part I will use this and what I get for my ground-rent lease to right these wrongs."

"You mean revenge, don't you? Revenge against whom?" asked Mr. Skye. "Do you mean to serve Hamilton and Duer as you did Tindall?"

Here was my moment to be careful in how I spoke—careful but commanding. I would need to convince them to follow me, but I would also need to convince them of my boldness, to show them I was determined and capable but not mad.

"It is precisely what I mean." I spoke with cool determination, the end result of careful deliberation. "It is they who conspired against us and continue to conspire against us. What is more, they conspire against the nation by trying to unmake the principles of the Revolution."

Mr. Dalton looked upon Mr. Skye with astonishment. Only Jericho Richmond acted as though what I proposed was of no moment. He set down his bowl, poured himself a whiskey, and watched his companions closely.

"You've lost your mind, lass," said Mr. Skye, the harshness of the words belied by his gentle tone. "No one here blames your wanting it, mind, but you can't take revenge against Alexander Hamilton. How will you do it?"

"I know precisely how," I said. "It was the subject of my novel. I wrote of how a man sought revenge against speculators, and I believe the principles I worked upon in my novel can apply in actuality."

"But it is pointless," said Mr. Dalton. "Even if it were possible to hurt these men in any significant way, what should we gain by doing it?"

"Let me explain to you," I said. "Listen carefully, for you will need to convince at least some of your whiskey boys to sign on. And why should they not? We are all hurt by this tax. If we can take just three or four more men with us, we shall be able to avenge ourselves and maybe even preserve the ideals of the Revolution. We can save our country from its own government."

Mr. Skye, the only one present who was familiar with the machinations of my lost novel, slowly nodded his head. "When you told me of your fictive story, I thought it remarkable in how very plausible it was. The scheme was audacious, yet it might actually have worked. But when you speak of saving the country, I am far more skeptical. If this thing were to be done, you might destroy the country in saving it."

"What of it?" I asked. "If this is our country—if it has become nothing but a haven for callous rich men and the lapdogs who would enforce their policies of greed—why should we not risk its destruction?"

"Because we're all of us patriots," said Richmond. "Does that answer your question?"

"What does it mean to be a patriot?" I asked. "You love the America in your head and your heart, but is that the same America that takes from poor men money they don't have so rich men can have a corrupt bank? Is that why you fought in the war? Is that why Andrew fought? Is that why your friends died? They died for liberty, not so that oppression might spring from nearer tyrants. Hamilton's bank is not just the newest incarnation of their greed, it is a beast that threatens to destroy everything we believe in."

"But would you really wish to see the nation brought to its knees, reeling in chaos?" asked Skye.

"We all of us here believe in liberty and freedom and republican government," I said, "but does that mean we must obey any government that claims to uphold those principles while, at the same time, openly and brazenly pursuing a course of subjugation? Less than ten years after the Revolution, and look at what we have wrought: greed, oligarchy, corruption, and slavery. It is better this nation be crushed, better we destroy this false beginning and begin anew in the hopes of doing things properly. Is that not preferable to permitting something rotten and insidious to dress itself up as glorious and just? If we do nothing, if we take our little share of wealth and turn our backs now, in future generations, when rank corruption masquerades as liberty, it will be upon our shoulders. True patriots will then ask why we who were there to witness our nation at the crossroads did nothing."

I had not planned to make so impassioned a speech, but now that the words had come out, I knew they were true. And from the looks upon their faces, I knew my friends believed them too.

Dalton said nothing for a long time. Then, at last, he looked at Skye. "You think it possible we can do this thing she speaks of? Not that it ought to be done, but that it *can* be—that the four of us and a few more, so small a number, can do it?"

"I do," said Skye. "It won't be easy, but why can we not do whatever we wish? Why can we not do whatever our minds conceive of?"

These men had changed the world once before. They had fought in the most important revolution in human history and redrawn the boundaries of government power for all time. Who was to say they could not do as much again?

Jericho Richmond set down his glass. "The two of you are under her spell. If this woman tells you to ride your horse off a cliff, will you do it?"

"Mr. Richmond, what have I done that you would speak to me so?" I demanded. "I thought we were friends."

"We are," he answered, "but I will not throw myself into the maw of your madness for no better reason than revenge."

I poured myself a fresh mug of whiskey. "No, I suppose not. But will you throw yourself into the maw of my madness if doing so would make you very wealthy?"

I now had his attention. "Perhaps. If you convince me your plan might work."

I began to speak, explaining to them the plan I had constructed, its dangers and nuances, and how it should leave us avenged, the country righted, and our efforts rewarded with great wealth. I spoke at length, at first fearing I'd said too much and not parsed out the information slowly or gently enough, but questions soon began to arise, from both Dalton and Skye and then even from Jericho. I made certain the whiskey continued to pour. By the end of the evening, my scheme had turned from an idea to a rebellion.

Ethan Saunders

I was now torn between my two goals, for if I was to discover the truth behind these threats against Mrs. Pearson, I would have to go to New York and learn more about Duer's scheme and how the upcoming launch of the Million Bank related to these threats against Hamilton's bank. Yet, how could I leave Philadelphia when Cynthia was under siege from her own husband?

It was Lavien who helped to resolve this dilemma. A few days after the dinner at the Pearson house, he summoned me a little after noon to Clark's Inn on Chestnut, across from the Statehouse, at the sign of the Coach and Horses. I was pleased with the invitation, for I was hungry, and Clark's is always an inviting place to dine for the entertaining way in which they prepare their meat. It turns on a great spit over a hot fire, and the turning is done by a pair of yellow dogs who run steadily in a large wheel, like overgrown squirrels.

Leonidas and I arrived before Lavien, for I saw no sign of him, but we were in time for the dogs' final exertions, so soon there was hot beef, boiled potatoes, and freshly baked rolls to enjoy. Clark's had no whiskey, so I settled for rum, and Leonidas led us to a table that offered us a good view of the door. Lavien arrived in a quarter hour, accompanied by an aging man, perhaps near sixty, wearing a once-fine brown suit that was now, in places, faded and spotted. He had a very erect posture and strode in slow, deliberate steps, affecting, I thought, a kind of gentility that perhaps did not come naturally.

Leonidas and I were near done with our fine repast, well roasted by the Labradors, and we rose to meet the men.

"Ah," said Lavien. "I'm sorry to keep you, but I'm glad you are here. I want you to meet this man. Albert Turner, may I present Captain Saunders and his associate, Leonidas."

Turner bowed very deeply. "Yes, very good," he said. "Captain Saunders, yes. Of course, sir. Your name is well known to me."

Rarely could that be desirable. I bowed, and we all sat. Lavien called for drinks.

"I am always pleased to make a new acquaintance," I said, though it was a wretched lie. I could not have desired less to meet this man. "Yet I suspect there is some particular reason I have been summoned. Something out of the way of ordinary sociability."

"Mr. Turner lived in Philadelphia during much of the war," said Lavien. "Indeed, he was not always the greatest friend of the United States, for he served the British cause."

Turner smiled sheepishly once more, this time opening his mouth, and showing me that the better portion of his teeth were but a memory. "Many people did, you know, and had things gone otherwise we'd have been heroes. Merely the chance of history. You cannot blame a man for taking up the cause of his native land."

"All in the past," said Lavien, careful to affect an air of easy civility. "The war is over, and we have no interest in punishing one set of men because their consciences dictated a course of action different from another set."

"Exactly so," said Turner. The tankards of beer had now arrived, and he drank quickly and deeply, as if afraid he might soon be asked to leave and wished to take as much drink as he could first. The end result was a rather large spill on his coat, which he brushed at with evident embarrassment. "These questions of loyalty and allegiance during the war are but matters of curiosity now, though they were of the greatest import then."

I believed I now understood what this was about. It concerned Fleet. I stood up. "I told you, Lavien, that I didn't want you looking into this."

"Yes," said Lavien, "but I didn't listen. I see in you an asset to this government and to Hamilton, but as long as your name lies in shadow, the government cannot make use of you. It is my duty to ignore your wishes."

I would not dignify his flattery with a response. "Come, Leonidas."

Lavien stood. "Sit down, Captain Saunders. You do wish to hear this."

I did not like to be ordered around, but I knew from how he spoke that regret would eat away at me if I did not listen. I had no choice, really. I sat down.

"Mr. Turner," said Lavien, "is the British agent to whom you and Fleet were alleged to sell messages. It was his correspondence that was found in your things. He, of course, fled once he received word that you had been apprehended and only returned to Philadelphia after the war."

I stared at him and then turned to Lavien. "He can say nothing I want to hear."

"You believe that," said Lavien, "because you believe he will condemn Fleet, but it is not the case."

I felt myself biting the inside of my cheek, but I said nothing.

"Very right," said Turner. "I never had anything to do with you *or* Major Fleet. Yours were the names I was directed to use by my contact. I did not know why, nor did I care. It sounds rather unkind, I know, but it was war, and we did not trouble ourselves with such things. You were no better than I, I am sure, for it is easy to overlook the harm to innocents when you cannot see or know them."

It was true enough. "Go on."

"I was authorized to buy secrets from various contacts, and one of them insisted that I contact him using your names instead of my own. It was these letters that Mr. Lavien informs me were found in your things, though I cannot say how they made their way there. When I heard of your capture, I did not think of it, for I presumed that my contact was but the middleman, though I was surprised to learn that you and Major Fleet were real men. I always presumed they were noms de guerre."

"You are saying that our betrayal was planned?" I asked. "For how long did you use these names before we were accused?"

"Oh, six months at least. Maybe nine. Then we were betrayed, each in our own way."

Lavien leaned forward and then back. This was as much enthusiasm as he ever demonstrated. "For the betrayal to have happened in such a manner, it would have had to have been done by your contact. Who else could have known enough to ruin all involved?"

I did not like it that Lavien had proceeded without my permission, but I could not deny my excitement. This conspiracy had been the great mystery of my life, its principal turning point. It seemed that now I was to learn the truth behind it, and the truth would not condemn Fleet. "Did you know his name?" I asked, keeping my voice steady.

"I was not meant to," answered Turner, "but I was cleverer than he thought. He believed me nothing but a blunderer, and I suppose I was, but even so, I was no fool. And he was always too impressed with himself. Still is, I suppose, but vicious too. I have no doubt he would kill me if he were to see me, for though it would be but my word against his, and the war is long over, he would not like it if I were to tell the world what I know."

I tried to speak, but my breath caught. I tried again. "What is his name?" I did not need to ask. I already knew.

"His name is Pearson, Jacob Pearson."

I was on my feet and halfway out the door when I felt Lavien's hand around my arm, pulling me back to my table. He must have weighed a third less than I did, yet his strength was great, his weight perfectly proportioned. I do not know that I could have broken free of his grip.

"Wait." His voice was quiet but undeniably commanding.

"Do not tell me to wait," I answered, though I had stopped without meaning to. "You cannot preach caution to me. He destroyed my life, and now he destroys hers. He destroys his own *children,* for the love of God! How can you bid me wait?"

"You misunderstand me," said Lavien. "I do not ask you for restraint. Do you forget to whom you speak? I only ask you to wait."

"For what am I to wait?" I asked, my teeth nearly clenched.

"You are not thinking clearly," he said. "You have allowed your reason to be clouded by rage. You do not see what I see."

"And what do you see?" I demanded.

He looked over at Turner. "He's not telling us everything."

I glanced over at the old man, nervously twisting a ring around his finger. I had not visited any anger upon him. No, not so much as a single harsh word had I offered him, for I heard his original plea, and though I could not love a traitor, I could not condemn a man who loves his own country, even when it is in the wrong. I had said as much, and he had believed me, he had seen it in me. And yet he nervously twisted that ring about his finger. I looked at him, and he looked away. I now turned to Lavien.

"He's not telling us everything," I said.

I sat down. Lavien sat down. Leonidas had never arisen, yet he seemed to understand our mood at once. "There's more," he said.

I nodded. To Turner I said, "There's more."

Turner continued to twist his ring. His skin turned red. "I have told you all—all you can care about. Of course there are more secrets. I was a spy, and it was war. But I have nothing else to say that would concern you."

"There's more," I said. "Where shall we take him, your house, Lavien?"

"I cannot bring violence under the roof where my wife and children live," he said. "I am a different man at home. It must be that way."

"I live in a boardinghouse," I said. "We cannot question a man there."

"Rent a room here," said Leonidas. "It is a loud tavern. Nothing will be heard."

"Clever man," I answered.

"One moment," said Turner, whose expression had changed from terror to confusion and back again. "Mr. Lavien, you told me there would be a reward for my information, and no consequences so long as I told you the truth. I have told you nothing but the truth."

"I told you that you must tell us the entire truth," Lavien answered. "Captain Saunders believes you are lying. I believe you are lying. Leonidas believes you are lying. You may tell us everything now, or you may tell us everything in private."

"I have nothing more to say," answered Turner.

Lavien tossed a coin to Leonidas. "Be so good as to get us a room. As far away as possible from the main room."

Leonidas left to tend to his task.

Turner continued to glance about the room nervously. "You cannot force me to go against my will. I shall simply cry out."

"If you do that," I said, "we shall be forced to tell the crowd that you were a British spy during the war and that you participated in a conspiracy against patriots. We would not be able to save you from the mob even if we wanted to. If you want to live, you will try your luck with us."

"I choose not to." He stood but then sat down at once. I saw that Lavien had placed his sharp knife to Turner's back, at his kidney.

In a moment, Leonidas signaled to us that he had secured the room. Lavien said to Turner, "If you do not come with us quietly and easily, you will die. Do you believe it?"

He nodded.

"Good. If you come with us, if you cooperate, you will live. It cannot be any simpler."

The three of us rose and walked toward Leonidas, me first, then Turner, then Lavien. We went up a set of stairs and then another, and Leonidas led us to a room in the back. The doors to three of the other five rooms were closed, and we could hear the creaking of floors, the shuffling of furniture, the low moans of passion. The rooms here were used by whores, which was good. Customers would be used to the occasional strange noise.

The room itself was just fifteen feet by ten, but it would do. Once we were inside, Lavien locked the door. I gazed around at a small dirty mattress, a pair of chairs, a small table for drinks or food. Lavien pushed Turner into one of the chairs. He shut the window, and the room grew dark.

"I have not known Mr. Lavien long," I said to Turner, "but my impression, from my limited experience, is that you ought to be very afraid."

"If I tell you all," said Turner, "you will kill me."

"It is a possibility," said Lavien, "but not a certainty. It depends, of course, on what you have to say and how hard you make us work for it. But if you *don't* tell us, we will try everything to make you speak, and if you still remain quiet we will certainly kill you. You have all but admitted that there is more, so we have no reason not to pursue it."

Lavien used his knife to cut a strip of cloth from the stained cotton mattress cover.

"We'll not have the deposit on the room returned," said Leonidas.

"What are you doing?" Turner asked.

"A little trick I learned in Surinam," Lavien answered. "You cut off part of a man's own body, place it in his mouth, and then gag him. Let him sit with his own bloody flesh in his mouth for a time—it works best in the hot sun, but here will do—and he usually becomes cooperative. The men I learned from loved to use the penis. It is symbolic, but I find it too devastating. A man without a penis will often drift into despair. I like to use an ear."

Turner started to rise. "No, you won't—"

"Sit down!" Lavien cried. His voice was so hard, so commanding, it would have taken a man with a godlike will to resist. Turner sat down.

"Leonidas, hold his arms behind his back. Keep them still. I don't want him to move while I do this."

It was at this point that I began to consider precisely what was happening here. If Turner had information about events from all those years ago, I would need to have it, of course. I would not walk out of that room without it. On the other hand, I had seen with my own eyes not only Lavien's resolve but his ruthlessness. The night we met he would have mutilated Dorland had I not intervened. I could not object now to his frightening Turner or even striking him a bit. Slicing off the man's ear and placing it in his mouth, however, was of an entirely different order.

"Hold, Leonidas," I said. I turned to Lavien. "A word."

"No," he answered. "I do this my way."

"It is my past," I said.

"And it is my sense of justice. Am I to spare this man because you do not like what it takes to find the truth?"

"Yes," I said.

He shook his head. "Leonidas, will you help me?"

"Do not," I said.

Leonidas, however, ignored me. He stood behind Turner, held him tight, and drew a thin stream of blood.

"Last chance," Lavien said.

"You are madmen," said Turner. "I'll tell you. Don't cut off my ear."

Lavien backed up. "Leonidas, keep his arms where they are. If I think he's holding back, I'll ask you to dislocate his shoulders."

"It might require a few attempts," said Leonidas.

"Do your best. Now, Mr. Turner, tell us your secret."

He remained quiet for fifteen seconds. Thirty. Lavien shook his head. "You are wasting my time." He stepped forward, knife out.

"We killed him," Turner said. Were I to imagine such a scene, I would have thought Turner would shout these words, but he spoke them softly, as though he added a vaguely relevant bit of information to an ongoing conversation.

I stared at him. He did not make me ask him to elaborate.

"Fleet. He came back to Philadelphia looking for me, looking to clear his name. He was going to taverns, asking questions, getting close. The particulars don't matter to you, I suppose. You need only know that Pearson knew that Fleet was looking for him—for us—and he asked me to help. He didn't say what for, and I don't know that I would have done it had I understood. I approached Fleet. He was in a tavern, drunk and angry, and I asked him to step outside with me, for I knew a man who could answer some of his questions. We stepped into the dark, and Pearson struck him on the back of his head with a hammer. Then he stabbed him. Fleet was not killed in a drunken brawl. He was murdered by Jack Pearson."

Ethan Saunders

Later I would be unable to say what I meant to do. Nor did I know why I was allowed to do it alone. I left Clark's in a blur of movement, and it seemed to me I did not walk but was transported by some unknown magic to Fourth and Spruce, outside Pearson's house. Neither Lavien nor Leonidas had come with me. I never asked either of them, but I believe they concluded it was something I needed to confront on my own, in my own way, without words of caution or prudence.

Later I would chastise myself, not because of what happened but because of what might have happened. I am no Lavien, no master of martial prowess, but I did not fear Pearson. Perhaps I ought to have. He had killed in cold blood. I never had. I ought to have taken time—a day or two, perhaps—to consider what I wanted and then determine how to accomplish it. That would have been the correct approach, but I had no patience for it. Had I taken more time to consider—even five minutes—I would have reached one single inescapable conclusion. I could not allow Cynthia to live with him another day. No, not another hour. The time for caution was done.

As I approached, the house looked quiet, still. It was late afternoon—too early to see lights in the windows—so I do not know what would have given the house a lively look, but something seemed to me absent or missing. I took an instant to consider, came to no conclusion, and went forward.

I did not trouble myself to knock or ring. I tried the front door, found it open, and entered. I had made it only five feet into the hallway when I was approached by the surprised footman. In my mind I saw myself grabbing him, throwing him down, striking him, but I restrained myself. He was called Nate. I remembered that. I also remembered that he, like the rest of the servants, was loyal to Cynthia.

"Captain Saunders—" he began, but said no more. I had not cut him off with words, but he saw my face. I felt the rage burning on my skin. I cannot imagine what I must have looked like.

"Where is he?" I felt as though my teeth bit the words from the air.

"I am sorry," he said, his voice unsteady. "That is to say, he is abroad, if it is Mr. Pearson you mean. He is not here at present. I am sure if you return some other—"

"Damn you, where is he?" I took another step forward. He took a step back.

The poor fellow actually cringed. He worked for Pearson, lived with him day after day, and yet he cringed before me. I did not like it; I did not feel powerful or dominating. I felt like an avatar of rage, something not myself, and I did not care. I believe I might actually have hurt the poor fellow had things not suddenly changed.

"He's not here, Ethan." It was Cynthia who spoke. She was at the end of the hall, standing in the gloom, the space where the darkness of the hallway did not yet meet the light of the parlor. Were it half an hour later, the sconces would be lit, but now all was twilight, and she was little more than a silhouette, partially turned away from me. "He is gone. Again."

I balled my fists and unclenched them and stepped forward, but Nate stood in my way, which I thought courageous under the circumstances. On any other day, at any other time, I would not have wagered an egg for my chances against a strapping footman such as he, but not that moment, and he knew it. He feared me and he stepped in my way.

"Please keep your distance, sir. You are not yourself."

It was true enough. I looked past the tall fellow to Cynthia. "Where has he gone?"

"I don't know. He did not say, only that he was going, and he did not plan to soon return. What has happened, Ethan?"

I could not answer. I knew not how. "To New York again?"

"I did not know it was where he went before."

I thought to say that was what Mrs. Maycott told me, but I thought better of it. "I must find him. I cannot tell you why. Not yet. But I must find him."

She took a step forward. "I don't know where he's gone, but he seemed—he suggested he would be away again for a length of time. He did not expect to be home soon. He had his valet pack several suits, and he left hours before dawn."

The New York express coach, no doubt. I would have to go to New York. There could be no more delaying it. I would find Pearson and then—then I knew not what. Kill him? It was not my way. Bring him to trial? With what, a single British spy as witness—one who had only told us what he had under threat of torture and mutilation?

"Cynthia," I began. I moved toward her, but she stepped back.

"No, Ethan. You must stay away."

Can she imagine that would have deterred me? Did she imagine she sounded as though there were some issue of propriety? I did not believe it. I pushed past the footman and came to her. She retreated but did not run away, and so she stepped into the light of the parlor, and I saw what she meant to hide. She had been holding the left side of her face toward me, and only now did I see the right, mottled with red and purple and blues. He had struck her in the eye. Her husband had hit her in the eye as though she were a drunk in a tavern.

I cannot say I was filled with rage anew, for I had no more room for anger. If anything, my fury became purer, sharper, more easily directed and controlled. I would find him and I would stop him. I knew not how, but I would do it.

"Cynthia, you must leave him," I said, my voice calm and quiet and nothing but reason. I was mad with rage, but I would not let her see it. "Why did he hurt you?"

"Because he was angry," she said. "He has been angry since the night you dined with us. He had good cause to be angry, I suppose. But then, so do I. I know I must leave him, Ethan, but how can I? He is a devil, but you have seen what happens to a woman who lives upon the street, without money to her name. You have seen what happens to her children. Is living with one madman not better than subjecting my children to the scorn and abuse of a thousand strangers?"

I stepped closer now. The secret of her bruise was exposed, and there could be no reason to insist upon my distance. I took her hand, though I knew, and I believe she knew, I would attempt no further liberty. Even so, the warmth of her touch astonished me, as though I really understood for the first time since seeing her again that she was a living, breathing woman, not merely an animated memory. She was Cynthia, whose hair I might feel tumble into my hand, whose face I might caress, whose lips I might kiss. Not that I believed I would, but the sheer physical truth of her staggered me.

"Cynthia, what would you have me do? I cannot leave you be. I must do something to protect you and your children. Tell me and I will do it."

She turned from me but did not attempt to pull her hand away. After a moment, she squeezed it tighter. "There is nothing to be done," she said.

"Yes, there is," I said.

She turned back to me and pulled her hand away. "No," she whispered. "No, Ethan, I cannot let you speak so. I don't know if you mean a duel or something more nefarious, but I do not ask it and cannot countenance it. I hate him, but he is the father of my children, and I could not live thinking I had some part in such a thing."

I took her hand back. "I do not suggest it, but there must be a way to be rid of him without resorting to the unthinkable, and I shall find it. I shall go to New York and confront him there, and I shall resolve this."

"How?" she asked. Her voice was quiet, restrained. She did not believe I could do such a thing, and yet there was something akin to hope in her eyes.

"I have no idea," I said with a slight smile. "But I will surely think of something."

"Please wait a moment." Cynthia left the room and came back a moment later with an envelope. "I hope I do not insult you or take liberties, but I know your means are limited. You must have some money for your expenses."

"I cannot take it from you," I said.

"It is his money."

"Oh. That's another matter." I took the envelope and put it in my coat. "It's not greed, you know, but the pleasure of using his own money to defeat him."

Somewhere between the time I'd taken her hand and she left to bring me the envelope, Cynthia's footman had disappeared, giving us such privacy as we would like. I cannot report we much exploited it. I understood she felt far too vulnerable for me to declare my love, and I don't believe she required any such declaration to feel it. Instead, she wished me well, and, holding both her hands, I wished her the same. I dared not tell her of her father, not now. First I would rid her of her husband, and then I would tell her. I could not endure the thought of her having to live with Pearson, even to speak to him, knowing who he was and what he had done.

I could not think, however, how I would rid her of her husband. I had spoken the truth to her. I was not a murderer, and despite what he had done to Fleet, I could not kill him in cold blood. Were I to ask him to duel, I have no doubt he would reject me, even as I had rejected Dorland. It would be the rare husband who accepted a challenge from his wife's admirer.

I would go to New York on the express coach leaving in the small hours of the morning. I would find out everything I could about Pearson: what manner of business he was involved in, how it connected to Duer, and how it connected to the plot against the Bank of the United States. And once I knew everything, I would determine how to convince him to trouble his wife no more. Perhaps it would even be enough to destroy him while still preserving his money for his wife.

I was walking I knew not where when a thought came to me. I considered how much easier it would be simply to duel, how I had avoided doing so with Dorland, and how even Dorland, who had challenged me, seemed disinclined to duel. And then, at once, a question of no small significance occurred to me. If he was so disinclined to duel, why had Dorland challenged me?

Of course, there could be a thousand reasons. He may have believed his honor demanded it, and he may have been convinced I would not accept the challenge, but he did not know me very well. He only knew that I had served in the war, and what man, cowardly and so disinclined to duel, would risk to challenge a man he knew to be a soldier?

Suspicions gathered in my mind, and though I ought to have left him and his poor wife alone, I did not hesitate to approach his house and ring the bell. When his man answered, I said that I must speak to Mr. Dorland, and for the sake of decorum, I would do so outside his house rather than inside it. My intention here was of sparing his wife the discomfort of seeing me, particularly in her husband's presence.

I hardly believed the man would answer my summons, but indeed he came to the door, and if rather reluctant to step out of it, he remained slightly behind his footman, who was a good head taller. He peered out at me, his fleshy face pale. "What is it, Saunders? Why do you trouble me at my own house?"

"For God's sake step outside, Dorland. I have no intention of harming you, and what I have to say is for your ears alone. Our business cannot be the business of those belowstairs."

"It is not a trick?" he asked.

"You have my word as a gentleman."

"You are not a gentleman," he said.

"Then you have my word as a scoundrel, which, I know, opens up a rather confusing paradox that I have neither the time nor inclination to disentangle. Now step outside and give me five minutes of your time, and I'll not trouble you again."

I believe it was my impatience that carried the day. Had I been more unctuous and less urgent, he might well have been too cautious to leave his lair. My unwillingness to use any art must have bespoke my sincerity. I would have to recollect that trick for the future, I decided.

He stepped cautiously down his stoop and stood facing me, a good three feet away, close enough to admit conversation, too far for me to make, as he supposed, any sudden moves. He must have confused me with Lavien, for whom three feet would be as nothing. For me, it only made conversation more trying.

"Dorland, why did you challenge me to a duel?" I demanded.

"How can you ask me that?" Much of the rage he had demonstrated in our previous encounters, and which I had mocked, was gone. Now he seemed only saddened.

"I do not ask why you believed you had cause. I ask you why you chose to challenge me. Was it your own notion?"

He swallowed and looked away, then back. "Of course."

"Who put you up to it?" I asked, my voice gentle. "Who suggested that you challenge me?"

"Must someone have suggested it?" he asked, but he had, with several signs and gestures, already answered that question.

"You are wasting my time, Dorland, and trying my patience. Who suggested it?"

"Jack Pearson," he admitted. "It was he who told me about you and my wife, and it was he who told me to challenge you. He said you would never accept, and then I would be free to take revenge as I saw fit."

It is strange. I ought to have been outraged, but I'd already learned that day that Pearson had stolen Cynthia and murdered my best friend, so this news could offer me no new anger. If anything, I felt victorious, for I had pulled from the fabric of the universe this thread of truth, and I had yanked upon it. Life offers such small triumphs. We must rejoice where we can.

"I have only begun to suspect the depth of Pearson's villainy in deceiving you, Dorland. He had his own reasons for wishing to be rid of me, so he told you horrible falsehoods about your wife to prompt you to attack me. Only think of it. A man willing to ruin another's domestic happiness in order to commit a vicarious murder."

Dorland now came closer. "One moment," he said. "Do you mean to say that you and my wife—I mean, that—that you—"

"Oh, just say it, Dorland. Were she and I together? No, of course not. I have addressed her more than once, and she is lovely, but how could you ever doubt so good a lady as your Susan?"

"It's Sarah," he said softly, his mind elsewhere.

"What do I care about her name?" I asked. "You ought to pay more attention to her goodness and less to her preferring to be called one thing or another." It is well that Dorland was not so good at detecting a lie as I was. I saw no reason why I should not offer the lady this small comfort. I had made her life uneasy. Perhaps I could, with little effort, restore it.

"Why did you not say so before?" he asked me.

"Because you annoyed me," I told him. "You threatened violence, and then you performed violence. I saw no reason to put you at your ease, but I was wrong, for it harmed your wife, and she had done nothing to deserve it. I was foolish, and for that I am sorry."

He now stepped even closer and gave me his hand. "I must thank you," he said. "I wish you had told me sooner, but I cannot tell you the joy this news brings me now."

We shook hands and Dorland rushed inside, no doubt to see his good lady and apologize in a thousand ways. I could only hope the woman was clever enough to hold her tongue and accept.

I turned to head back to my rooms to prepare to leave the coming morning on the express coach, which departed at 3 A.M. I now had a new dilemma to ponder on my voyage. Even before I had met Kyler Lavien, before I had troubled myself with William Duer, heard from Cynthia, or known of a plot brewing against the Bank of the United States—before all of this, Pearson had been plotting to kill me. It was time to discover why.

Joan Maycott

Summer 1791

Our little log cabin, despite the damage from the fire, fetched far more than I would have supposed. I was not surprised that Skye's property, as prim and proper as he made it, brought in a fair amount, but by far the greatest wealth came from Dalton's share—not his buildings, which were excellent, or his land improvements, which were significant, but his stills, which were, in the West, close in nature to a mint and, for practical purposes, a license to manufacture money. Certainly there were concerns about the new excise tax, but no one truly believed that the distant government in Philadelphia, particularly now that Tindall was gone, would be effective in collecting it or in otherwise hampering the production of Monongahela rye. To make certain, Brackenridge, at our behest, made it clear that whoever bought Dalton's land and stills would also buy his whiskey-making recipes.

I will not burden the reader with the details of our return to the East. The money we procured from this transaction did not make us rich, but it gave us what we would need for the scheme. Mr. Dalton spoke to five of his whiskey boys, the five he considered most trustworthy and intelligent, and given that they now had no means of earning their living, they were content to throw in their lot with us, particularly when we could offer them both money in hand now and the promise of more to come.

Thus it happened that we relocated to Philadelphia in the early summer of 1791, renting a small house in the unfashionable but neat Elfreth's Alley. It was a narrow thing, with no room more than six feet in width, and it could have housed perhaps four comfortably, but we nine frontier folk made do. The men required a bit of abusing if I was to keep things neat. We could not have the neighbors gossiping about a woman living alone with eight men, so we put it about that Mr. Skye was my brother, and no more was said.

The arrangement did not last long. Our news in the West had been woefully behind the times, but soon after our arrival we were well acquainted with the doings of Hamilton's bank, which was producing a frenzy upon the streets of Philadelphia. Shares were slated to go on sale on July fourth—did not that alone show the contempt in which these men held American liberty?—and everywhere men schemed how they might best position themselves to obtain their portion. Bank stock was expected to soar almost immediately. It was a mania, a large-scale bribe with which Hamilton tricked people into funding his schemes, making them believe they would be rewarded for doing so.

These moneyed men thought themselves invincible, but I felt certain that destroying their bank would be none too difficult. I took some two weeks to study the matter, consult my books, and take long walks along the river, and so reformulated my plan. When all was in readiness, I presented it to my confederates, and though some finer points were unabsorbed, particularly by the whiskey boys, they agreed one and all.

In a few weeks' time it became necessary to establish a second base of operations in New York, and though they were reluctant to leave me on my own, I sent Dalton and Jericho, along with two of his whiskey boys, Isaac and Jemmy. Much that would happen next would depend upon their efforts, and I did not think they could possibly succeed for the better part of a year, but within a few months my men in New York had laid plans for the bank's destruction.

On July fourth, Hamilton's bank opened for business at Carpenters' Hall, and before noon its allotment of shares had been sold out. Soon they were trading at 20, 30, and 40 percent above par. It was reckoned an enormous success by the Treasury Department. The Federalist newspapers crowed with triumph. The poor of the city grumbled and observed in the bank the mechanism of British oligarchy, but the rich refused to see how they made a darling of their own destruction.

In New York, Dalton and his boys had done their part; it was now time for me to do mine. Accordingly, I was obliged to spend more of our little stock of money than I should like upon clothing, but I needed to look every bit the lady. I rented my own rooms in a fashionable house on Second Street, and I began to appear in public. I promenaded about High Street and struck up conversations with other fashionable women. I appeared at concerts and performances, sometimes with a handsomely dressed Mr. Skye as my escort. I let it be known that I was a widow of means, and that was all the recommendation I needed to enter society.

As my men in New York discovered, William Duer had more than a few accomplices in Philadelphia. Some of them were known as his agents, and the world presumed they acted upon his orders. Others, however, were unknown. Should they be discovered, their usefulness would come to an end. Their primary responsibilities were no more than to set themselves up as speculators in their own right with their own reputations, and then, when called upon, to soften or freeze trade as Duer required.

If a speculator wished to get the better of William Duer, he need only discover the identities of those hidden agents, learn their orders, and proceed accordingly. Given Duer's prominence, given that a sneeze or cough from his lips had the power to send prices soaring or plummeting, I was a bit surprised no one had previously attempted our scheme: to infiltrate the innermost sanctum of his operation and outwit him.

Yes, I suppose it required a singular focus to even think of such a thing, and the truth is, such an operation would be unlikely to yield significant results. Duer might be outwitted once and even twice, but upon the third occasion he would certainly begin to suspect betrayal. It required a unique set of circumstances, such as those belonging to our little band of whiskey rebels, that a single instance could suffice.

We waited until late August, when the worst of the convulsions from the bank launch had passed. On the morning in question, I arrived at the City Tavern in the company of Mr. Skye, whom the general company must have thought to be a trader. It was not unknown for speculators to bring a lady to their trading sessions, perhaps to impress someone of the delicate sex with the manly pursuit of financial chicanery. We took a seat at a table in the main room without attracting overmuch notice. We called for tea, and once we had been served, Skye slipped away, leaving me alone in this room full of panting, sweating, gesticulating men, too bent upon their own pursuits to notice that a lone lady sat among their number.

My wish had been to remain unnoticed until I desired notice, and then to be noticed indeed. Accordingly, I wore a cream-colored gown with a high neck and long sleeves. It was not my best color, but I believe its cut showed off my shape to advantage. I wished to be pleasing to the man who looked twice, not the one who looked once.

Here I was, then, at the very center of the Hamiltonian maelstrom. I looked about in disgust at the traders, who seemed in their slavering greed more beast than man, as though, like in a child's story, transformed by vile magic. I recalled such stories from my own childhood, but I would not tell any myself, not to my own children. That was what this room, these men, had taken from me.

Fifteen years before, in this very city, not a quarter of an hour's walk from where I now sit, men had gathered in the Pennsylvania State-house to ratify the Declaration of Independence. How they had been like gods. How they had put aside their petty differences and concerns, their all-too-real fears for their own safety and property and lives that they might carve from the raw stone of idea and history an empire of republican value. Now all was in decline, as good as ruined, owing to Hamilton and his policies of gluttony and oligarchy and corruption. Men like Jefferson and Madison might condemn these outrages, but their condemnation would do no good if the men and women of the republic did not fight for the principals of the Revolution.

As I looked at these men, how I hated Hamilton. More than Duer, more even than Tindall, I hated Hamilton, for what he had wrought. Duer who had lured us west, Tindall who had murdered my husband—they were but dogs. Hamilton was the master who had trained them, and I would destroy him and his work. So help me, I would destroy it all.

And so I readied myself to do so. Glancing about the room, I wondered if any manner of dress, or even no dress at all, could have distracted these legions of mammon. There were some dozen or so tables, at which sat between one and six men. Each had about him saucers of tea, dishes of coffee, tankards of beer, goblets of wine, or some jumble of all four. Papers and documents and books were strewn about, and little portable inkstands had been arranged. Quills dipped and wrote with such fury that they produced a hurricane of ink.

One man would speak to another and a third would lean forward and say, "Ho, what's that, selling such-and-such, are you? At what price? A good price!" And others would rise and shout and buy or sell and mark it down. And all this done with manic gestures to suggest that these were not men of business but men of madness, better suited for a house of lunatics than for this tavern where the fortunes of a newly born empire were to be set forth.

Not three tables separated me from Mr. Burlington Black, whom I knew, thanks to the excellent work accomplished in New York by Dalton and his boys. The plan was simple but no less cunning, particularly since Duer had executed it many times and remained undetected. He wished to purchase Bank of North America issues at a discount in Philadelphia and then sell them in New York, where the price remained untouched by a rumor that lowered the price in Philadelphia. Thus, the previous evening he had had it set about that the shares were trading at a deep discount in New York, which was untrue. This morning, Mr. Black, acting upon this rumor, would sell a fair number of shares well below market price. Duer did not worry about the loss, since he would buy enough to make up the difference in New York profits, and experience had taught him that he would be able to buy the shares back himself, and at only slightly more than Mr. Black had sold them in the first place.

In the past, Duer had attempted operations in which one of his agents sold and a second bought, but he had discovered (so I learned through Dalton's communications) that this entailed a significant risk: namely, that the world might remain oblivious of this bit of stagecraft. It was far more efficacious to recruit real speculators engaged in real efforts to earn money. He knew the inclination of these people to swarm like bees about good news and bad, so all he had to do was offer the right sort of pollen to attract their attention. In this case, Mr. Black would remind the world, through word and deed, of the rumors Duer and his agents had cast about. He would support the rumors with a willingness to shed his Bank of North America issues at any price and would watch while the other men in the room endeavored to unload their holdings. Then, purchases in hand, he or his man would take the next express coach to New York and trade there before word of the sell-off in Philadelphia reached those markets.

No one had yet noticed me, a quiet lady, as I sat alone in that most masculine of taverns, but I observed many men as they went about their business. I especially observed Mr. Burlington Black, upon whom so much depended. He was a soft-looking man of perhaps fifty, inclined to be stout, but his was a softness like the pliable fat of an infant.

I had been in place, sipping my tea slowly, when at last Mr. Burlington Black lumbered to his feet to show the world the unusual shortness of his legs. He then called to another speculator across the room.

"Mr. Cheever, correct me if I am mistaken, but did you not wish, the week before last, to acquire Bank of North America issues?" His voice was far deeper and steadier than I would have supposed. He was in appearance quite foolish but in utterance impressive. "I have some number of shares that I am ready to part with, if you are so inclined. If not—" He shrugged his shoulders to signal his indifference.

The Mr. Cheever to whom he addressed this speech, an elderly gentleman who rose to his feet only with the aid of a cane in one hand and a younger supporter lifting his elbow, readied himself and returned his address to Mr. Black. Like Duer's agent, he shouted across the large tavern room, but then I had already observed this to be the custom, close conversation and whispering being regarded as mean things. "You were not so ready to part with them two weeks ago, when I offered a reasonable price."

"I am merely shifting my holdings, as does any man," answered Mr. Black. "I believe you offered me some twenty-seven hundred dollars two weeks ago, and I stand ready now to accept."

Mr. Cheever, in return, barked out a laugh. "I've done too much business and seen you go about your affairs far too often. You know something about the issues, don't you? Some trouble at that bank, is it? I would not buy for *twenty-three* hundred."

The other men in the room continued to trade and go about their own business, but I could see that each one had one ear or eye upon this transaction, for it was also their business to sense when something might change, and there were signs of such a thing about to happen here.

Mr. Burlington Black swallowed hard, sending a wave of undulation along the wattle of his throat. "I shall sell you the portfolio discussed for twenty-one hundred dollars."

Now, indeed, trades fell silent and the other speculators turned to watch, for what happened next would determine if they would buy more of the bank's holdings or sell what they already possessed. Mr. Cheever peered at the other man with much skepticism. "I decline," he said, with the wave of a withered hand.

Silence befell the room.

Mr. Black, to his credit, reddened considerably and appeared extremely agitated. I know not if his response was from anxiety about the burden placed upon him or mere theatrical skill, but in either case he created the impression of a man most distressed. "Nineteen hundred," he said, his voice tremulous, "and you know you have a significant bargain."

A serving boy came in to collect some of the dirty saucers, and one of the speculators shushed him as he dared to clink dish upon dish.

Mr. Cheever evidently scented trouble. "I don't like your urgency, and I shall decline."

Now a gasp arose from the room. In but a few minutes, the value of these holdings had fallen by a third, and the speculators were for a moment frozen as they attempted to form their strategies. Those who owned issues from the Bank of North America plotted how best to relieve themselves of the unwanted things. Those who did not scrambled to determine how they might profit from this sudden shift.

It was at this moment, when all was in flux and no one knew yet what he would do, in the seconds before someone would decide to buy and send the main room of the City Tavern into a bacchanal of buying and selling, that Mr. Duer always made his move. I knew this from the dispatches sent by Mr. Dalton. He would rise and announce that he had faith in one of this country's great banks, and he would be glad to accept Mr. Black's offer. He would then gather to himself similar offerings, reduced by a third, and when he turned around and sold them in New York, he would be praised as a sagacious businessman who scented the wind far better than his brothers of that trade.

I rose from my chair. "I shall buy for nineteen hundred," I called in a clear voice.

It is difficult to say if my willingness to purchase or my being a woman produced more surprise, but there was a momentary outburst as all shouted at once, and an expression of terror and confusion washed over Mr. Black's face.

By the accepted rules of the City Tavern, Mr. Black could not pick and choose to whom he would sell, and his offer to Mr. Cheever, once rejected by that gentleman, might be fairly taken by any other. I had done what any man might do, and my actions might be condemned as improper because I was a woman, but they could not be rejected.

Mr. Black, however, must have weighed his options and determined that he could not sell to me at such a price. He turned a near purple color as he struggled to find some escape, and at last he shook his head, sending his cheeks to shuddering. "I must decline to sell. I do not trade with ladies." Then he decided he would make himself into a scoundrel if he must in order to save his trade and added, "Or with women, for that matter."

Once more, the floor erupted. Men called *no!* and *custom!* and *the rules!* One man shouted, "You must sell!" and received general approbation. Encouraged, he added, "If you do not, you are no longer welcome here. We cannot have a man who will not observe our customs."

This comment received general assent, and, at last, knowing that he had been backed into a corner, Mr. Black nodded. Indeed, he looked somewhat relieved. I supposed he had told himself he had done all he could and Duer could not reproach him.

I strode over to him, and Mr. Black offered me a bow. "I am unused to trading with ladies, and my passions overcame me. I beg your forgiveness."

I smiled and curtsied and shook his hand, to signal completion of the trade. It was done, and he could not now rescind without ruining his reputation. "It is no matter, sir. You have not harmed me. Indeed, you have served me well, for I know that these issues retain their full value. If I can find no one to buy them here, I doubt not I can sell them in New York, where my agents tell me they will sell quite readily."

I had not said this in anything above a conversational voice, but I knew I would be heard and the surety with which I spoke would destroy Duer's ability to perpetuate his scheme. It was not that my opinion carried any weight, for the traders did not know me, and I was only a woman, after all. Yet, the certainty with which I spoke would break the spell cast by Duer's agent's efforts, and no one would be anxious either to buy or to sell until more could be learned.

My business being concluded, I went back to my table and collected my things, making a show of preparing to leave. I hoped I would be stopped. I hoped my sagacity would, after this one trade, be enough to attract interest, but I could not be certain. If not, I would have to risk more trades, though there would be diminishing returns, for each new success would be regarded less with admiration and wonder and more with suspicion.

I need not have worried, for I felt a hand fall upon my elbow, and when I turned, my smile quite prepared, I met the eye of none other than Mr. William Duer himself. I had not known he was present and had not seen him arrive. I had hoped he would be on the scene to watch his little deception, and here he was, witness to my own. He stood before me, the principal villain of my life's woe, the man who had, through his conniving and greed, destroyed everything I loved. This man had murdered my child and my Andrew, and he now smiled at me.

"Madam, William Duer of New York at your service." He bowed to me. "Though I observe from a thousand little things that you are new to the business of trading, you have impressed me with your knowledge and your coolness. I wonder if you would honor me by joining me for a dish of chocolate upstairs, where the rooms are far quieter."

I met the monster's gaze directly. "Mr. Duer, I should be foolish indeed to neglect the attentions of a man so well regarded as yourself." And thus it was that we went upstairs together.

Ethan Saunders

I have never enjoyed traveling long distances by road. The movement of the coach prevents any reading or other amusement, and there is little to do that passes the time other than conversation with strangers, yet the quality of strangers in a coach is never high. Instead one must endure perpetual jostling, an ongoing merciless rump paddling, combined with rough swaying and shoving. In winter, when the windows must be closed against the cold, the stench is of stewing bodies, of breath and garlic and onion and unclean breeches. Above that is the smell, too, of old damp wood, wet wool and leather, and inevitable flatulence. It is an unkind experience.

The roads, at least, were clear. It had not snowed hard in several days, and the precipitation on the King's Highway had been well tramped down by previous expresses. Our coach was typical of the sort: a long enclosed cart capable of holding nine people, divided into four benches with leather curtains that could be drawn for the slender pretense of privacy. It lacked storage for our bags, so we were forced to set our allotted fourteen pounds' worth before us. The four horses that pulled us made good time, but even so there was little to do but watch the scenery pass.

Having Leonidas by my side did make matters pass more agreeably, for it provided me with someone to whom to whisper disparaging comments about our fellow travelers. And soon enough I discovered that I might gain at least something from the journey, for it turned out that, typical of this run between New York and Philadelphia, nearly every man aboard was a speculator traveling upon business. One of our companions, a tall man with narrow diabolical eyes that rested under bushy brows, asked me my business. I thought it a good idea to hold out bait and said I went to New York in order to put a lately deceased cousin's estate in order. I received some questions regarding how much money I'd been left and if I had any interest in investing in this fund or that project, but otherwise I did not excite much interest among my fellow travelers.

Soon these speculators forgot that we were even present, and they began to speak freely among themselves. Their talk centered largely around the price of six percent government issues. They were in agreement that Duer banked upon the decline of government securities and that his agents were shorting them significantly in Philadelphia. Beyond this, much of what they had to say regarded how cheaply loans were to be got, both from the Bank of the United States and the Bank of New York. This made investment in the funds logical, but one of the principal problems in doing so seemed to be that Duer was so active in shorting the funds that only a fool would buy when he might sell.

To ensure that this line of credit would continue, should there be a curtailing on the part of the two major banks, Duer had involved himself in a scheme to found a new bank in New York, to be called the Million Bank.

Leonidas and I barely risked exchanging glances. I showed no particular interest but merely asked how long this plan had been in the works.

The wart-nosed speculator turned to me. "If you have some interest in investing in the new banks, you may call upon me in New York. I can broker any investment you choose."

"I would need to know more before I could invest any money."

"You need only know that, if you hesitate, someone else will take your place—and willingly too. Interest in the banks has risen so high that investors are calling it a *bancomania*. I promise you that you will find my commissions to be very reasonable, but the Million Bank launches this coming Wednesday, so if you wish to benefit from this opportunity you will need to act quickly."

He handed me his card, and I pretended to look at it with interest.

One of the other speculators turned to me. "You may be sure he speaks the truth. If you do not act quickly, you may lose the opportunity. However, that may not be a good enough reason to invest."

"Why not?" I asked.

"The Bank of the United States was born under the guidance of the Treasury Secretary, who is a capable man, and the Bank of New York and the Bank of North America have stood the test of time. But these new banks are only ventures designed to make money for the first investors. There is no thought of the bank's future prospects, which, because neglected, must be poor. Take my advice and act with caution."

The wart-nosed man turned to his colleague. "I say, that was rather unkind of you, frightening off a customer. 'Tis rather rude to do that to a man who is sharing your coach."

"Is he not also sharing my coach?" the other asked.

The wart-nosed man pondered this question for a moment. "Perhaps so, but I stood to make money by enticing him. You stood to make none by dissuading him. That sort of thing—well, 'tis hardly better than vandalism."

"Some would call it integrity," I suggested.

"Whoever would say that never worked upon commission in his life," he answered.

We made excellent time and arrived that afternoon, very late, at the New Jersey side of the Hudson, where we concluded our journey by ferry. Arriving in full dark, we were greeted at once by the bustle of New York. I had abided in that city for some years after the war and always liked it, without wishing to call it my home. It was full of frenetic people who could be little troubled to speak to a stranger, though once you started conversing with a New Yorker, he could no more stop himself from speaking than a river can stop flowing. I have ever felt fondness for Philadelphia, and it is in many ways a far more gracious city in which to live, but I could not help but feel regret that the capital was no longer in New York, which I had ever thought, with its sharpish tone, the very place for a national seat. Of all the cities in America, it has the most European flavor, with its international fashions, its excellent eateries, its diversions, and its variety. The streets are peopled with speakers of a hundred languages, and the harbor is ever full, even in winter, with ships stretching out into a forest of masts.

Tired and in need of refreshment, we took ourselves at once to Fraunces Tavern and proceeded to secure our room. After washing, I went down to the taproom, a spacious and well-lit affair, where I called for a plate of boiled ham and bread and two bottles of their most agreeable wine.

Once we had completed our meal, I told Leonidas that we might do well to begin our work. "We'll go see Duer," I said. "He has ever been at the center of all of this. Perhaps he can tell us where to find Pearson."

"What makes you think he will tell you anything?"

I shrugged. "I will ask politely."

We then hired a coach and traveled to a more northern location on the island of Manhattan, a village called Greenwich, where Duer's palatial home stood with all the regal bearing of an old-world manor house. I understood that our trip might be for naught, for a man of Mr. Duer's prominence could well be abroad attending to business or social concerns, but we were fortunate and he was at home. The servant appeared reluctant to admit us, but I used the name of Hamilton, which proved a shibboleth not to be denied, particularly when Duer's own wife was cousin to Hamilton's lady. With Leonidas taken to the kitchens to learn what he could, I was shown to a commodious room identified as a study and offered refreshment.

At last the door opened, and I recognized the prim and slender form of Mr. Duer from our brief encounters at Philadelphia. There was no sign of the mysterious Mr. Reynolds, but now he was accompanied by a very tall creature, a man with large eyes of a sunken appearance, a hooked nose, and thin lips seemingly devoid of blood. His hair, the color of dirt, thinned considerably in the front, but hung loose and stringy in the back. He was, as I say, tall, though of a narrow and stooping frame, with hunched and rounded shoulders, and he appeared, for all the world, to be panting.

"Ah, Captain Saunders," Duer said. "I am so sorry I could not keep our appointment in Philadelphia, but it is good of you to call upon me here, though it's rather an extravagant gesture. A letter would do, perhaps?"

"My particular interests favor a visit." I kept my voice agreeable, but I met his eye with a determined stare.

"Yes, yes. But where are my manners?" he shouted to the universe. "Wherever are they? I must present to you my associate," he said, gesturing to the man I found increasingly troll-like, lurking still near the door, "Mr. Isaac Whippo. Whippo is something of a factotum in my service. I have found him to be indispensable in my work."

I expected the factotum to bow or acknowledge the kindness of his master. Instead, he picked at a piece of lint on his not-overclean sleeve as though I were not worth his interest.

Duer gestured for me to sit, and I did so, though Whippo remained standing, at first lurking near the door and then standing near the window, gazing out into the darkness like a pampered pet who wishes the freedom to relieve himself.

Duer steepled his fingers and gazed at me through the window of digits. "Yes, well, it is all a bit redundant. I suppose I must answer questions, but I don't see that I must do it twice."

"Twice?"

"Yes. That little Jewish man, Lavien, has already been here today. Now must I speak to you as well?"

"Lavien? How did he get here before I did? I took the first express after I last saw him."

"He rode," said Duer. "Upon horseback, I believe. Much faster than the express."

"And did you have a pleasant conversation with Mr. Lavien?"

"No, I did not. I don't like the fellow."

"Then you may have a pleasant conversation with me. Unlike Mr. Lavien, I do not work for the government or for Hamilton. I am here upon my own business. Lavien, I presume, was anxious to learn about information surrounding the bank."

I had intended to refer to the Bank of the United States, but Duer misunderstood me. "Yes, I told him I have no connection to any new banks. I would not invest in the Million Bank, and I pity anyone who does. It is doomed to fail."

"I have heard that you are intimately involved in the Million Bank," I said.

"It's a damnable lie," he said. "Someone makes free with my name. It happens frequently, I am sad to say. It is an unfortunate consequence of reputation that when my name is attached to a project it is often viewed as a sign of inevitable success. Thus there are men who will cast it about that I have smiled upon their undertaking to generate interest among the general populace. I fear it may be so in this case. Anyone who invests in the Million Bank is certain to lose his money."

"And what of the Bank of the United States? Did Mr. Lavien ask you about that?"

"What is there to ask?" He continued to peer at me through his fingers, which made it difficult to measure his face as I would like.

"Some sort of danger to the bank, perhaps?"

"Don't be absurd. The bank is already a monolith. Nothing can harm it."

"Not even the Million Bank?"

"It would be like a mouse assaulting a lion."

I decided I would set out my concerns directly and see what happened next. "Am I to presume from what you say that you have no designs yourself against the national bank, no effort in seeing it stumble or even fail?"

"What an absurd notion. Why should I wish to see it fail? The bank could not be more dear to me."

"Dear to you precisely how?" I asked. "The bank and government securities are quite closely bound together, and I have discovered your agents are selling government securities short. You are gambling upon the price of the stock going down, are you not? Your situation, as I understand it, would suffer considerably if the price should go up. It sounds to me that what is dear to you is the depression of our economy."

At last he moved his hands, that he might flick his fingers dismissively. "You have many excellent talents, I don't doubt, but you do not know a great deal about finance. Whippo, does Captain Saunders strike you as a financial man?"

Whippo slowly rotated his cadaverous head toward me. "'Tis not how he strikes me."

"Truly, you must not think of this as a play, sir, with a hero and a villain. An agent in my employ may or may not sell short, for he is my agent, not my servant. He may engage in any number of transactions separate from, or even contrary to, my own wishes. That he does so does not mean he acts according to my orders. I am an important man and very influential. I would not have you saying in public that I sell securities short."

"Nevertheless," I said, "on the express from Philadelphia, I heard a group of speculators saying just that."

Duer snickered and turned to Whippo. "He heard a group of speculators, quotha." Then, to me: "You cannot be serious that you come to me in order to relate idle gossip heard on a coach. That is not your business, is it?"

To my surprise, the speculator had taken control of the conversation with the tenacity of a terrier and did not mean to let go.

"Now, as to the reality of the matter," Duer continued, "I do not say what my agents buy or sell when they are about their own affairs. It is not for me to know. As for what I do, I prefer to keep that to myself, and I ask that you keep your suppositions to yourself as well. Any rumors you might spread could be very detrimental to my finances and, by extension, to America itself."

"You have been attempting to drive down prices," I said. "How can you say you do so for the good of America?"

"I am afraid this confusion originates from your own poor understanding of the markets. Let us say I do gamble upon the value of securities declining. Does that make me an enemy of the government? I think not. Prices are in endless shift, and if I am to wager they shall be down this moment, it does not mean I wish them to be down or expect them to remain down forever. It is but the natural ebb and flow of the market, and it is no more than what Hamilton expects—indeed, what Hamilton desires. Why else has his bank made credit so cheap, but that we might buy and sell and attempt to guess the end result? To say I abuse the markets by attempting to predict them is like saying a ship abuses the ocean by riding upon it."

I honestly did not know where his bluster and fabrication ended and where the truth began. This was not war, where secrets relate to tangible things like troop movements, army composition, and battle plans. This was the world of finance, in which even the nature of truth can twist upon the slightest wind. I did not pursue the matter further because I did not believe I could learn more from listening to Duer spin his tales.

"What then," I said, as though it were the natural consequence of what had come before, "can you tell me of Pearson?"

Duer allowed himself the indulgence of a brief frown, just a flicking downturn of the mouth. "Jack Pearson? What of him?"

"I would like it if you could tell me about your animosity toward him."

He had now returned to smiling. "Animosity, you say? I know nothing of it."

"It has been said that you are his enemy. That the financial difficulties he is currently experiencing are of your engineering. That you and Pearson are locked in some sort of duel to the death, and that he has already emerged as the clear loser."

Duer stood up, a slow, deliberate motion. His face was now set, like a man enduring pain. Whippo observed this with some alarm, as though I were using invisible witchcraft to harm his master. He took a step toward me.

"Who told you that?" Duer demanded.

"It is something I heard," I said casually. I finished my wine. "Have you more of this claret? It is really quite good."

"Mr. Duer asked you a question," Whippo said. His voice was deep and resonant but had the vague quality of the perpetually bored.

"Oh, I heard him. But I also asked a question. Regarding the wine." I handed Whippo the glass. "A bit more if you please, fellow."

Duer nodded at Whippo, and though the large man's face was set in a mask of smoldering resentment—narrow eyes, flat lips, flaring nostrils—he went to the sideboard and tipped the bottle, filling the glass almost to the brim.

Once the wine was in hand, I smiled like a contented pasha. "So, much better. Now, do sit, Mr. Duer. It is bad enough that Pantagruel there menaces me, but I cannot speak to you gentleman to gentleman while you tower above me."

Duer, perhaps wishing to regain the illusion of composure, returned to his seat. I sipped my wine.

"Now," I said, "what was your question?"

"Damn you, you drunk fool, where did you hear I was against Pearson? Who told you?"

"Ah, yes, Pearson." Lest my reader believe that I was actually inebriated, I should point out that much of this behavior was in the order of a ruse. It served my purpose to have them believe me far more drunk than I was.

I emptied my glass to the point where I could hold it comfortably without spilling. While I did so, I considered what lie would best suit my purposes. It was clear that Duer and his factotum both believed it a terrible thing that rumors of this sort should be spread. I could not tell them I had intercepted coded messages between parties I did not know. At the same time, I did not want to tell them I had heard rumors cast about in a tavern or on the express, since doing so would alarm them, and while causing an alarm was an arrow I might later want to pull from my quiver, i was not yet ready to do so. For the nonce, I wished to calm them.

"The gentleman's wife," I said at last. "When I saw Mrs. Pearson at the Bingham house, she expressed some concern about the nature of her husband's business with you."

Duer let out a breath. Whippo unclenched his fists.

"Wives are apt to speak of what they do not understand," said Duer. "They believe they know better than their husbands and consider all new ventures to be ruinous ones."

"What, then, is the nature of your business with Pearson?"

"I cannot tell you that," said Duer. "What business I did with Pearson is all in the past. I told you as much. I have no knowledge of his current troubles other than what I hear, the same as any man."

"And where is Pearson now?"

"I have no idea," said Duer. "I believed him in Philadelphia, but if you have come looking for him, I presume it must not be the case."

"And where did he go when he disappeared previously?"

"I have no knowledge of that either."

"Do you have any immediate plans to do new business with Pearson? You need not tell me the nature of the business, only the day."

Duer smiled. "It would be foolish to do business with a ruined man."

I rose. "Then I shall waste no more of your time," I said.

Leonidas met me at the coach, and together we made our dark, uneven way back to New York. It was a closed coach, but it contained a small window by which we could observe the coachman, and I noticed that he looked back at us more than once. Since beginning our journey, Leonidas and I had spoken only of trivial matters, but it seemed to me that the coachman hung upon every word.

"What did you learn?" Leonidas asked at last, clearly impatient with my silence.

I cast a quick nod toward the coachman and then said, "Oh, nothing of import. He was tight-lipped, but it hardly mattered. I always know when a man is concealing something, and he was not. And you? Did you hear anything from the servants?"

I suspected he had something he wished to tell me, but I shook my head ever so slightly. He understood my meaning and said that he had learned nothing.

When our coach arrived at Fraunces Tavern, we climbed down, but then I turned to the coachman. "What were you offered?"

"Sir?"

"By Duer's man. He offered you money to report upon anything we said. How much?"

He shrugged, caught but unwilling to deny it. "He offered me a dollar."

I handed him some coins from the fund Mrs. Pearson had given me. "Here's two dollars. Report back that I said nothing, only made you stop the coach so I could vomit at the roadside."

He nodded. "Thank you, sir."

Leonidas and I went and warmed ourselves by the fire. "Did you learn anything of moment?" Leonidas asked me. "What are his plans? Is the scheme the short-selling of stock?"

"I don't think so," I said. "Duer is playing at something he thinks very clever, but I don't think it's selling bank stock short."

"How can you know that?"

"Because whenever he spoke of it, his discourse became theoretical, saying *a man may do this* or *my agent might do that*. He defended what he neither admits nor denies doing. He spoke about it in the most obviously evasive manner, and so could not have been more obviously hoping I would believe the shorting of issues was his goal. He was trying to lead me down a path to one thing and, by inference, away from another."

"From what?"

I shook my head. "I can't be sure. Did you learn anything in the kitchens?"

"Possibly," he said. "Some major event is afoot with the servants. Things are to be made ready for early Wednesday morning. The coaches are to be prepared and food ready for an early meal. There will be a large and early breakfast at the house. It has all been discussed and planned with the greatest urgency, yet no one knows the occasion."

I slapped my hand upon the table. "Oh, poor Mr. Lavien. He shall be behind us now, for we know what Duer intends and when he intends it."

"We do?"

"Do you not remember what the men in the express told us? The Million Bank launches on Wednesday. Duer plans to have his agents come to the house for one last strategy meeting and then descend upon the launch. He considers it vital that the world have no faith in the Million Bank, because, if I am correct, he means to take control of the bank on its first day. We have until Wednesday, then, to learn why. We have to find out if this is just another financial maneuver or if it is connected to dark schemes in Philadelphia."

Leonidas looked significantly brighter. "It must be very satisfactory," he said, "to know you have so well retained the old skills."

"Oh, well, you know," I said modestly, but it pleased me more than I could say that he should notice.

"But was that a clever move, paying the coachman such as you did? He might just as well report your bribery to Duer."

"If he tells Duer what he overheard, Duer will think I know nothing and will never learn anything. He will cease to regard me seriously."

"And if he tells Duer that you paid him to lie?"

"Then," I said, "we will have stirred up the hornet's nest, and we shall be able to watch the results. Always better to be involved in chaos of your own making, Leonidas. We know almost nothing and are set against powerful forces, but as long as they are reacting to what we do, the advantage is ours."

Joan Maycott

Autumn 1791

Within a few months of our arrival in Philadelphia, even Jericho Richmond, the most cynical of our band, began to think success was likely, if not precisely assured. William Duer may have been intrigued initially by the mere novelty of a female speculator, but soon enough he came to regard me as a sage advisor as well. I should like to have been able to offer him advice on how to invest, and have that advice bear fruit, but I am no more prescient than any other mortal, and I had no abilities beyond those provided by keen observation and common sense. Accordingly, I did the next best thing. Already having one of Dalton's whiskey boys close to Duer, I could receive word on the speculator's plans and then advise him to do what I knew he intended. If I could not predict the market, I could at least predict the investor, and he, hearing his own ideas parroted back, believed me brilliant, for I reflected back to him his belief in his own sagacity.

It was important that I also know the history of the investor. When I met with Duer I questioned him as closely as I dared. My interest would always have to be that of an adoring woman, not a counting-house clerk, and yet it was the details of the ledger book I craved. Indeed, Duer dropped a few hints of some past exploits I thought could be useful, and accordingly I visited the Library Company, that marvelous institution founded by Benjamin Franklin, and conducted some researches into old papers.

In reviewing the accounts of the old Board of Treasury, which functioned between the end of the war and the establishment of the Constitution, I learned that when William Duer had run the board he lent himself some $236,000, and only a careful review of the records, one conducted with knowledge of the cheat, made clear that the money had never been returned. Duer had stolen from his country, and apparently no one knew it.

I had found what I most sought, a key to Duer's ruin. It was a primed pistol, ready for me to discharge when the time was right.

Duer was, as near as I could tell, quite dedicated to his wife, Lady Kitty, the daughter of William Alexander, the famous Lord Stirling, hero of the Revolution. Yet after our first meeting he asked me to meet him again the next day at the City Tavern, where we might discuss further my insights into speculation. I cared little for his reputation or the feelings of Lady Kitty, so I agreed immediately. As we were stepping out onto the street, however, we were joined again by Reynolds, who continued to eye me with suspicion.

"I'm certain I know you from somewheres," he said to me.

"Mind how you speak to a lady, Reynolds," said Duer.

"I'm not looking to be impertinent," he said, "but I am to look after you, and I'm telling you I know her."

I had to make a decision, for if I denied knowing them, my falsehood might later expose me. Thus I smiled at Duer. "You sold my husband a ground lease in the West some years ago."

Reynolds colored. "By God, that's it! You're Maynard or Mayweather or something of that sort."

"This is Mrs. Maycott," said Duer. "Now, if you're done—"

"That's her! The one what Tindall said killed her own husband!" Reynolds shouted.

An expression of understanding crossed Duer's face. I don't know how much he had heard of the incident, but if he dealt with Tindall he would have had some notion of his perfidy.

He looked at me with a very contrite face. "I never did hear the full story, but my understanding was that Tindall treated your family unkindly and then attempted to lay the blame upon you."

I bristled at his use of so limpid a euphemism for murder, but this was not the time to resolve such things. Instead, I said, "I suppose none of us could be surprised that Tindall dealt with himself so harshly, given the crimes upon his conscience."

As it happened, accusations of murder had never surfaced in the Tindall affair. Perhaps Phineas ultimately lacked the resolve to deliver his confession, and the sheriff decided that a wound to the back of the head was consistent with a hanging. After Brackenridge had humiliated Tindall before the sheriff (a man who did not scruple to talk about his supposedly private conversations), it was widely rumored that Tindall had murdered both Andrew and his own man and, after attempting and failing to blame me, had taken his own life rather than face the humiliation of a trial.

I met his gaze. "Those events are in the past."

Duer took my hand and held it softly. "For my own part in that wretched affair—"

I shook my head. I did not want to hear a meaningless apology from him. "You did no more than sell us a lease. You cannot be responsible for how Tindall behaved."

"Of course not," he said, "and yet some small part of the affair must be set before me."

"No," I said. "It is noble that you say so, but it is not true."

"Wait one moment," said Reynolds. He stepped close to me, crowding me with his massive form. I believed I could actually feel the heat emanating from him, and his smell, like that of a bull, filled my nostrils. "I don't like this at all."

Duer pushed him back. "Mind yourself, Reynolds."

"I think I'd rather mind you and her. She always was a cagey one, this lady. You forget I rode out to Pittsburgh with her. She's one of those women who must always have her own way."

"Is there another kind? Ha-ha! You'll forgive me, madam."

I smiled in deference.

"You don't think it a bit odd," Reynolds said, "her appearing here, making nice with you after what you done—"

"That will be enough, Reynolds," Duer barked. "Silence yourself—now!"

Reynolds took a step back as if struck, though his face showed no expression of pain, just puzzlement. He wished to know what I did with Duer, and I could see he did not believe for a moment that our meeting was by chance or that I was so quick to forget the injury the speculator had done me. Even then, I could see behind his dark eyes, so obvious in their brooding, that he searched not for a way to protect Duer but to turn my unlikely presence to his own advantage.

I began to meet with Mr. Duer at the City Tavern whenever he did business in Philadelphia, which amounted to at least one protracted visit every two weeks. Though men wondered at the nature of our friendship, no one wondered aloud in our presence.

As I repeated to Duer his own ideas, handily reported to me by my man in his service, the speculator began to grow increasingly sanguine about my opinions. Thus, after meeting with him for the better part of two months, I decided it was time to begin pushing him in the direction I so desired. Duer made it a point to introduce me to a number of his associates—perhaps he wished them to believe our relationship was of a more intimate nature than it was, or perhaps he wished to impress them with his marvelous pet, the thinking woman—and so I came to know a number of men in Duer's circle.

The circle itself was a curious thing. His most important project that autumn was a loose confederation of traders he called the Six Percent Club. Its principal object, as all its members knew, was to establish control over those government issues yielding six percent interest. There was value in monopoly for its own sake, of course, but Duer's scheme was more far-reaching. When the Bank of the United States launched, investors could only buy scrip, the ownership of which allowed them to make the four subsequent payments necessary to own actual bank shares. Not until those four payments were complete would the scrip holder actually be a shareholder. Two of those payments were to be made in specie, but two were to be made in six percent issues.

Hamilton's intention in doing this was actually quite clever. Create a demand for government securities in order to increase the trade and, consequently, the value. Duer's plan was equally clever but far more diabolical. Control the flow of the six percents, make them impossible to obtain, and the original bank investors cannot hope to turn their scrip into actual shares. Their scrip becomes worthless, and they must sell it—to members of the Six Percent Club. It was his intention that by the end of the next year, his cartel would control both bank scrip and the six percent issues required to redeem it.

There was one added dimension, however. The Six Percent Club consisted of both agents whom Duer publicly acknowledged and those he did not. There were men who bought and sold with Duer's money, and those who bought and sold with their own. Not all in the latter category, but certainly many of them, were nothing more than stooges, men Duer sacrificed to manipulate the market. If he wanted prices to go down, he would send the unwitting agents out to sell. If he wanted prices to go up, he would send them out to buy. That their investments would ruin them mattered nothing to him. He did not see himself as directing a skirmish but rather the final battle of a long war. When it was done, he might have ruined the markets, but he would own them. He might have ruined his reputation, but by then it would not matter.

Much of this I learned from our man in Duer's employ in New York, and much I learned from my own observation. Duer liked to keep me on hand, as a kind of sign of his power, a charming woman with a considerable knowledge of finance. Never, not once, did he suggest he wished for a greater familiarity with me, though at times he might touch my arm when he spoke or place a hand upon my back. It was intimacy of a sort, certainly, and it took all my will not to recoil, but it was far less than I had feared he might demand.

Too, he discovered that my presence disarmed potential victims. I was a refined lady, and who would attempt chicanery in front of me? Only once did he ask me to participate in one of his ruses. Late in 1791, a man began to appear regularly at the City Tavern, a local landowner of some significance named Jacob Pearson.

Pearson would sit quietly during trading and then strike up conversations with other traders, explaining loudly that they had made terrible mistakes. He said he had observed the markets since their inception in this country and knew an error when he saw one—and a good trade as well. Yet he himself refrained from trading.

"Why do you think he behaves thus?" Duer asked me.

"Because he in fact knows nothing of the difference between a good trade and a bad one. He wishes to benefit from the markets but is too proud to admit knowing nothing."

"Precisely," Duer said. "He is quite perfect for our purposes."

Duer sent the man a note, saying he wished to meet but that the meeting must be private, lest the world know of their business. Thus it was we arranged to meet in the back room of another tavern, where we could discuss these matters in private.

"Will he not be confused by my presence?" I asked Duer.

"That can only work to our advantage," he said.

From a distance I'd found Mr. Pearson to be an unlikable person, loud and vain and pleased with himself to an unreasonable degree. In close conversation, I found him even more unpleasant, but because of, not despite, a kind of native charm. A man of a certain fading beauty, he displayed with Duer a self-confident expansiveness, but with me he used a predatory charm. It was the alluring gaze of a predator. I felt at once that Pearson was a dangerous creature—not to us, perhaps, but to those in his power. For myself, I did not fear him, but I did immediately despise him.

To this man, Duer explained that he needed someone to help him alter the market, someone who must buy and sell with his own money. When he profited, he would keep what he earned minus a small commission. When he lost, he would be reimbursed.

Some men, Duer had explained to me, reacted quite harshly to this suggestion, not liking the idea of behaving dishonorably to other traders, but that was what made Pearson so perfect. He was a stranger to the trading community and had no concerns about betraying his brothers. More to the point, he wished to learn the secrets of trade, yet he had nothing but contempt for those who had learned the secrets through the usual slow and persistent means. Duer offered him an opportunity to demonstrate his inherent superiority, wrapped in the protective cloak, so he would believe, of the undisputed master.

It began slowly. Duer had Pearson make a few trades he knew would prove sound, and these enticed Pearson's appetite. While he profited, Duer also directed Pearson to lose a few thousand dollars on a single trade, and Duer did not hesitate to return the funds with all speed and cheer, demonstrating that he was as good as his word and Pearson had nothing to fear from his losses. Within six weeks, Pearson was making a name for himself on the Philadelphia floor as a canny investor. No one knew he was Duer's puppet, and no one knew he was doomed.

Part of the difficulty of attempting to corner a market is that it does not take long for buyers to recognize that someone, even if they don't know who it is, consistently snaps up an issue when it comes to market. Thus, the prices of six percent securities began to rise, which made them more expensive and harder to obtain. Men who already held them understood an attempt at a corner was under way and so were understandably reluctant to sell.

The best way to bring more issues to market was to convince holders that they did not know all and that someone else knew more. Thus it was that Duer and Pearson executed a simple but effective deception. At the City Tavern, Duer arrived and announced he wished to sell six percents and buy four percents, rated less valuable for the simple reason that they yielded less interest. Yet the price of six percents was high, and the other speculators drew the obvious conclusion that Duer anticipated that six percents had peaked and that four percents were undervalued and poised for a sudden increase.

Pearson, per prior arrangement, accepted Duer's offer to sell. It was a perfect deal, since Pearson would simply return the six percents back to Duer later in the day. Pearson, who had begun to attract some notice, then announced that he would buy four percents from anyone who would sell them, and that he no longer wished to purchase six percents. Within a few days, the price of four percents soared while six percents declined. Duer's other agents, those acting with his money, snapped up the six percent issues now on the market. Pearson continued to buy four percents at a newly inflated rate, a rate they would likely never see again, but this rate kept the four percents high and the six percents low. It was for this reason, and no other, that Duer continued to drive Pearson, and anyone who would follow him, to keep buying. When it was all done, Pearson had committed himself to more than sixty thousand dollars of four percents, issues whose value was wildly overinflated and would crash without warning.

"I doubt the whole lot is worth more than forty thousand," Duer said to me, "and that is under the most optimistic of circumstances. If Pearson tries to sell them in anything but the smallest increments, he shall drive the price even lower. Of course, much of this will depend on how the other buyer chooses to act."

"What other buyer?" I inquired.

"I haven't been able to determine his identity, but there is another trader attempting to obtain four percents. It hardly matters, though. If the price goes down a little or a lot—or even stays high—it is nothing to me."

"But what of Pearson? Have you not ruined him for more purchases?" I asked.

"Not at all. He is like the drunkard who must have more wine. He has a taste of victory, and he will not let a little loss affect him. Indeed, he does not even know yet that he has lost. I believe I can extract another fifty or sixty thousand dollars of losses from him before he begins to grow suspicious, and by then it will be too late."

While Duer delighted in his deception, I plotted mine. Duer now trusted me entirely, and soon it would be time for me to lead him to his own destruction.

After the phenomenal success of the initial opening of the Bank of the United States and the wild trade in scrip, a number of other banks began to make preparations to launch, and though they had no real means of sustaining themselves, they hoped that public enthusiasm for new banks would prop up what would be otherwise empty ventures and sustain operations until the banks could become self-sufficient.

The most unlikely of these ventures was something called the Million

Bank, as much a political as an economic scheme launched by Hamilton's old political enemy Melancton Smith, with the aid of New York governor George Clinton, a fellow Hamilton-hater. I would never find a bank launched for worse reasons by more inept men. Anyone involved would be likely to incur Hamilton's anger, and I knew at once it was just the thing I required.

I saw Pearson as the perfect vehicle to lead Duer to the Million Bank, but I was not entirely certain how to convince him of my idea without incurring his suspicion, or perhaps his scorn. I therefore decided I would need to be more intimate with his family and arranged on several occasions to be introduced to Mrs. Pearson. I had anticipated a dour creature, someone cold either from a cruelty compatible with her husband's or a weakness that made her subject to it, but it turned out that Mrs. Pearson was a pretty woman, with fair hair and blue eyes, lively and full of wit and good humor. Yes, there was an unmistakable sense of sadness in her. Given the nature of her husband, I could hardly be surprised.

Mrs. Pearson soon became my particular friend, and I enjoyed the times I spent with her. It had been a long time indeed since I'd had a close friendship with another woman, and Cynthia was for me the perfect companion: warm and intelligent, but streaked with a melancholy and cynicism that left her with no patience for the empty platitudes that pass for conversation in polite society. She had never known the hardship of the West, but she had known her own sort of hardship and seemed like a sister to me. Yet I lamented the connection, for while we grew ever more attached, I was searching for an opportunity to destroy her husband—an action that must also destroy her.

One afternoon, while we drank tea in her parlor, I observed that Mr. Pearson was at home, and I had the distinct impression that he was listening to our conversation. I pushed the talk toward private matters, in particular the happiness I had known with my late husband. "Is it not a wonderful thing," I said, "to have a husband with whom you can enjoy so much likeness of mind? Above all things, it is necessary to contentment that one's spouse be agreeable."

At once Cynthia's face clouded over and I heard a creak upon the floorboards of the adjoining room. Pearson crept closer, hoping to hear her response.

"I am sorry you lost your husband," said Mrs. Pearson. "It sounds as though there were never two more compatible people."

I had long since sensed that she and her husband were far from companionable, and so I did not press the issue. I had what I wanted—Pearson's secret attention—and I meant to press the attack.

"I wish I could understand other men as well as I understood my husband," I said to Mrs. Pearson. "It is on that score I wished your advice. You know I am friends with Mr. Duer?"

"The world knows it," she said, her words containing more than what was spoken, though I know not what else. I flattered myself it was no more than curiosity.

I put my hand to my mouth. "I hope no one suggests anything improper."

She shook her head. "One need only look upon the two of you. He regards you more like a daughter, I believe, than anything else."

"I am glad to hear you say so. He is a clever man, and I have learned a great deal from him, but he is, I am afraid, rather dismissive of some of my ideas. You say he treats me like a daughter, but sometimes he treats me like a child. I wish to present a proposal to him, one I believe could make him a great deal of money, but I must suggest it in just the right way, lest he dismiss it out of hand."

Mrs. Pearson began to offer up much sage advice on soothing male pride, but I only pretended to listen. My heart beat hard in my chest. I could only hope this scheme would work, because if it did not, I would have to take a much more direct approach, and the more Pearson believed the idea his and not mine, the greater my chance of success.

All this concern was for nothing. As I left the house, Pearson came after me, not precisely racing but walking in his slow, methodical, stiff manner. His chin was raised, his eyes heavy and vaguely sleepy. He clearly wished to appear seductive. In that moment, I hated him more than I hated Duer or Hamilton.

"You will forgive me, madam," he said, "but inadvertently I overheard what you said to my wife. It is true that Duer may not take your proposal seriously, but you may be assured he will take it seriously from me. He has learned to trust me."

"Indeed he has," I said.

He placed one of his large hands on my elbow, perhaps because he had seen Duer touch me thus. I hated when Duer touched me, and yet I did not fear him the way I feared Pearson. Duer was merely a vile self-centered villain. Pearson, I was beginning to understand, was a beast.

"You must tell me what you have in mind," he said, "and if I like it, I shall present the idea to Duer. If he wishes to implement it, we shall tell him whose idea it was."

"Why, that is generous of you," I said, offering him my most gracious smile. "Shall we return to the house and discuss it?"

"By all means."

I looked up and there, at the window, was Mrs. Pearson peering down at us with concern in her eyes. At first I thought she suspected I had some evil design upon her husband, but then our eyes met, and I realized her concern was for me.

In my madness to destroy Duer and Hamilton, in my hatred for Pearson, I had refused to think of Mrs. Pearson, that lovely, intelligent, and oppressed creature. I had refused to consider her children. They too would be destroyed with Pearson; when Duer and Hamilton and the rest came undone, the innocents would be undone with them.

I had come much too far to turn away on such an account. I could not refuse to fight a war because there might be innocents harmed. Innocents were harmed during the Revolution, and no one would say the war was not worth fighting. Even so, at that moment I took a silent vow. I would break Hamilton and Duer, yes, and it was now a foregone conclusion that Pearson would be dashed upon the rocks as well, but I would protect Mrs. Pearson and her children from the worst of it. God help me, I would not become what I despised.

Ethan Saunders

A new morning met me in New York. Leonidas and I breakfasted together, and I informed him we would waste no time in pressing forward. To that end, I said we would spend the day—unless something
of greater interest revealed itself—in the Merchants' Coffeehouse,
which I knew from my time living in this city to be the financial center of New York. At the corner of Wall and Water streets, the Merchants' was a handsome structure in the New York style, bold on the
outside, spacious within. The taproom of this establishment was commodious and comfortable, with several fireplaces and a surplus of candles to keep the place well lit. It was filled by a wide variety of
gentleman, most of whom appeared to me to be too old and too fat to
warrant much respect.

Leonidas garnered a few curious looks from those uncomfortable
with the notion of socializing with Negroes, and he suggested he return

to our rooms. I would not let him go. "I need to have someone to speak to. I do better thinking when I can speak my ideas aloud."

"Then you may hire a whore to sit and talk with you, if it is all the same."

"Don't be so sensitive. You are like a jilted lover. In any event, you must know by now that you are more than a person with whom I can engage in dialogue. You are proving to be a very capable spy yourself, Leonidas."

He appeared pleased with my saying it. "But what of the looks? The traders don't like a Negro here."

"Even stronger than their dislike is their greed and indifference. If there were one of those instructional books, an *Every Man His Own Spy* or something of that nature, one of the chapters would certainly instruct you to act, everywhere you go, as if you belong there. That, more than anything else, will keep you safe. Now, let us see what sort of trouble we can cause. You there." I grabbed a passing trader. "Is it true that the Million Bank launches next week?"

He snorted. "Yes, but what of it? The Million Bank is a sham, a scheme rooted in political mischief and greed. No one but a fool will waste his money upon it."

I affected a look of surprise "Are you certain? I know for a fact that Duer means to invest heavily. Can the great Duer be mistaken?"

Something changed upon the man's face. "You are certain of that?"

"From the man's lips himself," I said.

"Then for God's sake, tell no one else," he said, and hurried off.

"There will always be a storm," I told Leonidas. "You may be rained upon or cause the rain yourself. I very much prefer the latter."

"What do you imagine he prefers?" Leonidas asked, pointing to a table across the room.

Drinking coffee, with an expression of utter seriousness, was my old friend Kyler Lavien.

He was alone at his table, so Leonidas and I sat down to join him. "Good afternoon, Leonidas, Captain Saunders. What are you doing here?"

"You know what I'm doing here," I said. "I'm looking for Pearson."

He smiled. "I understand that you have good reason to do so, and he has good reason to fear your finding him, but that doesn't explain why you went out to Greenwich to see Duer."

"You know about that?"

He leaned forward. "I know about everything, at least in the end. I want you to stay away from Duer."

"Duer is my best chance of finding Pearson. There is something improper in their dealings, but they do business together somehow, and, at least for Pearson, it is a desperate business. If I stir things up for Duer sufficiently, Pearson will emerge."

"If I can find out anything about where Pearson is, I shall tell you."

"I appreciate that," I said, "but I trust you won't mind if I continue to look on my own."

"As it happens, I do mind. There are things in play now—delicate things. I cannot risk your acting on your own."

"Then bring me in," I said. "Tell me what you do."

"I have not permission for that. You of all men must understand that I am in a difficult position. Were it in my power to trust you, I would. But I must act alone, and you must stay away from anything involving the Million Bank, stay away from anything involving the Bank of the United States, and stay away from Duer." He rose. "You and I have been friends, Saunders, but do not test me on this. You know what I am capable of. Good day."

Leonidas watched him leave. "He is unhappy."

"Rather unkind of him to take out his frustration on us, don't you think?" I signaled the boy to place our orders, but he did not come over. Instead, an older man in a very dirty apron manifested himself and came to our table. "Are you named Saunders?" he asked.

Leonidas stiffened considerably in his chair. I don't know what he made ready for, but I suppose after ten years in my service he knew that any time a stranger recognized me, it might well mean trouble.

I told the man I was indeed who he thought, but there was nothing threatening in him. He was, in fact, naught but smiles. "Very good, sir. I'm meant to inform you that your orders, sir, for drinks only—spirituous drinks, you understand—are to be paid for at no charge to you. May I send you a bottle of our best claret, sir?"

"Yes, that would be very good. Better make it two," I said.

"Ah, very good, sir. Your wine shall be with you anon." He bowed and retreated backward for a few steps, as though afraid I might attack him if he turned away.

"Duer means to keep you drunk," Leonidas said.

"Obviously."

"He is clearly afraid of the damage you might do to him."

"Certainly."

"And what shall you do about it?"

"Drink his wine and then do the damage."

To the accompaniment of some very good wine indeed, we spent several hours watching small trades transpire about us. At 3 P.M. there was a mass exodus into one of the Merchants' long rooms, where an auction in government securities was conducted by a man named John Pintard. It was a raucous and loud affair, and things happened far too quickly for me to understand who sold and who bought. Duer did not himself attend, but I noticed the unusually tall Isaac Whippo standing toward the back of the room, carefully observing each transaction.

After this, we retired back to the taproom, as did many of the speculators. The auction seemed to be only the most orderly and organized of the day's activities, for the real trading took place afterward in comfort and semiprivacy.

Whippo left after the auction, which I considered to my advantage. I did not want him around to see me work my business. It had been of some value to sit and watch, to listen to men talk. It was an even greater advantage to invite them to talk with me, using the excellent free wine as an incentive. I decided it would be wrong of me, very wrong, not to use Duer's assault upon my perceived weakness against him, and I spread it about that I was willing to share my bounty with any man willing to share information about Duer. No one precisely lined up, but as soon as one man left my table, another was willing to take his place. I listened to what each had to say and would ask the occasional question about Pearson, though this yielded little fruit. Some knew who he was and had seen him in New York, though not recently. Some asserted he worked with Duer, but none could say to what end or in what capacity.

I did hear a great deal about Duer, though, much of it contradictory. The Million Bank was indeed upon everyone's lips, and while most men had absorbed the message Duer wished them to receive—that this project was a fiscal disaster in the making—I was also pleased to hear repeated back to me the very rumor I had spread that morning: that the Million Bank was poised to be a major enterprise, and that Duer himself had invested heavily.

I had been at my project almost two hours, and growing weary of it, when a shadow crossed over my table and a vaguely familiar voice greeted me. The man himself was uncompelling in stature, losing his hair precipitously, and dressed finely in a new suit of light blue material. It took a moment, but then I recognized him, for I'd met him at the Bingham house. This was the new senator from New York, Colonel Aaron Burr.

"I'd hoped to make your acquaintance once again," he said, and sat without waiting to be invited.

I presented Leonidas to him, who nodded and spoke a few pleasant and forgettable words, as was his habit when I treated him as an equal. Burr looked at the bottle of wine, having clearly heard rumor of my bottomless supply. I called for a fresh glass and a fresh bottle.

With wine in hand, he appeared ever more relaxed. "What brings you to New York, Saunders? I hear you have been making inquiries of Duer. Are you making inquiries for Hamilton?"

"I'm merely curious," I said.

He knew an obfuscation when he heard one, and I had no doubt he had issued more than his share. "Then you are not upon Treasury Department business?"

"I am upon personal business," I said, as though this were but more casual conversation. "Tell me, have you seen Jacob Pearson here in New York?"

"I *have* seen him in New York, but not recently. Are you hoping to create a reunion of our little circle from the Bingham house?"

"What do you mean?"

"Well, the two of us, Pearson, and that delightful Mrs. Maycott."

This was interesting. "She is in New York?"

"Oh, yes, she has rooms in a boardinghouse on Wall Street. You must be careful, though. A rich widow is always an attractive target, but her Irishman doesn't let any suitors too close."

It was tempting to jump to conclusions, but I could not know that this was the same Irishman I'd met outside the Statehouse. New York was more full of Irishmen than Ireland. "Have you met this guardian?"

"Oh yes. Very imposing fellow. Not young, but tall, hairless as an egg, and smelling of whiskey. I would not recommend crossing him."

The charming and beautiful Mrs. Maycott, who claimed to be my best friend in this affair, was in league with the bald and giant Irishman from the Statehouse. This was disturbing news indeed.

"As for Pearson," he continued, "that is a more difficult matter. They say he is hiding from the Treasury Department, though no one knows precisely why. I suppose that is why Freneau is passing his time here in New York. He must wish to find Pearson as well as you, though I imagine for different reasons."

"Philip Freneau?" said Leonidas. "Jefferson's newspaper man? What has he to do with all of this?"

"I don't know," said Burr, "but if you wish to know, I can think of no better method of discovering the truth than asking him. He is sitting across the room."

Fortunately, he had the good sense to do no more than gesture with his head. I looked over, and there indeed was a gentleman I recognized. I could not disguise my astonishment. I knew the man's name and I knew his face, but I had never before associated the one with the other. It was the frog-faced man whom I had seen watching me all over Philadelphia. He sat behind a pillar so he was mostly obscured, and he was looking away at the moment, but every few minutes he glanced in my direction. He took a lazy note on a piece of foolscap. The man who had appeared everywhere I went was Jefferson's newspaper man.

"He has been following me for some time," I said to Burr. "Have you any idea why?"

"I imagine it is because he believes you can lead him to a story for his newspaper, and if it is for his paper, it must be something to make Hamilton look poorly."

"Do you know the man?" I asked.

"Not well, but I know him a little. I've had a few social interactions."

"Is he a physical man?" I asked. "Does he possess courage?"

"Not that I've seen," said Burr.

I glanced at Leonidas. He said, "Good."

Not long after that, Mr. Burr excused himself. Leonidas and I entertained a few more speculators in search of good claret and dropped a few more hints about the Million Bank, but I kept my eye on the froggy Mr. Freneau. At near eight o'clock, he left the Merchants', and Leonidas and I followed him. There could be no guarantee that his path would provide an opportunity for us, but as it turned out, the streets were quiet and poorly lit, and it was no difficult task to find our moment.

We approached him quietly from behind, and Leonidas turned his shoulder outward and slammed hard into Mr. Freneau's back. Leonidas then stepped back—men are more indignant if they know they are knocked down by a Negro—and I moved forward to take his place. "I do beg your pardon," I said, picking up Mr. Freneau's leather bag, which he had dropped as an inevitable result of Leonidas's expertly placed blow. It was dark and thus easy for my fingers to explore inside, extract a thick package of folded papers, and slip them into my own coat. "Your bag, sir," I said, holding it out.

He snatched the bag with great irritation. "You did that purposefully."

"For what reason," I demanded, "would I knock down a stranger on purpose?"

"Come, Saunders. You must know by now I've been keeping my eye on you."

I gasped. "Can it be?"

"You may choose to play games," said Freneau, "but I think it time we dealt openly."

Being in possession of Freneau's documents, I could not help but think the advantage was mine, so I invited him to join me in the taproom of Fraunces Tavern. I was happy to escape the cold, and we made ourselves comfortable near the fire. Before I could call for refreshment, the publican came forth to inform me that Duer had made the same arrangement with him as with the owner of the Merchants'. I therefore asked him to send me two of his best bottles of wine. I did not want them for myself, only to make Duer pay and to make him believe I depended more on his generosity than I did.

"Now, then," I said to Freneau, "perhaps you will tell me what you wish of me."

"You know what I wish. I wish to know what Duer and Hamilton are up to."

"They are not up to anything together."

"Together, separate, it hardly matters. You will find it is all of a piece. Now, out with it. There has been something brewing for some time. I've long felt it. This is an election year, you know, and my readers must have the truth."

"Perhaps you should first tell us what you know, since I too must have the truth. You say what you know, and then I will add what I can."

Freneau pressed his lips together in satisfaction, which made him look all the more froggish. "I know Duer plans to gain ownership of the Million Bank. He puts it about that he thinks the scheme will fail, but it is only so he and his agents can obtain more shares themselves."

"What is the harm in that? Many predict the bank won't survive, but if Duer wants to invest in it may he not do so?"

"Duer lies. He warns everyone away from the Million Bank launch, and then he plans to move in with his agents to gain a controlling share. What happens then? It's a new bank. It is regarded with interest and enthusiasm. The value of its shares rise, and, inevitably, the value of the shares of other banks falls. It may be temporary, but it happens. But if a man controls enough of one bank he can then use the artificial value of the inflated price of shares to buy up a controlling interest in another bank. In this case, Duer thinks he can use the Million Bank to take over the Bank of the United States. When he is done, the most venal man in America will hold in his hands the nation's finances, and Hamilton will have all but handed his bank over to him."

"It is a fantasy of Hamilton-haters," I said. "Why should Hamilton wish to sacrifice the bank, the thing of which he is most proud, by surrendering it to Duer?"

"Hamilton wishes to erase the difference between the government and the moneyed interests," said Freneau. "He wants to out-British the British, to build a corrupt nation, run by the rich, who use land and people as a factory for their greed."

"It must be pleasant to believe one's own lies," I said.

"I have proof enough." He patted his bag. "I can demonstrate what sort of a monster Duer is. His agents in Philadelphia and Baltimore and Charleston short government issues, and the word spreads, so the price declines. His agents in New York and Boston then buy them at a reduced price."

"But how does that aid him?" I asked. "One set of agents loses money, the other set gains. Does that not eliminate, or at least reduce, his profits?"

"It would," said Freneau, "if the agents shorting were using Duer's money. No, these are more like partners, convinced that they are sharing risks and rewards with the great man. They don't know it, but Duer sacrifices them in order to gain what he imagines to be ultimate wealth."

"Is Jacob Pearson such a man?" I asked.

"He is," Freneau said. "Duer has quite devastated Pearson's holdings, but the man is too big a fool to see it. What remains of Pearson's wealth will be put into the Million Bank, and then Duer will offer to help with Pearson's new debt in exchange for his Million Bank shares."

"That can't be the only means by which Duer aims to get control of the bank."

"No," said Freneau. "He has other agents, men who will, in fact, use Duer's money, to buy on the day of the launch."

"Do you know who they are?"

"I have that information," he said, patting his bag again. "But it is time for you to give me something."

"I've heard a rumor that Pearson is in New York. Do you know if that's true?"

"I have heard he is, but I have also heard he does not wish his whereabouts known."

"So you can tell me nothing of it?" I pressed.

"Nothing," said Freneau, "but one never knows when new information may be acquired. Make me your friend, sir, and I shall keep your questions in mind."

I was distracted, thinking of Pearson, of his hitting Cynthia, of his fist striking her face. I thought of him threatening to harm his own children. I had thought Freneau could tell me, but he knew nothing. If he deceived me about anything, I believed, it was about the likelihood he might yet discover the information I wanted. "Very well," I muttered.

"Tell me about Kyler Lavien," said Freneau.

That brought me back to the conversation. I did not know how much Freneau and the Jeffersonians knew about Lavien, but anything was too much.

I looked at him and did my best to appear puzzled. "Who?"

"Don't attempt to make me into a fool," he said.

"How could I attempt myself what nature hath wrought to perfection?"

Freneau sat straight. "Do you break your word in order to protect a scoundrel like Hamilton?"

"I've grown somewhat fond of Hamilton," I said. "I discover he is a decent man, and I'll not help a bloodthirsty jackal like you libel his name because you refuse to recognize that he and Duer, however much they may once have been friends, are now set against each other. Can you not advance the cause of your democratical republicanism with the truth? If you can't, perhaps it is not worth advancing."

Freneau chose to act as though I'd said nothing. "I asked you to tell me about Lavien."

"I cannot tell you of a man I've never heard of. Is he the French ambassador? Perhaps Jefferson knows him from all that time he spent in Paris, buying wines and furnishings, while the rest of us fought a war."

Freneau, unflatteringly, allowed his eyes to bulge. "I'm sorry I told you anything. I wish I could take back my words."

"And I wish all children of the world might be given the gift of beautiful flowers. Now be gone, you tedious man, and trouble me no longer."

Freneau stood. "You will regret using me so."

"I don't think so," I said. "I think, in fact, I will look back on this abuse with pleasure. Now, please go before I ask my man to knock you down again."

Leonidas grinned at him, and that proved the final argument. He stood, cast us a resentful glance, and left the tavern.

I had hoped to find Pearson tonight, but my hopes had been dashed. Even so, it was hardly a disastrous evening. Indeed, I had every reason to be pleased with myself, and with this in mind I took the papers from Freneau's bag and proceeded to see what he had to teach us.

Joan Maycott

Autumn and Winter 1791

Back in his house, while his wife attempted to walk noiselessly one floor above us, I sat with Mr. Pearson in his library. He poured me a glass of wine, and I sat in an armchair while he sat across from me on the sofa. I had a curious role to play, part child, part speculator, part seductress, and I was suddenly uneasy, aware of the noises of the street outside us, the clicking of the clock in the room, the distant barking of a dog. I sipped the wine so it would redden my lips, and then I began.

I spoke of the Million Bank, describing it as, yes, another bank attempting to capitalize on the public's new mania for banks, but also far more. Under the correct circumstances, it could become the most powerful financial institution in the new country. It only required daring leadership. It require men who were willing to see the times for what they were, times of unchecked possibility, times in which destiny might be shaped by the bold and the clever.

Pearson, who imagined himself such a man and was indeed looking at my wine-darkened lips, hung upon my every word, so I told him how I believed a relatively small group of investors, if they could but command enough money, might attempt to take the whole initial stock offering; imagine, I said, what a cabal might do if it suddenly and for a relatively small investment found itself in control of a bank.

He stopped staring at my lips long enough to ask me how that might happen.

I explained that I thought a new bank might use the initial euphoria that followed its launch to take over another, more established bank, such as the Bank of New York, or even—for men of true audacity—the Bank of the United States.

Mr. Pearson finished his drink and poured another. He stared out the foggy window for a long moment while he worked his lips soundlessly, as though having a long and somewhat contentious conversation with himself. At last, apparently having won the argument, he turned back to me.

"You chose not to present this to Duer?"

"I did not wish to impose upon our friendship. He asks me for advice, yes, and values my opinion, but it did not seem right that I should offer to direct his affairs."

"Let us be honest, Mrs. Maycott. That is not the reason at all. I think it is time for you to be direct with me."

"Sir," I said in protest. What had I done, I wondered, to tip my hand? Had I grown too lax in my deception? Had one success after another led me to lay down my guard? "If you have any reservations about what I say, you may feel free to disregard it. I remind you that it was you who wished me to speak."

He laughed, loud and barking. It sounded either forced or seething with madness. "You bring it to me because you understand the way things are. Duer's success is but a fluke, but I have had to build my achievements one brick at a time. He is nothing but a rich speculator, but you know a man of vision when you see one."

I was on uncertain ground here, there could be no doubt of that, but at least I was not myself the subject of his suspicion. I masked the sound of my exhalation of relief. "Mr. Duer is my friend, and I have the greatest respect for his successes."

"Of course, of course." He laughed again, though this time less like a lunatic, and waved one of his big hands through the air. "But different men have different talents, and not everyone can be a visionary. Not everyone can be bold enough to see what is invisible to others."

"That is most certainly true. Can I then conclude you think this is something that could be effected?"

"I think it can. It only lacks a man with both means and ambition enough."

"It requires something else, of course. It requires capital, and only a handful of men in the country have enough to attempt such a thing. And, if I understand how things stand, there is only one man with the means who might be willing to try."

"I will speak to Duer," he said.

Understanding full well the value of a coup de théâtre, I said, "Then you must not mention my name. I do not go to him directly because I fear he will not take me seriously, but if you tell him the idea is from me, he may wonder why I did not trust him. It must be our secret."

"But what do you gain if I take the credit for your idea?"

"I gain the satisfaction of feeling clever."

Several days later, Mr. Duer and I sat in the City Tavern and he told me of what he understood to be Pearson's scheme. His voice was strangely flat, and I wondered if I had somehow wandered into a trap. Did he know I had been deceiving him? Yet I could not back away now. I listened as he described my Million Bank scheme back to me in all its blunt, insane glory.

"Do you think it possible?" he asked me.

I pretended to give the matter a great deal of consideration. "I do think so, yes."

He rubbed his hands together. "The trick will be how to shift Pearson away from attempting to order me about. It is a brilliant idea, but he would not know how to go about it. It is only by the strangest of flukes that he would even think of it before I did."

"You need not worry," I said. "Pearson likes to present himself as brilliant, but he is all bluster, and he knows it. You will make him do as *you* wish by letting him tell you that he is doing as *he* wishes, even while he follows you about as though led by the nose. You need only tend to his pride, and he will give you all you need."

Duer smiled at me. "You are an astute observer of human nature. I should very much hate for you to be my enemy."

I sipped my tea and said nothing. Over Duer's shoulder, the scarred Mr. Reynolds smirked at me, and I could not help but wonder if he had been working on Duer, convincing him to doubt me. It was only a matter of time, of course, until Reynolds or circumstances proved to Duer that he'd been foolish to be so open with me, but I was almost certain that the time was not yet here.

Joan Maycott

December 1791

It was when the scheme to take charge of the Million Bank was under way that we first became aware of Ethan Saunders, who was to become so significant an actor in the events that followed. Since I had formed my friendship with Duer, he and his followers had redoubled efforts to gain a controlling interest of six percent issues. There were now two fairly significant irons in the fire, and when we met one evening at Pearson's house to talk of these things, it was I who raised the question for the first time.

"At some point," I said, "these activities are going to attract Hamilton's attention, are they not?"

"Oh, that is nothing," said Duer. "I can tend to Hammy. All he requires is a kind word, and he shall be satisfied. To know him is to understand he is more dog than man."

Duer and I had more than once discussed Pearson's need to exaggerate his own importance, but Duer was frequently guilty of the same sin.

When Hamilton's name came up, he would pretend to a closeness and influence for which I had never seen evidence. This above all concerned me, for if Hamilton were to discover Duer's activities too early, Duer would indeed be ruined but Hamilton would walk away—perhaps not unscathed but relatively intact.

"I think she's right," said Pearson, scenting Duer's blood. He was now significantly in debt because of his involvement in Duer's schemes, and he had borrowed recklessly from the Bank of the United States, in order to continue losing money and to have enough to invest personally in the Million Bank launch. There were rumors about town that he had even begun to sell off some of his real estate holdings, and if that was the case he was more precariously poised than I had realized or intended. If he fell from the precipice now, I had no notion of how I would save his wife and children, other than to give them money of my own.

"Mrs. Maycott is always sensible," said Duer, "but that does not make her right."

"Hamilton has invested everything—his heart, his soul, his reputation, his career—into the Bank of the United States and the American financial system," I said. "I cannot believe he will ignore suspicious activity simply because you are behind it, William." I did not say what we were all thinking, yet the world knew: During the crisis that followed the bank's launch, Hamilton had ignored Duer's advice against stabilizing the market and had achieved calm at the expense of Duer's profits.

"Well, what can he do?" asked Duer. "He can request that we stop, but he has no power to direct us."

"If he knows too precisely what we plan, he can thwart us," I said.

"And how would he learn what we plan?" Duer asked.

It was Pearson who spoke the name, saying it as if it were something vile, a bitter pill that, lodged under the tongue, blossoms foully in the mouth: "Ethan Saunders."

"Who is that?" I asked. At that point, I'd not before heard the name.

"What?" said Duer. "Ethan Saunders from the war? Was he not cashiered from the army as a traitor?"

"He left under a cloud, yes," said Pearson, "but Hamilton chose never to bring forth official treason charges. He was guilty, and everyone knew it, but no one could be troubled with it. The war was nearing its close, but he was Washington and Hamilton's pet, and I cannot imagine Hamilton will not use him now. I have seen him about town of late. He's become a drunk and a womanizer—the sort of man you cannot look on without wanting to destroy."

"Then it seems unlikely that Hamilton would engage his services," I observed.

He looked at me a long moment, and I must admit it made me extraordinarily uncomfortable. "Must you always contradict me?" Pearson asked.

"These things concern me," I said, attempting to keep my voice calm. "We do not discuss what we had for supper last week but what must be done next. I do not contradict, Mr. Pearson. I participate."

"Yes, yes, you are a clever woman and all that," he said. "But you must remember that I am a man, and that makes me cleverer. You are, at best, a parlor trick."

Duer rose to his feet and looked to me like a little boy who needed to relieve himself but knew not where to do it. "I do not wish to involve myself in what must be a private dispute. You will excuse me for a moment."

Seeing me abused, Duer wished to absent himself and so be rid of the discomfort.

I forced a pleasing smile at Pearson. My face was bright and full of nothing but admiration and congeniality. "We have no disagreement," I said. "Mr. Duer may sit back down, and you, sir, may continue. We are all friends here."

Duer looked not at me but at Pearson and, seeing something he liked, or at least found agreeable, he returned to his seat.

"With your leave," Pearson said to me.

"Of course," I answered easily.

And with that he continued as though there had been no disruption. "Saunders is not what he was, but Hamilton will bring him in, because he is here and because he was said to have been the cleverest spy of his day. I'm sure he wasn't, but that is what they said of him. Besides, he owes Hamilton a debt for not bringing him up on charges. Hamilton would have to be a fool not to use a man who must regard him as the greatest of benefactors."

"So what do you propose?" asked Duer, obviously exerting some effort to sound easy and natural. He did not wish to have Pearson explode before him as well.

"I'll tend to Saunders," said Pearson. "As it happens, I observed him not two weeks ago leaving a low sort of place with the wife of an acquaintance of mine. A word whispered in his ear will encourage this man, Dorland, to remove Saunders for us. Once he is fled or otherwise gone, Hamilton will have no spy at his command. If he learns what we plan, it will only be when it is too late."

In truth, I did not consider this matter as important as Pearson seemed to. Whatever his experience had been with Saunders, it had evidently been unpleasant in the extreme, so if he wished to remove this potential asset to Hamilton, I would not object.

Once I was done speaking to the gentlemen, I went upstairs and found Mrs. Pearson in the sitting room. She was upon the sofa, reading from *Pilgrim's Progress* to the children, who sat listening in rapt fascination. The fire reflected against her pale skin, and she seemed almost to glow.

Upon seeing me, she closed the book. "That's enough for now, children. I would like a word with Mrs. Maycott."

I expected groans and complaints, however halfhearted, for it is a time-honored tradition that children protest when story time ends. These children, however, unfolded themselves from the floor and quietly left the room. They were afraid and overdisciplined, and I knew it was not Mrs. Pearson's hand that had rendered them so.

Once we were alone together, Mrs. Pearson rose and shut the door to the sitting room. She poured us wine and then sat near me on the sofa, that she might speak in low tones.

"I hope you will not be angry if I tell you I overheard some of what you spoke of with the gentlemen."

"Of course not," I said.

She, however, was not quite ready to begin. "I envy you, the way you move among them as an equal. You are so beautiful, and yet they don't treat you as though you were a plaything. How do you gain their respect?"

"I gain it by demanding it," I said.

She turned away. "I cannot demand respect from Mr. Pearson."

"I know," I said quietly. "I know what things are like here, Cynthia. Don't think I haven't seen it. And—and I mean to help you."

She looked at me with great intensity, and I could not tell if it was surprise or hope. "Help me how?"

I shook my head. "I don't know yet. I don't know, but I will help you, Cynthia. You have my word. When this is over, you shall be the better for it."

She turned back to me. "When what is over?"

"The business I do with your husband and Mr. Duer."

She smiled at me. It was a strange thing. Mrs. Pearson was fair, and I dark; her eyes the palest blue, mine a heavy green; her features tiny and delicate, mine sharp and prominent. No one would ever have called us alike, and yet, for an instant, I felt as though I looked in a mirror. I knew that smile, in its stark cynicism and cold, penetrating understanding of the truth. "You command their respect, but you blind them with charm too."

"I don't take your meaning."

She smiled again, though this time it seemed to me more forced. "I don't know what you are doing with them, but I know it is not what they think. No, do not say a word. I don't want you to lie to me, and I don't want you to tell me the truth, lest Mr. Pearson force me to tell him. I don't know Mr. Duer, and I have no opinion of him, but I know my husband, and I shall not interfere with you."

I swallowed hard and attempted to show no reaction at all. "Is that what you wished to say to me?"

"No," she whispered. She turned away again, facing the window; with her voice low and the crackling of the fire, I could hardly hear her. Yet, against the odds, her words made their way to me and somehow were clear. "I heard a mention of Captain Saunders, and I want to know what was said."

"Can it be you know him, this man said to be a traitor?"

"I knew him during the war. He was no traitor, and he was my father's friend."

"And *your* friend?" I asked.

She nodded. "I was to marry him." She faced me now, but her voice was so low it was almost indistinguishable from breath. "Things went very wrong. My father died, and Ethan—had to flee. They accused him of crimes he could not have committed, but the world thought him guilty, and he could not endure that the taint should fall upon me also. I have never believed for a moment he did anything wrong. Ethan Saunders is the most astonishing man I've ever known."

"He is now in Philadelphia," I said.

Her eyes went wide. "What?"

"He is in town, and your husband means to harm him."

She took my hand. "You don't mean to let him, do you?"

I shook my head. "Oh, no," I said. "You may depend upon it. I had never heard of Ethan Saunders before tonight, but he sounds like the sort of man worth protecting." I meant it. Without having met him, I liked him already, perhaps because we had both suffered at the hands of an ungrateful government. At the same time, I could not help but wonder if he might prove to be of some use to me.

I have to admit I was extremely curious about this Saunders, and also quite sanguine about what he could mean for our project. My man in Duer's employ in New York had proved vital, but the rest of the men had been forced to endure months of inactivity, trusting in me as I cavorted with Duer, hoping I knew what I was doing, worrying that instead of bringing down our enemies I only strengthened them.

Learning more about Saunders would give us something to do. One at a time the boys went out to observe him, to see what sort of man he was, to see if he was a threat or an asset. I longed to see him for myself, but most of the public places he frequented were not the sort in which I could hope to blend unseen.

The first time I saw him was at the Duck Pond on a cold and sunny Sunday afternoon. Skye had been observing him and, believing he would be present for some time more, sent a boy to fetch me. When I arrived, I watched him from a distance, walking the perimeter, observing the ladies with predatory interest. He seemed to be particularly attentive to ladies who traveled in groups with no gentlemanly accompaniment.

"What do you think of him?" asked Skye.

"He's very handsome," I said, "and very drunk. I doubt he could be much of a threat to us, and I'm not convinced he will be much of an asset."

"Best to be safe," said Skye.

"It is always better to be safe," I agreed. "Does he have anyone close to him, someone we could approach?"

"There are not many, but I do believe there is someone," Skye said.

"Then it is time we began to pay this someone to keep us informed."

Ethan Saunders

The next morning, Leonidas and I ordered a pot of tea sent up to my room, and with daylight streaming upon my small table, we continued to look over the dozens of pages I'd taken from Freneau. The man had been busy, I will say that much for him, for he had not only several pages of closely written notes but many letters he had evidently borrowed or stolen. These were from and to Duer, and covered many tedious details, some too convoluted or elliptical to be deciphered, but others quite clear. Duer, the letters indicated, was indeed planning on taking control of the Million Bank and using its moment of ascendancy to absorb the Bank of the United States.

Freneau's documents made clear that Duer had organized a group of traders into what he called a Six Percent Club. These men conspired to bring down the price of the six percent issues that Duer might then buy, obtaining a near monopoly. With the issues out of circulation, their value would rise, increasing Duer's wealth. Moreover, Bank of the United States scrip holders needed these issues to pay out their shares. If they could not obtain the six percents, they would have to sell the scrip, most likely at a discount. Thus Duer hoped to gain a monopoly on Bank of the United States scrip. He imagined that by the end of the year, he would be the only significant holder of either. He would, in effect, own the American economy.

"Is it not enough to be rich?" Leonidas asked me. "What drives a man to a wealth that will crush all others?"

"It is the dark side of liberty," I said. "A man is not hindered by what cannot be done, so twisted men like Duer apply that liberty to their greed."

"But can he actually take over the bank?" asked Leonidas.

"No," I said. "I don't think so. There are too many variables, too many things he must juggle. But he can do great damage to the economy, to Hamilton, and ultimately to the country in the process."

"So what do we do?"

"We stop him."

"Lavien said not to."

"He is wrong. Perhaps he is too cautious. He doesn't know what we do."

"Then why not tell him?"

"Because this is my fight, Leonidas. Our fight. Duer's scheme makes a sacrifice of Pearson, and I have sworn to protect his wife. I may hate Pearson, but I must drag him from Duer's fire if I am to save his wife from penury. I cannot trust that Lavien will see things my way. First we stop Duer, then we tell Lavien what we know."

He nodded.

My mind was churning, thinking of a thousand things that might be done. "Would you return to Duer's mansion?" I asked him. "Learn some more from the servants about his plans for Wednesday."

After Leonidas set off for Greenwich, I took some lunch in the tavern and, rather than sit and drink Duer's free wine, decided to take a turn about the city to consider my next move. I had not visited New York in several years, and it continued to improve from the sorry state in which the war had left it. Everywhere were new buildings, or buildings under construction, even in winter. Streets that had been no more than muddy alleyways during the war were now lined with magisterial homes. Here and there were old ruins—abandoned houses and barns and, along the river, docks—remnants of the city's past struggles. These, I had no doubt, would soon enough disappear, lost to new construction and commerce.

I had traveled no more than a block or two from the tavern when I felt that the same shadow had been lurking behind me too long. During the war I had many times been in Philadelphia or New York or other occupied regions, and I was always alert to being followed. It is not a skill one forgets. Thus I sped up, and, feeling that my pursuer must also be speeding, I immediately turned around and headed back.

In doing so, I nearly collided with a tall and decomposing wreck of a man.

"Why," I said, "'tis Isaac Whippo. Fancy seeing you here. I did not know this was the best part of town to pursue boy buggery." Why I had taken such a strong dislike to the man eluded me, but I had, and that was enough for now. Perhaps it was because of his absurdly sinister appearance, perhaps because I felt I could treat him badly and get away with it.

Duer's strange man glared at me but said nothing.

"You may tell Duer that if he wishes to know what I am about, he need only ask. He need not send a cadaver to come spying after me; it is something I don't like."

"And I don't like you," he said.

"Don't say so, my good pudendum. Bit of a term of affection in Philadelphia. Strange place, that, but still. As I rather like you, I must shout it to the world." I then raised my hands and called out to all who passed, "This man is my very dear pudendum!"

Big men, small men, great men, and disentombed men—there is no great difference. Most enter into situations thinking they will have to face this conflict or that. It has ever been my experience that if you present an alternative completely foreign to their expectations, it will end the encounter entirely. So it was with my friend Mr. Whippo. He skulked away like the mummified thing he was.

After being followed by Mr. Whippo, I thought it best to disappear from the street for a short period of time. I therefore chose to divert myself with a visit to Dr. King's celebrated exhibit on Wall Street to view his living menagerie of creatures. It turned out to be a cramped house of the most unspeakable odor, full of small cages in which raged a variety of unhappy creatures, including a pair of sloths, a pair of porcupines, monkeys of all descriptions, and even a male and female of the species known as orangutans. These were very tall, hairy creatures of a ginger color with uncannily long arms and lugubrious faces. Dr. King himself, making a proprietary pass through the exhibition hall, informed me that these creatures were every bit as intelligent as Negroes, but all my efforts at communication failed, and I ultimately decided his conclusions were overly optimistic.

Once it grew dark, I returned to Fraunces Tavern and sent one of the serving boys upstairs to find Leonidas. He had, he told me, been there for several hours but knew not where to find me, so he had chosen simply to wait. His visit to the Duer mansion had proved to be of little value. He had spoken to the serving staff once again and found them eager to gossip about their master, but in the end they had little to say that we did not already know. The six agents in Duer's employ were to gather at his house for a meeting at eight o'clock on Wednesday morning, and from there they would proceed to Corre's Hotel, where the Million Bank's initial stock would be sold.

As he spoke I sensed a presence nearby, someone listening to our conversation. When I looked up I beheld Philip Freneau, who approached our table looking very pleased with himself. He sat down and stretched his legs out before him comfortably. "You asked if I could find Jacob Pearson," he said. "It turns out that I can. You are impressed, I can tell. Of course, I have no intention of telling you where he is, but I thought you might be interested to learn that *he* now knows where *you* are."

I said nothing. Leonidas leaned forward, his face only inches away from Freneau. "Are you implying that you are attempting to make certain some harm befalls Captain Saunders?"

He shrugged, apparently quite unafraid of Leonidas. I do not know I would have been so unafraid had he leaned in that way toward me, but Freneau merely smiled. "Oh, no. I am not a violent man and would never promote violence in others. I merely thought you might wish to know that Jacob Pearson appeared, to my eyes at any rate, quite agitated to learn of your presence."

"What do you want, Freneau?" I asked. "I thought our business was done."

"And it would have been done had you dealt with me honestly, but it seems that's not your way, is it, Captain Saunders? Perhaps it is simply not the Hamilton way. I should even have been content to lick my wounds had you only dealt with me as dishonestly as I had at first thought, but when I returned home, I found you had been far more treacherous than I had suspected. You stole documents from my bag, and I would like them returned."

"Stole from your bag?" I asked. "Good Lord, am I now a thief?"

"You stole them, and I want them back, and if you don't return them to me you shall be very sorry, sir. I have given you but a hint of the harm I can do you."

Leonidas poured himself a glass of wine. He was, of course, usually abstemious in his habits, but he knew well enough how to affect a cool demeanor to menacing effect. "Mr. Freneau, please take my advice," Leonidas said. Even I found his calm unnerving. "Stand up and leave. We have nothing of yours and nothing you want. If Captain Saunders feels threatened, he will call upon me to protect him. You do not want that."

Freneau's face did seem to blanch, but he held his ground admirably, I had to admit. "Captain Saunders, I can do you genuine harm, and I don't mean revealing your whereabouts to a man who hates you already. I can harm you in ways you would not care to think of, as regards your friend and slave. You know of what I speak. Now, return to me the documents you stole, and we shall forget this conversation ever took place."

Could he know about my liberating Leonidas? I'd told no one, but I was not so naïve as to believe that such information, like all information, could not be bought and sold, if only someone recognized its value. I felt suddenly frightened. The issue at hand was of an act of generosity I had performed, but I understood full well how Leonidas, if the news was presented in a biased manner, might misunderstand my actions.

Seeming to understand my thoughts, Freneau smiled at me. "It is amazing how a man might visit an attorney and not trouble to learn he is a Jeffersonian in inclination."

"Whatever he tells you," I said to Leonidas, "is misleading at best. He cannot have all the facts, so let him speak, and we shall sort it out when the rascal leaves us be." I attempted to sound confident, but I could not hide from myself the feeling of rapid descent from a precipice.

Leonidas stood again and looked at Freneau. "You have nothing to say to interest me."

"Oh, you will want to hear this," Freneau assured him.

"No, I won't. Go," Leonidas said.

I smiled at Freneau, seeing I had defeated him. Leonidas's loyalty would win out over any trivial detail.

Freneau stood. "Very well." He replaced his hat. "I see I am beaten." He began to walk off but stopped short. "You must know you are a free man, Leonidas, and have been for weeks. Saunders took the trouble to free you, but he did not take the trouble to mention it?" He turned quickly, as if afraid of some punishment leaping out at him, and departed our company.

Leonidas and I watched him go, carefully avoiding each other's gaze. It seemed to me impossible, given the momentousness of what was just said, that the others in the taproom paid us no mind, yet no eyes fell upon us, and our crisis came without notice. Men gathered in their clusters and drank and spoke and laughed. Life continued all around us, and yet it seemed we were upon a stage, a great light flooding down on us.

At last I turned to look at Leonidas, whose dark eyes were narrow and bloodshot and intense. "Do not say anything else," he warned.

I leaned back in my seat. "Do make yourself easy, Leonidas. I had hoped to make this a surprise when our task was completed, but I see I must tell you now in order to avoid any resentment. A greater sense of ceremony would have been welcome, but now this will have to do. Yes, I made arrangements with a lawyer. Congratulations, sir, you are a free man." I raised my glass to toast him.

It was a bittersweet moment, for I hated to let him go, but his freedom was long overdue. I hoped he would, in turn, look upon me in friendship and gratitude. This was not, I told myself, the end of my connection with Leonidas.

Yet the look on his face remained dark, harsh, unforgiving. He glowered and his breathing had quickened, and I understood something had happened, something terrible and unstoppable. "I have been a free man for weeks, and you did not tell me?"

"Well, I meant to, but then this business with Cynthia arose, and I could not spare you. I thought it best to postpone."

He sucked in air as though he'd been slapped. "You did not trust me to continue to help you of my own accord?"

I stammered like a man explaining away a whore to his wife. "Of course I trusted you, but it hardly seemed necessary to make any big announcements when we had so much with which to concern ourselves. A month or two could hardly make a difference."

"You had no right to hold a free man in servitude."

"I think you are taking this out of context," I said. "You were only free because I freed you. It's not as though I captured you in the African jungle."

"It doesn't matter how I was freed. I was free and you continued to hold me," he said, rising to his feet. "It is unforgivable."

"No, no, no, you are focusing on the wrong things. I have reformed, Leonidas. I have freed you. I understand that this is a confusing moment, but you will sort it out. Sit. Have a drink. Let us talk about your plans."

He remained quiet, in a pose of consideration. His face returned to its more customary sable, and his eyes returned to their traditional oval shape. He blinked at me a few times. Then he said, "I am going upstairs to collect my things, and then I am leaving."

"What?" Now I stood. "You cannot leave me now. I am in the thick of it. You said I ought to have trusted that you would remain by my side, and now you threaten me with leaving."

"I make no threats but a pronouncement. I cannot remain with a man who would use me so. Had you told me before, I would stay, but you did not. Goodbye, Ethan."

I opened my mouth to speak, but he had already turned and I would not demean myself by calling after him like a jilted lover. Instead I sat and poured myself some of Duer's wine. I sat and waited. I watched as he descended the stairs once more, and I watched as he turned to the door without once looking back toward me. I watched as he walked out into the cold New York night, leaving me entirely alone on the eve of crisis.

Joan Maycott

January 1792

I'd thought to go alone and might well have done so. It was not that I did not trust the man I was to meet. In this whole affair, he seemed to me among the most honorable, perhaps curiously so. It was not a question of fear but one of power. Would it make me seem more powerful, I wondered, to go alone and thus show him how secure I felt, or to bring a man with me and show him I had more men in my orbit than he had seen? In the end, I chose the latter. The time had not yet come—if it *were* to come—to let him know how few we were. It hardly mattered, for we had achieved much and would, I believed, achieve all. The smallness of our numbers made us adaptable and agile, but to an outsider it might make us appear weak.

In earlier meetings, he had met Dalton and Richmond, so I brought with me Mr. Skye, who accepted the assignment with solemnity. Now it was dark, and we sat in our hired coach—I'd had Skye hire the plainest one he could find—on the side of a quiet street in an indifferent neighborhood. It was modest, but not poor, and by no means unruly. It was one of those parts of town where men labored hard for their few dollars and held to their homes with pride.

It was not yet nine, the hour of our meeting, and Skye and I sat in the dark. He sat perhaps closer to me than he ought to have, and I could smell the scent of him: leather and tobacco and the sweet hint of whiskey that clung to them all, all the whiskey rebels.

"What are his loyalties?" Skye asked, after a long silence. He spoke quietly, almost a whisper, though I did not think such discretion was necessary. I did not think he believed the question necessary either. He spoke so as to have something to say.

"Right now I think he's loyal to himself," I said, "which means as long as we continue to pay him, he will serve us. We have to be careful, however, not to push him too far or make him fear that anything he does will hurt someone he cares about. I suspect no amount of money will make him do harm."

"No, of course not, else you would not have recruited him. His limitations are why you trust him."

I laughed. "You are wise."

"And you are impressive. More impressive than I can say." I felt him take my hand. "Joan," he said, "so much has happened—to both of us—and I would never imagine that you could put your grief for Andrew aside. Yet you are alive, a vibrant woman, and I should be a strange sort of man were I not moved by your courage and leadership—and, yes, beauty."

I resisted the urge to pull my hand away from his. I could not afford to offend him, to make him feel ashamed. I must be honest also and say that his attentions were not without their appeal. Skye was older than I was, but charming and learned and attentive. He never bristled at my leadership. Andrew, for all that I loved him, had regarded me with a mixture of admiration and tolerance. He humored me as much as he admired me. Skye, though it pained me to admit it, understood me in many ways better than my husband ever could have.

Yet I could not imagine giving my heart over to another man. Something had been taken from me when Andrew was murdered, and I did not want my armor pierced. And there was more. I did not know what would come, but I knew I must be unfettered. Those around me had broken all the rules of human decency to bring me low, and I would not be bound by any rules in striking back at them. I would not be deterred, not by loyalty nor affection nor love, from doing what must be done. Most of all, I did not want him because I did not love him the way he loved me, or believed he did. I wanted his friendship and loyalty and affection, but I wanted nothing more.

"You know it cannot be," I said to him. "You are in my heart, and I am in yours, but that is as far as we may go. There is too much, far too much, that lies before us."

He removed his hand and said, after a moment of attempting to master himself, "Will revenge bring us happiness?"

I let out a bark of a laugh. "It is too late for happiness. Revenge shan't bring it. If I am to speak honestly, I do not think it will even bring satisfaction. How can it? Revenge is the emptiest of enterprises, do you not think so? Days and weeks, perhaps years, to plan and execute, and then, once it is over, what have you? It is put together as meticulously as the artist crafts his work, but there is no painting or sculpture or poem to stand as testament to the labor. There is only the sensation, and that sensation must always be hollow."

"Then why do you do it?" he asked. "Is it only for the money you hope to earn?"

"I should like the money," I said, "but it cannot motivate me. I do it for the same reason you do—because it is my duty. Having conceived of it, having understood it could be done and that it ought to be done, *not* doing it would destroy me."

"Doing it may destroy us as well."

"Yes, it may. But that sort of destruction I can accept."

I parted the dusty curtain of the coach and saw him emerging from his little house. A few minutes sooner might have avoided the conversation with Skye, but I suppose it was well to have it done with. I had turned Skye away but not hurt him. That should keep him content for a little while.

Out the window I saw the man approach the equipage with a cold determination, a man in perfect control though full of perhaps violent emotions. His stride was easy enough, however, as though I were there to take him to an appointment he anticipated with pleasure, or at least contentment. He opened the door and folded his large body into the coach. He nodded to me and Skye, and then took a seat across from us. He was a handsome man with good teeth, perfect and easy in his manners. In a new nation of rough men and rugged manners, it seemed ironic that in him I should find so complete a gentleman.

He looked at Skye. "Yet another associate."

"He is with me," I said, "but I'll refrain from introducing him. I prefer to avoid names where I can."

"I'm sure that is sound." He waited a moment, then said, "I suppose it was inevitable you would come for me."

"We do pay you, and quite well," I said.

"And I do not complain, though I harbored the hope that I might continue to be paid well in exchange for doing nothing."

"I must say I hoped the same," I said, "but things are changing."

He took a deep breath. "What is it you ask of me?"

"I want regular reports," I said. "I want them sent every day. I want to know what Saunders is up to, what he plans, what he knows, and what he believes he knows."

He took in a deep breath. "I don't much like it."

"You should have thought of that before."

"Suppose I simply choose to defy you?" he said.

Mr. Skye leaned forward. "That would not be the wisest course."

I shook my head at the man, vaguely coquettish, vaguely maternal. "It is too late for that, don't you think? You are a man who believes in the value of keeping his word. Is that not why you are here? Captain Saunders did not keep his word to you. He promised to emancipate you, and yet he has not. He does not deserve your loyalty."

"No," said the slave called Leonidas, "he does not deserve it. And yet it is surprisingly hard to let it go."

"You know who we are," I said, "and you know what we have promised. Our enemies are his enemies, it is just that he does not know it, and if we deceive him, it is only to prompt him to do as he would choose himself, if he but knew all."

He nodded. "I'll do it, but if I think he will come to harm, I will not help you. If that is the case, I shall tell him everything, and then I shall be your enemy."

"You are more loyal than he deserves, but I think you'll find that we deserve it as well. When it is all over, you shall see. We will be reconciled."

Leonidas nodded again. Without another word, he departed from the coach.

Through the curtain I watched him return to the house, for I wished to be sure he did not try to follow us, and Skye watched me watch him. That is, I suppose, why we did not see the man approaching from the other side of the carriage. He opened the door and joined us, taking Leonidas's seat almost before we knew he was there.

I knew the scent almost before I knew the face, and in an instant I thought how very ironic it was, for to itemize the odors, they were nearly the same as Skye's—tobacco, whiskey, animal hides. But there was more too. This man stank of old sweat, of clothes infrequently changed, of urine and alley assignations. He carried about him the coppery smell of blood and an indescribable but instantly recognizable scent of menace.

Even in the dark I could make out the wide swath of scar that stretched across his face. "Well, if it ain't Joan Maycott and John Skye," Reynolds said. "I hope I ain't interrupting anything too important or private. I hear talk about you, Skye."

"How did you find us?" Skye asked. His voice rose in excitement and fear. He had not learned, as I had, to mask his emotions. Give no power, no authority, when it is yours to withhold.

"I've been following your lady friend here for some time, trying to figure out what she's about. It ain't been easy, and I'll be honest with you, I still don't know what you are up to. I couldn't get close enough to the coach to hear much."

"So you know of nothing against me," I said. "Now, I suggest you get out of the coach before I inform Mr. Duer how you've treated me. He will not love to hear of this rudeness."

"Duer?" Reynolds waved a hand in the air. "He'd be through with me if he knew, no doubt about it, but you won't tell him. I don't know what you're about, but I know you don't want him to know you're having secret meetings with Saunders's darky. Things ain't what they seem, Joan. They ain't at all. Now, I don't care much. I admire a pretty and clever woman; my own wife is plenty pretty but not so clever. On the other hand, I don't much admire Duer. Never have. But he pays me, so you see my difficulty. If only I had some—shall we call it incentive?—to keep me from mentioning what I seen."

"What sort of incentive?" Skye asked.

"I think a hundred dollars ought to keep my curiosity buried."

"For a hundred dollars, I'd want your curiosity buried forever."

"Forever is one-fifty. Bit more. One hundred only gets you a temporary situation."

I did not like it but had no choice. "Give me a few days to get the money,' and I shall pay you the larger sum. I hope, however, you are as good as your word. We can deal with this amicably and financially so long as no one is exceptionally greedy, but if you think this a well you can return to again and again, I cannot answer for your prospects. As it is, I will need to conceal this arrangement from some of my allies, men who are not so willing to seek compromise as I. I conceal it, you understand, for your benefit."

"I take your meaning," he said, "and I will call upon you again soon. Good evening, madam; Skye."

He departed the coach, and I ordered the driver to move on lest we get more visitors. Skye said, "He will not be content. Not for long. There is no forever for a man like Reynolds."

"No," I said. "Of course not."

"Then why did you agree?"

"Because I hope one hundred fifty dollars will buy us at least a little more time. And when he asks for more, we will give him more. If he asks for two hundred or five hundred, we will give it to him, as long as it is likely he will remain quiet."

"He has too much power over us," Skye said.

"We have one advantage, however. He does not know we need only a little more time. We have to hope his greed and his belief in his own cleverness give us the time we need."

———

It was a new year, and I believed that Duer, Hamilton, and the Bank of the United States had only a few more months left. They did not know it, but the ice beneath them was cracking, and all would soon fall into oblivion.

Duer increasingly found that he did not wish to be without my advice, so he rented for me a set of rooms at a boardinghouse in New York upon the Broad Way. When he was in New York, he wished me there too, though we did not travel together. I was not permitted to visit him at his home or to meet Lady Kitty. Cynics will believe that he and I must have crossed beyond the boundaries of propriety, but it was not the case. It might be that he desired me, perhaps he even believed he loved me— or loved the woman he thought me to be—but he did not seek to break his marriage vows. He did not even hint that he longed for such a thing. I provided him with something else, but even I was never certain what. Perhaps I did not wish to know.

Pearson was but one man among many, more than a dozen that I knew of, whom Duer deceived to ruin, though none of them knew it yet. Some of these men each believed himself to be Duer's closest friend in the world. Each had no idea that within weeks he would be revealed to be worth nothing, his money sunk into Duer's colossal dreams. Duer would talk around these things, never addressing them directly. I would listen, and I would assuage his guilt by telling him of his greatness and his ambition, how what Washington was on the battlefield, Duer was on the trading floor. Had Washington won liberty without sacrificing some of his beloved soldiers? Of course not. When men play at grand strategy, I told him, they can weep for the pawns they sacrifice, but they must sacrifice them still.

"Your vision of grandeur is too great for small men," I told him one day. "In any glorious enterprise, in any historic rise to power, there must be men who suffer for the greater good. If you are to show this country, this world, your vision of what financial greatness can be, are you to stop because some lesser men might get hurt? Perhaps on the surface such a sacrifice might seem noble, but if you are truly willing to turn away from your destiny because it makes you a little uneasy, it is cowardly and selfish—and I know you are not those things."

He nodded. "You are very wise."

"And once you have achieved your final victory, you can be generous to those who were hurt because they were foolish enough to lie down where you needed to step."

"It is true," he said. "I can make amends later."

I felt nothing but contempt for him as he planned to help later those he harmed now, but I could also not help but wonder if I was any better than he. After all, was I not willing to let Cynthia Pearson suffer now and help her at some future date?

In the meantime, Duer might have struggled with his feelings of guilt, but he also laughed at men like Pearson, men who were ruined and did not know it. Yet, Duer was ruined too, and he did not know it either. He owned more and more six percent issues, but he had borrowed far more than their value, and he continued to borrow. He borrowed from the banks, and when they would give him no more, he borrowed from the moneylenders. When they would give him no more, he turned to the poor and the desperate.

"It's really quite marvelous," he said. "I cannot gain control of the six percents or the banks without ready money, so where is it to come from? Why, now I borrow from little people—tradesmen and shopkeepers and cart men. A few dollars here and there for a promise of absurd interest payments. I shall never make good, but that is no matter. Once I have the banks, there will be no one to hold me to account. They may complain about their interest, but it is of no matter. And I am not a bad man, you know. I shall give them back what they lent me, but no more than that, I think."

This was too much. It was one thing to cheat speculators, men who knew they must go into trade with their eyes open. If they were too foolish to see for themselves what Duer did, they had no one but themselves to blame. They must be devoured by the beast they hoped to ride. But now for him to turn his sights on the laboring poor, to squeeze their pennies out of them so he could keep his operations afloat? It was too much.

"There must be some alternative," I said.

"Oh, don't you worry," he said. "I have thought it through carefully."

"When you own the economy, the workingmen and women of the

city cannot be hobbled with debt. They will be a drag upon everything."

"You worry too much, my dear," he said. "And you are all goodness, which I love. But you must trust me on this. The poor shall not miss their pennies, and there are always more where their first came from. They must work a little harder is all."

I smiled at him to show him my approbation. At what point, I wondered, does silence become complicity? At what point must the enemy of evil take responsibility for the harm done in the fight against evil? I did not know, and I dared not think of it. I would only think of poor Ethan Saunders, whom I had turned into my puppet. He would act as I wished, never knowing it was I who wished it, and he would make certain that Duer failed.

It was during this trip to New York that Mr. Pearson himself came to visit us while we sat in the parlor of my boardinghouse. I do not think he knew I was with Duer when he arrived and he seemed surprised, perhaps even disappointed, to see him. In Pearson's mind, he could trust me entirely, but Duer was always an object of suspicion—as he should have been. Duer, after all, was an untrustworthy man.

I think my landlady must not have told Pearson I had company, for he strode into the room manfully, but on seeing Duer begin to rise his body slackened. If I had not been watching him closely, measuring any sign of disposition—for it was now how I watched everyone—I might not have seen it, but there it was. The corners of his mouth twisted, his shoulders drooped, his arms dropped slightly, and he bent just a little at the knees.

He and Duer greeted one another—Pearson's enormous hand circling Duer's tiny one—but his eyes were upon me. There was something pleading there, but I could not tell what he wished from me. At first I believed he wanted me to dismiss Duer, but I soon decided it must be something else. I think even he, himself, could not have said what he wanted, but he somehow believed I would be able to provide it.

"What brings you to New York?" asked Duer. Pearson was, to his core, a Philadelphia man, and I, certainly, had not known him to travel to other cities. More to the point, I believed Duer considered me, when we were in New York, his exclusively. He did not like to share me, and he would have resented doing so with someone so beneath him as Pearson—a man ruined in everything but his understanding of his ruin.

The men returned to their seats, and Pearson brushed at his breeches. It seemed to be a nervous compulsion rather than a response to any dirt from the streets. "I am having difficulties in Philadelphia."

I spoke to take charge of the conversation for him, to make him believe I was attempting to mind his interests. "What has happened, sir? Is something wrong?"

"I'll tell you what's wrong," he snapped, though not at me. He was looking directly at Duer. "I have sold off nearly everything I own. I have done everything you asked me to do, and I am nearly a hundred thousand dollars in debt. All I have to my name are these blasted four percent securities, and they lose value every day. I would have suspected something ill on your part long ago had there not been others buying them up, but this might have been only some other fools following your lead. They are worthless. I might as well use them to kindle my fires, for all they are worth. And the men I speak to—they say they will never again rise in value—that they long ago reached an unrealistic peak."

Duer smiled. "Jack, we've talked about this. The four percents are nothing. You must regard them as nothing. Your debt is nothing. It shall be paid back."

"It must be paid back now, Duer. You promised me that if I did as you asked, you would cover my losses. I've sold my properties. I've borrowed money from the Bank of the United States."

"And all will be made easy," said Duer, "but you know we must wait."

Pearson rose to his feet. "There is no *we*, Duer. It is I who wait."

I rose too and put a hand upon Pearson's wrist. "I know a man such as you, who honors his name in the world of business, must hate to owe what you cannot pay, but you understand that the money is spoken for. Mr. Duer intends to use it to gain control of the Million Bank. Once that bank is launched, he shall take the Bank of the United States. It is hard, but you must be patient."

He bit his lip like a child and shook his head, but he sat again, allowing me to do the same. "It is not about patience," he said. "My creditors are after me. I've left Philadelphia because Philadelphia is too hot."

Duer laughed. "That is nothing," he said. "Send a list of these creditors to my man Whippo. I shall dispatch notes upon the next express explaining that I vouch for you and give my word that you shall make good within the quarter. No one will trouble you."

It was true enough. A note like that from William Duer was almost specie itself. One more set of debts that would ruin him.

"That answers well enough for the baker and the grocer and the tailor," said Pearson. "I don't think it shall satisfy Hamilton."

"You owe Hamilton money?" Duer asked.

"Not Hamilton the man," snapped Pearson. "I owe the bank. You urged me to take out a loan, and I don't even know where that money has gone. Your honey tongue did its magic, and now it is all gone. But Hamilton has sent his spy around on behalf of the bank loan. It seems the bank is restricting credit, calling in loans, and as I never respond to any of the letters, they've put a man upon me."

"That Saunders fellow?" I asked.

He shook his head. "No, Hamilton has a new spy, a little Jewish man called Lavien, and he is the very devil. He has the tenacity of a terrier. One day he waited in my parlor for six hours hoping to see me; my servants tell me he was as impassive as an Indian brave. There is something in his eyes. I met him once, and I felt as though I were speaking to a man who had visited Hell itself and spat out its fires with contempt."

Duer attempted a dismissive smile. "Tell my man Whippo your creditors' names."

"And what of Hamilton's man?" I asked. I did it on behalf of Pearson, so he would think me his ally, but also because I wished to know. I could not have Hamilton and this new spy of his put a stop to things before the final blow was struck.

"I'm sure it is nothing," said Duer. "You may ignore it."

"I think," I said, "it might be better if you were to limit your time in Philadelphia until the Million Bank launch."

"I had hoped to go to a gathering at the Bingham house next week."

"By all means, go," I said, "but do not linger. Go and stay for a day or two, if you must, but do not remain too long, not until after the launch. Then everything will be made easy."

Pearson left the room, and I walked Duer to the door, to put him at ease. I saw now how things must be. I could not save Cynthia Pearson entirely. I did not know if I could save her house and the great wealth she had long enjoyed, but I would save her from total destruction.

Once Duer was out the door, I turned to find Pearson in the foyer, his arms stretched behind him while one of the serving girls helped him on with his coat. He dusted it off once it was upon him and turned to me. "I don't know how you can trust that man. He is the devil."

"He's not," I said softly. "He is brilliant, but perhaps not as effective at explaining himself as he might be." I could not have told a bigger lie, of course. Duer was a fool, but quite good at getting people to do what he wished. That had ever been his secret. He understood no more about finance than anyone else and less than many.

"You do know I am fond of you, do you not?" I asked him. My tone was sweet but not flirtatious. I hated myself for even the suggestion that I would seek to harm Cynthia in this way, but I could not have Pearson abandon the scheme—not now. If he left, others might follow, and then Duer would fall far too soon. Perhaps Pearson need not ruin himself with the Million Bank launch. I might find a way—Saunders, perhaps—to make certain he did not lose the last of his wealth there. But for now I needed him to remain steadfast.

He seemed stunned by my question. He took a step forward and held my hand. "Why, Mrs. Maycott, of course I do."

I hated his vile touch. His oversized hands hardly seemed to belong to a human body, and yet I smiled. "I know Duer better than almost anyone, I think. Do you not agree?"

He continued holding my hand, but we had moved from the amorous to the financial, and he perhaps forgot he still touched me. "It does seem that way."

"He parses out information a little at a time. I shall tell you what he will not. Do not sell your four percents, Mr. Pearson. No matter how low the value falls, no matter how much you lose on them, do not sell them. They will come back. I swear to you, they will come back, and if you will hold on, your patience will be rewarded and you will not only not be the loser for your efforts, you will profit. Duer tells no one this because he does not wish anyone to act upon it, but you have the right to know."

He enveloped my other hand in his meaty paw. "I know not how to thank you, madam. Not only for the kindness of putting my anxieties to rest, but for showing me I have not been a fool."

I pulled away, I hope not too abruptly. "It is our secret," I said. I wished him gone and breathed with relief when he left the house, though the relief was illusory. I had taken a chance. I had risked my position, the wealth of my band of whiskey rebels, and even the scheme itself, for if Duer suspected, even for a moment, that I was anything other than a clever admirer, I should be out, and, once out, I would be powerless. Yet I had no choice. I had reluctantly turned a blind eye while Duer ruined one speculator after another, even when he sent his men out to the street to ruin tailors and fishmongers, but I would not let him ruin a wife and mother who had befriended me. I would not do it, and I could only hope I—and my friends—would not suffer for my loyalty.

Back in Philadelphia, a general discontent fell over the house at Elfreth's Alley. When I returned after my first New York visit of the year, I found Dalton out but Richmond and Skye home, clearly angry with one another.

"You are spending too much time with Duer," Richmond said to me.

I sat in our narrow gathering room on the ground floor. There was a small sofa and several chairs. Skye had brought me tea, which I sipped, but neither of them would join me. Skye sat across the room, watching Richmond as he paced like a caged tiger at a county fair.

"Have you forgotten why we came here?" I said. "Duer and Hamilton stole from us the money owed us and lied to us, that we might trade it for misery and deprivation in the West. Then, once we turned that misery into success, they took it away again—their theft disguised as a tax levied upon those with no money. I spend time with Duer not because I delight in his vile company but because I want to destroy him and save the nation from Hamilton."

"Fine goals, those," said Skye, "and I rejoice in them, but there's more too, let us not forget. We get not only revenge from this but compensation too. Our Joan has already more than tripled our holdings."

"At what cost?" Richmond said. "She cleaves so close to Duer, I doubt she herself knows whose side she's on. Tell me, Joan, do you care more for the country and for justice, after this tripling of holdings?"

Did I not know better, I would have thought Richmond had become jealous, but that was not it at all. He had always been cynical, had always been opposed to any project other than licking our wounds and finding the best possible hole in which to hide ourselves. He accused me of the worst because he feared the worst.

Skye rose to his feet. "You'll apologize," he said.

"Please sit, John," I said softly. I turned to Richmond. "You grow tired of doing nothing, I know. The time for action will come, and if it does not there's no helping it, but one way or another it will be over soon enough. It will be over by March or April, I promise. We will have revenge, the whiskey tax will be repealed, Hamilton and Duer will be destroyed. Then we may go our separate ways, if that is what you wish, but we will have money with which to do it. I know it is hard to be patient, but you must persevere. There is no other choice."

When a man's blood is up, there is nothing quite so infuriating as good, solid reason. Richmond grabbed his coat and left the house at once. After a moment of silence, Skye walked over to me, took away my cup of tea, and left the room. He came back in a moment with a bottle of wine and two glasses. He set them on the table, poured two glasses, and sat directly across from me.

"You've got to give Richmond something to do," he said. "He will go mad, and he will drive me mad. He's always been more beast than man. Not in the brutal way we often use the term, but he is meant for doing and action, for being outdoors and finding his own food. Sitting about in a house all day attempting to draw no attention to himself is no life for him."

"We may need him yet," I said, "though I pray God no. If things come to a crisis, we'll be glad of him, and he'll be glad to be of use. It cannot be helped that he is too uneasy to wait quietly for that moment. You seem to have no complaints, John."

" 'They also serve who only stand and wait,' " he quoted, "and cook dinner and clean the house." He attempted a smile.

I sipped my wine and closed my eyes. Behind me the fire burned; I loved the feel of the heat on my neck. I had been in a carriage all the day before, and now to be upon a comfortable sofa with a glass of wine seemed the height of luxury.

I was able to enjoy my peace only a moment, however, before the door flew open hard and loud. I leaped up, knowing not what to expect, but fearing either we had been discovered by Duer for what we were or that Richmond was back, somehow more angry than before.

The door was now open. The wind stirred up the fire, sending it into a rage, and snow blew into the front room. Dalton stood in the doorway, looking massive and vibrant. A huge grin broke out under his red mustaches. "I was hoping you'd be back, girl. We've got some good things brewing."

"What is it?" Skye walked toward Dalton, for no other reason, I believed, than because it gave him something to do, something unrelated to his awkward conversation with me.

"It's that Saunders fellow," he said. "He's hooked for certain now."

"What do you mean?" I demanded.

"You know that Pearson's fled town?" Recollecting himself, he shut the door and then walked over to the calming fire to warm his hands.

"I saw him in New York," I said. "He's hiding from creditors."

Dalton nodded. "His wife suspects something. She sent a note to Saunders."

I felt something spring to life inside me. "What sort of note?"

"Now, how would I know the answer to that?" he asked.

"Get it," I said. "Go to his boardinghouse, and if he isn't home yet, get it. Pay the landlady what you must to give it to you and keep her mouth shut. Promise her more each week she helps us. She'll not betray us if she thinks there's more money to be had."

"Why do you want to delay him?" Skye asked. "He'll find out in the end."

"That's precisely why." To Dalton I said, "When you pay the landlady, give your name as *Reynolds*. Make sure she hears the name and knows it. When Saunders finds out, as he must, he will begin to look to Duer."

Dalton sighed. "I hope you know what you're doing, Joan. If Saunders stops Duer too soon, it's all for nothing."

"We need to make sure we can hobble Duer when we need to, so we'll set Saunders to sniffing around, but after the wrong things. It will make Duer uneasy and more eager to trust me. We had been thinking of using

Saunders only to keep Duer from growing too powerful too quickly, but now I see he can be much more than that. Through Saunders we can manipulate Hamilton. We can make certain he learns nothing before we are ready, and everything when we wish it."

The two men left, and I was alone in the house, suddenly feeling content and at ease. I could not say why, precisely, but I felt certain that all was now in hand, or soon would be.

Ethan Saunders

I was on my own. So be it. I have worked alone in the past and I would do so again. Alone I would prevent William Duer from taking control of the Million Bank. I would have to remove from the game six men in the space of one morning, and to do that I would need to learn who they were, where they lived, and the nature of their personal arrangements. It would be difficult but eminently possible.

I began to go through Freneau's papers anew. Freneau had taken detailed and useful notes regarding Duer's scheme with the Million Bank. It was not clear to me why Freneau had not yet revealed his discovery to the public, and I could only conclude that rather than save the nation from a dangerous financial collapse, he would much prefer to see that collapse transpire. With Hamilton humiliated, Freneau would then be in a position to explain it. Fortunately, however, I was in a position to prevent that collapse from taking place. The key lay in Duer's agents, and I studied Freneau's papers to learn what I could of them, including their names and where they lived. I gleaned a little more from a few of the letters—this one was unmarried and lived alone, that one had a wife and two children. They were small details, but they might make all the difference.

Time not passed in discovering the details of Duer's agents I spent in the Merchants' Coffeehouse, where the air trembled with expectation—in part, I own, through my own machinations, for I never failed, when given the opportunity, to whisper that the Million Bank launch was imminent and that William Duer himself thought it the best investment of the season. Though cooler heads still regarded the new bank as a foolish venture, destined for failure, there were a number of traders—some of them clearly new to the world of speculation—being drawn into a *bancomania*.

At each turn, I congratulated myself that I did so well on my own. I'd had Leonidas with me almost the entire span of my disgrace and had regarded him as indispensable. I was not quite prepared to say I was better off without him, but I did well enough. I was lonely, yes, and I hated, truly hated, that I had no one with whom to share my thoughts, but I managed.

Duer did not show himself at Merchants', and I saw no sign of Reynolds or Pearson, but Whippo did his job as he moved from table to table, predicting gloom for the Million Bank and attempting—unsuccessfully, I thought—to undo the damage I did by speaking constantly of Duer's enthusiasm.

It was not the only time I saw Whippo. I was down by the docks, returning to my room after researching the address of one of Duer's men, when I observed him from a fair distance speaking in animated terms to a grocer. I watched while the grocer shook his head. Whippo spoke some more and the grocer shook his head once more. Whippo's color rose; he waved his hand excitedly as he spoke. This time the grocer nodded and then grinned, the way a man does when he achieves some small victory over a social superior. He disappeared into his shop and returned a moment later with a purse, which he gave to Whippo. In return, Whippo handed the grocer several small pieces of paper. They shook hands, and Whippo wandered off.

I then approached the grocer and introduced myself rather vaguely, but inquired immediately of his business with Whippo.

"What?" the grocer asked. "You want a bit for yourself?"

"A bit of what?"

"The loans. That fellow's master, Duer, is borrowing at six percent."

"It is a fair rate, but nothing to get overly excited about," I said.

"Six percent per week."

The very notion was absurd—it was as though Duer was giving money away—and I could not think what it meant.

I left the grocer immediately and headed toward Fraunces Tavern, but my path was blocked. There, before me, was the cadaverous form of Isaac Whippo. He stood with legs apart, his sunken chest thrust outward and his head back. He glared at me as though he had some hope of intimidating me. And perhaps this time he did, for my good Mr. Whippo was not alone. By his side stood a rough-looking fellow, broad in the shoulder, uncouth in manner. It was James Reynolds, who looked at me with a very unsavory expression.

"What pit of vomit have you crawled from?" Whippo inquired.

"Why, good afternoon to you too, my friend," I answered. "Your eyes are looking particularly hollow today. How *do* you accomplish that?"

"I notice you don't insult this gentleman," he said, gesturing at Reynolds.

"I would not insult a man with so beautiful a wife. It cannot be easy to have convinced such a gem to marry a man of your stripe."

"She's a slut," said Reynolds.

"Well," I said brightly, "that *is* good news."

"Enough banter, Saunders. Why are you following us?"

"I was not following you," I said. "I merely happened to see you and thought I'd ask that grocer about your personal and private business. You don't object, do you?"

"I advise you to stay out of my affairs," he said, "lest I ask Reynolds to keep you away."

"If he asks, it *is* something I'm paid to do," said Reynolds. "I think you may depend upon it. That is what I think."

"Do you know what *I* think?" I asked. "I think it is a bad policy to lend at six percent a week. Unless, of course, one's aim is to lose everything. You might wish to pass that along to Mr. Duer."

"Stay away from us and Mr. Duer," Whippo said, "or I'll ruin you."

"Too late, for I come already ruined."

"Then Reynolds will break you."

Reynolds snarled at me, showing a mouth of yellow teeth. No doubt feeling that their threats eliminated all possible retorts, they began to walk off.

"I'm also broken," I called after them, but they did not turn around, so busy were they in seeking out tradesmen to whom to offer their lucrative interest rates.

It was the evening before the Million Bank launch. It was early yet, perhaps half past four, but already dark. I had work to do, but not yet, and the sound thing would have been to retire to my room to sleep until the small hours of the morning. And yet I knew sleep would not be possible. The entire city was stretched taut with anticipation, waiting to see what would happen. Half the city predicted the Million Bank would be a disaster, the other half a wealth-generating engine. I did not know or care which, so long as the bank fulfilled its destiny without being controlled by Duer.

Too anxious to remain still, I decided to take a stroll about the city for an hour or two in the hopes I would become relaxed enough to sleep. Perhaps I had grown too arrogant, but I don't think so. Rather, I think it safe to say I misunderstood the malice of those against whom I had set myself. I walked north in the direction of the pleasure gardens and considered briefly taking a turn inside, though it was early in the evening and cold, which meant there would be little to distract me. Yet I looked at the gates as I passed, with their graceful stone arching and inviting, vaguely lurid statues of women, something wanton in their eyes.

I was, I suppose, too distracted, for I did not notice that of the conveyances upon the street, one—a covered cart—kept near pace with me. Cleverly it stayed behind me, where I was least likely to notice it, though notice it I did at last, when it pulled even with me, and I caught a glimpse of the driver. First I observed that he was better dressed than the drivers of such carts—he wore the spotless gray coat of a gentleman—

and, though he kept his face carefully pointed away from mine, there was something familiar about him. I quickened my pace for a better look. He turned away so I could see only the back of his head, but I observed his hands on the reins—massive, bestial hands—and so it was I knew him. It was Jacob Pearson driving the cart alongside me.

I stopped and stiffened, needing a moment's immobility to attempt to understand what this meant and what I must do. Then, being able to reach no immediate decision, I decided I would apprehend him now, and, once done, I would decide what to do with him. I tensed to spring forward when all went dark. A heavy leather bag had been thrust over my head. A pair of powerful hands gripped my arms just below my elbows and pressed them to my sides so hard they were pinned there. At once I smelled tobacco and sweat and sour clothes. Whoever had me was not only unclean but strong, far stronger than I, and though I did not wish to submit, I was not going to extricate myself from this encounter with violence.

It had all happened quickly—it would have to be quick if they were to avoid attracting the attention of others on the street. The man who pinned my arms to my side thrust me forward and into the back of the cart, throwing me down on the rough floor. It smelled of hay and manure; human beings were not the usual beasts conveyed in the vehicle, though that told me nothing. Whoever had me might easily have hired the cart from a farmer for the afternoon. The man who had me released one arm for an instant, grabbed my hair, and knocked my head against the floor. He did this hard but not brutally so. The impact hurt, and I felt a wave of nausea and dizziness. It soon passed, however, and when it did, even under the leather hood, I understood a few things. I understood that my assailant had pulled the heavy tarpaulin cover over us both, encasing us in smothering darkness. I understood that he acted alone and that he alone must concern himself with me while Pearson drove the cart, for otherwise he would not have needed to knock my head in order to buy a few seconds to cover us up in the flat of the cart. He now straddled me, placing his full weight upon the small of my back while he held my arms flat by the wrists. He said nothing, so I learned nothing of him that way, but among his many unpleasant odors—and I thought it significant—I did not detect whiskey like the Irishman from outside the

Statehouse. So that was the third thing I understood. Whoever had me pinned to the bottom of this cart was the same man who had attacked me at my home in Philadelphia and had been shot at by Mrs. Deisher.

"Good evening." I attempted to alter my voice. My words were hard even for me to hear, lost in the leather hood and the tarpaulin and the rumble of the wheels upon the road. "My name is Mr. Henry Rufus, and I cannot help but think you have taken me by mistake."

"Shut up, Saunders," he answered. "I'm not an idiot."

I knew that voice. I could almost place it, but the noise of the road and the muffling made it impossible for me to put the sound with its owner. "Look, what is it you want with me?"

"Quiet yourself," he said again. "I'll not speak with you. There's no point, and you've a devil's tongue. Pearson will tell you when he's ready."

When he's ready turned out to be perhaps an hour later. We drove for some time, and I could detect little except that the sounds from our surroundings grew fainter and less frequent. We drove someplace unpopulated—neither surprising nor comforting. At last the cart stopped. We remained motionless for a moment, and I listened to my own breath in the hood and my assailant's heavy breath over me, and beyond that something else: the lapping of water against the shore. Next I heard a rapping, like a cane against wood. It struck four times, no doubt a signal, and the man atop me eased up the weight upon me. He raised the tarpaulin, letting in a refreshing wave of cool air. Next he grabbed me by one arm, now less concerned that I might attempt to run away. I knew not where I was, so how could I run? He pulled me from the cart and onto the ground, where my other arm was gripped hard by a second man.

"Mr. Pearson, I imagine," I said. "I am so very flattered that you would trouble yourself to call upon me, but I must inform you that we would be much more comfortable at my inn than here. I have a most agreeable line of credit, at least with the wine."

He said nothing. Perhaps he wished to torment me, but I don't think so. I believe he was afraid. I believe he knew it was dangerous to engage in conversation with me and would not risk it. I made several further attempts, but he said nothing. We walked, first upon grass, and then upon soft dirt. Wet dirt, I believed. Then we walked briefly along a stone path.

They led me next down a set of slick stairs. More clearly now I heard the sound and smelled the tang of a river: waters both clean and stagnant, the scent of dead fish washed ashore. The air was cool and wet, and soon I was walking in the mud. At last one of the men pushed me forward, and there were subtle differences—a shift in the darkness, the disappearance of the wind—that led me to believe I was now in an enclosed space, a room of some kind, except the earth beneath us was still wet and I could hear the river just as distinctly.

The stronger of the two men—that is, not Pearson—pushed me to my knees, and held me down. Pearson then began to bind my arms behind me with heavy rope. Next he bound my feet together at the ankles. I felt him fumbling with the ropes, and though he pulled hard to make certain his knots were tight, I knew he was inexperienced in these arts.

Once this operation was complete, they pulled me to my feet once more. With a sharp tug, the hood was yanked from my head, and I stood in near-total dark. Only inches from my face I observed the malicious grin of Pearson; by his side, also grinning, but in the easy simple way of dogs, was Reynolds.

"So this is all Duer's bidding," I said, "and you, Pearson, are but one of his puppets?"

"I work for Duer," said Reynolds, "but I am willing to serve other men when time allows. At the moment I work for Mr. Pearson."

"And the evening my landlady chased you away from her house, were you in Mr. Pearson's service then too?"

"Aye," he said.

My eyes having had a moment to adjust, I now looked around me. All was still in darkness, but in shades of gray I determined a few things, none of them encouraging. The earth was wet mud, and it caked my stockings and breeches from when I'd knelt. All around me were the iron bars of a prison, though this cell was very small, not four feet in length or width, wide enough for a man to sit but never lie down. It was perhaps seven feet in height, and there was a single iron door that opened along a square stone slab. The cage rested only inches from the river, and above us was blackness. I smelled the decay of old wood; perhaps we were under a disused pier.

Pearson saw my appraising glances and chose to answer my unspoken questions. "It's an old dock, used by the British during the occupation, but it was damaged in the war and has never been repaired. A friend of mine, a British colonel, told me of this cage, and I wondered if it might someday become useful."

"A friend of yours," I said, "a British colonel? How shocking."

"You may make all the quips you like, but I have you and may do with you what I wish."

"And what do you wish?" I asked. "Why go to all this trouble?"

"Tomorrow," he said, "the Million Bank launches. Duer wishes me to invest heavily, to deploy my own agents to buy as much as we can, keeping the share within the circle of his acquaintance. I know he has tried to dissuade investment in the launch, but you have been singing its praises. I wish to know why and what you have in mind."

"What I have in mind," I said, "is making certain Duer does not gain control of the bank. Listen to me, Pearson. Keep your money out of the Million Bank. You'll lose everything. That bank will fail in a matter of months."

"Duer doesn't think so."

"Duer doesn't care," I said. "The Million Bank can be destroyed in half a year, and it won't matter to him. All he cares about is controlling the bank for now, using the credit such action will grant him to gain control of the market for six percents and, later, the Bank of the United States. But you didn't know that, did you? He convinced you to use your own money in lowering the price of six percents, so he could buy them cheaply. He convinced you to buy four percents to raise the value so others would come flocking to sell their six percents in order to buy four percents. But now the four percents are worthless. Don't lose even more in the Million Bank."

He paused, just long enough for me to see that my words disquieted him. "And why should I believe you? Why should I take your advice on any of these matters?"

"For the sake of your wife," I said. "The only reason she has not fled from you is because a woman and two children enduring poverty exposes herself to more dangers and abuse even than living with you. I could not endure to see her living in poverty *and* with you."

He did his best to appear untroubled. "Well, we shall see. I will wait an hour or so after the launch before deciding what to do, and then, based on what I have learned, I will come back and see if you have, perhaps, been withholding important information from me."

Here Reynolds took a step forward. "If I may, Mr. Pearson," he said, "it is my experience that it is always a poor decision to leave an enemy alive—particularly a sly one like Saunders here. Now, I don't have nothing against him. He lives or he dies, it don't signify one way or the other to me. If I'm paid to hurt him or kill him, that's what I do. But leaving him here? It's just foolishness. If he escapes, he's going to make your life very difficult. Mine too, likely."

"Likely," I agreed. "I hate to agree with him in a matter so detrimental to my well-being, but Reynolds is right. It's bad policy to leave me alive."

Pearson spat upon the earth. "I'll not be goaded into giving him what he wants."

"You're mad if you think what Saunders wants is death," Reynolds pointed out. "He is playing a game with you. He is attempting to convince you to leave him be. Don't give him what he wants."

"What he wants is to keep something from me, and if he believes it will aid my wife, I have no doubt he is foolish enough to prefer to die than speak the truth. All these soldiers with their romantic notions, they all want death. But he shan't get it without telling me everything first." He turned to me. "This little jail makes for an excellent means of revealing the truth. My friend, the British colonel, told me of its operation. This door, as you shall see, is far too heavy for any one man to open and close, though we shall lock it all the same. You will be bound within, unable to move your arms or legs. You will be cold and hungry and thirsty, and, when the tide comes in, you will suffer tremendously. The water will not drown you, but come up to your waist perhaps. Very unpleasant in January, I should think. You will have no means to relieve yourself but in your breeches. When I return in a day, or perhaps two, I will find you desperate, demoralized, and pliable."

"Don't leave me here," I said. "Kill me now, or you will regret it."

"Listen to him," Reynolds said.

"I do listen to him," Pearson said. "He tells me he knows something he wishes for me never to learn. I will find out what it is. I will let the cold and the river and his own misery extract it from him. Finish with the rope."

With my ankles tied together and my wrists bound behind my back, I was already in a poor state, but now Reynolds placed a small ball of cloth—fortunately not too dirty—in my mouth and held it in place with a strip of the same cloth, tied around my head. I have never loved being gagged, for it is a most dreadful feeling, and the idea that I would remain that way for a day or two was unbearable.

I watched as Pearson and Reynolds left the little cage and, together, pushed hard against the door. It did, indeed, seem to take all their energy to get the heavy door to move. They leaned into it, their backs bent, and, pushing from their legs, managed finally to put the door into place. Breathing heavily from his exertions, Reynolds now took a metal chain and wrapped it through cage and door, securing it with a lock. It seemed a needless precaution, but I supposed they wished to make certain that, even should I be discovered, I could not be easily rescued.

Pearson gazed at me from the other side of the cage. "Your easy manner suggests you think yourself in possession of some secret, but you will not escape this prison. No one ever has, not one. Do you believe you can accomplish what all who came before you could not? You have no secret advantage, and you shall no more escape than did the others."

I shrugged to show that I did not much mind or, perhaps, that I conceded his point without truly believing it. The two men stepped into the night, and though I thought it would be Pearson who turned around to gaze at me, he did not. Instead, it was Reynolds who briefly stopped and stared. In the dark, I could understand neither his expression nor his meaning, if he meant to convey one, only that he looked for a moment and then walked on, leaving me alone and cold and bound.

What a terrible situation. If only there were a clock visible so I could time myself to see how quickly I managed to extricate myself, how much better would I be able to recount the story later. Yes, I faced my challenges with a certain confidence, but then I had many advantages, which perhaps Mr. Pearson did not trouble himself to consider. First: I had been captured many times during the war and had, each time, escaped when I chose. Second: He had never before, most likely, captured a prisoner, let alone one with my record for escape. Third: I did not believe the universe was ordered such that he could triumph over me so entirely.

Thus, once I was certain they had left me alone and my actions would go unobserved, I began. The first step was to place my hands before me, and this was easily accomplished, though by no means as easily as it had been ten or fifteen years ago, when I was younger and more flexible. I sat upon the earth and slowly, with some discomfort, put the loop of my arms under my bottom. I then folded my legs and, straining considerably at the shoulders, pushed my arms up. I felt an unpleasant popping, and for a moment feared I had dislocated something, which would have answered my arrogance nicely, but it was merely the straining of underused joints. I gave one last push and my hands were now in front.

When taking a prisoner, if you wish to be certain he does not escape, I highly recommend tying the thumbs, for they are invaluable in freeing oneself from ropes. In addition, when binding the ropes, be certain that the wrists are as close together as can be managed. If the prisoner is clever, he will keep his wrists as separated as he can contrive without drawing attention to this fact. This I had done, so when I began to work at the ropes, they were already quite loose and pliable. It would have been far easier had I not been gagged, for I might have used my teeth, but I had slack enough to angle my right wrist toward my body and use my thumb and index finger upon the left wrist. My task was not to untie the rope, for the knot was well constructed, and I could not easily do so. Rather, I pulled at it, expanding the slack as much as I might. I then gripped it hard and pulled upward with my right wrist, backward with my left. The rope burned into my flesh, but soon it was just below the knuckles, the widest portion of the hand. Experience had taught me that even the tightest of ropes might then be moved piecemeal, if not all at once, but in this case one great shove answered the business and the rope came free.

Using my free hands, I now immediately untied the gag about my mouth and then slid the remaining rope off my wrist. The ankles were no more difficult, and only required that I remove my boots to be free of that burden. Now, before I replaced the boots, I removed from within them my useful little picks and began to work at the lock upon the iron door. This was no challenge and the darkness no impediment, since the picking of locks is done by feel and sound. In a moment I heard a click, and the lock fell away.

I was pleased with myself, and with good reason, but I still had one great object before me: the door. I placed the lock picks back in my boot and attempted to push the door open. It did not move. I thrust my shoulder into it, and the door reverberated wildly but did not move. I lay down upon my back and attempted to push it with my feet, but again nothing. Pearson had said it required two men at a minimum to move it, and that appeared to be the case.

I took a moment to consider my circumstances. All, of course, was not lost. In the morning, I would have a better sense of my surroundings. I might hear others walking nearby and call to them. I might, if necessary, replace the lock and pretend to be bound when Pearson and Reynolds returned. Provided I could convince them to open the door, I would then have the advantage of surprise.

These were options, but they were not agreeable options because, more than simply wishing for freedom, I wished for immediate freedom. I had work to do, and if I were not free, Duer might well succeed in taking for his own the Million Bank. Should he do that, he would at worst take possession of the Bank of the United States, at best produce a financial panic. I needed to get out of this cage, and yet I could think of no means of doing it without the help of at least one other person. Gone were the days when I might hope for the sudden and fortuitous arrival of Leonidas.

I sat upon the earth, thinking I should enjoy sitting before the cage began to flood. I considered everything, certain I had not neglected some path to freedom, but forcing myself to turn everything over again and again. It was all I thought of, and it was what I was thinking of when I saw three figures emerging from the dark. One was tall and broad, one quite small—a woman, I thought—and it was not until they were only feet away did I recognize them as Reynolds, the Irishman from the Statehouse, and Mrs. Joan Maycott.

Joan Maycott

January 1792

It was early evening. Having already eaten my dinner, I was in my room alone, reading quietly and sipping at a glass of watered wine, when my landlady knocked at the door. I had a visitor below, but he was of the sort she could not admit to her house, lest she receive complaints from the other tenants. I immediately apologized that she should be troubled by such a person and descended the stairs. I remained calm in my demeanor, though in truth I was very anxious, for I feared my visitor might be one of the whiskey boys, having encountered some trouble dire enough to risk visiting me in my home.

I knew not if I should be relieved or dismayed to find Mr. Reynolds on my stoop, leaning against the stone rail and spitting tobacco juice into the street. He looked at me, grinned, and took off his hat. "A moment of your time, Mrs. Maycott."

"I cannot imagine it would be anything but a moment wasted."

"No need to be so harsh to a man come maybe to help you," he said. "Maybe, I don't know, but I got a feeling I might. You've seen enough of me, I think, to know I'm loyal to no one and nothing. If it pays, that's all I care for, so here's a chance for me to make some money, if I know you right."

"Know me right about what?"

"About Captain Saunders. He stands against Mr. Duer and so do you."

"You misunderstand me if you think I'm not Mr. Duer's friend."

"And you misunderstand me if you think I trouble myself one way or t'other. I work for Duer, true, but he ain't no friend of mine. And you forget what I know already, so do you want to help Saunders, or do you want to leave him where he is?"

"Where is he?"

"Where he can't get out," Reynolds said, "and at Pearson's mercy, which ain't a great place for him."

"Are you telling me he's somehow been abducted?"

"Not somehow. I helped capture him, and now I'm willing to help you set him free, if you want to pay for what I know."

"You were paid by Pearson to abduct him, and now you wish to be paid to free him?"

"Clever, ain't it?"

I would not comment on that point. "Where is he?"

"Can't tell you that."

I had, perhaps, erred in making Saunders so vital to my plans, for things with him were coming undone rapidly. I had only just received word from his slave that he had been forced to break with Saunders. It appeared that Saunders had freed Leonidas without bothering to tell him, and Leonidas believed that he could no longer stay by Saunders's side. His logic was that if he did not respond with appropriate resentment, Saunders would begin to grow suspicious. It was perhaps true, but hardly convenient.

Leonidas had assured me their rupture would in no way interfere with Saunders's ability to thwart Duer. His capture by Pearson, however, was another matter. If Saunders was tucked away in some basement or garret somewhere, he would not be able to act against Duer in the morning, and nothing right now was more important than keeping Duer from taking control of the Million Bank. If he had the bank's credit at his disposal, he could conceivably be too powerful to be stopped, and we would not only have failed, we would have aided our enemy in achieving a wealth and power never before conceived of. It would not stand.

"How much?" I asked.

"Twenty dollars."

"Agreed."

"Too quickly agreed, in my opinion. Fifty dollars."

"I don't like you very much, Mr. Reynolds."

He shrugged. "Nobody seems to. But in the end, they pay me."

Reynolds informed me that I would need the help of another man in retrieving Saunders, so we stopped by Dalton's boardinghouse and he joined our little party. Next, Reynolds led us north to a deserted pier, one abused and abandoned by the British during the war. Underneath it we found a diabolical little cage, and therein was Captain Saunders, sitting against the far wall, his arms folded. A chain and picked lock lay at the door, a scattering of abandoned ropes lay strewn in the sand.

"I told Pearson it was a mistake to leave Saunders unattended. Look at him."

"I'm still imprisoned," he observed, his tone dry.

"Not for long, eh?" Reynolds said. "I've brung these folks to offer up their services in freeing you."

Saunders looked at us but did not move. "Freeing me? And not, let us say, killing me, which I should very much object to?"

I could hardly be surprised at his suspicion, and had he known to what extent I hoped to manipulate him, I could not doubt his anger; even so, it pained me—surprisingly—that he should be so suspicious. "Hardly, Captain. I have told you before that I believe we both stand for the same things."

"What about him?" He gestured with his chin toward Dalton. "He abused me and threatened me outside the Statehouse. He told me a sharpshooter would murder me if I did not act as he wished."

"There's no point in holding a grudge, lad," Dalton said. "Perhaps this rescue will even things for us."

"Mr. Dalton did not yet know you to be an honorable man." I had anticipated certain concerns on Captain Saunders's part, and I'd troubled myself to construct some plausible stories during the journey here. "We believed you one of Duer's men at the time. Only later did we understand our error. Come, let's get you out of there, and I shall tell you everything on the way back to your room."

Mr. Dalton and Reynolds both planted their feet firmly in the earth and grabbed hold of the bars of the door. Captain Saunders bent over, gripped hold of two bars slightly beneath their positions, and pushed. The door moved slowly but steadily, and in a few seconds was open wide enough for the captain to slip out with relative ease. As we walked to the carriage, he maintained a silent if agreeable demeanor, as though there were nothing unusual in our little outing, but I watched his eyes. Even in the dark he it was plain that he scanned each of us slowly and carefully, taking full measure of our moves, weighing our intents. I don't know that I would have made an effort to manipulate him had I understood him to be quite so vigilant, quite so clever.

When we reached our transport, I asked him, if he would not object, to ride alone with me in the carriage, and when he assented I sent Reynolds and Dalton up to ride with the coachman. Dalton would understand, and Reynolds was being well paid for his discomfort.

Once we were seated, he turned to me. "Reynolds works for Duer, for Pearson, and for you?"

"Reynolds will work for who will pay him. He took money from Pearson to imprison you, and then came immediately to me because he believed I would pay for your release."

"Perhaps it is time you told me why you cared to pay for my release."

"I thought we were friends," I said. "It is no more than I would do for any friend."

"Please, Mrs. Maycott, do not attempt to manipulate me. How do you know the big Irishman? Dalton, you called him."

"I know him from the West, and I am proud to call him my friend as well. He and I are patriots, Captain. Just as I believe you do, we stand against Duer, who is a vile man whose ambitions will undo the country if he is not checked. He has already stolen from the nation. Is he now to be allowed to bankrupt it?"

"Stolen? What do you mean?"

I had held on to this little bit of knowledge, but now seemed a good time to use it. Save something too long, and it becomes worthless. If, despite all that had happened to him, Saunders was still to attempt to thwart Duer tomorrow, I would need to use everything I could muster. "Before the ratification of the Constitution, Duer served as director on what was then called the Board of Treasury. It was a powerful position and he was a trusted man, yet he abused that trust. He procured for himself $236,000, which he has never returned."

Saunders said nothing for a moment. "You have proof?"

"It can be proved," I said, "though I can offer you no documentary evidence. I doubt not that Hamilton could prove it, had he the will, but of course he is Duer's lapdog."

I knew that Saunders disagreed and my accusation irritated him, but he was careful not to let himself be distracted. "Why did Dalton—and I presume you—wish to keep me from searching for Pearson?"

"Because of Mrs. Pearson," I answered. "Duer's men were threatening her to keep her quiet. Duer wanted Pearson's money invested in his schemes, and he feared that if Pearson was apprehended by Treasury men, he would be forced to repay his loan rather than lose more money in Duer's projects. I could not risk harm to Mrs. Pearson." These were more lies, but I could not tell him the truth: that we had all along manipulated him, hooked him like a fish and pulled him where we liked.

"Many ladies care for their friends," he said, "but few employ giant Irishmen and secret sharpshooters to aid them in their efforts."

"Then they have never lived on the border," I answered. I don't know that my answer satisfied him, but it silenced him long enough that I was made to explain no more before arriving at Fraunces Tavern.

"You are a mysterious woman, Mrs. Maycott," he said. "I am not a fool, and I know you will not tell me what you wish to keep secret, but I must beg you to be more open with me. You say you are my friend and we stand together, yet you tell me little or nothing. You have saved me from, at the least, an unpleasant day or two in that cold cage, and quite possibly from an even more terrible fate. I am grateful, as you must know. But I am not content."

"The time has not come for you to know more," I said. "But soon."

And so he departed. If he recollected that I had promised to tell him everything in the carriage, he did not hold me to it. I believe I understood him well enough to know he did recall and chose not to attempt to hold me to a promise he knew I would never keep.

Ethan Saunders

It was now half past nine. I had lost several hours, but no more than that. My plans to thwart Duer were as solid as ever, and my hatred of Pearson equally strong. What could he do to me that would make me despise him more than I did for what he'd done to his own wife? As for Mrs. Maycott, her actions tonight, her association with the whiskey Irishman, only confirmed that she was a more significant actor in these affairs than she would admit, but for the moment, at least, she appeared to be an actor who favored my success and Cynthia's safety.

There was but one person in New York who could now answer my questions, so after cleaning myself and concealing the bulk of my injuries, I went to the home of Senator Aaron Burr, where his girl directed me to a local coffeehouse, and there I found him, holding court for a large group of political clients—or perhaps men to whom he was a client. I hardly knew, but I was quite gratified to see him gesture to me to take a seat and indicate that he would be with me when he could.

Soon Burr rose and came over to my table. There were still men where he'd sat, but they seemed to have enough to say that they did not require his presence at the moment.

"How may I help you, Captain?"

"It is rather important, I'm afraid, and I must keep it between the two of us. I had hoped you might be able to tell me more about Joan Maycott."

"I know little of her myself," he said. "She appeared upon the scene less than a year ago. She is a fashionable lady, a wealthy woman, and a widow. She and her husband traded his soldier's debt for land out west, where he made something of a success as a whiskey distiller, but after he died she returned to the East. If pressed, she will speak against Hamilton's whiskey tax on this account." He shrugged to indicate he had no more to add.

"When did she move to the West?"

"I don't know," he said. "She mentioned to me once having lived in New York with her husband during the ratification of the Constitution, so it could not have been so long ago."

I thought about this for a moment. "How did her husband die?"

"She has never chosen to speak of it, and a man is never inclined to inquire too deeply of a dead husband to a pretty widow. There is no shortage of opportunities for a man out west to meet his death, and yet . . ." His voice trailed off.

"You have the impression that there is some bitterness there," I proposed. "That she believes there was an injustice."

His eyes brightened. "That is exactly right." He looked over his shoulder.

"I see you must return," I said. "Thank you for your time."

He wrinkled his brow. "But I have told you nothing."

I shrugged, and that seemed to be enough for him. We rose and shook hands. He pretended not to see how badly cut and scraped was my hand and went back to his men. As he did so, I thought about how interesting he was. He could not be ignorant of my reputation, of the things said about my past, and yet he chose to attend to me in public. He could not help but notice that hardly a day went by that I did not have some injury. It seemed to me that Burr was a man like myself, one who enjoyed courting a little bit of scandal, so long as it was only a little bit. I hoped this tendency would not lead him into any great difficulties.

In the meantime, though he thought he had told me little, he had in reality explained a great deal. Mrs. Maycott and her husband would not have traded war debt for land had they not been needy, and yet she returned from the West, after only a few years, a wealthy woman. I did not think any amount of success as a whiskey distiller could have produced significant money in so short a span. Either she and her husband had, in that time, inherited a fortune or there was far more to her past than she was making public. One thing seemed certain: Something terrible had happened to her husband out west, and if he had traded his debt for land, it seemed to me likely he had traded, directly or indirectly, with the largest and most energetic architect of these exchanges: William Duer.

I had hired a horse in advance, so I had little to do but pass the time. I dared not sleep, lest I fail to awake in time. I therefore waited impatiently until, when the clock struck one and the rest of the world was abed, I rode out to Greenwich Village and Duer's estate, where I did some naughty things to make that speculator's life uncomfortable, and did them without being seen or heard. I returned late, nearly four in the morning. There was no point in attempting more sleep. I would have to begin in an hour or two at the most, so I sat in my room, drank a bottle of port, and rehearsed over and over again what I must do.

Perhaps I fell asleep for a quarter hour or so, but when I heard the watchman call out four of the clock, I roused myself, splashed my face with cold water, and set out to make my mark upon William Duer.

The plan was simple. I would visit Duer's agents one by one, and then visit Corre's Hotel, usually a venue for music and now the place where the Million Bank was due to launch. Perhaps I would see Duer there, perhaps not. I did not know which I hoped for. If Duer did not show, perhaps Pearson would not show either. If Pearson did appear, he would see Duer's plan already in disarray and would refrain from investing. All of which, of course, depended upon my doing what yet needed doing.

So thinking, I headed out into the cold morning.

Speculators are an early rising lot, so it was not yet five when I visited the first of my agents, Mr. James Isser, whose removal I believed would be done without difficulty. He was a young man who lived in a busy boardinghouse on Cedar Street. My observations indicated that many men came and went from the house with regularity, particularly in the early morning hours, so, having secured a key from a chatty maid who did not mind the pockets of her skirt, I was able to enter the premises and ascend the stairs to his rooms without notice.

I knocked upon his door and heard a faint scuffling from within. A moment later the door opened a crack and there stood a small man, a bit too fond, perhaps, of beef and beer for his young age. His eyes were red and narrow and rather dull.

"You look sleepy," I said, and shoved him hard in the chest.

He stumbled backward into his room, so I stepped in, closed and locked the door, and punched the man in his soft stomach. I did so not to be cruel but to keep him from crying out.

Quickly, I took a burlap sack from my jacket and slipped it over his head. He started to cry out again, and though I had no wish to hurt him, I had my own difficulties to think of, so I struck him once more in the stomach. I did this in part with distaste, for I am not a brutal man, and later, I knew, I would regret hurting an innocent. I always did, but in the moment I only acted.

"My advice," I said, my voice even and calm, "is that you not speak."

I grabbed his arms and tied them behind his back. He hardly resisted, not having any notion of who I was or what I wanted. I believe it never quite occurred to him that he ought to fight me. Having immobilized and blinded him, I now placed a gag in his mouth, imposed over the sack.

"Mrs. Greenhill's husband has sent me to you, Mr. Jukes. It is a matter of revenge, for it is a cruel thing, cruel indeed, to violate a man's bed with his wife."

He mumbled and grunted, no doubt telling me that he knew no Mrs. Greenhill and was not Mr. Jukes. I, of course, pretended I could not understand him.

"You are to leave that married woman alone, you rascal. This shall be your last warning." Having finished my task, I departed. Upon his inevitable discovery, he would tell his tale, and it would be perceived as a simple misunderstanding. When all of Duer's agents suffered from such misunderstandings, it would be clear that something more sinister had transpired, but by then it would be too late.

I shan't describe each encounter, for I used the same technique four times with the four unmarried agents. I had planned my course in advance so I could move with all deliberate speed from one to the next.

The remaining two agents were married men with children in their homes, and I would not break open their houses and assault them where they lived. To do so would be dangerous and unseemly. Instead, I dealt with each according to his personality.

Mr. Geoffrey Amesbury liked to go by coach each day to his place of work. This day he would take a coach to Duer's estate, so it was no difficult thing to pay his regular coachman to fall ill and pay a substitute to take him to be robbed. The thieves I hired—a visit to the area of Peck's Slip was all that was required to find them—would take his money and his clothes and separate him from his coach, but he was not to be harmed.

The final victim, Mr. Thomas Hunt, lived in a large house with his wife, four children, and an elderly mother, so there could be no safe and easy way to detain him at home. Because I could not determine how he intended to get to Mr. Duer's house, I was forced to deal with him somewhat more creatively.

Mr. Hunt was in the prime of his manhood, tall and well made with thick brown hair and the sort of face that women find pleasing. It is not surprising that a man of his stripe had married a pretty lady, and he was known to be dedicated to his wife, but such was his regard for the gentle sex that his dedication was too large to be contained by a single woman, no matter how worthy. I suspected it must be so, and a little idle coffeehouse gossip confirmed my suspicions.

Thus it was I procured the service of a handsome woman from a local bawdy house. When Mr. Hunt left his home at eight in the morning, he was approached by the lady I had hired. She stopped him on the street and made some polite inquiries of direction, and then, once the conversation had begun, asked if he were not Thomas Hunt, the well-known speculator, who had been pointed out to her so often. She spoke those words as though she regarded stock trading as only slightly less remarkable and heroic than minotaur slaying. She had, she said, a large sum to invest and she knew not what to do with it, and perhaps so great and successful a man as he could advise her on how best to order these troublesome dollars. He told her he would be happy to advise her on the matter and would call upon her tomorrow, or perhaps even later today, but that this moment was for him bespoken. Alas, she answered, she was but in town for the day before she returned to Boston, and required an agent in New York immediately. If he could spare just half an hour she would be eternally grateful. He removed his watch and studied it with great anxiety but, once he had taken the time to calculate his duties and responsibilities, found he did have half an hour to give her, though no more.

I watched from a safe distance as the lady led him to an empty house, one for sale, the use of which she had acquired for the day. Left to his own devices, Mr. Hunt would be occupied well past half an hour, I had no doubt. A man means to dally for but a short time, but when he is with a willing lady the hands of the clock move at a most unreliable pace. A quarter hour becomes two or three. One's morning appointment is forgotten as noon comes and goes. Should these events come paired with a bottle or two of good claret, then so much the better. Mr. Thomas Hunt would not be available for Duer's service, and he could blame no one but himself.

Thus it was no great matter to procure a bucket of beer and a tankard and find a comfortable place to sit while watching the door to the house I had rented, to make certain that Mr. Thomas Hunt, hunter of whores and dollars, remained where I intended. Yes, it was cold, and yes, flurries of snow fell upon me and into my beer, but I did not mind. I was a man hardened by the trials of revolution, and a chill in the air meant nothing.

So it was that at fifteen or twenty minutes to nine, still enough time for him to arrive at his destination without much difficulty, the door to the house flew open, and Mr. Thomas Hunt emerged, hurriedly putting his arm through the sleeve of his greatcoat. My good whore, not so much dressed as her man, with her shift falling off her shoulder, tried to hold him back, but Mr. Thomas Hunt brushed her off, and rudely too, more roughly than I like to see women treated. Mr. Thomas Hunt, it was now quite clear to me, was a bad man, and though I had better than half my beer remaining, and leaving it upon the street meant I could forget ever again seeing my deposit, I nevertheless heeded the call of duty and sprang forward.

"Great God, sir!" I called out. "Mr. Hunt, Mr. Thomas Hunt, I say, you are in danger, sir. Go no further, take not another step, Mr. Thomas Hunt, for your life is in the balance!"

He looked up and saw me running toward him, running with concern plastered upon my face, and he must have recognized in me the countenance of a revolutionary hero, for he paused in his tracks long enough for me to catch him.

"Thank Jesus, you're safe," I breathed, holding on to his arm. "They are coming, and you must hide." I began to lead him back up the steps to my rented house.

Now he resisted. "Who are you, sir? Who is after me? Of what do you speak?"

I faced the not inconsiderable problem of having no idea of what I spoke. I struggled within myself for an answer. I don't know that I took more than a few seconds, if that long, and then I gestured toward the street with my head. "Men you have cheated," I said.

He was a speculator, and it seemed to me likely that he'd cheated someone. Indeed, he blanched, and without further explanation he moved toward the entrance of the house. Inside, the foyer was stripped of paintings and decorative objects, but the wallpaper and the floor covering, painted like Dutch tiles, were still there, and the house seemed a bit sterile if not precisely empty. Our footsteps echoed, however, as we pushed farther inside.

At the end of the hallway stood the whore, waiting to see what happened next. "I tried to hold him," she said, sounding bored by her own words, "but he wouldn't be held."

I'd no time to signal her to keep her silence, and she'd not read the commands upon my face or even the irritation that came after. As for Mr. Thomas Hunt, he looked between us and in an instant understood that the danger he faced came from me and from no other quarter. He attempted to push past me, shoving hard into me with his shoulder, but I held my ground and held Mr. Thomas Hunt fast, taking his arm in my grip.

"Just keep your peace and be still, and nothing will happen to you," I said.

"Whoreson," he answered, only not in a calm and quiet voice, as it might appear on the page. No, it was loud and shrill and full of fight and fire, more like "**Whoreson!**" I suppose, and he—the true whoreson if one of us must be so nominated—made to stick his fingers in my eyes. It was unexpected, vicious, and resourceful. He came at me, his fingers extended like an eagle's talons. If I had not thrust a knee into his testicles, I would be a blind man today.

Like his companion before him, Mr. Thomas Hunt found himself tied quite handily, his arms behind him. I had no need of his silence, we having the house to ourselves, so I concentrated only upon his hands and feet, and with him so detained, I dragged him into the front sitting room and put him upon a settee, the house being sold with some furnishings intact.

"Keep him here until two P.M.," I said to the woman. "Then you may let him go." To the man I said, "When she unties you, lay not a finger upon her in vengeance, or she will come to me and I will make you pay for it."

"If I am to be kept prisoner," he said, "may I have the woman's services at least?"

He was a practical man, and I could not fault him for it. "If he's still interested at two this afternoon, let him enjoy himself. And then," I added, for it never hurts to let a man know that his enemy understands how things lie, "he may return to his wife."

Rumors of the impending success of the Million Bank had been spreading throughout the city for some weeks, so I cannot say with any certainty that if I had not hindered Duer he might still have stumbled. As it happened, he arrived at Corre's Hotel nearly an hour late, at almost eleven o'clock. I never heard what happened at his home, but I imagined the scene. First, perhaps, Duer would be tapping his foot, waiting impatiently for at least one of his agents to show himself, yet not a one appeared. Then a servant would come running inside with the most horrific announcement. It would seem that every carriage in the house had suffered a breaking of the wheels, and, the doors to their stables having been thrown open, the horses had all wandered away. Oh, such carelessness, and on so important a day too! It was almost as though some malevolent spirit had visited Greenwich in the middle of the night to effect the chaos. With no other option, Duer and his man Whippo would be forced to find what horses they could and ride to the city. I suppose they had been in hopeful expectation of discovering their agents in place, handily purchasing every bit of stock available, their own lateness costing nothing more than the pleasure of observing a successful operation. Their arrival proved to them an unhappy truth.

Corre's Hotel was packed full of the angry and the agitated, a mob to be contained by a table at which sat three cashiers, far too few for the demands put upon them. The Million Bank had hoped to launch successfully, but not so frantically, not with the verve and enthusiasm that had marked the launch of the Bank of the United States the previous summer. Yet here was a throng of angry, pushing men, each hoping to buy riches cheap.

New York was a city of foreigners, and on hand to purchase stocks were Germans and Dutchmen and Italians and Spaniards and Jews. There were the confident and loud speculators who haunted the Merchants' Coffeehouse, but there were other men too, more timid men of more respectable businesses who, having watched the excitement of Hamilton's bank, hoped now to profit for themselves. There were also men of a lower order, men who perhaps brought their life savings in the hopes of, in a single moment, changing their lives forever.

It seemed the only significant group not to be found in this hodgepodge was Duer's agents. In the press of men, I observed this absence with some satisfaction. I was abandoned and alone, beaten and abused, despised by the world, but I had done my duty for my nation.

From across the room I observed a new face enter into the lobby of Corre's. It was Pearson, looking overwhelmed and a little bit like a child who has lost his minder in a crowded market. Did he know I'd already escaped his prison? I doubted it. And there he was, a man I hated above all others, the man who had murdered my greatest friend, ruined my life, married the woman I loved, and made her life into an unendurable torment. Here he was, having freshly imprisoned me, come to invest the last of his money, but upon scanning the room, it was clear he was dismayed by what he saw. All was madness and chaos, with no sign of Duer's agents or Duer himself. Pearson and I were separated by perhaps fifty feet and perhaps a thousand men, but for an instant, across the press of bodies and the cries of impatience, our eyes locked.

I cannot claim to understand what crossed his face—perhaps something like surprise and horror. He must have understood several things at once: that I had escaped his inescapable dungeon, that I was far more dangerous an enemy than he had reckoned, and that things would be different from now on. He also must have understood that money invested in the Million Bank was money lost. He understood that trusting Duer had been a colossal error. And he understood something else: that knowing what I did about who he was and what he had done—to me, to Fleet, to his own wife—I had still given him good advice. He stared at me now, nothing but derision and contempt upon his face for the man who had saved him, and then he left.

I wanted to follow him. I knew not when I would get a better chance, but it seemed to me the wrong choice. I needed to wait and see how the launch proceeded, make certain Duer did not find some way to turn everything to his advantage. I had outwitted him, yes, but until all was over, I could not be certain he had no tricks to extricate himself.

Not long after, I observed Duer himself. Actually, it was the remarkably tall Whippo I saw first; Duer was more easily lost in the throng. I had not seen their arrival, but they now moved through the crowds, who did not welcome them with enthusiasm, as they cried out the names of their associates—calls that went unanswered. Duer stared in dismay at the long lines to approach the cashiers, but having no other choice he queued up in one, Whippo in another.

They had not been standing fifteen minutes, however, and were seemingly no closer to the cashier's table, when the announcement went out that the bank was fully subscribed. Those who had waited without success were thanked for their interest and asked to vacate the premises. Some men walked off in triumph, others in despair; a sizable number, who had come after reading reports in the newspapers and thinking this something they should not miss out on, wandered off in resignation. Duer and his man did not leave at all, but remained like dazed horses amid the battlefield carnage.

I stood near the door, leaning against the wall, watching events unfold. Duer's mouth tightened into a little bloodless line. For a moment I thought he might weep like a child.

During these confusions, Mr. Isser, the first agent I'd detained and a man apparently well versed in the art of untying knots, came rushing into the hotel. He found Duer at once and began explaining something to him. I imagine he gave a somewhat jumbled version of events—an improbable tale of assault and detainment, of mistaken identity and capture and escape. They talked for only a moment, and then Whippo began to look about the room. I don't know what he looked for, but it was not long before his eyes found mine and locked on with an intense but unreadable expression. His lips trembled as though he stifled a laugh. Something passed between us that I did not understand. He looked as though he understood what I had done and approved of it.

It was gone in an instant. He turned away, and I was left to ponder the strange and wonderful events. Duer had been thwarted, and the threat against the Bank of the United States averted. Having saved Cynthia Pearson, and perhaps the republic, I was content to depart.

Ethan Saunders

I considered it a successful day and returned to Fraunces Tavern, where I found Lavien in the taproom sipping a cup of tea and writing a letter on a piece of foolscap. His hand was slow and deliberate, his letters neat and precise. He almost did not need to blot.

He set down the quill and looked at me. "I asked you not to interfere with the Million Bank launch."

I sat at his table. "I recollect something about that." I called for a bottle of wine. "*Don't obstruct government business,*" I said to Lavien. "Something on that order, yes?"

"You disobeyed the orders of the Treasury Department."

"Well, yes," I said, "but I don't work for the Treasury Department. Your suggestions are taken into account but do not direct my actions, any more than mine direct yours. I have no obligation to anyone or anything except honor, love, and vengeance, and I have attempted to fulfill those three as best I can."

My wine arrived, along with two glasses. I set one out for him and expected him to push it away. Instead, he poured for both of us.

"I suppose that's so," he said. "I don't know what chaos you've brought down on us, but it was nicely done." He raised his glass to me.

"Why, thank you very much."

"I believe you've now learned where Pearson was during the time of his absence, and your actions today suggest you know what he was up to."

"He was here in New York," I said. "You knew that as well. As to what, he was engaged in business for Duer that had to be kept secret because of his horrible debts in Philadelphia. He was shorting six percents and driving up the price of four percents so Duer's other agents, his real agents, could buy cheap, and he was making arrangements to invest in the Million Bank. The money invested in the six percents is gone, but I spared Cynthia the final ruin of Pearson's sinking his remaining funds into the Million Bank."

"There can be no doubt you saved her from ruin. Even if the Million Bank succeeds, its shares are already devalued. It oversubscribed today, in no small part thanks to your rumormongering. It oversubscribed by a factor of ten, so shares have been diminished by a factor of ten. The Million Bank will have to do well or else every investor will be a loser."

"Then perhaps Duer will thank me too."

"He will not. He did not need the shares he owned to possess their value but to control the Million Bank itself. He cared nothing for trading those shares and turning a profit on them, he wanted the wealth of the Million Bank as a whole. If anything, the devaluing would have aided him in buying up shares from disappointed investors, but to do that he would have already had to possess a significant portion, which, thanks to you, he doesn't." Lavien sipped his wine. "It must be difficult for you, though. You said your obligations were to honor, love, and vengeance. You have certainly fulfilled two of those today. You have demonstrated your honor and your love for Mrs. Pearson in defending what is left of her fortune, but what of vengeance? To protect her, you must save him."

I could not tell if he was chastising me, teasing me, or encouraging me to act. "Pearson's time will come, I have no doubt."

Lavien grinned, and I felt a coldness wash over me. "Nor do I." After a moment he said, "Leonidas came to see me. He wished to take his leave."

I took a drink. "It was a bit of a debacle—not so well handled as I might have liked."

Lavien's face softened, and for a moment he seemed to be just a man, full of kindness and concern. "I'm sorry you've lost him. I understand his anger, but I think it is out of proportion to your crime. You did him wrong in not telling him sooner that you had behaved justly, but you did behave justly. He ought to have seen that. In the end, he will."

"Thank you. Kind of you to say."

He looked at my glass of wine and smiled. "In balance, I'd say the re-form is going well. I must be sure to tell my wife what a wonderful effect she's had upon you."

To that there could be no response.

"Well, I suppose we should make arrangements to return to Philadel-phia," he continued. "Our work here is done. We'll ride back together, leaving early this morning by express, your expenses paid for by Treasury. In the meantime, we have work to do."

Had he then risen, I believe I would have risen with him—or at least begun to do so before I recollected myself. Yet, he did not command me, and he never had. I was not so tired from lack of sleep, not so addled with wine, that I failed to recollect that I was my own man. "I know we are not precisely opposed, but I do not work for you or for Treasury. I have my own business to attend, and that begins with Pearson."

"If you'd like," he said, "I can slit his throat before we leave."

His words were so calm and easy, I believe he would have done it had I given him the word. And how easy it would have been. Perhaps that was why I reacted so strongly. I did not want him to offer again. "I am not going to murder him."

He leaned forward. "Then what are you going to do, jeer at him? Point and laugh? There are things in motion, and you are not on the margins, Saunders. This is no longer a case of hoping to find out what some minor British functionary is up to, so that six months into the fu-ture some tiny bit of intelligence you've gathered can be placed together with a hundred other tiny bits in order to reach a conclusion that can be acted upon six months later."

"Do you dare to insult the work I did?"

"Never," he answered. "But it was a long war, and events unfolded on a large scale. Now we have not the luxury of time. You are in the thick of it, whether you like it or not, and waiting to see who Pearson contacts in two weeks is not an option. He must be dealt with now."

"Why is it your concern? Duer is struck down by my hand. The threat against the bank is finished."

He shook his head. "We don't know what the real threat was, but I can assure you it was not Duer's effort to take over the Million Bank. At best, that was but a portion. The threat is still real, and we cannot lose a day in our pursuit of it."

"I do not work for you," I said, "and I do not work for Hamilton."

"Yes, you do," he said. "Hamilton does not know it yet, but you do, and when all this is over, he will see what you've done and you will have what you've wanted—not only reform but redemption. When I first met you, I thought you were nothing but a useless drunk."

It ought not to have stung. I presented myself as nothing more, and yet I did not want to hear it. "And now?"

"And now," he said, "I find you are a useful drunk."

I pushed the bottle away, but not the glass. Then I looked him full in the face. "I want to help you. The devil take me, I want to help Hamilton, though I never thought I would utter such words, but first I must help Cynthia. That is my obligation and my desire. It is the air in my lungs, and I cannot breathe if I turn from it. You must see that."

"I do see it, but I see what you don't. You can rid Cynthia of her husband in a single stroke, and only we shall know of it, yet you won't do it. I understand why, but if you won't do it in a single stroke, we must do it strategically. Pearson has bound himself and his fortune to larger schemes, and if you want to be rid of him, we must deal with Duer and the threat to the bank. We must discover the plot and bring down the plotters, and somewhere, amid all that chaos, I believe Pearson will be dealt with. You believe it too, I think, and I know you long to be part of this, to bring down Duer with me. You simply cannot endure the torment of taking your eye off Pearson. I promise you, you may turn away from him, and he will not trouble you. He is done in Philadelphia. He is in exile. He can't hurt her now, and, if we do this right, he will not hurt her again."

I could see the reason in what he said, and I did not mind that he'd thrown in a few very kind words about me. This was Kyler Lavien, perhaps the most powerful man—if only secretly so—in the employ of the most powerful man in Washington's administration, and he begged me for my help. I would have hated to turn him away, but perhaps I did not have to. Perhaps he was right. I had no notion of what to do about Pearson. I would go, instead, with Lavien and see what came of his methods.

"What do we do?"

He grinned that evil grin again. "We've only a few hours before we take the express back to Philadelphia, so in the meantime we see Duer. We find out what he means to do next, and then we report to Hamilton. In keeping Pearson from utterly undoing himself, you may have completed your New York business as a private citizen. Now you are upon Treasury business."

At near seven, Duer received us in the parlor of his Greenwich mansion. He seemed as unflappable as ever, cool and friendly, a man at ease in the comforts of his own home, and he was alone: no Isaac Whippo in sight and no Reynolds. He showed us a painting he'd purchased and pointed out his window to a new pair of hunting dogs. Not a care in the world, and certainly not a thought for that pesky business with the Million Bank.

At last we sat but, unlike our last visit, no offer of refreshment was made.

"Now, how is it I can assist you gentlemen? Always at the service of the Secretary of the Treasury and his men."

Lavien leaped right in. "I have heard that your plans to acquire a controlling interest in the Million Bank came to nothing."

Duer kept his speculator's smile in place. Let the building collapse around him, Duer would not flinch. "I never entertained such a scheme. I thought very ill of that project."

Lavien scowled. "And now I hear that your agents move to acquire

Bank of New York issues, and you continue your efforts to control government six percents."

"You perhaps think you observe much from your little perch in the Merchants'," Duer said, "but you are new to the world of trade, and you may not understand all you see. I beg you to leave my business to me. I have politely entertained your interference, but you must understand that Colonel Hamilton will not thank you for troubling me."

"I understand it is time for you to be honest with us," Lavien answered. "No more prevarication, if you please."

"I must object, sir," he said, with a bit of a nervous laugh. "You speak to me as I am unused." Duer turned to me. "Do you not think a more civil tone is in order?"

"I shall tell you what is in order," said Lavien, with surprising harshness. "Forthrightness, sir. I must know of your plans. I want to know everything about your schemes, with the banks and with the government issues. I want it all and I want it now, and then Treasury will decide if you can be permitted to continue."

Duer flushed but attempted to laugh it off. "Oh, a businessman never reveals such things. I'm sure you understand."

"I don't give a fig for your schemes," said Lavien. "And you, sir, do not wish to stand in my way."

"Now, wait a moment—"

"No," Lavien said, his voice hard but quiet. "There is no negotiation. I am telling you what will happen, not proposing an arrangement. The time for subtlety is done. You will tell me what I wish to know, or I will find out my own way and you shan't like it."

Duer's face, which had gone white, suggested he did not doubt it. No one looking upon Lavien could doubt it. The man appeared to be himself in every way, and yet somehow he had metamorphosed into a devil. There was a hardness in his eyes, a hooded quality to his brow.

"I am happy to make open inquiries," Lavien said, "to spread about what I know and collect the information I require from others, laying open your schemes, as I understand them, to all. I presume you do not wish that."

Duer continued to gaze upon Lavien but said nothing. I believe this man, who had made his way through the world with lies and manipulation, could not now speak when faced with the sheer unmovable force of a man who would not, under any circumstances, allow himself to be convinced, charmed, or manipulated.

Lavien turned to me. "We will now go to the Merchants' Coffee-house. We will announce what we know about Mr. Duer and offer a reward for anyone who will tell us more. Surely if we get enough men together, each saying what he has heard from the man himself and each finding himself contradicted, then we shall know all."

Before I could rise, Duer spoke. "No, no, wait. I will tell you, but you must promise to keep everything I say a secret."

Lavien said, "I'll promise nothing. I'm not a gossip, and I'll not go about speaking of your business idly, but I'll speak of it as needs must."

Duer shook his head, as though exasperated at Lavien's stupidity. "I think the value of both six percent securities and bank stock will rise. I am patriot enough to invest in my country, and if you wish to persecute me for that, go ahead. Yes, I have tried to convince the world that I do otherwise, but that is the curse of my success. I am watched too closely, and my plans would be thwarted should they be uncovered."

"That is all?" asked Lavien. "What about your Mr. Whippo buying up money so dearly—taking those absurdly expensive loans from grocers and peddlers?"

Duer shrugged. "I require cash. It is a steep rate of interest, but it shall be repaid by and by. Hammy has made sure of it, by extending credit through the bank so readily. That is all, Lavien. A man who attempts so much at once, in an economy as small as ours, must have cash, so I raise cash. Would you destroy me for that?"

Lavien smiled. "If you had said as much sooner, we could have avoided the bickering."

"You must understand that a man of trade must keep his secrets."

"And a man of the government must sometimes discover them." Lavien rose from his chair, and I did the same. In the hall, I observed Whippo as he came out of a room, a pair of heavy books tucked under his arm. He stopped and looked at me, and I thought he should say something accusing. Instead he shook his head, as though with a recollected amusement, and laughed softly. "Pudendum," he said. "Very witty."

———

As we rode back to the tavern, Lavien sat in silent contemplation. I did not think he was withholding anything from me. As we rolled past the dark countryside between Greenwich Village and New York City, and he stared into the darkness, I honestly believed he forgot I was beside him. He might even have forgotten that he himself was there. Perhaps he was back in some dank Surinam jungle.

"It is still our plan to return to Philadelphia?" I ventured at last.

"Yes," he said, his voice thick.

I thought of Cynthia Pearson, whom I would soon see. "So, our work is done here?"

"It would seem so. Duer is acquiring both bank stock and government securities. He is interested in hoarding, not trading what he has for quick profit. That is why he is willing to borrow money at such exorbitant interest rates."

"But he will have to pay the interest, and even if he makes a fortune in his venture, he will have a hard time making enough to cover his loans."

"It is more complicated. The bank issues that are in circulation are not yet fully paid for. They are bought in several payments, and those payments have not yet come due. The bank will accept specie for some payments, but it will only accept six percent government securities for others. Do you understand now?"

"Duer will control government securities, which bank scrip holders need to make their payments, and because they will be off the market, the prices of six percents will soar while bank scrip values plummet. Duer will then sell off a small portion of the six percents so he can raise enough money to buy a controlling interest in bank scrip, which will now be cheap since holders can't get six percents to pay them off. And in that way, means to gain control of the Bank of the United States."

"Yes," said Lavien. "That is why we are going back to Philadelphia. We have, I believe, discovered the nature of the threat against the Bank of the United States. We know its author and his means. We now need only to discover how to stop it."

Joan Maycott

January 1792

There are signs, irrefutable signs, that a moment in history is coming to a head. I was not aware that I knew to look for these signs, and yet, when one manifested, there could be no mistaking them. And so, when I was awakened in the darkest black of night by my landlady's very agitated serving girl, who moaned, rather than said, that a man was below to visit me, I understood at once that events had accelerated. I had passed through a threshold from one era to another.

I dressed quickly and allowed the girl to lead me down the darkened staircase to the parlor, where candles had been lit hastily and where the fire from the evening before burned low. For all the girl's rushed attention, the room was still thick with shadow, not at all the sort of place a widow ought to sit alone with a late-night caller. She seemed to know it, and once she showed me in, she lurked behind me, unwilling to leave me unless asked to do so. I, too, was not certain I wished to be left with my caller, but I had no choice and sent the girl away.

Pacing before the low fire, looking drunk and unkempt, was Mr. Pearson. His cravat was loose, his shirt torn and stained with wine, and the right sleeve of his jacket was tattered as though it had been caught in some brutal machine that had mysteriously spared his hand.

I could not pretend to be surprised to see him so. This was the day of the Million Bank launch, and all had gone far better than I could have imagined. I'd known of Ethan Saunders's plans to sabotage Duer's efforts to gain control of the bank and had done all I could to make certain he would succeed. Pearson, in his jealousy and cruelty, had almost destroyed those plans, but fate and good fortune had turned Reynolds, that brute, into my ally.

I now approached Pearson and thought to hold out my hands, but I could not summon the energy to pretend to care for him. In his state, I doubted he would notice. "Sir, this visit is most unexpected. I hope nothing terrible has happened."

"The Million Bank was a disaster," Pearson said.

"I could not have known," I told him. "I proposed it because I thought it would subscribe. No one could know how much it would oversubscribe."

"I did not invest," he said.

I could not help myself. I clapped my hands together. "Oh, thank the Lord!"

His eyes glistened with moisture, for he mistook my concern for his wife as something meant for him. "We've all been foolish. We've all arrogantly believed that our cleverness elevated us above the madness of the markets, which no intellect can ever truly predict."

"I have tried to advise you the best I can, but I am relieved you had the foresight to avoid the Million Bank, even if the rest of us did not."

"It wasn't foresight," he said, rather bitterly. "It was Ethan Saunders. He warned me off, even while I—I was unkind to him. He gave me good advice for my wife's sake."

"I hope you will recall my advice regarding the four percents," I said.

He smiled somewhat bashfully, as though embarrassed to speak on this point. "Already the price has begun to rise. In this matter you were surely correct. But as for Duer, I think we all misjudged him. You see it too, I think. He is about to topple. No one has ever been so overextended as he, because he'd been counting on taking the Million Bank. Now I don't see how he can survive."

"I cannot say." I wanted to choose my words carefully. I did not wish to make myself sound more prescient than I ought to be, nor did I wish to expose my lack of loyalty to Duer. "He has a great many resources, and he is clever. But the failure of his Million Bank plan is a serious blow, and I believe things may have now entered the realm of uncertainty."

"The only reason I am not now hounded by creditors is because Duer vouches for me. Once Duer falls, I will not be far behind. Given his failure today, it may already be too late for me. I must retreat."

"To where?"

"I have a house off the King's Highway between here and Philadelphia. In Brighton."

"I'd heard you sold it."

He smiled. "It is what I meant people to hear."

"How long do you intend to stay there?"

"Until Duer falls," he said, "or until he recovers unequivocally and can vouch for me or, better yet, pay me what he owes."

I smiled at him—brightly, I hope—for I was thinking of how events might fall, and a safe haven on the Philadelphia road seemed to me just the thing I needed. "Would you object if I were to visit you there?"

He bowed. "I shall never object to your company."

I chose not to tell him I was inclined to bring friends, nor that my friends were rough men from the frontier. Best to leave that out for now. When he stood facing Mr. Dalton, I had no doubt Pearson would keep any objections he might have to himself.

Ethan Saunders

We rode the express coach, but it took us nearly four days to return to Philadelphia. Three hours after crossing the ferry to New Jersey, we were struck by a malicious snowstorm that slowed our movement to a crawl. We were forced to stop for the night at the dismal town of Woodbridge, having progressed no more than thirty miles. I should like to say we fared no better the next day, but that would be presenting things in too pleasant a light. Our equipage struck a gap in the road and overturned near New Brunswick, a town even more miserable than Woodbridge. Two of our fellow travelers, both speculators, were hurt quite badly, one breaking his leg and being in serious danger of dying. The carriage was fixed by late morning of the third day and the roads were somewhat clearer, but muddy, and our progress was slow. We stopped for the night in Colestown—tantalizingly close to our destination—and arrived in Philadelphia early the next morning.

Lavien rode off at once to report his findings to Hamilton. I had other business and walked from the City Tavern, where we wearily departed from our coach, to the Pearson house. I had no intention of knocking upon the door, but I wanted to see it, I wanted to get a sense from the outside that all was well within. Perhaps, I told myself, I would catch a glimpse of her at an upstairs window. Perhaps she would see me as well. Our eyes would meet and a thousand unsaid things would pass between us.

As I approached the house, I felt the cold air pierce my greatcoat; it had the eerie chill of foreboding. There was a large cart parked outside, and a dozen or more laborers were in the process of removing furnishings. I watched as three men carried a heavy oaken writing desk.

I rushed to them. "Hold. What happens here? Where is Mrs. Pearson?"

One of the men turned to me. He was a burly fellow, the sort usually found down at the docks. He was no doubt glad of the work, hard to come by in the heart of winter. "Don't rightly know, but ain't no one living in there, if that's what you're asking."

"What do you mean?"

"The house has been sold. We're working for a Mr. John Becker, what's bought it. He's marked the furnishings he don't want, and we're taking them to store for the auction."

I took a step closer, chilled at once by a thousand possibilities, but one above all else. I should have followed Lavien's first advice. I should have let him cut Pearson's throat when we were in New York.

It took a moment, but I found my voice. "When did this happen?"

He shook his head. "Can't tell you. We started work here this morning, but I can't say when the house was sold."

I got from the man the location of his employer, and went to see this Becker, but he was of little help. He bought the house, he told me, through a broker, and while he had been in negotiations for some time, the deal had only been finished two days earlier. As for Mr. Pearson, he had no knowledge of where to find that man—or his wife.

With no better notion of what to do, I took myself back to the City Tavern and began to question men at random if they had heard anything of Pearson. I forced myself to remain calm and easy, and merely presented my questions as though I had business with the gentleman. "I am searching for Jacob Pearson," I said, "in order to conclude a transaction begun sometime earlier. Can anyone here direct me to him?"

"Good luck, friend," said one man. "He's run from his creditors. Sold his properties in town, or else they were taken from him. Sold his house in Germantown and the one in Bristol. He's gone for good."

"I hear he went to England," said another.

"I heard it was the West Indies," said another, "but he killed his wife and children first."

"He did not kill them," said another man. "He sold them to pirates. That's what my footman told me, and Harry is never wrong about such things."

Such things? Was there a category of things that included selling one's family to pirates? Not that I believed the tale. The rumors were ugly, but when a man flees, his fellows are always eager to believe the worst, and while I thought little was beneath Pearson, and I feared for Cynthia's safety, this story, at least, I could dismiss. But that brought me no closer to the truth, so I called for a pen and paper and wrote at once to Colonel Burr, begging him to make inquiries for me. It seemed futile, but I could think of nothing else to do other than lament that I had let Pearson slip through my fingers. I vowed that, given the chance, I would not do so again.

I staggered out of the City Tavern, hardly able to continue my search, not knowing where I might go. I accepted that after four days of punishing road travel, I needed my rest, so I returned to my lodgings, threw myself upon my familiar bed, and slept perhaps five hours. By the time I awoke and arranged myself, it was dark, approaching six o'clock, and though it seemed unlikely I should meet with success, I decided to try Hamilton at his office.

The Treasury building was not locked, and Hamilton was not yet gone. He agreed to see me in short order, and I went into his office and took a seat before him. He looked tired himself, haggard and uneasy, as though he had been awake several nights in a row. Nevertheless, he forced himself to smile.

"Apparently," he said, "you did not heed my warning to stay away from the inquiry."

"Apparently."

He smiled again. "Mr. Lavien tells me you performed extremely well. You thwarted Duer's efforts to take command of the Million Bank. Had he succeeded, it might have had disastrous consequences for the economy."

"I am glad to hear you approve." And, strangely, I was. It is easy to hate a man we mistakenly believed wronged us, for it gives us the opportunity not to consider our own prejudices or mistakes. It was true enough that, even if I had been wrong about his sins of the past, I had reason enough to suspect him, and even so, I could not help myself; I enjoyed his praise. I knew not if I admired the man, if I wished somehow to return to a different time, or if it was Hamilton's own proximity to Washington that excited these feelings, but they were there, regardless of their source.

"And then," he continued, "there is the matter of the money that you reported missing. It does indeed look like Duer took $236,000 from the Board of Treasury. It is too early to tell for certain if we can prove it, but I have my man Oliver Wolcott inquiring into it, and thus far we believe there may be cause to bring action against him."

"And until such a time, what shall you do?" I asked.

"It seems that Duer and I are at odds. He is attempting to control six percent securities, and he is attempting to control bank scrip. The Million Bank was a setback, but he yet appears to have ample funds, thanks to the greedy fishmongers and milliners of New York. Nevertheless, I can make things hotter for him. I have directed the bank president to begin calling in short-term loans and restricting new ones, which should effectively shrink the entire credit market. In addition, I am dispatching my agents to every trading center in the country. I can try to thwart his plans. If he is a threat to the bank, as Mr. Lavien believes, he is a threat we can contain by freeing up six percents at a reasonable price. That will allow bank scrip investors to continue to maintain their holdings. It is a slow process, so for now we must wait."

I cleared my throat. "Have you heard anything of Pearson?"

He nodded. "He has sold his house and fled town. They say he has sold his other properties out of town as well, though I cannot confirm that. I know of nothing else, but I understand your connection to this matter, and if I hear more I will let you know."

"Have you no suggestions?"

He gazed upward in thought. "Perhaps you should ask your slave to inquire. There are networks of information among the Negroes that can be useful."

"Of course," I said, wishing to say no more on this topic.

"Now, Captain, I have much work to do. If you will excuse me." He spoke suddenly in clipped tones, like a man saying one thing to avoid saying another. It put me in mind of his relationship with Reynolds, which I could not help but suspect as being the source of his ill ease.

"Are you well, Colonel? You appear perturbed."

"I am overtaxed," he said rather curtly, "and you have been dismissed."

I rose from my chair, strode across the room, and opened the door. Outside was dark. Most of the clerks had retired for the evening and the candles had been snuffed, but a few oil lamps burned still, and in the gloom I could see a man waiting for Hamilton's attention. I could not at first see his face, but then he turned and I knew him at once. It was Reynolds.

Was he here as the man who threw me into Pearson's dungeon or the one who rescued me? I was in no mood to find out on *his* terms. He was just then turning to me, a foolish grin upon his face, and I swung out with my fist. I am no man of action, I have said so, but even I can throw a good punch at an unready opponent. Reynolds, however, was apparently always ready. He reached out with his hand and caught my punch. I felt my fist slam hard into the bones of his hand, and the pain echoed up my arm to my elbow. He hardly moved.

"That's unkind," he said.

Hamilton was out of his chair and rushed over to the doorway. "What happens here?"

"The captain here took a swing at me," said Reynolds.

"Captain Saunders," Hamilton shouted, sounding less like an army officer than a Latin master, "you will leave at once!"

My fist was still entangled in Reynolds's meaty hand, which held on

with a firm unchanging grip. I felt myself start to perspire. "This man attacked me in New York."

"I told ye," he said. "It were just business. I was paid to, and so I did.
And I made it right, didn't I?"

"Where's Pearson now?" I asked.

"Don't know. I haven't seen him."

"So you are back to working for Duer?"

"Reynolds's business is not your concern," said Hamilton. To the
beast he said, "Let go of his hand. Captain Saunders is now leaving."

"I demand to know what you do with him," I said.

"Who are you to demand?" Hamilton answered.

Reynolds let go his grip. I said not another word but strode from the
building, too angry to devise another option. Hamilton had secret dealings with Reynolds. I had long known that, though not why. Surely it
wasn't possible that the animosity between Hamilton and Duer was a
mere illusion, meant to confuse his enemies. Hamilton had dedicated
himself to government service at the expense of his personal economy. It
was conceivable he would do terrible things, even destroy his own brainchild, the bank, rather than remain poor forever, but I did not believe it.
Hamilton would never sacrifice the bank for anything, let alone greed.
And, in any case, Leonidas had seen Hamilton pay Reynolds, not the
other way around.

Reynolds had made it clear that he would hire himself out to other
men to perform other tasks, unsavory tasks. Hamilton had Lavien, but
he'd made it clear he was uneasy with Lavien's scrupulous view of duty,
which meant that whatever business Hamilton had with Reynolds was
something he did not wish discovered by the world.

I did not know what any of this meant, but I was determined to find
out. There was but one man in the world to whom I could pose a question on Hamilton's character, and I meant to ask him immediately.

There are few things in this world for which I am prepared to show reverence, it is true, but for this appointment I would show all the respect I
could muster. I'd refrained from drinking the previous night, and so I
awoke Tuesday morning well rested and easy. As the time for the visit ap-

proached, I dressed myself quite neatly, making frequent use of the mirror to make certain all was in order.

Rather than risk soiling my pumps and stockings with filth from the street, I hired a coach to take me the distance to Sixth and Market, where the great mansion stood. It was one of the first houses in the city, owned by merchant Bob Morris but now rented to his distinguished tenant. As I approached the door, a liveried Negro held out his hand for my invitation.

"I do not have an invitation," I said.

"Then you may not enter."

"My name is Captain Ethan Saunders," I said. "I must speak with him, and I must do so in this manner. I cannot have the world know I conferred with him, and so it must be a public and seemingly vacuous exchange. He will certainly see me if he knows I am here. Will you present my name to him?"

It was evident to me that he did not know if he ought to, and yet he seemed to sense the force of my request. Asking another usher to take his place, he disappeared into the house for several minutes. When he returned, he told me that I might proceed.

I was ushered inside an antechamber, all red and gold furnishings, filled with some of the first people of the city as well as visitors from the several states and even a few foreign dignitaries. None knew my name, and though I knew many of theirs, I was not present to make idle chatter, to gossip, or find my social footing. I merely stood by the window and made small conversation, for I was called upon to do it, with an Episcopalian bishop named White.

At precisely 3 P.M. the doors to the receiving room opened, and we queued up obediently. On the left, another liveried man announced each guest's name. This servant was not a Negro, since his role including reading, and a literate Negro might offend Southerners.

I was situated approximately in the middle of the queue, and so it came to be my turn. I handed my card to the servant, and he loudly proclaimed, "Captain Ethan Saunders!" I felt my stomach drop, the way it does before a man rushes into battle. I was full of fear, yes, but also exhilaration. And I felt shame, for all at once I saw the last decade of my life unfold before me as nothing but a string of drunken days and debauched encounters, as unsavory as they were unwise. I had once, long ago, been singled out for special notice by men who saw my particular talents as a means to serve rather than as an excuse never to achieve. Yes, I had been dealt some blows, but what excuse had I to surrender to failure and despair?

Such were my feelings when I turned to my right where President Washington stood, dressed in formal finery in his velvet suit and gloves, ceremonial sword at his side. I had not seen him close in many years, and time had not been kind to him. His skin had grown dry and papery, slashed with broken red veins. His eyes appeared sunken, his mouth winced with the pressure of false teeth, whose pain was already legendary. On top of it all, he appeared surprised.

As he did on the battlefield, he took his surprise manfully. He shook my hand and bowed slightly, and I proceeded to the circular room where I took my place alongside the other guests.

According to the custom, the doors closed at precisely half past three, and the President began to make his rounds. I had heard of the tedium of these events, but until it is experienced, it is impossible to believe that the human mind, free of the shackles of primordial tradition, could devise a ritual so designed to salt out the lifeblood of human fellowship.

Clockwise, the President turned to each of the guests, bowed, and exchanged some inconsequential words. If he knew the man, he might ask of his family or, more in Washington's character, of his land, its crops and improvements. If he was a stranger, he might speak of the weather or some development of trade or infrastructure near the man's home. These exchanges were not precisely whispered, but they were kept quiet to maintain the fiction of privacy.

As the President approached, I could little contain my distress. Perhaps he would refuse to speak to me. Perhaps he would condemn me as the failure I had become. Perhaps he would upbraid me as a traitor, for how could I know if he had ever learned the truth of those charges leveled so long ago? I held my ground and hoped I displayed no more signs of my terrible anxiety than the sweat that beaded along my brow.

The President turned to me and offered me a stiff bow. He smelled of wet wool. "Good afternoon, Captain Saunders. It has been too long."

I was upon business, and though I revered him as much as any, I would not insult him by showing it. "Hamilton," I said. "Can he be trusted?"

Washington showed no surprise. He must have intuited the purpose of my visit, and he would have certainly already determined on a course of action. His mouth twitched slightly in something like a grin, and his lips drew back over his false teeth. "He may be trusted absolutely."

"What if appearances are against him?" I asked.

"Have you been listening to Mr. Jefferson's supporters?"

"I've seen things for myself. I have seen certain associations."

He nodded. "What do you believe?"

Eyes were upon us now. This little exchange, brief though it was, had already consumed more than the usual allotment of time. The men in the room could hear at least part of what we said, and they knew this was not a wooden exchange of pleasantries. No, there was a seriousness, an urgency, that I had not bothered to mask, and neither had Washington. But it was too late to retreat. It was too late not to accomplish what I had hoped. Let them listen. Let them wonder. It would mean nothing to them, yet it would mean everything for me.

"I believe he is, on balance, honorable," I said, "even if I cannot comprehend his actions."

"He is my closest advisor, and he is to be trusted. He might lead himself into Hell, but he would never lead another." He made another poor attempt to smile, and I cannot say if it pained him more than me. "And what of you, Captain Saunders? Are you to be trusted?"

"Was I ever, sir?" I asked.

No hint of a smile this time. "Oh, yes," he said. "The world never thought ill of you. People thought you saw your duty as a game, a lark, but I knew better. I knew you hid behind the jollity a fierceness you dared not display. If you wear it on the surface, you become something else."

"Something like Lavien," I said.

He nodded. "Precisely." With that he turned to bow to the next guest, and in a room of dozens of men I felt utterly alone.

Even in my perplexity, I was not unmindful of important things. I returned to my boardinghouse to change my clothing to something less formal. I would need to pursue this thing to the end.

That night when I walked past the Treasury building, I could not but observe a light in the window of what I believed to be Hamilton's office. I approached and inquired of a watchman, who told me the Secretary was indeed yet inside. I withdrew and retreated to the shadows, planning nothing more than to wait for him, perhaps follow him home and speak to him there. I suppose I could have entered the building and walked into the office, but the truth was I preferred lurking in the shadows and trailing men across empty streets. It made me feel useful and involved.

Hamilton was well known for his long nights, so I was relieved when he emerged less than an hour later. I had a good view of him from across the street, and I was astonished by the look on his face—a kind of furtive, guilty, sneakish look I did not like.

I followed as he traveled away from the center of town and toward areas I knew to be most unlike those favored by fashionable gentlemen. Our Secretary of the Treasury, in short, was heading toward Southwark.

Before he reached the house, I had guessed his destination, for I had been to this neighborhood before, and in Hamilton's wake too. This was Reynolds's home, and it was here I expected to find answers. Philadelphia was, in general, a city of well-lit streets, but in these poor neighborhoods, a homeowner's duties were often neglected, and I was easily able to ensconce myself in shadow mere feet from the stoop. I was no Lavien, who I suspected could glide above leaf and twig, but I moved silently enough and only men on their guard could have detected my approach.

I watched as Hamilton knocked on the door and waited to see Reynolds's brutish face. Perhaps, I thought, I should confront the man, let him know he was exposed, that I was no longer fooled by his pretense of honor and rectitude.

Indeed, I had gone so far as to step forward when the door opened, and it was not the beastly James Reynolds who stood there but the lovely Maria.

She smiled at him and placed a hand upon his face.

He removed it. "I ought not to be here," he said. "Your husband—"

"Did not my husband write you and beg you to visit me? He left Philadelphia this morning upon some mission for his master. Think nothing of my husband."

"How can I think nothing of him?" Hamilton said. "He presses me for money because you and I have been together, and then, when I leave you alone, he begs me to return to you. Must I not believe that he will press me again?"

"Hush," she said. "Come inside. We will discuss it."

He followed her in and closed the door. As to whether or not they would do much discussing, I was in doubt, but there it was. Hamilton, with his children, his devoted wife, his staunch morals, had been drawn into a sordid affair with this woman. At once I understood this lady and her husband, she beautiful and he wretched. He'd told me his wife was a slut, and I could only presume the funds Hamilton paid Reynolds were a sort of compensation for the services she provided the Treasury Secretary. Did Hamilton not see that they both used him?

He did not see—or, rather, he saw and could not stop himself.

Ethan Saunders

Hamilton had fallen victim to the pleasures of the flesh. I could hardly blame him for showing human frailty with a creature as lovely as Maria Reynolds, and I could hardly blame her, with her brute of a husband, for preferring a dalliance with one of the most powerful men in the nation. He traveled a dangerous course, however. I believed Washington, that Hamilton would never sacrifice the good of the nation to feed his own desire, but he might well destroy himself.

I would do what I could for him. He had proved he would do what he could for me, and it seemed only just. In the meantime, I would continue to pursue Cynthia and her husband. I had been unable to find anyone in the city who knew for certain where they had gone, and I needed to enlist someone who possessed connections I did not.

The next day, cloudy and dark and windy, I went to Southwark, where the bulk of the town's Negroes made their home, and proceeded to ask directions, for I knew those streets indifferently well. Among the clusters of Negroes gathered by their market, hawking their roots and meats and bowls of pepper pot, white men such as myself are regarded with considerable suspicion, but I believe it is generally considered unwise to neglect their inquiries. Indeed, a few smiles and coins made it clear that I wished nothing but kindness, and within a few hours of beginning my project, I found the place for which I searched.

It was a neat little house of exceptional narrowness, but pleasing and well maintained. I knocked upon the door and was greeted quickly by a pretty Negress with large eyes and skin the color of drinking chocolate. She appeared momentarily alarmed, no doubt unused to white men on her stoop, but I smiled, removed my hat, and bowed. "You are Mrs.—" I stopped because I did not know Leonidas's surname. It was customary for slaves to take the names of their masters, but I could not imagine Leonidas doing so. "You are married to Leonidas?"

She nodded. Then her face bunched in a spasm of fear. "Has something happened?"

"No need for alarm. I know nothing of him, good or ill. I had hoped to find him home, but I intuit from your words that he is not."

Her concern melted away, and I admired again her attractive features, dignified in the Negro mold, and also her unmistakable strength of will. Leonidas had done well in marrying a woman who, I had no doubt, both appreciated and matched him.

"And who are you?" she asked. It was a rather strong way to talk to a white man she did not know, but I would not trouble myself over that.

"I do beg your pardon. I am Captain Ethan Saunders." I bowed once more.

"You're him?" she asked. She gazed upon my face. She looked me up and down the length of my body, like a side of beef presented for sale. And then she laughed in a way I did not like at all.

We sat in her neat little parlor, sipping tea. She told me her name was Pamela but seemed reluctant to present to me the surname Leonidas had chosen. It was no matter, for she treated me graciously, even though I suspected something else lay just beneath the surface. Mrs. Pamela served an agreeable tea and some sweet oat cakes with bits of raisin in them. They were quite tasty and wholesome.

"These are good cakes," I said.

She nodded her thanks.

"The raisins—a nice touch. Raisins make everything better, I think. Some prefer plums, or even apricots, but when it comes to dried fruit, I shall always take raisins."

She said nothing.

"Pamela." I tried again. "I like the name Pamela. It is very pretty."

This kind observation solicited no response.

I tried again. "From Spenser, I believe."

She stared at me.

"He is an English poet."

She scratched the bridge of her nose.

"He wrote *The Faerie Queene*," said I.

She blinked.

"It is," I attempted, "a very long poem. Long and dull."

More blinking.

I began to fear that I had misjudged blankness for determination and that my friend Leonidas had married a stupid woman. I supposed he knew best his own domestic felicity, but I feared Mrs. Pamela must make for dull company.

"My husband told me about you," she said at last.

"And what did he say? Nothing too unflattering, I hope. Ha-ha!"

She took a sip of tea. "He told me you were a wastrel and a scoundrel, but that you have a sentimental heart for so selfish a creature."

"Your husband has ever been an excellent judge of character," I said, now feeling nostalgic for the Spenser discourse. And the raisins.

"He told me that you are, by nature, the sort of man who would despise the practice of slavery, but you held on to him for as long as you could because it was the only way you could conceive of to keep from spending your days alone. Is that true?"

"I cannot say," I told her, suddenly feeling warm. "Mrs. Pamela, I did not come here to make you uneasy."

"Then for what did you come? Why do you trouble us?"

"That is something I must discuss with your husband."

This answer must have offered some offense, for the good woman did not trouble herself to respond. Thus we sat in silence for near the better part of an hour, though she was so good as to refill my teacup two times. By the time the front door of the house opened and closed and footsteps approached, I was quite ready for a chamber pot. Leonidas entered the room, still wearing his greatcoat, flakes of snow freshly melted upon it. He had removed his hat and still held it in his hand when he noticed me. I grinned at him. He looked at me, and never had I observed such a look of rage upon his face—and never on anyone's face outside of warfare. His dark face twisted; his eyes widened and then narrowed.

"What are you doing here in my home?" His voice was calm; perhaps that was what made me so easy.

I stood. "I beg your pardon. I do not mean to disturb your domestic peace. I should never have troubled you if it were not important—if someone's convenience other than my own were not at issue."

He appeared to give the matter some thought. He took another step toward me and sniffed like a beast. "You haven't been drinking. Have you at last reformed?"

"I suppose I have. It is amazing how people can change for the better."

"I'll not believe it."

"Leonidas, I know you are angry with me, and if I cannot truly understand the depth of your anger, it is only because I cannot know what you have known. I shall not attempt to justify my actions or place them in context, to help you see what justice must: that on balance I have treated you well, and better than you could have hoped for from another."

"How dare you—"

I held up my hand. "I do not care to hear it. Not because it is just or unjust, but because Cynthia Pearson is in danger, and I need your help. Her husband has absconded with her and her children, and no one knows where. I had hoped you might inquire among the servants and see if you might learn what others cannot."

"You come to me for a favor? I want nothing from you."

"Can you not recognize a plea not for myself but for a woman's life and for the life of her children? You would hold a grudge against the life of two children?"

"Leonidas," his wife said softly. "You must not be stubborn to the point of cruelty. You need not like him to help him in this."

"I will not have him stand here and pretend his motives are something other than selfishness. He claims to want to help others, but it is only desire that motivates him." To me he said, "What are the names of these children?"

It was true that I did not know, but I saw no need to demonstrate that he had so successfully taken my measure. "Julia and Dennis," I said, very quickly too.

Leonidas said nothing for several long moments. Then, finally, he nodded. "If I can learn anything, I shall let you know."

I stepped forward with my hand out. "You are a good man. I knew I could depend upon you."

He only stared at my hand. "It does not mean we are friends. It only means I will not let others suffer because you have earned my enmity."

I sniffed. "Right. Well, thank you, even so."

"If I have more to say to you, I will go to you. You are not to return to my home. Not under any circumstances. Now leave."

The two of them followed me to the door, as though I could not be trusted to find it, or to leave without helping myself to some of their goods on the way. Leonidas opened the door. I stepped through and turned, removing my hat and bowing.

The lady of the house met my eye, daring me to turn away. "I do not find Spenser at all dull," she said.

Her husband slammed the door.

Hamilton had not brought me into government service, not really, but here I was, speaking to him, to Washington, working alongside his principal spy. I could not ignore what I knew, and I could not leave him to his own peril.

That being the case, the next day I rose early, just after nine in the morning, dressed myself neatly, and strolled to the Treasury offices on Third, where I casually asked to have an audience with the Secretary. He saw me almost immediately, and I took a seat across from him in his small spare office.

"How can I help you this time, Captain?"

I coughed into my fist. "I wonder if there has been any progress in your dealings with Duer."

He leaned back in his seat. "When this matter is resolved, I want you to come see me. I wish for you to work with Lavien, if you think you can do so. You've proved your worth to me, and you seem to have mastered yourself considerably. This is the second time you've been here without the stench of drink upon you."

"I am flattered, and you may depend upon me, but why must we wait?"

"Because at the moment there is nothing for you to do—either for you or Mr. Lavien. I am in touch with my men in New York, and I know what Duer plans. He is still attempting to control the six percents; he is still borrowing dangerously. And he is about to learn that we have begun proceedings against him for the money he embezzled while upon the Board of Treasury. The word will spread—on its own or with our help— and it is but a matter of weeks, perhaps only days, until Duer collapses and the bank is safe. You have played no small role in this, Captain, and I am grateful. You may be certain I will do all I can, in addition to offering you employment, to make certain the world knows you and Fleet were falsely maligned those many years ago."

"Lavien told you."

"He did."

"If all this is true, why do you keep me at arm's length now?"

"You are of no use to me," he said. "I cannot depend on you."

I tried hard not to show my anger. Or was it my shame? "What do you mean?"

"I mean you ask about Duer because you are interested and involved, but it is not what is upon your mind. You want to find Pearson, the man who destroyed you, killed your friend, and stole the woman you loved. You want to find his much-abused wife and children. The Revolution is won, and while I don't doubt your patriotism, I do not expect you would be able to put any assignment I might give you before your duty to Mrs. Pearson. Find her, bring her to safety, and then you may come work with me."

I stood up and bowed. "I see you are a man who understands the human heart." I returned to my seat.

He turned away. "When it comes to our passions, we do as we must."

I coughed again. "It is upon that subject that I have come, in part, to see you. I've spoken to no one, and to my knowledge I am the only other person who knows about this. I say this first to spare you the pain of asking. I must advise you to end your liaison with Maria Reynolds. Her husband is closely connected with Duer. I do not know that your dealings with his wife have any bearing on these other matters, but I need not tell you that this is a powder keg that could explode in your face."

He remained still for a moment. "How did you learn of this?"

"I followed you."

His face turned dark at once. His fists clenched and unclenched like a baby's. "You followed me?"

"Colonel, Reynolds was waiting outside your office. My man had already seen you giving him money. I had to know the connection."

He nodded. "He discovered my intimacy with the lady several months ago and has been allowing it to continue in exchange for money, money I truly don't have. It has been a nightmare, but I know not what to do about it. He presses me whether I see Maria or not."

"And so you might as well see her."

"To be blunt," said Hamilton, "I am not entirely certain that she did not begin to attract my attention with this scheme in mind. She is very beautiful."

"I have seen her."

"Then you know. She is lovely, but flighty and inconstant and—well, not particularly clever. Yet I cannot help myself. I vow never to see her more, yet I return."

"When it comes to our passions," I said, "we do as we must."

This time he met my gaze. His stare was raw with shame.

"Yet in this case you must not," I said. "If Jefferson or his minions were to learn of this, it would destroy you. They would destroy you. They would never believe—or they would pretend never to believe—that this is a mere personal impropriety, but portray it as evidence of a larger corruption. You must vow never to see her again."

He said nothing, but I knew he understood. I expected to feel some satisfaction in standing upon the moral high ground with Hamilton, but all I felt was sympathy and something not entirely unlike friendship.

I wish I could say that the next several weeks were productive or eventful, but they were not. I spent my time doing little but attempting to find Pearson and having no luck. I made regular visits to the City Tavern and other establishments that catered to businessmen. I spoke to anyone with whom the Pearsons had a personal connection, including the mighty Bingham family, but no one could say where they had gone. Burr in New York wrote me to say no one had seen Pearson and promised to write again if he learned anything. I received regular updates from Lavien and Hamilton on Duer, as he slid toward destruction. Around the city, construction slowed as the Bank of the United States withdrew its loans to protect itself, but the loans were for the most part being repaid, and Hamilton felt confident that the bank was safe. I saw no more of Mrs. Maycott, and I could only imagine that she herself was satisfied with Duer's current troubles. I heard nothing from Leonidas.

For the most part I continued my efforts at reform. I did not eschew drink entirely, for a man must not die of thirst, but I was temperate, if not precisely frequently, then certainly more often than before. I admit, however, that one afternoon at the City Tavern I had far too much wine and began demanding of anyone who would listen that I had grown weary of waiting for information. I would go to New York, I said, and find Duer and demand he tell me where I might find Cynthia Pearson. A kindly young trader escorted me to the door, and I made my way home myself.

That would have been the end of the incident, but the next afternoon Mrs. Deisher announced that a delivery had been made to me—a crate of ten bottles of good Spanish sherry. The accompanying note was from William Duer, and it announced that he hoped I knew how well my efforts had served him, and the wine was a gift of gratitude. The words were spare and to the point, yet there could be no doubt of a kind of gloating. Perhaps he had been in town and learned of my drunkenness. It hardly mattered, for I would not be goaded into anything, even regret, by a man such as he, on the brink of ruin.

I was still contemplating these developments, and sampling one of the bottles—for it ought not to be wasted—when Mrs. Deisher announced that I had a visitor below. She appeared out of sorts, and when I went into the parlor I saw Leonidas standing with his back to me. He wore a fine new suit, and he held a handsome leather hat in his hands, and yet for all this grand appearance he looked somewhat abashed. His eyes were cast to the ground, and his fingers worked uneasily at the brim of his hat.

He turned to me, his face grave. I noticed, for the first time, lines forming about his eyes, as if he had aged five or ten years since last I saw him. "Good afternoon, Ethan."

"I did not expect you to come calling." I kept my voice calm and even, yet how my heart leaped to see him. Not since the war, not since I had studied under Fleet's tutelage, had I known a friendship like his, and to think that it was over, that Leonidas could not forgive me, nearly staggered me. Yet I would not show it. I could not.

"I never intended to call, but I thought you would wish to hear what I have to say. You asked me to inquire into the Pearsons, and I did so, though until now I have learned nothing of import. But just this morning I received a visit from one of the former kitchen maids who heard, if somewhat belatedly, that I was willing to pay for information. In exchange for two dollars she told me that she knew their fate with absolute certainty."

I stepped forward. "Well?"

He closed his eyes, as though bracing himself, and then looked at me boldly, as would a man offering a challenge. "It seems that Pearson has taken his family west, to Pittsburgh. They hired a guide and a team of animals, packed up a minimum of belongings, and departed."

"Pittsburgh." I whispered the word and then sat.

Falling into old habits, Leonidas poured me a glass of Duer's sherry and then sat across from me. His hands were on his knees, and he leaned forward paternally. "I know the woman, and she is not prone to fabrication. If she says she is certain, I believe it must be true. I am sorry. I know this is hard news."

I drank down the sherry at once. "I'll go after her."

He rose, refilled my glass, and handed it to me anew, this time nearly to overflowing. "Do you think that's wise? I understand that you feel the need to save her, but is that something for which you are prepared—a wilderness conflict with a man as willful as Pearson?"

I drank half my glass. "Are you mad? You think I am not fit to confront Pearson in city or wilderness? She *depends* upon me to go after her. I must prepare at once. Thank you, Leonidas, for telling me. I know you are angry, but you have done the right thing." I finished the drink. Already I felt the sherry flowing through me, and with it the inexorable energy that came with the first warmth of drink, and I felt shame, a deep and burning shame, that what Leonidas had taken from our years together was that I was not the man to save Cynthia. How wrong he was. I would go at once.

Leonidas studied me as though attempting to take some measure. "I shall leave you to your preparations, then." He held out his hand for me to shake.

I took it, but a terrible unspoken truth hung over this parting. I saw the distress in his gaze, and I understood it for the same trouble I felt in my heart. Once, not so long ago, the two of us would have faced these difficulties together. Now I was alone. I dared not ask him to join me, and his pride would never let him volunteer. Perhaps when I returned, when all these troubles had passed, Leonidas and I could begin to build the friendship anew. Perhaps this was my test. Only once I'd proved I did not depend on him could he trust me enough to befriend me.

I went upstairs and began to pull things from my trunks, things I could not do without. I would have to travel light and travel fast. They were several people. Including children. They had animals carrying their packs. They would be slow. They had a significant head start, but I would travel by horse and do so alone or perhaps with Lavien. If I were swift and made do with little sleep, I could hope to overtake them.

I looked at the crate of wine upon my floor, the bottles still—for the most part—nestled in their straw. There was a time, and it was not so long ago, when it would have been enough to stop me, or at least slow me down.

I looked at the crate again, which bore the name of the vendor stenciled upon the side. At once I grabbed my hat and coat and headed out to the street. It was but half an hour's walk to reach the wine merchant, and I burst inside, demanding at once to speak to the owner.

It was later than I realized, and the man before me had been preparing to close his shop, but he needed only to look upon my face to understand that he would be better served saying nothing of this to me. This man, tall and balding and with a very red face, announced that he was Mr. Nelson, the owner. I put my question to him at once.

"I am Captain Ethan Saunders. You delivered to me a case of wine this afternoon."

"Yes, sir. I trust there was no trouble with it. It was among our finest Spanish."

"The wine was excellent, but I must know where it came from. Who placed the order?"

"Well, I don't know," he said, looking confused rather than sinister.

"Was it Mr. Duer of New York? Did he write to you?"

"No one wrote to me," he said. "A man came in and placed the order directly. A big and very black fellow he was, but very polite and speaking like a white man. He didn't give his name, and I didn't need it. He paid me with good money, and as there could be no harm in sending a man a crate of good wine, that was all there needed to be between us."

I hardly heard the rest, for I wandered from the shop. Why had Leonidas done these things? There could be no other explanation but that he was attempting, by various means, to manipulate me for Joan Maycott. I would either collapse into drunkenness or drop everything to chase the Pearsons to Pittsburgh. All of which meant I would not do what I had threatened in public to do—go to New York and confront Duer.

Now I understood everything, or at least enough. I understood why Leonidas had fled once he learned of his freedom; he could not bear to betray me once he learned I had not betrayed him. I understood why he had been so cruel to me when I visited him at his home—there could be no friendship between us while he served my enemies. Most of all, I understood how much I had been manipulated—how much we all had.

The ground was icy, and the sun had by now set, casting the city in darkness. Still, I ran. I ran past pedestrians and pigs and cows and carts and cart men who shouted at me to watch where I went. I was called a brute and a damned fool, but I did not care. I ran until I reached Lavien's door, and I pounded and pounded and pounded until the miserable old woman answered and I pushed past her at once without a word.

Lavien sat at dinner with his wife and children and looked up at me in alarm.

"We must go," I said. "We must go to New York. Now, at once."

He rose. "What has happened?"

"The whole time we were wrong. We thought to prevent the collapse of the bank, but we have done everything conceivable to bring about the bank's destruction. It wasn't Duer, it was us. *We* are the plot against the bank."

He set down his knife. "What are you talking about?"

"We were so convinced that Duer was the danger that we did not see the obvious truth. It is Duer's *failure* that will destroy the bank. That is why they don't want me to go to New York. They don't want me to see Duer, to understand how much in debt he is, how precarious is his situation. If he goes bankrupt, he could well bring the country with him."

Lavien remained still for a moment. Then he said, "We must see Hamilton."

Eliza Hamilton made us tea while I sat in Hamilton's study. He remained impassive while he listened to us. Only a tapping foot gave away his agitation. I explained to him what I had concluded, and why I had concluded it. He understood. He insisted I wait, however. The night was too dark to ride out now, the roads too covered in snow. I would leave, I said, an hour before dawn, and ride by the lights of the city until the sun rose. Hamilton then began to write out another letter, this one for Duer.

"I am explaining all to him," he said. "I hope to appeal to his better nature. You must do the same. You must augment this letter as best you can, but you must convince him to reverse course. He will have to sell what he can, clear out what debt he can. He will have to sacrifice his dreams of conquest in exchange for an opportunity to avoid complete ruin and ignominy."

"I cannot imagine Duer accepting such a trade," I said.

He nodded, his quill still making its methodical way across his heavy sheet of paper. "Neither can I. Nevertheless, it is the choice he will have to make. He must understand the consequences of ruin. He cannot be allowed to be exposed as a bankrupt. He cannot allow the public to know of his debts. If that happens, if he is exposed, he is ruined, and that will produce a chain of events so devastating I cannot endure to think of it. England survived its South Sea Bubble because it was an old and large and entrenched economy, but France, where modern finance was new, never recovered from its simultaneous Mississippi Bubble. If Duer is exposed, we will be lucky to—like France—see no more than our economy ruined and our people pauperized. Banks will fail, so merchants will fail, and then farms. And then starvation. And that is the best we can hope for. I dare not think of how much worse it could become, but the resulting turmoil could put an end to our system of governance."

He paused in his writing.

I had been staring at the fire, thinking of all those with whom I now knew Leonidas to be involved, but most of all Joan Maycott. I knew she hated Hamilton and had some grievance with Duer, but could this be what she wished? Could that lady and her whiskey-smelling associates truly wish to see the destruction of American republicanism in its infancy?

"You will have to offer him something if he is to agree," I said. "Duer never acts, not even to save himself, if he cannot see something shining and glittering at the end of it. You may have to promise him some kind of quiet bribe, money with which to live when all is settled."

Hamilton hastily scratched a few words onto the page and then began to blot. "No. I cannot have it be said, when all is finished, that I paid this man a reward for his work of nearly destroying the nation. Even if Duer understands what he has done to himself, and even if he understands that a quiet reversal is his only hope, he will later feel resentment. He will tell himself he was tricked and bullied into giving up his scheme, and so he will complain of it to all who will listen. I cannot have Jefferson's republican faction learning that, in essence, I've bribed a scoundrel for nearly ruining the nation." He now looked at Lavien. "You will have to make certain he agrees to everything. You understand me."

Lavien nodded. "He will agree."

I understood their meaning. "You don't think the Jeffersonians will use it against you if you start breaking Duer's fingers?"

"They will use it against me if I have boiled beef for my dinner," Hamilton said. "What matters is the force of their argument. The populace will forgive a politician who uses rough means to accomplish a good end. They will never forgive a man who makes secret payments to a villain."

When the letter was dry, he folded it, placed it in an envelope, and handed it to me along with a letter of credit from the government of the United States. He said I was to do what I must—trade horses, buy horses, it did not matter. Spend any amount to get to New York with all due haste.

"But keep your receipts," he added, "so the ledgers will balance."

Even in the midst of crisis, he could not help being himself.

Joan Maycott

March 1792

Things began to happen not precisely quickly, for events were spread out over several weeks, but certainly with a kind of consistency that, looked at later with the eye of history, would certainly give the impression of rapidity. Duer attempted to proceed with his plan to control six percent securities, but his failure with the Million Bank was a public setback. News spread that Duer's schemes had failed him, and so finally there was tarnish upon his name.

Soon thereafter the Bank of the United States began to restrict credit, calling in loans, including a number belonging to Duer that were difficult, if not impossible for him to meet. Then the last blow was struck. The Treasury Department itself had conducted an inquiry into Duer's actions on the old Treasury Board—the ones I had myself discovered— and found the $236,000 he had illegally appropriated. Duer objected and wrote to Hamilton, begging forbearance, but these were only delaying tactics, and now it was but a matter of waiting for the inevitable.

The great speculator no longer made appearances at the Merchants' Coffeehouse. He could ask none of his agents to do his bidding. All either faced their own ruin or would not be touched by Duer's new ignominy. Instead, he barricaded himself in his house in Greenwich Village and, I could only imagine, attempted to convince himself that even the most severe of storms would, in the end, pass. A man who had endured as much as he would endure this.

He did venture out now and again for private business, and one such time, near the end, he came to see me. I received him in my parlor. Unlike Pearson on the day of the Million Bank launch, Mr. Duer appeared neatly dressed and well groomed and, were someone not to know his circumstances, he would never suspect him to be in any danger. I could only see him as the buzzard circling the dying form of a corruptible nation.

He sipped a glass of sherry and smiled at me, inquired how I had been keeping myself and what news I had to report. I made small talk, of course, but in the end I was forced to return the subject to his own concerns.

"I do not like to repeat the unpleasant news I hear in the papers," I ventured, "but you and I have ever been too friendly for me to pretend there are no such reports abroad."

"You need not concern yourself with me," he said. "I shall weather this. There are always moments of crisis in a speculator's life. This is but a distraction."

I sipped my sherry but never once took my eyes off him. "I should like to know how you will extract yourself from these difficulties."

He looked at me, seeing something new in me, perhaps. He might have, for I was growing weary of disguise. Indeed, I could hardly imagine a reason to remain in disguise. "Your tone, madam, suggests you do not think you will see me recover."

"You owe more than half a million dollars by my estimate, and that assumes you will liquidate your items of real value, including your house. Creditors such as the Bank of the United States are not easily put off, and I don't think the coopers and bakers of the city from whom you've borrowed will be any more forgiving. Indeed, you may have more to fear from them than you do the law."

He said nothing for a long moment, as if waiting for the words that would erase what I had already said, the words that would turn everything into a great joke. "I—I cannot understand why you would speak to me so."

"I only tell you the truth. You do not hate the truth, do you?" I set down my drink, folded my hands in my lap, and looked at him until he looked away.

"Is it the money?" he asked. "Is that what this comes to? You fear I shall soon be worthless, and so you scorn me?"

"Even in your moments of distress, you are nothing but a creature of greed. You think there is nothing in the world but money, sir? You think we care for nothing but wealth? It means nothing to me. Have I ever asked you for so much as a penny? No, never. I have never wanted anything from you, and yet you did not notice it."

He wiped his hands on his pants. "I do not know how to respond to this. I must go." But he did not stand.

"When you first sought my company," I continued, "I thought you must press me for the most intimate of favors. Did you know that, if I had been made to choose between giving in to you and incurring your displeasure, I would have given in? That is how much I wanted you to regard me well, to trust me. But you did not want the pleasures of the flesh. You wanted only to feel clever and important, and I had to do no more than praise your ideas and confirm your sense of self. And now you are ruined, ruined beyond redemption, and nothing can save you. You have debts such as have never been seen on this continent, such as could never be paid by any American, and if the mob does not take you out for a hanging, you shall die in debtor's prison."

"Mrs. Maycott," he said.

I would not wait. I would say what I had to while I could. "What I find particularly ironic is that during the Revolution, I am told, you were a true patriot. You had not yet let the rot of greed eat your heart to nothingness."

"Why would you torment me by saying these things? What have I ever done to you that you would hate me so?"

"What have you done? Do you not remember? You sat in my house and lied to me and my husband. You used your influence and knowledge and trickery to convince us to trade our war debt for worthless land on the frontier, to be tormented by your partner, Colonel Tindall. I saw Tindall die, you know. I saw him strung up myself, with my own eyes." This was not strictly true, but as I saw Duer sink into deeper and deeper reaches of terror, I could not resist a little theatrical elaboration. "You have thought nothing of ruining lives for your wealth, and your greed led to the death of my husband—and, yes, the child in my womb— murdered by your partner. All this death and destruction can be set at your feet, for you lied to us about what lay in store for us. That is why I have done it, and now you know. I tell you for the simple reason that there is nothing for you to do. Knowing won't save you. Your knowing can't hurt me. I've committed no crime you can prove. Yet, even if your knowing put me in danger, I would tell you, for it is important you understand that your ruin is not some random mishap. You suffer from the direct consequences of your ambition. You are undone in repayment for all these crimes and, I have no doubt, a thousand more, the knowledge of which I have been spared."

Mr. Duer rose slowly. He looked at me imploringly, as if I still had some power to undo what had been done. "I have never known such wickedness," he said in a slow, deliberate voice. "Perhaps I have not always been honest in my dealings. What of it? I am a trader. It is what I do, and what I am. But I have never taken pleasure in the destruction of others. That you revel in my suffering is unspeakable."

"I take no pleasure in it," I said. "I take my revenge not out of desire but out of duty. How could I live with myself if I let you continue? I have dedicated my life to your destruction, and though seeing it may give me satisfaction, it gives me no pleasure."

It would also make me and my partners wealthy, but I chose not to mention this part, for there he could still do me harm. Instead, I merely rang the bell and told the girl that I believed Mr. Duer had taken enough of our time.

My conversation must have effected a change in Duer's behavior, one notable to his underlings, for the next morning, just as I began to make preparations to abandon my New York lodgings for good, I was approached by Mr. Reynolds. He had clearly known better than to call on

me and so had been loitering outside my boardinghouse. I stepped outside to enter a hackney, but before I could reach it Mr. Reynolds stepped
out before me and bowed slightly.

"Good morning, madam. Nice weather today, ain't it?"

"What can I do for you?"

"Well, to be honest, you can give me a bit more money."

"You have already been paid well for your silence," I told him.

"It's true," he acknowledged, "but I spent that money, so I'll be wanting more."

I looked at him sternly. "I cannot be held accountable for that."

He showed me his yellow teeth, and he seemed to me like an overgrown dog who has eaten his master's dinner. "It's looking to me like you
can. You bought my silence once; I'm guessing you'll do it again. Oh, I
know, I made certain promises, but from where I'm standing, there
doesn't seem to me a lot you can do about it."

He squared his shoulders and hovered over me, and he was far taller,
far broader, and undoubtedly far more vicious than I saw—or at least
more violent. Yet I would not allow myself to be intimidated by such a
brute. I had faced down worse than he. It is what he did not understand,
would never understand—that there were limits to what can be accomplished by physical menace. "Mr. Reynolds, I did not buy your silence, I
rented it, and the time for which I required it has now passed us. You
may now tell Mr. Duer what you like. I imagine he is out of sorts, which
made you uneasy and is why you have come back. You feared the period
in which you might apply to me would be drawing to a close, but it has
already done so."

He put his face near mine, as if we were lovers, and I smelled his scent
of whiskey and tobacco. "I hope you ain't testing me, because I mean to
try your words."

"I have told him myself," I said. "He knows I've acted against him. I
do hope he doesn't owe you much money."

Reynolds stepped back. "He pays me by the quarter, and he ain't paid
me yet this year."

I brushed past him and allowed the coachman to open the door for
me. "You shan't see the money." I stepped in and looked out the window
at him. "I do hope you earn more than one hundred and fifty dollars a

quarter," I told him. "If that's the case, you've been a loser for your efforts. Good day, Mr. Reynolds. For your own safety, let this be the last time I see you."

And indeed it was, for I left New York that evening and made my way to the point of rendezvous with most of the others in my band. Only three remained in New York to protect the mission from Saunders. Having done so much to aid us, he could still do us harm if he managed to divine our scheme. In Philadelphia, my agents had done everything possible to lead him astray, but it was yet possible he might come to New York, so the remaining men were there to make sure he attempted nothing that would harm us, and, if he did, to use appropriate measures to stop him.

Ethan Saunders

The watchman had only finished crying out three in the morning when Lavien and I presented Hamilton's letter at the government's stable. We were given two stout well-fed beasts and, a bit earlier than agreed, we began to make our way. We rode in silence; the cold and the dark and the urgency made talk seem trivial. When dawn trickled orange into the eastern sky, we quickened our pace. The horses were sure-footed in the melting snow, and we rode hard.

We traded horses in Princeton and were at the ferry in New Jersey by two in the afternoon. Once upon the New York side of the river, we took the Greenwich Road to Duer's mansion. It had not snowed there, and the roads were dry, so we made good time. When we arrived there was a gathering of people outside Duer's palatial estate—maybe as many as a hundred—and they looked angry. Some appeared to be Duer's brothers of the speculation trade, dressed in fine suits and handsome coats, their own excellent carriages parked nearby. Alongside them were poor women in tattered dresses, their hair covered with rags. A boy with a dirty face clutched the hand of an angry father. A Negro man in homespun looked somewhat dazed, as though he'd been struck in the head. Some stared at the house. Some shouted at it. One man, aging and one-armed, with the look of an old soldier, held a rock that he clearly meant to throw.

Lavien and I exchanged glances, but we did not speak. We did not need to. We had come prepared to do what we must to make Duer see reason, to make him begin reversing course. We were prepared to make him, through kindness or cruelty, begin writing letters to creditors and merchants and traders. We had not come prepared for this. We had come prepared to stop his ruin. We had not come prepared merely to witness it. It seemed we were too late.

We rode around to the stables and were admitted by the liveried servant once we showed him Hamilton's letter. I did not know if he could read, but he seemed impressed with our earnestness. Once inside, we demanded to see Duer, and if the servant we spoke to was put off by our haggard looks or the dirt of the road upon us, he did not comment. He seemed to have troubles aplenty of his own and absently led us to the parlor.

I helped myself to some wine from the sideboard, while Lavien gulped from a pitcher of water flavored with oranges. Duer, however, did not keep us waiting long. He pushed into the room after we had been there for less than ten minutes. His suit was rumpled, as though he had slept in it, and his hair was wild. Streaks of redness shot across his eyes.

"This is all the result of your meddling," he said. "You and Hamilton and the rest of you. Have you no idea what you've done?"

"What is happening?" Lavien asked. "It may be we can reverse things."

He could not have believed it, but it was something to say. I felt a chill run through me, for I heard something in Lavien's voice I thought unimaginable. I heard fear.

"How can you not know?" Duer sneered at him. "Word of this absurd lawsuit has gotten out, and the rumor is I am to be ruined. Now my creditors gather like starving birds, ready to pick at me until there is nothing left."

Lavien began to pace back and forth. He put a hand to his temple. "How vulnerable are you? How much do you need to make this go away? Can you placate some of your creditors and thus make the others leave you be?"

"How vulnerable am I? I am entirely exposed, that is how vulnerable I am. And you know full well that no creditor will be satisfied until he is paid."

"Can you not even cover your most immediate debts?" I asked.

"My debts were never designed to be covered," he said. "I am engaged in *business*. But now that the government has seen fit to interfere, all is falling to ruin. Your drawing back the bank's credit, and now, with the absurd suit for money I supposedly owe, Hamilton has pulled the rug from under me."

"What is the difference between what you have and what you owe?" I asked.

"I don't know. Not too much above eight hundred thousand."

I walked over to Duer and shoved him so he fell back into his chair. "Listen to me, you greedy turd. You had better think of a way to escape bankruptcy. There are some very dangerous people who wish to see you fail, and we cannot let them have their way."

Perhaps because he sensed an opportunity, he appeared unconcerned by my violence. "I cannot avoid it unless you know of some source willing to give me the money. The bank, perhaps. Yes, that's it. The bank can lend me the money. Give it to me outright, perhaps. It is a great deal of money, I know, but surely it is worth it to save us from such confusion."

"It cannot happen," Lavien said. "Lending you that money would be as good as ruining the government. Once word escaped, Washington and his administration would be seen as no better than corrupt British ministers raiding the treasury for their friends."

"We had better think of something," I said. "The crowd sounds angry."

Outside his window, we heard angry calls—*We want Duer! He has got our money!*—over and over again. One group had started a poetic cry of *Put Duer in the sewer,* hardly euphonious but certainly concise in its meaning. I peeked out the window and saw an old woman, bent over at the waist, leaning upon a walking stick and looking upward. "I want my five dollars!" she cried.

"Good God, man," I said to Duer. "You borrowed five dollars from a stooped old woman? Have you no shame?"

"She would have had no complaints when I paid her what I owed."

"You were never going to pay," I said. "You never could pay."

"How could it have worked when the government itself is against me?" he demanded. "Hamilton pretended to be my friend, but it was he who has brought this upon me. Hamilton restricted the credit. Hamilton prosecuted me about old debts. If my fall brings about the ruin of the nation, it will be upon Hamilton's head."

"You are like a murderer who blames his victim for provoking him," I said. "Hamilton restricted credit because there was too much of it, prompting greedy men like you to abuse the aberration. He has prosecuted you for your crimes because to do anything else would be dishonest. If Hamilton is to blame, it is for not crushing you sooner and harder. Perhaps then you would never have had a chance to attempt a scheme foolish beyond reason."

"But it made such sense," he said. "And she convinced me it would work."

"She? Joan Maycott?" I asked, but I believe I already knew this was her treachery.

"Yes. I know what you will say, I ought not to have taken advice from a woman, but she seemed to know what she spoke of. So charming and clever. How could I know she hated me, blamed me for her husband's death? Whippo pushed me toward this too, and where is he now? He's abandoned me, that's where. He stole as much of my silver as he could carry and then slipped out in the night just ahead of the crowds."

"You've been manipulated, Duer," I said, "and we along with you. Now I want you to collect your ledgers for me." I turned to Lavien. "You'll need to determine how much he owes and to whom. Maybe we can put it out that he has the means to repay his debts. If we can but calm the crowds, we can perhaps calm the markets before they panic."

"I'm no money man," Lavien answered. "I may understand some of how these mechanisms work, but I can't speedily interpret such things."

"I'll help you," Duer volunteered, "in exchange for a promise of government assistance and an end to this absurd lawsuit, of course. Yes, we must forget about that."

"No," said Lavien. "You won't bargain your way out of this. We will have to bring in a few clerks from Treasury to review your books, and the best we will be able to do is see to it that you pay first those who need it most. I don't know if that will accomplish anything, but we must try."

Lavien's words were punctuated by the sound of shattering glass. A rock flew into a window in a room above us, then another to our left, and then in the room we currently occupied. We could now hear clearly the cries of the crowd. "Bring us Duer! Our money or his head!" Several angry men waved muskets. One held a blazing torch.

"Christ," I said. "They could burn the building down."

"We've got to get him someplace safe," Lavien said.

"Where?"

"There's only one place," Duer said. "I've known it all morning, but I would not say it to myself until this threat of violence. I cannot see Lady Kitty burned out of her home. You've got to take me to jail. Debtor's prison is my lot now. The mob must see me taken there so they will leave my family in peace."

And so we did. We ushered him out of the house and drove him south to the City Jail on Murray Street, which also acted as the city's debtor's prison. During the stretch of the journey we were followed by an angry mob, which called after us with withering insults. Duer sat tight-lipped, his eyes clenched almost shut as, I could only imagine, images of his failed aspirations paraded before him. We were strange pied pipers, for as our coach progressed, it drew larger and larger crowds, and when we reached the prison, I feared we must be arrested for orchestrating a riot.

Duer's crossing the threshold of the City Jail seemed to act as some sort of signal—his ruin was complete so no restraint was now required. Men rushed into the Two Friendly Brothers' tavern across the way to fortify their indignation with strong drink. Accordingly, food began to fly in our direction: eggs and apples and oranges, oyster shells, and old hard rolls. Lavien and I made it inside the jail without much harm, but Duer was struck in the forehead with an old egg. The sulfurous yolk, rotten and reeking, trickled down his face, but as we led him inside the stone edifice, he did not bother to wipe it away.

Outside the prison, stones and dead animals and fruit continued to strike the walls, a dull cannonade of impotent rage. Duer was ruined, worth less than nothing, and yet not without assets or ready money, and he had little difficulty in securing for himself the finest accommodations in the building, a pleasant suite of rooms upon the third floor. The turnkeys behaved like obsequious publicans and were rewarded by Duer for their courtesy. He sat on a chair in his little sitting room, head in his hands, his face now cleaned of the earlier yolk.

"I shall pay them back," he said. "Every last one I shall pay back."

"With what money?" Lavien asked.

"I shall pay them back," Duer said.

I rubbed my face, rough with beard stubble. "Yes, yes, when the money fairies visit you in the night and dust your bed with banknotes, you will pay them back. I understand. But what will happen to the markets now that your ruin is under way?"

He stared at me as though slapped. I don't believe he had fully accepted the truth, even though he had been struck in the face with a rotten egg, even though he sat at that moment in City Jail, vowing to pay his creditors. Until I said the word, I do not believe he fully understood that this was not merely an unseemly diversion on the road to triumph. This was, indeed, the road's end.

Duer looked at me. "I told you if you ruined me, you would ruin the country. Did I not say so? Go now to Merchants' Coffeehouse, and what shall you see? Men scrambling to sell their bank scrip and government issues. The prices shall plummet, and as I am made to sell off my holdings, six percents will plummet too. You men have ruined me, but not only me. You have ruined all of us."

"There it is," Lavien said. "This is what they wanted from the beginning and we have given it to them. Now we must ride back, as fast as we can. Our only hope is to reach Philadelphia and make certain Hamilton gets the information before the news hits the markets. Things were always much farther along than we suspected, and there is nothing we can do here. It is up to Hamilton. He can position his men to buy, and buy at decent prices. He can use the power of the Treasury to prevent a complete disaster. What happens in New York will be harmful, but the center of finance in this country is Philadelphia. If word of this reaches the Philadelphia markets before we do, it may be too late for Hamilton to stop it."

"To stop what?"

"The collapse of our economic system," Lavien said.

"Everything but four percents," said Duer, who appeared to be relieved of his misery for a moment in order to lecture us on money things. "They've been undervalued, and I believe the collapse of six percents will revive them."

"Is that enough to keep the markets from collapsing?" I asked.

"No. Oh, the irony of it. I had thought to ruin men like Pearson by having them gorge themselves on four percents, but if he now sells at the right moment, he shall be rich and I shall be penniless."

I hoped, for Cynthia's sake, Pearson would know that right moment, but we could wait to hear no more. We were out the door and pushing our way through the angry crowds. They had no knowledge of who we were and how or if we were connected to Duer, but they were angry, and only by holding ourselves erect and pushing back when assaulted, did we manage to get to our carriage unscathed.

There was no time to return to Greenwich for our horses, so we found the public stables and, using Hamilton's credit, gained access to the best horses we could find. From there we made our way to the ferry and waited to make the interminable passage to the New Jersey side.

We sat astride our horses on the flat ferry, listening to the waves of the river lap at the sides. While icy winds blasted us, Lavien looked at me. "You have never been comfortable doing precisely what I say. Not without argument or debate."

"Still, you have a certain regard for me."

"I hope you prove it merited. We have been watched and followed all day—to Duer's mansion, to the stables, to the ferry. There are at least three of them, and by their rough look I believe them whiskey men. They did not take the ferry with us, which is too bad, for I should have

knocked them into the river and been done with it. They will find another boat across, however. Are you prepared for violence?"

"Certainly. Just as long as it is not visited upon me."

He nodded grimly. "You will have to do as I say. It is no longer a question of strategy. I believe it is one of survival—ours and the nation's.
Above all else you must keep that in mind. This is as important as any intelligence you ran in the war. If we do not reach Hamilton before the
news, I cannot guess the devastation that will befall this union."

We came off the ferry, riding hard under a sky hooded with gray
clouds foretelling not snow or rain but merely a kind of gloom. The road
was free of ice, and I thought we started well. I was mistaken, for we had
not gone more than five or six miles before we heard the sound of men
behind us. Three of them, bent over, spurring their horses to catch us.

"Whiskey men," I shouted, but it was not necessary. Lavien must
have recognized them, for he already had taken a primed pistol from his
pocket; now he turned and fired off a shot, all done seemingly without
thought or exertion. It could not be, I thought, that such a shot could
find its target, but one of the men threw up his hands—I know not if in
pain or from the impact—and fell from his horse.

I took out my primed pistol and fired too. I was never much of a shot
from a moving horse, and aiming behind rather than forward made matters even more difficult, but I was determined to fire true. I turned to
glance at the riders to see who would make the better target. There were
two men, one far taller than the other, and it was then that I recognized
him. The taller one was Duer's man, Isaac Whippo. I aimed at him rather
than the other, purely out of irritation, but the shot went wide. Distant
as he was, I saw him glower at me cadaverously.

Lavien returned his pistol to his pocket and drew a knife from his
belt. From his moving horse, he took the blade between his fingers and
tossed it with a hard thrust from his arm. Shooting out, it twirled like a
whirligig, spiraling through the air until it struck the shorter of our pursuers in the sternum. Even above the roar of thudding hooves, I heard his
groan, less a cry of pain than an exhalation of despair, the sound of a man
who knows he is to die.

I had fallen behind Lavien, so I spurred my horse forward, ignoring
the smoking of my spent pistol in my saddlebag, and dared another look

behind me. Isaac Whippo had slowed somewhat, perhaps dispirited and no longer liking his chances quite so well as he once did.

I turned to Lavien. "He may lose heart. We've all but gotten away."

It was not to be, however, for though he kept his distance, he did not leave off the pursuit. I could only presume that Lavien had no more guns or knives about him, for he did not attempt to lose this last man. Then I saw why this third man remained in pursuit even though we had bested his fellows. Up ahead, a quarter mile down the road, were two more whiskey men, their horses blocking the road. We were trapped.

"Stop," Lavien called, and he pulled up on his reins. The men in front and Whippo behind were at enough of a distance that he would have time for at least a brief conversation before they were upon us. We brought our horses to a pause by the side of the road. Following his lead, I quickly tied mine to a tree, and then dashed into the woods behind him.

"That was Duer's man," I said. "He was with the whiskey men."

"I know," he said, in a breathy low voice as he half ran, keeping his pace both swift and stealthy. "There is a clearing in the woods. I saw it through the trees maybe half a mile back. We'll make for that spot, keeping out of sight of the road."

"What if they kill our mounts?"

"There are always more horses," he said. "Their own, for instance. They won't need them once they're dead."

I did not know why we should want a clearing, of all things, and I did not want to abandon the animals, but here was a situation in which I knew Lavien to be my superior, and I would not argue.

I ran hard. Unused to continuous physical exertion, almost at once I felt a stitch in my side and a burning feeling that rose in my throat and extended to the tip of my tongue. The blood pounded in my ears, and my eyes darted back and forth for any sign of danger, but as near as I could determine we were not yet seen. More than once I almost fell over in exhaustion, but Lavien continued to run hard, and I would not be the one to drag us down. Somehow I found the strength to keep pace—nearly, for I lagged ten or fifteen yards behind—until we came out in the clearing that Lavien had seen from the road.

It was perhaps a fifty-foot circle of flat earth pocked with mounds of dirty snow. There were signs that men had slept here recently—footprints and the bones of a small animal, perhaps a rabbit or a chicken—and a stink that suggested they had not wandered far to use the necessary. Nearly at the center was a small stone circle in which they had made a fire, and there were still pieces of wood there, some but blackened coal, others reasonably fresh.

I stood still, panting and holding my side, which now flared and fired and set forth cannonades of pain.

"Good," said Lavien in a low voice, as he stooped to examine the stone circle. "This will do. There's enough wood left to burn well."

He handed me his pistol, took a tinderbox, and began to relight the fire. "You'll find powder and balls in my travel bag. Prime the weapons."

"Are you mad? They'll see our smoke."

"Captain, that is what I wish. We haven't time for evasion. We've got to get to Philadelphia, and that means we need to fight them. If we want to do it quickly and without fear of sharpshooters, we must engage them on our terms. We will draw them here."

I readied the firearms, though I did it slowly and clumsily. My hands shook from the exertion of the chase and the running, and I kept searching the woods for any sign that the whiskey men had found us before we wished them to. There was no point in doing so. These were border men who stalked bears naked and slept in trees for days, waiting to pounce upon deer. If they knew we were here and wished us dead, we would be dead already.

Lavien quickly lit the fire, poking at it until it burned vigorously. He then went over to the nearest tree and broke off several small twigs, which he put upon the blaze.

"They're moist, and will make the fire produce more smoke." He gazed about him and took one of the smaller pieces of wood from the fire, a rounded branch not more than a foot long, and narrow enough to easily hold in the hand, and lifted it like a torch. "This way," he said, gesturing away from the road.

"Why do you want that?" I asked.

"You will see why," he answered, in a grim tone that suggested confidence but no satisfaction. "We must not let this fire go out."

I followed him out of the clearing. We moved back several feet, that we might not be seen, or not seen easily, from the vicinity of the fire. He held his torch behind a tree and squatted, his other hand in his bag, his eyes wide and unblinking.

"Let us hope they are as rushed as we are," he said quietly. "These Westerners are good hunters, as stealthy and deadly in their own way as the Maroons of Surinam."

"I understand," I said.

"If we die, we do not get our message to Hamilton."

"And we'll be dead. That is undesirable in itself." I felt tension, urgency, and anxiety for what must come next. It was not precisely fear, though there was fear in it. I am not one of those men who go into battle with nothing but courage in his heart. I felt fear aplenty, but enough other things that it was merely one flavor of the stew.

"I've no doubt," he continued, "that they have good shots among them, and they could pick us off, if they choose, before we even sensed they were near."

"I said I understand, damn you."

He grinned at me. "Just making certain."

He muttered something under his breath. It sounded like a prayer, and it sounded like a foreign language, though I know not know if it was Hebrew or the heathen Maroon tongue.

Then he was silent and there was little else but silence, the silence of the woods in winter when men have come tramping through moments before. There was a rustle of dead branches and birdsong, sporadic but distant. I heard the click of speedy animal claws not far away—perhaps a hearty squirrel that had not slept for the winter or had awoken early.

In a few moments one of our pursuers walked into the clearing. He was an older man, missing an eye, of average height but thin build, with fair hair and pale skin, somewhat blemished with freckles and the scars of smallpox. His clothes looked several sizes too big for him, and he comported himself with the shambling attitude of the habitual drinker.

The one-eyed rebel looked at the fire and then turned back the way he had come and let out a whistle, the kind that sounds precisely like a man trying to sound like a bird. In a moment, Whippo and the third whiskey rebel walked briskly into the clearing. Soon the trio was circling the fire, speaking in low tones, attempting to make sense of it, read some logic into its presence, some indication of our location.

Whippo turned, not precisely toward us but close enough, facing a deep thicket of wood. Hands upon his narrow hips, he called, "I know you're in there, Saunders. Why not come out and talk things over? You're taking it all a bit hard. I suppose it's our own fault, making you think us so ruthless. We're not violent men, just clever ones. We need not be at odds."

Lavien looked at me and put a finger to his lips, as though I would need to be told.

"It's been but a game," Whippo called out. "You and I being enemies, Saunders—I never felt it. If you knew who we were, and the wrongs we've suffered from Hamilton and Duer, you would join with us. We know you're no aristocrat like those fellows. The violence that's been done today is our fault. I'll own it. You come out now, and we'll talk. We'll parley. We'll lay down our weapons." He squatted to the earth and set his gun upon the hard ground.

I watched him with such intensity that I did not at first see Lavien pull his hand out of the bag. Only when he held his object against his little torch did I see it and understand. It was a ball of cast iron, as shiny as silver, a bit larger than an orange, with a pair of decorative horns molded onto it, as though it were a bull or a devil. From between the horns rose a wick.

It took me a moment to recognize the object, for I had not seen one since the war. It would appear that Lavien had thought to bring with him a grenade.

He held the wick to his torch and let it burn. And then he held it in his hand. My eyes must have registered concern because he looked at the wick and then at the men, to tell me he dared not toss it too soon.

That wick seemed to me the slowest ever made. It felt as though we waited for long minutes, though it could only have been a few seconds. I lived in fear that the men would see us and come running, they would lose interest and wander off, or sense a trap and flee. I feared that Lavien would misjudge and wait too long. Indeed, the wick grew shorter and shorter, and it took every bit of self-control I possessed not to shout at him, to tell him to throw it, for love of God.

It burned with a fiery glow and a faint hiss, and when it seemed to me that Lavien had waited too long already, he tossed the metal ball so that it landed just before the fire, bounced slightly, and came to rest within the little blaze. I knew not if I should be more impressed with his aim or his cleverness. Had the ball landed before them, they should have seen it and fled. Instead, the three men looked at the fire, certain they had seen something move, yet unable to find any sign of aught new upon the scene. The one-eyed man squatted down and peered into the blaze, bringing his face in very close.

Then came the flash.

The grenade burst in terrible cry of fire and heat and screaming metal. It sent out a rain of fire and dirt and broken branches. Leaves and wet lumps of snow fell from the skies. Birds took flight. Unseen animal feet scurried. I turned away and threw myself to the ground, though Lavien did not move or turn away. He must have known, to the inch, the grenade's range. When I turned back, Lavien was already standing.

"Give me the pistols," he said.

I did so, and he walked toward the clearing. Two of the men were dead, beyond any doubt. One body was entirely without its head, another nearly torn in two, missing an arm not to be seen anywhere. The dirt had turned a mottled black, and little mounds of snow were spotted pink with blood.

Astonishingly, Isaac Whippo was still alive. The grenade must have blasted away from him, for he sat upright, holding one arm, dangling and clearly broken, in the other. His face was wet with blood, and one eye was injured and closed, perhaps ruined. I had mocked this man, sought to belittle and humiliate him, and now he rocked back and forth, slowly, deliberately, like an old man with his pipe.

"He might yet live," I said softly.

"No," said Lavien. "He won't." He raised his pistol and fired it into Whippo's head.

I turned away, though I saw the flash of the powder and the smoke of the barrel. When I turned back, Whippo's body lay upon the ground, folded and still. A staggering revulsion coursed through me, for what I had seen and for Lavien, this little fount of heartless violence.

Lavien stepped to me and took me by the shoulders. He made me face him, made me look into his dark eyes, small and hot. "Understand me," he said in a low voice. "I have now murdered a wounded man. That's how important this is. It isn't about money or pride or power. It is about the future of the most audacious experiment in human liberty ever attempted. I do not want this government to do what I have just done. I take it on myself."

I swallowed. "You Jews have a fine history of taking sins upon yourself."

He looked in the general direction of the road. "You're a funny man. Let's go."

Ethan Saunders

It was growing dark, but that would not matter, could not matter. We would ride through the night, at a slow crawl if need be, if that would get us to Philadelphia before the trading began. We rode swiftly, clinging to every last second of daylight, and with the violence behind us, the violence I would not permit myself to think of, it did indeed seem as though we could get there before dawn. The roads were good, and there was no sign of rain or snow. We would arrive in time and Hamilton could perform whatever magic was required to calm the City Tavern crowd. It was too late to prevent some damage in New York, but he could send agents there, as well as to the other trading cities, who would buy at Treasury's direction to stanch the bleeding.

I thought of what we would do, not what we had done. I had no wish to recollect the whiskey men torn apart by Lavien's grenade, or Isaac Whippo executed, or charming Joan Maycott, who had engineered death and plotted to ruin a nation. I tried not to think of these things, and for the most part I succeeded. I thought mostly of the cold and discomfort and the growing dark. After sunset, as our pace slowed, we took turns holding a torch to light our way.

We rode on in silence, the cold bludgeoning us, numbing us. Our arms ached from holding the reins, from holding the torch. Our legs and backs were stiff and wretched. The skin on the insides of my thighs burned and itched. Onward we rode. I did not take out my watch. I would not. I would ride in the dark as fast as I could, and that would be enough. Knowing that I made good time or ill would not matter to me.

I don't know that I fell asleep. Not precisely. My mind, however, went elsewhere as we made our way in that slow, deliberate, careful pace. It was black of night, no end conceivable, as though we were to ride in the cold, barren darkness forever. And then, toward the east, I saw the first rouging of the sky.

We had not spoken in hours. Now Lavien turned back to look at me. "We shall be at Hamilton's office before seven o'clock. We've done it, Saunders. We've done all that men could do, and that will have to be enough."

We rode on, picking up the pace with the rising of the sun. In ten minutes, we were trotting. Five minutes after that, we were in a full gallop. The road showed signs of a nearby town, spotted now with farmers' shacks and outbuildings and a tavern where I wished, dearly wished, we might stop for tea and warm punch and the freshly baked bread that perfumed the air. It was an abstract wish, for what I truly wanted was to complete my task, to take my news to Hamilton and then rest. To eat my fill of food and drink and then lie down and let sleep overtake me and not wake for a day or more. Next I would find Cynthia. And then, with no urgency upon me, with the schemers on the run, wallowing in the filth of their own ruined plots, I would track them down one by one and make certain they knew justice.

We rode hard, leaning forward in our saddles, no longer troubled by pain or fatigue or cold. The chill wind and the beating of the hooves drummed in my ears, but I felt gleeful and giddy. I turned to Lavien. I said, "You know, in the midst of all this madness—"

That was as much as I said, because all went wild and the sky twisted from the top to the side, and the ground corkscrewed around to meet my face in a slap of cold earth that came hard and fast, making my teeth rattle. The blood trickled from my mouth, my nose. I felt the most dreadful of pains, those that come from a blow to the head.

I never heard the shot that killed my horse, but I heard the next one. It must have been only an instant after the one that brought me down, but I was already upon the ground, stunned and feeling pain reach out with its first tentative, exploring tendrils. There was a second crack and Lavien's beast reared up, threw him off, and collapsed upon him.

I thought how foolish they had been to shoot at me first, but it did not seem to matter. Not yet. And then I remembered that they had a marksman among their number, one of Daniel Morgan's men, and they'd shot our horses, not us. It could not have been an accident. We'd killed five of their men the day before, and they still took pains to keep us alive. But then again, it occurred to me they could not know. No one could have traveled faster than we had. If news was coming, it was not yet there.

Lavien was upon the ground some fifteen feet ahead of me, his horse atop his lower body. Blood—I presumed the animal's—pooled around him. He did not move. Lavien lay in the muck of the King's Highway, perhaps dead, perhaps dying. I was determined I would go to him, and was attempting to clear my head when I heard the voice.

"Can you stand?" asked the voice.

I knew not if he'd been standing there, ten feet behind me, all along, or if he'd approached while I lay in my daze. I could not see him easily in the glare of the sun, but I could determine that he was a large man, riding like an ancient warrior upon his beast. It was the Irishman.

"I asked if you can stand."

"Lavien's hurt," I said. I pushed myself to my feet and found that yes, I could stand. I was dizzy and my head ached, and I wished to Christ I had someone or something to lean against, but I would not tell him that. I wiped at my bloody nose with my sleeve. It bled but was not broken.

"He's hurt," I said again.

"We'll see to him," the Irishman answered. Dalton.

There must have been other men, men who used the glare of the sun and my own disorientation against me, for a hood came down over my head, and I felt rough hands grab me and begin to tie my wrists together behind my back. Hands moved me so a tree was to my back, and I was made to sit. The blood still ran from my nose, and it trickled over my lips.

From a distance I heard voices. They said, "His leg is broke," and "We'll need a litter," and "To the house." I heard Dalton's Irish accent, and I heard another man who sounded like a Scot. I thought, It's still early. If we get to Philadelphia by ten or eleven o'clock, we might yet salvage all, but I did not know how that could happen. I was dazed and bound and hooded. Lavien, it seemed, had broken his leg, and what was I without Lavien? I was a mind without a body, an arm without a fist.

Time passed, I knew not how quickly or slowly, but I felt its agonizing, excruciating pace. I feared not for myself. These people wanted us alive—or at least had no will to kill us. What was life to me, though? We had done what we had done because Lavien believed, believed to his soul, that the survival of the country depended upon our arriving in Philadelphia in time for Hamilton to quiet the markets. He'd set aside his humanity, murdered a helpless man, because he believed if he did not get to Philadelphia in time, Duer's ruin would be the spark to ignite the destruction of a new fragile nation. I could not simply allow myself to be held, to live passively while the forces of destruction won out.

At last I felt hands lifting me to my feet. They were soft hands, and I smelled the flowery scent of female flesh. "Come, Captain Saunders," said Mrs. Maycott. "Let's come this way."

"Lavien," I croaked. I was thirsty but would not ask for drink.

"He's hurt," she said. "His horse fell on his leg. It's broken, but Dalton says it's a clean break. He knows a bit of surgery from the war, and from the West too. He's already set the bone, which he says will heal well enough in time. They've borne him back to the house."

"What house?" I walked slowly, as she guided me, daring to trust her leadership.

"It's not half a mile east, by the river. It's lovely, actually."

"What do you want with us?"

"As our men in New York seem not to have detained you, we must do it ourselves. We only want to keep you as our guests," she said. "Until, perhaps, this evening, when all will be too late for Hamilton. Then you may go."

I said nothing, which she seemed not to like. She said, "There were two groups sent to stop you. Five men in all. How did you get past Mr. Whippo and the rest?"

I shook my head. "Never saw them. Must have outrun them without knowing it."

I heard skepticism in her voice but did not pursue it. "You might have outrun Whippo's men, but what of Mortimer? He and his partner should have intercepted you in New Jersey."

I shook my head. "Never saw them."

She sighed. "I suppose all will out. For now, let us get you to the house."

I did not answer. There was nothing I could say.

We walked and walked and then the dirt, made treacherous by rocks and malevolent tree roots, gave way to packed gravel. Our feet crunched along this for a few minutes, and then Joan led me up a set of steps, and I heard the sound of a door opening. Now I went up one flight of stairs and then another. I sniffed the air, trying to learn something of my surroundings, but I could smell nothing but the wetness of the sack and my own blood.

I heard another door open, and then I was pressed down in a chair. The door closed, and a lock turned. My hood came off.

I was in a small room, empty of furniture except for the chair upon which I sat. Marks on the floor and walls suggested that the room had previously contained more furnishings and wall hangings, but these were now gone. I could not help but wonder if they'd been removed for my sake, for fear I should turn a chair or a portrait into a deadly weapon.

Before me stood Joan Maycott, looking pretty in a gown of pale pink with a white bodice. She smiled, and perhaps it was the sunlight that streamed through the windows, but I saw the lines about her eyes. For the first time she looked like a woman past her youth.

"Oh, look at you." She gently wiped at my face with her handkerchief. The fabric felt hard and rough and hot.

"So, this is it," I said. "This is what you were after all along. You wanted to ruin Duer, and you made me help you."

"Duer is evil," she said, as she wiped blood from my upper lip. She had a gentle touch. "He deserves ruin."

"And the bank?"

"The bank in an instrument of oppression," she said. "Its shares will collapse in the coming panic, and they shall never recover. Hamilton gave birth to his whiskey tax to fund the bank without giving a single thought to the damage it would do—that it does yet."

"And what of the country itself?" I asked. "Have you thought of that?"

"I've thought of little else," she said. "I'm a patriot, Captain Saunders, just like you. This country began in a flash of brilliance, but look what has happened. The suffering of human chattel ignored by our government, a small cadre of rich men dictating our national policies. In the West, men die—they die, sir—as a consequence of this greed. This is not why my husband fought in the Revolution. I suspect it's not what you fought for either. Now I fight to change it."

"And what if something worse comes from the chaos?"

"Then the world will have to wait for just governance," she said. "Better anarchy than an unjust nation that masquerades as a beacon of righteousness. That would be worse than outright tyranny."

"Well," I said. "That is certainly interesting, and you clearly have the better of me. I wonder if you would consider untying me, and if I could impose upon you for some food and drink. If I am to be your prisoner, I should like at least to be a comfortable one."

"I would ask for your word that you make no mischief, but I somehow don't think you would consider yourself bound by it. What do you think?"

I thought at first that this question was addressed to me, but then I realized she spoke past me, to someone I had not yet noticed.

"Captain Saunders is a man of honor, but it is his own unique sort. He would not consider himself bound by his word if, by breaking it, he believed he might do a greater good." The man came and stood near Joan Maycott, where I could see him. It was Leonidas.

I could not be surprised to see him there, not after he had attempted to trick me with a case of sherry into a drunken expedition to the western frontier. Even so, it left me uneasy.

He turned to Mrs. Maycott. "I beg you give us a few minutes."

She nodded and took herself from the room. Once she was gone, Leonidas removed a knife and cut free the ropes binding my hands. The freedom of movement felt wonderful, and I rubbed at my wrists.

"Now it's your turn to free me," I said.

"You had me wait longer than I would have wished. It is time for me to return the favor." He suppressed a smile and, mad though it was, I could not help but feel that it was good to see him, even under these circumstances, for now I understood that though he had betrayed me he had not abandoned our friendship.

"My God, Leonidas, why would you join with them?"

"Money," he said. "I did it for money and the promise of freedom."

"But you were free!" I shouted.

"Yes, but I did not know it. Ethan, do you not hear your own words? What good is my freedom if I and the world know nothing of it? I have a wife, I will have a family, and we must have liberty. Mrs. Maycott offered me enough money to live free, and she promised no harm would come to you."

I said nothing, for I could neither forgive nor condemn.

"You need not worry," he said. "I've visited with Mr. Lavien, and he is well. His leg broke clean and should heal, and without fever. Neither of you will be harmed. What Mrs. Maycott says is true."

"There's still time," I said. "You could let me go."

He shook his head. "No, Ethan. I won't. Beyond the money, I believe in the cause. It is better to burn down the edifice than let it rest on a rotten foundation."

I sighed. "Can I get something to drink at least?"

"Don't expect a glass bottle." He left the room, and came back in a few minutes with a wineskin and a small pewter cup. "I would not trust Lavien with even this little, but I don't believe you can do much damage with these."

"I never thought to drink wine from pewter," I said.

"It's whiskey," he said. "Drink as much as you like. The drunker you are, the more comfortable we shall be."

I resented Leonidas's implication, but I nevertheless poured a drink. Before even a few minutes had passed, however, I heard a rattle at the door to my room, which arrested me from my efforts to excuse my inaction. The door swung open. I expected to see Leonidas or Mrs. Maycott or perhaps even Dalton. It was Lavien.

He stood upon one leg, the other was out before him, held straight by a splint and wrapped in a thick sheath of bandages. He used a long rifle as a crutch. His face was drawn and pale beneath the darkness of his beard, but his eyes were bright with pain and, I thought, with the delight of his disregard for it.

"Are you prepared to leave?" he asked me. He pulled back his lips in something like a sneer—or, perhaps, a wince.

It took me a moment to find words. "I must say, I'm touched that you troubled yourself to rescue me."

He managed a sort of shrug. "I don't think I can get down the stairs by myself." His voice was easy, as though he discussed something of import, but I felt his gaze on me, urgent and desperate, and something else, something greater and hotter and more intense. This, I understood, was Lavien's place and Lavien's time. He was a cannonball, fired toward Philadelphia, and no wall, no flesh, no fire would stop him.

I pushed myself to my feet and stepped out into the hall, and the mirth and wonder drained away. There, upon the floor, lying at the sick angles of the lifeless, was a man, pale and bloodied, his eyes wide as the face of oblivion. I'd not seen him before, but he was a rugged-looking fellow, probably handsome while he'd been alive. Now his throat had been opened, and for the first time I noticed the knife tucked into Lavien's belt.

"Christ. Who's that?" I asked, keeping my voice low.

Lavien did not spare a glance, but then why should he? I could only be speaking of one man. "A marksman. They called him Jericho. He's probably the one who shot our horses. Now he's dead. Let's go."

"How are we going to get out of here? How are we going to get past the whiskey men?"

His eyes grew harder, darker. His lips turned ruddy with anticipation. "We will kill anyone who opposes us."

"Hold," I hissed, suddenly feeling as though I held conversation not with a man but with a raging storm. "I am not going to kill Joan Maycott. And Leonidas is with them."

He nodded. "I've seen him. I am fond of Leonidas, but I'll kill him if he opposes me."

"My God, Lavien, is it worth it? All this killing? To save Hamilton's bank?"

"How many times must I tell you it is not about the bank?" he breathed. "It's about averting chaos, riot, and bloodshed and another war of brother against brother. This country is a house of cards, and it will not take much to bring it down. Now let's go."

He moved down the hall, hopping on one foot and using the butt of the rifle to balance himself, and yet he moved more quietly than I did. We came to the first set of stairs. I scouted down and saw no one on the second-floor landing and reported back to Lavien.

"I think they're all downstairs," I said. "I heard some faint voices."

He nodded.

"Whose house is this, anyhow? Where are we? Who is helping them?"

"I heard them say we are just outside Bristol," he said.

A chill spread through me. Not here, I thought. Why must it be here? "The Bristol house. Pearson put it about that it was sold, but it wasn't; they were here all the time. Cynthia and the children are likely here. For God's sake, be careful with your fire."

Lavien nodded, and I knew at once that he already knew, or suspected, that this was Pearson's house. He'd simply neglected to tell me.

We took the steps slowly, one at a time. Lavien steadied himself, silently pressed his rifle butt to the stair below us, and swung down. He repeated this over and over, never making a noise, not even letting the stairs creak. At last we made it to the second-floor landing. Before us stood the stairs to the first floor; to the left, a wall on which hung a large portrait of a puritanical sort of man; and to the right, a corridor with two doors on either side and one at the end. As we stood there, the door at the end opened, and we faced a man in his fifties, graying and bearded, strangely elegant. I recognized him at once. He was the Scot I'd met at the City Tavern.

He saw us and his eyes went wide with surprise and terror. From behind me, Lavien pushed forward, taking a massive leap off his good leg, landing upon it again, using the rifle to balance himself but somehow keeping it from banging against the floor. In two such impossible strides, he was upon the old fellow, gripping his throat, pressing him against the wall, and taking out his knife.

I hurried over. "Stay your bloody hand," I cried in as loud a whisper as I dared.

I could not see his face, so I did not know how he responded, but he did stop. "You said not to kill the woman or Leonidas. You said nothing of this man."

"We don't have to slaughter them. We only have to get away from them. They're not fiends, Lavien, they're patriots. They may be misguided patriots, but they do what they do for love of country, and I won't hurt them if I can help it."

"I haven't the time," he said in an exasperated breath. "We haven't the time for stealth or cleverness. We've only time for violence." So he said, but he still did not kill the poor man. He continued to squeeze his throat, and his face began to purple behind the gray of the short beard, but Lavien did not strike with the knife.

My heart beat so hard I felt the reverberation in my clavicle. Fists clenched in rage, I struggled to think of something to spare this man, this schemer who had been set against me for weeks. My mind was soft and spongy and would not answer when I called. There had to be something, I told myself, and without knowing what I would say, I began to talk. It was always the best way.

"Do you remember, Lavien, when we had our first talk that night at your house? Do you remember how you told me Hamilton described me to you?"

He nodded. "He said you could talk the devil himself into selling you his soul."

"Then let me do it."

"He didn't say you could do it with all speed," Lavien hissed.

"Let me try, damn it." I felt the faintest hint of optimism, but terror too, for if he gave me this chance, I did not know how to use it.

He lowered the knife and eased his grip on the Scot.

"Did you hear all that, or were you too busy being killed?" I asked the man.

He nodded vigorously, which for the sake of convenience I chose to understand meant he had heard.

"Good, then. Now, I've just saved your life, fellow. That's usually worth something. Is it worth something to you?"

"It is," he managed in a Scottish brogue, "but I'll not betray my friends."

"Oh, there's no betrayal in the works. I promise you that. We only want a way out of here. That's all we want."

"It's a betrayal, for you'll run to Hamilton and tell him all."

I shook my head, desperate for something. "It's too late for that. It's already too late, but this man, this man with a beard just like your own, only darker with youth, his wife is due to deliver unto him his first child, and we must hurry. You would not want, I think, to be the cause of him not being at her side when she gives birth. You are not so base as that, are you?"

"You'll have to do better than that," said the Scot, "if you want to talk the devil into giving up his soul." I could not blame him. It had been a weak effort, but given he knew I attempted to trick him, none but a weak effort would do.

"Right, then," I said to Lavien. "Best to kill him."

"Hold," he gasped, throwing forth his arms, much as I had predicted. "I'll help you. The front door is locked, but take my key." He dug into his pocket and came forth with a heavy brass key, which he handed to me. "They are all in the back sitting room, by the kitchens. They'll not hear you."

"Good Scot," I said, and shoved him into the room. There was a key to that room on the inside lock in the door. I removed it and locked him in. I suppose he could have still done harm, banging upon the floor or some such thing, but I believed we'd scared him sufficiently.

I turned to Lavien. "Far better than murder, don't you think?"

"It took too long," he muttered, and then gestured forward with his head. I was to scout the stairway. I crept down and faced the front door. There was a sitting room forward and to my right, and behind that a private room of some sort, and behind that the kitchens. I heard voices emerging from the back of the house.

I returned to Lavien with this intelligence. He nodded. "Once we make it out of the house, we head around the left to the stables. I've seen no sign of servants—perhaps Pearson can no longer afford any—so we should be able to get horses. Then we need only ride hard to Philadelphia."

"How are you going to make it to Philadelphia on a broken leg?"

"I can only do my best. If the pain should make me lose consciousness, however, you will have to finish the task yourself."

I studied him. His face was utterly placid, but for an instant I recognized it was a mask he wore to disguise the agony he felt. "You are a frightening man," I said.

The trek to the bottom of the stairs was terrifying, for we were most vulnerable, but we made it with good speed and little noise. Lavien rested against the banister while I went to the door. The adjacent sitting room's windows faced west, and there were no windows at all in this room, so the foyer, with its dark wallpaper and uncovered floors, was gloomy. Even so, once I took out the key the Scot had given me, I did not even have to try it to realize it was far too big for the lock. Its thick brass glinted like a winking eye in the dark room. He'd tricked us.

"It looks like the devil wins this one," said Lavien.

"Better to kill everyone in case they turn out to be not nice. It's not as fast as a key, but I can try to pick the lock."

I stooped down, preparing to remove my boot and retrieve my picking tool when I saw a presence from the corner of my eye.

"Oh, why trouble yourself," said a voice, vaguely familiar, and even before I could identify it, a thrill of terror ran through me. Somewhere, at the base of my consciousness, I knew that things had taken another turn, become more dangerous and more unpredictable. For a fleeting instant I kept myself from looking, as though I could prevent this encounter simply by not seeing it, but the instant passed and my head turned. There upon the top of the stairs was Jacob Pearson. He stood with his wife directly before him, however. Lavien, were he so inclined, could not toss his knife to eliminate him. He had one arm around her waist, held in that tight grip I had experienced myself, the other against her back, and her eyes were wide and moist and, even from a great distance I could see they were red from crying. He did not have to tell me for me to know there was a gun pressed to her.

Cynthia met my gaze, and I could see in her all the hope, all the expectation she placed in me. I would get her out of this. I would protect her. I had no idea how, but I would make it happen.

"No doubt you thought yourself too clever, but I've bested you before and will do so now," he said.

"You would bring your wife and children into the middle of this violence?" I said. "You are more of a wretch than I thought."

"The children are safe," he said. "They're with my sister. My wife—well, she deserves no special consideration. You'll be pleased to know she's tried to run away several times. No doubt to go to you, so the two of you can live in adulterous poverty and turn my children into an object of scandal. I think it's safe to say that Cynthia does not know what is best for her."

She smiled a sad smile at me. I knew what it meant. She was trying to be brave, to be ready should some chance present itself. I intended that it would.

"After you escaped from the prison under the pier," said Pearson, "I was prepared to kill you when I had the opportunity, but now I won't have to. I believe the big Irishman will take care of it for me when he sees what you've done to his man. I wish you'd killed the other, but one will have to do. That bitch of a widow made us all swear this way and that not to harm you unless our lives were in the balance, but I don't believe Dalton will honor her word now. Ho! Dalton! Irishman, come here quick!"

I heard footsteps running toward us, and I glared at Lavien. If he were to take his chances with Pearson, it would be now, but I met his eye. "Stay your hand," I said. "If you hurt her, I'll kill you myself."

He did not react, but I had not expected him to.

Now Leonidas came into the foyer, squinting as his eyes adjusted from the well-lit rooms of the back of the house to the gloom of the front. "What is this?" he demanded.

"I called for the Irishman, not the nigger, though there is little enough difference," said Pearson. "Get the Irishman. They've killed Richmond. I believe Dalton will want his revenge."

Leonidas looked as though he'd just learned of the death of a parent. His eyes grew wide with horror. "Oh, Ethan, why have you done it? Dalton's a good man, but he won't let this go."

I would not defend myself, not even to say that this time it was not Ethan Saunders who took a bad situation and made it worse. Things would sort themselves out or I would die, but I would not allow my final words to be a speech of equivocation.

Mrs. Maycott walked into the foyer, followed closely behind by Dalton. The space was now crowded. Five of us stood where two or three might comfortably remain. Pearson led Cynthia halfway down the stairs but then stopped, remaining distant.

Dalton looked us over and shook his head, not bothering to hide his amusement. "They're determined, I'll say that for them. Now, back to their rooms. Where's Skye and Jericho? We'll need their help."

"Skye's been locked in a bedroom." Pearson spat. "They've killed Richmond. Murdered him in cold blood."

Dalton's face turned pale and his lips, instantly bloodless, quivered as though he were a little child. Then, in an instant, his face turned cold and hard and frightening in its cruelty. He underwent a second metamorphosis, to something ugly and fierce, something that wanted vengeance. He stepped forward, then stopped. He swallowed. "Is it true?" he asked quietly. Then, when he received no response, he screamed the same words. *"Is it true?"* It was loud, ringing, like the roar of a deranged lion, and from his coat he pulled two pistols, primed. He held them aloft, not quite sure what to do next, and then he turned on us.

Joan said, "No, Dalton," and stepped before him, but he pressed a hand hard to her breasts and shoved, and she staggered down the hall, losing her balance, falling upon her knees.

Leonidas took out his own pistol and pointed it at Dalton. "Fire your weapon, and you're a dead man," he said.

"For God's sake, Leonidas, if you're going to kill him, do it before he shoots me, not after. But I beg that no one shoot anyone. Look you, if you have eyes. That man there on the staircase, holding a gun to the back of his wife. He is the one who tells you we hurt your friend. We did not. It's true we locked away your man Skye, but we did not hurt him, and he will tell you so himself." I tossed Joan the key to Skye's room. "Go unlock him and ask. Why should we kill one man and let another live? We would not. If this man, this known liar and thief, says your friend is dead, I doubt not it is because he did the killing himself."

I did not know if they believed it, but it would buy us time, which was the best we could hope for at the moment.

Put away the knife, I mouthed to Lavien. To my astonishment, he obeyed, though I had no doubt he could have it out again in a matter of seconds, should he so desire. For now, however, he would give me my chance to take the devil's soul after all.

I reached down and helped Lavien to his feet—to his foot. Whatever pain he had suffered, he appeared no more disabled than he had been before. I handed him his weapon, and I believe he made a good show of himself by using it as a crutch and doing nothing more.

"I don't deny we wish to escape," I said to Joan, "but that is how the game is played. You make your move, and we make ours. That is all. But that man," I said, pointing to Pearson, "would hold a woman hostage—his own wife—which is as base a thing as a man can do. He killed your friend for no other reason than to lay the blame upon us."

Lavien turned to Dalton and pulled his knife from his belt. It meant that he would be the target of the first fire, for a man cannot aim at two enemies at once. I had not a moment to spare, so I thrust out my leg into Lavien's one good one, and he slipped out from under himself, landing upon his broken limb. I cannot imagine the pain, but he made not a noise, though his face twisted in agony, or perhaps shock. Or perhaps relief, for as he landed, Dalton's pistol fired, unleashing its thunder crack and black smoke and sharp scent into the little space. The ball passed through the air where Lavien would have stood, blasting instead into the front door. There was a second blast—just an instant after the first—and wood splintered and sunlight shot into the gloomy foyer as the door swung open on its hinges. That, at least, was a bit of good luck, if we lived to take advantage of it.

I thought back to that night in Helltown, that night that now seemed so long ago, when I had been prepared to let Dorland kill me. I had stood in the cold and the filth of the Helltown alley and considered that I might yet talk my way into living, but I held my tongue.

I would not stay quiet this time. The air smelled of powder and my eyes stung with smoke. Just behind me, a door lay open, and sunlight seeped into our little gathering storm of violence. This would likely end in more deaths. There were far too many people in the room for whom

I cared—maybe the only people on earth for whom I cared—and I would not let it go that way. I had been built from my foundation with a capacity to deceive, and here, if ever there was one, was a time for deception.

"Hold!" I cried. "Hold! Let there be no more violence."

Dalton pointed his other pistol to Lavien, who lay prostrate upon the ground, and I stood directly in his path.

All this time Cynthia had stood a mute statue; I had hardly dared to look upon her. A weapon had already been fired, and there was like to be more. I would not have my own resolve softened by her fear. But now Cynthia spoke up, and her voice, though wavering, had a kind of clarity that surprised me. "It's true. My God, it is true. I knew he was cruel, but I never thought he could kill a man in cold blood. He walked up to him, and your man—he suspected nothing."

Was ever anyone so in love as I at that moment? Did ever man, since the fall of Eve, so rejoice in the lies of woman?

"Shut up," Pearson hissed at her. "It's not true," he said to the others, but if Cynthia had just spoken the most convincing of lies, her husband had the misfortune of sounding entirely false while speaking truth.

Leonidas trained his gun upon Pearson. "Let the lady go."

"But they lie," he said.

"You make a better case," Leonidas said, "if you are not holding a gun to a woman."

"She is my wife. I may use her as I wish."

"Let the lady go," Joan said, and her voice was hard and angry. Somehow Cynthia, held upon the stairs by her husband, a gun to her back, had become the most important thing to everyone in the room—not the dead man upstairs, not the two prisoners who had gotten free, not the open door to freedom that lay behind us.

He released his grip and Cynthia ran down the stairs and toward me. Our eyes met and she, for but a fleeting instant, nodded at me, and I knew that this was the moment when she must prove herself. She must be the woman she had always wished to be, or she would fail me. I dared to hold her eyes for a long important moment, and I hoped it would be enough for her to understand.

"You stupid bitch," I snapped. "This is all your fault."

She took a step back, the hurt on her face so real—or so seemingly real—it nearly broke my heart. "Ethan, I am sorry."

"I told you no one gets hurt. I told you that."

She shook her head. "I could not stop him," she said. Tears began to well up in her eyes. "I tried to stop him, Ethan, but I could not. I tried. You should have been there for me, but you weren't, and I could not do it alone."

"Oh, shut up," I said. "I never should have trusted you."

Dalton had heard enough. He turned now on Pearson. While, in general, I do not care to see unarmed men viciously assaulted, here was a case in which I could make an exception. Dalton darted up the stairs, grabbed Pearson under his armpits, and lifted him high in the air as if he weighed no more than a baby. Dalton then locked his elbows and hurled Pearson—whose mouth was open in terror too primal for noise—through the air and hard against the wall separating the foyer from the sitting room. He struck with a sharp agonizing crack, spun slightly, and then landed with his feet against a narrow chair, his head toward us, though it was cocked at the most unnatural of angles.

Cynthia let out a moan and covered her mouth. Leonidas whispered something under his breath. Dalton took a moment to admire his work and then ran up two flights of stairs. Above, I heard him wail.

I turned to Joan. "I am sorry it ended thus. Yours are good people, with your own sense of honor, and I do not doubt you've been wronged. I wish we were never opposed."

She shook her head. "So much bloodshed."

I stepped to her. "It never ought to have been like this. Joan, you are better than this. You are so much better. Imagine what you might have done had you only tried your hand at creating rather than destroying." I touched her face. "Imagine what we could do together. Joan, you and I must be together."

Cynthia rushed forward. "Ethan, are you mad? You promised it would be me. You swore you loved me."

"You silly woman," I said with a laugh. "How could I love someone like you?"

Leonidas let out a throaty laugh and began to clap his hands. "I must say, I am remarkably impressed. You cannot have practiced this, and yet it is so easy and natural."

Joan turned to him. "What do you mean?"

Leonidas laughed again. "I have seen it a hundred times, though never when the stakes were so high. It is Ethan Saunders being Ethan Saunders, when lies and false notions and absurd claims roll off his tongue; we all watched him. But now I look up and see his point. Even I, who ought not to have been fooled, was caught up. Do you not notice someone is missing?"

And indeed he was. I could not say when Lavien had slipped away. I had made a point not to look at him myself, hoping that if he was invisible to me he might be invisible to all. Joan Maycott now rushed to the door and looked out into the morning light. I moved behind her, prepared to place my hand over her mouth should she try to call to Dalton, but she made no effort. She stood there in confused silence. Far away, upon the distant King's Highway, appeared a single awkward figure upon a gray horse, riding hard and fast like Paul Revere, to save a country that was not even his own native land. I did not believe that there would ever be ballads sung of this ride, but oh, how worthy, how glorious, it was. And it had been made possible by my actions, which I could not but like.

Cynthia once more collapsed into my arms. She trembled, and I could not be surprised. She had witnessed more violence in a few minutes than most women see in a lifetime. Her husband, however foul a man, had been killed before her eyes, killed upon false pretenses and owing to her own machinations. It would not be easy for her in the days to come, but I meant to help her all I could.

For her part, Joan Maycott looked hardly less stunned. "I underestimated you, Captain Saunders. You too, Cynthia. I thought you were but a victim, but you are clever enough to deserve the captain." She took out a watch and studied it. "Your friend may yet save the bank."

"You appear less distraught than I would have thought," I said.

"Even if Hamilton can save the bank, Duer's ruin is accomplished and cannot be undone, and his fall will be a terrible blow. There will be panic and chaos, and the Hamiltonian plan may not be utterly demolished, but it will be discredited. I had four goals, Captain Saunders: to destroy the bank, destroy Hamilton, destroy Duer, and enrich myself. Even if the bank survives, Hamilton's career will end, and with the collapse of the market for overvalued six percent securities, I will profit handsomely on my own four percents, whose value will rise. By the way, Mrs. Pearson, you husband was a principal owner. I advise you to sell them the moment they rise above par. They won't stay there long."

"She is good in defeat," I said to Leonidas.

"And what are you like in victory?" she asked. "Do you think to apprehend me and my men?"

"No," I answered. "Lavien may have felt otherwise, but he is gone, and I don't believe Leonidas would permit it. For my own part, I do not want to see you plotting more against the nation, but I would not see you in prison."

She nodded. "You and Cynthia may take horses from the stables, but I beg you get gone."

"It *is* Mrs. Pearson's house," I said.

"Perhaps this is not the time to stand upon ceremony," said Leonidas.

Joan Maycott's man was dead upstairs, and there were five more dead on the King's Highway. She would learn of it soon enough, and I would not be there. "Right. We shall get gone and allow you to make your escape."

Cynthia, ashen and trembling, clung to me as we made our way from the house. We did not look back to wonder what Leonidas or Joan or Dalton would do next. We went to the stables, found beasts to our liking, and rode hard to overtake the rather sluggish Lavien, who struggled mightily with his leg. I left Cynthia to ride with him, and I went on ahead to Philadelphia to deliver the news to Hamilton, that he might act swiftly and with great skill to save the nation. Thanks to me.

Joan Maycott

July 12, 1804

It took twelve more years to gain the full revenge I wished, though, if truth be known, it was not so sweet as I imagined. My schemes in 1792 came to far less than I had hoped and cost me far more than I would have believed. So many of our whiskey boys dead—all because we underestimated Kyler Lavien and Ethan Saunders. I bore those men no ill will, however, and never sought to strike back at them. They did what they believed to be their duty, and they did it without malice. In particular, I could never have sought to harm Captain Saunders. I had the feeling his path and mine would cross again, and though we were never what one might call friends, when it happened we bore each other respect.

Mr. Dalton and I parted ways shortly after I collected on my investments in Duer's failure. He went west again, this time to the territory of Kentucky, where he established a large still to make whiskey in the new style. He intended to use his money to pay his taxes until such a time as the whiskey excise was revoked. Men are strange. Having done so much scheming and violence, in the end he was content to retire to private life and let political affairs sort themselves out in their own time.

Mr. Skye, however, remained faithful to me, and with his help I was able, in the end, to complete my revenge.

The markets did not collapse because of Duer's failure, for which I blame Lavien's frenetic ride to Philadelphia. The bank did not fail. Hamilton sent men to the City Tavern and fast riders to Boston, New York, Baltimore, and Charleston, and with the power of the Treasury Department they bought depressed issues and soothed frightened speculators. I caused a panic, not a failure. I staggered a nation—I, a border widow whom the great and powerful had used as their plaything—but I did no more than stagger it. The nation did not collapse or fly apart or buckle under the weight of its own corruption. It merely stumbled and regained its footing. I did not even bring down Hamilton. His reputation was tarnished by the panic and by Duer's ruin and provided fodder for his enemies, but he was more determined than I would have imagined, and I saw it would take more than a panic in the markets to destroy him.

If anything, he was emboldened. He continued to pursue his whiskey tax, and the men of the West grew ever more angry and restless. On the one side were government men who would demand that distillers pay money they could never have had. On the other, the angry populace led by David Bradford and shored up by angry men with frontier spirit and an American belief in their own rights. Between these two forces the wise, amiable Hugh Henry Brackenridge stood for the ordinary man, tried to negotiate peace, and was nearly hanged for his efforts. Hamilton led an army of thirteen thousand men—the size of the entire Continental force in the Revolution—into the West against a rebellion that he could not, despite his best efforts, locate. There were no insurrectionists to fight, so some twenty men were rounded up and two sentenced to die, though they were both, in the end, pardoned.

Secretary Hamilton had been determined to stretch the limits of federal power, and Colonel Hamilton did just that. In the war, it is said, he longed to command an army, and in peace he created a conflict so he could have his wish. I cannot say if he took any satisfaction that the enemy he pursued was entirely of his own manufacture, and mostly in his own imagination.

I could not remain in Philadelphia or anywhere else I was known, but I was not done with revenge. I would not act so rashly as I had once, but I would act. Two years later, I delivered a series of anonymous letters, informing Hamilton's republican enemies of his affair with Maria Reynolds, and if I embellished his crimes, suggesting he used federal money to pay off the lady's husband, I will not apologize. Hamilton was not above dirty tricks, and I saw no reason to be above them either. The affair ruined Hamilton for public office and made it impossible that he could ever stand for President. It would be enough for the time being.

After more than ten years had passed, I dared to impose upon my friendship with an old associate of Hamilton's, Aaron Burr, previously the senator from New York and now vice president of the United States. He and Hamilton had once been friends, but they had ended up on opposite sides of the Federalist divide. Burr was well known for showing preference for the ladies. He was a handsome man, though not tall, and already his hair was beginning to recede, but he never failed to charm, and I always enjoyed his company.

It had seemed for so long, particularly in the wake of the Maria Reynolds affair, that Hamilton would destroy himself. Yet, as the years went by, Hamilton moved from one disaster to another and always survived, always remained in the public eye, always voiced his long-winded opinions publicly and vociferously. I began to whisper in the vice president's ear of the many wrongs Hamilton had done him, the terrible things Hamilton said of him. A man of Mr. Burr's stamp could not long endure insults.

Burr arrived at my front door the afternoon of July 11, 1804. His hair was wild, his clothes stained with mud, his hands shook. "I ought never to have listened to you," he said, standing on my stoop. "I've killed him."

I could not suppress a smile. "Come inside."

He stepped in but turned to face the door. "I cannot stay. I must flee. I'll be wanted for murder."

"Nonsense. You are the vice president."

"This is a nation of laws, Mrs. Maycott. Being the vice president will count for nothing. Why did I ever listen to you and allow this petty squabble to escalate? *He insults your honor,* you said. *He mocks you in print,* you said. *He will not duel,* you said. Well, he did duel, and I've shot him."

"Is he dead?" I asked.

"I don't think so. Not yet. But he will be soon. He was shot in the hip and bled tremendously. It was a terrible wound. He cannot live long."

"He was a monster. He is one, so long as he lives."

"He threw away his shot," said Burr. "My God, he fired first and threw away his shot, and I, cool as you please, aimed directly at him. I am not a good shot. I never thought I would hit him. I only wanted him to see my earnestness."

"I will not have you regretting it. It is no more than he deserves for what he did to Andrew."

"Who is Andrew?" asked the vice president.

"It doesn't matter now. Not to you. Hamilton brought this upon himself, and you cannot be blamed. The world will not blame you. Hamilton is hated, and you will be loved for this."

This turned out not to be the case at all. Hamilton's scandals, his British leanings, his Federalist schemes, and his insane plan to march on South America at the head of an army, a New World Bonaparte—all these things were forgotten. Hamilton in death was recast as a hero. Once word of the duel circulated, one would think the vice president had dug up the body of George Washington and shot it full of holes at Weehawken.

"Why did you lead me to this?" Burr cried out. "Oh, never mind. I haven't the time to hear why or how. I shall flee at once, to South Carolina, I think, to be with Theodosia."

This was his daughter, whom he loved beyond all else. It is nice for him that he had someone to whom to turn in his dark hour.

And so he left me. I thought about seeking out the dying Hamilton, to confront him with what he had done and all he had to answer for, but if he were alive, he would be in pain and he would be prayerful. He would beg my forgiveness like a dying Christian, and it would only plant in me feelings of regret. I had no interest in that, so instead I returned to my sitting room, where I read a charming novel called *Belinda* by Maria Edgeworth. It was amusing but slight, as novels were becoming. I thought, as I often did, that perhaps I should attempt once more to write one of my own, but I could not help but feel that novels had missed their chance. They were but silly things, and nothing I had to say would rightly belong in one.

Historical Note

As with my previous historical novels, this is a work of fiction based on genuine events. Unlike the previous novels, this book intertwines fact and fiction more liberally. Necessarily this note contains "spoilers," so I recommend holding off until you've finished your reading.

In previous novels I have always tried to focus more on major historical events and trends rather than on historical figures, but it is difficult to write about the Federalist period without including at least a few canonical figures. Though the principal characters in the novel—Joan Maycott and Ethan Saunders—are fictional, many of the people within these pages are real, and I've done my best to portray them with at least reasonable accuracy. Readers will, of course, be familiar with Alexander Hamilton, but other figures from history include William Duer, Hugh Henry Brackenridge, Philip Freneau, Anne Bingham, and James and Maria Reynolds. Aaron Burr, as most readers will know, did shoot Alexander Hamilton in a duel on the plains of Weehawken (thus becoming the first sitting American vice president to be involved in a scandalous shooting incident), though it is a matter of some controversy as to whether or not he shot Hamilton on purpose or if Hamilton threw away his shot.

Hamilton's pet project was, indeed, the Bank of the United States, and while William Duer's reckless trading habits brought about the first American financial panic in early 1792, I've fictionalized the matter of the plot against the bank. The historical buildup to the Panic of '92—the machinations in government securities, the attempt to overtake the Million Bank, and Duer's bankruptcy—are all a matter of record. I've merely made Joan and her Whiskey Rebels the cause of these events.

This novel, in many respects, details the events that led up to the Whiskey Rebellion of 1794, which numerous historians and novelists have dealt with in much depth. The insurrection was indeed caused by an onerous tax levied upon whiskey, a commodity more used for trade and consumption than generating revenue, by Alexander Hamilton, who was eager not only to raise money but also to test the new power of a strong federal government. Conditions on the western frontier were every bit as brutal as I describe, and probably more so.

Acknowledgments

Historical fiction is never written in isolation, but this novel has been a far less solitary project than anything I've done before. My previous historical novels have focused on relatively minor and under-researched events, but attempting to get a handle on the Revolutionary War and Federalist periods, the founding fathers, New York, Philadelphia, and western Pennsylvania of the late eighteenth centuries, and countless other subjects has been one of the most challenging projects of my career. Thus I'd like to begin by thanking those who made the research possible.

In Philadelphia I was very fortunate to receive the help and support of many wonderful people and institutions. Many thanks to The Library Company of Philadelphia, with its amazing collections and people, especially Wendy Wolson, Sarah Weatherwax, Phil Lapsansky, and John C. Van Horne. I must also thank the Historical Society of Philadelphia, perhaps less gregarious, but with an invaluable collection. I was delighted by how much helpful, specific, and scholarly information I received from

Philadelphia's many living historians, especially Mitchell Kramer. Jack Lynch, my old friend and walking eighteenth-century encyclopedia, provided much help and pointed me to much-needed resources. Bernice T. Hamel, a total stranger, literally pulled me off the street to help me with research on the Man Full of Trouble tavern, and Paul Boni also provided much help on my research into eighteenth-century tavern life. I also received help from Edward Colimore and from the National Museum of American Jewish History.

My research in Pittsburgh was made a pleasure thanks to Animal Friends of Pittsburgh and Robert Fragasso of the Fragasso Group. Robert was remarkably generous with his time and resources. I would also like to thank Lisa Lazor at the John Heinz History Center.

In New York, many thanks to Joseph Ditta of the New-York Historical Society. For whiskey, I am in debt to Gary Regan and Mike Veach. I was very lucky in my research on the Bank of the United States to have the generous help of the world's foremost authorities on early American banking: David J. Cowen, Richard Sylla, and Robert E. Wright. Carl G. Karsch helped me understand the logistics of the Bank at Carpenters' Hall. Unfortunately I was obligated to remove numerous sections with Thomas Jefferson; nevertheless I must thank Jeff Looney of Monticello for his input and advice.

I'd also like to thank the hospitality of the many coffee shops which I've made my homes away from home: the late and lamented Café Espuma, where this book was first conceived; Ruta Maya in downtown San Antonio, where I worked on the early drafts; and Olmos Perk, where the book was finished and polished.

I am indebted to those whose ears I bent during Thrillerfest 2006, especially Joseph Finder and Leslie Silbert. And I am eternally grateful to the early readers of this very long manuscript: Billy Taylor and Sophia Hollander.

As always, I am grateful for the help and support from my phenomenal agent, Liz Darhansoff. If this novel is worth reading, it is only so because of the hard work and insightful, creative, and encouraging (if sometimes unwelcome) advice of my extraordinary editor, Jennifer Hershey, as well as that of Dana Isaacson. I suspect myself of having more typos than the average writer, so thanks to Dennis Ambrose at Random House and Janet Hotson Baker, my copy editor. I hope I am not jumping the gun, but assuming my publicist will once more be Sally Marvin, I will thank her in advance for her wonderful and tireless work. If it's not Sally, then I'll be content to thank her for her work in the past. Because of the necessary chronology of the publishing schedule, publicists don't get the public praise they deserve.

For reasons that need not be stated, I must thank my family for their love and encouragement, and my cats for their therapeutic value and for making sure I never overslept.

The Whiskey Rebels

DAVID LISS

A Reader's Guide

A Conversation with David Liss

David Anthony Durham is the author of the novels *The Other Lands, Acacia, Pride of Carthage, Walk Through Darkness,* and *Gabriel's Story.* His website is davidanthonydurham.com.

David Anthony Durham: This is your first historical novel to be set in the United States. Was it a difficult transition to make from Europe?

David Liss: It was difficult in a number of ways for a number of reasons. My other books have been set in the seventeenth and early eighteenth centuries, and this one was set in the late eighteenth century. Historians mark the dividing line between the early modern period and the modern period as 1750. Although it's a fairly arbitrary line, I do feel that people are much more modern at the end of the eighteenth century than they were at the beginning. Then of course there is the issue of writing about people and events with which many readers will already be familiar. And certainly American culture is very different from even English culture. So, yes, there was an enormous amount of research to do and an awful lot I had to learn.

DAD: Some of your previous books were populated with with lesser-known figures from history, such as Jonathan Wild in *A Conspiracy of Paper* and *A Spectacle of Corruption,* but in *The Whiskey Rebels* you have a large cast of canonical figures, including Hamilton and Washington. What was that like?

DL: I tend not to like to write novels that are overpowered by names, places, and events with which a reasonably knowledgeable reader is likely already familiar. I've always been interested in trying to get inside a time and understand and express what it would have been like to be alive during a significant or transformative historical moment. I'm less interested in recasting the historical record in fictional form. I have nothing against that sort of historical fiction, and there are many fine examples of it, but I just don't like to write it. In my other books, I've written about moments in time that are largely populated by figures with whom most modern readers will be unfamiliar. With this book, it would have been disingenuous to write out figures like Hamilton, Burr, Washington, and William Duer. If you were involved in the world of finance in New York or Philadelphia in the early 1790s, you would come across these people. The early American republic was a small world by today's standards.

As for what it was like, I have to say I prefer to write about purely fictional figures or at least very minor historical figures. It always felt to me disrespectful in some way to write about people such as Hamilton, to manipulate them as though they were completely made up. Also, I like having the freedom to take a story or character in any direction I want it or him to go. If I suddenly decide that the best way to make the story work would be for Hamilton to shave his head and grow a beard, I don't have the freedom to make him do that.

DAD: Can you say more about recreating a historical moment, and how you accomplished this in *The Whiskey Rebels*?

DL: When I think about the function of the historical novel, I tend to think about what it can do that history cannot. I think if you want simply to learn about the root causes of the Whiskey Rebellion or the Panic of 1792, there are numerous excellent works of history that you can reference that can provide all the important information you need. On the other hand, fiction can attempt to recreate the human experience of these events, the emotional context and specific subjectivity of living through such pivotal moments. It is all guesswork, of course. We can never really know how people in the past experienced their lives, but it is great fun, and interesting to try.

DAD: Your books generally have a crime or thriller or mystery aspect to them. Is that an integral part of the storytelling process for you?

DL: I think it is an integral part of the storytelling process for all traditional, narrative-driven fiction. I don't like to think of myself as being limited to one particular genre, but I do employ many elements from mysteries and thrillers. I think those elements have been around as long as the novel has been around. When you think of the great early examples of the novel, you will find there is mystery and suspense in them, even if these are not what you would think of as mystery or suspense novels. *Tom Jones* is driven by the central mystery of the identity of Tom's mother. *Pride and Prejudice* is driven by the suspense of who Elizabeth will marry. Narrative plots thrive on mystery, tension, and uncertainty. In my case, I often write about financial history, and so I tend to use these techniques because people are trained to believe they find finance dull, and I need to show in bold strokes what is at stake for the characters and their world if things go wrong for them.

DAD: What is it about financial history that so appeals to you?

DL: I wrote about finance in my first novel, *A Conspiracy of Paper*, because the transformation of the British economy in the early eighteenth century was a large part of my graduate school work at the time. I had no idea that I would keep writing about finance in other times and places. I think what I like about it is that how major financial endeavors are managed and mismanaged tells us so much about the times. The Panic of 1792, for example, is entirely different from the South Sea Bubble. The early United States was, despite covering a lot of space, a small world economically. It made it easy for a small group of bad actors to wield undue influence in the market. I am drawn to showing how in each unique time and place people tend to make the same sort of overreaching errors, though the nature of those errors and how they play out are always very different.

DAD: Is it a coincidence that your novel about a major American financial panic was published during a major American financial panic?

DL: No coincidence. I crashed the economy in the hopes it would help me sell books. Does that make me greedy or simply aggressive? I just don't know.

DAD: Your novel suggests that the events you write about had the power to destroy the early United States. Is that an exaggeration?

DL: I don't think so. We tend to see the history of this country in progressive terms. There was the triumph of the Revolution, the triumph of the Constitution, the slight hiccup of the Civil War, but that was good because it ended slavery, and now here we are. The truth is so much more complicated and treacherous. One of the things that really drew me to write about the early republic was the tentative, fragile, and paranoid feelings of the time. Many people genuinely believed the country could never survive after Washington died or stepped down. Others were already horribly disillusioned with the Constitution, which they thought was oppressive and established a new kind of federal tyranny to replace the one they'd defeated in the Revolution. There was talk in New England about succeeding over slavery, and the South was, of course, twitchy whenever the issue of slavery was raised. The Westerners, whom I write about in this book, experienced firsthand the consequences of the centralization of government. The ideology of the Revolution was that the people have the right to direct access to those who govern them, but they were finding the government in Philadelphia no more responsive than the government had been in London. The right blow in the right place could have ended everything.

DAD: Joan Maycott suggests at one point that it would be better to destroy the early American republic than let it continue in a flawed state: "Is that [destruction] not preferable to permitting something rotten and insidious to dress itself up as glorious and just? If we do nothing, if we take our little share of wealth and turn our backs now, in future generations, when rank corruption masquerades as liberty, it will be upon our shoulders. True patriots will then ask why we who were there to witness this nation at the crossroads did nothing." This is strong stuff, and she is a sympathetic character. You wrote those words, but do you agree with them?

DL: There are so many things I find brilliant and inspiring about the founders and the Enlightenment ideals they managed to crystallize into a working government. I continually marvel at the intelligence and flexibility built into the Constitution. On the other hand, all these things in all their greatness has tended to produce a kind of reflexive posture of rectitude in American culture. America is a shining beacon of freedom, and therefore if America does it, it must be good. Of course, no country is right all the time, and this one, like all others, makes mistakes. The principles upon which it was founded can't be used as a shield to ward off self-reflection. I think Joan's anger is just and her desire to strike back reasonable, but I don't think she was right. It is hard not to wish that the founders would have had the courage to push back against slavery, or would have been more modern on issues of gender equity, but that is simply not the world they lived in. I think it much more healthy to see our country as a work in progress rather than as something that was cast in stone at the beginning. That is, after all, how the Constitution was designed.

DAD: Why did you choose to write the novel from two first-person perspectives? Was it hard for you to write from the perspective of a woman?

DL: For me, the hardest thing about getting a new novel under way is figuring out the right voice for the book. I played around with a lot of ways to tell this story before deciding on the two first-person voices. It was the one that felt most comfortable.

As far as writing a woman goes, I don't think I would have the courage to write a story from the perspective of a contemporary woman, but I took shelter in the murkiness of the past. I did lots of reading on what life was like for women at the time. I read as many journals and letters as I could to get a feel for a woman's perspective on early American politics and on life in the western frontier. I don't know if I got it right, but it is an honest effort, and once I did the background work, those chapters were comfortable for me to write.

DAD: Ethan Saunders, like many of your characters, has a number of unlikable qualities. Why do you often write about flawed protagonists?

DL: I find flawed characters so much more interesting than square-jawed superhero types who always know the right thing to do and then do it without hesitation. I'm not entirely sure why, but I knew almost from the beginning that I wanted his story to be one of redemption, and for that to be possible, Ethan needed to be in a bad state at the beginning of the story. It is also fun to write about a character who is a drunk, womanizing, self-aggrandizing social misfit. I know in my own reading that it is often much easier to identify with and root for a flawed character so long as there is some basic human element to sympathize with and latch on to.

DAD: We began by asking you about the shift to an American setting. Do you plan to return to this period or these characters?

DL: I would say that it is a possibility but not a certainty. I feel that if I were to bring some of these characters back, I know exactly the story I'd like to bring them back into, and I think it would be something I'd very much enjoy writing. On the other hand, this book took me longer to write than anything I've ever done, and I'll need some time off before I even consider such an undertaking again.

Questions and Topics for Discussion

1. Andrew Maycott believes "The American novel, if it is to be honest, must be about money, not property. Money alone—base, unremarkable, corrupting money" (page 30). Do you agree? By his definition, is *The Whiskey Rebels* an American novel? Why or why not?

2. Captain Ethan Saunders implores us, "Look beneath and you may find several things that surprise you" (page 63). If we take Ethan's advice and look beneath or past his scheming, his impropriety, and his status as a "ruin of a man," what do we find? How and why are honor and reputation intertwined?

3. Through her reading, Joan Maycott discovers: "When my empathy for a character led me to weep or laugh or fear for her safety, I spent hours determining by what means the novelist had effected this magic. When I cared nothing for suffering and loss, I dissected the want of craft that engendered such apathy" (page 23). How does David Liss engender empathy or apathy for his characters? Did you sometimes feel both empathy and apathy for the same character?

4. En route to the Pennsylvania frontier, Phineas tells Joan "The West changes you. . . . I'm what the West made me, and you'll be what it makes you" (page 84). Is this true? If so, how does the frontier change Joan? Phineas? What does this say about free will and choice in relation to place and circumstance?

5. Examine the characterizations and the roles of women in *The Whiskey Rebels*. What similarities do you find? What differences? Are they victims?

6. Mr. Brackenridge defines himself as a patriot—one who "does not make the principles of his country conform to his own ideas" (page 188). How else is patriotism defined or demonstrated in this book? How would you define patriotism? Who else in *The Whiskey Rebels* is then a patriot?

7. Thomas Jefferson, Alexander Hamilton, William Duer, and Joan Maycott have varied theories on the American economy, the Bank of the United States, and the excise tax. For instance, the Bank is either a great boon for the nation, a terrible disaster for the nation, or an opportunity to be exploited. Talk about their differing perspectives in relation to the events of *The Whiskey Rebels*. Who do you think is right? Do these debates continue today?

8. Discuss the principle of justice and its relation to revenge, integrity, inequality, and the law in *The Whiskey Rebels*. How does Joan Maycott justify her revenge against Alexander Hamilton?

9. Why does Captain Saunders not allow his slave, Leonidas, to purchase his freedom and later "simply neglect[s] to inform" him that he is a free man? What does liberty mean to Captain Saunders? Joan Maycott? Leonidas? Cynthia Pearson? The newly formed United States?

10. Lavien believes "It is only in the eyes of one another that inequality lies" (page 94). Who else, besides Lavien, serves as a moral arbiter in the novel? What examples of presumed superiority and/or civility can be found in *The Whiskey Rebels*? What examples can you find of an impossible tension between greed and civility, wealth and humanity?

Here's a preview of

DAVID LISS'S

new novel

THE DEVIL'S COMPANY

chapter one

—

IN MY YOUTH I SUFFERED FROM TOO CLOSE A PROXIMITY TO GAMING tables of all descriptions, and I watched in horror as Lady Fortune delivered money, sometimes not precisely my own, into another's hands. As a man of more seasoned years, one poised to enter his third decade of life, I knew far better than to let myself loose among such dangerous tools as dice and cards, engines of mischief good for nothing but giving a man false hope before dashing his dreams. However, I found it no difficult thing to make an exception on those rare occasions when it was another man's silver that filled my purse. And if that other man had engaged in machination that would guarantee that the dice should roll or the cards turn in my favor, so much the better. Those of overly scrupulous morals might suggest that to alter the odds in one's favor so illicitly is the lowest depth to which a soul can sink. Better a sneak thief, a murderer, even a traitor to his country, these men will argue, than a cheat at the gaming table. Perhaps it is so, but I was a cheat in the service of a generous patron, and that, to my mind, quieted the echoes of doubt.

I begin this tale in November of 1722, some eight months after the events of the general election of which I have previously written. The rancid waters of politics had washed over London, and indeed the nation, earlier that year, but once more the tide had receded, leaving us none the cleaner. In the spring, men had fought like gladiators in the service of this candidate or that party, but in the autumn matters sat as though nothing of moment had transpired, and the connivances of

Parliament and Whitehall galloped along as had ever been their custom. The kingdom would not face another general election for seven
years, and in retrospect people could not quite recollect what had engendered the fuss of the last.

I had suffered many injuries in the events of the political turmoil,
but my reputation as a thieftaker had ultimately enjoyed some bene-
fits. I received no little notoriety in the newspapers, and though much
of what the Grub Street hacks had to say of me was utterly scurrilous,
my name had emerged somehow augmented, and since that time I had
suffered no shortage of knocks upon my door. There were certainly
those who might now stay away, fearing that my exploits had an unpleasant habit of attracting attention, but many more gazed with favor
upon the idea of hiring a man such as myself, one who had fought
pitched battles as a pugilist, escaped from Newgate Prison, and shown
his mettle in resisting the mightiest political powers in the kingdom. A
fellow who can do such things, these men reasoned, can certainly find
that scoundrel who owes thirty pounds; he can find the name of the
villain who plots to run off with a high-spirited daughter; he can bring
to justice the rascal who stole a watch.

Such was the beer and meat of my trade, but, too, there were those
who made more uncommon uses of my talents, which was why I found
myself that November night in Kingsley's Coffeehouse, once a place of
little reputation but now something far more vivacious. Kingsley's had
been for the past season a gaming house of considerable fashion
among the bon ton, and perhaps it would continue to enjoy this position for another season or two. The wits of London could not embrace
this amusement or that for too long before they grew weary, but for the
nonce Mr. Kingsley had taken full advantage of the good fortune
granted him.

While during daylight hours a man might still come in for a dish of
coffee or chocolate and enjoy reading a newspaper or hearing one read
to him, come sundown he would need a constitution of iron to attend
to dry words. Here now were nearly as many whores as there were
gamers, and fine-looking whores at that. Search not at Kingsley's
for diseased or half-starved doxies from Covent Garden or St. Giles.
Indeed, the paragraph writers reported that Mrs. Kingsley herself
inspected the jades to ensure they met her exacting standards. On
hand as well were musicians who played lively ditties while an unnat-

urally slender posturer contorted his death's head of a face and skeletal body into the most unlikely shapes and attitudes—all while the crowd duly ignored him. Here were middling bottles of claret and port and Madeira to please discriminating men too distracted to discriminate. And here, most importantly, were the causes of the distraction: the gaming tables.

I could not have said what made Kingsley's tables rise from obscurity to glory. They looked much like any other, and yet the finest people of London directed their coachmen to this temple of fortune. After the play, after the opera, after the rout and the assembly, Kingsley's was the very place. Playing at faro were several well-situated gentlemen of the ministry, as well as a member of the House of Commons, more famous for his lavish parties than for his skills as a legislator. Losing at piquet was the son of the Duke of Norwich. Several sprightly beaux tried to teach the celebrated comedienne Nance Oldfield to master the rules of hazard—and good luck to them, for it was a perplexing game. The great brought low and the low raised high—it all amused and entertained me, but my disposition mattered little. The silver in my purse and the banknotes in my pocket were not mine to wager according to my own inclinations. They were marked for the shame of a particular gentleman, one who had previously humiliated the man on whose behalf I now entered a contest of guile and deceit.

I spent a quarter of an hour walking through Kingsley's, enjoying the light of countless chandeliers and the warmth of their fires, for winter had come hard and early that year, and outside all was ice and bitter cold. At last, grown warm and eager, with the music and laughter and the enticements of whores buzzing in my head, I began to formulate my plan. I sipped at thinned Madeira and sought out my man without seeming to seek out anyone. Such was an easy task, for I had dressed myself as a beau of the most foppish sort, and if the nearby revelers took notice of me they saw only a man who wished to be noticed, and what can be more invisible than that?

I wore an emerald-and-gold outer coat, embroidered almost beyond endurance, a waistcoat of the same color but opposing design, bright with brass buttons of some four inches in diameter. My breeches were of the finest velvet, my shoes more silver buckle than shiny leather, and the lace of my sleeves blossomed like frilly blunderbusses. That I might go unrecognized should anyone there know my face, I also wore a massive wig of the wiry sort that was fashionable that year among the more peacockish sort of man.

When the time and the circumstances seemed to me as I wished them, I approached the cacho table and came upon my man. He was a fellow my own age or thereabouts, dressed very expensively but without the frills and bright colors in which I'd costumed myself. His suit was of a sedate and dark blue with red trim, embroidered tastefully with gold thread, and he looked quite well in it. In truth, he had a handsome face beneath his short bob wig. At his table, he contemplated with the seriousness of a scholar the three cards in his hand and said something in the general direction of the ample breasts belonging to the whore upon his lap. She laughed, which I suspected was in no small degree how she earned her master's favor.

This man was Robert Bailor. I had been hired by a Mr. Jerome Cobb, whom it seemed Bailor had humiliated in a game of chance, the outcome of which, my patron believed, owed more to chicanery than fortune. The tale I had been told unfolded accordingly: Subsequent to losing a great deal of money, my patron had discovered that Bailor possessed the reputation of a gamer who misliked the randomness of chance as much as he misliked duels. Mr. Cobb, acting upon his prerogative as a gentleman, challenged this Bailor, but Bailor had insolently excused himself, leaving the injured gentleman with no option but perfidy of his own

Needing a man to act as his agent in these matters, he had sought me out and addressed his needs to me. I was, according to Mr. Cobb's instruction, to manufacture a battle of cards with Bailor. Mr. Cobb had employed me to that end, but I was not the only one in his pay. So, too, was a particular card dealer at Kingsley's, who was to make certain I lost when I wished to lose and, more importantly, won when I wished to win. Once I had succeeded in humiliating Mr. Bailor before as large a crowd as I could muster, I was to whisper to him, so that no other ears might hear, that he had felt the long reach of Mr. Cobb.

I approached the red velvet cacho table and stared for a moment at Bailor's whore and then for another moment at Bailor himself. Mr. Cobb had informed me of every known particularity of his enemy's character, among them that Bailor had no love for the gaze of strangers and loathed a fop above all things. A staring fop could not fail to attract his notice.

Bailor set down his three cards upon the table and the other two players did as well. After a smirk, he gathered the pile of money to himself. He slowly raised to me a pair of narrow eyes. The light was such that I could observe their dull gray color and that they were well lined with red, sure signs of a man who has been at play too long, has enjoyed his spirits overmuch, and is vastly in need of sleep.

Though somewhat hampered by bushy brows and a flattened nose with wide and flaring nostrils, he also possessed strong cheekbones and a square chin, and he was built like a man who enjoyed riding more than beef or beer. He therefore had something commanding about him.

"Direct your eyes elsewhere, sir," he told me, "or I shall teach you the manners your education has sadly omitted."

"Och, you're a rude one, ain't you, laddie?" I said, affecting the accent of a Scotsman, for in addition to fops, I had been made to understand that Bailor detested North Britons, and I was fully outfitted to attract his ire. "I was only having a wee peek at the lassie you've got 'pon you. Perhaps, as you're not using her for aught but a lap warmer, you might lend her to me for a spell."

His eyes narrowed. "I hardly think you would know what to do with a woman, Sawny," he answered, using that name so insulting to Scotsmen.

For my part, I pretended to hold myself above such abuse. "I ken I wouldn't let her turn stale while I sat playing at card games. I ken as much as that."

"You offend me, sir," he said. "Not only with your odious words but with your very being, which is an affront to this city and this country."

"I canna answer for that. Your offense is your own. Will you lend me the lassie or no?"

"No," he said quietly. "I shan't. What I shall do is challenge you to a duel."

This drew a gasp, and I saw that a crowd had gathered to watch us. Some twenty or thirty spectators—sharply dressed beaux with cynical laughs and their painted ladies—pulled in close now, whispering excitedly among themselves, fans flapping like a great mass of butterflies.

"A duel, you say?" I let out a laugh. I knew what he meant but pretended to ignorance. "If your honor is so delicate a thing, then I'll help you see who is the man of the two of us. Have ye in mind blades or pistols, then? I promise ye, I am equally partial to both."

He answered with a derisive bark and a toss of the head, as though he could not believe there was still a backwards creature who dueled with instruments of violence. "I have no time for such rude displays of barbarism. A duel of the cards, Sawny, if you are willing. Do you know cacho?"

"Aye, I ken it. 'Tis an amusement for lassies and ladies and little boys who haven't yet the hair on their chests, but if it is your amusement too I'll not shrink from your wee challenge."

The two gentlemen who had previously sat at his table now vacated, standing back that I might take one of the seats. I did so and, with the greatest degree of subtlety, glanced at the dealer of cards. He was a squat man with a red birthmark on his nose—just the fellow my employer, Mr. Cobb, had described to me. We exchanged the most fleeting of glances. All progressed in accordance with the plan.

"Another glass of this Madeira," I called out, to whatever servant might hear me. I removed from my coat an elaborately carved ivory snuffbox and with all deliberate slowness and delicacy took a pinch of the loathsome stuff. Then, to Mr. Bailor, I said, "What have ye in mind then, laddie? Five pounds? Is ten too much for ye?"

His friends laughed. He sneered. "Ten pounds? You must be mad. Have you never been to Kingsley's before?"

"It's me first time in London, for all it matters. What of it? I can assure ye that my reputation is secure in my native land."

"I know not what back alley of Edinburgh from which you come—"

I interrupted him. "'Tis not right you address me so. Ken ye I'm the Laird of Kyleakin?" I boomed, having only a poor notion of where Kyleakin was or if it was a significant enough place to have a laird at all. I did know that half the North Britons in the metropolis claimed to be laird of something, and the title earned the claimant more derision than respect.

"I have no concern for what bog you call home," Bailor said. "Know you that at Kingsley's no one plays for less than fifty pounds. If you cannot wager such an amount, get out and cease corrupting the air I breathe."

"Fie on your fifty pounds. 'Tis no more than a farthing to me." I produced a pocketbook, from which I retrieved two banknotes of twenty-five pounds each.

Bailor inspected them to ascertain their legitimacy, for neither counterfeit notes nor the promise of a dissolute laird of Kyleakin would answer his purposes. These, however, came from a local gold-smith of some reputation, and my adversary was satisfied. He threw in two banknotes of his own, which I picked up and proceeded to study, though I had no reason to believe—or to care—if they were not good. I merely wished to antagonize him. Accordingly, I peered at them from all angles, held them up to the burning candles, moved my eyes in to study the print most minutely.

"Put them down," he said, after a moment. "If you haven't yet reached a conclusion, you never will unless you summon one of your highland seers. More to the point, my reputation is known here, yours is not. Now, we begin with a fifty-pound bet, but each additional wager must be no less than ten pounds. Do you understand?"

"Aye. Now let us duel." I placed my left hand on the table with my index finger extended. It was the agreed-upon signal to the dealer that I wished to lose the hand.

Even in such times when I often played at cards, I never much relished cacho, in which a man must make too many decisions based entirely on unknown factors. It is, in other words, a contest of chance rather than skill, and I have little interest in such. The game is played with a shortened deck—only the ace through the six of each suit in-cluded. Each player is dealt a card, he makes his wager, and then the circle is repeated twice more until each player possesses in his hand three cards. With the ace counting as a low card, whichever man has the best hand—or, in this case, the better hand—is declared winner.

I received an ace of hearts. A poor start as, in this simple game, hands were often won simply by a high card. I grinned as though I had received the very card I most desired and threw ten pounds into the center of the table. Bailor matched my bet, and my confederate dealer presented to me another card. The three of diamonds. Again, a poor showing. I added another ten, as did Bailor. My final card was the four of spades; a losing hand if I ever saw one. We both put in our ten pounds and then Bailor called me to lay my hand flat. I had nothing of value; He, however, presented a cacho, three cards of the same suit. In a single hand he had unburdened me of eighty pounds—approximately half as much as I might hope to earn in a year's time. However, as it was not my money and I had been instructed to lose it, I could not much lament its passing.

Bailor laughed as rudely as a puppet-show villain and asked if I wished to further mortify myself by playing another hand. I told him I would not shrink from his base challenge, and once more I signaled the dealer that I wished to lose. Accordingly, I soon lost another eighty pounds. I now began to affect the countenance of a man agitated by these events, and I grumbled and muttered and gulped angrily at my wine.

"I would say," Bailor told me, "that you have lost this duel. Now be gone with you. Go back north, paint yourself blue, and trouble no more our civilized climes."

"I've not lost yet," I told him. "Unless you are such a coward that you would run from me."

"I should be a strange sort of coward who would run from taking your money. Let us play another hand, then."

Though I may have had some initial reservations about my involvement in this deception, I began now to develop a genuine loathing of Bailor, and I looked to his defeat with great anticipation. "No more of these lassie wagers," I said, opening my notebook and taking out three hundred pounds' worth of notes, which I slapped down on the table.

Bailor gave the matter a moment's consideration and then matched my wager. I placed my right hand on the table with the index finger out—the signal that I would now win, for it was time to present this man with his unhappy deserts.

I received my first card, the six of clubs. A fine start, I thought, and added another two hundred pounds to the pile. I feared for a moment that Bailor would grow either suspicious or afraid of my bold maneuver, but he had offered the challenge himself and could not back down without appearing a poltroon. Indeed, he met my two hundred and raised me another hundred. I matched the bet quite happily.

The dealer presented our next cards, and I received the six of spades. I attempted to hide my pleasure. In cacho, the highest hand possible is that of three sixes. My employer's man meant to assure my victory. I therefore put in another two hundred pounds. Bailor met the wager but did not raise it. I could not be surprised that he grew uneasy. We had now both committed to eight hundred pounds, and its loss would surely hurt him a great deal. He was a man of some means, I had been told, but not infinite ones, and none but the wealthiest of lords and merchants can relinquish such sums without some distress.

"You're not raising this time, laddie?" I asked. "Are ye beginning to quake?"

"Shut your Scots mouth," he said.

I grinned, for I knew he had nothing, and my Scots persona would know it too.

And then I received my third card. The two of diamonds.

I strained against the urge to tell the dealer he had made a mistake. He had meant to give me a third six, surely. With so much of my patron's money on the table, I felt a tremor of fear at the prospect of losing. I quickly calmed myself, however, recognizing that I had been merely anticipating something far more theatrical than what the dealer had planned. A victory of three sixes might look too much like the deception that we, indeed, perpetrated. My collaborator would merely give Bailor a less distinguished hand, and our contest would be determined by a high card. The loss for my opponent would be no less bitter for its being accomplished by unremarkable means.

All about us the crowd had grown thick with spectators, and the air was warm with the heat of their bodies and breath. It was all as my patron would have wished. I glanced at the dealer, who gave me the most abbreviated of nods. He had seen my doubt and answered it. "Another hundred," I said, not wishing to wager more as my store of Cobb's money grew thin. I wished to have something left should Bailor raise the bet. He did so by another fifty pounds, leaving me with fewer than a hundred pounds of Mr. Cobb's money on my person.

Bailor grinned at me. "Now we shall see, Sawny, who is the better man."

I returned the grin and set forth my cards. "Not so bonny as I would like, but I've won with less."

"Perhaps," he said, "but this time you would have lost with more." He laid down his own cards: a cacho—and not only a cacho, but one with a six, five, and four. This was the second highest hand in the game, one I could have bested only with three sixes. I had lost, and lost soundly.

I felt a dizziness pass over me. Something had gone wrong, horribly wrong. I had done everything Mr. Cobb had said. The dealer had shown every sign of being Cobb's man. I had delivered the signals as planned. Yet I must now return to the man who hired me and report that I'd lost more than eleven hundred pounds of his money.

I glanced over at the dealer, but he would not meet my eye. Bailor, however, leered at me so lasciviously that I thought for a moment that he wished for me, and not his whore, to return with him to his rooms.

I rose from the table.

"Going somewhere, Sawny?" one of Bailor's friends asked.

"All hail the Laird of Kyleakin," another called out.

"Another hand!" Bailor himself shouted. "Or shall we call this duel concluded, and you the loser?" He then turned to his friends. "Perhaps I should take my winnings and buy all of Kyleakin and cast out its current master. I suspect I have quite a bit more than I should need upon this very table."

I said nothing, only wanting to escape from the coffeehouse, which now smelled to me intolerably of spilled wine and sweat and civet perfume. I wanted the shocking cold of the winter night air to wash over my face, that I might think of what to do next, contemplate how things had gone wrong and what I might say to the man who had entrusted me with his wealth.

I must have been walking far more slowly than I realized, for Bailor had come up behind me before I had reached the door. His friends were in tow, and his face was bright, flushed with victory. For a moment I thought he meant to challenge me to a duel of another sort, and in truth I would have welcomed such a thing, for it would have eased my mind some to have the opportunity to redeem myself in a contest of violence.

"What is it?" I asked of him. I would rather let him gloat than appear to run. Though I was in disguise and any behavior I might indulge would not tarnish my reputation, I was still a man and could not stomach flight.

He said nothing for a moment, but only gazed upon me. Then he leaned forward as if to salute my cheek, but instead he whispered some words in my ear. "I believe, Mr. Weaver," he said, addressing me by my true name, "that you have now felt the long reach of Jerome Cobb."

DAVID LISS is the author of *The Devil's Company, A Spectacle of Corruption, The Coffee Trader,* and *A Conspiracy of Paper,* winner of the 2000 Edgar Award for Best First Novel, as well as *The Ethical Assassin.* He lives in San Antonio with his wife and children.